A Treasure House
of Chinese Fables

A Treasure House of Chinese Fables

Translated By:
Chi Him Chiu

Copyright © 2006 by Chi Him Chiu.

Library of Congress Control Number: 2006905874
ISBN: Softcover 1-4257-2330-6

All rights reserved. No part of this book may be reproduced or transmitted in any form or by any means, electronic or mechanical, including photocopying, recording, or by any information storage and retrieval system, without permission in writing from the copyright owner.

This is a work of fiction. Names, characters, places and incidents either are the product of the author's imagination or are used fictitiously, and any resemblance to any actual persons, living or dead, events, or locales is entirely coincidental.

This book was printed in the United States of America.

To order additional copies of this book, contact:
Xlibris Corporation
1-888-795-4274
www.Xlibris.com
Orders@Xlibris.com
35259

Contents

*The Book of Changes
1. The Ram 47

*The Book of Odes
2. Asking for Guidance from Passersby 48

*Guanzi
3. Job in a Stable 48
4. Mistaken Identity 49

*Annals of Yanzi
5. The Duke Jing Prays for Rain 49
6. Cherish the People 50
7. Killing Three Warriors with Two Peaches 51
8. Temple Mice 53
9. A Wine Seller 53
10. The Golden Jug and the Decree Written in Vermilion 54
11. The Groom's Wife 54
12. Selling Horse-Meat as Beefsteak 55
13. The Duke Jing and the Art of Oneiromancy 56
14. Yanzi as an Envoy to the State of Chu 57
15. The Tangerine and the Trifoliate Orange 57
16. Prices of Artificial Limbs and Shoes 58
17. Zhuzou Lost the Bird, Zhuzou Must Be Punished 59
18. The *Roc* and the *Chilo Simplex* 60

*A Commentary on the Spring and Autumn Annals
19. At One Fling 61
20. A Paper Tiger 62

21.	Sensual Pleasures and Noble Ambition	62
22.	Take a Risk	63
23.	Paying the Debt of Gratitude	64
24.	Lost in Wonder	64
25.	Forgetting One's Ancestry	65
26.	A Rooster Pecking its own Tail	66
27.	The Power of Tears	66

*Master Sun's Art of War

28.	A Snake called *Shuai Ran*	67
29.	Two in Distress make Trouble Less	67

*Mozi

30.	Wu Mazi seeks Advice	68
31.	The Frog, the Fly and the Rooster	69
32.	Silk Dyeing	69
33.	Blocking the Thief's Exit	69
34.	The King of Chu Loves Slender Waist	69
35.	The King of Yue loves Heroic Soldiers	70
36.	Compasses and the Square	70
37.	God Kills the Dragon	70
38.	Help Cane a Child	71
39.	Gong Shu Ban Makes a Magpie	71

*Shenzi

40.	Flying Dragon	72

*Shizi

41.	Meng Ben's Constant Valour	72
42.	Wu Maqi Buys the Poisoned Wine	73
43.	The Deer	73

*The Book of Shangjun

44.	Dongguo Chang Seeks the Title of Nobility	74

*Wulingzi

45. The Snail of Zhongzhou 75
46. Bullrush 75

*Liezi

47. The Man of Qi 76
48. The Man of Song 76
49. Liezi as Archer 77
50. Shang Qiukai 78
51. Liang Yang 80
52. Seagull 80
53. Blow Hot and Cold 81
54. Yin 81
55. The Litigation 82
56. Befuddlement 83
57. The Return of a Native of Yan 84
58. *Chilo Simplex* 85
59. The Foolish Old Man Who Removed the Mountains 85
60. The Sun and Two Children 86
61. Zhan He goes Angling 87
62. Bian Que 88
63. Zheng Shiwen 89
64. Xue Tan 90
65. Han-e 90
66. The Story of Yu Boya and Zhong Ziqi 91
67. Yan Shi Created a Man 92
68. Ji Chang 93
69. Zao Fu 94
70. The Kunwu Sword and the Fire-wash Cloth 95
71. Power and Destiny 96
72. Ji Liang's Illness 97
73. Presenting Sunshine to the King 97
74. Guan Yinzi and Archery 98
75. The Shis and the Mengs 99
76. The Mulberry Girl 100
77. Song Yuanjun and the Two Acrobats 101
78. Real Worth is more Valuable than Looks 101

79.	Niu Que and the Highwaymen	102
80.	Ai Jingmu	103
81.	A Lamb Going Astray at a Forked Road	103
82.	The Dog and Yang Bu	104
83.	The Secret of Immortality	105
84.	Man, Fish, and Wild Goose	105
85.	A Beggar's View of Disgrace	106
86.	A Contract	106
87.	A withered Firmiana	106
88.	Suspicion	107
89.	The Man of Qi	107

*Zhuangzi

90.	The *Roc*	108
91.	Skin Salve	108
92.	Play the Lute to a Cow	109
93.	The Shadow	110
94.	Zhuang Sheng's Dream and the Butterfly	110
95.	The Chef Ding	110
96.	Keeping a Tiger	111
97.	An Untimely Slap	111
98.	The Oak Tree as the God of the Land	112
99.	Zhi Lishu	113
100.	Mutual Help and Relief in Adversity	114
101.	Bosom Friends	114
102.	The Death of Hundun (Chaos)	115
103.	Zang and Gu Lost their Sheep	115
104.	Bo Le's Guilt	116
105.	An Easy Thing to do	116
106.	Lun Bian	117
107.	Crude Imitation	117
108.	The River God	118
109.	A Frog in a Well	118
110.	In Attempting to walk like a Swan, the Crow loses its own Gait	119
111.	Zhuangzi	119
112.	Zhuangzi and his Wife	120
113.	The World-weary Human Skeleton	120
114.	The Marquis of Lu	121

115.	Catching Cicada	122
116.	The Ferryman	122
117.	The Officiant and the Sacrificial Pig	123
118.	The Duke Huan of Qi and the Ghost	124
119.	Dumb as a Wooden Chicken	124
120.	Uncanny Workmanship	125
121.	Dong Yeji	126
122.	The Tree and the Goose	126
123.	The Fox and the Leopard	127
124.	Lin Hui	127
125.	A Monkey and the Forest	128
126.	Zhuangzhou in Diaoling	128
127.	Beauty and Ugliness	129
128.	The Scholar	130
129.	The Cartographer	130
130.	The Stonemason and his Axe	131
131.	Wars on the Snail's Tentacles	131
132.	A Fish Trapped in a Dry Rut	132
133.	The Prince of the State of Ren	133
134.	Two Scholarly Thieves	134
135.	Sacred Turtle	134
136.	Afraid of one's own Shadow	135
137.	Learning to Slaughter a Dragon	136
138.	Zhuangzi and Cao Shang	136
139.	Under the Black Dragon's Jaw	137

*Gongsun Longzi

| 140. | Gongsun Long | 138 |

*Yi Wenzi

141.	A Self-effacing Huanggong	139
142.	The King Xuan as an Archer	139
143.	The King and the Pheasant	140
144.	The Farmer and the Jade	140
145.	A Matter of Names	141
146.	Different Names for *Pu*	142
147.	*Dao* and *Ou*	142

Xunzi

148. The Nest of Mengjiu 143
149. Sunlight Loving Fish 143
150. A Virgin and the Robbers 143
151. Juan Shuliang 143
152. The Tilting Wine Pot 144
153. Dong Yebi lost his Horse 145

Quezi

154. Bait of Cinnamon and Fishhook of Gold 146

In Response to the Questions of the King of Chu

155. Highbrow Songs Find Few Singers 146

Lu's Annals

156. A Man of Chu and his Bow 148
157. Recommend Qualified Persons for Service 148
158. Uprightness and Filial Piety 149
159. Cut Off One's Flesh to feed Oneself 149
160. The Monarch of Zhu and the Suit of Armour 149
161. Finches 150
162. Pursuing Rancidness at Sea 150
163. Drain the Pond to get the Pearl 151
164. Dan Bao and Occultism 151
165. Confucius lost his Horse 151
166. Penny-wise and Pound-Foolish 152
167. The Duke Huan called on Ji 152
168. *Jue* and *Qiongqiong* 153
169. The Men of Chu crossed the Yongshui River 153
170. Nick the Boat to seek the Sword 153
171. His Father was a Good Swimmer 154
172. The Prophecy of Guan Zhong 154
173. Solving the Unsolvable 156
174. Understanding a Man 157
175. False Reasoning 157
176. An Impeded Elbow 158

177.	Decisive Struggle	159
178.	Rongyi and his Pupil	159
179.	The Dragon Slayer	160
180.	Zihan and the Neighbours	160
181.	The King You and his Favourite Concubine	161
182.	The Eccentric Spirit of Liqiu	162
183.	Sinking a Well	162
184.	Three Pigs crossing the River	163
185.	The King of Song went Into Exile	163
186.	Self-deception	165
187.	Yang Youji	165
188.	Resurrection	165
189.	Sword Appraiser	166
190.	A Mouse-catching Dog	166
191.	A Net Open on Three Sides	167

*Hanfeizi

192.	Stay at one's Post	168
193.	The Duke Wu of Zheng attacked the State of Hu	168
194.	Cause for Suspicion	169
195.	When Mi Zixia fell into Disfavour	169
196.	He's Jade	170
197.	Guessing Game	171
198.	Bian Que	171
199.	The last Ruler of the Shang Dynasty	172
200.	Zihan	172
201.	Wang Shou	173
202.	Preoccupied	173
203.	Zip across the Horizon	174
204.	The Eye cannot see its Lashes	174
205.	Zixia and Zengzi	175
206.	Snakes in a Dried-up Pond	176
207.	Distant Water can't put out a Nearby Fire	176
208.	A Drunken Shao Jimei Lost his Leather Coat	176
209.	An Old Horse knows the Way	177
210.	Useless Talent	177
211.	A Daughter's Marriage	178
212.	Appraising Horses	178
213.	Xuyou's Self-imposed Exile	179

214.	Three Lice competed for Blood	179
215.	A Self-biting Snake	179
216.	A Ferocious Neighbour	180
217.	Wenzi shunned Sefu	180
218.	The Big Bell's Arrival	180
219.	Dreaming of the Cooking Stove	181
220.	The Deep Ravine in Shiyi	182
221.	Gold Pilferer	182
222.	The King of Yue and the Heroic Frog	182
223.	Making up the Number	183
224.	The Marquis Zhao of Han	183
225.	Merger, to Be or Not to Be	184
226.	Power and Influence	184
227.	Prayers of Husband and Wife	184
228.	A Beauty lost her Nose	185
229.	The Duke's Chef	185
230.	Buy the Casket without the Jewels	186
231.	A Singing Sheji	186
232.	A Mother Monkey on the Thorn's Tip	187
233.	A White Horse crossed the Checkpoint	188
234.	A Matter of Age	188
235.	Painting on a Pod	189
236.	Easier to Paint a Ghost than a Man	189
237.	A Solid Gourd	189
238.	A Child's Game	190
239.	Making a Pair of Trousers	190
240.	Bozi's Wife and the Soft-shelled Turtle	191
241.	Distorted Interpretation	191
242.	Buying Shoes	191
243.	Wearing Purple	192
244.	An Army of Justice	193
245.	More Haste, Less Speed	193
246.	Example is better than Precept	194
247.	An Apology	195
248.	Keeping One's Promise	195
249.	Kidding the People	196
250.	Confucianists do not Play Chess	196
251.	Ximen Bao as Administrator	197
252.	Why Gong Yixiu did not Accept the Fish	198

| 253. | Antilogy | 198 |
| 254. | Wait for Gains without Pains | 199 |

*Guoyu

| 255. | The Virtue of Poverty | 200 |

*Record of the Warring States

256.	The Magical Shooter	202
257.	Two Wives	202
258.	A Better Way to Kill the Tigers	203
259.	Bian Qiao and the King of Qin	203
260.	Persistent Rumours Shake the Strongest Confidence	204
261.	The Girl at the River Bank	204
262.	The Divine Tree	205
263.	Deception	205
264.	Paint a Snake with Feet	206
265.	Mud Man and Mahogany Man	207
266.	Talented People	208
267.	There is no Victor	208
268.	A Clever Rabbit has Three Burrows	208
269.	Don't Want to be an Officeholder	209
270.	Attacking the State of Di	210
271.	The Borrowed Majesty of the Tiger	211
272.	A Vicious Dog	212
273.	Mend the Fold after a Sheep is lost	212
274.	Elixir of Life	213
275.	A Frightened Bird	213
276.	An Aged Pedigreed Horse	214
277.	A Minor Sacrifice	215
278.	A Promise	215
279.	The King of Wei's Comment on Music	215
280.	A Lie, If Repeated Often Enough, Will Be Accepted as Truth	216
281.	Poles Apart	217
282.	Taming Dog	217
283.	Driving	218
284.	A Fervent Quest for Talent	218
285.	Salesmanship	219

| 286. | When the Snipe and the Clam Grapple | 219 |
| 287. | The Bride | 220 |

*Kong Congzi

288.	Angling	221
289.	Asperation	221
290.	The Wish of the King of Wei	222

*The Book of Mountains and Seas

| 291. | A Braggadocio | 223 |
| 292. | *Jingwei* the Mythical Bird | 223 |

*Notes on the Book of History

| 293. | Love Me Love My Dog | 224 |

*New Book

| 294. | Pestles Float on Blood | 225 |
| 295. | The King of the State of Guo | 226 |

*Huainanzi

296.	Mi Zijian	228
297.	A Shouter	228
298.	Thieving as an Expertise	229
299.	The Duke Mu of Qin	230
300.	A Chivalrous Man	231
301.	Overload	231
302.	Aggravation	231
303.	A Man of Ying sells his Mother	232
304.	Yanghu	232
305.	A Blessing in Disguise	233
306.	To Build or not to Build a City	233
307.	Tian Zifang	234
308.	Duke Zhuang and the Praying Mantis	234
309.	Monkey's Meat	235

*The Unofficial Biography of Hanshi

310. The Gatekeeper's Daughter 235
311. An Old Woman and her Daughter-in-law 236
312. Butcher Tu 237
313. National Treasure 237
314. Congratulation of a Different Kind 238

*The Historical Records

315. Call a Stag a Horse 239
316. Nail Drives Out Nail 240
317. To Lie on Faggots and Taste Gall 241
318. A Dog without its Master 241
319. Promising Young Man 242
320. Change of Attitude 243
321. A Silver Tongue 244
322. To Look on with Folded Arms 244
323. Gifted 245
324. Maosui 246
325. Besiege Wei to Rescue Zhao 247
326. A Single Word is Worth a Thousand Pieces of Gold 247
327. My Humble Opinion 248
328. Soaring up the Sky 249
329. The Funeral of a Horse 249

*The Book of Rites

330. Tyranny is Even More Dreadful Than Tigers 251
331. A Handout 251

*Xin Xu (New Foreword)

332. Quill and Down 252
333. Shengong Wuchen 253
334. Two-headed Snake 253
335. About Jade 254
336. Shooting at a Rock 255
337. Lord Ye Professed to Love Dragons 255

| 338. | Tianrao Left the State of Lu | 256 |
| 339. | Blighted Grains | 257 |

*On Imperial Gardens

340.	Flattery for Profit	258
341.	Three Bad Omens	259
342.	Dereliction of Duty	259
343.	Study by the Light of a Candle	260
344.	Sacrificed a Little, but Asked for so much	260
345.	The Foolish Old Man	260
346.	The Mantis Stalks the Cicada, Unaware of the Oriole Behind	261
347.	The Teeth are Gone and the Tongue Remains	262
348.	Figure of Speech	262
349.	The Owl is Moving to the East	263

*On the Laws of Nature

| 350. | A Sheep in Tiger Skin | 263 |

*New Commentary

| 351. | Make-Believe | 264 |

*The History of the Han Dynasty

| 352. | Prevention is Better Than Cure | 265 |
| 353. | Parochial Arrogance | 265 |

*Mouzi

354.	The Sound of Music	266
355.	The Likeness of Unicorn	267
356.	Live and Learn	267

*Lun Heng

| 357. | Born at the Wrong Time | 268 |
| 358. | Fowls and Dogs Turn Immortals | 269 |

| 359. | The Man with a Fur Coat | 269 |
| 360. | Frost in the Sixth Moon | 269 |

*The Book of a Recluse

| 361. | A Mascot | 270 |

*The Book of Jokes

362.	Parrot	271
363.	Divorce	272
364.	The Soup is not Salty Enough	272
365.	Holding Meat with the Teeth	272
366.	Shade the Eyes with a Leaf	273
367.	A Scrooge	273
368.	Meeting the County Magistrate	274
369.	How the Punt-pole Passed the City Gate	275
370.	Cooking the Bamboo Mat	275
371.	Glueing the Tuning Pegs	275

*Shenjian

| 372. | Driving Chickens | 276 |
| 373. | A Peephole View | 276 |

*Principles of Social Customs

374.	When the City Gate Catches Fire	277
375.	Itching to Have a Go	277
376.	False Alarm	278
377.	The God of Salted Fish	279

*The History of Later Han

378.	The Fallen Cooking Pot	280
379.	Covet Sichuan after Capturing Gansu	280
380.	The Pigs of Liaodong	281
381.	Tiger or Dog	281
382.	The Gentleman on the Beam	282

*Strange Tales

383. Ghost-catcher Song Dingbo 283

*On a Myriad Matters

384. A Matter of Opinion 284

*The Collected Works of Ruan Sizong

385. An Army of Lice 285

*The History of the Three Kingdoms

386. A Hearty Welcome 286
387. Too Happy to Think of Home 286

*Looking for the Gods

388. Boring the Rock with a Wooden Drill 287
389. Chinese Lute 288
390. The Mysterious Crane 288

*Bao Puzi

391. A Plum Tree on the Mulberry 289

*The Biographies of Gods

392. The Vicissitudes of Human Affairs 290

*Random Notes on the Western Capital

393. A Bright Mirror Hung High 291

*Fuzi

394. Ask a Fox for its Skin 292
395. Watching the Huge Legendary Turtle 292

396.	Relaxing in the Shade	293
397.	Looking for a Perfect Horse	293
398.	No Way to Meet an Urgency	293
399.	The Bird with Golden Wings	294

*The History of the Jin Dynasty

400.	Lying on the Ice	295
401.	The Old Man of the Eastern Suburbs	295

*Old Tales Retold

402.	Cutting the Mat to Sever Relations	296
403.	Fellow Victims	297
404.	White Crane	297
405.	Bitter Plum	298
406.	Perfect Poem	298
407.	The Sun is Closer to Us	299
408.	Imitating Pan Yue	300
409.	Turn Over a New Leaf	300
410.	Gone is the Music with the Man	301
411.	Kong Qun is Fond of the Bottle	301
412.	The Crane that Does Not Dance	302
413.	Feed on Fancies	302
414.	A Hot-tempered Person	303

*Tales of the Dead and the Living

415.	Falcon	303
416.	The Wooden Pillow of Jiaohu God Temple	304

*Confirmation

417.	The Parrot Put out a Fire	305

*The Garden of Strange Happenings

418.	Dancing Pheasant	305

The History of Song, One of the Southern Dynasties

419. The Maddening Spring 306

Stories by Yin Yun

420. Drill a Fire 307
421. The Dream of Yangzhou 307
422. World of Fantasy 307
423. Emperor Xiaowu's Notion of Donkey 308

A House of Gold

424. The Rich Man Wants Another Sheep 308
425. Saving the Drowning Man 309
426. A Scented Room for the Stuffy Nose 309

Liuzi

427. Appraising Jade 310
428. Yiqiu Lost a Chess Game 310
429. Miscalculation 310
430. The Big Tripod 311
431. Stone Cows Excrete Gold 311

The History of Wei

432. Breaking Arrows 312

The History of the Southern Dynasties

433. A Chosen Neighbour for the Price of Ten Million 313
434. Different Names for the Same Bird 313

The History of the Northern Dynasties

435. Killing Two Eagles with One Arrow 314
436. Wang Hao lost his Horse 314

*Tales of Funny Jokes

437. An Amnesiac 315
438. Purchasing a Slave 315
439. The Tiger and the Hedgehog 317
440. Boat Tower 318
441. Play on Words 318
442. The Fifth Sage 319
443. An Earthern Hat for a Fool 319
444. Salvaging the Black Beans 320

*The Dong Gaozi Collection

445. The Two Horses of Feilian 321

*The Dharma Park and the Pearl Forest

446. Hitting the Mosquito 322
447. Monkeys Rescue the Moon 322
448. Jealous of the Reflections 323

*Preface to the Inscription of the Orangutan

449. Drunken Orangutan 323

*The Complete Record in and out of the Imperial Court

450. The Key is Here 324
451. The Lion King and the Jackal 324
452. Horse Canon 325

*A Li Xiashu Prose Collection

453. The Osprey Catches the Fox 325
454. The Fledgling and the Old Ox 326

*The Collection of Yuan Cishan

455. In Praise of the Tiger and the Snake 328

*Dream on the Pillow

456. Gold Millet Dream 329

*The Liu Hedong Collection

457. The Hunter Plays Wind Instrument 330
458. The Biography of *Fu Ban* 330
459. Drowned for Money 331
460. The Elk of Linjiang 331
461. Tricks of the Guizhou Donkey 332
462. Mice 332
463. The Dogs in Guangdong Bark at the Snow 333
464. Globefish 334
465. Fake Medicine 334
466. The Huge Whale 335
467. The Horsewhip Trader 335
468. A Dragon Banished from Heaven 336

*The Han Changli Collection

469. On the Subject of Horse 338
470. The Biography of Mao Ying 338

*The Liu Yuxi Collection

471. Dim Mirrors 342
472. Medicine 342

*The Li Wengong Collection

473. A Rooster without Cockscomb 344
474. National Horse and Gallant Horse 345
475. The Phoenix lost Support 346

*The Biography of Prefectural Magistrate Nanke

476. A Dream 347

*A Mixed Collection of Strange Tales from Youyang

477. Flies 349
478. Partners in Crime 349

*Shenmengzi

479. A Roadside Well 350

*The Lize Series

480. Metamorphosis 350
481. The Wild Dragon 351

*The Pizi Literary Collection

482. Mistaken 353

*The Leisure Advocate

483. Money Can Move the Gods 354

*Slanderous Talk

484. Heavenly Roosters 354
485. The Wizard of the State of Chu 355
486. The Old Man of Qi and the Old Woman Next Door 356
487. What the Woman of Yue Said 357

*Notes on the Well-known Paintings of Successive Dynasties

488. Add the Finishing Touch 358
489. Double-barreled Move 359

*Elves and Goblins

490. A Seamless Heavenly Robe 359

*Poems and the Stories Behind Them

491. A Broken Mirror Joined Together 360
492. A Charming Face Among Peach Blossoms 361

*Wunengzi

493. The Venomous Bird and the Poisonous Snake 363
494. The Owl and Omen 364
495. A Handsome Young Man 365

*Views and Events in the Tang Dynasty

496. A Pedant 367

*Jade Hall Chitchat

497. A Cangued Tiger 368
498. Wild Geese 369

*Petty Talks of Dreams in the North

499. Passing Fish Eyes for Pearls 370
500. A Sichuan Monk Versus the Mountain God 371
501. *Mai Wang* 372

*Recent Events in Southern Tang

502. Beat the Grass to Startle the Snake 372

*Record on Passing the Wisdom of Buddha in the Reign of Jingde

503. Like a Parrot 373

*The Ouyang Wenzhong Collection

504. Practice Makes Perfect 374
505. A Leather-like Face 375
506. A Magic Mirror 375

507. The Bell 376
508. All broke into a Loud Laugh 376

*The Collected Works of Sima Wengong

509. Gathering Firewood 377
510. The Poison of Scorpion 378
511. The Food Cart 379

*Lessons in Statecraft

512. Will You Kindly Step into the Jar? 380

*Random Notes at Xiang Mountain

513. Tradition 381

*The Collection of Master Guangling

514. By Way of Analogy 381
515. Mistaken a Horse for an Ox 383

*The Complete Works of Wang Linchuan

516. Fang Zhongyong 384

*Mengxi's Sketches and Notes

517. Take Advantage of a Loophole 385
518. Dread the Toll of Bell 386
519. The Selfish Deputy 386
520. Miscalculation 387

*The Complete Works of the Two Chengs

521. Turn Pale at the Mere Mention of a Tiger 388

*The Seven Collections of Dongpo

522. Analogues 389

523. The Cuttlefish 390
524. Body Worms 390
525. Northerners go Underwater 391
526. The Frightful Appearance of Tiger 391
527. The Shepherd's Dream 392
528. Cunning Mouse 392
529. Dismiss the Physician and Reject the Medicine 392

*Dongpo's Sketchbook

530. Dependent on Others 394
531. Poor Scholars Talk about their Ambitions 394
532. Longevity 395
533. The Merchant of Liang 395
534. Words Between the Mouth and the Eyes 396

*Miscellaneous Literary Sketches about Aizi

535. Each One is Worse Than the Other 397
536. Same Age Next Year 397
537. Tracker Half Price 398
538. The King of Qi Wants to Build a City 398
539. Gongsun Long finds his Match 399
540. A Scholar in Yingqiu 399
541. Mistaking a duck for a Falcon 401
542. A Divine Animal Called *Xie Zhi* 401
543. Decapitate the Aquatic Animals with Tails 402
544. The Pleasure and Anger of the Dragon King and the Frog 402
545. Like Father, Like Son 403
546. Even the Devil is Afraid of the Villain 403
547. Opinionated 404
548. The Wisdom of Meat-eaters 405
549. The Mouth is the Door of Misery 406
550. A Surprising Move to Transport the Bell 407

*A Man of Letters Wielding his Trenchant Pen

551. Idolatry 408

*Random Notes in the Governor's Office

552. A Horse that Carries Three Thousand *dan* 410
553. "Colleagues" 410

*The Collection of Retired Scholar Houshan

554. The Brown Bear 411

*The Chicken Ribs Collection

555. Crows 412

*The Literary Circles of the Tang Dynasty

556. The Tiger Pays a Debt of Gratitude 413
557. The Cobbler and the Craftsman 413
558. The Mouth, the Nose, the Eyes and the Eyebrows 414

*Dao Shan's Straight Talk

559. Ancient Books in Exchange for Bronze Ware 414
560. Lifelike Painting 415

*Night Chat in a Secluded Study

561. Twaddle of an Idiot's Daydream 416
562. The Crane Spoils the Way of Nature 416
563. Prime Minister Zhang's Script Type of Calligraphy 417

*Reading at Leisure in a Secluded Study

564. A Matter of Verbal Parallelism 418
565. Shun the Character "Luo" 418

*Old Stories of Quwei

566. Accessible from All Directions 419

Selected Works of Qianyan

567. A Runner in the *Yamen* of Wu Prefecture 420

Notes and Data by the Only Man Awake

568. Where Does the Rice Come From? 421

On the Intellect of the East

569. The Intellect of the East 422

Sketches Penned in an Old Cottage Study

570. The Governor May Commit Arson with Impunity 425
571. The Magistrate Called the General Names 426

Of Tales in the Stillnes of the Night

572. Waterside Pavilion 427

Liu's Old Stories

573. Fortune-telling Department 428
574. The Guest and his Calling Card 428
575. The Cat and the Parrot 429
576. Do it Once More 429
577. Selling Medicine 429

Comic Tales

578. Beat the Monk 430

The Earth's Famous Historical Sites

579. Constant Grinding Can Turn an Iron Rod into a Needle 431

Of Tales in the Field

580. Loyal Magpie 432

581.	Same Bait Different Style	432
582.	The Moth Flying into the Flame	433

*Funny tales

583.	The Late Prime Minister's Distant Nephew	433

*Leader of the Five Lamps

584.	Danxia Burns the Buddha	434

*The Three Theories

585.	Sierra	435
586.	Bees North of the Huai River and Crabs South of the Yangtze River	435

*The Annals of the Song Dynasty

587.	Stand in the Snow to wait upon Master Cheng	436

*Extensive Coverage of Contemporary Events

588.	The Five Virtues of Scabies	437
589.	Scholar Qin Loves Antiques	438
590.	Insatiable Appetite for Human flesh	439
591.	Love "My Elder Brother"	439

*Bo Ya's Zither

592.	The Man of Yue and the Dog	440
593.	The Scoundrels Attach Themselves to the Demon	441

*The Master Shan Yuandai Collection

594.	A Talk on Cat	442

*Conversation with the Recluse Zhan Yuan

595.	Swallow the Dates Whole	442

*Tales by Nancun at Farming Intervals

596. Muddle Along 443
597. A Virtuous Mother Sends Back the Money 444
598. The Golden Hairpin 445
599. To Bark or Not to Bark 446

*Talking of the Outer City

600. The Spider and the Silkworm 446
601. The Robe Caught Fire 447
602. Old Woman Wang's Winery 447

*The Chengyibo Collection

603. Not a Product of Jizhou 449
604. Gong Gong Rams the Mountain 449
605. Rare Treasure 450
606. The Wizard and the Spirit 450
607. The Prince of Chu and the Owlet 451
608. A Pedigreed Horse 451
609. Three Merchants from Sichuan 452
610. Servants Contend for Household Management 453
611. The Magpies Clamour on Account of the Tiger 454
612. Yu Lizi Talks about Wisdom 454
613. Yu Lizi Laments the Crumbling House 454
614. A Nine-tailed Fox 455
615. The Wizard of Luoyang Arouses the Dragon 456
616. A Fake Tiger Faces a Fiercer Animal *Bo* 456
617. Anthill 457
618. The Musk Deer 457
619. The Stork Moves its Nest 458
620. Be Doomed to the Same Fate 458
621. The Taoist Priest Rescues a Tiger 459
622. The Catalpa and the Thorn Bushes 459
623. The Islanders Eat Snakes 460
624. Good-looking Clothes 461
625. A Deserted Son 461
626. Doctor Huan 461

627.	Zhuangzi Commiserates with the Beggar	462
628.	The Respected Old Man of Lingqiu	462
629.	A Broken Promise	464
630.	Butting Bull and Neighing Horse	464
631.	The Duke Ling of Jin is Fond of Dogs	465
632.	Hu Lizi Chooses a Boat	466
633.	Anlingjun	467
634.	The Dog as an Analogy	467
635.	Killing One Horse to Save Another	468
636.	The King of Song Loathes the King of Chu	469
637.	The Macaques	470
638.	A Man of Meng City Berates the Tiger	470
639.	Yu Lizi Admonishes Ji Xian	471
640.	Pangolin as Dragon	471
641.	People of the Dark Valley	472
642.	A Fungus	473
643.	To Know People	473
644.	Bu Wei Seeks Shelter	474
645.	No Difference Between "Fire" and "Tiger"	475
646.	Ju Meng Leaves for Yi Qu	475
647.	Que E Flees to Qin	476
648.	Replacing the Beam	476
649.	Cat, Mice and Chickens	477
650.	Coercive Measure	477
651.	A Nine-headed Bird	478
652.	Shi Kuang Tunes the Musical Instrument	478
653.	Wu Zhiqi and He Bo Go to War	478
654.	Chang Yang Learns Archery	479
655.	The Yue Craftsman	480
656.	Tu Longzi and Duli Confront Each Other in a Chess Game	480
657.	Yu Fu	481
658.	Ruo Shi	482
659.	Leopard Cat	482
660.	Jue Shu Trice Regrets	483
661.	The Man of Qi Curses at Meals	484
662.	Xuan Shi is Addicted to Wine	484
663.	As Luck Would Have It	485
664.	Li Ming Cries Over his treasure	485
665.	Man from a Remote District	486

666.	A Man of Wu and His Ape	486
667.	Sincere Advice and Flattering Words	486
668.	The Groom of Si Chengzi	487
669.	The King of Wu and the Mynah	487
670.	Tall Man and Short Man	488
671.	The Tiger and the Elk	489
672.	Morbid Impetuosity	490
673.	Gongsun Fuji	490
674.	The Dodder and the Climbing Fig	490
675.	In Dread of Ghosts	491
676.	Stealing the Dregs of Wine	492
677.	Ashamed to Use the Jade Wine Vessel	492
678.	The Leaves of Legume	493
679.	The Revered Mr Huang	493
680.	A Confucian Moralist	494

*The Complete Works of Song Wenxian

681.	Zi Liao Chooses a Mate	495
682.	Bei Gongzhi and the Legendary Luminous Pearl	495
683.	Dou Ziban the Hypocrite	496
684.	The Duke Jing of Qi	497
685.	Big Talk	498
686.	The Crow and the Chicks	500
687.	Liezong Zihong	500
688.	The Cat and the Leopard	501
689.	The Bear of Yangdu	502
690.	Quails	503
691.	The Pinworm and the Ascarid	504
692.	Drowning of the Mice	504
693.	The Human Exterior Conceals the Nature of a Monkey	504
694.	A Beast in Human Clothing	505
695.	Oxtail Civet	506
696.	A Fish-loving Man of Zheng	506
697.	A Scholar Fire Fighter	507
698.	Two's Company	508
699.	Disguise	509
700.	Harness the Pig to Plough the Land	510
701.	Wu Qi Abides by his Word	511
702.	To Tell a Lie	511

703.	An Arrow-maker	512
704.	Vanity	512
705.	Perspicacity	514
706.	A Hundred Thousand for the Precious Jade	515
707.	Mr. Shu	516
708.	Burn the House to Rid it of the Mice	516
709.	Right and Wrong	517
710.	Carve the Thigh to Hide a Pearl	518

*The Su Pingzhong Collection

711.	The Cats of Mr. Dongguo	519
712.	The Ears and the Earrings	519
713.	Wisteria and Vine	520
714.	The Golden Pheasant	520

*The Xunzhi Studio Collection

715.	The Wizard of Yue and the Demons	522
716.	Knowledge of Vehicle	523

*The Biography of Aliu

717.	Looking for a Leg of the Bed	524
718.	Aliu and the Saplings	524

*The Dongtian Collection

719.	The Biography of Zhongshan Wolf	525

*The Manuscript With Seven Subjects

720.	Play the Jackal to the Tiger	533
721.	The Game is Up	534
722.	A Poet Who Has Lost All Sense of Shame	535

*Tales of Life's Journey

723.	A Goose Feather Sent from a Thousand *li* Away	535

*Quanzi

724. The Elegance of One's Gait 537
725. In Search of a Master 537
726. The Scarecrow and the Water Birds 538
727. Admiring the Moralists 538
728. The Peacock and its Tail 539

*Follow-up Tales of Aizi

729. Being Serious 539
730. Unblushing Exaggeration 540
731. I'm the Rice 542
732. Amnesia 543
733. Marriage Between a Child and an Old Man 544
734. Crying in Advance 544
735. Biting Dogs 545
736. Castrating a Ram 546

*Hunranzi

737. A Gift from God 546
738. On Cultivation 547

*An Evening Conversation in the Mountains

739. In Dread of the Steamed Bun 548

*A Sketchbook

740. Hard Time for the Blind 549
741. Dispute over the Wild Goose 549
742. To Scratch the Itching Spot 550
743. The Chinese Character for Ten Thousand 550
744. The Tiger Cat 551
745. Stuttering Girls 552
746. Too Many Things to Worry About 552
747. Two Blind Men on a Collision Course 553
748. The Monster Put a Coat of Paint on the Mirror 554

749.	A Book of Model Paintings for Tian and Yang	554
750.	The Nao Scratches Where it Itches for the Tiger	554
751.	Portrait and the Man	555
752.	A Man of Chu Learns to Pilot a Ship	555
753.	Ten Families as Neighbours	556
754.	The Quilt on the Face	556
755.	Addicted to Broth of Entrails	557

*In Praise of Jokes

756.	Mispronounce the Characters for Life	558
757.	The Three Sages	558
758.	Wearing a Felt Cap on a Hot Summer Day	559
759.	A Scholar Buys Firewood	559
760.	An Unlined Jacket and a Lined Jacket	560
761.	To be Blind Has its advantage	560
762.	A Monk and a Sparrow	561

*Shu Juzi

763.	The Myna and the Cicada	561
764.	Black Pearl	562
765.	Release a Beast to Test its Nature	562
766.	To Be Original	562

*Jokes for the Refined Taste

767.	On the Strength of the Father-in-Law	563
768.	The Dog Has fallen Ill	563
769.	Gouge Out the Horse's Liver	564
770.	Borrowed Clothes	564
771.	Golden Eyes	565
772.	A Low Stool	565
773.	In Fear of the Flood Tide	565
774.	The Cat Offers birthday Congratulations to the Mouse	566

*Fun Garden

| 775. | To Borrow an Ox | 567 |

776.	The Target Helps Win the Battle	567
777.	Confucianist Moralists Revile Each Other	567
778.	Geomancy	568
779.	Biscuits made from Distillers' Grains	568
780.	The Monkey	569
781.	Cultivate the Land Together	569
782.	Be a Vegetarian	570
783.	This Monk Eats Shrimps	570
784.	A Table With Dew	570
785.	Selecting the Desired Numbers	570
786.	A Fall	571

*Godly Yu's Personal Stories

787.	Preoccupied with the Lambskin Coat	571
788.	Husband and Wife	572
789.	Disgorge at Someone Else's Gate	572
790.	Collecting the Paper of Song Dynasty	573
791.	Repairing the Leaking Roof	573

*The Fictions of Xuetao

792.	Bore a Hole in the Wall to Shift the Pain	574
793.	There is No End to Learning	574
794.	A One-egg Property	575
795.	The Surgeon	577
796.	A Crafty Disciple's Dream	577
797.	A Mouse's Trick in the Name of the Tiger	579
798.	To Cure the Humpback	579

*Xuetao's Pleasantries

799.	Lonesomeness	580
800.	Sour Wine	580
801.	The Quack Halts the Wind	581
802.	Sing the Praises of Others	581
803.	A Cat to Feed the Young Vultures	581
804.	Shaving the Eyebrows	582
805.	The Tiger Dreads Alms Begging	582

*The Finger Moon Collection

806. Untie and Tie the Bell 583

*Five Assorted Subjects

807. Getting Rich With Two Skills 584

*Humorous Buddhist Allegories

808. Good Friends 585

*Discourse at Random of Things Past and Present

809. Remonstrate Against Twig Snapping 586
810. A Person of Talent and Virtue Practises Physiognomy 586
811. Eating Meat as Punishment 586
812. Taboo 587
813. Looking for the Grave of Seventy-two Generations Ago 587
814. The Revered Mr Chen Abstains from Alcohol 587
815. Expose the Town God to the Sun 588
816. Haunted Houses 588
817. Shen Zhou 589
818. He and Yu Befriend One Another with a Bottle of Vinegar 590
819. Zheng Yuqing 590
820. Three Hundred Jars of Mashed Pickled Vegetables 590
821. Show Off Before a Superior Man 591
822. The Cat with Five Virtues 591
823. A Nice Guy 592
824. To Save a Meal 592
825. Busy Monks 592

*The House of Jokes

826. Giving Birth to a Child is Easier 593
827. Three's Company 594
828. New Bed and New Trousers 594
829. Teaching and Learning 595
830. Riding a Horse on Board the Ship 595

831. Pool Capital 595
832. Shrugging shoulders while walking 595
833. Sitting on the Fence 596

*An Extensive Collection of Jokes

834. Fraud 596
835. Too Subtle to Learn 597
836. On Whom One's Livelihood Depends 597
837. Going Straight or Walking Sideways 598
838. Investigation 598
839. A Taoist Priest Undertakes the Whole Taoist Ritual 599
840. Autumn Cicada 599
841. The Lotus Root and the Ship 600
842. To Prevent Suspicion 600
843. Drop Under the Sedan Chair 601
844. Tea and Wine 601
845. Where There is Money There is Life 601
846. No Transaction on Credit After Death 602
847. Unyielding 602
848. Talking of Giants 603
849. Praises 603
850. Deaf-mute Taboos 603

*Elegant Jokes Chosen with Care

851. Move House 604
852. Night Soil 604
853. The Hoe 605
854. Taoist Magic Mosquito Repellant 605
855. Salted Fish 605
856. Stealing an Ox 606
857. Venerable Sir 606

*The Latest Fad in Jokes

858. Zai Yu Slept in Daytime 607
859. The Hardest Object 607
860. The Tutor Accepts Bribes 607

*The Gem of Jokes for a Smile

861. Live on Others 608
862. Arrested for Being in the Spotlight 608
863. An Ox with Coins 609
864. Urge People to Practise Virtue 610

*A Sea of Million-dollar Jokes

865. A Common Pond Frog 610

*The Zhang Yangyuan Collection

866. A Country Bumpkin 611
867. Legacy 612

*Book Shadow

868. The Parrot and the Crested Myna 613

*The Collected Works of Tianjian

869. Strange Tale of a Bird Nest 614

*The Chunhantang Collection of Poems and Essays

870. The Biography of Old Man Yu 616

*Interpreting History

871. Rich Man 618

*Wu Guan Writes in an Outspoken Manner

872. The Pine, the Bamboo and the Plum 619
873. The Purple Swallow and the Golden Oriole 619

*The Book of Great Concentration

874. Good Physician 621

875.	An Expert at Planning and Management	621
876.	Driving out the Insects from the Mosquito Net	622
877.	The Sick Girl Tips the Decoction	622
878.	Wu County's Famous Physician	623
879.	The Good Man of Jiangli	623
880.	A Man of Chu Contracted Eye Cataract	624
881.	The Skill of Ice Engraving	624
882.	The Powerful Qin Si is Overpowered by a Guest	625
883.	Han Sheng's Prediction	625
884.	Seedlings and the Rain	626
885.	Human Feelings	626

*Ten Assorted Subjects

886.	Brambles	627
887.	The Pine Tree	628
888.	A Dog	628

*Random Writings in the Kanshan Pavilion

889.	Wandering Buffalo	629
890.	The Dongpo Meat	629
891.	The Coin's Eye	630
892.	A Couplet Pledge	630
893.	Money and Life are Joined	630

*After a Few Glasses of Wine

894.	When a Ghost Turns Out to be a Leopard Cat	631

*Random Conversation North of the Pond

895.	The Prime Minister's Grandson	632

*A Collection of Bizarre Stories

896.	Teasing One's Own Daughter-in-law	633
897.	Grow a Pear Tree	633
898.	The Taoist Priest of Laoshan	635

899.	Painted Skin	639
900.	Jia Fengzhi	642
901.	Current of Copper Coins	644
902.	The Mantis Catching the Python	645
903.	Berating the Duck	645
904.	The Black Beast	646
905.	Dragon	646
906.	Wolf Eating Human Flesh	647
907.	The Lion Cat and the Big Mouse	647
908.	Wolf	648
909.	Keeping Louse	649
910.	Shepherd Boys	649
911.	A Chivalrous Bird	650
912.	Elephant	651

*The Southern Mountain Collection

913.	On Birds	652
914.	The Biography of a Poverty-stricken Fellow	653
915.	A Blind Man's View	654

*A Collection of Baihetang's Literary Works

| 916. | Two Monks in the Remote District of Sichuan | 656 |

*Have a Good Laugh

917.	Black Teeth and White Teeth	657
918.	Physiognomy	657
919.	Yield to the Mouse and Hornet	658
920.	The Record of Contributions Kept at a Buddhist Temple	658
921.	The Mute Speaks	659
922.	Burn the Ants, Use the Neighbour's Winnowing Basket	659
923.	Man-eating and Without Spitting Out the Bones	659
924.	A Square Snake	660
925.	Exchange Fingers	660
926.	Uni-leg Trousers	661
927.	The Heart is on the Shoulder	661
928.	The Sparrow Entertains his Guests	662

929.	Ginseng Soup	662
930.	Don't Spoil the Tiger Skin	662
931.	Stealing a Sheep	663
932.	A "Crude" Moon	663
933.	Playing Musical Instrument	663
934.	Concealing the Thief's Garment	664
935.	A Heaven Without the Sun	664
936.	Expropriating Land	665
937.	No One to Grind the Ink Stick	665
938.	Writing an Inscription	666

*The Collected Works of Retired Scholar Meiya

939.	The Spider Combing Its Web	666

*As the Master Holds his Peace

940.	The Obsession to Hold a Government Post	667
941.	Mr. Perspicacious	668
942.	The Tiger Drowned Itself	669

*Pu Lizi

943.	The Deer and the Fly	670
944.	Carrying Tangerines into the City	671
945.	Pigweed Staff	672
946.	Taming a Horse	672
947.	Courtship of a Pedant	673
948.	Produce Flowers but Bear no Fruits	674
949.	The Proper Way to Love a Man	675

*Consonant Bell

950.	Coin Spirit	676
951.	The Hands of the Spirits	677
952.	The Village of Peach Blossom	679
953.	The City of Dung Beetle	682
954.	Tying Up a Tiger	685

955. Lost One's Position for a Coin 686
956. Learning the Art of Flattery 687

*Yuewei's Short Sketches from a Humble Cottage

957. An Evil Spirit at its Wits End 689
958. Sister Li Disguises Herself as a Ghost 690
959. Jiang Sanmang 691
960. Empty Words 691
961. The Ambition of a Wolf Cub 693
962. Tian Buman Upbraiding the Spirit 693
963. There's a Limit 694
964. Looking for the Stone Lions 695
965. The Tiger Metamorphoses Into a Beautiful Girl 696
966. Unable to Cope Without Help 696
967. Everything is as One Wishes 697
968. Drug Presented by a Crafty Man 697
969. How the Old Man Catches the Tiger 698
970. A Haunted House Changes Hands 699
971. A Bookworm 700
972. Two Tutors of Two Family Schools 700
973. Black Smoke 701

*The Collected Works of Qianyantang

974. Two Horses 702
975. Spectators Do Not Speak in a Chess Game 703
976. The Mirror 704

*The Posthomous Papers of Cui Dongbi

977. A Sham Doe Fetus 704
978. Yang's Tobacco 705
979. The Lotus Root Starch of Cizhou 705

*The Collected Works of Jian Songtang

980. A Mad Dog 707

The Luyuan Collection

981. The Tailor 707

Newly Engraved Comprehensive Collection of Jokes

982. Patch Up a Lie 708

In Aid of Conversation

983. Death by Mistake 709
984. Meeting the King of Hell 710

A Collection of Hearsays

985. No Cat is Good in the World 711
986. Cherishing the Donkey 711

The Collected Works of Youhuo Studio

987. The Horse with a Long Mane 712

A Collection of Poems and Essays from the Yinji Studio

988. Notes on Scorpion 714
989. Notes on Pigeon 714

The Complete Works of Ding An

990. Worrying about the Tree 715
991. God's Wish to Bestow Wine Failed 715

Casual Literary Notes of the Studio of Two Kinds of Autumn Rain

992. Debate about the Stones 716

*Qu Ting's Insignificant Talk

993. Phoenix Duck 717

*The Good Laugh Collection

994. Ancient Bricks 718
995. Don't Like Eggs 719

*The Comprehensive Collection of Jokes

996. Arresting the Spirits 720
997. The Spirit's Choice 721
998. A Buffalo Looking for its Phratry 722
999. A Lazy Woman 723

*The Yong An Sketchbook

1000. The Centipede and the Earthworm 724
1001. The Spider and the Snake 725
1002. The Wall Gecko and the Scorpion 725

*Recording a Variety of Events

1003. Wooden Eggs 726
1004. Traffic Accident 727

*A Collection of Merry Talks

1005. The Tortoise and the Magpie Become Sworn Brothers 728
1006. Two Mosquitoes Go for Brothers 729
1007. In a Trance 730

*With a Laugh

1008. Kill the Mule and Ride the Chicken Home 730

1009. "Tall Hats" 731
1010. Engaging a Teacher 731

*Witticisms

1011. Aliases 733
1012. Lepsima Saccharina 734
1013. Firestone 734
1014. The Maggots 735
1015. A Snake Seeking Ease and Comfort 735
1016. The Tortoise and the Crab 736
1017. The Earthworm Learns from the Snake 736
1018. The Fawning Dog 737

A Treasure House of Chinese Fables

The Book of Changes
This is a Confucian classic, a book of devination and philosophical thoughts. According to legend, King Wen of Zhou evolved the principles of *The Book of Changes* when he was imprisoned in Youli (now Tangyin, Henan Province). The book contains profound philosophical thoughts and has been the subject of study and research in later generations with diverse interpretations. Some of the brief sentences embody vivid philosophic theory, and may be regarded as fable in its rudimentary stage.

1. The Ram

A ram butted furiously against the hedge and both horns got entangled.

Had its horns not been caught, it would have gone on to butt against the wagon axle, vying with the wheel for supremacy.

Now that both its horns got stuck, it could neither advance nor retreat.

*

The Book of Odes
The first collection of poetry in Chinese history. The poems collected covered the interval from Western Zhou to the middle of the Spring and Autumn Period, a span of more than five hundred years. It contains dirges composed for sacrificial rites dedicated by the feudal princes to their ancestors, and folks songs from various states. Said to have been sorted out and selected by Confucius, there are three hundred and five songs all told. As Confucius and Confucianism were put on a pedestal from the Han Dynasty onwards,.*The Book of Songs* was also regarded as one of the Confucian classics.

2. Asking for Guidance from Passersby

Once upon a time, there was a man who intended to build a house. He did not know how to proceed, and went to the street corner to seek advice from the passersby. Soon a man came along. He was very old, leaning on a stick, but looked knowledgeable. He drew the old man aside. "Sir, I am going to build a house," he said. "Please tell me whether I should put up a big structure or a small one? Shall I use bricks and tiles, or stones and wood? And where should the house be located?"

This gave the old man a start. After listening to what he said, the old man replied, "Well, we haven't met before, have we? I don't know how many family members you have, and for that matter, how much money you intend to invest in this undertaking. It'll be difficult for me to give you any advice. Why don't you draw up a plan yourself instead of asking a stranger? We'll be talking sheer nonsense after all?" That said, he gave a loud laugh and left. Having no definite views of his own, this man thought he could rely on people he chanced to meet. As a result, apart from sighs and groans, he achieved nothing.

*

**Guanzi*
By Guan Zhong (?-645 B.C.), a statesman in the early Spring and Autumn Period. The book *Guanzi* contains various aspects of his words and deeds compiled and handed down by later generations. It touches on a variety of topics: politics, economy, astronomy, geography, agriculture, education, etc. Even such subjects as Taoism, the Confucian ethical code and the Buddhist doctrine are included. In between the pages a sprinkling of fables are found here and there. There are twenty-four volumes in all. Originally it numbered eighty-six chapters but only seventy-six are extant.

3. Job in a Stable

The Duke Huan of Qi arrived at the stable to look for a horse. He asked the junior official in charge there, "What is the most difficult job in the stable?"

The junior official could not find words to answer the question put to him, and Guan Zhong, standing near by, chipped in, "I was once a horse keeper myself, and I know putting up the tethering palings for the horses is the most difficult job in the stable. If you choose a curved shaft to begin with, then you must use the crooked pieces throughout. The trouble is, the straight ones are no longer needed. By the same token, if a straight rod is selected at the very start, then you will have to put all the curved ones aside."

4. Mistaken Identity

The Dike Huan of Qi went sightseeing on horseback. At sight of him, a tiger in the distance immediately prostrated itself.

The Duke asked Guan Zhong, "I rode a horse today on an inspection tour and a tiger was terrified upon seeing me and dared not move. Why so?" Guan Zhong replied, "I believe Your Highness must have ridden a piebald horse and raced towards the sun. Wasn't it so?"

"That's correct," said the Duke.

"A piebald horse with its mottled fur looks like a *Bo*. The *Bo* eats tiger and leopard. Fear must have caused it to freeze."

*

*Annals of Yanzi
By Yan Ying (?-500 B.C.) styled himself Ping Zhong, a high official of the state of Qi in the Spring and Autumn Period. A native of Yiwei of Qi, he had served under Duke Ling, Duke Zhuang and Duke Jing, and was the author of *Annals of Yanzi* which, in fact, was compiled by those who followed his teachings after his death, based on his words and deeds. The book consists of eight volumes, divided into two hundred and fifteen chapters, and contains quite a few fables, the most well-known being *Yanzi Sent to Chu as an Envoy, Counter the Questions of King Chu*, etc.

5. The Duke Jing Prays for Rain

The state of Qi was facing a serious drought, and Duke Jing called all the high officials to a meeting in order to find a solution. He said, "There has been a severe drought in our area. I was thinking of offering a sacrifice to the mountain god and praying for rain. Do you think this is the right thing to do?"

Yanzi warned against it. He said, "It isn't a good idea, as offering sacrifices will not solve the problem. The mountain god's body is made of stone, and covered with trees and grasses. There has been no rain for a long period of time, and the mountain god is losing its hair for lack of water, while its body has also been ravaged and scorched. Do you think it does not want the rain to come? If it had the power to bring rain, it would have done it long ago. That is why I say it will be futile to offer any sacrifices."

"Since this is the case," the Duke Jing said. "It might be better if I sacrifice to the river god instead, and pray to it for rain?"

"It won't do either!" replied Yanzi. "The river god considers water as its national territory, and the fishes and shrimps as its subjects. The drought has reduced the water level of springs. The river itself is drying up, and the river god's national territory correspondingly shrinks, which threatens to have all its subjects wiped out. Do you think it is not anxious? Should it be within its power to bring rain, it would have done so long ago. That is why I say it will also be useless to sacrifice to the river god."

6. Cherish the People

It was the coldest time of the year. With the roaring north wind and the large snowflakes whirling in the sky like myriads of feathers, the vile weather continued for many days. It was pitch-dark outside, and the plaintive cries of the people of Qi could be heard throughout the land. Hunger and cold had snatched away many lives, and corpses were seen everywhere.

The Duke Jing of Qi was wearing a silvery fox-fur robe, light, soft and comfortable. He was sitting inside a beautifully decorated pavilion, cozy and warm as springtime, enjoying the songs and dances. Nearby a red-hot charcoal fire kept the room warm, and on the table in front of him spread the choicest delicacies of land and sea, and top-quality wine. After drinking for a while, a film of sweat on Duke Jing's forehead was just becoming evident when in came Yanzi, his entire body covered with white snow.

"It's a bit queer," Duke Jing began. "Despite so many days of heavy snow, one doesn't even feel a little chill in the air."

"Do you really not feel any chill?" Yanzi countered, and Duke Jing smiled.

After a little pause, Yanzi said, "I've heard that in the past, whenever he enjoyed a good meal, the virtuous sovereign would think of his hungry subjects, and, whenever a warm robe was wrapped around his body, he would think of those who suffered from cold. But it is of course very difficult to carry it into practice!"

7. Killing Three Warriors with Two Peaches

Gongsun Jie, Tian Kaijiang and Gu Yezi all served under the Duke Jing of Qi. They were renowned for their courage throughout the length and breadth of the country, as each and everyone of them could kill a tiger with bare hands.

One day, Prime Minister Yanzi happened to pass by them, and he walked with small steps to show his respect to the warriors, but the three men ignored him.

Yanzi was infuriated and went to the court to see Duke Jing. Reporting the incident, he said, "I've heard that the warriors their virtuous sovereign kept understand the principle of righteousness, and adhere to proper propriety towards their superiors, so that rebellion can be prevented within the state. They become a force de dissuasion to the enemies outside, their accomplishments recognized by those above, and their courage admired by those under them. Theirs is a high prestige job, and they deserve liberal wages and benefits. The warriors now served under Your Highness, however, do not fit the description. They neither do justice to their sovereign, nor do they pay attention to the proper propriety towards their superiors. They will not be able to prevent rebellion within the country, nor will they deter the enemies from invading our land. In fact, they are the bane of the state and its people. We'll be much better off to get rid of them now."

Duke Jing said, "All three men possess immense physical strength. If force is intended, a match may not be forthcoming. On the other hand, if death is what we seek, assassination may not be the best way either."

"These three men may be bellicose, powerful, and defy mighty foes, but they lack the sense of comity," Yanzi said. He suggested to the Duke to give them two peaches with this instruction: "Share the peaches among you in accordance with the merits each one of you earned."

"Yanzi is a clever chap indeed!" Gongsun Jie looked up to the heavens and drew a sigh upon hearing these words. "He suggested to Duke Jing that we share the peaches in accordance with the merits each of us earned. If we refuse, our famed bravery will be at stake; on the other hand, if we accept, it will be difficult to share the peaches fairly and equitably, as there are more men than peaches. The only alternative now is to evaluate services of each and render rewards accordingly. I've defeated a boar in my first attempt, and on my second, I've killed a tigress. I consider myself to have contributed much, and so I should have a peach to myself without having to share it with anybody." Accordingly, he picked a peach and stood up.

Tian Kaijiang said, "Weapon in hand, I've twice repulsed the enemies' ferocious attack. Such contribution certainly deserves a peach all to myself!" So saying, he took the remaining peach and left his seat.

It was now Gu Yezi's turn to speak, "I once followed our sovereign across the Yellow River, and a big soft-shelled turtle snapped at the left side horse of our carriage, hauling it to the middle of the river, where the current was swiftest. Seeing this, I could no longer afford to swim at my own pace. I dived to the bottom of the river in hot pursuit. I was forced to go against the strong current, and covered more than a hundred steps before I could glide along with the swift river. I walked under the water for about three miles ere I caught up with the big soft-shelled turtle and killed it. I held the tail of the left side horse with my left hand and used my right hand to hold the head of the soft-shelled turtle up high as I vaulted sprightly to the surface like a red-crowned crane. Those at the ferry-crossing were taken by surprise and exclaimed, 'Ah, here comes the river god!' On closer look, they discovered it was my raised right hand with the soft-shelled turtle's head. Contribution like this should qualify me for a peach without having to share it with anyone! Why don't the two of you hand over the peaches?" He unsheathed his sword as he spoke, and stood up.

At this point, Gongsun Jie and Tian Kaijiang chipped in, "It is true we cannot compare with you in courage and contribution, and it was sheer greed and selfishness on our part to have appropriated the peaches. After what happened, if we still go on living, how can we still call ourselves brave warriors?"

They both committed suicide by cutting their own throats.

Gu Yezi said, "Since they are both dead, it would be the height of insensibility if I refuse to die. To humiliate other people with words in order to show off is to be devoid of righteousness. To be struck with remorse and yet do not have the courage to die is cowardice. Come to think of it, it would indeed be proper and fair for the two to share one peach; and myself get the other one." Gu Yezi was so ashamed of himself that he returned the peaches and cut his own throat also.

Thereupon the messenger returned to report to Duke Jing. "All three of them have committed suicide," he said.

Duke Jing sent his man to help put the appropriate garments on the three warriors and placed their dead bodies in the coffins. The funeral rites took place in the customary manner warriors deserved.

8. Temple Mice

The materials used in the construction of the temple of the village god were twigs, which made up the framework, and mud, which was daubed onto the framework. Mice liked to dig holes and live in this environment. Although ridding the place of mice was desirable, both fire and smoke could not be used, because the twigs inside the walls might catch fire. On the other hand, water might erode the mud walls and bring down the temple. Thus the mice were able to live in comfort and never in dread of extermination since they had the protection of the temple god. Come to think of it, there are such mice-like people in the state too.

9. A Wine Seller

Once upon a time, there was a wine seller in the state of Song. Inside his establishment, all the utensils and drinking vessels were kept spotlessly clean, and the tavern sign in the form of a streamer was hoisted high and eye-catching. Despite everything, however, clients were few and far between. It was believed that wine, when not sold in its proper season, would in time turn sour. He thought the situation very odd, and went asking his neighbours as to why it was so.

His neighbours told him, "Your dog is so ferocious. Whenever it catches sight of any visitor, it will rush head-on at him, barking furiously and even nipping at people who come near the establishment. Imagine just how anyone dare come to your door to get wine? I'll be surprised if your wine is not left to become vinegar!"

10. The Golden Jug and the Decree Written in Vermilion

After the state of Ji had been subjugated, the Duke Jing of Qi arrived there on an inspection tour, where he came by a golden jug. He took off the lid and found a piece of writing penned in vermilion ink, which read: "Eat only one side of the fish; don't turn it over and eat the other side; and don't ride on a horse of inferior strain." Upon reading the inscription, Duke Jing exclaimed, "That's exactly right! Not to eat the reverse side of a fish is to have an aversion to its offensive smell; and not to ride on a horse of inferior strain is to say it is unfit for a long journey." Yanzi, however, disagreed. He said, "It's not the correct explanation. Not to eat the reverse side of a fish means not to exhaust the people's energies, and not to ride on a horse of inferior strain is not to give way to the villians by the sovereign's side, who manipulate power for personal ends." The Duke Jing asked, "Since the state of Ji possessed such national treasure, why was it that it still could not avoid being annihilated?" Yanzi replied, "There are causes behind a country's downfall as a rule. I've heard that the sovereign's decree should be hung at the entrance of a street. The state of Ji, however, put the country's administrative maxim in a jug. How could the country not perish?"

11. The Groom's Wife

Yanzi was the prime minister of the state of Qi. One day, he was inside a coach while passing through a busy shopping area. The groom's wife, who was standing in front of the door at one side of the street, saw her husband sit in the high carriage drawn by a team of four horses, and proudly brandish his whip as he shouted at the beasts with his nose in the air. When the groom returned, his wife packed up her possessions and demanded a divorce. The groom was scared out of his wits and wanted to know the reason. His wife said, "Even though Yanzi is less than six feet tall, at least he is the dignified prime minister of a state, known to all the feudal princes. Today I saw him sitting in the coach, his head bowed and absorbed in thought, in appearance very humble. When I turned to look at you, a groom, you appeared so cocky and put on such a show, as you drove the coach with all your eight-foot stature. It goes against the grain for me to live with a conceited man." The groom was greatly ashamed of himself as he heard his wife's criticism. From then on, he was very careful about his behaviour whenever he was driving. Yanzi was surprised when he discovered the change in his groom, and tried to seek an answer. The groom told him the truth. Yanzi praised him for being amenable to good advice. Later, he recommended him to be a senior official in the government.

12. Selling Horse-Meat as Beefsteak

The Duke Ling of Qi liked to see women in men's clothes and let all his concubines, women attendants and maids in the palace dressed as men. Soon it became a vogue in the country. Duke Ling was very angry, and thought it an offence against decency. He ordered every official in the state, "Should any woman be found wearing man's clothes, her dress must be rent to ribbons, and her belt cut." Despite the ban, the fad went on unabated.

One day, Duke Ling was with Yanzi and he took the opportunity to seek his opinion, "I've issued a stern warning and adopted a rigid step, why is it that the practice has not stopped?"

Yanzi replied, "Has Your Highness ever noticed that, in some meat markets, they hung up the head of a cow in the shopfront, but sold horse-meat on the sly. The fact that Your Highness allows the palace women to put on the clothes of men but wishes the nation not to follow is tantamount to selling horse-meat as beefsteak. How can the ban be carried out? If one hopes those below not to mimic, one must first of all not set an example himself."

Duke Ling saw the point and followed his advice. Within a month the fashion died out.

13. The Duke Jing and the Art of Oneiromancy

The Duke Jing of Qi suffered from nephrosis and became bedridden for more than ten days. One night, he had a dream, in which he fought with two suns and was ultimately beaten. The next morning when Yanzi presented himself at court, Duke Jing told him, "Last night I had a dream during which I fought with two suns and lost. Do you think that was an omen of my imminent death?"

"Please summon the Oneiromencer at once," said Yanzi.

Yanzi then went outside the palace to wait for the oneiromencer. Soon the diviner of dreams arrived and Yanzi said to him, "The king had a dream last night during which he fought with two suns and lost. He wishes to know if it is an omen of his imminent death. He has requested your presence so that you can interpret the meaning as to whether it bodes ill or well."

"Shall I tell the king the reverse of what he believes in my interpretation?" the oneiromencer asked.

"Put it this way. You should say pathologically the king's illness is *yin*, and the sun is of course *yang*. Since one *yin* could not have overcome two *yang*, the king's illness will soon disappear. Yes, please proceed in this train," said Yanzi.

And the oneiromencer explained to the king the meaning of his dream in accordance with Yanzi's suggestion. As expected, the king's illness recovered three days after the meeting took place. The king wanted to give the oneiromencer a reward, but the latter refused to accept credit, saying, "It was Yanzi who taught me the method, and I've done nothing worthy of praise."

The Duke Jing again wanted to bestow a reward on Yanzi, but Yanzi said, "To be efficacious, my words must be spelled out through the mouth of the oneiromencer. If it was I who spoke, you would not have been convinced. That is why the honour belongs to the oneiromencer, and not to me at all."

Duke Jing was very pleased. He praised Yanzi, "Since Yanzi doesn't want to claim credit for himself, and the oneiromancer doesn't conceal the fact, it is but fair that both be equally rewarded."

14. Yanzi as an Envoy to the State of Chu

Yanzi was sent to the state of Chu as an envoy. The Chu people knew Yanzi was a short fellow and wanted to insult him. They constructed a small door beside the normal one, and waited for him in front of the small door. Yanzi read what was in their mind and resolutely refused to enter through the small door. He said, "Only an envoy sent to a country of dogs enters it through an opening for dogs. Since I am an envoy sent to the state of Chu, naturally I should not enter it by this small doorway seemingly for dogs." The welcomers saw that Yanzi was not an easy man to cope with, and they decided to let him go in through the normal entranceway.

When the king met Yanzi and noticed that he was short in stature, he was displeased and said, "Can't the state of Qi send someone else?" The implication was that why must the state of Qi send such an unseemly person. In a calm and unhurried manner, Yanzi replied, "The capital of Qi, Linzi, has a total of seventy five hundred families. With so many people, their sleeves spread out will form a shade, and wiping off their sweat drops makes it look like rain. The country is so overcrowded with people that you may describe the sight as side by side, shoulder by shoulder, one follows on the heels of another. How can you say the state of Qi is short of people?"

The king of Chu asked him, "If as you say, why should your king send you then?"

"The state of Qi draws a distinction when making a decision as to which envoy should be sent to what country, i.e. it dispatches a virtuous man to a virtuous king, and a less virtuous man to a less virtuous king. I, the least virtuous person, is therefore being sent to the state of Chu."

15. The Tangerine and the Trifoliate Orange

Yanzi was about to travel to the state of Chu as an envoy. When the king of Chu received this information, he said to the officials around him, "Yanzi is a man of Qi gifted with a silver tongue. I intend to humiliate him when he arrives. Do you have any suggestions?"

His attendants proposed, "When he arrives, we beg to have a criminal trussed up and brought past in front of Your Highness as you receive him. Your Highness will ask who the trussed-up man can be, and we shall answer that he is a man of Qi. Then Your Highness will continue to inquire about the nature of his criminality, and we shall reply that he is a thief. In this manner, he will be humiliated."

As Yanzi arrived in the state of Chu, the king gave a banquet in his honour in the palace hall. When they had become mellow with wine, several palace guards were seen escorting a criminal with hands tied behind his back across the hall.

From a distance the king saw what happened and asked, "Who is the person bound?" The guards replied, "A man from the state of Qi." "What law has he violated?" asked the king again. "theft!" the palace guards said.

The king of the state of Chu turned his head to look at Yanzi and said, "Are the people of Qi addicted to stealing?"

Yanzi stood up in a flash. In a severe tone he replied, "I've heard that the tangerine tree will bear the tangerine fruit when it is grown south of the Huai River. If it is replanted north of the River Huai, however, it will turn into the trifoliate orange tree. Despite their resemblance, the fruit each bears tastes strikingly different. Why? It is because the water, soil, and natural environment are all different. The people of Qi today will never steal when they reside in Qi; but they will learn to steal after arriving in Chu. It may be because the environment of Chu is condusive to stealing!"

Upon hearing these words, the king of Chu produced a forced smile and said, "It is futile to play jokes on a sage. I was thinking of humiliating Yanzi but, instead, I had brought redicule and contempt upon myself."

16. Prices of Artificial Limbs and Shoes

During the reign of the Duke Jing of Qi, corporal punishment was cruel, and it often happened that a man's feet were cut off. At that time, a new profession came into being, and that was the sale of artificial limbs.

One day, the Duke Jing, out of kindness, urged Yanzi to move to a better residential area. He said to him, "Sir, your house is too close to the market place. It is small and noisy. Why don't you move to a quieter place?"

Yanzi thanked him but said, "There is no need for that. The place was once my father's living quarters (Yanzi's father, Yanruo, was also the prime minister of the state of Qi). I have less merit and virtue than my deceased father, and this house is already too extravagant for me. Besides, it is close to the market and convenient if I need to get a thing or two in my spare hours during the day."

Duke Jing smiled and added, "Since you live near the market, do you know the prices of commodities, sir?"

"Of course I do," Yanzi replied.

"What prices of commodities are up, and what down, then?"

"Talking of up and down," Yanzi replied, "I notice that the prices of artificial limbs have risen on a day to day basis because the supply cannot meet the demand; and the prices of shoes seem to drop daily because the demand is slack."

Duke Jing's face fell upon hearing these words. As time progressed, the cruel corporal punishment of having a criminal's feet cut off was used less indiscriminately.

17. Zhuzou Lost the Bird, Zhuzou Must Be Punished

The Duke Jing of Qi loved to go bird-hunting, and Zhuzou was entrusted with the care of the birds he caught. One day, Zhuzou was careless and one of the birds flew away. This made Duke Jing very angry, and he ordered Zhuzou executed. Yanzi, by his side at the time the order was given, said, "Zhuzou has committed three crimes. Could you please let me enumerate them before the execution is carried out?"

Thus Zhuzou was summoned before Duke Jing, and Yanzi began to count his crimes. "Zhuzou," he said, "the king has entrusted you with the care of the birds, but you are negligent in the performance of your duty, and let one of the birds fly away. This is your first crime. Because you lose a bird, the king is obligated to kill a man. This is your second crime. You have created the impression among the states that the king values a bird and belittles the life of a scholar, and that is your third crime." This said, he turned towards Duke Jing,

"My good king, I've finished enumerating Zhuzou's crimes. Please proceed with the execution!"

Duke Jing, however, changed his mind. "Don't kill him," he said, "and thank you for the advice."

18. The *Roc* and the *Chilo Simplex*

One day, the Duke Jing of Qi asked Yanzi, "Is there an extremely large being in this world?"

"Yes, there is," replied Yanzi. "A certain bird called *roc*. Its feet move among the clouds, its spine is higher than the heavens, its tail lies across the sky, just the neck and the tail occupy the space between heaven and earth; when it spreads its wings, it is hard even to imagine how far they will reach."

Duke Jing then put to him another question, "Is there an extremely small being in this world?"

"Of course, there is," affirmed Yanzi. "In the East China Sea, there exists a kind of worm, which builds its nest on the eyelashes of a mosquito. It multiplies continually there, yet the mosquito does not detect its existence. I am afraid I don't have a clue as to its name. However, the fishermen who operate in the East China Sea called it *Chilo Jiaoming*, or *Chilo simplex*."

*

*A Commentary on the Spring and Autumn Annals
By Zuo Qiu Ming, dates of birth and death unknown. He lived at the end of the Spring and Autumn Period, and was once a court historian of the state of Lu. Tradition has it that the book *Spring and Autumn Annals* was actually a description of the main historical events taking place among the states as recorded by the court historian of Lu. Edited by Confucius, the content of the book is brief, and a number of commentaries has emerged in subsequent years as scholars tried to explain the text, the noted ones being *Gongyang*, *Guliang* and *A Commentary on Spring and Autumn Annals*. The former two paid particular emphasis on argumentation,

and used it to explain the text. The latter collected a large quantity of factual data and became the most important chronicles of the Spring and Autumn Period. The record began in the Duke Yin of Lu's first year (722 B.C.), and ended in the Duke Dao's fourteenth year (454 B.C.).

19. At One Fling

Sometime during the Period of the Warring States, the state of Qi launched an offensive against the state of Lu, and the Duke Zhuang of Lu decided to resist the aggression. Seized with an ardent desire to serve his country, Cao Gui, an ordinary citizen, requested an audience with Duke Zhuang. His friends and neighbours all advised him, saying, "Making war plan is the responsibility of the high officials, who consume meat every day. Why should you mingle yourself with them?" Cao Gui replied, "All the high officials are myopic people; they are incapable of thinking in depth and planning carefully."

Subsequently, Cao Gui sat with Duke Zhuang in the same war chariot, leading the army to meet the troops of Qi. While banners and pennons fluttered in the wind, both sides placed their troops in battle array. As the Qi side rolled the battle drum for the first time, signalling advance, the sound reverberated across the vast expanse of the open ground. Duke Zhuang signalled his men to do likewise, but Cao Gui halted him. The Qi side, seeing no response, began anxiously to beat the drum for the second time. It was only after their battle drum thundered for the third time that Cao Gui said, "Now is the time to advance." Accordingly, Duke Zhuang gave order to sound the first drum and go on the attack. Giving vent to their suppressed energy, the Lu army let out a loud shout and rushed towards the enemy. The Qi troops suffered a crushing defeat, and fled in disorder.

Thus the Lu side carried the day. Duke Zhuang wanted Cao Gui to explain the cause of their victory. Cao Gui said, "In battle, courage is of primary importance. With the first roll of drum, the courage of the troops is at their acme; if this courage is not brought into play, the second roll of drum will dampen their spirits; and with the third roll of drum, their courage will disappear. Since the courage of our troops was stimulated at the sound of the first drum, we were confident that we would win the battle."

20. A Paper Tiger

The Duke Mu of Qin sent his army to attack the state of Jin, and the Duke Hui of Jin led his troops to resist the enemy in person. Before the battle began, Duke Hui ordered his men to hitch the steed from the state of Zheng to his battle chariot. When Minister Qing Zheng learned of it, he said to the Duke, "In the olden days, local horses were used to pull the chariots as a general rule when going to battle. This was because those horses were accustomed to local environment and climate. After having been drilled, they became highly amenable. But now Your Highness have chosen a steed from the state of Zheng. In appearance, the horse seems sturdy enough, but in fact it is as weak as a cat. In the tense atmosphere of the battlefield, it will lose its habitus, and breathing difficulty will cause it to kick and neigh in confusion. If it comes to that, you will be caught in a dilemma; unable to decide whether to proceed or to retire. As you will then not be in a position to continue fighting, you will regret having chosen this steed."

The Duke Hui of Jin, however, turned a deaf ear to Qing Zheng's advice, and decided to harness the steed from the state of Zheng to his chariot and to do battle. As a result, when the war drum was sounded, and the battle began, the steed from the state of Zheng began to lose its nerves. It leaped and hoofed, and became unmanageable. The chariot was thrown into a mud pit and could neither go forward nor retreat. The Duke Hui of Jin was at his wits end and had to shout for help. However, before reinforcements arrived, he was caught by the Qin army and taken prisoner.

21. Sensual Pleasures and Noble Ambition

Chong Er, the prince of Jin, became a fugitive in the state of Qi. The Duke Huan of Qi had him married to a girl of noble birth, and bestowed on him twenty coaches. Chong Er was content with this blissful life, and no longer think of leaving the state of Qi. His subordinates, however, did not wish to stay there forever, and took steps to persuade Chong Er to run away, for which purpose they gathered under a mulberry tree to discuss the matter.

It so happened that a silkworm raising girl was up on the tree at that moment, and she reported what she heard to Chong Er's newly-wed wife, nee Jiang. Jiang immediately had the maid put to death, and said to Chong Er, "It is an excellent thing that you have the noble intention of going abroad to pursue your own ambition! I've already killed the girl, who knew your plan."

"Nothing of the sort," Chong Er flatly denied.

"Act quickly and flee! A true man steeped in sensual pleasures is apt to spoil his good name," Jiang urged him. But Chong Er did not believe it was a problem, and his wife had to enlist the help of his uncle, Zifan. Together they devised a plan to get him drunk, and have his subordinates carried him to the coach as they started off.

22. Take a Risk

With the restoration of his ancestors' once dominant position among the states in mind, the monarch of the state of Jin, Duke Ling, led his military forces to a place called Fu (now Yuanyang, Henan Province) inside the state of Zheng and stationed there. Then he proceeded to notify several small states to come and form an alliance. As he suspected the monarch of the state of Zheng to have colluded with the big state of Chu in the south, he had excluded it from becoming a member.

The news came to the ears of the monarch and officials of the state of Zheng, and they became extremely frightened at the possibility of the alliance's attack. Zijia, a senior official of Zheng, wrote a letter to the prime minister of Jin, Zhao Dun, to explain the difficult position of his country, saying it was placed between the two powerful states, Jin and Chu. He added, "Deer is an animal which, when threatened with death, will risk everything to find a sanctuary. If the powerful countries cannot convince us of their good intention and kindness, but intend to subjugate us by force of arms, then the only way open to us is to act like a deer, having the whole nation prepared to fight to the death."

Zhao Dun received the letter and, because he was afraid that the state of Zheng might be driven into a corner and thus determined to fight to the death, he persuaded Duke Ling to allow the state of Zheng to join the alliance.

23. Paying the Debt of Gratitude

During the time of the Spring and Autumn Period, Wei Wuzi, a high official of the state of Jin, had a favorite concubine, who was barren. When Wei Wuzi became ill, as a death-bed injunction, he enjoined his son Wei Ke to let her remarry. Later, when he was at the last gasp, he talked about letting his concubine be buried alive with him. After his father's death, Wei Ke did not allow the concubine to be buried with her husband, but let her remarry to someone else.

Long after that, when Wei Ke met the valiant general Du Hui of Qin in the battlefield, he saw an old man knotting clusters of grass together, which caused Du Hui to trip and be taken prisoner. That night, Wei Ke had a dream, in which the old man told him that he was the deceased father of the remarried concubine, and that he came to help Wei Ke catch the enemy general in order to pay the debt of gratitude.

24. Lost in Wonder

Ji Zha, the youngest son of Mengshou, monarch of the state of Wu, was an extremely shrewd young man in the Spring and Autumn Period. When Mengshou died, and the high officials of the state wanted him to succeed his father as king, he flatly refused to go along with their request. To enable the officials to support his elder brother as the king of Wu, Ji Zha left his own country to visit the other states.

The monarch of Lu had long heard of his good name and, when Ji Zha arrived there, he was very warmly received. As he was also known to love music and art, the monarch ordered the best musical and dancing troupes in the country to perform and amuse him.

The music of Lu had its origin in the *Book of Odes* compiled by Confucius, putting together the songs gathered from various states to become a collected edition. As the musicals were being performed, Ji Zha voiced his opinion as he watched. Not only was he able to point out from which state the songs originated, but he could also talk about their evolution, merits and demerits. Listening to his conversation, the high officials of Lu all admired his erudition.

Finally, the *Shao Huo* dance was performed to the music, which was so wonderful that Ji Zha rejoiced and applauded in admiration. "Exquisite!" he said. "It seems not even heaven can contain, nor the earth hold it. When a piece of music has attained to such high excellence, it has indeed reached its zenith. Even if there are other musical performances, I would rather not watch them."

25. Forgetting One's Ancestry

In the year 525 B.C., Queen Consort Mu of the King Jing of Zhou died. All states sent their representatives to attend the funeral rites and paid tribute to King Zhou. From the state of Jin, however, only two representatives, Ji Tan and one other came, and no tribute or gift had been presented. At the reception to welcome them, the King Jing of Zhou asked them, "Every prince paid tribute to the imperial court, why should the state of Jin be an exception?"

Ji Tan replied, "All the princes have received grant of territories and handsome reward from the imperial court, which enable them to pacify their own countries, and permit them to pay tributes to the Son of Heaven. The territories conferred upon the state of Jin, however, are in the outlying mountain area, where reward from the Son of Heaven cannot reach. Furthermore, we share common border with the minorities like the *Rong* (an ancient name for the peoples in the west) and the *Di* (a term given to northern tribes in ancient China). The imperative of preserving peace keeps everyone busy day in day out. How can we still have the ability to pay tribute to the imperial court?"

The King Jing of Zhou was greatly annoyed upon hearing these words, and he enumerated the events which had taken place before, beginning with the annihilation of Shang Dynasty (which was later renamed Yin Dynasty; c.1800-1200 B.C.) by the King Wu of Zhou and the large quantity of Yin's wealth that had been left in the state of Jin, and went on to relate how every successive dynasty had bestowed gifts on the state of Jin, which could all be found in the historical records. To conclude, he reprimanded him, saying, "Your ancestors were court historians in charge of the annals of the state of Jin, and these events were chronicled by them. How can you forget your own ancestors?"

26. A Rooster Pecking its own Tail

Bin Meng went on an excursion in the countryside, where he saw a rooster making a desperate effort to peck its tail, which completely bewildered him. He tried to find out the cause, and his attendants said, "May be the rooster is afraid of becoming a sacrificial offering."

Hastily Bin Meng returned to the city to report to the king of Zhou. He said, "Is it possible that the rooster is afraid of being offered as a sacrifice by men? . . ."

27. The Power of Tears

During the Spring and Autumn Period, in the fourth year of the Duke Ding of Lu (506 B.C.), Wu Zixu, as commander in chief, led the huge army of the state of Wu to attack the state of Chu, and occupied its capital Ying. Wu had an old friend by the name of Shen Baoxu. In the past, when Wu Zixu's father and elder brother were executed by the king of Chu, Wu had vowed to avenge their death. At that time, he said to Shen Baoxu, "I will certainly annihilate the state of Chu." Shen Baoxu replied, "You may annihilate the state of Chu, but I'll resurrect it." Now that the state of Chu had lost its capital, and King Zhao had fled, Shen Baoxu, as promised, went to Qin alone, hoping to draw the support of the Qin army.

At that time, the Duke Ai of Qin was on the throne. He was unwilling to send his troops at first, and so he accomodated Shen Baoxu in a hostel. Shen Baoxu said, "My sovereign has fled to the wilderness and hidden in the tussock without a place for the night at this very moment. How can I feel at ease and go to sleep here?" And he stood beside the main gate of the Qin palace, leaning on its walls, lamenting unremittingly for seven days and seven nights, refusing to take even a bite of cooked rice or a mouthful of water. The Duke Ai of Qin was greatly moved and summoned him to an interview, during which the Duke was overcome by his feelings as he sang the poem *Without Clothes*, which contained such sentences as "the king mobilizes the troops, mends the lances and dagger-axes, and shares a bitter hatred of the enemy with you." Nine times Shen Baoxu kowtowed to express his appreciation. Some time later, the troops of Qin set out, and the Wu army was defeated. Thus the state of Chu survived the attack which threatened its very existence.

*

*Master Sun's Art of War
By Sun Wu styled himself Changqing, originally from the state of Qi, a militarist strategist during the Spring and Autumn Period. The dates of his birth and death were unknown, but he lived at about the same time as Confucius. Once serving as general under the King Helu of Wu, he had led the Wu troops to attack the state of Chu and conquered it. *The Art of War*, which he authored, contains thirteen chapters, being China's earliest and the most outstanding book on military strategy. It was regarded as a military classic by later generations.

28. A Snake called *Shuai Ran*

There is a species of snake called *Shuai Ran* in Changshan. If you knock at its head, its tail will turn to aid and support it; if you strike at the tail, its head will come to rescue it; and if you beat its middle part, both the head and the tail will gather to second it.

29. Two in Distress make Trouble Less

There were a state of Wu and a state of Yue in China's Southeast region during the Spring and Autumn Period. As the monarchs of both countries equally sought hegemony, they had mobilized their respective people, urging them to join the army. As a result, there had been war for years, back and forth, as they became inveterate enemies.

Both states faced the ocean on the east, and it was customary for the fishermen to go fishing at sea. At one time, they were caught in a typhoon. With howling wind and torrential rain, the furious storm caused many boats to capsize. Some had their masts broken, others sustained damage to their hull bottoms. Only one big vessel successfully weathered the storm, and thus provided a sanctury for those who fell into the sea. Those rescued included both the Wu and the Yue countrymen. In the face of the typhoon menace, the people of both states no longer saw each other as enemies. Instead, they became as close as brothers. They elected a ship captain, and everyone was allocated work. One rowed, another steered the ship, cooperating in perfect harmony, all efforts directed towards a common purpose in their struggle with the typhoon. Eventually they were able to overcome the terrible ordeal and reach the shore.

*

Mozi
By Modi (468-376 B.C.), name of Mozi, a thinker and statesman of the Spring and Autumn Period. A native of the state of Song (although others believed he was from the state of Lu), he was the founder of Mohism. The book *Mozi* originally contained seventy-one chapters, a collection of writings penned by members of the Mohist school. Only fifty-three chapters are extant. Apart from recording Modi and his disciples' words and deeds, also included are some of the philosophical and scientific works of Mohist School in its later period. The book was compiled by later generations.

30. Wu Mazi seeks Advice

Wu Mazi spoke to Mozi, "You advocate love without distinction, which does not benefit humanity; I propose not to love mankind, but it too has not harmed the human race in any way. In either case, the effect is equally indiscenible. Why should you think you are right, and I am wrong?"

Mozi replied, "Let us cite an example, say, a house along the street catches fire. One of the neighbours gets ready to carry water and extinguish it; another neighbour, on the other hand, is ready to bring more lighted torches to help the fire grow bigger. Both of them have not yet carried out their intention. Who do you think deserves to be called a good man?"

Wu Mazi declared, "Needless to say, the neighbour who intends to fight the fire is a good neighbour, while the one who tries to pour oil over the flames is the bad one."

Mozi smiled and said, "That's correct. Although both of them have not yet done anything, it leaves no doubt in our mind as to who is good and who is bad, and that is also the reason why I think I am in the right, and you are erroneous."

31. The Frog, the Fly and the Rooster

Mozi's disciple Ziqin asked him, "Is much talking a beneficial thing?"

Mozi replied, "The toad, the frog and the fly never stop croaking and buzzing; they talk until their mouths parched and their tongues scorched, but is there any person who listens to them? The rooster, who is the harbinger of dawn, by contrast only crows a few times at daybreak, but arouses the whole world. What is the use of talking too much? Therefore I say, it is the timeliness, and not the number of words, that counts."

32. Silk Dyeing

Watching the workers in the dyeing mill dye the silk, Mozi sighed with feeling, "White silk, when steeped in the green dye, will turn into green silk; when steeped in the yellow dye, will turn into yellow silk. The colour of the silk changes in accordance with which dye the worker puts in. Five times it is dyed, and five times it changes colour. That is why silk dyeing requires great care. And not only the dyeing of silk works in this manner. By the same token, problems of corrupting influence exist in running a state."

33. Blocking the Thief's Exit

A rich man built a mansion with many courtyards and very high walls. After the enclosing walls had been constructed, he had only a small door opened. Once, a thief slipped through the door, and the rich man closed it behind him. As a result, the thief's exit was blocked and had to give himself up.

34. The King of Chu Loves Slender Waist

The king of Chu loved people with slender waists. Consequently, all the ministers restricted themselves to one meal a day. After the meal, they hastened to exhale and tighten their belt, leaning on the wall as they stood up slowly. One year later, all the ministers had grown very pale and thin, and weak in their limbs.

35. The King of Yue loves Heroic Soldiers

The king of Yue, Gou Jian, loved heroic soldiers. He often urged his officials to exert their best effort so as to foster the spirit of heroism in their soldiers.

On one occasion, he sent someone to burn his own ship in order to test the soldiers' courage. When the flames sprang up, Gou Jian shouted at the top of his voice, "All the property and valuables are in the ship!" He personally beat the war drum, and urged the soldiers on to salvage the treasure.

The soldiers, upon hearing the roll of the drums, rushed into the sea of flames regardless of personal danger as they vied with one another to achieve top-notch results. In so doing, they threw into confusion the original formation and, as no one wished to be left behind, some one hundred men were burnt to death. It gave tremendous satisfaction to Gou Jian then, and he beat the gongs to withdraw the army.

36. Compasses and the Square

He who makes wheels always carries the compasses in his hands. He uses them to decide everything in this world as to whether it is round or not. He says, "Anything that coincides with the loci these compasses trace is round; anything that does not is not round. In other words, whether a thing is round or not round cannot escape me." Why is it so? It is because the rule to determine whether a thing is round or not is very clear and definite. The craftsman with his square in hand uses it to gauge whether a thing is square or not. He declares, "Anything that corresponds with the angle this square makes is square, otherwise it is not. In a word, whether a thing is square or not square is entirely clear to me." Why is it so? It is because the criterion is likewise very clear and definite.

37. God Kills the Dragon

On his way to the state of Qi in the northern region, Mozi met a soothsayer. The latter told Mozi, "God is slaying the black dragon in the north today and, as your complexion resembles the black dragon's, you must not go north." Mozi, however, did not believe him, and continued to travel north with a firm determination. When he reached Zihe River in Shandong Province, he ran into the rising tide. Crossing the river was therefore out of the question, and he had to turn back. The soothsayer said, "I told you before that you should not travel to the north." Mozi replied, "The fact is, the southern people cannot go north, and the northern people cannot go south. As far as complexion is concerned, there are dark-skinned people as well as fair-skinned people, but all of them cannot do as they desire. Supposing God kills the green dragon in the east on the first and second days, slays the red dragon in the south on the third and fourth days, slaughters the white dragon in the west on the seventh and eighth days, and butchers the black dragon in the north on the ninth and tenth days, then, according to your interpretation, the whole world must refrain from leaving the door. This is going against the will of the people, and making the streets desolate. Certainly, your words cannot be put into practise."

38. Help Cane a Child

Long, long ago, there was a family who had an overbearing son, a good-for-nothing. His father was exasperated at his son's failure to make good, and picked up a whip to lash him. An old neighbour saw it, and followed the father's example by beating the young man with a stick. "In beating you, I am only following your father's wish," he explained. Wasn't it preposterous?

39. Gong Shu Ban Makes a Magpie

Using bamboo splits and pieces of wood, and working at them with the care and precision of a sculptor, Gong Shu Ban created a flying magpie. He then sent it into the sky, where the magpie flew for three days without falling down. Gong Shu Ban believed it was a very ingenious piece of work, but Mozi thought otherwise, saying, "Although you have created a flying magpie, it cannot compare with the latches on both ends of the shaft made by the craftsman. With a piece of wood three inches long and, in a few moments, using his hands, he had it carved into something that enables the carriage to carry a load of fifty *dan* (each *dan* equals to 120 catties). Only things that are useful to men can be called ingenious. If it is useless to men, then it can only be termed inferior."

*Shenzi

By Shen Dao (c 395-c 315 B.C), a Ligalist in the Warring States Period. Originally from the state of Zhao, he had once given lectures in the state of Qi, where he enjoyed quite a good reputation. The book *Shenzi*, which he authered, had forty chapters, but was lost. Extant are seven chapters compiled by later generations.

40. Flying Dragon

The flying dragon is borne on the clouds, and the soaring snake passes through the dense fogs. As the clouds are scattered and the fogs dissipate, the dragon and the snake will fall to the ground and become like earth worms. This is because the clouds and fogs, which sustain and enable them to fly in the sky, have dispersed.

*

*Shizi

By Shijiao (c 390-c 330 B.C.), a thinker of the Warring States Period. It was said he had come from the state of Lu, though others believed he originated from the state of Jin. He was a contemporary of Mencius and allegedly was Shangyang's teacher. He had played a part in Shangyang's Reform Movement. When Shangyang was executed, he fled to Shu. The book *Shizi*, which he authored, contained twenty chapters, but had long been lost. The extant *Shizi* was compiled by later generations.

41. Meng Ben's Constant Valour

Someone asked the celebrated warrior Meng Ben, "Which do you value more, life or valour?"

Meng Ben's answer was, "Valour!"

The man asked again, "Which is more important, to be an official of the highest rank or to hold on to your valour?"

Again, Meng Ben's reply was, "Valour!"

Finally, the man put to him another question, "Which do you crave most, to be a millionare or a man of great valour?"

Meng Ben's invariable reply was, "Valour!"

The three things mentioned here, life, official position, and wealth were all precious to a man. They were things people generally pursued. But to Meng Ben, they were not enough to exchange for his valour. It was his unshakable faith that made him the bravest man in the army, as he could even subjugate an enemy as ferocious as a tiger or a leopard.

42. Wu Maqi Buys the Poisoned Wine

Wu Maqi was sent by the king of Chu to the state of Ba as an envoy. On his way to his destination, he saw a man carrying two loads of poisoned wine on a shoulder pole. He went forward and asked him, "What is the wine for?"

The man said, "It's poison and is used to kill people."

Once he heard this, Wu Maqi requested that he be allowed to buy all the wine. He did not have enough money with him for the purchase, so he supplemented it by giving away his carriage and horse.

Having bought the wine, he next poured it all into the Yangtse River.

43. The Deer

If the deer does not turn its head but only devotes itself to running at full speed, then even if you use a carriage with six horses to pursue it, you will not be able to even see the dust its running has raised. The reason of its being caught up and captured is its constant looking back for fear of being overtaken.

*

**The Book of Shangjun*
By Shangyang (c 390-338 B.C.), a statesman of the Warring States Period. A native of the state of Wei, his family name was Gongsun,

personal name,Yang, otherwise known as Wei Yang. Initially, he was an official in the family of Prime Minister Wei. Later, he entered Qin to peddle his idea to the Duke Xiao of Qin, and was put in an important position. The reform movement which he initiated boosted the economic development of Qin, and laid the foundation of Qin's growing power. Eventually, he was granted a title and given the territories in Shang, hence his name Shangjun, or Lord Shang, and Shangyang. After the death of Duke Xiao, Shangyang was framed by the feudal nobles and sentenced to be torn limb from limb by five horses with his head severed. He left the book *Shangjun*, which contained twenty-nine chapters, though only twenty-four of it remain. The other titles given to the book are *Shangzi* and *The Book of Shangjun*.

44. Dongguo Chang Seeks the Title of Nobility

In the state of Qi there was a man called Dongguo Chang. He had many wishes, among which was one that would enable him to become a millionare with riches unsurpassed by anyone. Once, his apprentice asked him to help out, but he refused, saying, "I'm hoping to use this money for a title or a reward." The apprentice was so infuriated that he left him for the state of Song. Now, what comments should we give on the matter? Since the things he craved had yet to come, why not complied with the request of his apprentice by saying that he would help him when he had the money.

*

**Wulingzi*
By Chen Zhongzi, also known as Zi Zhong, dates of birth and death unknown, a native of the state of Qi, and a very famous hermit. His elder brother was a high official of Qi and, as he thought it shameful to share his brother's emoluments, he withdrew from society and went to live at Wuling in solitude, hence the name Wuling Zizhong. Later, when the king of Chu sought him to be an official, he fled again, this time living incognito, and working as a gardener. The book *Wulingzi*, which he authored, was not recorded in *the Biographical Sketch* section in *the History of the Han Dynasty* and, for that reason, it was regarded by later generations as being a product of Wei and Jin scholarship.

45. The Snail of Zhongzhou

There was a snail in Zhongzhou (formerly Yuzhou, in Henan) which thought all its life it had accomplished nothing and, after cursing itself roundly, made up its mind to have a big go at it.

Now, if it were to go to Mount Tai, it would have to spend more than three thousand years on the road, it thought; on the other hand, if it were to turn south and go to Jiang Han, it would also take more than three thousand years to arrive there. It reckoned its own lifespan would afford neither journey, as it believed it would die soon.

Having reached that conclusion, it was overcome by grief and indignation, lamenting its misfortune for not in a position to realize its ambition. Eventually, it died on a heap of wormwood, and even the mole crickets and ants laughed at it.

46. Bullrush

Bullrush, also known as sweet sedge, grows under the rock, where it is dark and gloomy. Glittering and translucent in appearance, and bathing in the crystal-clear spring water, it looks carefree and content.

If it is transplanted to the land, sprinkled with dirty water, and exposed to strong sunlight, it will wither away in a very short tiime.

*

*Liezi
By Lie Yukou, dates of birth and death not available, a native of the state of Zheng and, according to legend, a Taoist of the Warring States Period. His life story was also vague, and his name appeared only in *Zhuangzi, Lu Buwei's Annals,* and *Record of the Warring States.* The original *Liezi* had long been lost, and the book we see today was a collection of thoughts and views which belonged to the two Hans and the era before the destruction of Chinese classics by Shih Huang Ti (221-207 B.C.) of the Qin Dynasty, and which many scholars believed were works of the Wei and the Jin eras, camouflaged as authored by Lie Yukou. The value of this book lies in the fact that it preserves a

large quantity of documents and materials of historical significance as well as the many folklores, myths, and fables it contains, which are brilliantly conceived, with profound message, and very popular.

47. The Man of Qi

In ancient times, there lived in the state of Qi (the vicinity of today's Qi County, Henan Province) a certain man who was haunted by the fear that the sky might fall and the ground sink, for in that case he would have nowhere else to go. He was so worried that he could neither eat nor sleep.

Someone tried to soothe him down by saying, "Your worry is unfounded. The sky after all is but a vast concentration of gases. How can it fall down? The ground, on the other hand, is made up of a crust of strong and heavy earth and rocks, which is incapable of sinking. To worry over something that will never happen is making much ado about nothing."

But still, the man of Qi could not put his mind at ease, and said, "Even though the sky may not fall, nor the ground sink, but can the sun, the moon, and the stars tumble down and crush people to death?" People thought such talk ludicrous, and endeavoured to explain it to him, saying, "The sun, the moon, and the stars are gasses that give out light. They follow the innate laws of things in motion, and will not fall to the earth; and even if they were to fall to the ground, they would not crush men to death."

This explanation worked well, for the man of Qi seemed to understand a little better as, from then on, he put his worry behind him.

48. The Man of Song

In the state of Qi there was a very wealthy man with the surname Guo, while in the state of Song there was a poverty-stricken man with the surname Xiang. Wherefore the man called Xiang went to the state of Qi to seek the man called Guo in order to learn the way of getting rich.

Guo told Xiang, "The reason why I am rich is because I am an adept in stealing. In the first year of my career as a thief, I was able to attain self-sufficiency; in the second year, I was already becoming rather wealthy; and in the third, I was really prosperous. Beginning that year, the financial assistance I contributed reached all my neighbours and fellow townsmen." Xiang was overjoyed to have learned the secret of Guo's prosperity. However, he only remembered the part about stealing, but did not ask the how and why of it. As he was anxious to put what he learned into practice, the moment he arrived at his hometown, he lost no time making his way into houses over walls and roofs, boring holes in walls, and helping himself to anything he could lay his hands on. Soon he was caught, convicted and punished. Not only did he not benefit by the undertaking, but even the little that he had before was confiscated. He thought Guo had deceived him, and went to the state of Qi to reprove him.

Guo asked him, "How did you do it?" Xiang acquainted him with the facts, and Guo exclaimed, "Alas! How could you violate the code of conduct, which a thief must follow, to such an extent? Now, let me tell you. I have heard about such things as favourable climatic and geographical conditions. I took advantage of the auspicious moment and the right terrain, with the help of wind, cloud, rain and dew, which these produced, the mountains and forests, swamps and marshes, to cultivate crops, build walls and construct houses, stealing crops, land, timber, animals, fishes and turtles from nature, which would not bring disaster, or cause trouble. All these things were not my own, of course; they were found everywhere in nature. As to gold, jade, and precious objects; grains, silks, wealth, and goods, they are accumulated by man, and not bestowed on him by heaven. Since you stole them, it was but right that you be caught, convicted and punished. Who could you blame for what happened?"

49. Liezi as Archer

Lie Yukou was exhibiting to Bohun Maoren his skills in archery. He pulled the bowstring to its full, placed a cup of water on his wrist before he let fly the arrow. He shot one arrow after another, every arrow hit right at the center of the target; one arrow just went out, another was immediately put on the bowstring. While he was doing this, he looked very much like a wooden statue.

Bohun Maoren said, "This is a common enough skill in archery. It can hardly show your forte when you are not shooting. Suppose we go to climb a high mountain together, step near the precipice, and stop at the brink of the bottomless abyss, can you still shoot with such accuracy?"

Thereupon Maoren ascended the high mountain, came near a precipice, and stood on the brink of a bottomless abyss. Taking a step further, he made an about-turn and went backwards towards the abyss, until two-tenth of his feet overhung the chasm. At this point, he waved to Lie Yukou to go forward. Lie was so terrified that he fell prostrate on the ground as sweat coursed down his back all the way to his heels.

Bohun Maoren said, "A man with superb skill will go straight to an extremely distant place with his eyes casting upwards at the blue sky, and downwards at the yellow spring, and never for a moment will he move a muscle of his countenance. Look at you, both your eyes have already exposed your timidity, and it is evident you are very weak at heart.

50. Shang Qiukai

Fan's son, Zihua, was well-known for the travelling swordsmen he kept. The people of Jin, be it high or low, all respected him. The king of Jin loved him. Although he had no official position, his status was far above the three highest-ranking officials in the imperial court. The two men, Hesheng and Zibo, were the Fan family's most honoured guests. One day, they went for an outing and, when night came, slept in Shang Qiukai the farmer's home. By midnight, the two were still talking about Zihua's prestige and influence, his power to bring about the death of those who lived, and resurrect the dead. To cause a rich man to go bankrupt, and a pauper to become a millionaire would only be the work of a moment. Shang Qiukai had a hard life, having to endure hunger and cold since childhood. He lay huddled up in bed by the north window while the above conversation was in progress, and distinctly heard what was being said. The next morning, he borrowed some provisions and, with a shoulder pole and two bamboo baskets, he set out for Zihua's residence.

Now, those who had any dealings with the Fan family were either noble or rich. They wore costly embroidered dresses, and sat in luxurious carriages. Some looked arrogant and proud, and walked with unhurried steps, as if they considered the whole world below their notice. When they saw Shang Qiukai, old and weak, sloppily dressed, haggard and half-starved, they inevitably held him in contempt, and tried their best to insult and humiliate him, pushing and shoving until they were tired of it. Shang Qiukai, it seemed, did not resent the indignity he received at all.

Thereupon they played another shabby trick on him. Ascended an elevated terrace with Shang, one of them said with an ulterior motive, "Anyone who jumps from here will receive a reward of one hundred ounces of gold." Everyone else in that group cheered, and Shang was enthused by it. He jumped without thinking, like a bird touching down from the sky. He reached ground without suffering any injury to his body. Those watching thought it was just sheer luck. Then they came to a river bend where the water was swift. "Down there you will find jewellery in abundance. If you dive into the current, you will get them," Shang was told. Again, he believed them. He splashed into the water and swam against the swift current. When he emerged, there was indeed a pearl in his hand. By this time, people began to suspect that he must have possessed some kind of Taoist magic, and Zihua allowed him to join the exclusiove club of the rich and powerful.

Not long after that, one day, when everyone was having their feast, the Fan family's storeroom suddenly caught fire. Zihua declared, "Anyone who enters the fire and gets the brocades out will receive a reward proportonate to what he has salvaged." Shang Qiukai fearlessly threw himself into the fire, as if nothing mattered much. In and out of the fire he went, and yet without so much as a little dust on his person, nor any hint of being burnt. Seeing what happened, all the people associated with the Fan family were convinced that Shang Quikai had the Taoist magic. They apologized to him, saying, "We did not know you possessed the magic arts, nor did we know you were an immortal. Please forgive us for being mean to you before. Just think of us as some idiots who could neither see nor hear. May we venture to ask how you came by the Taoist magic?"

Shang Qiukai replied, "I do not possess any Taoist magic. I myself don't understand all that happened. But since things did happen, I might as well tell you the truth. Not long ago, two of your guests lodged in my humble thatched cottage. I heard them talk about Fan's prestige and influence, that he could make the wealthy lose everything and the destitute rich. I was absolutely convinced of what they said and covered a long distance to come here. After my arrival, I found out what I heard was all very true. That was why I had always tried my best to follow your instructions, anxious lest I was not sincere and good enough. I've never thought about the consequences of my actions and nothing seemed to get in the way. It is only now that I know you were actually pulling my leg then. As a matter of fact, I had my doubts on those occasions, and only pretended to be calm and collected. Fortunately I had not either been drowned or burnt to death. When I recall those events, it is as if I experienced yet again the horror of being drowned or burnt. In future, I shall no longer be able to do such things fearlessly."

51. Liang Yang

Liang Yang was an experienced animal raiser. The king You of Zhou, anxious lest Liang's skills might be lost after his death, ordered Mao Qiuyuan to learn the art of animal husbandry from him. Liang Yang told Mao Qiuyuan, "I am only a lowly domestic servant. Where can I find any unique skill to pass on to you. I'm worried the king may think I've concealed anything from you, so let's talk about my experience in raising tiger. A tiger will be pleased if gratified, and irritated if defied. This is the common character of all animals. They do not get inflamed without cause. That is why I always take care not to provoke them. However, they should not be pampered or overindulged. Pleasure will turn into irritation in case of overkill, and vice versa, because it is not the right way. My method is to take the middle course, neither to overindulge, nor to provoke them. The birds and animals take me as their own kind. Living in my garden, they feel comfortable, and do not recall the forest or the great lakes. In other words, the animals in my garden do not wish to return to the remote mountains and the deep and secluded valleys. The reason is as I have mentioned."

52. Seagull

Upon the coast of the East China Sea there was a village. In the village there lived a youngster, who loved seagulls. Everyday he would paddle a small boat and go out to sea to look for seagulls as playmates. This went on for a long period of time, and the seagulls became well acquainted with him. Tens, and even hundreds, of them would gather, now hover above the boat in circles, now touch down and rest on the shipboard. Sometimes they even flew onto his arms, and remained there like intimate friends.

One day, when the young man returned home, his father said to him, "I've heard that you are in very good terms with the seagulls. How about bringing one back tomorrow?" The young man promised to do just that.

The next day, he paddled the little boat to the sea like any other day, but he was no longer his usual self. He looked nervous as he lay in wait for the seagulls. That day all the seagulls only circled above the boat, not even one of them would venture to come down.

53. Blow Hot and Cold

Long, long ago, a man, who was an expert in raising monkeys, kept a flock of these sprightly, mischievous primate mammals. The monkeys, though could not talk, understood perfectly well any commands their master cared to issue, and that made their master loved them even more.

Then came a year of scarcity when the farmers reaped nothing at harvest time, and acorn nuts, the food of the monkeys, were hard to get. What remained at home, the master reckoned, was not enough to last for the whole winter, and he decided to start a regimen of rationing. He knew, however, that it would not be plain sailing to carry out his plan unless he gave some thought to the matter. When evening approached, he summoned all the monkeys together, and told them, "Beginning tomorrow," he said, "everyone of you will only get three nuts in the morning, and four in the evening for your meals." When the new arrangement was proclaimed, all the monkeys grinned wryly and became unruly. Seeing that the monkeys manifested apparent discontent, the master paused to think. Then, his tone became conciliatory as he announced, "Ok, how about getting a four-nut meal in the morning for each, and three in the evening? Agree?" All the monkeys were greatly pleased by this announcement. They jumped and danced for joy, as if celebrating for victory.

54. Yin

Yin was a millionaire. However, his mind was completely occupied with worldly affairs, and in worrying about his family property. As a result, he was physically and mentally exhausted. He slept poorly at night, and usually with bad dreams, in which he more often than not became someone's servant, when he was being ordered about to do all kinds of manual work, taken to task at every turn, and even got insulted or beaten with a stick. At night, he moaned and groaned and shouted in his dreams till the break of day. Yin felt very uneasy, and called on his friend to seek advice. His friend said, "Your social standing should bring honour to your person but, since you are far richer than most people, your becoming a servant in dreams is quite natural, as it reverses joy and sorrow. Why, how can you be rich in the daytime, when you are awake, and again in dreams?" After the conversation, Yin relaxed his control over his servants, and tried not to worry excessively. In due course, he recovered from his illness, and his health improved.

55. The Litigation

During the Spring and Autumn Period, there lived a woodcutter in the state of Zheng. One day, when he was chopping firewood in the mountain, a red deer rushed out in a state of panic. He raised his axe and struck it head-on, killing it at one blow. He had intended to pick it up when he made the return journey, but he was afraid someone else might see it. So he hauled the red deer to a dry ditch, and covered it in a down-to-earth manner with plantain leaves.

But in his excitement who would have thought he should forget the very location he concealed the red deer. After spending a long time looking for it, he became quite confused and came to believe he had only dreamed about it. On his way home, he told everyone about the strange dream he had. An idler heard the conversation and made a mental note of it. Following the woodcutter's description, he went to the mountain in search of his quarry. Sure enough, the dead deer was discovered hidden in a ditch.

The idler was beside himself with joy at the discovery. He carried the deer on his shoulder, sneaked home, and told his wife, "A woodcutter talked about having killed a deer in his dream, but forgotten the place he had hidden it. Now that I've found it, he must have had a good dream indeed! Ha! Ha!"

"Don't rejoice too soon," his wife said, twitching her mouth. "I'm afraid it was you who had been dreaming, and it was about a woodcutter who came by a deer. Was there really a woodcutter like you said? If you truly got the deer, then you must be dreaming for sure."

The idler replied, "Anyway, I've found the deer. Who cares about what dream anyone else had?"

Now, let us talk about the woodcutter. When he returned home, he was still harping on his "dream". At midnight, he had a veritable one, in which he remembered the precise spot where the deer was concealed, and he also saw the idler who had stolen it. The next morning, he followed the trail shown by the dream, and found his way to the idler's home, where he noticed the red deer hanging in the central room. A dispute followed, and they grappled with each other all the way to the court.

The judge, having found out the real situation, said to the woodcutter, "It was a fact you came by the deer, but lied that you dreamed about it. When you really had a dream, in which you saw the deer being taken away, you thought it was a reality. And you," the judge turned around to face the idler, and said to him, "You have found a deer, but your wife believed you were dreaming. Great stuff! That proves you all have been dreaming. Nobody actually came by any deer at all. But since we have a red deer here, why don't you halve it and share with each other?"

When the king of Zheng learned about the litigation, he laughed merrily and said, "The judge must have been dreaming too."

56. Befuddlement

A man surnamed Pang of the state of Qin had a son, who was very intelligent as a child but, when he grew up, he acquired a strange illness, which made him incapable of differentiating one thing from another. Singing might be mistaken for crying, and white for black; a savoury dish to him might be unpalatable, and sweet turned out to be bitter. If a msitake was committed, he might think just the opposite. In a word, all objects within his purview, such as heaven and earth, the four directions, fire and water, chill and fever, etc.etc., were turned upside down. A man under the surname Yang told Pang, "There are many learned gentlemen in the state of Lu who possess occult powers. Why don't you pay them a visit?" And so the man surnamed Pang proceeded to Lu. On his way there, he passed the state of Chen, where he met Lao Zi, and he told the latter of his son's illness and its symptoms. Lao Zi said, "How do you know your son has contracted the illness? These days people have become befuddled about right and wrong, bemused as regards gains and losses, and because there are so many people suffering from the same illness, nobody ever comes to realize the truth. Moreover, the befuddlement of one man will not endanger the whole family; the befuddlement of one family will not endanger the whole village; the befuddlement of one village will not endanger the whole state; and the befuddlement of a state will not endanger the whole world. If the whole world become befuddled, there will be no more people to get befuddled; and if everyone in the world gets befuddled like your son, then the truth is only you yourself is befuddled. Where is the borderline between sorrow and joy, voice and countenance, sweet and foul, right and wrong? Who can make the distinction? Even what I have just said may only be the words of a bemused person, and the gentlemen of Lu are far more befuddled than I am. How can you expect them to relieve others of befuddlement? You will be far better off if you immidiately shoulder the provisions and begin your journey home."

57. The Return of a Native of Yan

A man, who was born in the state of Yan but grew up in Chu, decided to return to his native place at his old age. He passed the state of Jin on his way home, his fellow traveller fooled him by pointing to a city and said, "This is the city of Yan." The moment he was told this, he became very sad.

The same person again pointed to a temple of the village god and said, "This is your native place's village god temple." He heaved a deep sigh upon hearing this.

Then, they came to a house, and the man said, "This is what your ancestors have left." Thereupon he found himself in agony with tears dripping down his cheeks.

Next, they came to a grave and, when the man said, "This is the grave of your ancestor," he could no longer contain his feelings and cried without restraint.

His fellow traveller burst out laughing, and said, "I've only been fooling you. We are actually still in the land of Jin." This made him feel rather abashed.

At last, they arrived in the state of Yan, and saw the actual Yan's city and town, his native place's village god temple, and his ancestors' house and grave, but he no longer had the same sad feelings as he previously did.

58. *Chilo Simplex*

Living near the river bank was a species of very tiny insects, which people called *Chilo Simplex* for lack of a more appropriate name. They descended in large numbers on the eyelashes of mosquitoes without knocking against one another, and the mosquitoes could not detect their movements. In fact, even Lizhu and Ziyu, famed for their ability to see the fine down of birds in autumn, could not see their bodily form, though they might stare with eyes wide open and brows raised; so also were Shikuang and Guoyu who, with their expertise in tonality and sharp ears, could not hear any sound emanated from them, though they pricked up their ears and bowed their heads. Only the Yellow Emperor and Rong Chengzi, who lived at the peak of Kongtong Mountain, and who fasted for three months until they attained the realm of spiritual stupor and wasted bodily, if they focused their eyesight, could notice that the *Chilo simplex* crowded together in lump or mass, in appearance similar to the hills on Song Mountain and, when they held their breath and listened carefully, could hear sort of *huhu* sound like the crash of thunder.

59. The Foolish Old Man Who Removed the Mountains

The two mountains, the Taixing and the Wangwu, covered an area of seven hundred *li*, and rose to a height of ten thousand *ren* (about twenty-six thousand metres). There were once located to the south of Jizhou, and to the north of Heyang.

The Foolish Old Man lived in the northern mountain. He was fast approaching ninety years old. Right in front of his house was the mountain, and he had to make a detour once he left his house, which, to say the least, was very inconvenient. This was the reason why he had made up his mind to remove the mountain and hew out a path to the outside world. His wife expressed some doubt about the possibility, "With your feeble physical strength, it is difficult even to level a small hill, let alone the two mountains Taixing and Wangwu." The Foolish

Old Man did not contradict her; he headed his sons and grandsons to start digging the earth and chiselling away the stones. Then he loaded them into the wicker baskets and carried them to the Bohai Sea. The son of his neighbour, a widow, then only seven years old, also came to offer his assistance. To and from the Bohai Sea, the round-trip took them from winter to summer.

In the river bend, there lived an old man called Zhisou. He thought the attempt was ridiculous, and came to dissuade the Foolish Old Man, saying, "You are crazy! You are old and weak; it would be too strenuous for you even to pull out a weed. What can you do to these earth and stones?" The Foolish Old Man was displeased, and retorted, "You are too obstinate, and not even as good as the widow's son. Even if I should die, there is my son here. My son will have grandson, and my grandson will give birth to his own son. Thus the line will continue forever, sons and grandsons, without end. On the other hand, the mountain will not add an inch to its height. How can you say it cannot be levelled?" Zhisou was struck dumb and stared in bewilderment at this refutation. And the Foolish Old Man continued to chisel away the mountain.

The mountain god heard their conversation, and was afraid the Foolish Old Man would not stop digging. He went to report to the Jade Emperor. The Jade Emperor was moved by the Foolish Old Man's unswerving determination, and ordered the two sons of the god of unusual strength, Kua-E, to shoulder the two mountains away. One was unloaded at the northern side of Shuozhou, the other at the southern side of Yongzhou. From then on, south of Jizhou and the Han River, there was no longer any mountain to obstruct the flow of traffic.

60. The Sun and Two Children

Confucius went to the east to do some sightseeing. On the way he met two children engaged in an argument, and he asked them why they did so.

One child said, "I'm of the opinion that the sun is nearer to us at dawn, but as the day goes on, it moves further and further away. By noon, its position is the farthest." The other child, however, thought the sun was farther away in the morning, while becoming nearer at noon.

One child said, "At sunrise, its size is as big as the canvas top of the carriage; at noon, it shrinks and is only as big as a dinner plate or the rim of a rice bowl. When an object is farther away, it looks small; when it is nearer, it appears bigger. Isn't it so?"

The other child refuted him, saying, "When the sun first comes out, the air is a little cooler; while at noon, it is as hot as if we immerse ourselves in a tub of boiling water. Isn't it a fact that when the sun is farther away, we feel cool, but when it is nearer, everything warms up?"

Confucius heard all the arguments, but could not decide who was right. The two children jeered at him, "Who says you are the most learned person alive?"

61. Zhan He goes Angling

Zhan He used a silk thread as fishing line, bent a needle to become a fishhook, had a fishing rod made from the slender bamboo pole grown in Chu (today's Hunan and Hubei provinces), and he split a grain of rice as bait. He used this fishing gear in lakes where the water was deep and swift, and was able to catch fish as big as a carriage, yet his fishing line did not snap, the hook did not become straight, and the rod did not bend. The king of Chu was greatly surprised at the news. He summoned Zhan He to his presence in order to know the truth.

Zhan He told the king, "When my father was around, I once heard him said, 'Pu Qiezi used a frail bow and a thin string to shoot an arrow. He watched how the wind blew and with a single arrow he shot down two black-naped orioles flying in the clouds. The reason was his single-mindedness, and the even handling of his strength.' I therefore applied this theory to my angling. It took me five years to master the technique. When I brought my fishing gear to the river bank, my mind had no distracting thoughts apart from complete concentration on the fish. As I threw my line into the water and let sink the fishhook, I took care to act equably, and never overreact. At that moment, nothing in the outside world could disturb my mind. The fish took the bait on my fishhook as dust or bubbles in the water, and without suspicion they swallowed it. This is the theory of the weak defeating the powerful, and counterbalancing the heavy with the light. If Your Majesty will apply this theory in government, the whole world will be within your grasp. There will be nothing to worry about then." As he listened to Zhan He, the king nodded his head repeatedly as he said, "An excellent idea! An excellent idea!"

62. Bian Que

Gonghu of the state of Lu and Qiying of the state of Zhao fell sick, and they went together to consult the celebrated physician, Bian Que. Bian Que gave them medical treatment, and they soon recovered from their respective illnesses. Bian Que told Gonghu and Qiying, "Your past affliction was due to invasion from outside, which spread to the internal organs of the body. They were curable with the use of medicine. But you have contracted another disease, which accompanied your births, and which lodged inside your bodies as you grew up. I propose to have them treated now. What do you think?"

The two men replied, "We should like to hear you describe the symptoms."

Bian Que then said to Gonghu, "You possess intelligence enough and to spare, but weak in temperament. As a result, you are rich in strategem but, because of your vacilating nature, poor in execution. Qiying, on the other hand, is somewhat deficient in intelligence, but he is strong in temperament. In consequence, he tends to make arbitrary decisions. Suppose I undertake to swap your heart for his, each of you will then inherit the other's good points to remedy his shortcomings. That will be beneficial to both sides."

Thereupon Bian Que gave poisoned wine to both men, which made them unconscious for three days as if they were dead. He opened their Chests, took out their hearts, exchanged one for the other, and applied some efficacious medicine. When they came to, they were none the worse in appearance. Having said goodbye to Bian Que, they returned home.

And Gonghu went to Qiying's home to live with the latter's wife and children. They did not know him, however. On the other hand, Qiying proceeded to Gonghu's residence, and lived under the same roof with Gonghu's wife and children. They, too, did not know him. In desperation, the two families took the matter to the court, and Bian

Que was invited to arbitrate the case. Bian Que told them how it all began, and the lawsuit was dropped.

63. Zheng Shiwen

Huba was good at playing the stringed instrument. When he played, birds would follow the rhythm of the music and fly in harmony with it, and the fish would dance. A musician named Shiwen from the state of Zheng heard talk about it, and he left home to learn the art of playing musical instruments from Shixiang, who was also a musician. Three years' practice, however, did not enable him to play a complete and presentable movement. Because of that, Shixiang did not want him to continue, and said, "You can go home now."

Shiwen put down the musical instrument and sighed, saying, "Not that I do not know how to adjust the strings, and play a complete movement. The problem is, my mind is not on the strings of the instrument, and my goal is more than to play a complete movement. When the feel is absent, the musical instrument will not display what you wish it to demonstrate, and that is why from the beginning, I have never been able to let loose my inhibition and go all out to manipulate the strings of the musical instrument. Please give me a few more days, and see how things work out."

Not long after that, Shiwen again went to see Shixiang. "Have the skills of your performance improved?" asked Shixiang. "I believe I've grasped the subtlety of it now. Please let me try a tune on it," replied Shiwen.

Thereupon he began strumming his stringed instrument in earnest. As he came to the tune on spring, he stroke at the *shang* string (corresponding to *re*, the second note in the sol-fa musical scale) to produce the musical sound of southern *lu* opera, and instantly people could feel the warmth that associated with springtime. Then suddenly a cool breeze arose, and the picture of an open country appeared with its meadow and trees, and fruit in abundance. It was an autumn scene. While the autumn song was in progress, he turned to strike at the *jue* string (corresponding to *mi*, the third note in the sol-fa musical scale), and the tune changed so that one felt like experiencing the awful atmosphere of autumn. The breezy warm weather woke up all things on earth, and all manifestations of nature returned with spring. As he was playing the summer tune, he suddenly plucked the *yu* string (corresponding to the sixth note in the sol-fa musical scale), so that from the intense heat of summer, one experienced the return of winter frost and snow with its frozen ponds and rivers: it was a severe winter. Then he plucked the *zhi* string (corresponding to the fifth note in the sol-fa musical scale), and the scorching sun melted all the solid ice. The bitter winter gave way to hot summer. As the movement neared its end, he chose the *lu* tune, as it were, to complement the other four strings. By now the breezy wind began to gently blow; auspicious clouds lingered around, and sweet dew fell from the sky. It was as if one had suddenly witnessed the springs gushing out luscious wine. Shixiang clutched at his heart and stopped breathing, enthralled from start to finish, and so excited was he that he danced with joy. Finally he lavished his unreserved praise on Shiwen for his plucking skills, saying, "Your play is splendid. Even the skills of Shikuang and Zouyan could not have surpassed you in perfection. They can but hold their plucked or wind musical instruments in the hands or under the arm, and followed you as your pupils."

64. Xue Tan

Xue Tan learned the art of singing from Qin Qing. Scarcely had he acquired the skills when he took leave from his teacher and returned home, thinking he had already mastered all the techniques. Qin Qing did not stop him. On the contrary, he prepared a farewell dinner at roadside outside the city. As they were drinking, Qin Qing sang a very sorrowful song as he softly beat time. The sound of singing caused all the trees to vibrate, and even the flitting clouds in heaven halted their movements. Having heard him singing, Xue Tan immediately apologized to his teacher, requesting Qin Qing to let him go back and continue his study. Since then, he never again talked of his desire to go home.

65. Han-e

One day, the space in front of the city gate of the capital of Qi was packed with a dense crowd, who were listening with bated breath to the song a girl was singing. The sound of singing was mellow and full, the tune was sweet and touching, and it could be heard from afar. Many people were entranced by it. The girl, a talented singer, came from the state of Han, and her name was Han-e. She arrived in the state of Qi without a penny to her name, and had to go singing in the streets in order to support herself.

The people of Qi had never heard such wonderful voice, and her singing created a great sensation throughout the city. As Han-e lodged herself in the inn, quite a few enthusiastic fans came lingering by its gate, and remained there for a long time. When Han-e was about to leave Qi, all neighbouring people earnestly begged her to stay. To express her appreciation, she sang once more inside the inn. In so doing, not a few people were moved to tears. It was simply unbelievable that such beautiful voice could exist in the world. A sizeable contribution was subscribed towards her travelling expenses. After Han-e left the inn, it was said her mellow and full voice did not dissipate for a long time. It lingered around the beams for three days.

66. The Story of Yu Boya and Zhong Ziqi

During the Spring and Autumn Period, there was a famous musician named Yu Boya. His contemporary, Zhong Ziqi, was adept at interpreting the meaning of musical sound. Once, Boya was playing the dulcimer alone. He was describing his interests and predilection for music. When he was "aiming at the lofty mountains", Zhong Ziqi exclaimed in delight. "Good!" he said. "Majestic and solemn, reaching to the sky, like the Tai Mountain!" Boya, seeing that the musical sound his stringed instrument produced could expose his ambition, immediately changed the tune to "aspire after the flowing water". As soon as Zhong Ziqi heard it, he was again pleased, and said, "Excellent! Vast and mighty, for ever surging forward, like the ocean and river!" Boya knew he had met someone well-versed in music and very perceptive. He changed his tune again and again but, no matter what he thought, what subject matter he put into his music, Zhong Ziqi was able to interpret accurately. When Boya arrived in Tai Mountain, he was greeted by torrential rain, and had to take refuge under a big rock, which made him very sorrowful. Overcome by his feelings, he played one tune after another. Zhong Ziqi, however, was able to know what was in Boya's mind at the end of every song. Finally, Boya threw away the dulcimer, sighed with emotion, and said, "Well! Well! You are very adept at interpreting the sound of music, and can read what is in my mind. How can I conceal the music, and not let you know my aspirations?" Later, people combined "aiming at the lofty mountains" and "aspire after the flowing water", and shortened it into "Lofty Mountains and flowing water", which means a bosom friend, or a friend keenly appreciative of one's talents.

67. Yan Shi Created a Man

The king Mu of Zhou was touring the western part of the state. After passing the Kun Lun Mountain and nearing theYan Mountain, he suddenly decided to return to the capital. He was still on the way when he met a craftsman, who came to present his handiwork. His name was Yan Shi.

King Mu received him and asked, "What skills do you have?"

Yan Shi replied, "Your Majesty may apply whatever tests. I've made something though, which I'd like Your Majesty to see."

King Mu said, "Good, bring it along with you tomorrow, so we can view together."

The next day, Yan Shi again called on the king. As king Mu received Yan Shi, he saw standing with him there was another man, and he asked, "Who is that man that accompanies you?"

Yan Shi replied, "This is the man I've fashioned, and he will present his performing skills."

King Mu was amazed to see the artificial man, so like a genuine one when he walked, bent his body, or raised his head. How ingenious! Shook his chin gently, and he would sing a melody; stirred his hand, and he would rhythmically danced. As a matter of fact, he could perform kaleidoscopic change, and do whatever you asked of him. King Mu thought he was truly human, and invited his favorite concubines to watch his performance together. When the show was about to end, the artificial man even rolled his eyeballs towards the king's concubines, flirting with them.

King Mu was furious. He thought Yan Shi had deceived him, and he wanted to punished Yan Shi. Yan Shi was so frightened that he dismembered the artificial man at once, and showed all its parts to king Mu, who discovered the components were in fact leather, wood, vegetable glue, raw lacquer, all of which bonded together, and painted in white, black, red, or green colour. King Mu examined the artificial man's liver, gallbladder, heart, kidneys, spleen, lungs, intestines, stomach, his muscles and bones, tendons, his four limbs, joints, skin, hair, teeth, and found them all man-made. They were true to life though, and complete in every detail. He let all the parts be assembled again, and restored the figure he saw when they first met. Then he had his heart removed, so that it would not talk; had his liver extracted, so that it would not be able to see things; dislodged its kidneys, so that it would not be able to walk.

By this time, king Mu was convinced of Yan Shi's truthfulness and, in high spirits he praised him vehemently, saying, "The skills of man can indeed compare with Nature which created everything. Both have achieved similar result!"

68. Ji Chang

Gan Ying was a good archer in ancient times. The moment he fitted an arrow and pulled the bowstring, the animal he aimed at would surely fall and, if it was a bird, it would drop to the ground. His student, Fei Wei, who learned archery from him, was even more brilliant.

There was another man called Ji Chang, who took archery lessons from Fei Wei. Fei Wei said, "You must first of all learn not to blink your eyes before you can talk of shooting an arrow."

Back in his home, Ji Chang lay on his back under the weaving machine of his wife, his eyes stared at the treadle, which moved up and down. For two years he disciplined himself in this way, until he could stand the stab of an awl's pointed end without blinking.

Then he told Fei Wei of his achievement, but Fei Wei said, "It is not enough, because you still have to drill your eyesight. You should be able to view a small object as if it were big, and to see a minute body clearly. When you have reached that state, then come and let me know."

When Ji Chang came home, he took a hair from the oxtail and attached a louse to it before hanging it at the window. Facing south, he focussed his eyes and gazed at it. In ten days, the louse seemed to be growing bigger and, in three years, the louse became as big as a carriage's wheel. From then on, anything bigger then a louse would appear to him like a hill. Ji Chang used an ox horn from the state of Yan to make a bow, and applied the arrow shaft made of northern bamboo to shoot the louse. The arrow went through the heart of the insect, but the hair on which the louse had been attached was intact.

Again, Ji Chang told Fei Wei about his remarkable feat. Fei Wei was so impressed that he danced for joy. Patting the former on the chest, he said, "You have got the knack of archery at last!"

69. Zao Fu

The name of Zao Fu's teacher was Tai Dou.

From the very beginning, when Zao Fu took driving lessons from Tai Dou, he had been very polite, very modest. Three years had gone by, and Tai Dou did not so much as utter a word, but Zao Fu was even more respectful and prudent than before. Then Tai Dou began to teach him, saying, "It was said in an ancient poem: 'The son of a good bow maker must first of all learn how to weave a winnowing fan; the son of a good blacksmith must begin by learning to sew a fur coat.' You must watch carefully how I manoeuvre and, when you can act as I do, you may then hold in your hands the six halters of a carriage drawn by six horses, and drive it."

Zao Fu replied, "I'll certainly follow my teacher's instructions."

Tai Dou next erected wood piles on the ground as path in accordance with a man's pace. That path was so narrow that it can hold only a single foot. He asked Zao Fu to tread on this path. To and fro he had to run without falling down.

Zao Fu followed his teacher's instructions and practised diligently. In three days, he had already mastered all the techniques.

Seeing how fast he learned, Tai Dou exclaimed, "You are smart and nimble, and have mastered the skills very quickly! Generally speaking, anyone who wishes to become a carriage driver must go through this process. Previously you walked a lot, and that must rely on the strength of your legs. The legs and the heart always work in concert, but it is the heart which controls the movement. If we extend this theory to cover carriage driving, then the halters of the six horses and the bits must be arranged to a nicety, the horses' speed and breathing must be uniform and harmonious, the horses must not run too fast nor too slow. To attain all the above, the reins must not be kept excessively tight, nor must they be too loose; they must be just right. Only when one truly understands this principle can one's hands manoeuvre with ease, and in an appropriate manner. That is to say, in our mind we already know what to do and, in order to do it well, it must be done in such a way as to conform to the horses' temperament. In so doing, we will be able to act according to our rule, backwards and forwards, going in a straight line or turning a corner, and no matter how far we go, what distance we cover, our strength will always be sufficient to cope with the situation. The secret of driving lies in the horses' bits, which in turn affect the halters. What benefit we have in the halters will pass to the hands that hold them. Thus the state is reached wherein what the heart wishes the hands accomplish. If we can realize all this, there will be no need to use our eyes, nor do we have to lash the horses with our whips. You will feel very much at ease, just sitting straight with six halters in perfect order without confusion, and the twenty four hoofs touch the ground where they should; be it advancing, retreating, or turning around, all perfectly matched and rhythmical. There will not be extra space to allow wheels to cross into, nor excess room for the horses' hoofs to encroach on. You will not be aware of the danger of high mountains and deep valleys as you advance, nor the wilderness' openness because, to an experienced driver it makes no difference. And that's all I can say regarding my driving skills. I hope you remember them well."

70. The Kunwu Sword and the Fire-wash Cloth

When the king Mu of Zhou mounted a large-scale offfensive against the Western Rong (an ancient name for the peoples in the west), the latter presented His Majesty with a Kunlun sword (a double-edged sword) and a piece of fire-wash cloth. The sword was only about twenty three inches long, but the steel was of good quality, solid and strong.

Tinged with red, the blade would cut clean through a piece of jade as though it were mud. The fire-wash cloth possessed another mysterious property: if it was begrimed, it must be put in a fire to remove the dirt. In the blazing fire, it would turned red as the fire, but the original colour of the grime remained. After it had been, as it were, tempered by the fire, the dirt could be gotten rid of with a few shakes and it would look as white as snow. A man who called himself a prince did not believe there was such a piece of cloth. Xiao Shu, however, said, "The prince is excessively self-confident. He is arbitrary and unreasonable."

71. Power and Destiny

Power was arguing with Destiny about who had contributed more. Power asked Destiny, "What's your contribution that can compare to mine?" Destiny replied, "What makes you think you can stand on a par with me?" Power boasted, "Life and death, poverty and wealth, elite or otherwise, all of these are within my power to give." Destiny said, "Peng Zu's intelligence was not equal to Yao Shun's, and yet he lived to a ripe old age of eight hundred; Yan Yuan's talent surpassed most people, but died in his eighteenth year. Despite Confucius' preeminence in benevolence and virtue, he was stranded in Chen and Cai (states in Zhou Dynasty); king Zou of Yin was certainly a lesser man than Weizi, Jizi, and Bigan, who were officials in his court, but he was the monarch nonetheless. They were others like Jiza, who was considered a wise man, but who had never been granted a title or rank of nobility; Tian Heng of Qi, having killed his king, grabbed all the power in court. Boyi and Shuqi were starved to death in Shouyang Mountain, and Jisun's wealth outstripped that of Liu Xiahui's. If indeed it was within your power to control all those things, why should someone had such a long life while other, so short; the virtuous was destitute while the traitor, prosperous; the wise was lowly, and the foolish became high officials?" Power refuted him by saying, "If, as you have just said, the existence of all those things were not of my making, were they under your control then?" Destiny replied, "Since the name is Destiny, what can my role be? As far as I am concerned, I'll let whatever is straight alone, and I will not interfere with whatever is crooked. Longevity, dying young, poverty and prosperity, noble and lowly, rich and poor, they are all fate, and since they are one's destiny, they do not concern me."

72. Ji Liang's Illness

Yang Zhu had a friend called Ji Liang. Ji Liang had been ill once, and in a matter of seven days, his illness became very grave. His sons all stood around his bed and cried, talking of calling the doctor. Ji Liang said to Yang Zhu, "My sons are all good-for-nothing. Why don't you sing a song to enlighten them?" Yang Zhu then began to sing. The words of the song were: "Since heaven does not show the way, how can man know what to do? Blessings from heaven have nothing to do with it, nor is it caused by man's sins. Can it be you, or is it me? Who knows? The doctor or the witch? How can they ever know?" When the song came to an end, Ji Liang's sons still could not fathom out its meaning, and they invited three doctors, Jiao, Yu, and Lu, to diagnose Ji Liang's trouble. Jiao, having examined him, said, "The cause is the fluctuation of your body temperature, the deficiency and excess not being well regulated, and crapulous, your indulging in sensual pleasures,—all help to bring about a state of anxiety, and set your nerves on edge. Your suffering does not come from heaven, nor is it the work of ghosts and goblins. Although it seems very grave, it can still be remedied." Listening to the diagnosis, Ji Liang commented, "This is an ordinary doctor. He can withdraw now." Doctor Yu then expressed his opinion. He said, "The illness is caused by congenital deficiency, and over abundance of milk after birth. This condition does not come in one day; it was the result of many years' neglect. Now that the disease has spread to the vital organs, it is hopeless." Ji Liang again pronounced his judgement, saying, "This is a good doctor. Please entertain him with a feast." The last doctor to see him was Lu, who said, "Neither heaven nor man, nor ghost or goblin, has caused your illness. As a life form, your body is influenced by the power of nature. Since you already know it is the influence of nature that lies at the root of your trouble, what benefit can either medicine or acupuncture bring?" Ji Liang exclaimed, "This is really a miracle-working doctor. He must be richly rewarded when he takes his leave." And Ji Liang's illness actually recovered without any medicine soon after that.

73. Presenting Sunshine to the King

Long, long ago, there was a peasant in the state of Song. His family was so destitute that he had to wear clothes made from woven sackcloth to pass the severe winter. When spring arrived, he went to work in the field. During the recess, he basked in the sunshine. It was the most comfortable moment in his life, for the warmth of the sun was the best thing he had ever experienced. Besides, he had no knowledge of the comfort of a heated mansion with spacious halls and extensive gardens, nor had he ever heard of warm silk patting robes and fox fur gowns in the world.

He turned his head and said to his wife, "It seems few know the warmth and comfort of basking in the sunshine. Suppose we were to present this discovery to His Majesty the king, we would probably be rewarded richly for it."

74. Guan Yinzi and Archery

Liezi was taking archery lessons and, when he hit the target, he invited Guan Yinzi especially for the purpose of asking his advice and comment.

Guan Yinzi asked him, "Do you know why you can hit the target?"

Liezi replied, "I've no idea."

Guan Yinzi said, "If you don't know, then it cannot be said you have mastered the art of archery."

Thereupon Liezi returned to his quarters to continue practising. Soon another three years had elapsed. He thought he had gained additional knowledge and went to see Guan Yinzi again.

Guan Yinzi repeated the question, "Do you know now why you can hit the target?"

Liezi replied, "I know it now."

Guan Yinzi said, "That means you are now qualified as an archer. You must bear in mind, and never for a moment forget, that this is relevant not only to archery, but the same principle is also applicable to running a country and cultivating one's moral character."

75. The Shis and the Mengs

In the state of Lu there was a man surnamed Shi, who had two sons; one loved the pen, the other loved the sword. The one who was versed in polite letters went to the state of Qi to sell his idea of running the country with the principle of justice and virtue to the king. The king of Qi adopted his suggestion, and invited him to be the prince's teacher. The other son who was adept in martial arts went to the state of Chu to present his art of war to the king of Chu. The king of Chu was very pleased, and appointed him to be a military officer. The emoluments of both sons enabled their family to become wealthy, while the rank of nobility brought honour to their parents.

It so happened that Shi's neighbour, surnamed Meng, also had two sons; one loved the pen, the other loved the sword. They were penniless and frustrated, and admired the Shis' prosperity very much. So they went to ask their neighbours' advice on the subject of position and wealth. The Shi brothers told them the truth.

Before long, one of Meng's sons travelled to the state of Qin to sell his idea of running the country with the principle of justice and virtue. The king of Qin, however, said, "This is the time when the princes all endeavour to annex the world. What I am trying to do now is to make the country rich and the military force efficient. The country will be ruined if I adopt the principle of justice and virtue to run the government." The king, therefore, ordered him castrated and expelled from the state.

The other son went to the state of Wei. He recommended the art of war to the king of Wei. The king of Wei said, "Our country is a small one. Moreover, it is sandwiched between powerful states. I have to fall in with the big states and pacify the small ones. That is a policy of peace and security. If I were to use military force, the day would not be far when my country would be ruined and destroyed. I'll not let you leave this country in peace, for you will then be able to go about influencing other countries, which eventually will prove disastrous to us." The king then gave order to have his feet chopped off before sending him back to the state of Lu.

Back at home, the two sons and their father beat their breasts and stamped their feet, blaming the Shi family for their trouble.

Shi said, "There is a common saying, he who seizes the opportune moment will be prosperous; he who loses the opportunity will be ruined. Although your sons have the same expertise as my sons, yet the results are quite different. This is because the opporune moment have not been located, and not because you have done anything wrong. The world is constantly changing, and the idea of right and wrong is not permanent. Things that were applicable before may have to be discarded today; and things that we dismiss today may prove to be useful in the future. Useful or otherwise, the fact is, nothing is immutable. That is why one must act according to circumstances, swim with the tide, so to speak. That is the only smart way. If one is not resourceful, even though one may be as knowledgeable as Confucius is erudite, and possess political skills as superb as Lu Shan's,—heroes though they were,—there is no scope for displaying one's abilities. How can one not be destitute then?"

Having heard the argument, the Meng brothers and their father suddenly saw the light and, their anger dissipated, said, "We understand the hows and whys now. There is no need to say more."

76. The Mulberry Girl

The Duke Wen of Jin left his palace preparatory to attacking the state of Wei. His son, Chu, threw up his head and burst into laughter. The Duke Wen asked why he laughed?

He replied, "There was a neighbour, who accompanied his wife to her parents' home. On their way, he saw a woman gather mulberry leaves. Smiling, he tried to strike up a conversation with her. As he did so, he noticed someone beckon to his wife. I laughed because of that."

The Duke Wen of Jin immediately saw the message contained in what his son had just said and, cancelling his plan to attack the state of Wei, he ordered his army to return. He was still on his way home when he learned that Jin's northern border was being invaded by enemy forces.

77. Song Yuanjun and the Two Acrobats

In the state of Song, there was an itinerant entertainer who planned to arouse the feelings of Song Yuanjun, the king of the state of Song. Song Yuanjun summoned him to his presence and asked him to show his artistic skills. He obliged by attaching two wooden poles twice as long as his bodily height on his legs, now walking briskly, now sprinting ahead. Then, in sequence, he threw seven swords to the air, caught them one by one as he tossed them, with five of them dancing above his head at all times, dazzling all eyes. Song Yuanjun was amazed as he watched, and rewarded him with money and silk on the spot.

There was another itinerant entertainer, who likewise was adept in juggling. After learning how the first entertainer had been rewarded, he took a leaf from the latter's book, endeavouring to use his acrobatic skills to arouse the feelings of Song Yuanjun.

Song Yuanjun was furious, saying, "Not long ago, someone flaunted his peculiar acrobatics before me but, in fact, those were of no practical use. It so happened I was in good spirits at the time, and rewarded him with money and silk. The one who is here now must have heard the news and come to swindle me out of the reward."

He ordered his subordinates to detain the entertainer, meaning to have him executed.

A month later, Yuanjun's anger subsided and he ordered the entertainer's release.

78. Real Worth is more Valuable than Looks

During the Spring and Autumn Period, Bo Le was considered an expert in surmising the worth of a horse by its looks. He had picked not a few pedigreed horses for the state of Qin. When he grew old, he recommended his friend Jiu Fanggao to the Duke Mu of Qin to take over his work.

The Duke Mu of Qin summoned Jiu Fanggao to his presence, and requested him to find a thorough-bred horse. Three months had passed before Jiu Fanggao reported he had found a pure-bred horse in Shaqiu. The Duke Mu of Qin inquired about the horse's looks, and he answered, "A yellow mare." The Duke Mu of Qin ordered the horse brought to him, and it was "a black stallion". Duke Mu was greatly displeased. He summoned Bo Le and reprimanded him, saying, "The expert you recommended is too incompetent. He could not even distinguish between a mare and a stallion, nor could he differentiate their colours. How can he be trusted to find a good horse!"

Bo Le sighed, and said, "That does prove his judgement of horses a thousand times better than mine. I certainly cannot be compared with him. What he sees is a horse's quality, and not its appearance. He pays attention only to those things he should see, but doesn't care about the things he needn't see. Compared with ordinary horse expert, his method is of course superior by far." Thereupon he asked someone to ride the horse Jiu Fanggao had chosen to appraise its worth. The result did prove the horse to be a rare and superb animal.

79. Niu Que and the Highwaymen

There was once a scholar by the name of Niu Que. One day, while he was driving his carriage across some remote, thickly forested mountain, he heard a whistle and lo, a pack of robbers emerged from the roadside, each with a gleaming frogsticker. They took away his carriage and horses, snatched all his money, and stripped off all his clothes. Having robbed him of everything, the highwaymen were about to leave him when they turned round and discovered Niu Que, sitting upright by the roadside, his appearance calm and without the slightest worry or apprehension. Quite contrary to expectation, he seemed very pleased with himself. The robbers felt rather weird, and asked him, "Hey, we have snatched away all your possessions, and a knife is placed in front of you, but you seem not to have the slightest fear. Why?" In a gentle voice Niu Que replied, "A carriage is for man to sit in, and the function of clothes is only to cover the body. Though you have taken them away, they really do not harm me at all. The sage never let mere worldly possessions spoil his morality." The robbers looked at each other, and burst into loud laughter as they said, "We never read any books, but we have heard of man who does not care for either money or profit, whom people called a sage. It is certain that you, being a sage, will inform against us, the non-sages, once you are in the presence of an official, and we had better kill you first." That said, the knife swiftly followed, and Niu Que had no time even to give a snort before he was dead.

80. Ai Jingmu

Long ago, there was a man from the east, whose name was Ai Jingmu. He was on his way to some other place when, because of exhaustion and hunger, he fell down on the ground, unable to move forward.

A robber named Qiu, who came from the district of Hufu (south of Dangshan, Anhui Province), happened to pass by. Seeing that Ai Jingmu had fainted because of hunger, he fed him with the food he brought for himself.

After eating three mouthfuls, Ai Jingmu recovered somewhat from his weakness and slowly opened his eyes. "Who are you? What's your profession?" he asked.

Qiu replied, "I am a native of Hufu, and my name is Qiu."

When Ai Jingmu heard this, he opened his eyes and said, "What! Are you the famous robber, Hufu's Qiu? Can it be possible that you feed me with your food? I'm a man of virtue and morality. I can't eat the food of a robber!"

Having uttered these words, he supported his body with his hands on the ground, and exerted his utmost to throw out the three mouthfuls of food he had just swallowed. Down from his throat came a cackling sound. He had used up his last strength and fell down, dead.

81. A Lamb Going Astray at a Forked Road

During the Period of Warring States, Yang Zhu undertook serious study and investigation in order to find out the logic behind everything in the material world. He had established his own school of thought, and was addressed as Yangzi, an ancient title of repect for a learned or virtuous man. One day, his neighbour lost a lamb, and requested people to help out, Yangzi's servant included. Yangzi asked, "Why are so many people needed for the search?" His neighbour replied, "It is because there are too many forked roads, and a thorough search cannot be carried out with a few people."

It was not long before everyone of the search party returned with empty hands. Yangzi asked, "Why was everyone unable to find the lamb?" His neighbour replied, "There are really too many forked roads, and every forked road again branches into more forked roads. As we don't know which way the lamb has escaped, there is nothing we can do but to call off the search."

The manner his neighbour talked had Yangzi lost in thought, and even his facial expression changed. For several days, he was unhappy. One of his students asked him, "A lamb is but a domestic animal and, besides, it is not yours. Since it cannot be found, you should forget it. Why can't you put it out of your mind?" Yangzi did not reply. Another student called Meng Sunyang told Yangzi's friend Xin Douzi about the situation. Xin Douzi learned from indirect sources what was in yangzi's mind, and he told Meng Sunyang, "Your master made a connection between the lost lamb and the difficulty of learning. Too many forked roads make the search for the lost lamb difficult; by the same token, there are numerous subjects in the field of study and diverse schools of thought. If one does not have the correct orientation in one's pursuit, one will get nowhere." His students suddenly saw the light. They admired their master's far-sightedness and brilliant understanding.

82. The Dog and Yang Bu

The younger brother of Yang Zhu, Yang Bu, left home wearing a white suit. Because of rain, he was drenched through, and had to borrow a black suit from his friend. When he returned, the watchdog did not recognize Yang Bu and barked at him furiously, barring him from entering the house. Yang Bu was very angry. He picked up a stick and wanted to beat the dog soundly with it.

Yang Zhu hastened to mediate, saying, "Don't beat the dog. Just think, if your white dog leaves the house and comes back turning into a black dog. Can you not mistake it for some other dog?"

83. The Secret of Immortality

Long ago, a man claimed himself privy to the Taoist magic of immortality. The king of Yan heard it, and a man was sent to learn his Taoist magic. When the king's messenger arrived, however, the man who claimed to possess the Taoist magic had died.

Thereupon the messenger came back to report to the king of Yan; and the king was infuriated. He blamed the messenger for being too slow to act, and wanted to kill him, because he did not arrive before the man was dead.

His officials remonstrated with him, saying, "Man worried about death most, and sought after life unremittingly. That man declared himself privy to the Taoist magic of immortality, but died before anybody else. How could he have taught the Taoist magic of immortality to others?"

The king of Yan, listening to the remonstration, suddenly realized the truth, and the messenger was pardoned.

84. Man, Fish, and Wild Goose

In the state of Qi, there was a noted aristocrat surnamed Tian. He had a thousand hangers-on at home, and was very extravagant.

One day, Tian spread a big feast in his spacious hall. His guests brought various gifts, which included fish and wild geese. The host was overjoyed, and said with emotion, "Heaven has been munificent. As you can see, all these fish and wild geese, are they not exist for our food and enjoyment?" All the guests echoed his views by nodding their heads. However, a twelve-year-old boy from the Bao family disagreed. He stood up and said, "I don't agree with what you have just said. Man is a species of the myriad of living things like all the others. Due to the diversity of size and intelligence, sometimes the weak stand as easy prey to the strong in the animal kingdom. But there is no such thing as one species lives for another. Though it is a fact that man does choose things that are edible as food, but that doesn't mean they are prepared by Heaven. The same situation may be found in nature, where the mosquitoes suck man's blood, the tiger and the wolf consume man's flesh. Can you say Heaven has created man for their food?"

85. A Beggar's View of Disgrace

In the state of Qi, there was a poverty-stricken man, who often begged in the city. Every city dweller disliked him because he came ever so often. As a result, he could no longer get any food to eat and had no other recourse but to muddle along in the stable of the Tian family, where he worked for the veterinarian as an odd-job man, just to earn a meal or two.

His townsmen teased him when they met, saying, "Follow the veterinarian simply for the sake of some leftovers. Are you not feeling ashamed of yourself?"

The beggar replied, "The greatest humiliation in this world is none other than to go begging. If begging is not beneath me, what shame is there to follow the veterinarian?"

86. A Contract

A man in the state of Song picked up a lost contract from the road as he was walking. He returned home hurriedly and had it hidden away. In the meantime, he furtively looked at the accounting items, and went about telling his neighbours, saying, "I'll soon become a rich man."

87. A withered Firmiana

The firmiana a man planted withered, and his old neighbour told him it was an evil omen. When he heard this, he instantly had the firmiana chopped down. The old neighbour, on the other hand, brought the withered firmiana back to his home as firewood.

The man was very annoyed, and said, "It turned out his real motive was to get the firmiana for firewood, and that indeed was his reason for telling me to cut down the tree. As he treated me like this despite our being neighbours, isn't it very dangerous?"

88. Suspicion

A man lost his axe. He looked for it everywhere, but it vanished without a trace. He suspected that the son of his neighbour was the culprit. Once he had this idea and looked at the young man again, it seemed his talk, his every movement, his expression, his attitude, all looked like those of a thief who took the axe. He concluded further that the ill-intentioned fellow was indeed the one who stole his axe.

The next day, he went into the hills to gather firewood. Under a tree, he suddenly discovered the axe he lost. He began to remember it was the day before, when he was here to cut firewood, that he had left the axe. As he returned to his home, he again scrutinized the young man's talk, his every movement, his expression, and his attitude, but it seemed none of those bore any semblance of one who stole his axe. Now he said, "Who doesn't have an axe at home? Why should anyone wish to steal somebody else's axe? From the very beginning, I had foreseen he was not the thief."

89. The Man of Qi

Long, long ago, there was a man in Qi who was eager to gain possession of gold. One morning, after putting on his clothes and donning his hat, he proceeded to the market place. Approaching the place where gold was on sale, he grabbed it and ran. Later, he was caught by government officials, who asked him, "There are so many people around. Why are you so bold as to grab people's gold?"

The man replied, "When I grabbed the gold, I only saw the gold, but aslolutely not the people."

*

Zhuangzi
By Zhuang Zhou (c.369-286 B.C), a thinker of the Warring States Period, a native of Meng of the state of Song (the northeast of Shangqiu, Henan Province), once a minor official of the government. He inherited the mantle of Laozi, developed his doctrine, and was the main representative figure of the Taoist school of thought during the Warring States Period. His work *Zhuangzi,* also known as *Nanhua Canon,*

contains thirty three chapters, divided into three sections, the In-section, the Out-section, and the Mixed-section. It is generally believed the In-section was authored by Zhuangzi himself, whereas the Out-section and the Mixed-section might contain the works of his disciples and other Taoist writings of later generations. Many fables, rich in imagination, lively in description, and humorous, are to be found in his book.

90. The *Roc*

The North Sea, or *Tianchi*, the Heavenly Pond, was situated in the North Pole, where neither trees nor grass were to be seen. Inside the Heavenly Pond, there was a fish called *kun*, an enormous fish, its body measuring several thousand *li* in width. As to its length, well, it was quite beyond anybody's guess. Later, the *kun* fish became a big bird, the *roc*, whose back towered like Mount Tai, and whose wings looked like clouds hanging down from heaven. It wheeled above the tourbillion, soaring as high as ninety thousand *li* in the sky, passing through the clouds, with its back to the heavens, and flew towards the south, all the way to the South Sea.

The little *yan*, or quail, who lived by the bank of *Tianchi*, and who had never known the immensity of heaven and earth, derided the big *roc*, saying, "Where is he flying to? I put on a spurt, but the most I can do is only ten or twenty metres high. It is actually a lot of fun flying among the weeds. I believe this is the ultimate height one can aspire to. Where can the big *roc* be flying to?"

As a matter of course, the myopic little *yan* could not have understood the aspiration of the huge *roc*. People now use the phrase "a *roc*'s flight of 10,000 miles" to encourage one to have high aspiration, to face the future with courage, and not be satisfied with the existing state of affairs like the little *yan*, who had no gumption to move forward.

91. Skin Salve

A man in the state of Song had produced a skin lotion to prevent frost crack. Relying on its protection, his family had rinsed cotton fibres in the water for a living for generations. A nonlocal man heard of it and came to him, offering a hundred silver dollars for the formula. To discuss the offer, he convened a family meeting, during which he said, "Our family has been rinsing cotton fibres for generations without making much profit. If we sold our secret formula now, we can get a hundred silver dollars all at once. How about selling it? Please tell me what you think."

When the transaction was concluded, the nonlocal man went to see King Wu, who began to manufacture it. Sometime thereafter, the state of Yue mounted a large-scale offensive against the state of Wu, and King Wu commissioned him to lead the army and defend the country. It was the twelfth month according to the lunar calendar, and the north wind was piercingly cold when the two armies met on the river. The soldiers of Wu applied the lotion to their hands and feet for protection, thus preventing frost crack from happening. As a result, every man was a lively dragon and an active tiger, and the soldiers of Yue fled at the mere sight of the oncoming force. King Wu was overjoyed and the man who introduced the lotion was granted a piece of land.

It was the same skin lotion for the prevention of frost crack, but some got land as a reward for it, while the other could only rely on it for their livelihood as cotton fibre rinsing hands. The distinction was brought about by their methods of application.

92. Play the Lute to a Cow

In ancient times there was a distinguished musician of great attainments, whose name was Gong Mingyi. Gong Mingyi was adept in playing the lute. When he played, it was as if he were in ecstasies, often oblivious of himself. The musical sound he produced was very sweet and pleasing to the ear, as he used the notes to create a harmoniously elegant atmosphere. The listeners were led into the realm of art. People who heard his music would involuntarily put down what they had been doing, inclined their ears and listened attentively. Once, it was the third month of the lunar year, springtime, and he was in the open country. A pleasant breeze blew gently, hundreds of flowers were in full bloom, the grass looked like a green carpet, and it was full of life in every corner. Suddenly he saw a big castrated bull grazing leisurely, and he thought, "My music has brought excitement to many people. Can I likewise move this bull?" As he was thinking, he went closer, plucked the strings of the lute, and played a beautiful melody. However, despite a serious Gong Mingyi and an exquisite tune, the big bull continued grazing with lowered head, completely indifferent to his music.

93. The Shadow

The lighter shade at the rim of the shadow was called *Wang Liang*. *Wang Liang* asked the shadow, "Previously the man walked, and you followed. Now he stopped, and you also stopped. When the man sat, you sat simultaneously; when he stood up, you stood up likewise. Why, haven't you your own personality?"

The shadow replied, "My existence depends on somebody else's support. Actually even my supporter has to have something to rely on to appear as he is. The relation between me and my supporter is similar to a walking snake and its horizontal abdominal scales and, as the cicada, which has to use its wings on its back in order to fly. How do I know why everything exists as it is, and why not?"

94. Zhuang Sheng's Dream and the Butterfly

Zhuangzi once dreamed that he morphed into a butterfly, which could fly at will, and was so happy that he did not know a Zhuangzhou existed. When he woke up, he was surprised to find himself turned into Zhuangzhou. He was not sure whether it was zhuangzhou who dreamed himself morphed into a butterfly, or was it the butterfly which dreamed it had turned into Zhuangzhou. Evidently Zhuangzhou and the butterfly were distinctly different. What had been said above referred to the change and differentiation of things.

95. The Chef Ding

During the Period of Warring States there was a chef called Ding. He was adept in slaughtering cows. When he was in the process of dismembering a cow, he would sometimes used his hands to push it down, sometimes leaned with his shoulders, sometimes stamped on it, and yet sometimes propped it up with his knees. Only the *chichi* sound of the knife at work could be heard, followed by the *shuashua* sound, denoting that the meat and skins were being detached from the bones. The king Hui of Liang was watching on one side. He praised him highly, "Ha, you are wonderful!" he said. "Your skills have reached such a flawless and perfect state!"

The chef Ding said, "In my work, I always tried to master the cardinal principle. In this case, I first learned the anatomy of the cow. As I cut up the carcass, my knife follows the space that exists between the tendons and bones, and separates them without any difficulty. A good chef has to replace his knife every year, an average one change it every month, because he uses his knife without regard to the animal's anatomy. The knife I used is over ten years now, during which time I've dismembered about a thousand cows. Despite frequent use, its blade is still as sharp as if it had just been whetted. There are always some space between the joints and, as the edge of my knife is thin and sharp, wielding it to and fro between the joints is easy, and even delightful."

The king Hui of Liang again praised him, "You have spoken well."

96. Keeping a Tiger

A man kept a tiger. He refrained from giving the tiger live objects to eat, as he feared it might arouse the tiger's desire to seek its prey. By the same token, he did not use a whole carcass to feed it, because he thought ferity might return when it tore the carcass up. He knew well when the tiger would be hungry and adhered strictly to the timetable of feeding. In a word, he tamed it in accordance with its animal nature. The tiger and man do not belong to the same species, yet the tiger follows the instructions of its tamer. It is because man understands its nature and conforms to it. Those who have been killed are the ones who provoked it by going against its nature.

97. An Untimely Slap

A man loved his horse to a fault. His love was such that he used his large wicker basket to hold the horse dung, and let a large conch with a riot of colours be utilized as its urinal.

One day, it so happened that a gadfly alighted on the horse's back to suck its blood. At sight of it, the man's heart ached so terribly that he instinctively slapped it without much thinking. The horse was frightened and shook off its rein and bit, and escaped. The man too had his head broken, and his body hurt.

This is an example of loving with all one's heart does not necessarily benefit the receiver; sometimes it results in harming him. People should be discreet.

98. The Oak Tree as the God of the Land

A carpenter, surnamed Shi, went to the state of Qi. When he arrived at a place called Quyuan, he saw an oak tree being worshipped as the earth god. The tree was so huge that it could give shelter to several thousand heads of cattle. Its trunk measured two hundred arm spans around, towering more than ten meters above the mountaintop, where it began to branch out, and several of its branches could be utilized in ship building. The place was crowded like a market place, as people gathered to watch the spectacular sight. The carpenter, however, continued to move on without so much as taking a look at the tree. The apprentice watched for quite a while before overtaking the carpenter, and said, "From the day I clutched the axe and followed you, my master, I've yet to see such good material. Why was it that my master did not stop and take a look. I don't understand." The carpenter replied, "Forget it, and don't mention it anymore. The wood is bootless. If it is used to construct a ship, the ship will sink; if it is used to make a coffin, the coffin will rot quickly; it is not suitable for tools, because it will break down fast; for door, one must take into account the resin; for pillar, it will be eaten into holes by worms. In other words, the wood is absolutely useless, and it is because of its uselessness, it is able to live such a long life."

Later, when the carpenter returned home, the oak tree appeared in his dream and said, "What do you use to compare me with? Do you take those trees that can be made into something to compare with me? Fruit trees like hawthorn, pear, tangerine, pomelo, etc. are picked when the fruits ripen, during which time the trees are treated roughly, the larger branches being broken, and even the smaller branches are being twisted about. Why? Because they can be utilized to make something, they have to suffer, and die a premature death. This is all their own fault, because they invite people to attack them. All things are the same. I've longed for being useless years ago, but there are still people who do not know and, for that reason, I have been chopped to near death. The fact that I'm still alive is proof enough that my uselessness is very useful indeed. Suppose I were to become useful, do you think I can live till now? Besides, you and I are equally objects, why should you look upon me as worthless, or I consider you as useful? After all you also are a bootless fellow. How can you judge me as a piece of worthless wood?"

When the carpenter woke up, he told the apprentice about his dream. The apprentice said, "Since he likes to be known as worthless, why then should he want to become the earth god?" The carpenter at once stopped him from saying further. "Don't say it anymore. He only lodges himself in the temple to avoid being harmed, and allows those who don't know him to tease and revile him. If it does not assume the role of the earth god, it cannot be said for sure it will not be cut down. His method of self-preservation is out of the ordinary. Making himself useless in order to protect himself. If we still insist on convention, will it not be wide of the mark?"

99. Zhi Lishu

Talking of Zhi Lishu, well, his lower jaw almost touched his belly button, his shoulders rose straight up over his head, the hair coil behind his neck pointed towards heaven, all the acupuncture points at his back faced upwards, and his thighs were level with both sides of his ribs.

Yet, despite his severe hunchback, he still lived tolerably well. He earned enough to support himself by sewing and washing clothes, and the grains he got everyday by sweeping the provisions store floors and sifting with his winnowing basket were enough to feed ten people.

Moreover, when the country went to war and the conscription law was enforced, his fellow countrymen had to think of a way to avoid being drafted into military service. During which time, everyone was constantly in a state of anxiety, yet he could rolled up his sleeves and stretched out his arms, walking up and down the street with a swagger. When the country required forced labour on a large scale, he could escape service by reason of his hunchback. Lastly, when relief provisions were allocated by the government to the handicapped, he received quite a large amount of grain and firewood.

If, even a handicapped man, by submitting himself to the the will of Heaven and be content with his lot, was able to support himself and eke out a living, how much more so it would be for anyone with a healthy body to extricate himself from all the spiritual shackles?

100. Mutual Help and Relief in Adversity

According to legend, several fish went travel together. They swam from the river, where there were rolling waves, to a small pond, where the water was limpid and the spring bubbled, and it was as if they had left a city bustling with noise and excitement to the quiet and beautiful countryside. They played and enjoyed day in day out without the slightest care in the world. Calamity, however, was approaching without being noticed,—all of a sudden, the spring dried up, and the water level of the pond dropped rapidly. By the time the fish discovered the approaching danger, it was already impossible to flee from the place. They lay at the bottom of the pond, which now became a piece of dry land, where their lives hung by a thread. Ah, how they hoped to be able to survive and return to the varied and colourful life of the river! They began to open their mouths and puff some wet breath on their companions, just to keep them awake and not fall unconscious. They tried hard to disgorge what little saliva available to moisten each other's body. By this method, they hoped to prolong their lives until the spring spouted water again, when they might yet return to the river.

101. Bosom Friends

Four men, Zisi, Ziyu, Zili, and Zilai, were chatting together. They said, "Anyone who can have "nothing" as his head, "life" as his spine, and "death" as his bottom, anyone who knows that life, death, being and not-being are an organic whole, is to be my friend. The four looked at one another, smiled a smile of understanding, and became friends.

Not long afterwards, Ziyu fell sick, and Zisi paid him a visit. "Great is the Creator!" he exclaimed. "He has made your body contract to such an extent." Ziyu hunched his back, the internal organs of his body and blood vessels pointing skywards, his face sinking below his belly button, his shoulders towering above his head, his hair coil targeting heaven, and the two opposing principles in nature, *yin* and *yang*, in disorder. However, his mind was at perfect ease, as if nothing had happened. Haltingly he walked to the well, looked at his reflection in the water, and said, "Oh, my! See how the Creator has modified my body." Zisi asked him, "Do you resent it?" "No," replied Ziyu. "Why should I be resentful? If my left arm should turn into a rooster, I would use it to herald the break of day; if my right arm should become a catapult, I would use it to shoot the osprey and roast it for food; if my buttocks should change into a brougham, and my vitality, a horse, then I would ride in it. It would save time looking for a carriage. After all, all things emerge at a historic moment; even death is but conforming to the mandate of heaven. If one can hang up one's fiddle anywhere and be content with one's lot, one will not be influenced by emotions of sorrow and joy, being free from worldly worries. External entanglements are the cause of man's inability to free himself. No man can act against God's will. It has always been so. What, then, have I to resent for?"

102. The Death of Hundun (Chaos)

The leading god of the South Sea was called Shu (swift), that of the North Sea was called Hu (sudden), and the one in the middle was called Hundun (chaos). Shu and Hu often met at Hundun's place, and each time they came, Hundun offered them a very friendly and thoughtful reception. Shu and Hu were very grateful and wanted to repay him for his kindness. They said, "Every man possesses seven apertures in the head; those are for sight, for hearing, for food, and for respiration. He is the only one without these organs. Let us bore them for him." They dug one hole a day. When seven days elapsed, Hundun died.

103. Zang and Gu Lost their Sheep

Zang and Gu both made their living by grazing someone's sheep. One put his sheep out to pasture in the eastern mountain, the other did so in the western mountain. In the evening, they both returned empty handed, and both said they had lost their sheep. A neighbour asked Zang, "How did you lose your flock?" Zang replied, "I was reading under the tree, and the sheep simply went away." The neighbour then called Gu to account, and Gu replied, "I was gambling for fun, and the sheep ran away."

Although the two young fellow had been doing different things, the outcome was the same: the sheep ran away.

104. Bo Le's Guilt

The horse was an animal which lived on grass and water the land provided. When they were happy, they would bill and coo; when they were irritated, they would turn around and kick one another with their hind hoofs. These were the only things they knew. When headwear was put on one, and had it harnessed to a carriage, it soon learned how to defy its master's command, such as knocking against the carriage curtain, breaking the crossbar at the end of a carriage pole, spitting out the rein, biting the halter, etc. etc. It was all Bo Le's fault to domesticate this animal that caused its mind to be warped, its behaviour perverted, acting like a thief.

105. An Easy Thing to do

Once upon a time, there was a stingy rich man. He was anxious all day long lest his property might be stolen. Because he was so worried, he had many rattan trunks, wooden cabinets and bamboo baskets made, into which he put all his gold, silver jewelry, and other valuables. Even so, he still felt worried, and so he locked every trunk, cabinet and basket with sturdy iron locks. To be on the safe side, he tied them firmly with ropes made of hemp before moving them to his room, where he made his rounds several times a day. All his fellow villagers said the rich man was smart and careful, not an easy thing to do under the circumstances.

One night, when the starlight was dim, a pack of thieves bored a hole through the wall and snuck into the rich man's room, where they made short work of all the trunks, cabinets, boxes and baskets. Some they carried on the back, others put on the shoulder. The only worry they had as they fled was some of the contents might drop on the way, thus exposing their whereabouts. However, seeing that every trunk, cabinet, box and basket was firmly tied and securely locked, they knew such worry was unfounded.

The next day, when the rich man woke up, he discovered the room empty. He was so angry that he fainted on the spot. When his fellow villagers heard about it, they all said the smartness of the rich man only benefited the thieves in the end.

106. Lun Bian

During the Spring and Autumn Period, the Duke Huan of Qi assigned Guan Zhong the task of making the country rich and the military forces efficient, for which purpose he carried out a series of reforms. The Duke Huan of Qi eventually became the most powerful chief of the feudal princes in the Spring and Autumn Period (770-476 B.C.) One day, when Duke Huan was reading in the hall, a carpenter called Lun Bian was wielding his large axe making a wheel down the hall. After a while, Lun Bian took a break and went up to the hall to have a little chat with the duke. He saw Duke Huan reading, and asked, "What is Your Highness reading?" "I read a book by the sage," replied the duke. "Is the sage alive?" Lun Bian asked again. "He is dead," Duke Huan replied. Lun Bian was disappointed and said, "In that case, the book you read is of no use." The duke was displeased. He said, "I was reading here, and there's no place for a carpenter like you to poke your nose into! If you can give me your reason for doing so, I may pardon you; if not, then I'll have you executed!" Lun Bian was calm. He said, "Let me take the making of wheels as example. It should be just right, neither too fast nor too slow. 'What the heart wishes the hands accomplish'. It is somewhat difficult to spell out the hows and whys, but in my mind I've grasped the principle. The principle I've come to understand cannot be passed to my son, who likewise cannot learn it from me. Now, I am a man of almost seventy, and yet I continue to make wheels, because our forefathers, together with the experiences that could not be expressed in words, would be dead at the same time. That's why I said what you read is just some useless dross which the ancients have left."

107. Crude Imitation

During the Spring and Autumn Period, there lived in the state of Yue a beautiful girl named Xishi. One day, Xishi suffered from epigastric pain. She walked in the street, her hands covered the pit of her stomach, and knitted her brows. Her neighbours saw and thought she was more beautiful than ever in her new posture, and people kept on singing praises. In the eastern village, there was a girl with very ugly looks. People called her Dongshi. When Dongshi heard people praise Xishi, she thought by mimicking her she would also become beautiful and win their approval. So she followed her example, walked in the street, her hands covered the pit of her stomach, and knitted her brows. People saw her and thought she was uglier than ever before. They all shut their doors, not wishing to see her anymore. Those met her in the street avoided her by keeping away from her. Dongxi tried to mimic Xishi, but she did not win any praise from the people; on the contrary, she had made herself even uglier.

108. The River God

The god of the Yellow River, Hebo, was bloated with pride. He thought no god in the world could equal his greatness. When he heard that the ocean god was also powerful, he remained unconvinced. That day, he rode the fierce wind to the east. It did not take long before he arrived at the North Sea. The sight that greeted him startled him: a boundless ocean, stretching away to meet the blue sky; to the east, or west, or south, or north, they all seemed shoreless. The sun rose from the sea, and sank to the sea during the day; and at night, the moon and the stars shone bright and glittering, and the sea became a world of lights. When the day was warm and windless, the sea was so blue that it looked like a piece of fine jade. When the autumn wind was blowing, mountainous waves rolled, howling like thunder, and seemingly touching the sky. As he noticed the vastness of the ocean, Hebo began to feel his own insignificance. He looked up at the ocean god, and could not but sigh with emotions, "I was too arrogant. I did not deserve it."

109. A Frog in a Well

A frog lived in a well which was not very deep. One day, a big soft-shelled turtle arrived at the well from the Eastern Sea. The frog complacently told the turtle, "As you can see, how happy I'm! If I like, I can leap to the curb; if I want to get in, I can enter the hole in the wall of the well and take a rest. To take a bath, the water reaches exactly to my armpits and cover my neck. To take a walk, the mud can only bury my toes and the insteps. The little insects and tadpoles cannot compare with me. I've exclusive control of all the water in the well, I can go where I like, free as the wind. It is really a paradise. Why don't you come more often and take a sightseeing tour?"

The soft-shelled turtle listened to what the frog had to say, and felt inclined to go in and have a look. Before its left foot entered the mouth of the well, however, its right foot tripped, and it had to retrace its steps. It told the frog, "The place I live in is called a sea. It is broader than a thousand *li*, and deeper than three thousand meters. During the great Yu's time (the reputed founder of the Xia Dynasty—c.21st to 16th century B.C.), there were floods nine out of ten years, but no one detected any rise in the water level; during the Shang Dynasty (c. 16th-11th century B.C.), there was drought seven out of eight years, but it was also hard to detect any decrease in water level in the sea. Regardless of the span in time and rainfall, the boundless sea is always a scene of rolling waves. I live in the sea. That's what I call real happiness!" The frog in the well was struck dumb with astonishment, and flushed with shame.

110. In Attempting to walk like a Swan, the Crow loses its own Gait

In the Period of Warring States, there was a young man called Shouling in the state of Yan. He had heard about the graceful gait of the people of the state of Zhao. He admired them so much that he went to the capital of Zhao, Handan, all by himself, to learn how the people there walked, despite the long distance, the high mountains in between, and the fatigue of travel. Every day he watched their pose, pondered on their peculiarities, and appreciated their beautiful walking manner. Soon, he began to follow behind other people, and imitated them. However, he could not master their art of walking no matter how hard he tried. He examined and analyzed his own deficiencies, and concluded that it must be because he had been accustomed to the Yan manner of walking, and thus difficult to correct it in a short priod of time. Having reached that conclusion, he decided to forget his native gait, and whole-heartedly learned from the Zhao people. He made a great effort, spent a lot of time, to learn the way the people of Zhao walked. But, in so doing, not only was he unable to acquire the new gait, he had forgotten his own walking style. In the end, he had to crawl instead of walk when the time came for him to return home.

111. Zhuangzi

Zhuangzi was angling by the Pu River when two persons wearing court dress approached him. They said they were senior officials of the state of Chu, sent by the king Wei of Chu to convey His Majesty's regards and invitation. "Our monarch invites you to assist him in administering the country," they said respectfully.

Zhuangzi, his hands holding the fishing rod, did not so much as turning his head. He said, "I've heard that the state of Chu had a holy turtle, already dead for three thousand years. The king of Chu wrapped up its shell and put it in a bamboo box, which is kept in the ancestral temple as a national treasure. Please tell me, supposing the holy turtle were to live still, would it rather be alive, though by doing so, it had to drag its tail and crawl in the mud, or be dead and its shell wrapped up to be revered and worshipped?" Without a moment's hesitation, the two officials said simultaneously, "Of course it would rather be still alive in the mud!" Zhuangzi said, "That's why I respectfully ask you two gentlemen to go back because, like the holy turtle, I would rather drag my tail and crawl in the mud, and be free!"

112. Zhuangzi and his Wife

Zhuangzi's wife passed away, and Huizi visited the bereaved to offer his condolences. When he arrived, Zhuangzi was sitting there with his legs crossed and a basin in hand, which he beat as he sang. Huizi felt rather resentful and said, "Your wife and you lived together for such a long time, bearing sons and daughters for you. Now that she is dead, even if you don't cry for her, why beat the basin and sing? This is going too far!" Zhuangzi responded, "It isn't as you think. When she died, how could I not feel the anguish of sorrow? But after much deliberation, I realized she was not a living thing to begin with; not only was she not a living thing, she did not even possess a body; and not only did she not possess a body, she didn't even have breath. The breath came about when the world was in a state of confusion and chaos, then it developed into a form, the form evolved into life, and now it shifted into death, just as the four seasons, spring, summer, autumn, and winter, which go round and begin again. She is now resting peacefully between heaven and earth; in fact, she was only going back to nature, where she originated from. If I still cried sorrowfully, it would mean I didn't understand the meaning of life and its evolution. That's why I do not cry anymore."

113. The World-weary Human Skeleton

On his way to the state of Chu, Zhuangzi saw a human skeleton, which had rotted, bone-dry and without gloss. However, it still retained more or less the human form. Zhuangzi rapped him with his horsewhip, and asked, "Was it because you had done bad things and still cravenly clung to life that you got into such a plight? Or, was it because you were killed by a knife or an axe while defending your country in a war of life and death that you got into such a plight? Was it because of some immoral act you were too conscience-stricken to face your parents, wife, and children, and you died of shame, that you got into such a plight? Or, was it because you couldn't make enough to feed and clothe yourself, so that you died of cold and hunger, that you got into such a plight? Lastly, was it because you had reached a ripe old age and died of senility that you got into such a plight?"

Having said all that was to say, Zhuangzi moved the human skeleton over to serve as a pillow, and he lay down to sleep. At midnight, the human skeleton appeared in his dream, and said, "Listening to what you said, you seemed like a persuasive talker. However, anything you mentioned only concerns the living, his burden and suffering, for the dead do not have such trouble. Do you like to hear me talk about the joy of being dead?"

"Good," Zhuangzi replied.

The human skeleton said, "A dead man has no monarch above, nor subjects below. He has none of the hardships in connection with the four seasons: spring, summer, autumn, and winter. He is at ease, free as the wind, sharing weal and woe with heaven and earth. It is a life the happiness of which even the emperor cannot have!"

Zhuangzi was unconvinced, saying, "Would you like me to ask Yama, the King of Hell, who is in charge of life and death, to restore your body, grow your bones, muscles, and skins, and let you return to your parents and wife, your fellow villagers and friends?"

The human skeleton tautly contracted his brows and puckered the bridge of his nose and said, "How can I abandon a king's life and go back to endure the suffering in the world of man?"

114. The Marquis of Lu

Once upon a time, there was a sea bird named *Aiju*, which perched in the suburbs of the capital of Lu. The marquis of Lu mistook it for a sacred bird, and led his officials to welcome it as a guest of honour. A banquet was spread in the Lu ancestral temple, where such ancient music as the *nine shao*, performed only at very solumn occasions, was played, and the three animals, beef, lamb, and pork, as sacrifices were presented for its food. However, such excessive attention only brought physical and mental suffering, and caused it to be confused and disoriented. It felt so sad that it dared not even eat a small piece of meat, or drink a tiny cup of wine. In three days, it died. The trouble arose because the marquis of Lu did not feed the bird in accordance with the need of a bird, but with that of his own life.

115. Catching Cicada

Confucius visited the state of Chu, and on his way he passed through a forest, where he saw a rickety old man using a pole to stick cicadas. He did it as if picking up things, and not a cicada had escaped.

Confucius was quite astonished, and he asked, "You are wonderful. Is there any secret of success?"

The old man said, "I've some tricks doing it. In May and June, when I was practising my arms, I put two sticky balls on one end of the pole. If it did not come off, there would only be a few escaped cicadas; if three sticky balls were put on it and did not come off, then the number of escaped cicadas would only be one-tenth; if five sticky balls were stuck and did not come off, then the situation is like picking up things, none would slip at all. I stood as steady as a tree stump; my arms which held the pole were just like dead tree branches. Although the world was so huge, and things were so numerous in it, I only concentrated my mind on the cicada's wings. I did not turn around, nor did I look left and right. I would not let anything to distract my attention. That's why no cicadas could avoid being stuck!"

Confucius wheeled around to speak to his disciples who stood by his side, and said, "There is a popular saying: when the mind is undivided, the thought will be highly concentrated. This is the principle the rickety old man teaches us."

116. The Ferryman

Yan Yuan told Confucius, "I once took a ferry to cross a lake called Shui Tan, and observed that the ferryman's steering skills had reached the acme of perfection. I asked him, 'Can everyone learn to steer a boat?' He replied, 'Of course. Anyone who can swim can steer a boat after a little practice. As for divers, they can steer a boat the moment they get one, even though they never see one before.' I asked him why was it so, but he refrained from telling me. Master, can you tell me the reason for it?"

Confucius replied, "A swimmer will become inured to the water condition after a little practice, and no longer feel afraid. As to those who are divers, the reason why they can steer the moment they get a boat, even though they have never seen one before, is because they take the deep pool as a hillock, and handle a capsized boat as if reversing a car. The danger of an overturned car or a capsized boat, a common sight, no longer threatens them, and that is why they can take it easy. One who wagers with tiles will show composure and presence of mind; one who uses the buckle of his belt as bet will feel a little uneasy; one who stakes with gold will be nervous and lose his head. The gambling skills are the same, and it is the import or weight of the stakes that affects a man's state of mind. That's why those who value mere worldly possessions have no end of misgivings, and are slow-witted."

117. The Officiant and the Sacrificial Pig

An official, who was in charge of sacrificial affairs, came to the pigsty fully dressed, and said to the pig, "Why should you be afraid of death? I'll take good care of you and feed you for three months. Ten days before the sacrifice, I'll bathe my body and purify myself. When you died, I'll use cogongrass to make a mat, and place your shoulders and hindquarters on a beautiful sacrificial basin with exquisite decorative pattern on it, and things like that. Are you still not willing to die?"

From the pig's standpoint, it will be better to keep it in the pigsty, feed it with rice or wheat bran; from one's own point of view, what brings satisfaction are wealth and rank in life and, in death, the hearse with engraved decorative pattern, and the coffin with painted ornamental design. From the pig's point of view, the cogongrass and the engraved decorative pattern on the sacrificial basin should be discarded; from the standpoint of oneself, only the vanity of wealth and rank while living, and the posthumous honour in death, will bring satisfaction. Is there any difference between the pig and the man after all?

118. The Duke Huan of Qi and the Ghost

The duke Huan of Qi went hunting in the marsh, where he crossed a ghost's path. He was so terrified that he held Guan Zhong, who was on the driver's seat, tightly, and nervously asked him, "Fatherly Zhong, did you see anything?" Guan Zhong said, "I didn't see anything!" When they returned, the duke Huan of Qi fell ill, and for several days could not leave the house. The scholar prince, Gao Ao, told him, "It is because you keep thinking about what happened the other day when you were hunting, and your worry caused the illness. How could a ghost harm you? The vital spirits of man, if scattered and do not come back, will make one feel weak and deficient in vital energy; when the vital spirits go upwards and do not come down, the person will feel a surge of anger. On the other hand, if the spirits go downwards and do not rise up, a person will become forgetful; if the vital spirits remain neither up nor down, but pent-up in the mind, a person will get ill." Duke Huan asked, "Now, are there ghosts?" The prince replied, "Yes, there are. In the ditch, there is the shoe spirit; on the top of a kitchen range, there is the hair coil spirit; indoors where dust acumulated, the thunder god lives. To the northeast of a heap of earth lives the *gui* spirit; to the northwest, lives the *yiyang* god. In the water, there is the baffling spirit; in the hills, the *xing* spirit; in the mountains, the *xie* spirit. In the wilderness, there is the vacilating spirit; in the swamp, the meandering spirit." The duke asked again, "Do you know how the meandering spirit looks like?" The prince replied, "The meandering spirit is as big as the hub and as long as the shaft of a carriage, wearing purple clothes and red hat. This spirit looks extremely ugly, and hates to hear the noise produced by the moving axle. Whenever it hears that sound, it simply holds its head and stands still. Anyone who sees this spirit will soon become the chief of all the princes." The duke gave a happy laugh when he heard this, and said, "What I saw was exactly this spirit!" Thereupon he adjusted his clothes and hat, and sat down with the prince for a good talk. The day was hardly over when his illness unknowingly disappeared.

119. Dumb as a Wooden Chicken

In the state of Qi, there was a man called Ji Shengzi, whose official duty was to train the king's gamecock. Eager to have his cock tamed successfully, the king of Qi often asked about the progress of training.

Only ten days had passed, but he was already impatient, and came to ask Ji Shengzi if the training had been concluded. Ji Shengzi replied, "Not yet." Then in another ten days, he again asked the same question, and Ji Shengzi had to give a similar reply, "Not yet." The king of Qi, upon hearing that the project had yet to bear fruit, was greatly irritated. But for the sake of the fighting cock, he did not reprimand Ji Shengzi. Thus another ten days had passed, and the king of Qi asked yet again, "Hasn't it been tamed by now?" Ji Shengzi replied, "It should not be long now." At the fortieth day, Ji Shengzi finally tamed the fighting cock. The king of Qi was overjoyed, and brought his rooster to contend with another rooster. Nobody expected Ji Shengzi's trained rooster to be dumb as a wooden chicken, for it did not respond to the other rooster's war cry at all. Its newly acquired disposition, steady and calm, had become the hallmark and a prerequisite to win all fighting bouts against its opponents. In the arena, any cock would be hopelessly frightened if it was seen present there. Who would dare to compete with it?

120. Uncanny Workmanship

During the Period of Warring States, there lived in the state of Lu a very skilful craftsman called Qing. Qing, with concentrated attention, used a piece of wood to make a *Ju*. Now, a *Ju* was a kind of musical instrument, in appearance like a bell, something difficult to design. When Qing completed his *Ju* masterpiece, people who saw it all thought it was probably made by the spirits. The monarch of Lu having seen it asked Qing, "What skills you've got to shape so exquisite a *Ju*?" Qing replied, "I'm only a carpenter. What skills can I have? I've learned something from my work though. Before I started to make the *Ju*, I would never sap my premordial vitality. I tried my hardest to keep the mind calm: keeping calm for three days, without thinking of high official positions and riches; keeping calm for a further five days, during which I refused to consider about honour, or being clever or stupid; keeping calm for another seven days, and I entered the realm of selflessness. At that juncture I went to the forest to examine the build and property of the trees, and the idea of *Ju* took shape. Then I got to work at once. Thus from the very beginning the *Ju* was made to conform to the principles and laws of nature. When people saw it, they all thought it was made by the spirits. Later, the same phrase came to mean uncanny workmanship.

121. Dong Yeji

Dong Yeji once drove his carriage to see the duke Zhuang of Lu. His carriage now went forward, now backward, and the ruts left by the wheels were so straight that they looked like lines made by a carpenter's ink marker; then it wheeled around, now left, now right, circling round and round, and the ruts made by the wheels looked as if they were drawn with a pair of compasses. Duke Zhuang was convinced nobody could equal the driving skills of Dong Yeji, and he ordered him to circle his carriage around a hundred times before returning to his starting point.

Yan He met Dong Yeji on the way, and he entered the palace to see the duke, asserting, "Dong Yeji's carriage will definitely turn over."

Duke Zhuang was annoyed by such comment, but he held his peace. A few moments later, Dong Yeji's carriage turned over as expected, and he returned with his spirits dampened.

Duke Zhuang asked Yan He, "How could you know that the carriage would turn over?"

Yan He replied, "His horse was exhausted long before the accident, but it was still made to risk its life running. It would be odd if the carriage didn't turn over."

122. The Tree and the Goose

Zhuangzi passed a remote mountain, and saw by the roadside a big tree that was luxuriant in branches and leaves, and so thick that it took several persons to encompass with outstretched arms. A group of lumbermen stood under it, carrying saws and axes, but did not seem to be ready for the chopping down of the tree. Zhuangzi was somewhat surprised, and asked them why, to which they replied, "The wood from this tree is worthless, and it can't be utilized." Zhuangzi suddenly saw the light, and turned around to tell his disciple, "No wonder it grows to be so thick and big, and so old. So that is how it is: the tree is good-for-nothing. In life, one should conduct oneself just like the tree."

It was already evening when he left the remote mountain. Zhuangzi went about in search of a village, and eventually put up for the night at a friend's house. Seeing that he had come a long way, his friend was greatly delighted, and told his son to kill a goose to prepare a feast for the guests. His son, knife in hand, asked his father, "Dad, am I to kill the one that honks or the other that does not?" The host replied, "A goose that does not honk is useless. Of course you should kill the one that does not honk first."

His disciple at his side whispered to Zhuangzi, "Previously we observed that a big tree in the remote mountain could stay around for so long simply because it is worthless; now, our host's white goose, on the other hand, will get killed because it is useless. How do you explain this phenomenon, sir?"

Zhuangzi smiled and said, "One should conduct oneself just between worthy and worthless, that is to say, one should appear right, but to be really wrong, so that nobody will ever catch one tripping."

123. The Fox and the Leopard

The fox with its rich and thick fur and the spotted leopard with its very beautiful decorative pattern make their homes in the dense forest of remote mountain, and live in cavern, place where few people tread. As a rule, they hide themselves in the daytime, and are active only at night, which demonstrates their vigilance and their instincts of self-preservation. Sometimes, even though they are very thirsty and hungry, and cannot but go out in search of food in the rivers and lakes, still they move with sedulous care. Yet despite their discreet disposition, they cannot escape the tragic lot of being caught in a net or a trap, not because they have committed any crimes or sins, but because they possess very valuable fur, which cannot but bring disaster to their door.

124. Lin Hui

The state of Jia had perished, and Lin Hui discarded his precious jade (a round flat piece of jade with a hole in its centre used for ceremonial purposes in ancient China) worth a thousand pieces of gold, then carried the baby and fled from the place.

Someone asked him, "Is this because of money? How much can a baby bring? Are you afraid of encumbrance? But a sucking baby is much more cumbersome. Why is it that you discarded a piece of precious jade worth a thousand pieces of gold, and fled with a baby?"

Lin Hui replied, "The jade came to my possession because of the consideration of benefit, whereas the child is our own flesh and blood. A connection based on utilitarianism will come to an end when poverty or disaster strikes; a relationship sealed by natural bond will love and protect one another even in the face of destitution or calamity. There is all the difference in the world between mutually forsaking and mutually loving and cherishing indeed."

125. A Monkey and the Forest

The forest was full of *nanmu, zimu* (Chinese catalpa), and *zhangmu* (camphor tree), tall and straight. A monkey which lived in this forest sometimes climbed up the perfectly straight tree trunk, and swung from one tree to another with the help of the wisteria. He was as free as the wind, and very complacent, convinced he was the king of the forest, where no one would dare to harm him, and that even expert archers like *Houyi* and *Pangmeng* would not be so bold as to throw a sidelong glance at him. Once, the monkey fell into a clump of brambles, where sharp thorns and sturdy vines abound. Panic-stricken, he was afraid to move, lest the sharp thorns should bleed him to death. He turned this way and that, trembling with fear, and looking very pathetic. He was searching for those tall and straight trees, but could not see any. Circumstances changed, and he could no longer put his ability to good use.

126. Zhuangzhou in Diaoling

Zhuangzhou once travelled to the district of Diaoling (in Fugou, Henan Province), where he did some sightseeing in an orchard. He saw a strange bird flying in from the south, brushing past his forehead, and touched down on one of the chestnut trees to take a rest. Its wings measured seven feet long, and its eyes were as big as one inch in diameter.

Zhuangzhou said to himself, "What kind of bird is this? It has big wings but cannot fly over long distance, a pair of large eyes but unable to see far." Lifting up the lower hem of his gown, he walked briskly over, catapult in hand, and hid himself, waiting for an opportunity to shoot at this strange bird.

At this juncture, he saw a cicada, which was chirping long and loud because it had found a cool shade, forgetting the danger it was in. A mantis quietly crawled near, concealing itself behind the leaves, ready to pounce on the cicada. The mantis was so sure of success that it went wild with joy, oblivious of its own precariousness. In the meantime, the strange bird was intently eyeing the mantis, ready to go into action. Little did it know, however, that its own life was now a target of Zhuangzhou's catapult.

This series of events gave Zhuangzhou a shock so terrible that he sighed, "Ah, so that's how matters stand. All living things are killing each other, taking advantage of each other, and at the same time attracting each other."

He was no longer bent on shooting the bird. Laying down the catapult, he turned round and went away. Nobody had expected the orchard keeper to run after Zhuangzhou at that moment, mistaking him for a chestnut thief, and giving him a dressing-down.

Because of the encounter, Zhuangzhou was very unhappy and stayed at home for the next three months.

127. Beauty and Ugliness

Yangzi was a noted philosopher in the early years of the Warring States Period. Once, he made a long and arduous journey to the state of Song. When evening came, he was at a roadside inn looking for a night's lodging. There were two young females in the inn at the time, one was pretty and charming; the other; vulgar and ugly. However, the ugly girl was being treated with respect, as if she were a noble lady, while the pretty one was looked upon with disdain, as if she were mean and degrading. Yangzi watched them for a long time, and felt rather strange, so he asked the waiter on the quiet. The waiter whispered to him, "The pretty one thought she's very pretty, but I can't see where her beauty lies; the ugly one thought she's very ugly, but I don't see where's her ugliness." Yangzi lowered his head and was lost in thought. After some time, he murmured to himself, "Oh, now I understand. A person who has done good deeds but does not think he does is welcome wherever he goes."

128. The Scholar

Zhuangzi went to see the duke Ai of Lu. Duke Ai said, "There are many Confucian scholars in the state of Lu, but few study your doctrine."

Zhuangzi responded, "I hardly see any in Lu."

Duke Ai said, "Almost everyone in the state of Lu put on a scholar's trappings. How can you say you hardly see any of them?"

Zhuangzi replied, "I've heard that a so-called Confucian scholar will wear a domed hat to show he knows about astronomy; put on a pair of square shoes to show he studies geography; have soft fur and loose girdles on, and adorn himself with jade to show his decisiveness. As a matter of fact, any gentleman who is well-versed in any such learning does not necessarily put on these trappings; on the contrary, those who wear these trappings may not really have any knowledge of Confucianism. If you don't believe what I said, why don't you publish an ordinance, declaring, "Anybody who does not know Confucianism but puts on the Confucianist's trappings will be executed without exception!"

Thereupon Duke Ai issued an ordinance to that effect. In only five days' time, nobody had the courage to put on a scholar's trappings anymore. Just at this junction, it so happened that a man with shipshape confucian scholar's trappings was seen standing at the duke's doorway. Duke Ai immediately asked him in to learn his thoughts on running the state. That man was found to be truly erudite, for he answered all questions fluently.

Zhuangzi said, "Large as the state of Lu is, only a single man can be called a Confucian scholar. How can you say there are many?"

129. The Cartographer

The king Yuan of Song asked his official historians to draft a map of the mountains, rivers, and land of the country, and one after another they came. After making obeisance and bow, they all stood there, behaving in an affected manner. Some pretended to prepare the Chinese ink, and half the men present were laymen. One historian arrived last. He was unhurried, neither humble nor pushy, cupping one hand in the other before his chest to do obeisance before going into his own room. The king Yuan of Song sent someone to keep an eye on him. They saw him unbutton his garment the moment he entered the room, sat cross-legged, bared his chest and rolled his sleeves, took up his brush and dipped it into the ink, and began to sketch the outline. The king of Song praised him highly, saying, "This man is good. He is a real cartographer!"

130. The Stonemason and his Axe

On his way to attend a friend's funeral, Zhuangzi went past Hui Shi's grave, and he turned round to tell his retinue, "In Yingdu (north of present Jiangling, Hubei Province), capital of the state of Chu, a man smeared a layer of white powder as thin as a fly's wing on the tip of his own nose, and let a stonemason used his axe to pare it away. Fast as the gale, the stonemason brandished his axe and, before you knew it, the white powder was gone with the sound. The nose, however, was unharmed. The man kept a straight face, as if nothing had happened. The king Yuan of Song heard about the event, and summoned the stonemason to his presence, and said, 'Can you perform it once more so that I can watch it.' The stonemason replied, 'It is true I pared the white powder from the tip of the man's nose. But, although it can be done, the person who could act in concert has died long ago.' Since the death of Mr Hui Shi I, too, could not find another person to act in concert, and no longer can I debate with other people and probe thoroughly into problems."

131. Wars on the Snail's Tentacles

Dai Jinren called on the king Hui of Liang, and said to him, "There is a small animal called snail. Has Your Majesty ever heard of it?"

The king Hui of Liang replied, "I did."

Thereupon Dai Jinren continued, "There was a state founded on the left tentacle of the snail, whose name was Chu; there was another state founded on the right tentacle of the snail, whose name was Man. Between them wars were often waged to compete for spheres of influence, and countless people died. The victorious party would pursue the vanquished party for more than a fortnight before withdrawing its troops."

The king Hui of Liang said, "Alas! This must be false."

Dai Jinren said, "Let your humble subject prove it. Now, Your Majesty, do you suppose there is a limit to the space between heaven and earth, and in all directions?"

The king Hui of Liang said, "There is no limit."

Dai Jinren continued, "Since Your Majesty already knows that the space between heaven and earth and in all directions is limitless, in one's imagination one can travel across the boundless universe at will without any hindrance. In the real world, however, the place one can reach will only be the Four Seas and the Nine Regions. If we compare them with the universe, are not the Four Seas and the Nine Regions in fact small like the snail, not worth mentioning?"

The king Hui of Liang replied, "That's very true."

Dai Jinren then said, "In the territory within our reach, there was the state of Wei. When the state of Wei moved its capital to Daliang, the state of Liang was born, and the state of Liang brought about the king of Liang. In this boundless universe, is the position of Liang any different from the state of Man on the tentacle of the snail?"

King Hui replied, "No difference at all."

Dai Jinren then asked permission from His Majesty to leave, and withdrew. The king Hui of Liang was left sitting alone, lost in a reverie.

132. A Fish Trapped in a Dry Rut

Zhuangzhou came from a family of scanty means. Once, he asked for a loan of grains from Jian Hehou. Jian Hehou was very stingy yet sensitive about his reputation. Since Zhuangzhou came to borrow from him, his reputation would be at stake if he should refuse. Therefore he feigned generosity, and said, "No problem. When I've collected the rent tax and other levies from the people, I'll let you have 300 pieces of gold for sure." Zhuangzhou knew Jian Hehou was unwilling to lend him the grains, so he related to him the incident that happened the day before. He said, "Yesterday, when I was on my way here, I heard someone crying for help in the street, and when I turned around, I saw a crucian carp in the dry rut. I asked the crucian carp, 'Why do you call me?' The crucian carp replied, 'I was originally a resident of the East China Sea, so unfortunate as to fall into this dry rut. Can you help me with a little water?' I said, 'Good! I'm going south to call on the king of Wu and the king of Yue, and I'll ask them to divert the water of Xijiang to relieve you.' The crucian carp suddenly changed his countenence, and said, 'Due to lack of water, I'm going to die soon. If you can help me with a little water, then my life will be saved. If I've to wait till the water of Xijiang is diverted for my rescue, it will be far better for you to go to the dried fish market to look for me!'"

133. The Prince of the State of Ren

A prince of the state of Ren made a huge fishhook, a very long fishline, and had the meat of fifty robust cows dried to make a bait. He squatted above the Huiji Mountain, threw his fishhook far out to the East China Sea. Thereafter, he concentrated his mind on his work as an angler. A year went by, but he did not get any fish.

Later, a big fish swallowed the bait. In pain, it pulled the fishline downwards all the way to the bottom of the sea. It thrust here and struck there, tossing and turning, up and down, struggling with all its miight. On the surface of the sea, white-crested waves surged and swelled sky-high, and the dashing of billows howled like the wails of demons and the moans of ghosts, heard from places as far as a thousand miles away.

The prince of Ren had the fish sliced, dried, and preserved when he eventually caught it. Everyone from east of Zhihe to north of Canwu all had so much to eat that they became tired of it.

In later generations, the garrulous were apt to get excited and rushed about telling the news. Those who used short pole and thin line day in day out, angling by the big and small ditches, with eyes on the mud fish, would never be able to catch a big fish, even if they wanted to.

134. Two Scholarly Thieves

Two Confucian scholars who made a living by breaking into the tombs and robbed the dead insisted on conforming to the Confucian etiquette in their every act.

One moonless night, the two again busied themselves with the graves in the wilderness all night. The learned man stood at the top of the grave keeping watch. He looked around for a minute, then, with clear articulation and a mellow and full tune, said, "The sun rises in the east, how goes the digging of the grave?"

The lesser scholar was already in the tomb. As he stripped the dead man of his clothes, he managed to reply to his companion at the same time, rather unhurriedly, "The skirt and short jacket have not yet been undone, but I discover a pearl in his mouth."

"Oh, take it out! In the Book of Songs, it was recorded,—" and the learned man sang, "Fresh and green is the wheat, growing on the hilly slope. While living, you refused to perform good deeds; in death, why keep a pearl in your mouth?—Are you not afraid it might be taken by someone!"

"The mouth closes too tightly, how am I to take it out?"

"Grip his hair, seize his beard, use an iron hook to slowly pry open his mouth, and cut his cheek with a knife, but take care not to touch the pearl."

135. Sacred Turtle

One day at midnight, the king Yuan of Song dreamed that a man with an unkempt appearance glanced at his door furtively and said to him, "I came from a deep pool called Zailu, and am sent by the large river god to the small river god on official business. While on my way, rather unfortunately I was caught by a fisherman named Yuqie."

King Yuan fetched someone to consult the oracle when he woke up. The oneiromancer said, "This is a sacred turtle."

King Yuan asked, "Is there a man called Yuqie among the fishermen?"

The officials on his left and right said, "There is."

King Yuan said, "Let Yuqie be presented at court."

The next day, as Yuqie was presented at court, King Yuan asked him, "What have you got in your recent fishing voyage?"

The man replied, "I've netted a white turtle with a diameter of five feet."

The king ordered Yuqie, "Present this turtle."

When the turtle was presented, King Yuan wanted to have it killed at first. Then he changed his mind, and wanted to keep it, off and on, unable to make up his mind. Eventually, he had the matter decided again by consulting the oracle. The result was, "It will be auspicious if the turtle is killed for use in divination." Thereupon he had the turtle split from both sides, its entrails emptied, and prepared for divination. Of the seventy two sessions it was used, none had failed.

Confucius said, "This turtle had the ability to enter King Yuan's dream, yet did not have the ability to evade Yuqie's net; it could fulfil all seventy two divinations with no failure, yet unable to escape having its shell broken and entrails taken out. From this one can see however farsighted and prudent a man may be, there will always be moments of weakness. Although one may have the ability to divine the unknown, still there will be unforeseen matters. In this world of ours, even with means and resources unlimited, one can never match the wisdom of the millions!"

136. Afraid of one's own Shadow

A man who was as timid as a mouse thought he must have crossed the devil's path whenever he walked on the street and saw his own shadow and footprints. He was so frightened that he began to run, thinking that by doing so he could shake off those terrible objects.

Quite contrary to his expectation, however, the faster he ran, the more footprints he made, and the closer the shadow followed. This made him even more frightened, and he put up a desperate effort to run even faster. In the end he died of exhaustion.

137. Learning to Slaughter a Dragon

So the story goes, that, in ancient times, there was a certain man called Zhu Pingman who was bent whole-heartedly on learning some amazing skills. He next heard about a certain person named Zhili Yi, who possessed the expertise of slaughtering the dragon. What a man! Needless to say, Zhu Pingman admired him in the extreme. He paid him a visit, requested Zhili Yi to be his teacher, so that he could learn the dragon-slaughtering skills. Zhili Yi promised to teach him for an exorbitant fee, and Zhu Pingman scratched together what he had to make up the number of one thousand tails of gold, which he handed to Zhili Yi as tuition fee, and began to acquire the knowledge of killing a dragon. Altogether he studied under Zhili Yi for three solid years. When finally it was time to leave happily for home after completing the course, he had hoped somebody would come and invited him to kill a dragon, so that he had the opportunity to show his amazing ability. But it was a long wait, and nobody came. Well, because there was no such animal as dragon in the world, and consequently no target for him to shoot. In the end, Zhu Pingman's outstanding skills did not have the opportunity to display even once.

Even though you may have acquired some amazing skills, it is of no use if impracticable.

138. Zhuangzi and Cao Shang

There was a man called Cao Shang in the state of Song, who was being sent as an envoy to the state of Qin. As he was about to set out, the king of Song awarded several carriages to accompany him. When he arrived at the state of Qin, he tried his best to flatter the king of Qin, and received another one hundred carriages as a result. Cao Shang brought his one hundred carriages back to the state of Song, bloated with pride.

As he met Zhuangzi, he boasted, "It is impossible for me to live like you in a poor, shabby alleyway, weaving straw sandals for a living. To be able to move the feelings of the king of a big country with ten thousand chariots, and received a reward of one hundred carriages, was what really showed my talent best."

Zhuangzi replied, "The king of Qin fell ill, and invited good physicians to come and cure him. Anyone who could cure him of his festered carbuncle and boils would receive a carriage as reward; one who would lick his hemorrhoid receive five. That is to say, the meaner the approach in the method of curing, the more carriages rewarded. Have you cured the king of his hemorrhoid? Why have you got so big a reward? Go to the devil!"

139. Under the Black Dragon's Jaw

In the ancient times, there was an adept young swimmer. Once, he went to swim in a deep pool beside the bank of the Yellow River. As he dove to the bottom of the pool, he discovered an unfathomable cave, from which flashes of light could be seen. He was curious and swam into the cave, anxious to ascertain as to the nature of this phenomenon. At the bottom of the cave, he saw a big black snake curling itself up to sleep. Under its jaw, there was a bright pearl, and the light in the cave came from this pearl. The young man sensed it must be a treasure of some sort, and so he swam over and removed it. Holding the pearl in his hand, he followed the original route to the bank, and went home.

As he reached home, he showed his father the pearl he got, explaining in the meantime the whole course of the incident. His father said, "It is not a snake. The name of this creature is black dragon; and only under the jaw of this species of dragon can you find the bright pearl. The black dragon is very ferocious. You are lucky it is asleep, or you might have been eaten long ago."

Later, people use the phrase "under the black dragon's jaw one acquired a pearl" to denote running the risk in order to overcome obstacles, grasping the theme, bringing out the best, or writing which brings out important points from a maze of facts.

*

*Gongsun Longzi
By Gongsun Long, a thinker of the Warring States Period. He was known to have been active around 270 B.C, though dates of his birth and death were elusive. A native of the state of Zhao, he was once the protégé of Lord Pingyuan. He was against the war of annexation waged

by various states, and was the leading exponent of the School of Logicians in the Mid-Warring States Period. His deeds were seen here and there in *Zhuangzi* and *the Spring and Autumn Annals by Lu Buwei*. The original *Gonsun Longzi* had fourteen chapters, only six chapters are now extant. The most famous debate which he put forward was the sophistry paradoxes of "a white horse is not a horse". He had made some contributions to the developemnt of logical thinking in ancient times.

140. Gongsun Long

Gongsun Long was the protégé of Lord Pingyuan, and Kongchuan was the descendant of Confucius. One day, Kongchuan and Gongsun Long happened to meet, and Kongchuan told Gongsun Long, "I already heard of your fame even as early as when I was in the state of Lu. I admire your wisdom and farsightedness, and have a high opinion of your moral integrity. I've long wished to become your disciple so that I may receive your instructions. I'm glad we meet at last. I've some reservations though, and that's your doctrine of 'a white horse is not a horse'. If you can abandon the doctrine of 'a white horse is not a horse', then please let me be your disciple." Gongsun Long responded, "My dear sir, you are wrong there. My doctrine came from none other than the proposition of 'a white horse is not a horse'. If I were to abandon it, what more could I have to offer? Come to me for instructions after I've nothing to instruct, will that not be ridiculous? The reason you come to learn under me is because you are inferior to me in knowledge and wisdom, but now you want me to give up the doctrine of 'a white horse is not a horse',—does that not mean you come to teach me first before asking for my instructions. To be one's master first before becoming his disciple is not the right way to proceed."

*

Yi Wenzi
By Yi Wen (c. 350-c. 285 B.C.), a thinker of the Warring States Period, and a citizen of Qi. He enjoyed equal popularity with Songxing, and together they were regarded as the representative figures of the School of Songyi, classified as an offshoot of the School of Logicians. Only two chapters of his book *Yi Wenzi* are extant. Characteristic of his writing is his eloquence, making use of fables to expound his doctrine with rather profound and moving result.

141. A Self-effacing Huanggong

In the state of Qi, there was a certain Huanggong, a man steeped in modesty. He had two daughters, both being the foremost beauties. And because his daughters were so pretty, he often said things the other way round, declaring modestly that his daughters were very ugly persons. In this manner, their ill reputation spread far and wide, so much so everyone believed that his daughters were ugly monsters. Because of that ill reputation, they all passed the marriageable age without a suitor.

In the state of Wei, there was a bachelor. Rashly he married the elder daughter, and found her to be a rare beauty. He told people, "My father-in-law relishes modesty, and always uses the word ugly to describe his daughters. Since my wife is so pretty, her sister must be beautiful too." From then on, all the young men vied with one another to send gifts and court her, and indeed her sister was among the most beautiful.

Huanggong's two daughters all possessed surpassing beauty, and that was a fact. To describe them as ugly did not conform to reality. They were words unfounded and imposed on them. The man from Wei in his rashness married an "ugly maiden", but it turned out to be a rare beauty within the boundary of the country. That was disregarding the bad reputation to garner a real treasure.

142. The King Xuan as an Archer

The king Xuan of Qi had a passion for archery. He took delight particularly in being commended by others for the ability to use a powerful bow. In actual fact, his bow required only a little over three hundred catties of strength to pull and stretch it, but he liked to boast before his high officials who followed him around. Those high officials knew how to play up to their king. One by one they would make a pretense of trying to draw the bow, and feign astonishment by stopping half-way and exclaimed, "Aiya! The bow requires at least a thousand catties of strength to pull it to the full. Nobody other than His Majesty could have the ability to do it!"

Actually, King Xuan only need apply some three hundred catties of strength to pull his bow. Throughout his living days, he was led to believe he had administered over a thousand catties of strength. Three hundred was the actual number, and one thousand was in name only, but King Xuan enjoyed having a false reputation at the expense of inconsistency with the facts.

143. The King and the Pheasant

In the state of Chu a man carried a pheasant on the road, and a passerby asked him, "What kind of bird is this?"

"It's a phoenix," the man with the pheasant told him a lie.

The passerby asked, "I've heard about the phoenix, but only see it today with my own eyes. Are you going to sell it?"

The man with the pheasant replied, "Yes." And the passerby handed over ten pieces of gold. The seller complained that it was too little and refused to part with his merchandise. Finally the passerby added another ten pieces of gold and the transaction was concluded.

The buyer was thinking of presenting the pheasant to the king of Chu. Unfortunately, the pheasant died overnight. The man did not regret the twenty pieces of gold he spent in acquiring the bird. What he regretted was he could not personally present to the king of Chu the "phoenix" he bought.

The news, nevertheless, began to circulate in the state of Chu, and spread like wildfire. Everyone thought it was indeed a phoenix that died, and felt very sorry for the loss. How good it would be if the precious bird could be presented to the king of Chu, they all said. In the end, the story reached the ears of the king of Chu, and he was very moved. He summoned the man, who was to have presented the pheasant in the first place, for an interview, and richly rewarded him. He received more than ten times the money he spent for the bird.

144. The Farmer and the Jade

A farmer in the state of Wei was tilling his little plot of land when he came across a piece of jade one foot long. He had no knowledge of jade, so he told his neighbour about it.

His neighbour, bent on tricking him out of the jade, said, "It's a queer piece of rock! It may not be auspicious to keep it at home. You had better put it back to the place where you found it."

The farmer had his doubts, so he kept it in a wing-room. During the night, the precious jade emitted light which illuminated the whole room. The entire family was struck with fear, and the farmer had to go and talk with his neighbour about what happened.

His neighbour tried to frighten him, "This is proof enough of the mischief it can do to you. Get rid of it quick, so that you will not be harmed."

The farmer, therefore, threw the piece of jade to a distant field hurriedly. Not long after that, his neighbour stealthily took the piece of jade and presented it to the king of Wei.

The king of Wei summoned a jadesmith to have it examined as soon as he got it. At one glance, the jadesmith immediately complimented His Majesty. Stepping back a few paces, he paused and told the king, "I congratulate Your Majesty on coming by such a unique treasure. I've never seen a precious stone like that in my life."

The king of Wei asked him to evaluate the price of the jade, but the jadesmith said, "That's a priceless treasure. Even if the most prosperous city were to be offered, it would only be enough to pay for a moment's look at it."

Thereupon the king of Wei rewarded the man who presented the jade, and bestowed upon him the rank of high official with its concomitant emoluments.

145. A Matter of Names

An old man, who lived by the roadside, named his houseboy as "Shanbo", meaning, good at fighting; and gave the appellation "Shanshi", meaning, good at biting, to his dog. And, because of those names, for three years, nobody came to pay him a visit. They were afraid that his houseboy might beat his guests, and the dog might bite.

The old man felt the matter uncanny, and asked his guests why nobody came to visit him. They told him the truth. Thereupon the old man gave his houseboy and his dog each a new name. From then on, guests came one after another in endless succession.

146. Different Names for *Pu*

In the state of Zheng, people called a piece of uncut jade *pu*, while in the state of Zhou, the same appellation referred to the uncured meat of vole, or field mouse.

A man from the state of Zhou brought with him a quantity of vole meat for sale. He happened to meet a trader from Zheng and asked him, "Do you want to buy some *pu*?"

The trader from Zheng replied, "I may." He wanted the man to show his merchandise and, in this manner, discovered it to be a quantity of uncured skinless vole. Needless to say, the trader from Zheng declined the offer.

147. *Dao* and *Ou*

In my home village, there was a man whom people called "uncle". He gave his elder son the name *Dao*, which was the Chinese character for robber; and his second son, *Ou*, the character meaning to beat up.

One day, his elder son was going out, and "uncle" tried to catch up. He shouted after him, "*Dao! Dao!*" A government official happened to hear it, and thought it was meant to alert people to catch the robber. He therefore tied up the elder son.

"Uncle" felt anxious and, without a moment's delay, called his younger son to explain to the official. Due to the urgency of the moment, he was unable to change his habit, and cried out, "*Ou! Ou!*" The governemnt official concluded he was calling people to beat up *Dao*, and accordingly beat him within an inch of his life.

*

*Xunzi
By Xunkuang (c.313-c.238 B.C.), a thinker in the last years of the Warring States Period, and a citizen of the state of Zhao. He once studied in the state of Qi, but later sought refuge in the state of Chu,

and became the magistrate of Lanling at one point. The book *Xunzi*, which he authored, contains thirty two chapters. In the book, he introduced, commented on, and summarized all schools of thought of the era before the Qin Dynasty (221-207 B.C.). The content of the book is broad, reasoning careful and deliberate, and fables are found here and there.

148. The Nest of *Mengjiu*

In the southern region, there was a species of pigeon, a bird called *mengjiu*. It often made its nest with feathers, and wove them together with material like hair. Then, it attached the finished product to the ears of the reed. When strong wind blew, the reed ears inevitably snapped, and the eggs were broken, the nestlings fell down, dead.

How did matter come to such a pretty pass? It was not because the nest was not well-built, it was because the nest was not built at the proper place.

149. Sunlight Loving Fish

Both *Tiao* (hemiculeer leucisculus) and *Ti* (anchovy) were the kind of fish that liked to swim on the surface of the water where sunlight could shine on them. When they were stranded on the beach, it would be too late for them to yearn for the great expanses of the ocean. Even though they could remember the disaster, and tried to be cautious from then on, it would have been all to no avail.

150. A Virgin and the Robbers

A young girl having necklace and jewellery around her neck, precious jade dangling from her waistband, and head full of gold ornaments, had the misfortune to cross the robbers' path as the latter descended from the mountain. She did not dare look straight into the face of the robbers. Trying to make a great show of obedience and courtesy, she behaved more like a servant girl than her normal self,—despite all this, she could not escape being looted and raped.

151. Juan Shuliang

To the south of a place called Xiashou, there was a man named Juan Shuliang. As a man, he was timid and foolish. Once, when he was walking in the moonlight and saw his own shadow as he bowed his head, he thought it was an apparition lying prone on the ground; when he looked up and saw his own hair, he concluded it was the apparition standing up. He was so frightened that he turned and ran. By the time he arrived at home, he had breathed his last.

152. The Tilting Wine Pot

Confucius brought his disciples to pay respects to the ancestral temple of the duke Huan of Lu, and discovered a queer-looking wine pot on the table. Confucius asked the temple attendant, "What manner of wine pot is this?" The temple attendant replied, "It is the wine pot the king put on the desk, much as a motto engraved on a tablet." "Oh, I know the role it plays now!" Turning around, he spoke to his disciples, "Bring some clean water, quick, and pour it into this wine pot."

His disciples scooped up a full dipper of clean water and had it slowly poured into the wine pot while watching with bated breath in deep concentration. They saw with their own eyes that the pot began to tilt not long after the water was poured in; then, when the water reached the mid-point of the pot, the pot stood upright of its own again. As the water continued to pour in so as to reach its mouth, the pot overturned with a bang, and fell to the ground. Everyone was baffled, and looked at Confucius with raised head. Confucius applauded as he exclaimed, "That's only proper. There is no such thing as being full and not upset!" Zilu asked him, "Master, may I ask, is there any principle involved with regard to this wine pot, which tilts when more empty than full, stood upright when half-filled, and upset when overflowed?" "Of course there is!" replied Confucius. "The principle is the same, whether it be the wine pot or the way a person conducts himself. Though smart and learned, one should know there are blind spots of foolishness and ignorance; even if one was the most meritorious, one should behave in a humble and courteous manner. One might be brave and valiant, still one should act as if one was timid and weak. One might be wealthy and strong, still one should be frugal and industrious. People often cited the virtue of even-handedness and making up for each other's deficiencies. All this springs from the same principle."

153. Dong Yebi lost his Horse

The duke Ding of Lu asked Yan Hui, "Do you think Dong Yebi's driving skills good?" Yan Hui replied, "His driving skills are not bad. But he will lose his horses despite his driving skills." The duke Ding of Lu was annoyed by his comment. Going back to his palace, the duke told the people around him, "So Yan Hui is a backbiting hypocrite after all." Three days later, the official in charge of the horses reported to Duke Ding, saying, "The horses hitched to Dong Yebi's carriage had run away. The two front horses freed themselves from the bonds and fled. Only the two horses in the shafts returned to the stable." The duke Ding of Lu stood up suddenly and spoke to his subordinate, "Take a carriage and ask Yan Hui to come." When Yan Hui arrived, the duke Ding of Lu said to him, "I asked you the other day, and you said that 'Dong Yebi's driving skills are not bad. But he will lose his horses despite his driving skills.' I can't fathom why you know this?" Yan Hui replied, "I was calculating from the way the man conducted his business and knew. In the olden days, when Song was emperor, he never exhausted the people's resources; formerly, when Zaofu was driving the carriage of the king Mu of Zhou, he never overworked his horses to the point of exhaustion either; and that was why Song did not lose popular support, and the running away of horses never happened to Zaofu. In the present case, although I must say the reins of the horses as well as the speed in connection with Dong Yebi's driving were all strictly correct, yet he let his horses go too far and dangerous a journey. As a result, all his horses were tired out. Even so, he still would not stop and let his horses take a rest, but continued on the road. I was just guessing from these circumstances that the horses would run away." The duke Ding of Lu said, "You spoke very well. Can you elucidate it further?" Yan Hui replied, "I've heard that, when a bird is hungry, it will peck fiercely; when an animal is hungry, it will scratch with its claws recklessly; when a man is destitute, the idea of fraud will germinate in his mind. From ancient times to the present, there has never been a case wherein the financial resources of the people had been exhausted and had not had to take the consequences."

*Quezi

By Quezi. Little is known about his life and deeds, but he probably lived in the Period of Warring States. His writings had long been lost to the world. The fable below was seen in *Taiping Yulan*, quoted in turn from *Quezi*.

154. Bait of Cinnamon and Fishhook of Gold

There was a man in the state of Lu who enjoyed angling, using the priceless spice cinnamon as bait, and a fishhook made from gold. The fishhook, again, was inlaid with silver thread and green jade, and the fishline was decorated with rare emerald. The manner he hold his fish pole and the posture he took were all correct. The catch of fish, however, was small.

*

**In Response to the Questions of the King of Chu*

By Song Yu (c. 290-c. 223 B.C.). A poet of the state of Chu in the Period of Warring States, he had once been a high official of the king Qingxiang of Chu. He was the author of the poems *Nine Apologies*, *Requiem*, and *Ode to the Wind*, *Ode to a Goddess*, etc. totalling ten articles. All writings other than the above were lost. *In Response to the Questions Of the King of Chu* was a piece of celebrated prose purportedly written by him, but textual research done by later generations discovered it to be the works of Han Dynasty scholarship.

155. Highbrow Songs Find Few Singers

When the king of Chu heard talk about Song Yu, he summoned the latter to the palace.

The king of Chu said, "Some people have a grudge against you, and they often talk about you behind your back. Probably it is due to your less than honourable behaviour."

Song Yu replied, "Formerly a man came to Yingdu to take part in a performance. He stood at the crossroads. First he sang the folk tune

The Song of the Rustic Poor, and there were thousands of people echoing. When he sang such popular tunes as *Sunshine* and *The Essence of Chinese Onion*, there were still several hundreds of people singing with him. When he performed the highbrow song *The Spring Snow*, those in the city could follow him were only tens of people. When he performed with exquisite skills, now singing at the top of his voice, now chanting in low pitch, fine and smooth, mild and roundabout, modulating and with endless variations, profound, beautiful, and moving, only a few could sing along with him. What do you think all this mean?"

The king of Chu shook his head, hesitated, and said, "I've not thought it over."

Song Yu said, "This means that the more elegant and highbrow a tune is, the fewer can sing along together. By the same token, my behaviour cannot be easily understood by mediocre people."

*

*Lu's Annals
By Lu Buwei (?-235 B.C), a statesman and thinker in the later part of the Warring States Period. A native of Yangdi (now, Yuzhou city, Henan Province), he was originally a big-time businessman. He gave financial support to help free the prince of the state of Qin, Yiren, who was held as a hostage in the state of Zhao at the time. Later, when Yiren returned to his own state and became the monarch of Qin (the king Zhuangxiang of Qin), Lu Buwei was put in the position of prime minister. When Yiren died, and his son Ying Zheng suceeded him (first emperor of Qin, 259-210 B.C.), Lu Buwei continued to be the prime minister. Because of his political view, which was at loggerheads with that of the monarch, Lu was released of his position, and later exiled to Shu (now Sichuan Province). Worried and apprehensive, he committed suicide.

Lu Buwei was a very rich and powerful man at the time, with three thousand hangers-on, and over ten thousand houseboys. *Lu's Annals*, or *the Lu Chronicle*, was compiled by the hangers-on, whom Lu assenbled, and totalled twenty-six volumes, one hundred sixty chapters. Its content dealt mainly with ideologies of Confucianism and Taoism, with a summary of different schools of thought before the Qin Dynasty, and that was the reason the book was classified later as the Eclectics.

156. A Man of Chu and his Bow

A man of Chu lost his bow, but refused to look for it. Someone asked him why he did not want to look for it, and he said, "A man of Chu lost his bow, and a man of Chu picked it up. Why should I go to look for it?"

When Confucius heard of it, he said, "Good. Suppose we get rid of the word 'Chu', retain only 'a man lost the bow, and a man got it'. Would that not be better?"

When Laozi heard it later, he said, "Get rid of 'a man', and retain only 'lost bow, got bow'. Would that not be better still?" It seemed Laozi had truly reached the ideal state of selflessness.

157. Recommend Qualified Persons for Service

The duke Ping of Jin asked Qi Huangyang, "The county of Nanyang has a vacancy for the position of magistrate. Do you think who can take up the post?" Qi Huangyang replied, "Jiehu can fill the vacancy." Duke Ping said, "Is not Jiehu your enemy?" Qi Huangyang replied, "What Your Highness asked was who could fill the position, and not who my enemy was!" Duke Ping commended him. "Good!" he said. Thus Jiehu was designated the magistrate of Nanyang County. In time, Jiehu proved himself to be competent, and loved by the people there.

Some time later, Duke Ping again asked Qi Huangyang, "The capital is in need of a military officer. Do you think who can fill this post?" Qi Huangyang replied, "Qi Wu should be up to the job." Duke Ping said, "Is not Qi Wu your son?" Qi Huangyang replied, "What your Highness asked was who was up to the job of military officer, and not who my son was." Duke Ping said, "Good!" And he designated Qi Wu as the military officer. Subsequently, Qi Wu proved to be a good choice, as he was praised all around.

Confucius heard about the matter, and said, "What Qi Huangyang said was indeed excellent! When recommending an outsider, the matter of whether he be an enemy or not should not come up; in recommending a family member, one should not consider whether he is one's son." Man like Qi Huangyang might be called a fair and square man.

158. Uprightness and Filial Piety

In the state of Chu, there was an upright and fillial man, whose name was Zhigong. His father stole a lamb from someone, and he reported it to the gevernment. As a result, his father was arrested and sentenced to death. Zhigong begged to die in the place of his father.

When the sentence was about to be carried out, he said to the executioner, "My father stole a lamb, and I reported him to the government. Is this not being upright and loyal? My father is to be executed, and I take his place. Is this not filial piety? To kill a man who is both upright and filial, I wonder whether there is anybody in the country who has not been punished."

When his words reached the ears of the king of Chu, it was decided that the execution be suspended.

159. Cut Off One's Flesh to feed Oneself

In the state of Qi, there were two brave and strong men; one lived in the city's eastern corner, the other lived in the city's western corner. One day, the two men met on the road, and they both said, "Let's sit down and have a cup of wine."

After a few cups, one said, "Let's get some meat for the wine." The other said, "There is flesh aplenty on your body, and on mine. Why get from sources other than our own." So they prepared the seasoning sauce, took out their knives, and cut each other's flesh to eat until they both died from it.

Bravery of this kind is far worse than without bravery at all.

160. The Monarch of Zhu and the Suit of Armour

The traditional method in making a war skirt was to use silks as the material, but Gong Xiji told the monarch of the state of Zhu, "To use silks as the material for war skirt is not as good as to use silk strings. The strength of the war skirt depends on its smooth and close stitching. Although the stitches can be very close when silk is used as the material, its finished product can be ripped open with half the force.

A war skirt made with silk strings, however, can not be torn even if you use all your strength to do it, once it has been smoothly and closely stitched."

The monarch of Zhu thought he was right, and asked him, "But, where can we get so much silk strings?"

Gong Xiji replied, "As long as the king continues to utilize them, the same shall be manufactured by the people."

The monarch of Zhu said, "That's good!" He ordered local authorities to use silk strings in making war skirts from then on. Sometime later, somebody vilified Gong, saying, "It is because Gong Xiji has got a lot of silk strings at home that he suggested to the monarch to use silk strings for war skirts!"

When the monarch of Zhu heard it, he was annoyed, and a new order was issued, requiring local authorities not to make war skirts with silk strings anymore.

161. Finches

The finches chased after one another, intimately enjoying life under the same roof. The mother bird fed its young, seeking pleasure together, passing the days happily, and thinking that the world was peaceful and safe. Suddenly the chimney of the fireplace cracked and fire shot through the opening, reaching the roof beam. The finches, however, looked unperturbed. Why was it so? It was because they did not know a great calamity was at hand.

162. Pursuing Rancidness at Sea

A man's body emitted a kind of rancidness that assailed one's nostrils, and his parents, brothers, wife, concubine, and friends could not stand it. No one would live with him, and so he went to stay at the seaside, all by himself, alone and friendless. However, there were people at the seaside who loved the foul smell, and who followed him whether it was day or night, and refused to be parted.

163. Drain the Pond to get the Pearl

Huantui of the state of Song enjoyed the official position as high as the minister of war, but had to flee abroad because of a crime he committed. The monarch of Song heard he had a precious pearl, and sent someone to make a detailed inquiry. Huan, the minister of war, said, "I've thrown it into a pond." The monarch, therefore, dispatched someone to drain the pond. The pearl, however, could not be found, and the ordeal proved too much for the fish. Alas! They were all dead.

164. Dan Bao and Occultism

That man, Dan Bao, devoutly believed in occultism. He longed to leave the world.

He refused to eat the five cereals and coarse grains planted by man, or to wear the clothes woven by man. He escaped to the deep mountains and forests, and lived in a cavern, in order to preserve what he called the heavenly instincts bestowed by nature.

In less than one year, he was eaten by the tiger.

165. Confucius lost his Horse

Confucius was tired out, trying to push on with his journey, and had to take a rest by the roadside. The horse he rode had escaped and, because it had eaten the farmer's crops, it was detained. Zigong came forward of his own accord to mediate, trying hard to reason with the farmer, but the latter would not listen.

A country folk, who had waited upon Confucius not long ago, said, "Let me try to talk him over." He said to the farmer, "The land you till is not in the East China Sea, and mine is not in the West China Sea either. We are actually next door neighbours. How can our horse not occasionally graze on your crops?" Hearing the man talk like that, the farmer was pleased and responded, "That's what I mean by tallking sense. He is not like the other one at all!" And he untied the horse and gave it back to him.

166. Penny-wise and Pound-Foolish

During the Period of Warring States, war broke out between the state of Yan in the north and the state of Qi in the east. The general of Qi, Dazi, stationed his army at a place called Zhouqin. He sent a messenger to the capital Linzi (east of Zibo City, Shandong Province) to report to the king of Qi, hoping that the king would allocate some money and provisions to reward the soldiers so as to encourage the meritorious and enhance troop morale. The king of Qi was unhappy upon receipt of the report. He did not like to have to shell out money and provisions, and even railed against Dazi for quite a while. As a result, the army of Qi was under-supplied, and suffered a crushing defeat at the hands of the state of Yan. Dazi, moreover, died in battle. The army of Yan went on to occupy seventy-two cities belonging to Qi. Finally, even the capital Linzi was lost, and the king of Qi fled in panic, taking refuge in Jucheng.

Eventually the army of Yan entered Linzi, rushed into the Qi palace, opened up the warehouses, took all the gold, silver and precious things, and transported them back to Yan. Because the king of Qi refused to allocate a little money to reward the soldiers, he lost the whole state. The loss was many times the amount for the reward of the soldiers. That was why he had been ridiculed by the people.

167. The Duke Huan called on Ji

The duke Huan of Qi, one of the five overlords in the Spring and Autumn Period, called on a scholar called Ji. He called on him three times in one day, but was unable to see him. The attendants of Duke Huan advised him, saying, "Your Highness is the monarch of a large country with ten thousand chariots, calling on a common scholar three times in one day. That certainly can be regarded as being courteous to the wise and condescending to the scholars. But three times should be enough!"

Duke Huan said, "That won't do. It's common for scholars to belittle high official positions and riches, and treat their sovereign without proper respect. But a sovereign, if he does not have the ambition to become the chief of the feudal princes, may likewise slight talent in the country. As for me, I dare not look down upon my career as the chief of the feudal princes, and that's why I must respect talent." And

Duke Huan made up his mind to continue his call upon Ji, until he fulfilled his desire to see him.

168. *Jue* and *Qiongqiong*

In the northern region of the country, there was a small animal called *Jue*. Its front feet resembled those of a mouse, and its rear feet, those of a rabbit. Due to the disproportion of the front and rear limbs, it could not walk with fast steps, or it would fall down, the more so if it tried to run. However, it often helped gather a kind of tasty sweet grass as food for a queer animal called *qiongqiong*. *Qionqqiong*, also known as *juxu*, is a wild animal very much resembling a galloping horse. Whenever there was an alarm or disaster, *qiongqiong* would carry *jue* on its back and fled.

In this manner, *jue* was able to make use of what he had, and utilized the forte of others to remedy his deficiency.

169. The Men of Chu crossed the Yongshui River

The men of the state of Chu planned a surprise attack on the state of Song, and they sent people to check the water level of the Yongshui River and to erect markers.

Not long afterwards, the water level of Yongshui River suddenly rose. The men of Chu did not know this, and continued to follow the markers when they crossed the river at night. As a result, more than a thousand persons were drowned. The army of Chu was convulsed with fear and utterly routed, much as the collapse of houses in the city.

The markers put up before could indeed serve as guide in crossing the river. Now that the water level had risen, the condition changed. The men of Chu persisted in following the markers as if nothing had happened, and that was the cause of their defeat.

170. Nick the Boat to seek the Sword

Once upon a time, in the state of Chu there was a man who crossed the river in a large wooden boat. The sword he brought with him fell into the water just when the boat was in the middle of the river. Hurriedly he took a knife and nicked a mark at the side of the boat, saying to himself, "This is where I've dropped my sword."

When the boat pulled in to shore, the man who lost his sword followed the mark on the boat and jumped into the water to retrieve his sword. As a matter of course, after half a day's work, he got nothing.

His fellow passengers derided him, saying, "The boat is moving on the surface of the water, while your sword remained at the same spot in the bottom of the river. This is no way to find your sword. Isn't it a little silly to do so?"

After some thought, the man who lost the sword realized his fellow passengers were right, and felt ashamed of his foolishness.

171. His Father was a Good Swimmer

A man was crossing the river when he saw someone tugging a child, and trying to throw it into the river. The child was crying loudly. People asked the man why he wanted to throw the child into the river, and the man replied, "Because his father is a good swimmer."

Even if his father was a good swimmer, did it necessarily follow that his son must be a good swimmer too? It was preposterous to deal with problems or manage things in this manner!

172. The Prophecy of Guan Zhong

Guan Zhong was severely ill, and Duke Huan paid him a visit, saying, "My Fatherly Zhong, your illness is serious. How are you going to guide me into the future?" Guan Zhong said, "In the state of Qi, the country folks have a proverb, 'When you are an official, you should not keep your opinion to yourself; and when you die, you mustn't let your ideas be buried underground.' Now that I'm about to leave the world, what more can you ask?"

Duke Huan said, "I hope you will not find a pretext for not saying anything."

Guan Zhong replied, "I wish my master would not be too close to Yiya, Shudao, Chang Zhiwu, and the prince of Wei, Qi Fang."

Duke Huan said, "Yiya killed his son, and had his son's flesh cooked in order to provide me with meat. What more is there to doubt his loyalty?"

Guan Zhong replied, "It's only human nature that a man loves his son. When a man could harden his heart and kill even his own son, what can't he do to his sovereign?"

Duke Huan said, "Shudao had willingly been castrated and entered the palace to serve me. What more is there to doubt his loyalty?"

Guan Zhong replied, "It's only human nature to love one's own body. When a man could ruin even his own body, what can't he do to his sovereign?"

Duke Huan said, "Chang Zhiwu could tell a man's life and death. He could even cure a man of his insanity. What more is there to doubt his loyalty?"

Guan Zhong replied, "A man's life and death are decided by destiny, and insanity is due to letting one's imagination run wild, so that the evil spirit can take advantage of one's weakness. If my master does not rely on destiny and thus maintain the normalcy of the mind, but believe in Chang Zhiwu's witchcraft, he will then have the opportunity to do whatever he likes!"

The duke further said, "The prince of Wei, Qi Fang, has followed me for fifteen years, and did not even go back to attend his father's funeral because of me. What more is there to doubt his loyalty?"

Guan Zhong replied, "It is only human nature to love one's own father. When a man could harden his heart and not go to attend his father's funeral, what can't he do to his sovereign?"

Duke Huan said, "I'll surely do as you ssid."

After the death of Guan Zhong, Duke Huan exiled all four of them. As a result, he soon found the food he ate not as tasty as before, the things he did not after his own heart, incidents of insanity broke out again, and the rules of the palace were not strictly enforced. Three years later, Duke Huan said, "Maybe our fatherly Zhong was too extreme after all. Who can say that every word of his is right?" He therefore had the four men recalled.

In the second year after the return of the four men, Duke Huan fell ill. Chang Zhiwu, upon emerging from the palace, said, "The master will die on such and such a day." Yiya, Shudao and Chang Zhiwu united to stage an armed rebellion. They obstructed the palace gate, built a high wall around it, and barred everyone from entering or leaving the palace. Everything they did was in the name of Duke Huan.

A certain girl climbed over the wall and entered Duke Huan's living quarters. Duke Huan said, "I'd like to eat something." The girl replied, "I can't get any food." Duke Huan said, "I'm thirsty, and should like to have some water to drink." The girl replied, "I can't get anything to drink." Duke Huan asked, "What's the matter?" The girl answered, "Chang Zhiwu emerged from the palace and announced, 'The master will die on such and such a day.' Yiya, Shudao, and Chang Zhiwu united to stage an armed rebellion. They obstructed the palace gate, built a high wall around it, and barred everyone from either entering or leaving. That's why I can't get anything. The prince of Wei has led the people of forty communities and headed for Wei."

All sorts of feelings welled up in Duke Huan's mind. He sighed as tears rolled down his cheeks and said, "Alas! How far-sighted the sage Guan Zhong is! If a dead man can feel, how am I to face the fatherly Zhong?" He covered his face with his sleeves and breathed his last in the king's resting place. Three months after his death, the body had still not been interred. The corpse began to rot and maggots crawled out of the door. Officials covered him with a door leaf made of poplar wood to fool public opinion. All this was because he did not listen to Guan Zhong's advice.

173. Solving the Unsolvable

A country folk from Lu presented a rope-knot to king Yuan of Song, and King Yuan proclaimed to the whole nation, "Let every man with skills undo the knot."

Nobody was able to undo the knot. A pupil of Nishuo asked for permission to try, but he could only partially undo it, and there was other component of the knot which he could not disentangle. He said, "It is not a matter of my failure. The fact is, it cannot be disentangled."

The king Yuan of Song asked the man from Lu whether it was indeed a fact that the knot could not be undone. The country folk from Lu said, "That's true. The knot was incapable of being disengaged. I was the one who made the knot, and naturally knew its secret; that man had not taken part in shaping the knot, yet he knew it was not possible to undo it. He is really a smarter man."

Man like Nishuo, who knew the knot could not be disentangled, had actually had the problem solved.

174. Understanding a Man

When Confucius was on the way between the state of Chen and the state of Cai, he was so destitute that even soup of edible wild herb was not easy to come by. For seven days, he had not a grain of food to eat, so he could only go to sleep in the daytime.

His disciple, Yan Hui, happened to find a little rice and began to boil it. When it was almost cooked, Confucius saw him grab the half-cooked rice from the earthern utensil to eat. After a while, the rice was ready, and Yan Hui invited Confucius to fall to. Confucius pretended not to have any knowledge of Yan Hui's grabbing of the rice which happened not long before.

As Confucius got up, he said, "I had a dream just now, in which my ancestor asked me to give them the cleanest possible cooked rice."

Yan Hui replied, "It won't do. Just now some dirt dropped into the earthern utensil, and foul the rice a little. Because it would not be good to throw it away, I use my hand to take it out and eat.

Hearing this, Confucius sighed, saying, "I trust my own eyes, but even what the eyes see cannot be trusted; what I rely upon is the brain, but even the brain is not trustworthy sometimes. You must know it is not easy to understand a man."

175. False Reasoning

There was a man known by the name of Chengzi in the state of Song. He lost a black garment, and went looking for it on the road. He saw a woman with black coat, so he held her tight and would not let go, demanding that she gave him the coat, saying, "I've lost a black garment."

The woman said, "Although you have lost a black garment, but the clothes on me are truly mine."

Chengzi replied, "If you are smart, you should give your clothes to me. What I've lost just now was a lined garment of soft plain-weave silk fabric, and yours is only an unlined garment of black cloth. Since you use an unlined garment in exchange for my lined garment, won't it redound to your advantage?"

176. An Impeded Elbow

Mi Zijian was on his way to become a senior official of Danfu, but he was afraid backbiters might influence the king of Lu so that he would not be able to do things according to what he believed in. For this reason, he requested the king of Lu to assign two trusted officials as his followers to accompany him to Danfu when he took his leave and set out.

All the officials in Danfu came out in full force to welcome their new superior. Mi Zijian ordered the two accompanying officials to record the event. The two were about to commence writing when Mi Zijian held and shook their shoulders ceaselessly. He would fly into a rage when the officials did not write to his satisfaction. The two were in a tight corner and asked to be released of their positions so that they could return. Mi Zijian said, "You have done too badly, so better go back at once."

So the two officials returned to report to the king of Lu, saying, "It is impossible to be Mi Zijian's clerical staffers."

The king of Lu asked, "Why?"
The two replied, "Mi Zijain often shook our shoulders when we were writing. If we did not write well, he would fly into a rage. The local officials all thought Mi Zijian's behaviour ridiculous, and your humble subjects had to leave him because of that."

After listening to the two officials, the king of Lu sighed with emotions and said, "This is the method Mi Zijian has adopted to help rid me of my mistakes! I've always stood in his way so that he could not do things as he wished. That has happened more than a few times in the past. If it were not for you two, I might commit the same mistake again!"

Thereupon the king of Lu dispatched a trusted follower to Danfu to inform Mi Zijian, saying, "From now on, Danfu should be regarded as a place owned by you, not by me. Anything that is beneficial to Danfu, you may have full powers to do as you think fit!"

177. Decisive Struggle

During the reign of the duke Zhuang of Qi, there was a warrior called Bin Beiju. Bin had a dream one night, in which a very powerful male, wearing a white silk hat with red decorative pattern embroidered on its band, a loose dress of textile, a pair of white shoes, and a sword in black scabbard at his waist, chided him angrily, and even went so far as to spit in his face. Bin awoke with a start, and realized it was only a dream. But the event made him unhappy throughout the night.

The next day, he invited his friend over, and told him, "I was brave and unyielding even as a boy. I've never suffered any setbacks or humiliation up to the age of sixty. Last night the man in the dream insulted me. I'm going to seek him out based on his likeness. If I can locate him, all is well; if not, I'll die for it in order to avenge an insult." From then on every morning he would go to the vital communications line with his friend and tried to find the man. Three days had passed but he could not find anyone matching the description, and so he returned home to commit suicide.

178. Rongyi and his Pupil

Rongyi left the state of Qi and was on his way to the state of Lu. As he arrived at the periphery of the city, it was already dark, and the city gate had closed. There was nothing Rongyi and his pupil could do but to sleep in the open outside the city. It was midwinter, and the weather was bitterly cold. At midnight, both men were so frozen they could not endure it anymore, and Rongyi said to his pupil, "If you take off your clothes and give them to me, I'll be able to live on; by the same token, if I strip and give my clothes to you, you will be able to survive. However, I'm a person of ability and the state needs me. From the standpoint of the people as a whole, I should value my existence, and should not die just like that. On the other hand, you are neither virtuous nor talented and, as your existence will not be of much benefit to the world, you should not overvalue your life. Why not take off your clothes and give them to me." His pupil replied, "I'm not a virtuous man, but not being virtuous cannot avoid being selfish. That's why I cannot give you my clothes."

As Rongyi heard this, he sighed, saying, "Alas! Moral principle no longer works." And he took off his own clothes and covered his pupil with them. In the end, Rongyi was frozen to death, but his pupil survived.

179. The Dragon Slayer

There was a man called Cifei in the state of Chu, who got a treasured sword from Gansui. On his return journey, he took a boat to cross the river. When the boat was in the middle of the river, it was surrounded by two flood dragons.

Cifei asked the boatman, "Did you ever see a boat surrounded by two flood dragons and the passengers and dragons both managed to survive?"

The boatman said, "Never saw it."

Cifei rolled up his sleeves and unsheathed his treasured sword, saying, "This is but a heap of carrion and bones. If I lay down my treasured sword in order to live, there will not be anything left in me worth loving by anybody." He then dove into the river to fight with the dragons and killed them both. And because of his heroism, the passengers were saved.

180. Zihan and the Neighbours

Shi Yinchi was sent by the king of Chu to the state of Song as an envoy. Zihan, the prime minister of the state of Song, had a banquet prepared in his residence to entertain Shi Yinchi. Shi saw that the environment of Zihan's residence was very beautiful, but the walls of his neighbour to the south were irregular and stretched all the way to the front portion of Zihan's hall; and the drainage ditch of his neighbour to the west was draining water all the time, passing by Zihan's house.

Shi Yinchi therefore asked Zihan, "Why don't you ask the two neighbours to move away?"

Zihan replied, "My southern neighbour is a family who makes shoes. I was thinking of asking them to leave once, but the young man's father said to me, 'Our family's livelihood depends on shoe-making, and I've lived here for three generations. If we move, the people of Song who are used to buying our shoes will no longer know where we live. If the shoes are not sold, the whole family will have no food to eat. I hope Your Excellency will take pity on us as it is a matter of livelihood.' For that reason, I did not ask them to move elsewhere. As to the western neighbour, their house is situated on high ground, while ours is on low ground. Water flows from high to low places as a matter of course, and passing by our house is but natural. That's why I did not have a reason to stop it."

When Shi Yinchi returned to Chu, the king of Chu was in the midst of making preparations for the attack of Song. Shi Yinchi advised the king, saying, "The state of Song should not be attacked, because its king is very wise, and its prime minister, very benevolent. Wisdom is apt to win support from the people, and benevolence will enable them to make proper use of personnel. If we attack the country, we may not succeed; on the contrary, we may become the laughingstock of all the people in the world!" The king of Chu was receptive to his advice and desisted from attacking the state of Song. He attacked the state of Zheng instead.

181. The King You and his Favourite Concubine

Feng Hao, the capital of Western Zhou Dynasty (c. 11th century-771 B.C.), was very close to the *rong* (an ancient name for the peoples in the west) people's territory. The Zhou Dynasty had an agreement drawn up with all the feudal princes. Tall towers, where big drums were deposited, were constructed by the sides of the main roads, so that the sound of drums could be heard far and near. Whenever the *rong* people invaded the country, drums would be beat, and the princes would come from every direction with their forces to save the Son of Heaven. Once, when the *rong* people again intruded into the territory, the king You of Zhou beat the big drum, which caused the princes to come with their army from all directions, and king You's favourite concubine, Baosi, was so thrilled that she laughed heartily. From then on, whenever king You wanted to win a laugh from Baosi, he would beat the big drum. This happened several times. Every time he beat the drum, the princes would hurriedly lead their men to his rescue. But there were no invaders. Later, when the *rong* people mounted a large-scale offensive, and king You in panic beat the big drum, no princes came with their army to his rescue again. Consequently, king You was killed by the *rong* people at the foot of Lishan (in Lintong, Shaanxi Province), and mocked at throughout the empire.

182. The Eccentric Spirit of Liqiu

In Liqiu, a village to the north of the state of Liang, there was an eccentric spirit, who was ingenious in masquerading as the son, nephew, or brothers of someone in the village.

It so happened that a drunken old man was on his way home and, as was its wont, the Liqiu spirit assumed the likeness of his son, pretending to support him but in reality to torment him.

Arriving at his own home, and when he became sober, the old man upbraided his son, saying, "I'm your father. Am I not being kind to you? Why did you torment me on the way home while I was drunk?"

His son knelt down and cried, "It's a sin! I did no such thing! I was in the east village to collect some payments. If you don't believe me, you can ask the people of the east village."

His father believed him, and said, "Ah! It must be the work of the eccentric spirit. I've been told such thing before. Tomorrow I'll go again to town to get drunk. If I meet the spirit again, I'll kill it."

And the old man went to town to drink the next day. His son was afraid that he might not be able to come home by himself, so he took to the road to get him. Upon seeing his son, the old man thought it must be the spirit again, and he unsheathed his sword and stabbed him to death.

The senses of the old man were confused by the spirit who assumed his son's appearance; as a result, he killed the son that was truly his.

183. Sinking a Well

The family of Ding in the state of Song did not have a well at home, and a member of his family must be sent outside the house to get water every day. Later, when a well was sunk, no one need be sent anymore, and they told everyone, "We sank a well, and saved a man."

Someone heard what they said, and began to spread it, saying, "The Dings have got a man out of digging a well."

Throughout the country everybody was talking about the matter, and soon it reached the ears of the king of Song. The king thought it queer, and sent someone to the Ding family to find out the truth.

The Ding family reported, "What was meant was saving a man's labour, not digging out a man from the well."

184. Three Pigs crossing the River

During the Spring and Autumn Period, Zigong, Confucius' disciple, went to the state of Jin on business. He passed the state of Wei, where a scholar was studying a history book. In the book it was written, "There were three pigs in the army of Jin that crossed the river." What was the meaning of this passage? Was there really pigs kept in the army of Jin? Three pigs crossing the river should not be a great event. Why recorded it in the history book? He was unable to reason it out when he heard Zigong had arrived in the state of Wei. He was very pleased as he knew Zigong was the disciple of Confucius, a learned man. He therefore went to him with the book for advice. Zigong, after reading what was written, said, "This was only a transcription error. It should be read as 'the Jin army crossed the river on a certain date'." The ancient people used the Ten Celestial Stems and the Twelve Earthly Branches (sexagenary cycles) to record the year, the month, and the day, and *ji-hai* represented a certain date. In the seal characters (a style of Chinese calligraphy, often used on seals), the two characters *ji-hai* and the other two characters *three pigs* were very similar. The transcriber might be careless and had them written incorrectly. The Wei scholar was enlightened when this explanation was offered, and expressed his gratitude again and again.

185. The King of Song went Into Exile

The state of Qi mounted an offensive against the state of Song, and the king of Song sent a messenger to gather intelligence about the enemy's position. The messenger came back and reported truthfully, saying, "The Qi troops have already pressed on towards the capital. The people are in a state of consternation."

The high officials on his left and right said to the king of Song, "That's what we called 'Worms breed only when the meat has already started rotting' (The news of the enemy's approaching has frightened the people out of their wits). Judging from the powerful and prosperous state of Song, and the small and weak state of Qi, how can this happen?" As the king of Song listened, he thought the messenger must be telling lies, and he was so enraged that he had the messenger executed.

Then, he sent another messenger to reconnoitre the enemy's movement. The messenger returned and reported as his predecessor did earlier. The king was as infuriated as before and had him put to death. In this manner, he killed three messengers in succession.

Soon, he despatched another man to do the scouting. This man found the army of Qi to have indeed drawn near to the capital, and the people were convulsed with fear, ready to flee. As he returned, he met his own brother on the way. His brother asked him, "The country is already in a state of emergency. Where do you intend to take refuge?"

The messenger replied, "The king has sent me to reconnoitre the enemy's position, but I never dream that the enemy is so near the capital, and the people so frightened. I'm rather frightened myself. My predecessors were all killed because they reported truthfully that "the Qi army has drawn near to the capital'. The situation at present is, if I report the condition as it really is, I'll die; if I tell lies, I'll likewise die when the enemy enters the city. What am I to do now?"

His brother said, "If you tell the truth, you will certainly be executed before the enemy enters the city. It will be better if you flee before the Qi army arrives!"

And so the messenger returned to delude the king, saying, "There is absolutely no enemy in sight, and the people all live and work in peace."

The king of Song was overjoyed. All the high officials said, "The deaths of the previous messengers are justified." This messenger was richly rewarded for his report.

Before long the Qi army broke into the capital city. The king of Song vaulted into the carriage and had to drive it himself to escape. By this time the lying messenger was living in comfort in some other country.

186. Self-deception

At the time Fan, an aristocrat of the state of Jin, became a fugitive, a commoner stole a bell amidst confusion, and intended to carry it away with him. Unfortunately, the bell was too big and heavy. So he brought a hammer, trying to smash the bell before moving it piece by piece to his home. (Copper was highly valued at the time. In those days, the coins were made of copper.) But the moment his hammer fell on the bell, it gave out a loud *clang*, which startled him. He was afraid other people might hear the sound of the bell and come to snatch it from him. The problem was, how to smash the bell and not let other people hear the sound? For a long time he cudgelled his brains for ideas. Finally, he got an ingenious notion: plugged both his ears tightly before pounding the bell with all his might. He was convinced if he could not hear the sound of the bell, others would not hear it. This was really the height of absurdity.

187. Yang Youji

In the palace of Chu, there was a white monkey, whom people called the sacred one. The reason it was so named was because a number of famed archers in the state had tried to shoot it without success. Later, the king of Chu invited Yang Youji to do the job. Yang Youji first examined and adjusted his bow, then brought the arrows with him. Before he shot, he took good aim at the target and, when he felt he was perfectly certain he could score a hit, he let go of the arrow. Sure enough, the white monkey was hit and fell from the tree immediately the sound from the bowstring was heard. The reason why he could hit the white monkey with only a single arrow was because Yang Youji had already mastered the skills, and was absolutely confident of his ability to achieve success even before he undertook the job.

188. Resurrection

Gongsun Chuo, a man of the state of Lu, told people, saying, "I can bring a dead man back to life." When people asked him how, he said,

"Previously I was able to cure a man of his hemiplegia. I'll now double the dosage for hemiplegia, and it'll be an efficacious medicine to bring a man back to life."

189. Sword Appraiser

A man whose job it was to appraise the value of a sword said, "A sword that was made with the alloy casting method will be hard and flinty if its colour is white; pliable and tough if yellow. If it shows a mixture of yellow and white, the sword will be hard and tough, yet pliable, and can be classified as a good sword."

Someone refuted him, saying, "Based on what you have just said, a precious sword which is white in colour will not be sufficiently pliable and tough; if yellow, not hard and flinty. If all this is true, then will the one showing a mixture of white and yellow be neither hard and flinty, nor pliable and tough? Besides, if it is too soft, its blade will easily be turned; when it is too hard, it will readily break. When a sword is either too soft or easily broken, how can it be called a good sword?"

There was no difference in the intrinsic quality of the sword, yet some believed it was a good sword, others thought it shoddy, all because of the angles from which the sword was judged. That's why one must have sharp ears and eyes as well as the abililty and experience with which to discern the good from the bad, and not listen to the nonsensical opinions of mediocre persons. Without the necessary experience and sagacious perception, and be able to render appropriate analytical judgement in every situation, one would be, as it were, deaf and blind, unable to distinguish between the merits of Tang Yao (a sage King of over 4,000 years ago who gave the throne to a capable and virtuous minister instead of his own son) and that of Xia Jie (name of the last emperor of the Xia Dynasty—a synonym of cruelty and oppression).

190. A Mouse-catching Dog

In the state of Qi, there lived a man who was a good judge of dogs. His neighbour asked him to get a dog that could catch mice. After a lapse of one year, he eventually found the dog of his choice, and brought it to his neighbour, saying, "This is a good dog."

The neighbour kept the dog for several years, but it did not catch any mice.

He told the dog appraiser, but the latter said, "This is really a good dog. What it likes to catch are animals such as roebuck, elk, wild boar and deer, and not mouse. If you wish it to catch mouse, you have to tie up its legs."

Thereupon the neighbour tied up the hind legs of the dog, and from then on the dog has no alternative but to catch mice at home.

191. A Net Open on Three Sides

The founder of Shang Dynasty (c. 1600-1046 B.C.), Tang, once saw a man spread his nets in every direction and prayed, saying, "From the sky, beneath the earth, and from all directions, whencesoever thou comest, all run into my net."

Tang said, "That's catch all in one net. Who would do that except Jie?"

And so Tang put away the nets in three directions, and left open in one direction only. He asked the man to pray again, saying, "Previously only spiders could weave the net with their legs, but now men have learned the weaving skills. O ye birds and animals, if you intend to turn left, please do so; if you wish to turn right, you are free to go; you may choose to fly upwards, or to bore a hole underground, just do as you like. I only catch those who are destined to die."

All states south of Han River listened and said, "Tang has bestowed his kindness even upon the birds and animals. He is indeed a benevolent man." And all the forty small states came over to pledge allegiance to Tang.

*

**Hanfeizi*
By Hanfei (280-233 B.C.), a thinker at the end of the Warring States Period, and the principal representative of the Legalists (a school of thought in the Spring and Autumn and Warring States Periods, 770-221 B.C.). He was born of a aristocratic family in the state of Han. A disciple of Xunzi, he had tried to remonstrate with the king of Han to carry out reform and become big and powerful, but without success.

He was sent to Qin as an envoy, where he was highly regarded by Qin Shi Huang (259-210 B.C.). Framed by Lisi and Yaojia, he was imprisoned and later committed suicide. The book *Hanfeizi* comprises twenty volumes with fifty-five articles. He epitomized the thought of the Legalist School and synthesized its component parts into an organic whole to become a theory. A large number of fables were found in his writings, some of which had become proverbs and allusions.

192. Stay at one's Post

The marguis Zhao of Han was drunk, feeling dizzy and sleepy, so he lay down on the bed to take a nap. Dianguan saw it and was afraid the marguis might catch cold. He took a garment and covered the marguis with it.

When the marguis woke up, he was very pleased, and asked his attendants, "Who was it that covered me with the garment?"

The attendants replied, "It was Dianguan."

When the marguis was sure of the facts, he immediately meted out punishments to both Dianyi and Dianguan—the former because he neglected his duty, and the latter because he overstepped his authority.

It was not that the marguis Zhao of Han was not afraid of cold, it was because he believed the harm done in the case of the violation of authority was much greater than the threat of cold weather.

193. The Duke Wu of Zheng attacked the State Of Hu

The state of Hu was contiguous with the state of Zheng, and the duke Wu of Zheng had long harboured the ambition of having it annexed. It was only because the state of Hu was vigilant against its powerful neighbour and combat-ready that the latter did not dare act rashly. Nevertheless, it was as if a piece of fat meat before his eyes, impossible not to make his mouth watery. Crafty as the duke Wu of Zheng was, he soon thought of an ingenious idea, and that was to marry his daughter to the monarch of Hu. In so doing, the state of Hu would think that the two states had become relatives and thus relaxed its vigilance. When the time was ripe, he would then strike. As a matter of fact, the state of Hu fell into the trap devised by duke Wu, and dropped its guard. All this, of course, could not escape the eyes of duke Wu. One day, he asked the high officials, "I'm going to war for land. Which country do you think I should attack?" Guan Qisi, one of his high officials, knew the duke had long wanted to attack the state of Hu, so he answered, "It would be feasible to attack the state of Hu." Who would have thought when the duke Wu of Zheng heard this, he instantaneously changed his countenance. In fact, he was so angry that he spoke in a harsh tone and with a severe expression, saying, "The state of Hu is our brother. How can you suggest that I send my forces there? What is your motive?" And he ordered his bodyguard to have Guan Qisi executed. The news reached the state of Hu, which had no idea it was only a ruse, and, being convinced of the good intention of Duke Wu, all defensive measures were dropped. The duke Wu of Zheng saw that the opportunity had finally arrived, and launched a surprise attack. Thus the state of Hu had become an easy prey for the state of Zheng.

194. Cause for Suspicion

In the state of Song, there was a moneybags. A torrential rain had brought down the walls of his house. His son said, "If we do not repair the walls, petty thief will be able to get in and steal." An old man, who was their neighbour, also echoed his idea.

That night, his house was broken into and a large quantity of their belongings was stolen. After the event, the whole family of the moneybags praised their son's foresight, but they cast a suspicious eye on their neighbour, the old man.

195. When Mi Zixia fell into Disfavour

Long, long ago, there was a man called Mi Zixia, whom the duke Ling of the state of Wei loved ardently. According to the laws of Wei, anyone found driving the monarch's carriage without permission would have his feet cut off. It so happened that Mi Zixia's mother fell ill, and someone arrived from a by-road to inform him. Thus Mi Zixia forged the order of Duke Ling and drove the duke's carriage home.

When the duke knew it later, he praised Mi Zixia, saying, "How filial he is! Because of his mother's illness, he disregarded even the penalty of having his feet cut off."

On another day, Mi Zixia and the duke Ling of Wei were enjoying themselves in the orchard, and the former picked a peach within his reach from the fruit tree. He found the peach delicious, so he gave the half of it which he did not finish to Duke Ling.

The duke Ling of Wei said, "How he loves me! He refrained from eating all of the delicious fruit and offered it to me."

However, when Mi Zixia grew old, Duke Ling's love thinned and, as he offended him, Duke Ling said, "That fellow once drove away my carriage on false pretences, and gave me the the remainder of the peach he could not finish."

196. He's Jade

In the Chu Mountain, Bian He of the state of Chu came by a piece of uncut jade. He respectfully presented it to the monarch, the king Li of Chu. King Li summoned a jadesmith to appraise it, the jadesmith said, "This is only a piece of rock." King Li thought Bian He a cheat, and cut off his left foot.

When the king Li of Chu died and King Wu succeeded him, Bian He again presented the uncut jade to King Wu. Like King Li before him, King Wu asked a jadesmith to appraise it. The jadesmith rendered a similar judgement, "It's a piece of rock." And King Wu believed Bian He a fraud, and cut off his right foot.

When King Wu died, succeeded him to the throne was King Wen. Bian He held the uncut jade to the foot of Chu Mountain, and there he cried for three days and three nights. When his tears dried up, blood came out. King Wen heard about it, and he sent someone to inquire about him, saying, "There are lots of people whose feet had been cut off. Why should you cry so sorrowfully?"

Bian He replied, "I'm not sad about my feet. I'm sad because a piece of precious jade was mistaken for a rock and an honest man looked upon as an impostor. This is the real cause of my sadness!"

King Wen asked the jadesmith to carve and polish the uncut jade carefully, which eventually yielded a piece of rare jade. King Wen called it "He's jade".

197. Guessing Game

Zhan He of the state of Chu sat inside the house while his disciple waited on him. Just then, the mooing of a cow echoed through the door, and his disciple said, "That's a black cow with white forehead."

Zhan He said, "That's correct. It's a black cow, but the spaces around the horns are white." He sent someone outside to make sure, and it was a black cow, whose horns were bound with white cloth.

It might seem brilliant to sit inside the house, seek popularity by saying something sensational, and indulge in some kind of guessing game but, in reality, it was the most foolish thing to do.

198. Bian Que

Bian Que, the miracle-working doctor, was in the midst of a formal visit to the duke Huan of Cai. He stood there for a moment, and then said, "Your Highness is ill, and although it has only just become apparent, if medical treatment is not administered in time, the illness may become serious."

The duke Huan of Cai said, "I don't have any illness." And Bian Que took his leave. After he left, Duke Huan said, "Doctors as a rule like to treat patients with no illness. They do it to show their medical skill."

Ten days later, Bian Que again visited the duke Huan of Cai, and he said, "Your Highness's illness has spread to the muscles. If it does not receive treatment now, it may get more serious." But Duke Huan did not heed his warning, and there was nothing Bian Que could do but to take his leave. The duke Huan of Cai appeared rather displeased.

In another ten days, Bian Que came again. He said, "Your Highness's illness has spread to the intestines. It will become worse if not treated promptly." But the duke again ignored his advice. As Bian Que left him, Duke Huan was even more displeased than ever.

A further ten days had passed, and whenever Bian Que saw Duke Huan, he turned and left. Duke Huan sent soemone to ask Bian Que why he left without saying a word, and Bian Que replied, "When the illness is only superficial, it can be taken care of by a decoction of medicinal ingredients or hot compress; when it is in the muscles, it can be cured by acupuncture; when it is in the stomach and intestines, the antipyretic method can be used; but if it spreads to the marrow, then it is in the hands of Death, and no human can do anything. Now that the manarch's illness has spread to the marrow, I've stopped requesting to attend to him."

Five days later, the duke Huan of Cai felt his body suffering from pains all over, and he sent people to locate the whereabouts of Bian Que, but Bian Que had fled to the state of Qin. Not long thereafter, Duke Huan died.

199. The last Ruler of the Shang Dynasty

In the past, King Zhou used the valuable ivory to make chopsticks, and Jizi felt perplexed and uneasy, for he was convinced, "The ivory chopsticks will not be used to pick up food from an earthen pot and, because of that, cups and dishes must needs be made of rhinoceros horn and fine jade. Once chopsticks of ivory and cups of rhinoceros horn are used, coarse food will no longer be on the table. People will eat the embryos of yaks, elephants and leopards. When the table is spread with exotic food from mountains and seas, people will not garb garments of coarse cloth and take their meals in the thatched cottage. They will put on their triple-layered embroidered dress in and out, live in spacious houses, and ascend higher buildings. I'v a presentiment of King Zhou's sad denouement, and that's why I feel uneasy and perplexed by King Zhou's extravagance."

Five years later, as expected, King Zhou constructed a meat garden, implemented the cruel punishment of ordering a prisoner to walk on a slippery metal beam kept hot by coal underneath, and often ascended the small hill piled up with the distillers' grains. Looking at the pool of good wine, he felt proud and self-satisfied. But King Zhou eventually paid a price: death.

200. Zihan

There was a country folk in the state of Song who liked to play up to people of power and influence.

Once, he came by a piece of uncut jade, and thought the opportunity of fawning on some rich and powerful person had presented itself. Without wasting time, he carried the precious jade to the government office, and presented it to the new official, Zihan, who had just assumed his position. Zihan obstinately refused to accept it. The sycophant smiled obsequiously and said, "Only a man of noble character and high prestige like Your Excellency is fit to have this precious stone for making utensil. Those greedy petty men are not up to it. I beg Your Excellency to accept it."

"Please say no more," Zihan warned sternly. "You take this jade as a treasured object. But it is most important for me to refuse your gift, as my honesty is priceless."

201. Wang Shou

Wang Shou carried a package of books on his back on his way to Eastern Zhou and met Xu Feng on the road. Xu Feng said, "Things are done by men. Anything a man does must fit in with the trend of the times, and be in accord with different situations. Knowledge must, therefore, also keep up with the times. What had been written down in the book was people's words, and words were expressions of men's understanding of the objective world. That's why a knowledgeable man does not store up books. Why do you still carry books on a journey?" Upon hearing this, Wang Shou immediately burned his books, and was as happy as a clam at high tide, dancing irresistibly.

202. Preoccupied

The king Xiang of Zhao learned driving from Wang Ziqi, and soon he tried to engage the latter in a contest. Three times King Xiang changed his horse, but three times he also lost.

King Xiang complained, saying, "You taught me how to drive, but you kept back the essential skill."

Wang Ziqi replied, "I've taught you everything. The problem was, you did not use it properly. Generally speaking, in driving, the most important thing is to let the horse feel at ease. To do so, the driver's mind must be concentrated on the horse, so that he can pick up speed and realize his goal. Today you set your mind on catching up with me whenever you lagged behind; and when you were in front of me, you were afraid I might catch up. In racing, naturally, it is either in front or behind. But Your Majesty had your attention on me all the time whether you were ahead or at my back. How could you get control of your horse? That was the real cause of your lagging behind."

203. Zip across the Horizon

The king Zhuang of the state of Chu had ascended the throne three years, but within those three years, he cut no figure. Neither had he issued an order, nor concerned himself with a single matter of state.

One day, The minister of war, while waiting on him in the palace, spoke in a metaphor, saying, "My great king, there was a bird which perched in the southern mountain for three years. It neither spread its wings and flew to the sky, nor roared out a song. Might I ask for the reason?"

King Zhuang smiled as he replied, "It did not spread its wings for three years in order to become full-fledged; neither flew nor cried in order to concentrate its mind on the people's conditions. That bird, although it did not fly before, will soar up into the sky with one start; although it did not cry before, will set the world on fire when it does. Please set your mind at ease. I understand your concern."

In half a year's time, King Zhuang began personally to administer the state affairs. He abolished ten obsolete laws, established nine new projects, executed five dishonest high officials, and reinstated six virtuous recluses. Henceforth, the state of Chu was well run.

204. The Eye cannot see its Lashes

The king Zhuang of Chu would like to attack the state of Yue, but Duzi remonstrated, saying "Why must Your Majesty invade the state of Yue?" The king Zhuang of Chu replied, "Because the country is politically in a mess, and its army is weak, which presents a good opportunity to subjugate it by force of arms." Duzi said, "Although your humble servant is ignorant, he is nevertheless very anxious about the matter. The wisdom of man may be compared to his eyes, which can see objects a hundred paces away, but cannot see its lashes. Your Majesty have lost several hundred *li*'s territory to the two states of Qin and Jin when your forces were defeated, that should be interpreted as a sign of weakness in our army. When Zhuangjiao rebelled and ran wild within the country, it could not be suppressed and eradicated, that's also a sign the state was politically in a mess. It is therefore not difficult to visualize that the same political instability and weakness in military forces exist in both countries. Under these circumstances, to send a punitive expedition to the state of Yue, is not the wisdom of which just like the pair of eyes that can see far but not near?"

This conversation caused the king Zhuang of Chu to change his mind and abandon his desire to invade the state of Yue.

Thus it can be seen that it is very difficult to accurately appraise the objective situation. The important thing is not to be able to see others clearly, but to know one's own self. That's to say, "To have a clear estimation of oneself is to have wisdom."

205. Zixia and Zengzi

One day, Zixia met his classmate Zengzi on the road and had an exchange of conventional greetings to show their affection towards one another. Zengzi suddenly discovered that Zixia had put on weight, and remarked, "It's not long since we met, and why have you suddenly become much stouter?" Zixia, in response to what he said, deliberately kept him guessing by saying, "It is because I've won the battle, and that's the reason why I've put on weight." Zengzi was truly a bit perplexed. He shook his head, and said, "I don't understand what you mean." Looking at Zengzi's baffled appearance, Zixia could not help smiling and said, "Now, let me tell you. As I studied the Confucius' doctrine of humanity and justice at home, I began to admire it very highly. But when I left home, I saw how wealth and position brought joy and pleasure to men, and yearned for them. My mind was continually nagged by these two opposing thoughts, and it was as if two armies fighting in the battlefield, for a time neither could get the upper hand. My mind was wandering as a result, and I had no appetite for food and drink, so much so that I became sallow and emaciated. But it is all over now. Confucius' humanity and justice have finally won against wealth and position. My mind is now peaceful and calm, and my body begins gradually to put on weight."

206. Snakes in a Dried-up Pond

The pond dried up, and the snakes must move elsewhere to survive. A small snake said to a big snake, "If you walk in front and I follow, people will take us to be two common snakes passing through, and they will kill you first. It is better we join our mouths, and you carry me on your back. In this manner, people will mistake us for some kind of gods." Thereupon they join their mouths, and the big snake carried the small snake on its back as they crossed the road. Sure enough, those who saw them hurriedly stood aside, and said, "They are gods!"

207. Distant Water can't put out a Nearby Fire

The duke Mu of Lu sent his sons either to the state of Jin or the state of Chu to serve as officials, and his motive in so doing was to unite the two big powers. Lichu, a high official of Lu, said, "Suppose we go to the state of Yue to beg somebody to come and rescue a son who is about to be drowned, he will not be able to save the son, even though the people of Yue are good swimmers. Suppose our house is on fire and we go to the sea to get water in order to put out the fire, the fire will not be put out, even though there is plenty of sea water. The reason is simple: distant water can't put out a nearby fire. The states of Jin and Chu, though strong and powerful, are far away from us, whereas the state of Qi is near at hand. If the state of Qi were to attack us, how could the states of Jin and Chu come in time to help us?"

208. A Drunken Shao Jimei Lost his Leather Coat

Shao Jimei was drunk and dozed off and, because he slept, his leather coat was stolen. The monarch of Song heard about it and asked him, "Even though you got drunk, how could you have lost the leather coat on your body?"

Shao Jimei replied, "Jie of the Xia Dynasty (c. 21st-c. 17th century B.C.) lost his country because of drunkenness. In *the Book of History* (one of the thirteen classics), the *Announcement to Kang* (a chapter in *the Book of History*) has said, 'Don't use the *yi* cup (the *yi* cup is a wine vessel) for wine.' Don't use it for wine is not to get drunk often. The Son of Heaven can lose his state by getting drunk, the common people likewise can lose his life by getting drunk once too often."

209. An Old Horse knows the Way

One year in the Spring and Autumn Period, the duke Huan of Qi led a huge army to attack the state of Shanrong to the north, and the state of Shanrong asked the state of Guzhu to sent reinforcements to help fend off the enemy. The monarch of Guzhu, Da Li-a, was a crafty, ruthless fellow. He instigated his subordinate, marshal Huanghua, to surrender pretendedly to the Qi army in order to lead the Qi soldiers into a maze valley, where Duke Huan encountered dangerously steep mountainsides in every direction without a trail, and howling winds scattering flying sands and moving stones everywhere. The chill entered into the very flesh of the men. The duke hastily looked for marshal Huanghua, but Huanghua had already slipped away. The Qi army was in a state of confusion, plunging forward on one side, dashing in on the other, trampling each other. Casualties were heavy, and the situation became extremely critical.

The duke Huan of Qi consulted with the prime minister, Guan Zhong, and Guan Zhong, after deliberating for a moment, struck on a brilliant scheme. He sent someone to select a few old stallions from the horses that were captured from the state of Guzhu, untied them, and let them moved freely, while the Qi troops followed at the back. The instinct and experience led the old stallions to eventually find the way to get out of the mountain, and the duke Huan of Qi was able to break the impasse. What followed was the Qi troops defeated the army of Guzhu, quelled the rebellion, and brought peace to the northern territory.

210. Useless Talent

A native of the state of Lu knew how to make a pair of straw sandals, and his wife could also spin and weave plain silk fabric. With these skills, they thought of moving to the state of Yue.

Someone told them, saying, "You will have to endure poverty if you move over to Yue."

"Why?" the man from Lu asked.

That someone replied, "A pair of sandals is made for a man to wear, but the people of Yue are used to walking bare-footed; plain silk fabric is spun for hats, but the people of Yue take delight in having their hair hanging loose, and prefer not to wear hats. That's why you will have to endure poverty despite your abilities, because the country you go to does not require your talents."

211. A Daughter's Marriage

A man of Wei, whose daughter was about to get married, inculcated his belief in her, saying, "After your marriage, you must make it a point to save money of your own. It is not uncommon for a wife to be cast off and sent home. To reach old age together is only a matter of luck."

When she eventually moved over to her husband's home, as expected, she saved for herself a lot of money over the years. Because of that, her mother-in-law thought she was too selfish, and instigated her son to have his wife cast off and sent home. Thus she brought back to her parents' home more than double the amount of her dowry. Her father was overjoyed to see her back. He not only did not regret the miseducation inculcated in his daughter, but exulted at his own prevision, because it resulted in the increase of wealth.

Today, many of the officials in power are men of this type.

212. Appraising Horses

Bo Le taught two of his students the expertise to know a horse that inclined to kick, and they both went together to Zhao Jianzi's stable to look at the horses. One of them pointed out a kicking horse, the other man stroked the horse from the rear upwards, did so again and again at its bottom, but the horse did not kick at the man. The person who said the horse would kick thought he had made a mistake, but the other man said, "You are not wrong. This is really a kicking horse. The fact is, the muscles and bones of its shoulders have been hurt, and the knees of its front legs are a little swollen. One must know that when a horse kicks a man, its hind legs are raised, and the center of gravity moves to the front part of its body. Because of the wound in the front legs, it will be difficult to support its body, and that's why it cannot raise its hind legs to kick. You are adept at knowing a horse that kicks, but not good eough at discovering its swollen knees."

213. Xuyou's Self-imposed Exile

Tang Yao (a sage king of over 4,000 years ago) gave the important post of administering the country to Xuyou, but Xuyou was unwilling to accept the heavy responsibility and exiled himself to live in the house of a common man. The common man was afraid Xuyou might steal his belongings, and hastily concealed his leather hat.

Considering Xuyou could refuse the gift of running a country, yet the head of a common family could not trust him with his leather hat and had to conceal it, it did seem the man was too ignorant to understand Xuyou.

214. Three Lice competed for Blood

Three lice on the fat pig had a quarrel, and another louse went over to them and asked, "What are you quarrelling about?" The three lice simultaneously replied, "We are fighting for the place that has more blood and meat!"

The other louse said, "Are you not worried about the imminence of the sacrificial moon (the ancient practice of offering sacrifices to the gods in the twelfth month of the lunar year, hence the term 'sacrificial' for the twelfth moon), when twitch-grass and firewood will be burnt to cook and offer your host as sacrifice to man's ancestors? Why are you not making good use of your time to suck blood, but quarrelling to no purpose?" So the lice stopped their bickering, gathered together to suck the blood of the pig desperately. As a result, the pig wasted away and, because of that, people did not kill it for sacrifice when the sacrificial moon arrived.

215. A Self-biting Snake

Hui, a poisonous snake, had two mouths on its body. Whenever they competed for food, the two mouths would bite one another. The internecine strife resulted in its own destruction.

The fight for power and money among the monarch's officials likewise would lead to the destruction of the country. They were kith and kin of the poisonous snake mentioned.

216. A Ferocious Neighbour

A man wanted to sell his house in order to get away from his ferocious neighbour.

Somebody told him, "Your neighbour has almost reached the limit of crimes tolerated by Heaven. Just be patient and wait a little longer!"

The man replied, "What I'm afraid of is he will make me his last crime before the limit is reached!" And he sold his house and moved away.

That was why people said, one should not have anything to do with matter that contained a dangerous element in it.

217. Wenzi shunned Sefu

Zhongxing Wenzi, who once was one of the six highest officials in the government of Jin, fled the country because of an offence he committed. When he passed a certain county town, his attendant said, "Isn't Sefu of this county your friend? Why don't you take a rest at his home? In so doing we can also wait for the other carriages to catch up." Wenzi replied, "Formerly this man used to send me the lute and psaltery because I loved music, and when he learned that I liked articles of personal adornment, he would present me with jade bracelet and that sort of thing,—all this had aided and abetted my mistakes. He is exactly the kind of man, adept at rubbing me the right way to obtain favour and realize his objective. Now that I've fallen so low, it is possible he will send me to somebody else as a gift." Having said that, he hastily left the place. No long after that, sure enough, Sefu intercepted and seized the two carriages belonged to Wenzi's attendant, and presented them to his king.

218. The Big Bell's Arrival

Zhibo of Jin wanted to subjugate a small country called Chouyou (in present Yu County, Shanxi Province). However, Chouyou was situated in a mountainous area, where the roads were difficult and dangerous to travel. Zhibo struck on a scheme: he ordered a big bell cast, and presented it to the monarch of Chouyou as gift. The monarch of Chouyou was overwhelmed by this unexpected honour, and prepared to have a road constructed, so that the big bell could be carried back by a wagon. His official Chizhang Manzhi remonstrated with him, saying, "It mustn't be done! It stands to reason that a small country should present to a big country with gifts, asking for protection; but now instead, a big country is sending present to a small country. That's very abnormal. When the road to transport the bell is constructed, and the bell comes in through it, the troops of Jin will certainly follow behind. That's why the bell must by no means be accepted."

However, the monarch of Chouyou turned a deaf ear to his advice, and the road was constructed as planned in anticipation of the arrival of the big bell. Chizhang Manzhi saw that the monarch did not follow his advice. He had the axle of his carriage shortened to enable it to pass through the small mountain path, and escaped to the state of Qi. Seven months later, the chariots of Zhibo passed through the newly constructed road without any hindrance, and the state of Chouyou was wiped out.

219. Dreaming of the Cooking Stove

When the duke Ling of Wei was still living, Mi Zixia was his favourite, and he dominated the government over major issues. A midget, at the time he was granted a visit to the duke Ling of Wei, remarked, "My dream has come true."

"What dream?" asked Duke Ling.

The midget replied, "I dreamed of a cooking stove, and that indicated my visit to the monarch."

The duke flew into a rage when he heard this, and said, "I heard that to visit the monarch, the dream must be about the sun. Why have you dreamed of a cooking stove while visiting me?"

The midget replied, "The sun illuminates the whole world, and no object can block its light; the monarch's lustre illuminates the whole country, and nobody can deceive him. That's why people say one will dream of the sun when one is about to meet the monarch. As to the cooking stove, well, when there is a man standing in front of it to take care of the fire, anyone behind him will not be able to see the light anymore. At present, it seems there is such a man taking care of the fire. If so, why can't I dream of the cooking stove?"

220. The Deep Ravine in Shiyi

Dong Yanyu was sent by the king of Zhao to Shangdi as an administrative official. That day he travelled to the mountain of Shiyi, where the ravine was deep and the current swift, the sharp-cut cliffs were like walls, and if you looked down, the depth seemed over three hundred meters, precipitous and scary. He asked the country people, "Did anybody ever come here before?" The people replied, "None." He asked again, "Did children, idiots, the deaf, women, and the lawless ever come here before?" The people answered, "Never." "In that case, did animals like cows, horses, dogs and pigs ever come here?" The people said none ever came. Dong Yanyu thought for a moment, then sighed with deep feeling, and said, "I know how to run the place now. If I enforce the laws already enacted to the letter, those who break them will be like falling into the deep ravine, death is certain, and people will take care not to break the laws. In this manner, the laws will be upheld. How can the the place not be geverned well?"

221. Gold Pilferer

In southern Chu, placer gold was found in the Lishui or Li River, and most people went gold washing secretly.

The imperial government had explicit order banning gold washing. Those who broke the law would be sentenced to have his body torn by five horses in the market place when he was caught. Those being punished were many, and the Li River was blocked with corpses, but gold pilfering did not stop.

There was no other punishment more severe than tearing the body limb from limb by five horses in the market place, but gold pilfering continued despite the heavy penalty. The reason was, some people did slip through the net by luck.

222. The King of Yue and the Heroic Frog

Gou Jian, the king of Yue, was in his carriage on the road when he saw a frog with a bulging body. Supported by the shaft in front, Gou Jian lowered his head and showed his respect to the frog. The driver asked him, "Why did you show respect to a frog?" The king of Yue replied, "The frog is so tough and full of courage. How can I not show my respect to it?"

The people and those in the army of Yue were all encouraged by the news, saying, "The king of Yue showed his respect to a mere frog. How much more so will he respect the people and soldiers who are courageous?" That year, the whole country, irrespective of their station in life, set great store by bravery, so much so that there was man who cut off his own head, and asked members of his family to present it to the king of Yue.

223. Making up the Number

In the Period of Warring States, the king Xuan of Qi liked to watch performance where the wind instrument, *yu*, was an inseparable part of the orchestra. He especially loved instrumental ensemble. Thus during that year he ordered a band of three hundred persons organized.

A scholar, Nanguo, not being successful in his endeavour to become an official, heard the news and came to enrol as a player of the wind instrument. The king was very pleased, and kept him in the band. Actually, this Mr Nanguo was not a player of the wind instrument at all. He only mingled with the team and pretended to play whenever the ensemble went into action. But even though he could not play, he was one of the three hundred musicians, enjoying the same official meal and salary as anybody else.

Later, when the king Xuan of Qi died, his son inherited the throne and became the king Min of Qi. King Min too loved the wind instrument, *yu*, but with a difference. He liked to listen to instrumental solo, and insisted on each playing independently by turns. Realizing that the situation was against him, Mr Nanguo hastily rolled up his swag and quietly left the place.

224. The Marquis Zhao of Han

The marquis Zhao of Han palmed his fingernail and told everyone in the court that he had lost it, pretending in the meantime to look for it everywhere with anxiety. Thereupon every official in the court hastily cut off their own fingernails to present to the marquis.

This was in fact a ruse of Marquis Zhao's, designed to test whether or not the officials were loyal to him.

225. Merger, to Be or Not to Be

After Jin disintegrated into three political entities, the kings of Wei and Zheng met again on one occasion, during which the king of Wei said to the king of Zheng, "In the beginning, the state of Zheng and the state of Wei were one country. It was later that the country was divided into two. I've now set my mind on merging the state of Zheng with the state of Wei again. What do you think of my idea?" The king of Zheng was restless after what he heard. He gathered the court officials to discuss the unreasonable demand of the king of Wei and to draw up the tactics to deal with it. His son said to him, "This is easy to cope with. You can just say to the king of Wei, 'If it is because the states of Zheng and Wei were originally one country and could be united again as one, we are thinking why not let the state of Liang merge into the state of Zheng.'" From then on the king of Wei no longer raised the same unjustifiable question.

226. Power and Influence

Jing Guojun became prime minister of Qi, and when he and his friends gathered and talked more often, his friend soon became rich; when he expressed sympathy and solicitude for his attendants, his attendants were regarded as important persons at once.

Just because the prime minister talked to certain people more often, or expressed sympathy and solicitude, people who were low in social station would be regarded as important persons, and some people even became rich. Needless to say, if he himself were to use his power in connection with his official position, how much more so?

227. Prayers of Husband and Wife

A couple in the state of Wei prayed together, and the wife said, "O Heaven! Please bless me with safety and bestow upon me a hundred strings of coins!"

Her husband said, "Why asked for so little?"

The wife replied, "If I asked more than that, you would use the money to get a concubine."

228. A Beauty lost her Nose

The king of Jing (another name for the state of Chu) had a fovourite concubine called Zhengxiu. Recently the king of Jing came by a beautiful girl, and Zhengxiu pretended to give her guidance by saying, "The king likes to see the pose whereby a person's mouth was covered up. Therefore, whenever you go near the king, do remember to cover up your mouth." Wherefore when the fresh beauty went to see the king, she made it a point to cover her mouth as she came near the king. The king of Jing was bewildered and asked the reason for her practice. Zhengxiu said, "She thought Your Majesty's body had a bad smell."

When the king of Jing, his favourite concubine Zhengxiu, and the beauty were about to take their respective seats, Zhengxiu urged the attendant again and again, saying, "Implement at once whatever the king's order is."

The king of Jing said, "Beauty, come forward." The beautiful girl covered her mouth several times as she came near the king. The king of Jing was furious, and ordered, "Cut off her nose." Thereupon the attendant immediately unsheathed his knife, and had her nose removed.

229. The Duke's Chef

During the reign of the duke Wen of Jin, a chef sent someone to present roast meat, but it was discovered the meat had human hair in it. Duke Wen summoned the chef and loudly reproached him, saying, "Are you going to choke me to death. Why left human hair in the meat?" The chef bowed till his forehead touched the ground. After kowtowing twice, he deliberately admitted his guilt, saying, "Your humble servant deserved to die. There were three guilts, all deserving the death penalty. First, I had the best sharpening stone, with which my knife was honed till it became as sharp as the precious sword *ganjiang*. However, although it could cut meat, it could not cut hair. This was my first guilt. Secondly, I used wooden sticks to pierce the meat, yet did not discover the hair. This is my second guilt. I carried a red hot stove, where the charcoal burnt bright, and the meat was roasted till it smelt sweet and appetizing, but the hair was not burnt. That was my third guilt. But I guess there may be someone in this hall who hates your humble servant." Duke Wen listened and thought it quite reasonable, so he said, "Right." And he summoned all the officials at one end of the hall, interrogated them one by one. In the end, he discovered the man who intended to frame the chef, and the duke Wen of Jin had him executed.

230. Buy the Casket without the Jewels

In the state of Chu, there was a jewellery merchant, who owned a priceless large pearl. A beautiful wooden box was created to keep it. The box used the rare timber—the wood of lily magnolia—as material, and had a very ingenious design and elegant style. Outside, it was engraved painstakingly with rose pattern, inlaid with sparkling pearls and jade, and surrounded by glittering emerald. It was fumigated with perfume until its unusual fragrance assailed the nostrils. He arrived in the state of Zheng with this precious object.

One day, this merchant from the state of Chu put his precious object for sale in the market. Those who saw it praised the magnificent box highly. A merchant of the state of Zheng offered to pay the Chu merchant's asking price, which was quite a big sum of money, and the transaction was concluded. The buyer opened the box and discovered the big pearl. He returned it to the Chu merchant, keeping only the beautiful wooden box. A bystander saw what happened, and laughed secretly at the ignorance of the man of Zheng, who apparently did not know the true value of the pearl.

231. A Singing Sheji

The king of Song had a long-standing feud with the state of Qi, and it became necessary for him to construct a military drilling ground whereby officers and men could be trained as a defensive measure in anticipation of an attack from Qi. Gui, a singer at the construction site, sang along as he worked. His voice was so beautiful that those who passed him would stop and listen, and the craftsmen too forgot their fatigue. When the king of Song heard about it, he summoned Gui for a citation. But Gui said, "My master sheji's voice is much better than mine." So the king of Song sent for Sheji, and let him also sing in the construction site. Despite Gui's commendation, however, Sheji's singing seemed to avail but little, for those who were walking no longer stopped to listen, and the craftsmen were beginning to feel fatigued. The king asked Gui, "It is not as you said, for the walking continue to walk, and the craftsmen become fatigued. It seems to me Sheji does not sing as well as you." Gui replied, "Will Your Majesty please examine the effect? At the time I was singing, the height of the wall only increased by four planks, whereas when Sheji sang, the height doubled and reached eight planks. Further, if you look at the hardness of the wall, you could poke five inches into that part done when I was singing, but only two inches that which was piled up when Sheji sang."

232. A Mother Monkey on the Thorn's Tip

The monarch of Yan loved dainty, delicate little things, and a man from the state of Wei catered to his wishes by saying, "I can carve a mother monkey on the tip of a thorn from the jujube tree." The king of Yan was very pleased and provided him with a generous official salary.

The king of Yan said to him, "Let me see the mother monkey you carved on the tip of the thorn from the jujube tree."

The man from Wei said, "If Your Majesty wishes to see it, you must refrain from going to the imperial harem for half a year, stay away from drinking and not eat any meat. In addition to that, you must wait till the drizzle just stop, at the exact moment when the sun emerges, and in the split second when the sky is in a twilight condition—at that precise instant, you will be able to see the monkey at the tip of the thorn from the jujube tree."

The man from Wei knew the king was incapable of fulfilling the conditions he raised. The end result was that the king provided for the man from Wei all for nothing, for he could never see the monkey he carved.

In a place called Taixia in the state of Zheng, a blacksmith learned about the matter, and he told the monarch of Yan, "I'm a blacksmith who makes carving knives. I know for a fact that no matter how dainty and delicate an object may be, it must be carved with the carving knife and, besides, the object carved must necessarily larger than the knife. If the tip of the thorn from the jujube tree cannot accommodate the blade of the engraving knife, how can one carve a mother monkey on it? That's why your Majesty only needs to look at the engraving knife of the man from Wei to know whether he can carve a mother monkey on the tip of the thorn from the jujube tree or not."

The king of Yan said, "It's a good idea!" He summoned the man from Wei at once, and said, "What kind of tool you used to carve the mother monkey on the tip of the thorn from the jujube tree?"

"A Carving knife," the man from Wei replied.

The king of Yan then said, "I'd like to see your carving knife."

The man from Wei replied, "I'll get it from my house." And seizing the opportunity to save himself, he fled.

233. A White Horse crossed the Checkpoint

Er Shuo was a well-known sophist in the state of Song. His theory was based on "a white horse is not a horse" premise which Gongsun Longzi had advocated. With this premise, he argued heatedly with all contenders at Jixia, and won all the debates brilliantly. However, when he complacently rode his white horse about to pass the checkpoint, he was barred by the soldiers there from crossing it unless he paid the horse tax. Again he used his "a white horse is not a horse" theory but, despite his eloquence, the soldiers' principle was simple: no tax, no pass. In the end, Er Shuo had to follow the regulations and paid the tax, which made him rather depressed.

234. A Matter of Age

In the state of Zheng, two persons were arguing who was older. One man said, "I was born in the same year as Tang Yao (a sage king of over 4,000 years ago)." The other said, "I'm of the same age as the elder brother of Yellow Emperor (a legendary ruler)!" It was an endless debate, as each stuck to his guns, neither would give way. Well, the truth was, whoever could talk untill the other side was left without an argument, he would be declared the winner.

235. Painting on a Pod

A guest who was not a relative painted a picture on the pod for Mr Zhou. The work took him three solid years. Mr Zhou noticed that it was like a pod with a coat of paint, and felt very angry.

The man who drew the picture on the pod said, "Please construct a wall four metres high and bore a window of eight square inches in size; then wait until the sun rises. Place the painted pod at the window, and see the painting on its surface."

Mr Zhou did as he said, and looked at the painting on the surface of the pod from afar. There were figures of dragons, snakes, animals, and carriages, complete in every posture. Thereupon Mr Zhou became happier.

The painting was indeed done with consummate skill and meticulous care but, much as a pod with a coat of paint did, it served no useful purpose.

236. Easier to Paint a Ghost than a Man

A painter, who came to paint for the king of Qi, was being asked, "What object is the most difficult to paint?" The painter replied, "The dog and the horse are the most difficult."

"What is the easiest?"

The painter replied, "Ghosts are the easiest. That is because people have an intimate knowledge of the dog and the horse. They appear before us almost all the time, and are difficult to paint exactly as they are. People will notice the slightest difference at once if there is any. That's why I say they are the hardest to paint. As to ghosts, they are intangible. Nobody ever saw them. However you draw them, it makes no difference at all. That's why I say they are the easiest."

237. A Solid Gourd

There was a recluse called Tian Zhong in the state of Qi. Qugu, a man of the state of Song, went to see him and said, "I've heard, sir, that you are a man of high moral integrity, that you want to leave the human society, and that you don't want to have to depend on others to live. I've here a big gourd. It is as solid as a rock. Its outer shell is so thick and hard that no hole can be bored into it. I'm now present it to you, sir."

Tian Zhong said, "The most precious attribute of a gourd is that it can be used to hold things. Now the outer shell of your gourd is so thick that a hole cannot be bored into it, and that is to say it cannot be opened to hold any object. Moreover, it is as hard as a rock, and that means it cannot be split to make a scoop. What good is this gourd to me?"

Qugu said, "You are perfectly right there. I'll throw it away by and by. Now, sir, you intend to leave the human society to become a recluse. That will not do any good to the state. In fact, you are not much different from the hardest gourd!"

238. A Child's Game

When children played, they take the dust as food, watery mud as soup, and a piece of wood as a chunk of meat. But when they are tired of playing, they will go home in the evening for supper. The reason is because those simulated food and vegetables are only dust and watery mud, they can be so treated in a game but cannot be eaten like real food.

Singing the praise of the men and their deeds that have been eulogized since ancient times is good to listen to, but not realistic. Extolling the benevolence and righteousness of past kings but unable to run the country well, is similar to the children's game, entirely useless and should not be taken as real in the administration of a state!

239. Making a Pair of Trousers

Bozi, a man from the state of Zheng, bought a new piece of cloth, and requested his wife to make a pair of trousers for him. His wife asked him, "What manner of trousers do you want me to make?" The husband replied, "More or less like the pair of old trousers I wear." The wife put the new piece of cloth on the floor, twisted and rubbed it again and again, washed it, until the piece of cloth became worn-out ere she began making it stitch by stitch, using her husband's old trousers as pattern. When it was finished, as expected, they looked exactly like the pair her husband was wearing. Her husband almost fainted when he saw them, not knowing whether to laugh or to cry, saying, "Is this the new pair of trousers?" The wife replied, "That's right! It was done according to your wish, and similar to the pair of your worn-out trousers!"

240. Bozi's Wife and the Soft-shelled Turtle

The wife of Bozi, who came from the state of Zheng, went to the market. She bought a soft-shelled turtle and brought it home. When she was crossing the Yingshui, or Ying River, she thought the turtle must be thirsty, and released it into the river to drink. The result: the turtle escaped as soon as it was put into the river.

241. Distorted Interpretation

During the Spring and Autumn and the Warring States Periods, one night in the Chu capital, Yingdu, a scholar was wholly absorbed in writing a letter to the prime minister of the state of Yan. As he wrote on, the lamp suddenly became dim, and the words were hardly discenible. Without turning his head, he ordered his servant, "Raise the candle." The meaning was very clear. Regrettably, however, he was concentrating on his writing, and the words "raise the candle" were written into the letter by mistake while he was ordering the servant. The words had nothing to do with the content of the letter at all.

The prime minister of the state of Yan, upon receipt of the letter, read the words "raise the candle". At first, he was baffled, then gradually he thought he understood, and soon became very pleased, saying, "The man was deliberately being obscure, but I do understand it. He is hinting at running the country by promoting honesty and openheartedness. To promote honesty and openheartedness, one must recommend men of talent and integrity to be the state's officials." Thereupon the prime minister at once conveyed the meaning of the words "raise the candle" to the king of Yan. The king was overjoyed. He drew up state policies based on the meaning of the words, and the state was well run thenceforward.

242. Buying Shoes

During the Spring and Autumn Period, there was a muddle-headed man in the state of Zheng, who went to buy a pair of new shoes in a downtown shoeshop. Before leaving home, he measured the size of his foot with a ruler, and used a string to mark the measurement. But he was in a hurry, and carelessly left the string that stood for the measurement at home. As he arrived at the shoeshop, he fumbled all his pockets for quite a while only to discover that he had left it behind. Anxiously he said to the shopkeeper, "I've forgotten to bring the measurement of my feet, and it is difficult to make comparison. Allow me to go back and get it."

Rashly he returned home, and hurriedly he came back to town. By that time it was already dark, and the shoeshop had closed. He was despondent. He had made the journey twice, but still could not get the new shoes he wanted to buy. A kind-hearted man heard him sigh and asked him, "Who do you buy the shoes for? Why take so much trouble?" The muddle-headed man became even angrier when he heard what the man say. He reproved the man, saying, "I buy my own shoes. What's that to do with you?" The kind-hearted man was baffled and said, "If it's yourself, why do you need the measurement? Can you not just try them on your feet?" But he disagreed, "How can my feet be as dependable as my measurement?"

243. Wearing Purple

The duke Huan of Qi loved purple clothes and residents of the entire city followed his example. As a result, the price of purple clothes increased dramatically. A piece of purple clothes cost five times its equivalent in plain colour. Duke Huan was worried and he asked Guan Zhong, saying, "I like to wear purple clothes, but they are very expensive now. Yet, even so, it is difficult to stop the people from wearing purple. What do you think I should do?" Guan Zhong replied, "If you are bent on changing the prevailing habit, why not put away your purple clothes for a while. You can also tell the people around you, saying, 'I hate the odour from the purple dyestuff.' And whenever people with purple dress come to pay you a visit, you can tell them, 'Please step back a little. I hate the odour of the purple dye.'" The duke Huan of Qi said, "I'll try your idea." Sure enough, not even one of the court officials wore purple that day. The next day, there were none wearing purple in the entire city. By the third day, the whole nation could not see a person with purple dress.

244. An Army of Justice

Both the state of Song and the state of Chu had made up their minds to fight on the bank of the River Hong, or Hongshui. The soldiers of Song had already lined up, while the soldiers of Chu were still crossing the river. The right minister of war, Gouqiang, stepped forward and told the duke Xiang of Song, saying, "The Chu soldiers were more numerous than the Song soldiers. The Song army should attack when the Chu army is half way across the river and not yet lining up. In this manner, the Chu army's defeat is assured."

But the duke Xiang of Song said, "I heard man of moral integrity said, 'Do not overkill; do not capture grey-haired old soldiers; when people are in a dangerous situation, do not push them over the cliff into the chasm; when people are in difficulty, do not forced them to desperation; and don't attack an army that has yet to line up and fight. Now the army of Chu are still half way across the river and, if we push forward, it will be contrary to the path of justice. We should let the Chu army cross over and line up in battle array before we beat the drum and attack."

The right minister of war said, "My dear monarch, people are the foundation of a country! When the people of Song cannot even protect their own lives, what more can we talk of justice?"

Nevertheless, the duke Xiang of Song insisted on his own opinion, and said to the right minister of war, "Go back to your troops at once, otherwise I may have to court-martial you." Thus the right minister of war, Gouqiang, had no alternative but to return to his troops. Duke Xiang waited until all the Chu soldiers had crossed the river and lined up before beating the drum to attack. As a result, the Song army suffered a crushing defeat, and Duke Xiang himself was severely wounded in the thigh. He died three days later. That was the disastrous consequence of his admiration for justice.

245. More Haste, Less Speed

Once, the duke Jing of Qi went sightseeing in the East China Sea. Out of the blue, a courier arrived from the capital by a swift horse and reported to Duke Jing, saying, "The prime minister Yanying is seriously ill. He is on the verge of death, and beg the monarch to return posthaste, or else it may be too late."

The news startled Duke Jing, and he stood up in a flash. At that moment, another courier arrived, urging him to return immediately.

Duke Jing's mind was weighed down by anxiety. He shouted as he walked, "Prepare the carriage, and get Hanshu to drive for me. Be quick and back to the capital."

As he set out, Duke Jing's mind was afire with impatience while sitting in the carriage. He complained that the carriage did not go fast enough and, after several hundred paces, he took over the reins, trying to drive himself.

He did so for another several hundred paces before he bemoaned the slowness of the horses anew, and simply left the carriage to run by foot. Well, Duke Jing thought even with such good carriage and swift horses, and a skilful driver like Hanshu, he could still run faster all by himself.

246. Example is better than Precept

The king of the state of Zou liked to wear hats with long decorative ribbons and, when his subjects saw it, they all imitated him by having long ribbons on their hats as decoration. The ribbons were embroidered with elegantly beautiful pattern, and the price was high. The king, when he came to know it, was very worried, and he asked the officials around him why the ribbons were so expensive. His attending officials said, "It's because the monarch likes to decorate his hats with ribbons, which the people imitate, that the price of ribbons has gone up."

After learning what his officials had to say, the king of Zou made it a priority to cut off the ribbons on his hat before riding his carriage out on a tour of inspection. The people noticed there were no ribbons on the manarch's hat, and the custom quickly faded.

Since it was not feasible to force the people to stop wearing hats with long ribbons, the king cut off the long ribbons on his own hats instead, setting an example for them to follow. That was to say, putting himself to some inconvenience prior to have the people followed of their own free will.

247. An Apology

Sheng Buhai was a distinguished member of the Legalists in the period of Warring States. For fifteen years he was the prime minister of the state of Han.

One day, the king, Marquis Zhao of Han, said to him with a heavy heart, "It's really very difficult to put the legal system in place!" "What's there so difficult about?" replied Sheng Buhai arguementatively. "First of all, the legal system demands meting out the proper rewards and penalties, avoiding the practice of favouritism, rewarding the meritorious, and appointing people on their merits. But just look at what you did. You have often privately granted the requests of your relatives, or fovourite officials, despite the existing laws. You have acted with partiality, defeating the end of justice, and asked other people to uphold the laws. That of course is not an easy matter." Marquis Zhao blushed and nodded his head, saying, "I'm grateful for your instructions. From now on, I understand how the legal system should be put into practice."

Some time later, Sheng Buhai's cousin arrived in the capital seeking some official appointment. Sheng Buhai went to the king asking for the favour of an official title. The king lowered his head and kept quiet. After a while, he said, "That seems not what you have taught me before, isn't it? Should I violate your teachings, open a back door, and destroy the system of law, or should I follow your teachings and refuse to open the back door?" A blush of shame spread over Sheng Buhai's face when he heard the king's words. He prostrated himself before the king and offered an apology.

248. Keeping One's Promise

Zeng Shen's wife was going out, and her son cried, wanting to accompany her. She told her son, "Please go back. I'll kill a pig for you when I come back."

The moment his wife returned from the market, Zeng Shen immediately wanted to catch and kill a pig. His wife halted him, saying, "I was only kidding the child."

Zeng Shen said, "How can you kid a child? A child is ignorant of the way of the world. They learn from their parents, listening to their instrucions. If you tell them a lie, that is equivalent to teaching them to lie to others! When a mother lies to a son, the son will no longer believe in his mother. That's not a good way to educate a child!"

After he finished talking, he went to kill and cook a pig for the child to eat.

249. Kidding the People

Whenever the king Li of Chu discovered the presence of the enemy, he would beat the drum to convene the people in order to defend the city. One day, King Li got drunk and, his mind in a haze, picked up the drumsticks and beat the drum. When the people heard the sound of drum, they clustered around all in a fluster. Hastily, King Li sent his men to stop them and convey the message: "King Li got drunk and, his mind in a haze, picked up the drumsticks and beat the drum. He was only kidding." Thereupon all the people returned home.

Several months later, the enemy launched an attack, and King Li beat the drum to call the people, but the people thought it was the king kidding them again, and did not come to defend the city as in previous occasions. It was only after King Li altered the original order, and adopted a new alarm signal, that the people's confidence was restored.

250. Confucianists do not Play Chess

The king Xuan of Qi asked Kuangqian, "Do the Confucianists play chess?"

Kuangqian replied, "They do not play chess."

The king Xuan of Qi asked, "Why is it so?"

Kuangqian replied, "In chess, the formidable man is considered honourable. The winner must kill this villian, and that is equivalent to killing the honorable. From the standpoint of the Confucianists, this is something that causes harm to justice, and that is the reason why they do not play chess."

King Xuan asked, "Do the Confucianists shoot at birds?"

Kuangqian replied, "They do not shoot at birds. Because to shoot at a bird, one must do it from the earth to the sky. That is like the inferiors going against the superiors, eventually going to hurt the monarch. From the standpoint of the Confucianists, this is causing harm to justice, and that is why they do not shoot at birds."

The king Xuan of Qi again asked, "Do the Confucianists play musical instruments?"

Kuangqian replied, "They do not play musical instruments, and it is because the small string produces high-pitched sound, and the big string, on the contrary, produces low-pitched sound. That is as if the old and the young had their places reversed, and the social ranks turned upside down! From the stanpoint of the Confucianists, this is also something that brings harm to justice, and that is why they do not play musical instruments."

King Xuan said, "You are right."

251. Ximen Bao as Administrator

When Ximen Bao took over the administration of Ye (north of Anyang, Henan Province), he was self-denying and public-spirited, not even the smallest object would he take for himself. He would not fawn on the high officials around the king's person. Those officials therefore came together to slander him before the king.

As the administration of Ximen Bao reached a full year, the king took back his official seal and position when he came to turn over the taxes he had collected to the king. Ximen Bao supplicated, saying, "I did not know how to administer the place before. Now that I've learned the knack of it, will my king please give back to me the official seal so that I can continue to run the place. I promise if I'm not equal to the job, I'll submit myself to the penalty of decapitation." The Marquis Wen of Wei could not bear to take away his official position, and so the seal was returned to him. When Ximen Bao took over the adminisration of Ye for the second time, his style of governance underwent a dramatic change. He began to bleed the people white with ruthless taxation, and to fawn on the high officials near the king with the best effort, giving away large amount of money. At the end of the year, when Ximen

Bao again reported to the king, the king was overjoyed, and came out to welcome him in person. Ximen Bao said to Marquis Wen, "Last year I administered Ye for my king, and the king wanted to take away my official seal; this year I did it for the high officials around you, and you commended me. I cannot be the administrator now." He surrendered his official seal and was ready to leave. Marquis Wen, however, would not accept it. He said, "I did not understand you before, but now I do. Please try your best to administer the place of Ye for me." In the end, Marquis Wen did not take back the official seal from Ximen Bao.

252. Why Gong Yixiu did not Accept the Fish

Gong Yixiu held the position of prime minister in the state of Lu. He liked especially to eat fish, and everyone in the country fell over each other to present fish in an attempt to curry favour with him. But Gong Yixiu refused to accept them.

His disciple tried to persuade him, saying, "You like fish, sir, and yet you don't accept them from the people. Why do you insist so?"

Gong Yixiu replied, "It is prcisely because I like fish that I'll not accept the fish. If I accept the fish from the people, I'll have to give in to their demand at the crucial moment; if I give in to the demand of others, then I'll have to distort the law to do it; and for a law-enforcement official to be guilty of law-breaking activities is to court the danger of dismissal from office. Suppose I were to be dismissed from the office of premiership, the people would certainly not continue to send me fish, even though I like fish very much. By that time, I would not be in a position to buy fish myself either. If I do not accept the fish now, I'll not run the risk of bending the law to suit private interests; not to bend the law to suit private interests, I'll not be dismissed; not be dismissed, I'll then be able to provide myself with fish with my own official salary, even if my love for fish remains unchanged all through my life."

253. Antilogy

A man was simultaneously selling a spear and a shield in a busy marketplace. First he shouted, "Come and see! My spear is keen and sharp, and it will break any shield in the world with a stab, no matter how strong the shield may be. There is no other spears that can compare with this.!" A man in the crowd of spectators was moved by his eloquence and about to buy the spear when he gave a big pat on the shield in hand and continued, saying, "Look, here is my shield. It is the strongest shield ever made. Even the keenest spear will not be able to break it!"

At this juncture, a clear-headed man came forward. He took over where the man had left off and raised a question, "Suppose I use your spear to attack your shield, what will be the result?" The man who was selling the spear and the shield was agape and tongue-tied, not knowing what to say. Surrounded by a jeering crowd, he dumbly fixed his gaze at the spear and shield in his hand, looking very much put out.

254. Wait for Gains without Pains

In the Spring and Autumn Period, there lived in the state of Song a farmer, whose field had a big tree at its fringes. One day, a hare suddenly came along as he was turning the soil in his field. It was probably in a panic as it ran desperately over, knocking itself against the roots of the big tree, and broke its neck. After rolling for a while, it straightened its legs and died. The farmer was overjoyed. He got together his plowing implements, picked up the hare and returned home.

The next day, he came to the field anew. He thought, tilling the land was hard work. If he could sit down and wait for the hare to knock itself against the tree, that would give him time to rest comfortably, while the hare he got could be sold for money, with which he could live a better life. From then on, he had no desire for work. Everyday he would sit under the tree, waiting for the hare to knock itself against the tree. However, he did not see that happening anymore, and it became a standing joke when the story became known in the state of Song.

*

*Guoyu

It was believed in the past that the book was culled from material found in *the Spring and Autumn Annals,* and was called *the Unofficial Spring and Autumn Annals.* Reported to be authored by Zuo Qiuming, it was actually put into the form of a book in the Period of Warring States, and people were still editing it even until the time the king Xiang of Wei was on the throne. There are twenty-one volumes in all, recording the anecdotes of the eight states,—Zhou, Lu, Qi, Jin, Zheng, Chu, Wu, Yue,—with one hundred and ninety six items. The book is distinguished by its insistence on the description of characters. It fills up the gap left by *the Spring and Autumn Annals.*

255. The Virtue of Poverty

Shu Xiang, a senior official of the state of Jin, went to pay Han Xuanzi a visit. At that time, Han Xuanzi was anxious about his poverty, but Shu Xiang congratulated him for being poor.

Han Xuanzi said, "Although I'm a senior official, I do not possess the corresponding wealth. For that reason, I cannot vie with the other senior officials in maneuvering capabilities. The matter has kept me on tenterhooks. What are you congratulating me for?"

Shu Xiang replied, "In the past, senior official Luan Wuzi was so poor that he had only less than seven hectares of land and did not have a complete set of sacrificial utensil to offer sacrifices to his ancestors. But his noble character was known to everyone in the society, and his law-abiding and just attitude has won universal acclamation. As a result, his fame spread farther than all the other princes. All the princes were willing to be his friends, and even the *rong* (name given to the people of the West in ancient times) and the *di* (name given to the people of the North in ancient times) people were convinced of his good intention. For this reason the state of Jin became peaceful and prosperous. He has done his best in executing the law, and calamity was averted. When his son, Huanzi, took over his official position, he became presumptuous and extravagant, insatiably covetous and gluttonous, lawless and unbridled, a loan shark to accumulate wealth by unfair means. Such behaviour would have led to disaster and incurred the wrath of heaven, but his father's moral integrity and influence had come to the rescue, and he had successfully avoided the calamity and died in peace. Then it came to Huanzi's son, Huaizi, who, as a matter of fact, had intended to change his father's way of doing things, and to restore his grandfather's morality and style. It should have been possible for him to evade harm to his person, but the sins of his father, Huanzi, got him into trouble, and he had to leave for the state of Chu as a refugee in the end. There were others such as senior official Xizhi, whose wealth could equal half the state of Jin's national riches, and the number of whose servants and private warriors, half the number of Jin's army. He relied on his wealth and high position, and became arrogant and domineering. In the end he could not escape the fate of being killed, his corpse publicly exposed in the court hall, while his whole clan was exterminated in Jiangyi. Had it not been the case, and judging from the fact that his family had produced five senior officials and three ministers in several generations, his clan's power and influence would have been great indeed. When his clan was exterminated, no sympathy was forthcoming from any quarter. Today you have attained the status of Luan Wuzi's destitution, I believe you will be able, like Luan Wuzi, to develop the moral excellence, and that is why I come to congratulate you. If you are worried only by your deficiency in wealth and not your inability to establish your moral character, then I should come to condole rather than congratulate you."

Having listened to what Shu Xiang had to say, Han Xuanzi bowed his head and saluted him, saying, "I'm old and near death. Fortunately your teachings help me to stay alive. Such favor should not be for me alone. I believe beginning from my ancestor Huanshu to every generation thereafter, all would be indebted to you."

*

*Record of the Warring States
The book was a compilation of the views of the officials of various states and those went about selling ideas during the Period of Warring States. There were a number of other titles by which it was once called. Liu Xiang in the last years of Western Han revised and compiled it into thirty-three chapters, and the present name began to take shape. It was a book of important historical materials, recording the political and military activities of various states during the Warring States Period. At that time, idea-selling and ingenious arguments were much in vogue, and stories were often woven to illustrate the advantages and disadvantages, right and wrong, of a given situation, and to explain political proposition. As a result, many lively fables were left behind for us to enjoy. The fables in this book and the book of *Hanfeizi* each had its own emphasis. *Hanfeizi* used fables to explain his philosophical ideas, while this book emphasized the application of strategy.

256. The Magical Shooter

There was an eminent archer in the state of Chu called Yang Youji. One day, he was doing target practice and, as none of the arrows missed its mark, the crowd surrounded him applauded in unison. Yang Youji himself was encouraged by the enthusiasm. A passerby, taking note of what happened, said, "Good shot! The young man is promising and worthy to be taught." Hearing the remark, Yang Youji was annoyed, saying, "Everybody else acclaims my marksmanship, and you just say I am worthy to be taught. Please give me your advice then!" The man said, "I cannot teach you. But carry on your practice." At this juncture, a man asked Yang Youji, "Can you hit the centre of a willow leaf within a hundred paces?" Having said that, he had the willow leaf painted black and asked Yang Youji to take aim. Yang Youji stood at a distance of more than a hundred paces. Then, he drew the bow and set the arrow, released it, and hit the target. Thereupon another person requested Yang Youji to shoot at three leaves placed at three levels. He obliged; thrice he shot, trice his marksmanship was confirmed. All the spectators clapped their hands in applause. The passerby who voiced his opinion before again said to Yang Youji, "Judging from the fact that you can achieve perfect score on the willow leaves, your skill is not bad. But if you continue like this, you will be exhausted. By that time, can you still achieve perfect score?" Yang Youji was enlightened by these words and said, "I understand what you meant now. A good archer should know when to take a rest. He should also study intensively in order to perfect his skill."

257. Two Wives

A man of Chu had two wives, and another guy with evil intent tried to seduce them. First, he approached the older wife, but met with sharp rebuke. Though disappointed, he did not give up, but turned to the younger one instead. Unbelievably, this time he succeeded. Some time later, the husband passed away. Someone said to the guy who once seduced the wives of the man of Chu, "That's your opportunity. Now, are you going to marry the older one, or the younger one?" "Of course the older one." "The older one once upbraided you, while the younger one had promised to be good to you. Why do you still desire to marry the older one?"

"Well, when she was somebody else's wife, I was hoping she would accept my advances but, now that she will be my wife, I wish she would rebuke anyone who tries to seduce her."

258. A Better Way to Kill the Tigers

Guan Zhuang and his brother, Guan Yu, were hurrying on with their journey in the dense forest of a remote mountain, when suddenly from the foot of the mountain they heard the howling of angry tigers. Hastily they hid themselves behind a big rock, and from that vantagepoint they saw two fierce tigers of variegated colours fighting for a carcass. Guan Zhuang's interest grew, and he unsheathed his sword, ready to go forward to kill the tigers, but Guan Yu caught him by the hand and stopped him, saying, "Don't be too hasty. Tigers were voracious and cruel animals. To compete for the carcass, they will fight fiercely for it. As they fought on, the small one will die and the big one will be wounded. By that time, will it not be killing two birds with one stone?"

Just as expected, Guan Zhuang had an easy job. Moreover, he earned the good reputation of being the killer of two tigers.

259. Bian Qiao and the King of Qin

Bian Qiao, the well-known physician, had an audience with the king Wu of Qin. King Wu told Bian Qiao the state of his illness, and Bian Qiao promised to take care of it.

The attending officials around King Wu, however, advised him, saying, "Your Majesty's cause of trouble is located in front of the ear and under the eye. It won't be easy to get rid of it. If it is not done well, you may end up deaf and blind."

King Wu's confidence was shaken by these words, and he decided not to let Bian Qiao take care of his illness.

As Bian Qiao had already got ready to look after the king's illness, he was very angry upon receipt of the message. He threw the stone needle used for treatment on the floor and sighed, saying, "The king had an understanding with the physician who knew how to cure a disease, but was thwarted by those who did not know. If one runs a country in such a vacillating manner, that country will be ruined in no time."

260. Persistent Rumours Shake the Strongest Confidence

When Zeng Shen was living in Feiyi of the state of Lu, another Zeng Shen bearing the same surname and given name killed a man. Someone came to tell Zeng Shen's mother, saying, "Zeng Shen killed a man!"

Zeng Shen's mother said, "My son could not kill anyone." Then she continued to weave her cotton cloth.

After a while, another persom came to announce, saying, "Zeng Shen has killed a man!" Again, Zeng Shen's mother calmly carried on her weaving as before.

Sometime later, there was yet another man came and said, "Zeng Shen has killed a man!" This time, Zeng Shen's mother was overcome with fear. She quickly threw away the weaving shuttle, climbed over the wall and fled.

261. The Girl at the River Bank

A bevy of girls lived together at the river bank. Among them there was one whose family was poverty-stricken. The rest of the group talked over the matter and decided to throw her out.

As she was about to leave the place, she said to the girls, "It was because I couldn't afford a lamp and often had to borrow the light here that I used to come early, have the floor swept, and the mat spread. Why should you grudge the use of a little surplus light that shines on the four walls? Suppose you just let me use the surplus light, what's that to you? I believe at least I am of some benefit to you. Why do you want to drive me away?"

After discussing the matter among themselves, the girls thought she was right, and let her stay.

262. The Divine Tree

Did you ever hear of a divine tree in Hengsi?
There was a doughty young man in the locality who wanted to wager with the divine tree. He said, "If I win, the tree must lend me its divinity for three days; if I lose, the tree can punish me." Having said that, he pulled out the gambling paraphernalia. Using his left hand, he threw the dice for the tree; and using his right hand, he threw it for himself. The result was, the young man had won. So the tree lent him the divinity.

Three days later, the tree demanded the return of its divinity, but the young man acted shamelessly. The tree withered on the very day the young man went back on his word. In seven days, the tree died.

263. Deception

Zouji, the prime minister of the state of Qi was seven feet tall, a fine-looking man, mighty and handsome. Every morning after he woke up and put on his clothes, he would carefully examine himself in the mirror. Then he would ask his wife, "Compared with the revered Mr Xu north of the city, who is more handsome?"

His wife replied, "Of course it's you. How can the revered Mr Xu be compared with you?"

The revered Mr Xu north of the city was known as a handsome man. That was why Zouji still lacked self-confidence despite his wife's assurance, and had to ask his concubine the same question, "Compared with the revered Mr Xu, who is more handsome?"

The concubine replied, "How can the revered Mr Xu compare with you?"

The next day, a guest arrived. At the reception party given by Zouji, he again asked the guest during their conversation, "Compared with the revered Mr Xu north of the city, who looks more handsome?"

The guest replied, "The revered Mr Xu is not as gook-looking as Your Excellency the prime minister."

In another two days, the revered Mr Xu himself paid Zouji a visit. After carefully examining the revered Mr Xu's features, Zouji felt he was actually not as handsome as the revered Mr Xu. When the revered Mr Xu left him, he picked up the mirror again to look at himself. The more he looked, the more he was convinced the revered Mr Xu was far handsome than he.

That evening he lay on his bed thinking about the matter, "My wife says I am handsome because she loves me; my concubine says I am handsome because she is afraid; the guest says I am handsome because he has something to request of me." And he went to see the king Wei of Qi at dawn, saying, "It is a fact that I am not as handsome as the revered Mr Xu, but my wife loves me, my concubine is afraid of me, my guest has something to request of me, and they all say I am more handsome than the revered Mr Xu. Now, The territory of the state of Qi amounts to a thousand *li*, and there are one hundred and twenty cities. In the palace, all the women love Your Majesty; in the court, all the officials are afraid of Your Majesty; within the state territory, everywhere there are people who have something to request of Your Majesty. Based on my assessment, there must be lots of things Your Majesty has been deceived."

The king Wei of Qi said, "Well said!" Thereupon he ordered rewards be given to any official or subject who can point out the shortcomings of the king.

264. Paint a Snake with Feet

In the olden days, in the southen region where the state of Chu was situated, an aristocrat, accompanied by his servants and attendants, was on his way to offer sacrifices to his ancestors. After the ceremony was over, the aristocrat bestowed upon the servants and attendants a pot of wine as reward. However, there were more men than wine, and it was difficult to decide who should, and should not, drink. After much discussion, they struck on a solution: everyone should draw the picture of a snake, and whoever finished first would be the winner. Thereupon everyone began to draw on the ground. Soon someone had finished drawing the snake. While all the others were still busy, this man picked up the wine pot and get ready to drink. With his left hand on the pot, he said complacently to himself, "I have time still to draw two feet for the snake." So saying, he added two feet to the snake. He had never thought that before he finished drawing, someone else had already done so. That man wrested the wine pot from him and said, "It goes without saying, a snake has no feet. Why do you append two feet to it?" As he said this, he raised the wine pot and began to drink. The man who was trying to append two feet to the snake had no alternative but to look on while the winner drank the wine.

265. Mud Man and Mahogany Man

Mengchangjun, or Lord Mengchang, received an invitation to visit the state of Qin. While he was getting ready to go, thousands of people advised him against the journey, fearing that he might be detained by Qin, but he refused to listen. Su Qin, the famous persuasive talker, also asked Mengchangjun for an audience, trying to influence his decision. But Menchangjun was getting a little impatient and said, "I've learned all that happened in this world. The only things I've not heard are those about ghosts and goblins."

Su Qin said, "Your humble servant dares not talk of happenings in the human sphere, but only some events in the spiritual world."

Mengchangjun, therefore, granted him an audience. He then told Mengchangjun, "On my present journey, I passed Zishui (in Shantong Province), or Zihe River, where I heard the conversation between the mud man and the mahogany man. The mahogany man told the mud man, 'You were originally the mud on the western bank, kneaded into the human form by man. When the eighth moon arrives and, if there is a downpour and the Zishui rises suddenly, you will be washed away.' The mud man replied, 'That's not so. As I was the mud from the western bank originally, I'll return to the western bank as mud if the worst comes to the worst. You, on the other hand, are another story. You were once only a piece of mahogany wood, which man carved into the human form. If there is a downpour, and the Zishui rises suddenly, you will be driven by the current and drifted to nobody knows where.' At present, there are strategic stockades and impregnable passes everywhere in Qin. If you go to Qin, it will be like going into the mouth of a tiger, and it is difficult to predict whether you can get out again." Mengchangjun cancelled his trip to Qin after he heard what Su Qin had said.

266. Talented People

Chun Zikun recommended seven persons to the king Xuan of Qi in a day. King Xuan said, "I've heard that within an area of a thousand *li*, if one can find an able man, that can be considered men of talent come out in multitudes; and in a hundred years if you can find a sage, that too can be considered as sages come forward in succession. Now, you recommend seven persons in one day. Don't you think there are far too many talents?"

Chun Zikun replied, "It should not be viewed in that way. Take for example, birds of the same species usually gather together; and animals of the same kind too usually travel in a group. If you go to the marshes to seek radix bupleuri (the root of Chinese thorowax) and platycodon grandiflorum (the root of balloonflower), you will not be able to locate it in a lifetime, but if you seek them in the northern slopes of Mount Gaoshu and Mount Liangfu, you will easily load a whole cart back. Birds of a feather flock together, as the saying goes, and I believe I can be classified as a talented man. To me, it is like getting water from the river, or fire from a flint, if Your Majesty wants me to recommend men of talent. I'll recommend more people in the future, and not only these seven persons."

267. There is no Victor

Han Zilu was the fastest courser in the world, and Dong Guoqun the swiftest wily hare on the planet. Once, the hunter let loose his dog to pursue the hare, and the wily hare fled in front like an arrow shot from the bowstring, while the hunting dog ran after it like a whirlwind. They raced round the mountain three times, then climbed over five high mountain ranges, and for several days they sped forward, until both were exhausted. In the end, the wily rabbit died in front, and the hunting dog behind it. At this juncture, a farmer came along. He picked up the dead rabbit and the dead dog, brought them home, skinned them and had them cooked for food.

268. A Clever Rabbit has Three Burrows

Mengchangjun, prime minister of the state of Qi, had an hanger-on called Feng Xuan, who was sent to his fiefdom, Xuedi, to collect debts. Mengchangjun instructed him to buy anything that was needed at home after he received the payments. Feng Xuan, upon his arrival at Xuedi, announced to the tenant farmers that all debts were cancelled, and burnt the certificates of indebtedness in the presence of all. The tenants were very grateful to him, and shouted, "Long live Feng Xuan!" Returning to the capital, Feng Xuan reported to Mengchangjun, saying, "you instructed me to buy anything required at home. I observed that be it jewellery, dogs and horses, or beautiful girls, everything was in abundance. The only thing short was benevolence and justice, so I bought back benevolence and justice." After he knew what actually happened, Mengchangjun was greatly displeased but, as there was no help for it, he said, "Don't say anymore about it!"

Not long after that, Mengchangjun's premiership was taken away from him by the king of Qi, and he left the capital to live in Xuedi, where the people brought along the old and the young to welcome him. It was then he began to see the motive of Feng Xuan, and said, "I've now seen the benevolence and justice you bought." Feng Xuan replied, "A clever rabbit has three burrows, and they are all for the purpose of staying alive. You have only one burrow at the moment, and can hardly lay your head on the pillow and just drop off to sleep. Let me dig another two burrows for you." Sometime later, Feng Xuan again used his resourcefulness to find "a second burrow" and "a third burrow". When all was done, he came back to report, "All three burrows are ready; you can sleep without any anxiety now."

269. Don't Want to be an Officeholder

A man in the state of Qi met the recluse, Tian Pian, and said, "I've long admired your superior judgement. You don't want to be an official, and are content to be a common person."

"Where do you get all this?" Tian Pian asked.

The man of Qi replied, "I heard it from the woman who is my next door neighbour."

"What did she say?" Tian Pian asked again.

The man of Qi replied, "The woman who is my next neighbour once declared she was not going to marry anyone, but now she has seven children despite the fact she is not yet thirty. Well, if she doesn't want to get married, that's her choice. The thing is she has more children than those women who do! Now, you also said you didn't want to be an official, but you have an official salary of one thousand *zhong* (grains, equal to 384,000 kilograms) and over a hundred attendants. If you are not willing to be an official, that of course is your choice, but the fact is, you are richer than those who are officials!" Tian Pian immediately offered his thanks and left after he heard what the man of Qi said.

270. Attacking the State of Di

Tian Dan, a general of the state of Qi, intended to lead his army to attack the state of Di. Before he set out, he went to see Lu Zhonglian, a eminent man of noble character. Lu Zhonglian told him, "If Your Excellency go to attack the state of Di, there will be no prospect of success."

Tian Dan replied, "Formerly in Jimo, when there was only an area of five *li* left in the inner city, seven *li* from the outer wall, and only the ramnants of a rabble army under my command, I was able to defeat several thousand elite troops of Yan, and recovered the lost territory of Qi. With the powerful army under my command at present, is it possible that I cannot defeat a small state like Di?"

He did not listen to Lu Zhonglian's advice, but rode in his chariot and led his army to attack the state of Di. For three months the battle dragged on, but he was unable to take the city. There was in circulation a nursery song which ran like this:

"His helmet is as big as the winnowing fan,
His long sword props up his chin like a hand;
Sighing, the state of Di the general fails to take,
While bones pile up like a hill in his barrack."

When Tian Dan heard the nursery song, he was afraid that he might incur the wrath of the monarch, and visited Lu Zhonglian again. He said, "You have predicted, sir, that I could not succeed in the battle against the state of Di. Why is it so? Please enlighten me as to the reason."

Lu Zhonglian replied, "When you were in the city of Jimo, Your Excellency wove the straw sandals together with the soldiers while sitting and, implement in hand building the city defence with them while standing, sharing their joys and sorrows. You often guided your soldiers by saying, "Where can we go in the future if our country is destroyed, and our homestead occupied by the state of Yan? We shall no longer have a home. Where can we go then?" At that time, the superiors and the inferiors were of one mind and one soul. The general was ready to die, and the soldiers did not cling to life cravenly. As they listened to the general, they were moved to tears, and roused themselves up in action, having the same enemy and hatred, and preparing to fight to the death agaisnt the army of Yan. It was these brains and drive that had defeated the Yan army. Now, however, the situation has changed. Your Excellency possess a fiefdom in the east side of the state of Qi; in the west, you have a hunting garden; around your waist, you wear a gold belt which only high officials are allowed to wear; and you ride in an elegant carriage galloping freely between Zishui and Shengshui (in Shandong Province). At this moment, there is only one thought, and that is enjoying life to the fullest, and not the determination to fight to the death. That's why I said Your Excellency would not be able to take the state of Di."

After listening to Lu Zhonglian, Tian Dan was fear-stricken and said, "There is indeed such thought in my mind. You have judged most accurately, sir!"

The next day, Tian Dan proceeded to the frontline, inspecting the troops attacking the city, and inspiring their fighting will. When the attack began, Tian Dan rushed to the battlefield, braved the rain of stones and arrows, and personally beat the drum to boost the soldiers' morale. As the courage of the Qi army redoubled, the city of Di was eventually broken into.

271. The Borrowed Majesty of the Tiger

All throughout the Period of Warring States, the state of Chu remained a comparatively powerful country. Once, the king Xuan of Chu asked his high officials why its senior general, Zhao Xixu, was feared in the north, and nobody knew how to reply. At this juncture, a high official called Jiangyi stepped forward and said, "I've heard of a story like the following: A tiger, which roamed about to find food, caught a fox. The tiger wanted very much to eat the fox, but the cunning fox told the tiger, 'You mustn't eat me. The God in heaven has sent me down the earth to take care of all animals. If you eat me, it will be against the wish of heaven; and if you still don't believe me, well, why don't you follow me and walk around, and see whether it's true that all the animals will run away at the sight of me." The tiger believed what it said, and followed behind the fox. Sure enough, all the animals hastily ran away at the mere sight of them. The tiger did not know that the animals were afraid of itself, but thought they were afraid of the fox." Having related the story, Jiangyi added, "Your Majesty has a territory of five thousand square *li* and an army of one million. You have handed over the armed forces to Zhao Xixu, and he is therefore feared in the north as a matter of course. Just as what the animals feared was the tiger, not the fox, what is feared in the north is not Zhao Xixu but Your Majesty and Your Majesty's army."

272. A Vicious Dog

The dog was very good at looking after the door, and its master loved it ardently. The dog, however, often urinated into the well. One day, a neighbour saw it doing it again, and intended to tell its master. The dog hated this neighbour very much, and so it barred the door, barking and biting recklessly. All its neighbours were frightened as they could not find a way to enter the door to tell its master.

273. Mend the Fold after a Sheep is lost

During the Period of Warring States, the duke Xiang of Chu put the self-seeking and wily court officials in important positions. The country was politically corrupt, and became weaker and weaker with each passing day. Zhuangxin, a high official, was very worried and advised him not to idle away his time in pleasure-seeking to the neglect of state affairs, or else the state of Chu would be in danger of perishing. The duke Xiang of Chu, however, refused to listen; on the contrary, he upbraided Zhuangxin. A few months later, sure enough, the state of Qin launched an attack on Chu, and Chu was defeated. Duke Xiang was very remorseful for not following the advice of Zhuangxin, and expressed his regrets to Zhuangxin, asking for his advice in running the country. Zhuangxin told him a story:

Once upon a time, there was a man who kept a flock of sheep. One morning, the owner found that his flock was one sheep short, and subsequently discovered a breach in the fold, which explained the loss of his sheep. His neighbours advised him, "Mend the fold immediately, so that no more sheep will be lost." But he replied, "The sheep has already gone, what use is there in mending the hole." Because he did not care for advice, he lost another sheep the next morning. The owner became anxious, and mended the hole at once. As the sheep fold was solidly mended, none of the sheep got lost again from then on.

Zhuangxin used the story to persuade the duke Xiang of Chu to administer the country well and remedy past mistakes.

274. Elixir of Life

A man presented an elixir of life to the king of Chu, and the receptionist brought it to the palace. The imperial guard asked him, "Can the medicine be taken?"

The receptionist replied, "Yes, it can." And the imperial guard grabbed and swallowed it. The king of Chu was furious, and ordered the imperial guard executed.

The imperial guard requested someone to explain it to the king, saying, "I asked the receptionist whether it could be taken, and he said it could; that was why I took it. I was innocent, the one who committed the crime was the receptionist. Why should he say it could be taken? Moreover, the man who presented the medicine said it was an elixir of life; if Your Majesty kill me as soon as I take it, what kind of elixir is this? This should be called the medicine of death! If Your Majesty executes me because of it, doesn't it clearly indicate that the man who presented the elixir of life was deceiving Your Majesty?" Thereupon the king of Chu decided not to execute the imperial guard.

275. A Frightened Bird

During the Period of Warring States, there was a well-known archer named Geng Lei in the state of Wei. One day, as he followed the king of Wei on a sightseeing tour, he saw a big honking wild goose approaching from the east. Geng Lei said, "I need only make a false show of shooting to bring the wild goose down and present it to Your Majesty." The king of Wei was rather sceptical, but willing to let him try.

It was not long before the wild goose reached the sky overhead. Geng Lei pulled the bowstring to its full, acting as if he were shooting, but without an arrow on it. As he let go, the bowstring *twanged*, and the wild goose fell down from the sky. The king exclaimed with admiration, saying, "Your skill is marvellous!" Geng Lei replied, "It has nothing to do with my marksmanship. The fact was, by listening I knew the bird had been wounded, and the wound hurt, as it was flying very slowly. Its cries were sorrowful, and it was because it had broken away from the flock. When it heard the sound from my bowstring, it hastily flew higher in order to dodge it. The exertion caused a sharp pain to the wound, and it was unable to keep up any longer and fell down."

276. An Aged Pedigreed Horse

There was an old pedigreed horse, so old that it had lost all its teeth. It was forced to do odd jobs, pulling a heavy salt cart to climb the lofty Taihang Mountain.

The old horse carried the heavy load with lowered head, and step by step moved along the rugged mountain road. Its four limbs trembled with fear as it trod on the rocks; a slip threw it to the ground, and it was held down under the shafts. It tried to get up, but its front legs lost balance and it dropped down yet again, wounding its knees and hoofs badly. There were only a few hairs left on its tail. Sweat mixed with blood fell on the stony road, forming small puddles. As the cart came to a steep slope, the aged horse pulled and rolled with all its might but the cart would not move, and the cart driver's whip came down like rain on its back.

Just at this moment, Bo Le, who rode in a carriage, came head-on towards them. He examined the aged horse carefully, came down from his carriage, caressed the back of the horse, where scars of wounds strung together like beads, and began to cry aloud. Then he loosened his linen robe to cover its trembling body. The aged horse looked at Bo Le, its eyes brimming with tears. As it did so, it suddenly sneezed and, raising its head it gave out a long neigh. The neighing was earth-shaking and heaven-battering, soaring straight up into the sky. It had met a man who truly understood itself at long last.

277. A Minor Sacrifice

Someone used a rope to make a loop and caught a tiger by its paw. The tiger stamped with rage as it bit its paw off and escaped. The reason why the tiger did it was not because it did not love its own paw but, after weighing the pros and cons, it decided not to save the paw at the expense of the entire body.

278. A Promise

The duke Wen of Wei had an engagement with the administrative official of the mountain forest to go hunting in the forest on a certain day. It so happened that on that day he had a dinner party and, besides, it suddenly began to rain, but the duke Wen of Wei insisted on going as scheduled. His attending officials on his left and right advised him, saying, "You have been very happy drinking today, and it is raining outside. Why must you insist on going?"

The duke Wen of Wei said, "I've an engagement with the administrative official of the mountain forest to go hunting there today. Although we have a very lively party, but I should not break my promise and stay away so casually." So saying, he braved the rain, bringing his attendants with him.

The feudal princes in all the other states heard about the matter and, as their trust in Duke Wen deepened, the state of Wei began to grow ever stronger.

279. The King of Wei's Comment on Music

The duke Wen of Wei and his mentor Tian Zifang were drinking and discussing about music in the palace.

The duke Wen of Wei said, "The sound from this bell doesn't seem very harmonious; the note from the left side is a little too high." Tian Zifang smiled.

The duke Wen of Wei asked him, "Why did you smile?"

Tian Zifang replied, "I've heard that the interest of a sagacious monarch lies in the understanding and education of his subordinates and in the rectification of the officialdom; whereas a fatuous monarch is indoxicated with vocal music. Seeing that Your Majesty was so unmistakably discriminating in the area of vocal music, I was afraid you might neglect to understand and educate your subordinates!"

The duke Wen of Wei said, "Well said! I'll certainly listen to your advice with an open mind."

280. A Lie, If Repeated Often Enough, Will Be Accepted as Truth

During the Period of Warring States, the state of Qin and the state of Chu joined forces and attacked the state of Wei. Wei did not have the resources to resist, and had to ask for help from the nearby state of Zhao. The state of Zhao, however, made it a condition that the prince and high official of Wei, Pang Gong, must be sent to Handan, the capital of Zhao, to serve as hostage, before it could come to the rescue. As there was nothing the king of Wei could do, he accepted the condition and sent prince Pang Gong to Handan.

Pang Gong knew the king of Wei was easily swayed by one-side story, so before he left, he said to the king of Wei, "If someone tells you there is a tiger in the main road, do you believe him?" The king replied, "I won't believe him." "If a second person tells you there is a tiger in the main road, do you believe him?" Pang gong asked again, and the king replied, "I won't believe him." "If a third person also says there is a tiger in the main road, do you believe him?" Pang Gong asked for the third time. The king of Wei replied, "I'll probably believe him." Pang Gong said, "It was obvious there could not be any tiger in the main road, but since three persons all said there was, a lie was accepted as truth. Now, the city of Handan is farther from the state of Wei than the main road. When we arrive in Handan, those speak ill of, and attack, us at our back will certainly not be three persons. I hope Your Majesty will not believe them." Later, when Pang Gong returned from Handan, sure enough, the king of Wei had already heard a lot of bad things about him, and believed them. He no longer trusted the prince, and did not wish to see him anymore.

281. Poles Apart

During the Period of Warring States, the king of Wei intended to attack the capital of the state of Zhao, Handan, but the court official Jiliang thought that should not be carried out, and he told a story to illustrate his point and to dissuade the king from doing it:

"When I left the capital to come here, I saw a man driving a carriage northwards at the foot of the Taihang Mountain. He told me, 'I'm going to the state of Chu.' I said, 'The state of Chu is in the south. Why do you go north?' He replied, 'My horse is a good horse.' I said, 'Your horse may be a good horse, but this is not the way to Chu!' He replied, 'I have with me a lot of money.' I said, 'You may have a lot of money, but this is not the right direction to the state of chu!' He replied again, 'My driver possesses very good driving skills.' I believe the more advantages he enumerated, the further he would be from the state of Chu."

The king of Wei listened and understood what Jiliang was trying to convey. Originally, when the king of Wei made the decision to attack Zhao, he was also thinking of the favourable conditions the state of Wei had, such as more troops, brave generals, and abundant provisions and fodder, etc. However, the chief enemy of Wei was Qin and not Zhao at that time, to invade Zhao would be contrary to the main direction of attack. Thus the king of Wei accepted the view of Jiliang, and cancelled the plan to invade Handan.

282. Taming Dog

Zhuzi, a high official of the state of Qi, kept a dog. The dog was extremely ferocious, and nobody had the courage to scold it in a loud voice. Whoever dared to do so, he would be bitten.

A guest volunteered to bring the villianous dog under control. First, he stared with his eyes fixedly upon it, then he upbraided it slowly. At this point, the dog was not moving at all. After a while, he shouted at it loudly, and the dog no longer bit anybody.

283. Driving

The disciple of Wangliang was driving a carriage, claiming that those hitched to his carriage were horses with enormous speed and staying power. On the way, he met the disciple of Zaofu. Zaofu's disciple told Wangliang's disciple, saying, "Your horses will not be able to cover a thousand *li*." Wangliang's disciple asked him, "The horses are thousand-*li* horses, including the two in the middle. Why can't they cover a thousand *li*?" Zaofu's disciple replied, "It's simple. The reins of your horses are too long." Compared to other things like driving, the length of the rein might only be of minuscule importance, a small matter, but nevertheless could thwart the horses' endeavour to complete the thousand *li* journey.

284. A Fervent Quest for Talent

During the Period of Warring States, the state of Qi took advantage of the internal turmoil of the state of Yan to launch an aggressive attack, and occupied several of its cities. When the king Zhao of Yan ascended the throne, he was determined to re-energize the country and avenged himself. To do this, he first invited men of wisdom and valor to his side, and recruited qualified personnel.

One day, the king Zhao of Yan asked Guowei, a man well-known for his virtue, for sound strategy, and the latter related a story. He said:

In ancient times, there was a monarch who yearned to get a thousand-*li* steed (a horse with enormous speed and staying power). For that purpose, he was willing to pay a thousand pieces of gold. Yet for several years, he was unable to get what he sought. A minor official came forward and offered himself to help accomplish it. After several months' search, he obtained information that a certain family had such a thousand-*li* steed. However, by the time he called at his house, the horse was already dead, so with five hundred pieces of gold he bought back the bones of the dead horse instead. The monarch was infuriated, and upbraided him for wasting money, but he said, "My intention is to let the world know that Your Majesty will not balk at paying the price of a live horse, since you are willing to pay five hundred pieces of gold for the bones of a dead one. It will not be long before someone calls with a thousand-*li* steed." Sure enough, within a year, the monarch got several genuine thorough-bred horses.

As Guowei finished the story, he added, "If Your Majesty is sincere in getting men of virtue, why don't you begin with me? When men of talent see that a person like me is being put in an important position, they will come one after another." Thereupon the king of Yan formally acknowledged Guowei as his teacher, and had an official residence constructed. Later, a batch of able and virtuous personages such as Leyi and Zouyan arrived at the state of Yan as predicted.

285. Salesmanship

A man spent three days in the market trying to sell his steed, but no one took any notice of it. The man therefore went to see Bo Le, an eminent appraiser of horses, and said, "I've a fine horse for sale, but nobody came to look at it although I've been in the market for three days. I'm hoping that you can help by going to look at my horse, walking around the horse a few times, and casting your eyes once more on it before you leave. I'll pay you for your day's trouble."

Bo Le accepted the request, and walked around the horse a few times, looked at it, casting his eyes on the horse again before he left. By so doing, the price of the horse immediately rose ten times.

286. When the Snipe and the Clam Grapple

During the Period of Warring States, there was a time when the state of Zhao was bent on attacking the state of Yan. Sudai, a persuasive talker, arrived at Zhao, intending to persuade the king of Zhao not to send his army into battle. Upon seeing the king Hui of Zhao, Sudai spoke slowly, saying, "On my way to your great state during my present trip, I saw a clam lying on the beach with its shells open, basking in the sunshine. A long-legged snipe noticed the exposed tender meat, quietly stepped over, and stretched its pointed beak to peck, knowing it was most palatable. To its surprise, the reaction of the clam was swift; it immediately shut the two leaves of its shell with all its might, and the beak of the snipe was tightly nipped. As the water bird could not loosen the clam's grip, it said, "Just wait and see. If there is no rain today and tomorrow, you will be scorched to death." The clam, not to show its weakness, replied, "Provided you cannot free your beak today and tomorrow, you will also be starved to death." The two of them went on arguing, neither would give in to the other; a fisherman came along, and caught them both." Sudai paused for a moment, then continued, "Now that the state of Zhao is bent on attacking the state of Yan, the state of Yan will no doubt resist. As the two states are fighting each other, it will be the state of Qin, which has the ambition to expand its territory, that will profit by it like the fisherman."

287. The Bride

In the state of Wei, a man was taking a wife. The moment she was aboard the festooned vehicle, the bride asked, "Whose horses are they at the sides of the carriage?"

The driver replied, "They were borrowed."

The bride then instructed the driver, "You can whip the horses at the sides, but not the ones that are harnessed to the shafts!"

When the carriage arrived at the door and she was about to alight, she instructed the servant who accompanied her, saying, "Be quick and extinguish the fire in the stove, so that there will be no fire hazard."

As she entered the house and saw the pestle and mortar, she again said, "Move the pestle and mortar under the window. It hampers people coming and going here."

Listening to the way she talked, her in-laws all could not help laughing.

Actually the three sentences she uttered were quite regular, but why did she get laughed at? The reason: those words were not appropriate to a new bride; she had spoken a little too soon!

*

Kong Congzi
By Kongfu (c. 264-c. 208 B.C.), a descendant of Confucius, who lived in the state of Wei. Towards the end of Qin, when Chenshe rose in

revolt, Kongfu too joined the insurgents against the reign of Qin, and was engaged as a learned scholar. Later, he resigned because of eye disease, and returned home, during which he wrote *Kong Congzi*. The book, totalling six volumes, was a collection of the words and deeds of Confucius' offsprings: Zisi, Zishang, Zigao, Zishun, etc. At the time of Emperor Xiaowu, Han Dynasty, Kongzang produced a continuance of one volume appended thereto, so that the book was handed down as a seven volume work. The book was not mentioned in *Bibliographical Sketch: the History of the Han Dynasty* (prepared by Ban Gu), hence the scepticism that it might have been written by Wangsu and his disciple, who lived in Wei of the Three Kingdoms (A.D. 222-265).

288. Angling

Zisi lived in the state of Wei. A man of Wei angled at the bank of Yellow River and got a big elopichthy bambusa, so big that it could filled a whole cart. Zisi asked the angler, "The elopichthy bambusa is very hard to get. How did you get it?" The angler replied, "When first I began angling, I only put on a bream as bait, and the elopichthy bambusa did not so much as cast a glance at it; then I changed the bait and put on half a pig, and the elopichthy bambusa came and swallowed the hook."

Upon hearing what the angler said, Zisi heaved a deep sigh, saying, "Although the elopichthy bambusa is hard to catch, but it is gluttonous, and eventually died because of it. Some scholars might have lofty ambition, but they hankered after an official salary, and in the end lost all standing and reputation."

289. Asperation

Kong Chuan, a Confucius' descendant, was travelling for pleasure and reached the state of Zhao. Zouwen and Jijie were two proteges of gentleman Pingyuan (a famous official of Zhao in the Period of Warring States) of Zhao, and Kong Chuan's good friend. When Kong Chuan was about to return to the state of Lu, his friends in the locality all went out of the city to say goodbye to him. As Kong Chuan set out on his way, Zouwen and Jijie were rather reluctant to part, and insisted on accompanying him for a distance. The result was, they were together for three days before they took leave of each other. As they separated,

Zouwen and Jijie all shed tears, but Kong Chuan only saluted with joined hands, turned his head, and started off without looking back.

Kong Chuan's disciple asked Kong Chuan, "Master, you and the two gentlemen are good friends. When you were leaving, they seemed rather reluctant to part, not knowing when you could meet again and, for that reason, they all shed tears. But, master, you only made a bow with hands folded in front; your words seemed without feeling. Doesn't it show that you are rather cold and indifferent to your friends?"

Kong Chuan replied, "At the beginning when I became associated with them, I had the impression they were true men, but later I discovered they were sentimental fellows. A man should aspire after a great career anywhere in the world. How can we behave like pigs and deers, forever shut up in a pen?"

The disciple said, "In that case, do you think the two gentlemen's tears showed their true feelings?"

Kong Chuan replied, "These two are good and honest men, and the feelings they showed are true and sincere. The question is, they do not have enough animal spirits. Their wishywashy weakness will show whenever problem arises that requires resolute action."

290. The Wish of the King of Wei

The king of Wei said, "I've heard that once a Taoist priest reached the peak of Huashan, he will become an immortal. I'm willing to do that too."

Zishun told the king of Wei, "Since ancient times, there is no such thing as immortality. Such wish can never be realized."

The king of Wei said, "I've heard that it's true and reliable."

Zishun replied, "Well, I don't know the source of your information. Have you heard it from the mouth of the immortal Taoist priest himself, or is it just hearsay? If it is hearsay, then it must be something absurd and false; if you have heard it from the mouth of the immortal Taoist priest, where is he now?"

The Book of Mountains and Seas
It was a masterpiece in Geography of ancient China. It is believed that the part concerning the mountains must have written before the Period of Warring States; the portion dealing with the seas might have been completed a little later, say, in the Qin, or Han Dynasties, as part of the writings contained place-names of Qin and Han. The book is rich in content, dealing with history, nationalities, religion, mythology, natural resources, medicine, etc., from ancient times to the Zhou Dynasty. It contains many stories of mythology, which can be treated as fables, of which "A Braggadocio", "Jingwei the Mythical Bird", "Archer Houyi", etc., are well-known.

291. A Braggadocio

In ancient Chinese mythology, so the story goes, Kuafu was a giant. He noticed the sun moved from east to west every day and pursued it until he stood right in front of it. The heat of the sun scorched him so terribly that his thirst became unbearable, and he yearned for water badly. He went to the Yellow River and the Wei River to quench his thirst, and the water of both rivers were exhausted thereby. As he was still feeling thirsty, he proceeded north to the great lakes, but before he reached there, he died of thirst and lay at the roadside. The cane he used to lean on was discarded on the ground and became a forest of peach trees.

292. *Jingwei* the Mythical Bird

In ancient times there was a mountain in the east called Mount Fajiu. On the mountain there were lots of three-bristle cudrania where a certain kind of bird perched. In appearance the bird looked like a crow, with marking on the head, white beak, and red claws. The bird's name was *jingwei*. According to legend, Nuwa, the youngest daughter of Yandi (supposedly lived from 2737-2697 B.C.), otherwise known as Shennong, a legendary ruler supposed to have introduced agriculture and medicine, once swam in the East China Sea and was drowned, whose corpse could not be recovered. Her spirit lived on to become the bird *jingwei*, which made daily trip to West Mountain, where it carried some pebbles or sticks or grass back and threw them into the sea, in a vain attempt to fill it up. But as the East China Sea was a vast expanse of water, boundless, and unfathomably deep, it was an impossible task for a little bird. *Jingwei*, however, toiled on without interruption, its one desire being to fill up the abyss of hatred and disaster.

*

Notes on the Book of History
By Fusheng, whose dates of birth and death remained blurred. He was a scholar in early Han Dynasty who had the reputation of being the earliest lecturer on the existing *Book of History*. He was once the department head of the imperial college in the Qin Dynasty. During the reign of Emperor Wen of Han, Chaocuo, sent by the emperor, learned *the Book of History* from him. *Notes on the Book of History* was a treatise on the meaning of *the Book of History*. It was said the book's author was Fusheng, but textual research by subsequent scholars indicates that it might have been written by Fusheng's disciples, Zhangsheng, Ouyangsheng, etc., who had collected what they knew from various sources to form a book. The extant copy is rather fragmentary, an episode here and there, with the exception of one chapter: *The biographical Sketch of Hongfan Wuhang*. A four-volume work compiled in Qing Dynasty with one volume of addenda exists today.

293. Love Me Love My Dog

Jifa, the king Wu of Zhou, having defeated the king Zhou of Ying, called his officials together to discuss the matter of stabilizing the situation and consolidating the reign of Zhou, so that the people could live and work in peace. The first to speak was Jiang Tai Gong (also known as Jiang Shang, or Jiang Ziya), who said, "I've heard that 'the love for the man extends even to the crows perching on its roof; the dislike for the man extends to the corner of the wall that belongs to him.' What does Your Majesty think?" By quoting the statement, Jiang Tai Gong was saying: If you loved the man, you should also loved the crows on his roof; if you didn't love him, even casting a glance at his house was superfluous. The king Wu of Zhou understood well what Jiang Tai Gong was driving at, but he thought it was not a good solution, and asked Zhao Gong. Zhao Gong, after a little ponder, said, "Those who are quilty should all be executed, those who are not guilty should be left alone." King Wu thought it was no good either, so he went to solicit the opinion of the duke of Zhou (brother of king Wu, first ruler of Zhou Dynasty). The duke of Zhou said with a severe tone, "The people of Ying should have a normal life so they can keep the mind on their work. Make friends with all who are benevolent, and live together in peace." The king Wu was convinced that was the best way, and so he adopted the opinion of the duke of Zhou.

*

New Book
By Jiayi (200-168 B.C.), a native of Luoyang, and a writer and political commentator of Western Han Dynasty. During the reign of emperor Wen of Han, he was the department head of the imperial college. Later, he became one of the three highest-ranking officials in the imperial courts of the king of Changsha and the king Huai of Liang. He was saddened by the death of king Huai, who fell from the horse and died. His excessive grief brought about his own death. During the Ming Dynasty, his essays and poems were compiled into a book entitled *The Jia Changsha Collection*. *New Book*, ten volumes, was his political essays.

294. Pestles Float on Blood

In remote antiquity, the Central Plains (comprising the middle and lower reaches of the Huanghe River) was ruled by Yandi Shennong. For many years the political environment was clean and just, and the people lived in harmony and peace. Later, when Yandi became old, all the feudal princes seized the opportunity to rise up against each other, in the process putting the people in harm's way. Among the princes, Huangdi (Yellow Emperor) had the upper hand, as his military strength was superior, and became Yandi's mortal threat from within.

To uphold his rule, Yandi decided to mobilize all the military forces under his control against the princes, in an attempt to prevent further fragmentation of the country. In the meantime, Huangdi was actively making preparations to overthrow the reign of Yandi. Internally, he set up an honest and enlightened government, reorganized his military forces, developed production, and appeased public feeling; externally, he liaised with various feudal princes to establish an united front, and had a group of brave and resourceful men trained, ready for a final showdown with Yandi.

In the spring that year, a bloody battle between the two powerful military forces was unfolded in the open field in Zhuolu, Hebei Province. The intensity of the battle was unprecedented. The wind rolled up the yellow sand, obscuring the sun, while the men howled and the horses neighed, shaking the entire wilderness. Deaths were numerous and corpses piled up like a mountain. So profuse was the blood shed that the wooden sticks in the hands of the soldiers floated on the blood stream. After three decisive battles, the victory of Huangdi was complete. He ascended the throne as the new ruler who replaced Yandi.

295. The King of the State of Guo

Formerly, the king of the state of Guo (one of the feudal princes in Zhou Dynasty; in today's Shaanxi Province, but moved to Henan later) was overbearing and capricious, perverse in temper, and loved to listen to the flattery and sycophantic talk of the fawning officials. Practically deaf to all earnest advice, he hated those who remonstrated with him. Those who failed to watch his every mood would run the risk of being exiled. The country was in a state of confusion, the people were destitute, and voices of discontent were heard everywhere. As a result, the state of Jin seized the opportunity to launch an attack, and took the country at one fell swoop. Panic-stricken, the king of Guo fled.

That day, they arrived at a bleak and desolate swampy land. As they stopped to take a rest, the king of Guo felt parched and told the driving attendant, saying, "I'm very thirsty and should like a little water to drink." The attendant handed him a canteen of diluted wine, which he drank and said, "I'm also feeling hungry and should like to eat something." Again, the attendant brought forth some dry meat and provisions, which the king ate with relish. As he enjoyed the food, he asked, "Where did you get all this?" "I prepared them early on," replied the attendant. "Why have you kept all this?" "Because I knew you would need them on the way when you became an exile." "You knew I would be an exile?" "Yes, I did." "Why didn't you remonstrate with me if you knew?" "Because you only liked sycophantic talk and flattery, but disliked good advice that cut into the present-day corrupt practices. I'd have remonstrated, but I was afraid as I did so I might die before the country was ruined." The king's face turned alternately blue and red, apparently about to lose his temper. His attendant immediately corrected himself and apologized repeatedly, saying, "I was wrong to say that; I was wrong to say that." Thereupon the king's gloomy countenence brightened up a little. After a while, the king calmed down, and he again asked the attendant, "How did I get into such a plight?" The attendant changed the tone of his voice and replied, "Your Majesty does not understand. It was because you had extremely keen intelligence and sound judgement." The king of Guo did not see the point, so he asked, "A man of keen intelligence and sound judgement should be able to live his own life, why have I to flee?" "Well, that's because all the feudal princes in this world are villianous, and only you are intelligent and sound in judgement, which make them jealous, and they will not rest until you are dead. That's why you have to flee." The king of Guo thought that explanation very reasonable, and was greatly pleased. With his hands leaning on the shaft, he could not help smiling and said, "Ai! Is this bitter fruit the result of keen intelligence and sound judgement?" Having said that, he alighted from the carriage and stepped forward barefooted. He found a place in the mountain and settled down. As he had been on the road for many days since he took to his heels, he was both hungry and exhausted. With his head on the leg of the driving attendant, he fell asleep. The attendant waited until he was sure the king was really sleeping, then took a piece of rock to replace his leg, and slipped away. The king of Guo eventually was starved to death in the mountain, and became a delicious meal for the ferocious birds and the violent animals.

*

Huainanzi
by Liu An (179-122 B.C.), a writer and thinker of western Han Dynasty. He was the grandson of Liu Bang (whose dynastic title was Han Gaozu, 247-195 B.C. founder of the Han Dynasty, 206 B.C.-219 A.D.). Inherited the title *king of Huainan*, he later committed suicide because of his part in the rebellion which had been discovered. *Huainanzi* was the title of a book on philosophy, known also by the name of *Huainanhonglie*, compiled and written by his guests and the occultists whom he convened. The contents of the book include the doctrines of Taoist, Legalist, and the Yin-Yang Schools, and that was why the *Bibliographical Sketch: the History of Han Dynasty* had it classified as

the Eclectics, a school of thought flourishing at the end of the Warring States Period and the beginning of the Han Dynasty.

296. Mi Zijian

A guest of Mi Zijian's introduced another man to see him. After the man left, Mi Zijian told his guest, "Your friend has three shortcomings: First, he looked at me and laughed; that's frivolous and not being serious. Second, he did not address me as master; that's betraying the principles a master abides by. Third, not being intimate with one another and talked a lot irrespective of topics, that's lacking in manners."

The guest replied, "He looked at you and laughed, that's upright; without addressing you as master, that's being understanding and without parochial prejudice; talked about everything under the sun at the first meeting, that's being truthful."

It was the same as far as the man's speech and deportment were concerned. One was of the opinion that the man's behaviour was noble; the other thought he was a villian whose character was despicable, and the reason was, each man had a different point of view.

297. A Shouter

Gongsun Long was an eminent scholar during the Period of Warring States. When he was in the state of Zhao, he used to tell his students, saying, "I'll not accept anyone as student without ability of some sort,."

One day, in came a young fellow with clothes worn to the threads, ready to acknowledge him as his master. Gongsun Long asked what his ability was. The young man thought for a moment, then answered, "My voice is loud and clear, and I can utter a resounding shout." The students nearby all laughed at him, thinking that he was only joking with the teacher. Gongsun Long looked around and asked all those present, "Is there anybody who can shout aloud here?" Everyone laughed even more vehemently, and the reply was, none. Gongsun Long beckoned to the young man and said, "Well, I accept you as my student." All those who were there looked at each other in astonishment, unable to understand.

Sometime later, the king of Zhao sent Gongsun Long to the state of Yan as a persuasive talker. As they arrived hurriedly at a big river, they saw to their dismay that the water was vast and boundless, and the ferryboat was at the opposite bank. Everyone was anxious to cross the river but could find no solution for it. The young man, however, went calmly to shape his hands into a speaking trumpet and, through it, he gave a big shout towards the other bank. His resonant voice reached the other side and, as the boatman heard the call, he padled the boat over at once.

298. Thieving as an Expertise

General Zifa of Chu liked to enlist men of special ability. A petty thief, who was good at stealing, sought an audience with him, saying, "I've heard that you are enlisting men of special ability. I'm a petty thief in a city of Chu, and am willing to serve under you as a runner who possesses the expertise of thieving." When Zifa heard this, he hastily put on his clothes, wore his hat, and did not wait until his clothes were buttoned up and his hat put right, he was already on his way to respectfully receive the petty thief.

The people at his side tried to dissuade him, saying, "This thief is a notorious robber; why should you be so respectful to him?"

Zifa replied, "This is something you don't comprehend."

Not long after that, the state of Qi launched an offensive against the state of Chu, and Zifa led his forces to defend the country, but every time he sent his troops, they were defeated. This happened thrice. Despite racking their brains for a solution and quite a number of ways were devised, the able and virtuous high officials were unable to turn the table; on the contrary, the forces of Qi seemed to become even stronger with the fighting. At this juncture, the petty thief came in to suggest, saying, "I've some insignificant skill, and am willing to go to the army of Qi for Your Excellency."

Zifa said, "Good!" And without a second word, he sent him off to the Qi army.

At nightfall, the petty thief went into the military camp of the Qi army, and stole the curtain of the general's carriage, which he carried back and presented to Zifa. Zifa returned the curtain to the Qi army and added, "Our soldiers found your general's carriage curtain when they went to cut firewood in the mountain. I've sent a special messenger to return it to you."

The next day, the petty thief again went to the military camp of the Qi army and stole the pillow of the Qi's general. Zifa sent a messenger to return it as before.

The third day, the petty thief yet again went to the military camp of the Qi army and stole the general's hairpin. Zifa, accordingly, sent a messenger to return it.

When the soldiers of Qi heard about it, they were greatly shocked. The general and his officers talked over the matter and said, "If we do not withdraw today, that general of Chu may come to take my head." And he brought his army back to Qi.

That was why people said, there was no distinction as to big or small, light or heavy, in matter of skills and sorcery. It was the king who held the key and the way he used it! That was why Laozi said, "The imperfect is the stock-in-trade of the perfect man."

299. The Duke Mu of Qin

The duke Mu of Qin was on an inspection tour outside the capital when his carriage broke down, and one of the horses slipped away. Duke Mu pursued it to the southern foot of Mount Qishan, where he saw a group of men slaughtering his horse and cooking it for food. Duke Mu showed his concern by saying, "If you take only the horsemeat without wine, it will be harmful to your health. I'm worried about your health!" One by one Duke Mu urged them to drink before he left.

A year later, Duke Mu and the duke Hui of Jin went to war. The battle took place in Handi. The army of Jin surrounded the chariot of Duke Mu and, Liang Youmi, a high official of Jin, firmly held the horse hitched to the chariot of Duke Mu. It was clear Duke Mu would soon be held captive. Just at this crucial moment, the men who once ate his horse came to his rescue with three hundred men. They carried spears and halberds, and fought with the soldiers of Jin in a bloody battle. Eventually they defeated the army of Jin, seized Duke Hui, and returned with gongs beating and banners flying.

300. A Chivalrous Man

To the north of the state of Chu, there was a chivalrous man. He liked to intervene whenever any injustice arose. His children often advised him not to poke his nose into other people's business, but he just ignored them. One day, a band of robbers came to rob his family. It was sheer luck that he discovered the plot in time and was able to escape with the valuables during the night. The robbers, however, followed and caught up with him on the main road. At this critical moment, when he was hopelessly outnumbered, the people who once received his assistance rushed to his rescue. Eventually they fought off the plunderers, and he returned home more scared than hurt. He said to his children, "You often advised me not to meddle in others people's affairs, but you should know better now. Today I met with danger, and it was because of my chivalrous deeds that a disaster has been averted."

To understand only why one had averted a disaster, but not how to prevent it,—it seems to me the chivalrous guy does not know where the shoe pinches.

301. Overload

A man, who used his bullock cart to carry goods, overloaded his cart so that the axle was approaching breaking point. He tried to remedy the situation by adding another hitch pole to the axle, thinking it would make the cart safe. He did not know, however, that to add a hitch pole to the axle would only made matter worse, for it would only hasten the fracture of the axle.

302. Aggravation

The king of the state of Chu chased a rabbit with his penannular jade ring on him. The jade ring broke because he ran too fast. To prevent the jade ring from breaking on collision, he wore another penannular jade ring. As a result, the rings broke even more easily as they collided with one another.

The politics of a state in turmoil is very much the same.

303. A Man of Ying sells his Mother

There lived in the capital of Chu, Yingdu, a man who brought his mother to the market to sell. Beseeching the buyer piteously, he said, "The woman is old. I hope you will take good care of her. Please don't let her suffer!" His behaviour was intrinsically treacherous, but he still tried to win a little good reputation out of it.

304. Yanghu

Yanghu was making trouble in the state of Lu, and the king of Lu ordered the city gate closed in order to capture him. In the meantime, a notice was pasted up: "Anyone who catches Yanghu will receive a reward, and anyone who lets him escape will be severely punished." Yanghu was encircled ring upon ring, and despairingly he held the sword to his cheek, ready to kill himself. The city gatekeeper rushed forward to stop him, saying, "The world is huge, and where can't you hide yourself? I'll let you go."

Yanghu, therefore, carried his sword and dagger-axe as he ran with the people who surrounded him, looking for an opportunity to break the encirclement and escape.

The gatekeeper released him. But he was not very far from the city when he came back, caught the gatekeeper with his dagger-axe, and stabbed him in the armpit. The gatekeeper chided him, saying, "It was not because you were my kinsman that I ran the risk of decapitation to let you go, but now you returned kindness with ingratitude, and even went so far as to hurt me. It was but just you met with misfortune!"

When the news reached the king of Lu, he was infuriated. He questioned closely as to which gate the criminal had run away from, and sent men to arrest the gatekeeper. The king of Lu was of the opinion that any wound incurred must have been caused by the man's struggle with Yanghu, and therefore should be richly rewarded, whereas the unhurt man must have let Yanghu go, and should be severely punished. This was a case of trying to bring harm to a man but, instead, resulted in his benefit!

305. A Blessing in Disguise

There lived a family near the frontier fortress. In that family there was an old man whom people called Old Man Sai (old man in the frontier fortress). Old Man Sai had a son, who was a good rider. One day, his horse suddenly disappeared into the desert. All his neighbours felt bad for him, but Old Man Sai only said, "The horse's disappearance may prove to be a good thing." Several months later, his horse came back from the desert of its own accord, bringing with it several fine horses. All the neighbours again came to congratulate him, but Old Man Sai only said, "This may prove to be a disaster." Not long after that, the old man's son fell from the back of his horse while galloping. The bones of his leg had been broken and, although it was subsequently healed, the fall left him a cripple. All the neighbours, again, came to console him. But Old Man Sai said, "This may yet prove to be beneficial." One year later, a war broke out in the frontier area. The armed forces of the minority people broke into the fortress, and all able-bodied men in their prime were drafted into the army. The fighting was very intense, and nine out of ten soldiers died, but Old Man Sai's son was not among them on account of his crippled condition. The two of them—father and son—took care of each other at home and lived on comfortably.

A good thing can turn into a bad one under certain conditions, and vice versa. That's why one should not regard anything as rigid and inflexible.

306. To Build or not to Build a City

Jing Guojun intended to build a city in his own fiefdom, Xue. Many people tried to dissuade him, but he refused to listen. He even went so far as to order the receptionist, "Stop transmitting messages from the guests!"

A man from the state of Qi wanted to see him, saying, "I only speak three words. If I speak more than that, you can boil me."

Jing Guojun received him after he heard him. The man hurriedly entered. After doing his obeisance, he stood up and, without rhyme or reason, said three words, "Big fish sea", then he left without further ado.

Jing Guojun did not understand the meaning of these words and urged him to stay, saying, "I should like you very much to elucidate."

The guest said, "How dare I jest my life away with you like that!"

Jing Guojun said, "You have come a long way, sir, and the purpose of your visit is to convince me. Why don't you say it now?"

The guest said, "Big fish in the sea cannot be caught by the fishnet, nor can it be affected by a fishing line. However, if it swims ashore, and out of the water, then, even insects like mole crickets and ants can bully and humiliate it. The state of Qi is at present your sea! If you leave the state of Qi, don't you think you can still preserve your fiefdom, Xue?"

Jing Guojun thought what he said made sense, and nodded again and again, saying, "Right! Right! You are absolutely right!" And he gave up his intention to build a city in his fiefdom, Xue.

307. Tian Zifang

Tian Zifang saw an old horse on the road, and his thoughts and feelings were aroused. He heaved a sigh, and asked the man who led along the horse, "What kind of horse is this?"

The man with the horse replied, "It was originally a horse your family kept, but it has grown old and weak and useless, so I bring it out for sale."

Tian Zifang said, "Coveted its strength when it was young, but discarded it when it grew old. This is what a benevolent and virtuous man will not do."

Thereupon he redeemed it from the man with five bolts of silk.

308. Duke Zhuang and the Praying Mantis

Duke Zhuang was out hunting, and a tiny insect raised its legs to stop the wheel of his carriage. He asked the carriage driver, "What kind of insect is this?"

The carriage driver said, "That is what we commonly called the praying mantis. It only knows to go forward but never to retreat, taking the enemy lightly and acted rashly, not knowing its own limits."

Duke Zhuang sighed with feeling and said, "If it were a man, it must be the most courageous and skilful person in battle!" He ordered the carriage driver to turn the carriage around and dodge it.

309. Monkey's Meat

A man of Chu cooked a pot of soup to entertain his neighbours. Everyone thought it was dog meat and ate with great relish. When the host told them that the main ingredient of the soup was in fact the meat of monkey, everyone lay prone on the floor and threw up until everything was disgorged. This illustrated the fact that they never actually knew what was the taste of the monkey meat soup.

*

*The Unofficial Biography of Hanshi
By Hanying, dates of birth and death unknown. He had served three courts under the emperor Wen, the emperor Jing and the emperor Wu of Han. A writer, he later became one of the three highest officials in King Changshan's court. Author of *The Official Biography of Hanshi* and *The Unofficial Biography of Hanshi*. However, only ten volumes of the latter are extant. Pithily and exquisitely written, they preserved quite a number of ancient legendary stories.

310. The Gatekeeper's Daughter

Ying was the name of a gatekeeper's daughter in Lu. Once, while she was twisting hempen threads with several of her companions at midnight, she suddenly began to cry.

Her companions asked why she whimpered, and she replied, "I've heard that the prince of Wei is not a person of talent and virtue, and I'm worried. That's why I cried."

Her companions said, "Whether or not the prince of Wei is a person of talent and virtue is a matter for the feudal princes to worry. What has it to do with you? Why should you cry because of it?"

Ying replied, "When I heard about it, my thoughts were different. Previously, when the minister Huan of the state of Song offended the king and had to flee to the state of Lu, his carriage came rolling over our vegetable plot and spoiled the vegetables. In addition, his horse ate a lot of the plants. I later heard the gardener said that that year's proceeds decreased by about half. And there was the king of Yue, Goujian. When he led his troops to attack the state of Wu, all the feudal princes sent presents to him because they were afraid of the power and influence of Yue. The state of Lu likewise presented a bevy of beautiful girls, among whom was my elder sister. My brother was so mentally tormented that he died on his way to see my sister. It was of course the state of Wu that was being threatened by the troops of Yue, but my brother died because of it. From this we can see that fortune and misfortune are interconnected. Now that we know about the prince of Wei being a bad man, who loves wars and military exploits, how can I not feel worried when I still have three younger brothers?"

311. An Old Woman and her Daughter-in-law

There was a family whose daughter-in-law was virtuous and friendly with all the old women in the village. One night, a large chunk of pork on the kitchen range suddenly disappeared, and the old mistress of the house suspected her daughter-in-law might have been the cause of it. So enraged was she that she obstinately wanted to send her daughter-in-law back to her parents.

Early the next morning, the young woman went to say goodbye to all the old women in the village, bringing her cloth-wrapped bundle along with her. Everyone was indignant upon learning the reason for her departure. Among them was an old woman who said, "Take your time. I'll make your mother-in-law ask you to come back in person."

The old woman found some old rags and had it bound into a torch. She then went to the family in question and spoke to the mother-in-law, saying, "Last night, God knows where the two dogs with a piece of meat came from. They fought for the meat in front of my door and one of them was bitten to death. I'm here to ask for some live cinders to start a new fire so I can cook the dog meat."

When the mother-in-law heard what she said, her anger dissipated as she suddenly realized the truth. Hastily she went after her daughter-in-law and asked her to come back.

312. Butcher Tu

The king of Qi prepared for his daughter a very generous dowry, intending to marry her to a butcher called Tu. Tu, however, declined on ground of ill-health. His friend felt sorry for him, saying, "It looks like you will grow old and die in this stinking slaughterhouse! Why did you decline this marriage?" Tu replied, "The daughter of Qi's king is too ugly." His friend said, "How did you know about it?" Tu replied, "I knew it from my experience with the meat I sold." His friend was rather baffled, and said, "What are you driving at?" Tu then told his friend about his own view, saying, "In the course of selling beef, I know if the meat is good, it will sell fast and in great quantity, and there is always not enough to meet the demand. If the meat isn't good, even if you add something extra, nobody will pick it up. Now, the king of Qi offered so generous a dowry to marry his daughter off, it must be because his daughter is ugly."

Later, in a chance meeting with the daughter of the king of Qi, his friend realized that the daughter of the king was indeed less than beautiful.

313. National Treasure

The king Xuan of Qi and the king Hui of Wei met at the suburbs and went hunting together. The king of Wei asked the king of Qi, "Do you own any treasure?"

The king of Qi replied, "None."

The king of Wei said, "A state like mine, so small; yet I've ten pearls of one inch in diameter each, whose light can brighten up twenty carriages. How can a big state like yours with ten thousand chariots be devoid of treasure?"

The king of Qi replied, "The treasure I value are somewhat different from yours. I've an official called Tanzi, whom I sent to guard the South City, and no Troops of Chu dare come to harass; not only that, the twelve princes whose fiefdoms I conferred in Sishui and its vicinity all came to pay tribute. I've another official called Panzi, whom I sent to defend Gaotang, and the people of Zhao no longer dare to come fishing along the southern bank of the river. I've yet another official named Qianfu, whom I sent to guard Xuzhou, and more than ten thousand people of Yan and Zhao arrived from the north gate and the west gate to pledge allegiance. I've still another official named Zhongshou, whom I sent to take care of the thieves and brigands. Since then, no one pockets anything found on the road. Because of them, all lands within and beyond a thousand *li* are lighted up, which is far more than the twenty carriages you mentioned." The king of Wei was abashed, and left feeling rather unhappy.

314. Congratulation of a Different Kind

One day, during the reign of the duke Ping of Jin, the storehouse where national treasures were kept caught fire, and all the officials either drove their carriages or spurred their horses as they hastily arrived to help extinguish the fire. It was only after three days and three nights of hard work that the fire was put out. Prince Yan, however, brought along a bolt of silk to congratulate the duke, saying, "How fortunate it is!"

Duke Ping flew into a temper, saying, "That was a place where jewellery and precious jades were kept, and those were the most valuable national treasures! When the storehouse caught fire, all the officials either drove their carriages or spurred their horses here to help salvage what they could, but you brought along a bundle of silk to congratulate me. Why? If you can explain it, I'll let you off; otherwise I may have to take away your life!"

Prince Yan said, "How dare I do so without a reason! I've heard that a king stocks his treasure in the state, a prince stocks his treasure in the people, and a businessman stocks his treasure in a chest. At present the people are haggard and half-starved, and do not even have homespun cloth and short garment to cover their body, nor coarse food to fill their stomach. The people are destitute and possess nothing, but exorbitant taxes and miscellaneous levies are unremitting. My king, you had put away half the collection in your store, and that was why Heaven had torched and burned it. I have also heard that formerly Jie the tyrant ruled the country with an iron hand, bled the people white with ruthless taxation, and the people were so overwhelmed with grief that eventually he was killed by Tang of the Shang Dynasty, and held to ridicule throughout the world. Today Heaven sent down a fire to your storehouse of treasure, and it was indeed your good fortune! If you still do not wake up and continue as before, you may not be able to escape being held up to ridicule by our neighbouring states!"

Duke Ping said, "You have spoken well! From now on, I'll stock the treasure among the people."

*

*The Historical Records
By Sima Qian (c.145 or c.135-? B.C.) styled himself Zichang, a historian, writer, and thinker of Western Han Dynasty. A native of Xiayang (To the south of Han City, Shaanxi Province), he was the son of court historian Sima Tan. He later succeeded his father's position. He received the punishment by castration for defending Li Ling who surrendered to Xiongnu, an ancient minority in China. After his release, he became a senior official of the Imperial Patent Office, and wrote energetically. *The Historical Records* was the first comprehensive history that utilized a form of historical record that centered on individuals and their performances (as opposed to annals or chronicles); it was also the first biographical literature. A lot of textual research had been carried out on historical figures and events. The book influenced the the science of history and literature of later generations in a profound and far-reaching way. It is an immortal masterpiece.

315. Call a Stag a Horse

After the death of Qin Shi Huang, or First Emperor of Qin (259-210 B.C.), succeeded him was his second son, an imbecile. Wherefore Zhao Gao, the prime minister, was all the more reckless and unbridled. Zhao Gao was an ambitious schemer. In order to remove those who disagreed with him and further consolidated his control of court affairs, he hatched a notorious plot, staging a farce that was later known as calling a stag a horse.

One day, Zhao Gao presented a stag to the second son of the First Emperor, saying, "Will Your Majesty please look at this horse." As the Second Emperor of Qin saw it was clearly a stag; he smiled and said, "The prime minister has made a mistake. It is a stag, not a horse." At this juncture, Zhao Gao looked around and asked the officials nearby, "Do you think it's a horse or a stag?"

Among the officials, some were cowed by Zhao Gao's power and influence, but they did not wish to tell lies and so kept quiet. Some seized the opportunity to please Zhao Gao and said it was a horse. Some refused to distort truth and act in a perverse way, so they said, "It's absurd. Why call a stag a horse!" Zhao Gao had the names of the people who told the truth put in his bad books. When the time came for revenge, he would strike a vicious blow. It was of course intentional for Zhao Gao to call a stag a horse, all for the purpose of consolidating his power and the realization of his ambition.

316. Nail Drives Out Nail

As a boy, Xiangyu already showed signs of his unusual talent and great ambition. He possessed great strength and could lift a huge tripod of bronze which weighed several hundred catties. He did not love books, nor did he like swordsmanship. His uncle, Xiang Liang, criticized him, saying, "You have neither learning nor skill. What can you do when you grow up?" Xiangyu replied, "It will be quite enough to know just a few words and be able to remember people's names. As for swordsmanship, even if you are good at it, you can only deal with several persons; what use will that be? What I want to learn is the ability to deal with tens of thousands of people." Xiang Liang knew he had high asperations and tanght him the art of war. Later, Xiang Liang fled to Wuzhong (Jiansu and its vicinity) with Xiangyu to avoid being caught by the authorities because he had killed a man.

That year, The First Emperor of Qin visited Huiji (Shaoxing, Zhejiang Province). As he passed Wuzhong, the people lined the streets to welcome him. Xiang Liang and Xiangyu also mixed themselves with the crowd to watch the fun. As Xiangyu saw the great fanfare and the large number of people waiting on Qin Shi Huang wherever he went, which was awe-inspiring, he told his uncle, "I can step into his shoes and replace him." Xiang Liang covered his mouth at once and scolded him, "Don't talk nonsense! That's asking for the extermination of the entire family which extends to the nine degrees of kindred." From then on, Xiang Liang was convinced Xiangyu was an extraordinary person.

317. To Lie on Faggots and Taste Gall

During the Spring and Autumn Period, it was very often for the state of Wu and the state of Yue, whose geographical positions lay on the southeast, to go to war with one another. One year, the state of Wu defeated the state of Yue, and the king of Yue, Goujian, was encircled ring upon ring on the mountain of Huiji. To survive, he adopted the suggestion of his high official, Wen Zhong, acknowledging allegiance to, and feeding horses for, the king of Wu. Large quantity of valuables were also presented, and even Goujian's wife was sent to attend on the king of Wu. The king of Wu noticed that Goujian was extremely obedient, and set him free.

Back in his own state, Goujian was torn with grief whenever he thought of the humiliation. To avenged himself, he dispensed with all the extravagance he used to have, and slept on the faggots every night, while a gall bladder was hung beside him, which he licked whether he was standing or sitting in order to taste the bitterness of the bile. As he tasted it, he would asked himself, "Goujian, have you forgotten the humiliation you have suffered?"

To make the country prosperous and powerful, Goujian personally tilled the land; he ate coarse grains and wore simple clothes, condescending to the men of wisdom and the scholars, and courteous to the guests from abroad. After several years of pioneering work, the state of Yue gradually became strong and, in the end, Goujian was able to avenge himself by defeating the state of Wu.

318. A Dog without its Master

During the Spring and Autumn Period, the great thinker, Confucius, travelled with several of his disciples around various states, endeavouring to present his doctrine of administering a country to the princes, thereby realizing his own asperation. As the fame and prestige of Confucius were considerable, many of the high officials of these states were envious lest their own positions should be affected. Some of them vilified him before their sovereigns, and some simply expelled him from the country. Consequently, Confucius was not able to stay and secure an official position, although he had been to many states.

Once, he arrived at the state of Zheng and got separated from his disciples. As he did not know the way, he could only stood indolently by the city gate. Confucius' disciples became anxious as they lost touch with their master, and began to look for him everywhere. One of his disciples, Zigong, tried to find out from the people of Zheng whether or not they had seen Confucius when someone said, "At the city gate there was an old man, whose forehead looked like the sage king Tan Yao, whose neck can be likened to Gaotao, the chief judicial officer for the legendary ruler Shun, and whose shoulders are similar to Zichan's, while below the waist, he is three inches short compared with Yu the Great (2276-2177 B.C. founder of the Xia Dynasty). He looked very tired, like a dog without a master. He must be Confucius."

Hastily Zigong went to the city gate and, sure enough, there he found Confucius. He told his master how one of the Zheng people described him. Confucius laughed heartily and said, "It does not matter how a man looks, but the description that I appear like a dog without a master is most appropriate."

319. Promising Young Man

One day, Zhang Liang was crossing a bridge when he saw an old man wearing a simple suit. The old man walked until he stood in front of him. He intentionally flung the shoes on his feet under the bridge and asked Zhang Liang to pick them up for him. At that instant Zhang Liang was stunned and the idea of hitting the old man flashed through his mind, but he stopped short of doing it on account of the man's old age. He went down the bridge to get the shoes and knelt down to put them on the old man's feet. The old man smiled, but left without a word. After a while, the old man turned around and said to Zhang Liang, "Well, the young man is promising and worthy to be taught." That was to say, he thought the young man could be taught to become a useful person. He then fixed a date with Zhang Liang for their next meeting, agreeing that five days hence at dawn they should come to the same bridge. On the fifth day, Zhang Liang arrived early in the morning, but the old man was already there, and Zhang Liang was criticized for being late. They agreed to meet again in another five days' time. Unfortunately, Zhang Liang again arrived later than the old man, and the old man postponed their meeting for another five days. This time Zhang Liang arrived at the bridge before midniight. When the old man later came, he was very pleased. He passed on to him *The Taigong's Art of War,* urging him to study well, so that he could assist emperors and kings to make great contributions and accomplish great tasks.

320. Change of Attitude

During the Period of Warring States, Suqin, a native of Luoyang, initially advanced a proposal which called for the six other states (Han, Wei, Zhao, Qi, etc.) to ally with Qin individually. He went to the state of Qin to sell his idea to the king Hui of Qin, but the king refused to adopt his proposal. After staying in Qin for a period of time, his money was exhausted, his clothes worn-out, and he was haggard as he returned to his home in Luoyang. His wife, seeing he was in such a sorry plight, did not bother to step down from her loom, his sister-in-law did not offer him a meal, and even his own mother did not heed his presence. Suqin felt terribly ashamed and, from then on, he was all the more determined to study hard and do something worthwhile.

Sometime later, Suqin began to advocate the alliance of six states against the state of Qin. The first leg of his journey brought him to the state of Zhao, where his idea was accepted, and he was conferred the title of *Wu-anjun*. In time all six states supported his idea, and he was made the common prime minister of the six states. That year, Suqin wore the seal of prime minister of the six states and proceeded to the state of Chu. As he passed through his native land, Luoyang, and alighted from his carriage for a home visit, his parents had already prepared a band, spread a feast, and went to as far as thirty *li* to welcome him. His wife dared not raise her head to look him in the eye, and his sister-in-law knelt on the ground and crawled towards him to apologize. As Suqin observed the demeanour of his family, all sorts of feelings welled up in his mind, and he asked his sister-in-law, "Why do you change from arrogance to humility?" The sister-in-law's reply was, "Because your position is now high, and you have more money!"

321. A Silver Tongue

Zhangyi was one of the Political Strategists during the Period of Warring States (475-211 B.C.). His career began when he was a scholar of little means. Eventually he attained the eminent position of prime minister in the state of Qin, all because he had a silver tongue.

When he was still a poor scholar, he once went to the state of Chu to sell his idea, where he was entertained by the prime minister of Chu. Unfortunately, during his visit, a round flat piece of jade with a hole in the centre in the prime minister's home was stolen. The prime minister's servants suspected Zhangyi, and had him bound and hung up, beaten until his flesh was torn to shreds, then expelled him. Zhangyi struggled to crawl back home. His wife was very angry when she noticed his plight, and scolded him, saying, "Humph! If you had not been so meddlesome, and did not go selling your idea everywhere, you wouldn't have suffered such humiliation." Zhangyi opened his mouth and asked his wife, "Will you please see if my tongue is still there?" His wife smiled and said, "Of course it is." Relaxed, Zhangyi gave out a deep sigh and said, "That puts me at ease."

322. To Look on with Folded Arms

The state of Han and the state of Wei fought one another for over a year without any sign of reconciliation. The king Hui of Qin was thinking of playing the mediator, but first he tried to solicit the opinions of those around him. Some of them said it would be beneficial to mediate, others thought just the opposite. The king Hui of Qin was still undecided when Chen Zhen came to Qin, and the king said to him, ". . . The states of Han and Wei have been fighting each other for over a year now without any sign of conciliation. Some people said I should mediate, others opposed it. I've not made up my mind yet. I hope you will think over the matter for me in addition to what you have been doing for your own master."

Chen Zhen said, "I don't know whether anybody has told Your Majesty the story of Bian Zhuangzi killing the tigers? Bian Zhuangzi saw two tigers; he unsheathed his sword, ready to kill them. Guan Shuzi stopped him, saying, 'The two tigers are just in the middle of eating a cow. They will definitely fight over it and, as they do so, the stronger will be hurt while the weaker will probably die. If you wait until they are both wounded and go forward to kill them, you will reap the reputation of killing two tigers at a stroke.' Bian Zhuangzi thought the opinion plausible, and he waited patiently. After a while, as espected, the two tigers began to fight, and the stronger was hurt while the weaker died. Bian Zhuangzi seized the opportunity, went forward, and killed the wounded tiger, resulting in the brilliant achievement of killing two tigers all at once. At present, the states of Han and Wei are fighting each other; they do so for over a year now. It is conceivable that the stronger state will suffer a considerable loss of strength and resources, and the weaker one is near exhausted. Wait till they are both severely crippled and go forward to attack, you will then reap the benefit of defeating two states all a once. That's similar to what Bian Zhuangzi had done: killing two tigers at a stroke."

The king Hui of Qin commented, "Well said!" He did not go forward to mediate. Sure enough, Wei, the sronger state, was seriously weakened, and Han, the smaller state, was near extinction. Qin seized the opporunity to launch an attack, and decidedly defeated them both.

323. Gifted

During the Period of Warring States, Mengchangjun, or Lord Mengchang, was a man of high prestige, and anyone with some ability or skill would go to him for support. He would put them under his care, and they were called the hangers-on. At its height the number of hangers-on was over several thousand people.

The king Zhao of Qin heard his name and sent his messenger to invite him to come to Qin. Mengchangjun brought his hangers-on with him and arrived in Qin, where he was made prime minister by King Zhao. In Qin, someone said to the king that Mengchangjun was an aristocrat of Qi, and that he would always have the interest of Qi at heart while doing his job as the prime minister of Qin. That would not redound to the benefit of Qin. The king Zhao of Qin believed what he said, and removed Mengchangjun from office. In addition to his dismissal, he was imprisoned and lined up for execution.

Mengchangjun sent someone to ask King Zhao's favourite concubine for help. The concubine, however, wanted a white fox-fur robe worth a thousand pieces of gold in return. Mengchangjun had only one such fox-fur robe, which he had presented to the king Zhao of Qin on another occasion. Wherefore one of his hangers-on, who was gifted with the talent of mimicking the bark of a dog and an adept in stealing, snuck into the king's wardrobe to steal the fox-fur robe, which he gave to the favourite concubine in exchange for his release. To escape to Qi, Mengchangjun had to pass the frontier checkpoint of Hangu. It was nighttime, and the official in charge must wait until the cock crowed before opening the gate. It was then the hanger-on who was gifted with the ability to crow like a cock that was useful. When he crowed, every cock in the vicinity followed his lead and crowed with him. The official in charge opened the gate and Mengchangjun was able to flee from the state of Qin, albeit in a hurry-scurry manner.

324. Maosui

During the Period of Warring States, Zhao Sheng of the state of Zhao, titled Pingyuanjun, or Lord Pingyuan, took in, like Mengchangjun of the state of Qi, many hangers-on, and among them was one known by the name of Maosui. He lived in the mansion for three years, but nobody ever took any notice of him. That year, the armed forces of Qin encircled the capital of the state of Zhao, Handan, and the king of Zhao despatched Pingyuanjun as an envoy to Chu to ask for help. Pingyuanjun tried to select twenty persons from his hangers-on of thousands to accompny him, but could only find nineteen of them, one person short. At this juncture, Maosui recommended himself, affirming his willingness to make up the number.

Pingyuanjun did not understand him, saying, "Anyone gifted with talent will, naturally, be like an awl, even if you concealed it in a bag, its pointed tip would show at once. You have been here for three years, but nobody ever praises you for anything. You had better not go this time." Maosui replied, "The reason for my request is to beg you put me into your bag. Had I been put into it, the awl, which I am, would certainly have shown through the bag long ago, and not only its point." In the end, Pingyuanjun relented.

When they arrived at the state of Chu, Maosui used his wisdom, courage, and silver tongue to compel the king of Chu to agree on signing an alliance of resistance between the two states, and despatching their troops to rescue the state of Zhao immediately. It was then Pingyuanjun discovered Maosui's outstanding ability. He heaved a sigh and said, "Your silver tongue, sir, could equal the mighty army of a million men." And Maosui became an honoured guest from then on.

325. Besiege Wei to Rescue Zhao

During the Warring States Period, the state of Wei sent its troops to attack Handan, the capital of the state of Zhao. Zhao's situation was critical, and it asked for help from the state of Qi. The state of Qi despatched its senior general, Tianji, and Sunbin to head the rescue team. Tianji would have sent his troops directly to the state of Zhao to relieve Handan, but Sunbin said, "To resolve the dispute between two parties, the best way is not to be drawn directly into the conflict. Now that the state of Wei is attacking Zhao, their best men must have been sent to the front line, what remains in the country is only the ramnants of a rabble army. Why not let us take advantage of this gap, lead our men to attack the capital of Wei, Daliang (in Kaifeng, Henan Province), occupy their vital communications line, and assail whichever place is weakly defended. In that way, their main force outside the country will certainly leave the state of Zhao alone and hurry back to rescue their own state. If we do so, we shall not only remove the threat to the state of Zhao, but severely teach the state of Wei a lesson, aren't we?" Tianji thought Sunbin's idea was good, and launched an offensive against the state of Wei, encircling its capital. The armed forces of Wei, as expected, withdrew from the encirclement of Handan and rushed back to help rescue Daliang. At this juncture, the troops of Qi was waiting midway for them. An intense battle broke out in Guiling, resulting in the resounding victory of the army of Qi.

326. A Single Word is Worth a Thousand Pieces of Gold

One day during the Period of Warring States, in front of the city gate of Xiangyang, the capital of Qin, the whole town turned out to see the manuscript of a book on display. What kind of book was it? How could it have so strong an attraction? The fact was, a large quantity of gold was put beside it, and a notice was there with these words: "Can anyone point out any mistake in the book? Anyone who can delete one word, or add one, will immediately receive a thousand pieces of gold as a reward."

It turned out this was a game the prime minister of the state of Qin, Lu Buwei, played. As a matter of fact, Lu Buwei did not have much learning; he was originally a merchant. He used his money for political speculation and eventually got the position of prime minister with tremendous power and influence. At that period of time, all the powerful aristocrats in other states kept thousands of learned hangers-on with far-reaching results. In the mind of Lu Buwei, a mighty state like Qin without a corresponding culture and lagging behind the other states was something very inglorious. He therefore scouted for talents throughout the country, attracting them with big salary, and eventually got more than three thousand distinguished men. He divided the work among them based on specialization. In the end he completed a book with extremely rich content. Lu Buwei was very pleased with himself, and he entitled the book *The Annals of Lu Buwei*, and displayed it publicly to establish his prestige. Later, the phrase "A single word is worth a thousand pieces of gold" becomes an idiomatic expression, meaning an article or poem well written and with elegant language deserves high esteem.

327. My Humble Opinion

When the eminent general, Hanxin, was fighting energetically to seize state power for the king of Han, Liu Bang, he had once deployed his troops with backs to a river, and defeated the king of Zhao. Learning that the senior staff officer of the king of Zhao, Li Zuoche, had been captured by his men, he hastened to come forward and personally undid the rope that bound him, and invited him to dinner. The fact was, Li Zuoche was not an ordinary fish; he was an expert in strategic planning. The severe defeat of the king of Zhao was due to his tactical advice not being listened to. Hanxin's great courtesy was an integral part of his strategy preparatory to attacking the states of Yan and Qi. He was going to ask how the war should be conducted so that victory would be assured.

Li Zuoche said, "I've heard that a defeated general is not entitled to make a show of himself. I'm now a captive. How can I take part in the planning of important matters for the army?" Hanxin replied, "If the king of Zhao had lisened to your advice, I'm afraid the one captured would be me. Fortunately the king did not adopt your plan and thus I am able to ask for your instructions today. I am earnest and sincere; I hope you will not refuse my request anymore." Li Zuoche said, "I've heard that even a wise man sometimes makes a mistake, and a stupid person may once in a while have a good idea. I'm now giving you my humble opinion, a fool's little sincere advice."

328. Soaring up the Sky

During the Period of Warring States, the king Wei of the state of Qi went on a spree, living in the world of wine and women day and night, and did not attend to state affairs. The country was in a state of confusion, and the armed forces were like a heap of loose sand, utterly lacking cohesion. The princes of the other states, seizing this opportunity, often intruded into the country to snatch a little land here and there, and the state of Qi was facing a critical moment. The loyal ministers were extremely anxious. They lingered outside the palace, pacing up and down, but did not have the courage to enter it to remonstrate with King Wei. Just when they were at a loss as to what to do, however, there from afar came a small fellow, Chun Yukun the dwarf, a well-known figure in histroy. He smiled to the ministers and walked swaggeringly into the palace.

At the sight of the amusing Chun Yukun, the king Wei of Qi was all smiles. Chun Yukun said, "Nowadays there is an extremely gorgeous big bird with multicoloured plumage in the palace but, for three years, it does not fly, nor does it cry. Your Majesty, do you know what kind of bird is it?" King Wei knew he was talking about himself, and he said solemnly, "That bird may not fly at the moment, but when it does, it will soar up into the sky with one start; it may not cry now, but when it does, it will amaze the world with a single brilliant feat." Thereupon he began to put the state affairs in order and reorganize the armed forces. The princes of other states took notice and withdrew from the territory of Qi.

329. The Funeral of a Horse

The king Zhuang of Chu loved horses. He covered his beloved steed with luxurious silk, put it in a hall decorated with jade and gold, let it sleep in a summer bed with cool mat, and eat delicious dates. One of the overfed horses subsequently became too fat and died. The king of Chu ordered the ministers all come and pay their respects, intending to dress and lay its corpse in a coffin with an outer shell, and solemnize the occasion by following the funeral ceremony due to a high official. The ministers on his left and right remonstrated with him to refrain from so doing, but not only did he refuse to listen, he even went so far as to issue a general order, stating: "Anyone who dare to suggest to me anything with regard to the horse's funeral will be executed without exception."

Upon hearing this, Youmeng burst into the palace and wailed bitterly. The king of Chu was stunned and asked why he cried; Youmeng replied, "The horse that passed away was one Your Majesty loved most. For a state as big and powerful as Chu, it is a shame to solemnize the occasion of a horse's death with only a high official's funeral ceremony. The funeral ceremony of a king should have been adopted."

The king asked him, "According to your idea, what should be done then?"

Youmeng replied, "In my opinion, the coffin should be made of white jade, and the outer shell, of red sandalwood. Assign a large number of soldiers to dig a big grave, and mobilize men and women throughout the city to carry the earth. When the funeral takes place, the diplomatic envoys of Zhao should lead the procession by beating gongs, and the diplomatic envoys of the states of Wei and Han should sway and shake at the back to call back the spirit of the dead. Build a memorial temple, put up a memorial tablet for perpetual worship, and bestow the title of marguis with a fief of ten thousand families. By so doing, the whole world will know that Your Majesty belittles the people and values the horses."

The king of Chu said, "Is my mistake so great? Well, what should I do now?"

"That's easy. Make the top of the kitchen range the outer coffin, and the bronze caldron the inner one. Put in some pepper and cinnamon, ginger and garlic, cook it into a savoury stew, and let everybody eat to his heart's content."

*

*The Book of Rites
One of the Thirteen Classics. It was the selected works of various treatises concerning rites prior to the dynasties of Qin and Han. They are the primary data for those who study pre-Qin social conditions, customs and habits, and Confucian doctrine. Generally speaking, the

book was what Confucius' disciples and the disciples of his disciples had recorded. The definitive edition was compiled by Daisheng, a scholar of Western Han. As Daisheng's uncle, Daide, also studied *the Book of Rites*, the two were called Big Dai and Small Dai to distinguish them one from the other. The book is also known as *Small Dai's Book of Rites*.

330. Tyranny is Even More Dreadful Than Tigers

Confucius once drove the carriage with his disciples and passed Taishan, where he saw a woman wail before a new grave with great sorrow. Confucius held tight the handrail in front of the carriage, inclined his ear and listened attentively. Then he asked Zilu to inquire why she cried so bitterly. Walking over to her, Zilu asked, "Listen to your wailing, it seems to me there are more than one funeral arrangements, or aren't there?" The woman replied, "That's true. Previously my father-in-law was eaten by a tiger; later, my husband was bitten to death by a tiger too; now, my son also died in the mouth of a tiger. How calamitous the tigers are to our family!"

Listening to what she said, Confucius remarked, "Since the tigers here are so ferocious, why don't you and your family leave here and move to some other place?" The woman replied, "It is because there is no tyranny here, and that's why we risk the danger to stay on." Confucius sighed with emotion, and to his disciples he said, "Remember this, young men; tyranny is even more dreadful than tiger!"

331. A Handout

Sometime during the Spring and Autumn Period, there was a famine caused by crop failures, and many people died. A wealthy man, Qian-ao by name, set up a congee booth at the roadside and gave away food to the poor and hungry, but the real intention was to reap the good name of benevolence and righteousness.

That day, a man came from a distant place. He covered his face with his sleeve, and wore his cloth shoes with the backs turned in. He was terribly hungry and, his mind in a whirl, walked with unsteady steps. With food on his left hand, and soup on his right, Qian-ao went towards the hungry man and shouted, "Oh! Come and eat!" He was evidently arrogant and proud, and hailed the man as he would a pig or a chicken, all in the name of charity. The hungry man stared at him and said, "It was because I refused to eat handout food that I've got into such a plight." He moved on and did not so much as cast an eye at the food. He was later found starved to death.

*

Xin Xu (New foreword)
By Liu Xiang (c. 77-6 B.C.), a scholar of Confucian classics, writer, and bibliographer of Western Han. His original name was Gengsheng styled himself Zizheng, a fourth degree grandson of Liu Jiao, the king Yuan of Chu, Han Dynasty. During the reign of Emperor Cheng, he assumed a number of government positions. He once worked in Tianlu Pavilion, where he read and revised the books in the imperial library, and wrote *Classification*, which was the earliest book catalogue. He produced many books during his lifetime. *Xin Xu* originally had thirty articles, divided into eighty-three chapters, a greater part of which was lost by the early years of Song Dynasty. Zeng Gong sorted it out and edited it into ten volumes, which is the extant book. It recounts historical figures and their deeds starting from Shun, Yu to early Han Dynasty, supplementing other historical writings, and contains a number of quick-witted and thought-provoking fables.

332. Quill and Down

The duke Ping of Jin went sightseeing on the yellow River. As the boat came to the middle of the river, the rolling waves aroused in him all sorts of feelings, and he sighed, "Ah, only if there were prominent personages with me on this trip to share the joy together!" The boatman Gusang said, "Your Highness has committed a mistake there. The famous sword was made in Guyue, the precious gem was a production of Jianghan, and the beautiful jades came from Kunshan—these three treasures have no legs, yet they all come to Your Highness's side. If your Highness truly thirsts for talents, distinguished men will naturally come to you." After listening to the boatman, Duke Ping seemed a little resentful, saying, "There are three thousand hangers-on in my house. When I discovered there were not enough grains in the morning, I sent someone to collect rent the first thing in the same evening; I was afraid the grains might not be enough for the evening and despatched my man to collect all the city tax. Do you think that was not sufficient to prove I loved talented people?" The boatman Gusang replied, "Do you see the big swan flying high in the sky? Why is it able to soar straight into the sky? Well, it relies solely on the few quills. As to the fine hairs under its belly and on its back, their number will not affect the height of its flight. Are Your Highness's hangers-on the quills on the wings? Or are they the down under the belly and on the back?" The duke Ping of Jin was not able to reply to the boatman's question, and he just kept quiet.

333. Shengong Wuchen

The duke Ling of Chen was killed by Xia Zhengshu. To avenge his death, the king Zhuang of Chu sent a punitive expedition against Xia, killing him and got a beauty named Xiaji, whom he loved very much and intended to keep in the palace. His minister Shengong Wuchen remonstrated with him, saying, "This girl is the root cause of the ruin of the state of Chen. She committed adultery with several ministers since she came to the state of Chen. It was on account of her adultery with the duke Ling of Chen that the latter lost his life. Your Majesty must not court disaster by being intimate with her." The king Zhuang of Chu heeded his advice and put the matter aside. As he did so, the idea of marrying her began to enter Lingyin's mind. Again Shengong Wuchen spoke to him of the stake involved, and the idea of marrying Xiaji was also abandoned by Lingyin. Eventually, Xiangyin married Xiaji. After the king Gong of Chu succeeded to the throne, a war broke out between Chu and Jin and, in the battle of Yanling, the army of Chu was utterly defeated. Xiangyin died in battle, his corpse taken by the armed forces of Jin. Despite several representations made by the state of Chu, Jin refused to return it. Finally, Xiaji asked to be allowed to go to Jin for the corpse. As the king of Chu decided to let Xiaji go, it so happened that Shengong Wuchen was being sent to Jin as an envoy. Together with Xiaji, he engineered a plot to defect in secret. As Xiaji set out for Jin later, Shengong Wuchen fled on his way in disregard of his mission, and met Xiaji, all in accordance with the plan they had previously agreed on. They then defected to Jin together.

334. Two-headed Snake

When Sun Shu-ao was still a child, he went out to play on one occasion and saw a snake with two heads. He heard people say that anyone who saw a two-headed snake would meet with disaster. He therefore picked up a stone and killed the snake at once, and had it buried in a field far away.

As he returned home, Shu-ao held onto the lower hem of his mother's garment and sobbed. His mother was surprised and asked why he cried. Shu-ao said, "I saw a two-headed snake just now. I am afraid I am going to die soon and can no longer see mother." His mother hastily inquired, "Where is the two-headed snake?" Shu-ao replied, "I was afraid someone might see it, so I killed and had it buried." Caressing his head, mother was pleased, and said, "Don't be afraid, my son. You will not die. You have done a good deed, and Heaven will reward you for it." Later, Sun Shu-ao became a district magistrate and, even before he assumed office, the people throughout the state were already convinced of his benevolence and virtue.

335. About Jade

In the course of handling cases, the king of Liang encountered one that was difficult for him to decide, and he summoned the revered Mr. Zhu to his presence and asked him, "I meet with a case difficult to form a judgement. Half the officials thought punishment should be meted out, the other half believed the culprit should be set free. I'm at a loss as to what to do, and hope you can help decide what's best for the case." The revered Mr. Zhu replied, "I'm a mediocre person lacking in knowledge and experience. How do I know how to judge a case? Well, may be I just tell you something, and you can decide whether it is of help or not. There are two round flat pieces of white jade with a hole in the centre in my home; in colour, size, and brilliance, they are exactly the same, but one worth a thousand pieces of gold while the other only worth five hundred." The king of Liang was somewhat puzzled, and said, "Since they are the same in size and brilliance, how come one worth a thousand pieces of gold and the other only worth five hundred?" The revered Mr. Zhu continued, "If you turn them around and observed more carefully, one is thicker than the other by half, and the thicker one is worth a thousand pieces of gold." The king of Liang was very much enlightened when he heard this, and he praised him, "Excellent. You are saying that the more our policy be relaxed and lenient, the more people will support it." And the king of

Liang made it a point not to punish a man whose offence was marginal; and rewarded a man whose case was likewise marginal, and the people of Liang were entirely free from worry.

336. Shooting at a Rock

Formerly, Xiong Quzi was out walking in the street one night when he saw in the haze a rock, which he mistook for a tiger lying on the ground. With all his might, he pulled the bowstring and shot an arrow; the arrow went into the object completely, including even the feathers at the tail end of the arrow. But he discovered it was only a rock when he went over to look closer. He was very much confused and turned back to shoot another arrow, but this time the arrow was broken, and the rock did not have so much as a mark on it.

337. Lord Ye Professed to Love Dragons

During the Spring and Autumn Period there was a man by the name of Zigao, whose fiefdom was in a place called "Ye", hence people addressed him as Lord Ye.

Lord Ye had a predilection for dragons. At his house, there were images of dragon everywhere: the walls were painted with dragons, the doors and windows were engraved with dragons, the beams and pillars of the house were encircled with carved dragons, and even hooks and chisels were in the shape of a dragon. Some bared fangs and brandished claws, some in full feather, and they all made Lord Ye happy.

The true dragon in heaven was very pleased too when it learned that Lord Ye loved itself, and so it came down from above the clouds to pay him a friendly visit. This dragon was long and only its head could thrust in through the window, while its tail still dragged outside the central room. As Lord Ye had not seen a true dragon before, now that he saw a live one before his eyes, he only noticed the glittering scales around its body, a bloody mouth, and the bright red tip of its tongue sticking out, while the eyes looking at him were similar to two red lanterns. Lord Ye was so frightened that forthwith his countenance changed, as if the soul had left the body. He put aside all that he had been doing and fled in great haste.

Clearly, what Lord Ye loved was not the real dragons; what he loved was the images of dragons but not the real ones. If anybody only loves something in appearance but not in reality, we can say he is "Lord Ye who professed to love dragons."

338. Tianrao Left the State of Lu

Tianrao served under the duke Ai of Lu but was never given an important position. Because of that, he bade Duke Ai farewell, saying, "I'm leaving Your Highness and will be off to a distant place like a swan goose." The duke Ai of Lu asked him, "Why do you have to go?" Tianrao replied, "Has Your Highness not seen the rooster? On its head there is a bright-coloured cockscomb, handsome and elegant; on its legs, there are sharp spurs, magnificent and mighty; in the face of a powerful enemy, it fought with courage; it will call the chicks if there are food to share, kind and loving; and it is very punctual in keeping watch at night and heralding the break of day, honest and reliable. Yet, despite the fact that it possesses these five merits, Your Highness still wants to have it cooked and eaten, why? The only reason is it is near at hand and easy to get. Look at the swan geese, they come from a place a thousand *li* away, alight on Your Highness' gardens and ponds, eat Your Highness' fish and soft-shelled turtles, peck at Your Highness' grains and, although they do not have the five merits of the rooster, Your Highness values them. The reason is they come from a distant place, and it is not easy for Your Highness to get them! I'll now fly away like a swan goose."

The duke Ai of Lu urged him to stay, saying, "Please don't go! I'll jot down your words and memorise it." Tianrao replied, "I've heard that a man will not break someone's utensil while eating his food; and if one wishes to relax in a cool place, one will not snapped off the branches and leaves of the big tree. If you are unwilling to put a man of talent in an important position, why write down his words?" And Tianrao left the state of Lu for the state of Yan.

The king of Yan let Tianrao be the prime minister. In three years, the government began to function well and the people enjoy peace in the state of Yan, and there was not even a thief in the country. When Duke Ai heard of it, he was seized with remorse. To show that he regretted his past mistakes and tried to do better in the future, he lived alone in a wing-room for three months. In the meantime, he lowered the standard in such matter as dress and personal adornment. He said with deep feeling, "I was careless in the beginning, and it's useless to cry over spilled milk. How can a thing that's lost be back in one's possession again?"

339. Blighted Grains

An order issued by the duke Mu of Zou said, "Poultry must be fed with blighted grains only; milled grains are strictly forbidden." However, there were no blighted grains in the granary; and they could only be obtained by exchanging milled grains with the common people at the cost of two to one. Officials thought it made the feed even more expensive, so they asked Duke Mu to rescind his order and allow them to feed poultry with milled grains as before. Duke Mu said, "What do you know? The people, having fed their ploughing cattle, go to work in the fields under the sun with bare backs. How can the grains they work so hard to produce be given to poultry and the domestic animals? Milled grains are men's tip-top food; how can they be used to feed birds? It seems to me you are penny wise, pound foolish. There is a saying, 'Spillage is in the house.' Have you heard of it? It says that although a bag may be torn, the rice that spills remains in the house. As their sovereign, I'm the people's parents. Can you say that when the grains in the granary go to the people's home, they are not mine? Provided fowls only eat blighted grains, they will not waste the milled grains in our state. As to whether the milled grains are stored in the state granary or in the people's home, that's something I do not have to choose."

*

*On Imperial Gardens
By Liu Xiang The book was completed in 17 B.C. Originally it contained twenty articles, divided into seven hundred and eighty-four chapters. The greater part of it was lost by the beginning of Northern Song Dynasty, and only five volumes were left, which were edited and checked by Zeng Gong, who compiled it into twenty volumes, divided into six hundred and thirty-nine chapters. It recorded and classified anecdotes and old stories beginning with the Periods of Spring and Autumn and the Warring States to the Han Dynasty, mainly concerning the philosophy of the rise and fall of states using allegorical approach. To

a certain extent, it inspired and influenced the creative activity of novelists and writers of fables in later generations.

340. Flattery for Profit

Yanzi was already dead for seventeen years. One day, the duke Jing of Qi and his ministers were drinking. During the feast, Duke Jing was in high spirits and sought pleasure in archery. The arrow he shot missed the target, but there were roars of applause throughout the hall. Duke Jing pulled a long face, cast aside his bow and arrow, and retreated to the imperial harem sighing.

Xianzhang followed him, and Duke Jing said, "Xianzhang, I lost Yanzi seventeen years ago. Since then, nobody ever pointed out my mistakes. My arrow clearly missed the target today, but everyone in the hall applauded without exception." Xianzhang took up the conversation and said, "It was wrong of the ministers, of course. They did not have the intelligence to notice the mistakes of Your Highness. They were timid, and did not have the courage to offend Your Highness. There is one point which requires clarification though. I've heard that whatever the sovereign favours in the matter of personal adornment, his officials will put on the same; any food the sovereign likes, so will his officials follow. A small worm like the looper, when it consumes yellow food, its body will turn yellow and, if the food it takes is black, its body will turn black. Does Your Highness covets flattery?" The duke Jing was very pleased upon hearing this, and he said, "Well said! There is much substance in your argument today. It is as if you had become the sovereign, and I your subject."

Just at this juncture, the fisherman at the seaside arrived to present fish to the duke Jing of Qi, and Duke Jing took aside fifty of them to reward Xianzhang. As Xianzhang returned home, he noticed that the delivery cart of the fisherman was causing a traffic jam, and he held the hand of the driver and said, "Those who applauded the king in the hall when he missed the target are pleased that you come to present the fish. Formerly when Yanzi refused to accept the reward it was for reasons of helping the king. That's why he would point out any mistakes the king made without glossing them over. Nowadays the ministers fawned on the king to seek advantage even to the extent of shouting applause when he missed the target. I'm assisting the sovereign now. I've very little contribution to my credit, but receive so big a reward. This is against the principle Yanzi laid down, and comforming to the flatterers' selfish desire!" Xianzhang refused to accept the fish throughout.

341. Three Bad Omens

The duke Jing of Qi was out hunting. The moment he arrived at the mountain, he met with a tiger. As he went down to the marshes, he saw a snake. He felt somewhat uneasy, and summoned Yanzi to his presence when he returned. He asked, "I went out hunting today, and met with a tiger in the mountain and a snake in the marshes. Are these what people considered the bad omens?" Yanzi replied, "The state has three bad omens, but the ones you mentioned just now are not among them. What are the three bad omens? First, there is a man of virtue in the state but he has not been discovered; second, having located the whereabouts of the great man of virtue, he is not being used; third, he is being used but not being trusted. The bad omens I referred to are these three. As to the tiger Your Highness met, the reason is tigers live in the mountain; and the marsh likewise is where the snake has its hideout. It is absolutely normal that you saw them in the places where they live. How can these be called bad omens?"

342. Dereliction of Duty

Gao Liao served under Yanzi as an official for three solid years, and had always been cautious. One day, he was suddenly dismissed by Yanzi. Those at Yanzi's left and right felt greatly surprised by his action, and they asked him, "Gao Liao has worked under you for three years. He has never committed any mistakes. This being the case, even though you didn't want to give him a reward, why should you fire him? It seems what you did was a little too much."

Yanzi replied, "I'm a mediocre person, like a piece of wood with many bends and curves, which requires the flicking of the carpenter's ink marker, the whittling of an axe, and the shaving of a plane to shape it into a useful implement. Gao Liao has been with me for three years. He has noticed my shortcomings, but never mentioned them. What use is he to me? That's why I fire him."

343. Study by the Light of a Candle

The duke Ping of Jin asked Shikuang, "I'm already seventy years old, but still wish to learn a little something. Will it be too late?"

"Why don't you light a candle?" responded Shikuang.

Duke Ping said, "Where can you find a subject teasing his sovereign so casually?"

Shikuang replied, "How dare a blind subject like me teasing the sovereign! I've heard that a man who is studious as a juvenile is like the early morning sun which shines with great splendor. If he is studious in the prime of his life, he is like the sun at noon, whose illuminating power is immense. If he is studious in his old age, he is still as bright as a candle can provide. Although a candle has limited brightness, but if you compare it with groping in the dark, which is better?"

"Well said!" Duke Ping commented.

344. Sacrificed a Little, but Asked for so much

A neighbour of mine used a little box of cooked rice and a small crucian carp as his spring sacrifices to the land god. He prayed to the god, "I wish my poor low-lying land could yield a hundred cartloads of grain, and the rice plants in my narrow strip at the highland would grow well."

I laughed at my neighbour, for he sacrificed a little, but asked for so much!

345. The Foolish Old Man

The duke Huan of Qi was out hunting. As he pursued a deer deep into the valley, he met with an old man. He asked the old man, "What's the name of the valley?" The old man replied, "This is the Valley of the Foolish Old Man."

"Why is it called the Valley of the Foolish Old Man?" the duke Huan of Qi said.

"It was all because of me that it came to be called the Valley of the Foolish Old Man," the old man replied.

"From what I can see, you do not look like a foolish man. Why should it be called the Valley of the Foolish Old Man because of you?" Duke Huan still could not understand.

The old man replied, "Let me explain it to you! I used to keep a cow; it gave birth to a little calf. When the calf grew up, I sold it to buy a colt. A young fellow said to me, 'A cow cannot give birth to a horse!' As he said this, he led the colt away. My immediate neighbours learned about it, and they all said I was foolish. From then on the valley is called the Valley of the Foolish Old Man."

"Grandpa, you are really senseless," Duke Huan commented after he heard the story. "Why should you give the colt to that young man?" Having said that, the duke Huan of Qi left for home.

As he held court the next morning, Duke Huan related this incident. No sooner had Guan Zhong heard it than he adjusted his collar and bowed several times, saying, "That's my fault! If emperor Yao were still on the throne, and Gaotao still the prison officer, how could they allow anyone to take someone's colt away? If there was such an honest man being molested at that time, the old man would certainly not hand over his colt to the young fellow. It was only because the old man knew that at present there was no justice in a court of law that he let the young fellow take away the colt for nothing! Please let me return to rectify the situation so that the state will be administered in an honest and enlightened manner."

346. The Mantis Stalks the Cicada, Unaware of the Oriole Behind

Sometime during the Spring and Autumn Period, the king of Wu, Shoumeng, intended to attack the state of Chu. He warned the officials around him, "Anyone who dares to dissuade me will be executed without exception." A young attendant was very worried about the situation, but there was no way he could remosntrate with the king openly. Then an idea occurred to him. He brought with him a catapult every morning, getting his clothes wet with dew by running hither and thither in the garden for three straight days. The king of Wu was curious and asked him why he got his clothes wet every day. The attendant said, "I saw a cicada on the tree in the back garden, chirping aloud, unaware that a mantis was hiding behind. The mantis likewise did not know an oriole was nearby, stretching its neck and ready to snatch it. Feeling very complacent, the oriole itself was ignorant of the danger posed by my presence, for I was at the foot of the tree with a catapult. These three animals all focussed their attention on the immediate interest, forgetting the danger lurking at their back." After a moment's silence, the king of Wu commended him for his good speech, and cancelled the plan to attack the state of Chu.

347. The Teeth are Gone and the Tongue Remains

Chang Cong opened his mouth and asked Laozi, "Is my tongue there still?"

"It's there," Laozi replied.
"Do I have my teeth there?"
"They are gone," Laozi replied.
"Do you know why is it so?" Chang Cong asked.
"Is it not because the tongue is soft that it is able to survive, and the teeth are gone because they are too hard?" Laozi replied,
"Ha-ha, that's absolutely correct. All things in this world are the same!" Chang Cong said.

348. Figure of Speech

Someone slandered Huishi before the king of Wei, saying, "Huishi likes to use figure of speech in his conversation. If he is banned from using it, he will not be able to state anything clearly."

The next day, King Wei met Huishi and said to him,"Please speak plainly and straightforward from now on. Don't ever use figure of speech again."

Huishi replied, "Suppose someone does not know what a 'slingshot' is, and he asks you, 'What is a slingshot?' And you tell him, a 'slingshot' is like a 'slingshot'. Can he understand?"

"No," the king of Wei shook his head.

"That's right," said Huizi (Huishi). "If you tell him that a 'slingshot' is like a bow, its string is made of bamboo, and it is a kind of shooting apparatus. Will he understand it?"

"Yes," the king of Wei nodded.

"That is why. To use figure of speech is to make use of the things a person knows to inspire and enlighten him so that things unfamiliar to him will be more easily understood. If you ask me not to use figure of speech anymore, how can it be done then?"

The king of Wei thought for a moment and said, "You are right."

349. The Owl is Moving to the East

An owl came across a turtledove. The turtledove asked the owl, "Where are you going?" The owl replied, "I intend to go to the east." The turtledove was baffled, and asked again, "Why are you moving when everything is all right?" The owl replied, "The people here are disgusted with my hooting, and that's why I'm moving east." The turtledove replied, "If you can modify your hoots, then it will be okay. But if your hoots do not change, people will still hate them, even though you might move to the east."

*

*On the Laws of Nature
Yang Xiong (52-18 B.C.) styled himself Ziyun, a thinker, writer, and linguist of Western Han Dynasty, originally from Shujun, Chengdu, Sichuan Province. *On Laws of Nature* contains thirteen articles, mainly propagating the Confucian doctrine of respecting the sage and benevolent government, but he also raises the naive materialistic idea of "Where there is life, there will be death; where there is a beginning, there must be an end. These are the laws of nature." He advocated meticulous scholarship and extensive learning. A few fables were found in the book.

350. A Sheep in Tiger Skin

A sheep clothed itself in tiger skin.

When it saw grass it was delighted; when it saw the jackal and the wolf, it trembled, forgetting it had a piece of tiger skin on.

*

New Commentary
By Huan Tan (?-56 A.D.) styled himself Junshan, a scholar of Confucian classics; originally from Pei Guo Xiang (North of Huaihe, Anhui Province). The *New Commentary* with twenty-nine articles, which he authored, was lost long ago. Only one article is extant, which was included in the *Great Brilliance Collection*.

351. Make-believe

A man who heard that Chang-an was bustling and prosperous, and there were many public places of entertainment, yearned to have a taste of the place. While he was thinking about it, an idea occurred to him. He stepped outside the house, facing the western direction as he conjured up the city wonders, and laughed heartily, as if he were really inside a bustling place of entertainment in Chang-an, feeling very enjoyable and happy. After a while, he thought of the deliciousness of meat, so he went to a meat shop, standing in front of it and facing its main gate. As he alternatively opened and closed his mouth as if he were really eating, his expression was remarkably true to life.

*

The History of the Han Dynasty
By Bangu (32-92 A.D.) styled himself Mengjian, a historian and writer of Eastern Han Dynasty (25-220 A.D.); originally from Fufeng, Anling (northeast of Xianyang, Shaanxi Province). He was the son of Banbiao, an eminent scholar. He received imperial decree to compile a history book, for which he spent more than twenty years, and completed *The History of the Han Dynasty*. The uncompleted portion was later made up for after his death by his sister, Banzhao. It was the first dynastic history presented in a series of biographies, and it wielded very great influence on the compilation of history books in later generations, becoming the mode and style of history books written in biographical style. In the biographical portion, it was spiced here and there with fables.

352. Prevention is Better Than Cure

There was a family whose chimney in the kitchen was perfectly straight and pointing upwards, while the floor beside it was stacked with firewood. A guest arrived one day and said to the host, "You should adjust the position of your chimney somewhat, so that the upper part of it will bend a little to one side, and the firewood moved a bit further from the chimney. Otherwise the sparks from the chimney may drop on the firewood and become a fire hazard." But the master of the house turned a deaf ear to the warning.

Not long after that, the house of that family, as expected, caught fire. Neighbours hurriedly gathered to help, and the fire was put out at last. The master of the house slaughtered a cow, prepared wine, and spread a feast to thank those who assisted in the fire fighting, with the bruised and wounded occupied the seats of honour, but the guest who suggested modifying the chimney and moving the firewood further away from it had not been invited. Someone told the host, "If you had adopted the suggestion of the guest at the beginning, you would not have to spend money, and there would be no fire hazard. Today you arrange the seats according to the contributions of your guests to express your appreciation, but unfortunately you disregard the one who suggested a little modification to the chimney and the removal of the firewood, and only the bruised and wounded become your guests of honour. Do you think it is appropriate?" The host suddenly realized his mistake, and at once invited the guest who had given the suggestion before.

353. Parochial Arrogance

During the Han Dynasty, the territory of the country was vast and extensive, and it was the most powerful nation in the east. To the southwest of China there was a small country called Yelang. It was only about the size of a county, with sparse population and infertile land. Nevertheless, the king of this small country was extremely conceited.

The king was originally an orphan abandoned by his parents, who had him put into a big bamboo tube and thrown into the river, which drifted down the river with the tossing waves. A girl washing clothes by the riverside heard the faint sound of crying, had it retrieved and discovered the baby boy. The boy was later brought up by the girl and proved to be strong, brave, and outstanding as a man. At long last, he became the king of Yelang. However, as the king was brought up in an atmosphere of isolation, and did not have any knowledge of the wider world, he thought he was the greatest man on earth.

Upon discovery of such a Yelang nation, the Han Dynasty sent an envoy there on a diplomatic mission. As both sides sat down for business, the king of Yelang was so ignorant as to ask, "Which country is bigger, Han Dynasty or Yelang?" In his mind, he believed Yelang was definitely the bigger and stronger, otherwise why should the Han Dynasty be the one who initiated the diplomatic relations and send its envoy there?

*

Mouzi

By Mourong (?-79 A.D.) styled himself Ziyou, a scholar of the Eastern Han Dynasty; originally from Anqiu (Shandong Province). Learned even as a young man, he once gave lecture on *The Book of History*, and hundreds of people gathered, causing his reputation to spread throughout the district. Later, he became chief of the commissariat. The original two-volume *Mouzi* was already lost. Extant are only thirty-seven items scattering here and there in *The Great Brilliance Collection*. The contents are mostly plausible argument. There are people who believe that the book was written by some author in the Six Dynasties (Wu, East Jin, Song, Qi, Liang, Chen), passing off as Mourong.

354. The Sound of Music

Gong Mingyi played a tune of classic beauty and elegant taste to the cow, but the cow remained in the same posture, lying on the ground and grazing as before. It was not because the cow had not heard it, it was because the tune did not arouse its interest!

Later, Gong Mingyi changed his approach and play in a different way. He mimicked the sound of the mosquitoes, the gadflies, and the mooing of a calf looking for its mother, and the cow at once wagged its tail, pricked up its ears, and walked with long strides as it listened.

355. The Likeness of Unicorn

Formerly, a man who had not seen an unicorn asked another man who had, "What is the likeness of the unicorn?" The other side replied, "An unicorn is like an unicorn." The man said, "If I've seen the unicorn, why should I ask you? But you said an unicorn is like an unicorn, how am I to understand by that explanation?" And the man who had seen the unicorn elaborated, "The body of an unicorn is like the roebuck's, its tail like the cow's, its hoofs like the deer's, and its back like the horse's." Thereupon the inquirer knew the likeness of the unicorn at once.

356. Live and Learn

It was during the Han Dynasty that China began to trade with the minorities in the Western Regions. A trader happened to transport a batch of goods to sell in the Western Regions and brought back another batch on his way home. As his journey lay across the desert, he bought two camels to carry them.

As he returned, his neighbours all came to see him. One of the neighbours said to him, "The journey to the Western Regions must be arduous, and you must be very tired. See, even the horses you brought back were having such a hard time that their backs have formed two big lumps."

The trader laughed uproariously upon hearing this, and said, "They are not horses but camels, which are everywhere in the Western Regions. What you see on their backs are not lumps but humps which were inborn."

All the neighbours and relatives had not seen camels before, and the news began to spread from mouth to mouth until people nearby all came to see this weird animal. There were so many visitors that the trader's gate was almost burst by the huge crowd.

There was a school master called Mourong. When he heard the news, he immediately took the opportunity to exhort his students, saying, "A man of little knowledge was apt to make mistakes and become a laughingstock. He didn't know there was an animal called camel, and mistook it for a horse with lumps on its back. The only way to avoid making a fool of yourself is to acquire more knowledge through reading."

*Lun Heng

By Wang Chong (27-c. 97 A.D.) styled himself Zhongren, a philosopher of Eastern Han Dynasty and a native of Shangyu, Huiji. An avid reader even in his early years, he was once a student of Banbiao. Served as minor officials in a number of positions at one time or other, but retired at his old age and stayed at home. He devoted more than thirty years of his life to complete the book *Lun Heng*. It comprises thirty volumes, divided into eighty-five chapters. The book is the representative work of materialism and atheism in ancient China. It lashes out against both the Confucian doctrine and the superstition of Taoism in Han Dynasty.

357. Born at the Wrong Time

Once upon a time, a man in the Zhou Dynasty wished to become an official. He did not meet with such an opportunity, however. As days went by, he found to his sorrow that his hair was turning white, and that he was getting old. He felt very bad and sat down at the roadside, crying bitterly. Someone asked him, "Why are you crying?"

He said, "Many times Have I yearned to become an official, but never had the opportunity. Now I feel sad for my old age, as my wish to become an official is now dim, and that's why I'm crying."

The man inquired further, "Why have you not been able to become an official?"

The man of Zhou replied, "When I was young, I devoted my energy to poetry. After much hard work, I've cultivated the appropriate morality and the aptitude for writing, and hoped to enter government service, but then I learned His Majesty had a penchant for older men. When the king with a penchant for older men died, his successor preferred men with military skills. As I switched to learning military skills, it was rather unfortunate that the king who preferred military skills was dead by the time I had acquired them. Succeeded him was a very young king. He liked younger men. But by then I had become an old man. As things now stand, it is obvious I've missed all the boats throughout my life!"

358. Fowls and Dogs Turn Immortals

Liu An, the king of Huainan, devoted his time learning to cultivate himself according to the Taoist religious doctrine, and he invited all people in the world who knew some Taoist magic to come to him. Thus he gave up the throne in order to associate himself with the Taoist people. Because of his call, all the people adept in Taoist magic gathered in Huainan, and every imaginable description of divine decoctions and magic arts vied for his attention.

In time the king of Huainan attained perfection in Taoism and became an immortal, and all his domestic fowls and dogs also became immortals and followed him to heaven, so that there were dogs barking in heaven and cocks crowing among the clouds.

359. The Man with a Fur Coat

Yanling Jizi of Wu went sightseeing in the state of Qi and came across some money in the street. It was the fifth moon in summer, and the weather was rather hot. He looked around. Not very far from him there was a man wearing a fur coat with a sickle in his hand cutting firewood. He shouted at the woodcutter, "Come, pick up the money on the road!"

The woodcutter threw his sickle on the ground with a thud. With a stare he pointed at Jizi, saying, "Who do you think you are, condescending to look at me like that? From your appearance you seem noble and dignified, but why do you speak so boorishly? Don't you see I wear a fur coat to cut firewood on a hot summer day in the fifth moon; can such a man pick up money left on the road by other people?" Jizi realized then that he must be a man of virtue, and he apologized to the woodcutter, asking courteously what his name was, but the man did not appreciate his kindness. Coolly he replied, "You are one of those who judge people by their appearances. Is it really necessary to tell you my name?" Having said that, he walked away without further ado.

360. Frost in the Sixth Moon

During the Period of Warring States, Zouyan, a person with a literary reputation, was an official in the state of Yan. He was infinitely loyal to the king Hui of Yan. Jealous of his talent, someone spread lies and slandered against him. The king Hui of Yan believed the calumny, had Zouyan arrested and put into prison. Unjustly accused, Zouyan was extremely grieved and indignant. With his face towards the sky, he wailed bitterly in his cell. It was then at the height of summer, a day in the sixth moon. A gust of cold air suddenly descended from heaven, and the houses and trees were covered with frost.

*

*The Book of a Recluse

By Wangfu (c.85-162 A.D.) styled himself Jiexin, a philosopher at the end of Eastern Han Dynasty, and a native of Linjing, Anding (Present Zhenyuan, Gansu Province). A recluse, he had no desire to enter government service, devoting his entire lifetime to writing, and that was why his book was called *The Book of a Recluse.* It contains ten volumes, divided into thirty-six chapters, in which the fraudulent conduct of officials and despots towards the people and the prevalence of superstition in society are mercilessly exposed and criticized.

361. A Mascot

Once upon a time, there was a man called Siyuan. Following the usual practice, he kindled a fire in the field to begin hunting, and animals such as deers fled helter-skelter to the east to seek refuge. Siyuan chased them in hot pursuit, shouting aloud as he ran after them. A group of people who were driving pigs on the western side at that moment echoed as they heard him. As there were so many people shouting, Siyuan ceased chasing after his quarry and hid himself. An old boar whose body was covered with chalk, or white earth, happened to come his way. Siyuan became highly excited, thinking that he had come by a mascot in the form of a white animal. He brought it back to his house, drove away all the other domestic animals he kept, and let this old boar live in the pigsty all by itself. The old pig bent its body and raised its head, as if saying *ga-yi, ga-yi;* the melodious sound it made seemed to indicate it was quite happy and carefree. Because of that, Siyuan loved it even more. Not long after that, however, there was a storm, and the wild wind and torrential rain caused the chalk on the boar's body to come off and flow away with the water. As it now literally revealed its true colours, the old boar was so frightened that it cried like a regular pig. By now Siyuan had discovered that it was after all but a domestic boar kept at somebody's home. All this had happened because he pursued an object based on false assumption!

*

The Book of Jokes

By Handan Chun (132-? A.D.), otherwise known as Li, styled himself Zishu, a writer of Wei in the Period of the Three Kinkdoms (Wei: 220-265; Shu Han: 221-263; Wu: 222-280). A native of Yingchuan (Yuzhou City, Henan Province), he nevertheless came to live in Jingzhou. He was known for his wide range of studies. *The Book of Jokes* was China's earliest jokes collection. It recorded funny stories of all times, most of which contained taunts, and there were not a few fables, which were pregnant with philosophy, provoking deep thinking, The original book was long lost. Extant are only over twenty items, salvaged by Ma Guohan of Qing Dynasty and Luxun.

362. Parrot

Situ Cuilie of Han Dynasty recruited Baojian of Shangdang as his assistant. At the time Cuilie was about to see him, Baojian was very nervous, and he asked those preceded him what kind of etiquette must he follow. Someone told him, "Just follow the master of ceremonies."

At the day he met Situ, the master of ceremonies said, "Do obeisance."

Baojian followed his example and said, "Do obeisance."

The master of ceremonies announced, "Take your seat."
Baojian followed him and said, "Take your seat." Then he put on his shoes and sat down.

As he was about to leave his chair, he could not remember where he had put his shoes. The master of ceremonies said, "Your shoes are on the feet."

Baojian followed his example and said, "Your shoes are on the feet."

363. Divorce

Taoqiu of Pingyuan married the daughter of Bohai's Motai. The bride was very beautiful, bright and capable, and husband and wife were deeply attached to each other. Not long after their marriage, a baby boy was born to them, and they went together to visit the bride's parents. The mother-in-law was getting on in years, but she went out to see her son-in-law.

When the couple returned, the man wanted to divorce his wife. His wife was baffled as she could not understand the motive behind this sudden decision. Before she left, she asked her husband what offence she had committed. The husband replied, "Not long ago I saw my mother-in-law. I noticed signs of senility both as regards her appearance and manner, and she was very different from before. I was afraid you might grow old as she was, and decided to send you back. There was no other reason."

364. The Soup is not Salty Enough

A man stewed a pot of soup and ladled out some with a wooden spoon to find out the taste of it. He thought a little more salt would make it taste better, so he added a handful into it and tasted again. It was not sufficiently salty, and he put in another handful, then tasted it yet again. This went on and on until a whole earthen jar of salt was emptied into it, but the soup still tasted not salty enough. The man opened his mouth in wonder, and thought he was imagining things.

365. Holding Meat with the Teeth

A certain man was selling meat. As he passed a city toilet, he went in to relieve himself. The meat, in the meantime, was hanging outside it.

A certain other man stole the meat. Before he left, however, the owner of the meat came out to take possession of his property. The man who stole the meat held the meat with his teeth and said artfully, "You would certainly lose it by hanging it outside as you did. But if you do it like I'm doing, biting it with my teeth, how can it get lost then?"

366. Shade the Eyes with a Leaf

A poor scholar in the state of Chu came across a passage in the book called *The Huainan Prescription*, which said, "When the mantis endeavoured to catch the cicada, it hid behind the leaf called 'the cicada's ocular scale'. If one covers one's body with it, one will become invisible to others." He therefore went to the forest in search of this species of leaves. It so happened that he saw a mantis hiding itself behind a leaf, waiting for the opportune moment to catch the cicada. He was delighted and climbed up the tree to pluck the leaf. However, as he was sliding down the tree with the leaf in hand, the leaf got loose and fell to the ground. There were numerous leaves on the ground and, as his 'cicada's ocular scale' was one among many, he could not distinguish which one was the magic leaf he plucked. There was nothing he could do but to sweep all the leaves into several *dou*, or containers, and brought them home.

When he reached home, he began to put each leaf to the test. As he did so, he asked his wife, "Do you see me?" His wife replied, "Yes, I do!" He changed leaf after leaf until it was approaching dark and his wife was getting impatient with his questions. When he asked again, his wife angrily told him a lie as she replied, "No, I don't!"

The man was so happy when he heard these words, and he covered his body with the leaf, which he carried before him, and went to the market with the conviction that nobody could see him anymore. Armed with that conviction, he went about in front of people and get things that did not belong to him, resulting in his being caught by the *yamen* runner and sent to the county *yamen*, or governemnt office. The magistrate took over the case and, as he interrogated this scholar, the whole course of the incident was revealed. The magistrate burst into hearty laughter as he listened to the scholar. He thought the man must be an idiot and released him without punishment.

367. A Scrooge

Once upon a time in the Han dynasty, there was a childless old man who was very wealthy but extremely stingy. Ordinarily he cared little about his food and clothing. He rose up at the break of day and went to sleep when it was dark. As far as money was concerned, he was insatiable, and never let a copper coin slip from his finger. A beggar once asked him for alms and, against his will, he went into the house to get ten copper coins. On his way out, he put away one copper each step he took, and there was only five coppers left by the time he reached the door. He shut his eyes and handed over the five coppers to the beggar, but warned the beggar on second thought, saying, "I've given away all I have to you. You should not tell anybody under any circumstances, otherwise they may follow your example and come to me for money."

Not long after that, the old man died. All his possessions, including his house and the land, were confiscated by the government, and the money he owned went to the treasury.

368. Meeting the County Magistrate

A certain person wished to see the county magistrate. Before he went, he asked the people around him, "What is the thing the magistrate likes most?"

Someone told him, "The magistrate loves to read *The Biography of the Ram.*"

Later, as he met the county magistrate and the latter asked him, "What books have you read?"

"Only *The Biography of the Ram*," he replied,

The magistrate wanted to test his knowledge and asked again, "Who murdered Chentuo?"

"I've never murdered Chentuo all my life?" the man replied after a long pause.

The county magistrate realized he knew nothing, so he teased the man by saying, "If you did not kill Chentuo, then who was the one who murdered him?" The man was frightened out of his wits at this turn of events, and he fled at once, barefooted. Someone asked him why was he in such an awkward position, he shouted, "I went to meet the county magistrate, and he interrogated me about a case of murder. I'll never come again in the future unless there is an amnesty."

369. How the Punt-pole Passed the City Gate

In Shandong, a man carried a bamboo punt-pole was trying to enter the city gate. He held it vertically at first, but found it impossible to pass the gate; then he put it in a horizontal position, and discovered it was likewise not feasible. He was at his wits end, unable to find a solution.

A little later, an old man came up and told him, "I'm not a sage, but I've seen quite a lot of things. Why don't you cut the pole into two before carrying it into the gate!" Thereupon the man from Shandong cut the bamboo punt-pole into two in accordance with the old man's advice.

370. Cooking the Bamboo Mat

A man from the territory of Chu, Hanzhong (Hanshui River Basin) came to Wu Prefecture, Jiangdong (an area on the south of Yangtze River beyond Fuhu and Nanjing). At a Banquet honouring his arrival, a dish of bamboo shoot was presented. He found the dish very delicious, and asked what it was. Offhandedly a man said, "It's bamboo." Remembering the dish when he was home, and wanting his wife to taste the delicacy, he took the bamboo mat on the bed and cooked it. However, no matter how he cooked, the mat never became tender or soft. Disgusted, he said to his wife, "The people of Wu Prefecture are a crafty lot. How could they lie to me like that?"

371. Glueing the Tuning Pegs

A man of Qi went to the state of Zhao to learn to play *se* (a twenty-five-stringed plucked instrument, somewhat similar to the zither). He was not conscientious in his learning but, instead, only took note of the tuned positions which the man of Zhao had set. He had the tuning pegs glued, thinking that by so doing he would be able to play as the man of Zhao had done. Thus he brought his *se* back to Qi. However, three years had passed and he was unable to play even a tune. The man of Qi was baffled. Later, someone came from the state of Zhao, and he was asked why he—the man of Qi—was unable to play even a tune. It was then discovered how foolish the man's course of action was.

*Shenjian

By Xunyue (148-209 A.D.) styled himself Zhongyu, a native of Yingyang, Yingchuan (west of Xuchang, Henan Province). A historian and political commentator of Eastern Han Dynasty, he was the author of *Shenjian*, a five-volume work. Advocated Confucianism, and morality based on humanity and justice, he believed "A child needs to be brought up despite the goodness of its inherent character; law enforcement is required to bring around those who are born with evil nature", and ethics and punishment are both important in running the government.

372. Driving Chickens

A child was driving the chickens home. If he did it too hastily, the chickens would be frightened and run helter-skelter; if he was slack, the chickens would not move. When the chickens were heading north, and the child stopped them, they would turn southwards; if they were heading south and the child intercepted, the chickens would turn northwards. As the child went near, the chickens would become frightened; if he stood at some distance, the chickens would be carefree and without constraint.

In driving the chickens, one must wait till they are quiet and at ease. If they are fidgety, throw them something to eat to coax them. The important thing is not to be rigid and inflexible. When the chickens are calm and at ease, they will follow the same route and return home, and this is the best way to do it.

373. A Peephole View

A bird was about to fly past, and the bird catcher spread a net waiting for it.

A little later, the bird came and it was caught instantly. The bird catcher gathered up the net and found the bird entangled in the mesh. When he returned, he devised a net with only one mesh, brought it to the same place and spread it. Then he waited in high spirits.

Unfortunately, never again was he able to catch another bird.

Principles of Social Customs
By Yingshao, dates of birth and death unknown; a native of Nandun, Runan (north west of Xiangcheng, Henan Province). Originally the book *principles of Social Customs* had thirty-two volumes, but only ten are extant, contents of which deal with history of archaeology, social customs and habits, historical figures and their deeds, and strange tales.

374. When the City Gate Catches Fire

So the story goes. In ancient times, a man called Chi Zhongyu (In Chinese, it sounds like 'the fish in the moat') of the state of Song lived near the city gate of the capital. Once, the city gate caught fire, and all the people's houses in the neighbourhood were burnt down. The conflagration spread to Chi Zhongyu's house too. Not only was his house burnt down, even Chi Zhongyu himself was burnt to death. That was why someone said, "'When the city gate catches fire, the fish in the moat suffer from it' should mean 'when the city gate caught fire, a sudden misfortune befell Chi Zhongyu'", as he was burnt to death. There were others who said "the fish in the moat" did not refer to Chi Zhongyu. In ancient times, the city walls were surrounded by a moat called the city moat. In the event the city gate of Song caught fire, people would bring their water containers to get water from the moat to help extinguish the fire. If the fire was too strong, and numerous people drew water ceaselessly, the water in the moat would be exhausted, and the fish therein would die because they would be out of water. That was why people said, "When the city gate catches fire, the fish in the moat will suffer from it."

375. Itching to Have a Go

In the last years of the Period of Warring States, Jingke went to assassinate the king of Qin, and Gao Jianli accompanied him as far as Yishui River, beating the *zhu* (an ancient thirteen-stringed instrument) as he bid farewell to Jingke. When Jingke failed in his mission and died, Gao Jianli changed his name and surname, and became a hired hand. The work was hard and tiring, and it went on for a long period of time. When he heard someone beating the *zhu* in the master's home, he itched to have a go but could not, and so he told people, "The man's skill in playing the *zhu* is good at times, but bad at other times." Someone conveyed what he said to his master, saying, "The hired hand in your house knows music; he makes comments in private." Thereupon the master of the house asked Gao Jianli to play the *zhu* before him. Gao Jianli exhibited his skill then and there, and won universal applause. The master rewarded him with wine. As Gao Jianli withdrew to his own quarters, he took out his own *zhu*, put on a suit of new clothes and, taking on an entirely new look, he presented himself before the people again. Everyone was amazed and withdrew from the table to salute him, treating him as a guest of honour, and asking him to play the *zhu* and sing. Gao Jianli willingly obliged, and the songs he sang were so stirring they moved everyone to tears.

376. False Alarm

It was a day in the June Solstice when Yingchen, the county magistrate of Jixian, called in the chief clerk, Duxuan, and entertained him with a feast. A bow in red hanging on the wall of the room cast its reflection in the cup of wine, which looked like a curled up snake. Duxuan was frightened, but he did not have the courage to decline the wine offered by his superior, and so he braced himself and drank it. As he returned home, he had an unbearable stomachache, and no appetite for food and drinks. He ate very little, and soon became a mere bag of bones. No matter how often he went to see the physician, it was useless. One day, Yingchen arrived at Duxuan's home on some official matter. Duxuan's appearance prompted him to ask why the former was in such a bad shape. Duxuan said, "It was because I drank the wine with a snake in it at your house the other day. The snake had entered the stomach, and I was unable to cure it despite frequent visits to the physician." Yingchen pondered over the matter for a long time after he left Duxuan for home. As he looked up, he saw the bow on the wall, and everything became as clear as daylight. Once again he invited Duxuan for a drink, and arranged for him to sit in the same chair. As the wine was poured, Duxuan again saw the snake, and he was frightened more than ever. Yingchen said, "Don't be afraid. That is only the reflection of the bow on the wall, and no monster." All doubts had now dissipated and, with the ease of mind returned, Duxuan suddenly recovered from his illness.

377. The God of Salted Fish

In a swampy ground a man caught a roebuck. As he thought it unwise to bring it with him at once, he had it fastened to a tree with a rope and left it there. Not long after that, a trade caravan made up of more than ten carts passed though the place, and the roebuck was seen by an attendant. As there was nobody in sight, the man conveniently led the roebuck away. To avoid unforseen incident, he replaced the ruebuck with a salted fish. It was not long before the man who caught the ruebuck came back. He discovered that the ruebuck had gone, and in its place there was only a salted fish. He was rather baffled, as he was quite sure what he caught was a ruebuck. How could it have changed into a salted fish so suddenly? Moreover, the swampy land was desolate and uninhabited. There was no other explanation unless there was a god. Inexplicably, the news of a god of salted fish spread like wildfire, and more and more people came before the salted fish to ask for good fortune or medicine. Believe it or not, not a few said it was remarkably efficacious. Then a temple was constructed, in which the salted fish was consecrated. Several sorcerers were invited, and a tent was put up. With the beating of drums and the ringing of bells in all apparent seriousness, people within a radius of several hundred *li* gathered there at the news to pray and offer sacrifices. Several years later, when the man who left the salted fish there came to the place again and saw the singular phenomenon, he went into the temple to find out what happened. When he learned the truth, he laughed heartily and said to the devout men and women, "It was I who placed the salted fish there, and the ruebuck was also led away by me. How in the world could a god have anything to do with it?" So saying, he went into the hall and took away the salted fish. From then on, nobody believed there was a so-called god of salted fish, and in time the temple became dilapidated.

*

*The History of Later Han
By Fanye (398-446 A.D.) styled himself Weizong, a native of Shunyang (Zhechuan, Henan Province). A historian of the Song Dynasty (A.D. 420-479) of Southern Dynasties (A.D. 420-589), he had successively held a number of posts in the government Later, he was killed when

his part in the coup d'etat of Liu Yikang, the king of Pengcheng, was known. Before he wrote the book, there were already eighteen other compilers of the History of Later Han. Fanye learned widely from others' strong points, and drew up strict stylistic rules and layout, eventually becoming the most outstanding of all. The eighteen books written by other writers were all lost, and only Fanye's book remains, which is placed in the list of official histories.

378. The Fallen Cooking Pot

Mengmin styled himself Shuda, was a member of the Yang family in Julu.

When he lived in Taiyuan, he went into the street one day and, in a moment of carelessness, dropped the cooking pot he carried and broke it into pieces. He went on his way as before, however, without so much as casting an eye over it.

His behaviour greatly surprised Guotai, who wanted to know why. Mengmin replied, "Since the cooking pot was broken, it availed nothing to cast an eye over it?"

379. Covet Sichuan after Capturing Gansu

During the early years of Eastern Han Dynasty (25-220 A.D.), emperor Guangwu, Liu Xiu, had a senior general under him, whose name was Cenpeng. At that juncture, Gansu was occupied by Kuixiao, and Sichuan held by Gongsun Shu, both against Liu Xiu. Cenpeng, ordered by Liu Xiu, led a large forces to attack the two places, Xicheng and Shanggui, under Kuixiao. Kuixiao realized he could not withstand the attack and asked for help from Gongsun Shu. Gongsun Shu sent his senior general, Liyu, to the rescue. When Liu Xiu received the news, he wrote to Cenpeng, saying, "If you capture Xicheng and Shanggui, you may continue your triumphant advance, pushing onward to the south and attacking Sichuan. Nobody's heart is ever content. Once Gansu is seized, the next target is Sichuan." Accordingly, after Gansu was suppressed, Cenpeng moved southwards to attack Gongsun Shu. However, as his large contingent arrived at the neighbourhood of Chengdu, Cenpeng was murdered by an assassin sent by Gongsun Shu.

380. The Pigs of Liaodong

In ancient times, the pigs kept by the people of Liaodong (the eastern region of Liaonin) were all black. It so happened that the sow in a certain family gave birth to a litter of piglets. Among them one was white. The master of the house thought it was a rarity, and perhaps a good omen, and he brought the piglet to the capital, intending to present it to the emperor. When he reached Hedong (inside Shanxi Province), he discovered all the pigs there were white and, as he felt abashed about the whole affair, he turned around and retraced his steps.

In the early years of Eastern Han Dynasty, Pengchong, the prefecture chief of Yuyang, capitalized on his contribution towards the establishement of Eastern Han, always felt discontented and indignant. This led to the grudge against, and even an armed attack on, Zhufu, the governor of Youzhou. Zhufu wrote a letter to Pengchong, in which he criticized him for capitalizing on his own contribution, but ignorant of the great contribution of others. He related the above story *the Pigs of Liaodong,* obliquely compared Pengchong's opinion of himself to the attitude of the man of Liaodong with regard to his white piglet. He advised Pengchong to know his own limitations, to have a clear understanding of the situation and not to do things which would grieve his own people and gladden the enemy.

381. Tiger or Dog

Mayuan, or general Fubo, who lived in the early years of Eastern Han, was very strict with his sons and nephews. He had a nephew called Mayan, who loved fencing and archery, indulged in empty talk, and had an inclination to pour ridicule on others. Mayuan was an official outside the capital at the time, but he often wrote home to educate them. In his letter, he expressed his aversion to gossiping about other people, and warned his descendants to refrain from such behaviour. He took Long Bogao and Du Jiliang as examples and exhorted them, saying, "Long Bogao was faithful and honest. He was cautious in words, humble and striaghtforward, frugal and upright. I like him, respect him, and I urge you to learn from him. Du Jiliang had a strong sense of justice, ready to help the weak, and correctly distinguished between the clear and the muddy. When his father died, many went to console him and express their sorrow. I like him and respect him, but I don't want you to learn from him. If you learn from Long Bogao, you can at least abide by the laws and behave yourself, even though you might not be able to copy his example. People often say, 'even though you might not be able to successfully draw the swan, at least it would look more or less like a duck'. If you try to learn from Du Jiliang, you may become a frivolous man if you are not able to imitate him in the right way, and that is what people often refer to as 'setting out to be tigers but ending up as dogs'. That is the reason why I don't want my descendants to learn from Du Jiliang."

382. The Gentleman on the Beam

Chenshi, who lived in the time of Eastern Han Dynasty, came back to his native place Yingchuan when he was no longer young. One year, there was famine due to crop failures, and people's life became more difficult than ever. One night a petty thief slipped into his home and concealed himself on the beam in his room. Chenshi saw the thief, but he pretended to be ignorant of it. In the meantime, he called his son and grandson before him and sternly admonished them, saying, "A man must not fail to make a determined effort. A bad man is not necessarily bad by nature, it is the product of habits formed over a long period of time. An example is the gentleman on the beam." The thief was both frightened and ashamed. He came down from the beam, knelt before Chenshi and apologized, saying that he was not born a bad man, and assured him that he would not remain a thief anymore.

Chenshi believed that the thief was truthful. He knew he was forced by circumstances to go out and steal. He took some food and cloth and gave them to the man, and exhorted him to become a law-abiding citizen when he returned. The petty thief was very grateful as he took his leave. As news of the incident spread, social morals began to change markedly, and very few thieves were seen thenceforward.

*

Strange Tales
By Cao Pi (187-226 A.D.) styled himself Zihuan, emperor Wen of Wei, the second son of Caocao; originally from Qiaojun, Peiguo (Bo County,

Anhui Province). Ascended the throne as emperor on behalf of Han in the twenty-fifth year of Jian-an, and remained in the throne for seven years. Author of twenty-three volumes of *Collected Works*, five volumes of *Dianlun*, and three volumes of *Strange Tales*, etc., most of which were lost in subsequent years. The book *Strange tales* might have been supplemented, or even wholly written by author of later generations in his name, but it can no longer be ascertained.

383. Ghost-catcher Song Dingbo

In his youth, Song Dingbo of Nanyang went out one night and met a ghost. "Who are you?" he asked.

"A ghost!" the ghost replied.

"Who are you then?" asked the ghost in return.

"Also a ghost!" Dingbo lied.

"Where are you going?" asked the ghost.
"I'm going to the city of Wan," Dingbo said.
"I'm going to the city of Wan too," the ghost said.
And both of them walked together for several *li*.

"We walked too fast. How about carrying one another by turns?" suggested the ghost.
"Excellent!" Dingbo replied.

And the ghost carried Dingbo on its back and walked for several *li*.

"You are too heavy. Is it possible you are not a ghost?" the ghost was suspicious.
"I just died not long ago, and that's why I'm so heavy!" replied Dingbo. Then it was Dingbo's turn to carry the ghost. The ghost had almost no weight. They carried each other alternately three times.
"I've just died, and don't know what things ghosts dread most," Dingbo tried to make sure.
"Only don't like man's spittle," the ghost replied.

By this time they came to a river. Dingbo let the ghost cross it first. It made no sound at all as it did so. When it was the turn of Dingbo to cross the river, it was as if the hub of the waterwheel was turning under deep water.

The ghost asked, "Why are there noises?"
"It is because I'm just dead and have not yet been used to crossing water. Please don't take it amiss!" Dingbo said.

As the city of Wan was near at hand, Dingbo put the ghost on his head, and gripped it fast. The ghost raised a hue and cry, making the *zha zha* sound, and asking to be put down. Dingbo did not listened to him anymore. He went straight into the city of Wan. The ghost became a lamb when placed on the ground, and Dingbo sold it. He was afraid that it might turned into a ghost again, and so he spat on it. He got one thousand and five hundred coppers from the transaction. Thereafter, he returned home.

*

*On a Myriad Matters
By Jiangji styled himself Zitong, dates of birth and death unknown. He was a Wei resident during the Period of Three Kingdoms. The content of *On a Myriad Matters* was rather broad, but mainly on ceremonial dress, historical figures, and comments and analysis of military affairs.

384. A Matter of Opinion

Once upon a time, there were two men who happened to talk about the looks of the king of Wu. One said the king of Wu was very handsome, and the other believed the king was actually very ugly. Each stuck to his own view, and argued for a long time without being able to dissolve their differences. Finally, they all said, "If you look through my eyes, you will be able to decide whether he is handsome or ugly."

As a matter of fact, the king's looks remained constant. However, the impression each man had was entirely different. It was not because they argued wilfully for the sake of arguing; it was indeed a matter of different opinions.

The Collected Works of Ruan Sizong
By Ruanji (210-263 A.D.) styled himself Sizong, a writer of the state of Wei during the Period of Three Kingdoms, and a native of Weishi, Chenliu (Henan Province). He was once an infantryman, so people called him Ruan the footsoldier. Together with another six men, Jikang and others, they were given the name "The Seven Wise Men of the Bamboo Grove". The poems and essays he wrote were originally compiled into a collection, but later lost. *The Collected Works of Ruan Sizong* was put together by later generations. His famous article, written in prose, *the Biographies of Great Men* was written in an incisive style and biting sarcasm, attacking the so-called *gentlemen of rites* and their hypocrisy and shamelessness. The following, *An Army of Lice,* is a section of it.

385. An Army of Lice

Don't you see the state of affairs of the army of lice concealing in the crotch of the trousers? They flee to the deep seams of a trouser leg, and hide in the worn-out cotton fibres, thinking they are living in a propitious house. When they move, they do not have the courage to leave the edges of the seams; as they run, they do not dare to overstep the boundary outside the crotch of the trousers, fancying all their actions are in comformity with the moral standard, and fit in with reason. Nevertheless, as conflagration befalls the cities, big and small, and burns them to the ground, the army of lice will not be able to escape as well.

Under these circumstances, what difference in their conditions is there between those who regard themselves as gentlemen and the lice in the crotch of the trousers?

*

The History of the Three Kingdoms
By Chen Shou (233-297 A.D.) styled himself Chengzuo, a historian of Jin Dynasty, and a native of Anhan, Baxi (Nanchong, Sichuan Province). He had once been an official of the Kingdom of Shu Han (221-263 A.D.), later became an official in charge of compiling and editing national history in Jin. Famed for his talent as a historian, his most

outstanding work was *The History of the Three Kingdoms*, but there are other works as well.

386. A Hearty Welcome

In the last years of Eastern Han Dynasty, there in Gaoping, Shanyang (norhtwest of Jinxiang County, Shandong Province) was a man called Wangcan styled himself Zhongxuan. He was an eminent writer, being listed first among the "seven revered men of Jian-an". Wangcan had a very good memory, and anything he casually read only once would retain in his head. Once, he watched people playing chess. The chess-players inadvertently upset the composition of the chess game, and he was able to rearrange it without any msitake. He wandered to Chang-an when he was still a small boy. Caiyong, a leading authority in the literary world, had heard of him earlier, and came to admire the talent of this teenager. Caiyong's talent and learning were tremendous and, besides, he was in high position. He was considered a very influential man. His courtyard was as crowded as a marketplace, as his house was always full of guests. Once, Caiyong was entertaining his guests at home when the arrival of Wangcan was announced. In his haste, he put his shoes on the wrong feet. The situation was described in *The Biography of Wangcan*, a section in *The History of the Kingdom of Wei*, which says "as Wangcan's arrival was announced, haste had caused his shoes to be put on the wrong feet as the host went out to welcome him". Caiyong's guests were convinced the visitor must be an important one since their host was so respectful. When Caiyong entered holding the hands of Wangcan, they realized he was only a small boy, short in stature, and they were all amazed. "This is Wangcan, a talent unsurpassed, and I'm not as good as he," Caiyong said to his guests as he announced the arrival of Wangcan.

387. Too Happy to Think of Home

In A.D. 263, one of the three kingdoms, Shu, was wiped off the face of the earth by Wei, and its second monarch, Liu Chan, surrendered, becoming a captive of Wei. He was brought to the capital of Wei, Luoyang, where Caomao, the king of Wei, bestowed upon him the title of "the Duke of Peace and Happiness". From then on, he was only allowed to live comfortably and enjoy, but practically without any authority.

At that time, Sima Zhao had already controlled the political and military powers of Wei, and harboured the ambition of usurping the throne. He believed the existence of Liu Chan was a hidden danger, and tried to find a pretext whereby he could be eliminated. One day, Sima Zhao spread a feast for Liu Chan, during which he intentionally arranged for the songs and dances of Shu to be performed. The attendants of Liu Chan were moved by what they saw, feeling very bad as they recalled their mother country that had perished. Liu Chan, however, watched them with great interest, and without any expression of sorrow. Sima Zhao asked whether he missed his kingdom of Shu, but Liu Chan replied, "It's enjoyable here, and I don't miss the Kingdom of Shu at all." Sima Zhao realized he was indeed a mediocre man without ambition, and no longer worried about him. For that reason, Liu Chan was allowed to enjoy life as before.

The story appeared in an annotation of *The Biography of Liu Chan, the Second Monarch,* in *The History of the Three Kingdoms.* Later, the phrase came to denote someone who was satisfied with the existing state of affairs and reluctant to move forward, or forgetting one's roots or motherland for the comfort at hand.

*

*Looking for the Gods
By Ganbao styled himself Lingshen, dates of birth and death unknown, a historian and writer of the Eastern Jin Dynasty; a native of Xincai (Henan Province). During the reign of emperor Yuan of Jin (317-322 A.D.), he held the position of assistant official in charge of compiling and editing national history. *The Annals of Jin*, which he authored, was lost now. The book *Looking for the Gods,* which recorded uncanny stories of gods and spirits, was regarded as the representative work of its kind in Wei, Jin, and the Northern and Southern Dynasties (420-589 A.D.). The stories are mostly fabrications, allegorical in nature, using gods and spirits to reflect the human world.

388. Boring the Rock with a Wooden Drill

A man went to Jiaoshan in the middle of Yangtse River to cultivate himself according to the Taoist rules for seventy years. Laozi gave him a wooden drill, asking him to bore through a large rock. The rock was five feet thick. Laozi said to him, "When you have bored through this rock, you will attain perfection in Taoism and become an immortal." The man bored the rock ceaselessly for forty years, and eventually bored through it. As promised, he obtained the secret of making pills of immortality.

389. Chinese Lute

Caiyong of Eastern Han was a scholar who knew the temperament well. One year, he went to a place called Wujun, where the people used paulownia wood for cooking purposes. The raging fire was so fierce that the wood exploded. Caiyong heard the sound of the wood's explosion and was amazed, saying, "It is a piece of good timber indeed!" He requested his host to pull the wood from the fire and give it to him. He then used the paulownia wood to make a lute, the sound of which proved to be most melodious and pleasing to the ear. As it had a charred end, he called it "the charred-end lute".

390. The Mysterious Crane

Once, a black crane was wounded by a hunter and, as it could no longer fly towards the sky, it fled to Kuaishen's house. Kuaishen kept it with him and helped tend its wound. When its wound was healed, he released it.

Later one night, the crane alighted outside the door of Kuaishen. Holding high a candle, Kuaishen stepped out of the door. He saw two cranes, one male and one female, each with a precious pearl in its mouth, apparently as gifts to repay Kuaishen for saving one of them.

*

Bao Puzi
By Gehong (284-363 A.D.) styled himself Yachuan, Taoist name Bao Puzi; a medical scientist, chemist, and Taoist theoretician. Originally he was from Jurong, Danyang (Jiangsu Province). He was once a military staff officer, but later resigned his post and lived in seclusion in Luofushan making pills of immortality, hoping to become a celestial being. He was the author of *The Biography of Gods, Ramdon Notes on the Western Capital,* etc. *Bao Puzi* was divided into two parts, in and

out. The in-part contains twenty volumes, dealing with immortality, its medical practice, morphosis of ghosts and spirits, regimen and longevity, and so on. The out-part consists of fifty volumes, dealing with the gains and losses, success and failure of the human world, and comments on world affairs. It also synthesizes the doctrines of Confucianism and Taoism. The content of the book are mostly superstitious, weird and uncanny but, to a certain extent, it also unmasked the seamy side of the political and social conditions from Eastern Han Dynasty to the time of writing. The part concerning the making of immortality pills also preserves some of the achievements of natural science in ancient times.

391. A Plum Tree on the Mulberry

Zhangzhu of Nandun discovered a plum sapling while tilling his dry farm. In the normal course of events, he would have ploughed it away, but he was a little loath to part with it, and so he dug out the sapling, intending to transplant it at home. It so happened that something turned up which required his immediate attention. Before he left, he wrapped up the roots of the plum sapling with wet earth and put it in a hole found on the trunk of an old mulberry tree. Thereafter, he forgot all about it.

Later, Zhangzhu went to his post in a distant place. During his absence, people discovered a plum tree suddenly grew out of the mulberry tree and thought it must be some tree god. A blind man happened to rest under the shade of the tree and prayed, "If the mighty plum god will cure me of my blindness, I'll slaughter a pig as sacrifice to express my gratitude." By coincidence his eye illness recovered not long after that and, as promised, he killed a pig and brought it to the tree as sacrifice. The event was blown up out of all proportion, and people all said the tree was a god which could make the blind see again. The pious and devoted from far and near all came to ask for blessing in order to rid themselves of calamities. For many years the place was a scene of heavy traffic and sacrifices.

When Zhangzhu retired from his office and returned to his native land.later, he was rather amused by the sight and said, "That was the plum sapling I left at the time. Where in the world was the tree god?" Thereupon he chopped down the plum tree.

*

The Biographies of Gods
The stories listed in this book came from works of ancient writers. They were all legends about people who attained Taoist perfection and became immortals, numbering eighty-four persons in all. Although they were mostly old wives' tales, they became a source of literary quotations by poets and novelists alike in later generations and, in the process, enriched the stories. In Ming Dynasty, yet others augmented the number to ninety-two persons.

392. The Vicissitudes of Human Affairs

In Eastern Han Dynasty, a man called Wang Yuan was rumoured to have entered the mountain to cultivate himself according to the Taoist rules and became an immortal. Once, on the way to his destination Guacangshan, he passed the district of Wu, and lodged in the home of a man called Caijing. The Cais knew the revered name of Wang Yuan, and came out to welcome him. Wang Yuan stayed for a while; and then he sent someone to invite Magu, a female immortal. As he did so, a voice was heard from the sky, saying, "Magu will arrive in an instant." Two hours later, sure enough, Magu arrived. The Cais all turned out to watch and discovered a beautiful girl of eighteen or nineteen, who wore her hair partly in a bun with the rest falling to her waist. Her clothes were dazzlingly bright. She was gorgeous beyond what the world had ever seen. Magu said, "Before I came here, I've already witnessed the East China Sea thrice changing into mulberry fields. Not long ago, I went to Penglai the Island of Immortals, and noticed that the water in the East China Sea was much shallower than it used to be. Can it be that the East China Sea is about to turn into lands and hills again?" Wang Yuan sighed with feeling, saying, "The sage had said with foresight that it would not be long before a huge cloud of dust would rise yet again from the bottom of the sea!" The ancients believed the world rolled on in circles, the seas would become lands and the lands turned into seas after a number of years. Later, people used the phrase "the Eastern China Sea changing into mulberry fields" as a figure of speech to denote the vicissitudes of human affairs.

*

*Random Notes on the Western Capital

The book recounted past incidents and hearsays of Western Han Dynasty, and random notes on palace anecdotes, folk customs, festivals, etc. Because the stories were narrrated under the name of Liu Xin, a Western Han Dynasty scholar, Liu Xin was thought to be the author in the olden days, while Gehong was only the compiler. There were yet others who thought Liang Wujun was the author. Extant are two versions: one with six volumes, and another with two volumes.

393. A Bright Mirror Hung High

In the palace of Qin there was a precious mirror. It was square in shape, four feet in width, and five feet nine inches in height, and its surface was clear and bright. As one stood in front of the mirror, one's inverted reflection would appear in it. The most extraordinay feature of the mirror was that it could show a man's internal organs. If there was anything wrong in any position of the viscera, that portion would be plainly seen. If it was a woman who looked into it, one can gauge from the condition of her gall bladder's expansion and the heart's movement whether she conceived any wicked thoughts. It was said that Qin Shi Huang used to parade the palace girls before this mirror. Anyone found to have an expanding gall bladder and a moving heart would be executed at once, because she was considered a violator of palace ethics.

By the end of the Qin Dynasty, the country was experiencing widespread uprisings everywhere, and Liu Ban was the first to lead his troops into the city of Xianyang, the capital of Qin. He had seen the precious mirror, but dared not take it for himself. He had it sealed and stored in the government warehouse, waiting for Xiangyu to arrive. When Xiangyu arrived, his soldiers looted all the jewellry and burnt the Qin palace to the ground. From then on, nobody knew the whereabouts of the precious mirror.

Literary figures in later generations often talked about the precious mirror of Qin. It was regarded as an effective weapon and a symbol of authority against all evils.

*Fuzi

By Fu Lang styled himself Yuanda, originally from Linwei, Lueyang (Tai-an, Gansu Province); dates of birth and death unknown. He lived during the Eastern Jin Dynasty. A member of clan society, he was the second nephew of Fujian (338-385 A.D.), the emperor of Qianqin (351-394 A.D.), one of the 16 kingdoms formed in North China that existed concurrently with the Jin Dynasty. Having successively held the posts of general of the Eastern Garrison and governor of Qingzhou, he later surrendered to Eastern Jin Dynasty. He was killed for disobeying the powerful minister, Wang Guobao. Author of *Fuzi*, which contained six volumes, but the original was lost. The Compiled version of Ma Guohan of the Qing Dynasty can be found in *Yuhan's Lost Books series*.

394. Ask a Fox for its Skin

A man in the district of Zhou loved not only to wear fur coat, but also to taste delicious food. He intended to make a coat worth a thousand pieces of gold, and went to consult with the fox, hoping that it would present its fur to him. He also avowed that he would look for the lamb, asking it to present its meat as food for sacrifice. He had not finished talking when, one after another, the foxes all fled to the rolling hills, and the lambs too hastened to hide in the deep forest while calling their companions to follow.

395. Watching the Huge Legendary Turtle

There was a huge turtle in the East China Sea. It carried the Penglai Mountain on its head and swam about in the boundless sea. When it leaped, it could touch the clouds; when it dove, it could reach the bottom of the deep chasm. A red ant heard about it and was greatly impressed. It invited a swarm of red ants to the seaside to watch the appearance of this huge turtle. For over a month, the huge turtle remained hidden under the water. The red ants were very disappointed and intended to leave. Just at this juncture, there arose a violent storm, and the rolling waves surged, billowing against the sky, shaking heaven and earth with thunderous noise. The red ants were excited, saying, "This must have been raised by the huge turtle." A few days later, the wind subsided and the waves calmed down, and the thunderous sound was gone. In the middle of the sea, a newly-emerged mountain was faintly visible. It rose high above the clouds, moving slowly towards the west. The red ants commented, "The huge turtle carried the mountain on its head like a hat, floating on the sea or hiding under it. What different is it from us, each carrying a grain of rice on the head, wandering at leisure on a heap of earth, and concealing ourselves in the cave as we return to it? This is the way we live all along. Why then must we tire ourselves and travel several hundred *li* to come here and watch it?"

396. Relaxing in the Shade

A man of the state of Zheng could not stand the hot summer weather, and so he hid himself under the shade of a big tree to enjoy the cool. As the scorching sun climbed over the sky, the shadow of the tree moved, and he had to change his position also. At sunset, he returned to his original place under the tree.

When the moon rose from the east, he again followed the movement of the tree's shadow, for he was afraid the dew might wet his clothes. However, as the shadow moved further from the tree, the wetter his clothes became.

This man was smart in dodging the summer heat, as he took advantage of the cool under the shade of the tree during the day Trying to keep away from the dew by lingering under the shade of the tree at night, however, was a very silly thing to do.

397. Looking for a Perfect Horse

The duke Jing of Qi loved fleet-footed horses. He ordered the palace painter to draw a horse with extraordinary energy and vitality, a perfectly fine horse with no defect. He then sent someone to look for a horse like the one in the painting. However, he could not get one after a year and the expense of a thousand carriages because it was too divorced from reality.

398. No Way to Meet an Urgency

It was a common occurrence for Huizi not to have a fire in the stove for several days at a stretch because he was so poor. Wherefore he went to ask for help from the king of Liang, but the king said, "Can you wait till summer when the wheat is ripe for harvest?" Huizi replied, "When I set out on my way here, there was a big deluge in the mountain, and a man was drowning. He asked for my help repeatedly. I told him, 'I can't swim myself, but I'll send an urgent message to the king of Yue, asking him to get someone who can swim to come and help you. Will that be all right?' The man replied, 'I'll be saved with only the floatage of a wooden dipper at the moment, yet you want to go and seek help from the king of Yue, asking him to send a good swimmer to my rescue. Why don't you go down the chasm to find my corpse in the stomach of fish instead?'"

399. The Bird with Golden Wings

The duke Jing of Qi said to Yanzi, "The treasure I have now is sufficient to fill a thousand carriages, and ten thousand horses are needed to pull them. I'm now planning to get the hanging black precious jade of the state of Liang to add to my collection, putting together a whole array of gold vessels and jadeware. Do you think I can do it? Will that work?"

Yanzi replied, "I've heard of a distant place called Wanyu. There was a bird there known as the bird with golden wings. Local people called it fine jade hair. The bird was very fastidious in food. It would not eat unless it was the dragon's lung or the phoenix's blood. Because of its fastidiousness, it often had to go hungry and thirsty. As the prerequisite for its material life was beyond reach, it died soon after it was born, unable to live to the age it should."

*

*The History of the Jin Dynasty
It was a 130-volume work compiled by twenty-one historians during the Tang Dynasty. In A.D. 644, Taizong of Tang Dynasty ordered the re-compilation of the old history books of Jin compiled by various writers. Fang Xuanling and others spent twenty years to complete the work. Fang Xuanling (A.D. 578-648) was a statesman who helped emperor Taizong of the Tang Dynasty to bring about one of the most properous eras in Chinese history.

The two fables selected here were from *the Biography of Wang Xiang* and *the Biography of Wang Shen* respectively.

400. Lying on the Ice

In the Jin Dynasty there was a man called Wang Xiang, a filial son. His mother died of illness when he was still a child, and his stepmother Mrs Wang nee Zhu treated Wang Xiang harshly and often spoke ill of him. Incited by his stepmother, his father too was ill-disposed towards him, and would beat him at the slightest provocation.

Under these miserable circumstances, Wang Xiang slowly grew into a man. There was no resentment in his heart, even though his parents were harsh towards him; on the contrary, he was even more respectful and obedient towards his parents.

One year in winter, both his parents fell ill and became bedridden. Wang Xiang brewed liquid preparations with medicinal herbs and attended to their needs at bedside without grumble. One day, his stepmother complained of losing her appetite, and wished she had fish for a change. This was something hard to come by in the depth of winter. The river was frozen and the ice was three feet thick. Where could he get a fish? After struggling with himself for quite a while, Wang Xiang concluded the only way to fulfill her mother's wish would be to go down the water under the ice regardless of his own danger.

That day he arrived at the river bank. The howling wind was bitterly cold and the chill entered into the very flesh of men. He hit the ice with a thick stick, but there was not the slightest hint of breaking except the sound *dong, dong* as the stick came into comtact with the solid ice. As Wang Xiang thought of his seriously ill stepmother, he was in a stew. He took off his clothes and lay down on the ice, hoping that somehow his body heat would melt away the ice. Quite unexpectedly, as soon as his body touched the ice, it broke open, and two carps sprang out only to fall into Wang Xiang's hands. People were of the opinion that it was Wang Xiang's filial piety that had moved the heart of the gods.

401. The Old Man of the Eastern Suburbs

An old man in the eastern suburbs selected his living location based on the current political situation and prevailing circumstances. He lived in seclusion and tilled the land bordering the wasteland, where it was wild, dirty, but fertile. A man born in the land of frozen ice arrived from the icy valley and approached the old man for direction. The old man asked him, "Where do you come from?" The son of ice replied, "From the dry and cold land." The old man asked again, "Where do you intend to go?" He replied, "To a warm and sunny place." The old man said, "Those who go to the warm and sunny place must possess exuberant vitality and radiance. As you were brought up in a gloomy and cold land, even though you might wish to pursue the blazing sun, you would not be able to do it." The son of ice was baffled and asked, "Why is it so?" The old man replied, "Those who live in comfort and happiness are the people who go after the sweltering heat. The reason they can step into the hall of warmth and sun is because they possess charcoal as fuel. You are not one of them, that is why you should stop pursuing the flare and radiance."

*

*Old Tales Retold
By Liu Yiqing (403-444 A.D.), originally from Pengcheng (Xuzhou, Jiangsu Province) of Song (420-479 A.D.), one of the Southern Dynasties (420-589 A.D.). He was the younger brother of Liu Yu, Emperor Wu of Song, Southern Dynasties, and was bestowed the title of king of Linchuan. He loved literature by nature, and was a prolific writer. Among his books, *Old Tales Retold* was the most notable. The extant *Old Tales Retold* consists of three volumes, classified into thirty-six categories, mainly recording the anecdotes of historical figures from Eastern Han to Eastern Jin. The language is succinct, and the content thought-provoking. The stories in this book were the source of many classical allusions. The satire and metaphors therein make excellent fables.

Liu Yiqing was also the author of literary sketches such as *Tales of the Dead and the Living, Confirmation,* etc. They were all lost except a few pieces preserved in such book as *Extensive Collection in the Reign of Peace,* and expecially in Lu Xun's *Salvaged Stories of Ancient Origin.*

402. Cutting the Mat to Sever Relations

Guanning and Huaying were fellow students at the time of the Three Kingdoms. Once, they were working together in the vegetable garden and by chance hoed up a lump of gold in the ground. Guanning continued to work, regarding the gold as rubble, which was not worth a look. Huaying, however, picked up the gold and looked at it before throwing it away.

On another occasion, the two sat together on the mat reading. Outside the door, an official in his high carriage pulled by strong horses passed through. Guanning concentrated his attention on the book uninterrupted; Huaying, on the other hand, put down his book and went out to see. Thereupon Guanning cut the mat into two halves with a knife and sat separately from Huaying. Taking a step further, he expressed his desire to break with Huaying, saying, "You are not fit to be my friend."

403. Fellow Victims

Huaying and Wanglang fled from calamity in the same boat, and there came a man asking to be taken on board and flee together. Huaying refused to accept him.

Wanglang's opinion was different; he said, "As there is enough space in the boat, why must we refuse to take him in?"

Later, the bandits were approaching, and Wanglang had to forsake the man he thought of bringing with him.

But Huaying voiced his dissent then and there, saying, "The reason I have been hesitating at first was exactly because we were in a hurry. Now that you have promised to take him, how can you forsake him because time presses?" Finally, they brought the man along as intended.

People in the world later judged the morals of these two men based on this event.

404. White Crane

Master Zhi Daolin loved white cranes. When he was living in Maoshan to the east of Yan County, someone presented him with a pair of white cranes. Not long after that, the white cranes became full-fledged and endeavoured to spread their wings to fly. Zhi Daolin found it difficult to part with them, and so he had their wings clipped. However, by nature, cranes were birds that would flutter and soar high. Now that they could no longer fly, they would often turn their heads and look at their clipped wings, becoming depressed and despondent. The sight of their dejection moved Zhi daolin. He was filled with a thousand regrets and said, "As the white cranes have lofty asperation to reach the clouds, how can they willingly become pets of men?" And he made up his mind to take meticulous care of the white cranes. In time the wings grew to their normal state, and he let them fly away.

405. Bitter Plum

Wang Rong went out with a flock of children to play when he was seven years old. There was a large plum tree by the roadside with lots of fruit. Many children fell over each other in their eagerness to climb up the tree and pick the plum. Only Wang Rong remained where he was. Someone asked him why did he not join them. Wang Rong replied, "The tree grows near the high road with clusters of fruit unpicked. It must be because the fruit is bitter." The man went to pick one and taste it. Sure enough, the fruit was too bitter to swallow.

406. Perfect Poem

During the last years of Eastern Han Dynasty, while leading his troops on an expedition, Caocao went past a stone tablet. The tablet was Caoe's, and on its reverse side there was an inscription of eight Chinese characters, the meaning of each was, "yellow, silk, young, woman, daughter's son, ginger powder, mortar"; the pronunciation in Chinese was, "huang juan you fu, wai sun ji jiu". Caocao asked Yangxiu, an official in charge of literary matters, "Can you explain the meaning of these words?" Yangxiu replied, "Yes, I can." Caocao stopped him from speaking outright. It was only after he had grasped the meaning himself that he allowed Yangxiu to talk. Finally, Yangxiu explained, "Yellow silk is the same as coloured silk, put the two characters together, they become the character *jue;* the second group, young woman, when combined, make up the character *miao. jue miao* in Chinese means perfect or superb. The third group, *wai sun*, again, can be combined to build the character *hao*, meaning, good, which was made up of the two characters *nu* and *zi*, or daughter's son ('wai sun' in Chinese, or external grandson. The female side offspring is considered outside the Chinese family structure, hence the character 'wai' or 'external'). The last two characters simply mean the mortar for grinding ginger, or garlic, or any such substance, into fine powder. As ginger and garlic are pungent spices, the meaning is clear, the mortar receives pungent matter, which make up the Chinese character *ci*, meaning poem. The inscription is actually a riddle, and the answer to the riddle is 'perfect poem'." Yangxiu's explanation coincided with Caocao's understanding of the inscription and, for that reason, Caocao admired Yangxiu for his sharp mind, but he was at the same time jealous of Yangxiu's talent at heart. Later, he had him killed under a pretext.

407. The Sun is Closer to Us

During the reign of Eastern Jin Dynasty, the crown prince of Emperor Yuan of Jin, Sima Shao, was very talented even at a tender age. He was, moreover, very eloquent. One day, Emperor Yuan was trying to find out if there was any information concerning Luoyang, the old capital of Western Jin, from people who had just arrived from Chang-an. At that period of time, the five nomadic tribes from the north had invaded China, and Luoyang was also under their control. As Emperor Yuan listened to the report of the messenger, he was so heart-broken that tears coursed down his cheeks. Sima Shao was playing on his father's lap at the time, and what happened surprised him. He asked his father why was he crying, and Emperor Yuan explained to him why the dynasty of Jin had to move its capital to the South. After that, he asked his son, "Which is farther away from us, Chang-an or the sun?" Sima Shao replied, "the sun is farther, as I never heard of anybody coming from the sun, but often heard of people arriving from Chang-an." As Emperor Yuan listened to him, he felt rather amazed.

The next day, Emperor Yuan asked his son the same question before his civil and military officials. His purpose for doing so was of course to show how smart his son was. However, Sima Shao's reply was, "The sun is nearer, and Chang-an is farther away." At this, Emperor Yuan questioned him why his answer was different from the day before. Sima Shao replied, "As you look up, you can see the sun overhead, but you cannot see the whereabouts of Chang-an, and that's why I say the sun is nearer to us than Chang-an." Both civil and military officials gasped in admiration for the eloquence of the crown prince, convinced that he would be an enlightened ruler in the future, and emperor Yuan was even more delighted than he ever was.

408. Imitating Pan Yue

Pan Yue was good-looking in appearance and graceful in demeanour. When he was young, he used to carry a hunting slingshot under his arm out in Luoyang Avenue. If he was seen by women, he would be surrounded with joined hands.

Zuo Taichong was extremely ugly, yet he liked to imitate Pan Yue and go hunting. The experience, however, was quite different. The girls who happened to meet him on the road would invariably spit at him. On such occasion, he would return home feeling greatly embarrassed and dejected.

409. Turn Over a New Leaf

When he was young, Zhou Chu was fierce and tough, possessing a sense of justice, yet bellicose. At that time in Yixing, there was a flood dragon in the river and a ferocious tiger in the mountain, both brought harm to the people. The people there put Zhou Chu, the flood dragon, and the fierce tiger together, and called them "three pests".

To get rid of Zhou Chu, someone instigated him to go and fight with the dragon. The intention was to cause destruction to both sides. However, Zhou Chu went to the mountain to kill the ferocious tiger first before going down the river to pursue the flood dragon. The flood dragon emerged from the water sometimes, and at other times it submerged under it. As it swam, it did so for tens of *li*. Zhou Chu followed it closely without slackening. After three days and three nights, all the people thought Zhou Chu and the flood dragon must have died together, and they congratulated themselves. Contrary to their expectation, however, Zhou Chu had killed the flood dragon and came out unhurt. It was only when he heard how people celebrated the death of the flood dragon and himself that Zhou Chu realized how they had hated him, and it brought about his remorse. He went to Wujun to look for his two brothers, Luji and Luyun, intending to learn from them. Luji was not at home, and only Luyun met him. Zhou Chu related his own bitter experience and dejectedly expressed his desire to turn over a new leaf. He was also worried that he might not be in a position to do anything of merit on account of his advanced age. Luyun consoled him, saying, "The ancients believe one is even willing to die in the evening if he can hear the truth in the morning. You have a very bright future. The thing a man must worry about is his asperation. Why should a man worry about his name not being known?" After listening to Luyun, Zhou Chu made up his mind to start with a clean slate and in time he became a loyal official and dutiful son whom everybody looked up to.

410. Gone is the Music with the Man

Wang Xizhi was the most illustrious calligrapher in the history of the nation. He lived in the Jin Dynasty, and begot seven children, of whom Wang Huizhi and Wang Xianzhi being the most gifted. Wang Xianzhi styled himself Zijing, was also adept in calligraphy, enjoying equal popularity with his father. Wang Huizhi styled himself Ziyou, was a palace official. That year, Wang Huizhi resigned his post and returned to his native place, but unfortunately fell ill with his brother at the same time.

It was said that an occultist had mentioned at the time, "If there is another man who will take the place of the dying man, then the dying man can live on." Wang Huizhi expressed his willingness to die in his brother's place, and asked the occultist to assist him. The occultist said, "Both of you are going to die, so one cannot take the place of the other." Not long after that, Wang Xianzhi departed first, and Huizhi rushed to his brother's side. He did not cry, but only sat on the bier, took over the lute which Xianzhi once played during his lifetime, and prepared to play a tune to express his deep sorrow. However, despite his effort, he could not produce the tone tuning right. Wherefore he threw aside the lute, and said sorrowfully, "Alas, Zijing, gone is the music with the man!" Having said that, he fainted. A month later, he also passed away.

Later, the phrase "gone is the music with the man" came to mean "mournful over the deceased on seeing the thing left behind by him".

411. Kong Qun is Fond of the Bottle

Kong Qun, the minister of rites, was very fond of the bottle. Wang Dao, the prime minister, advised him, saying, "Why must you often drink to excess? Don't you see the cloth that covers the wine jug? Having been exposed to the vapour of the wine, it soon becomes corroded?" Kong Qun, shielding his shortcoming, quibbled, "Decomposition is not necessarily bad. Did you ever see the meat cured in distiller's grains? The longer it is left to decompose, the better its taste!"

412. The Crane that Does Not Dance

Yang Hu, a famous general in the early days of Western Jin, controlled the military affairs of Jingzhou as prime minister in charge of military matters. During the ten years as the military governor of Xiangyang, he led the army and the people to reclaim the wasteland for farming, hoard up grains and fodder, do everything possible to prepare for the elimination of Eastern Wu. Ostensibly, however, he remained in friendly terms with the defending general, Lu Kang, each guarding his own territory. As to the soldiers captured in previous battle, they could stay if they wanted to, or leave if they were so inclined. It was said Yang Hu used to catch cranes in the marshes of Jiangling at the time he was garrisoning Xiangyang; the cranes he caught were brought back and taught to dance. As the cranes were domesticated, he would take them before his guests to dance and amuse them. Yang Hu himself often praised the cranes he had domesticated, boasting how clever they were, and how exquisite their dancing skills. His guests, seeing that the cranes were so cute and human-like, tried to make them dance as well. The cranes, however, just loosened their feather, but not in the mood to oblige, as if they had become the divine birds which did not dance. "The crane that does not dance" is now a metaphor for an incompetent person; it is also used as self-effacing words.

413. Feed on Fancies

It was a hot summer day when Caocao led his troops and horses travelling across a loess area. It was a long and arduous journey, and the soldiers were exhausted. They all looked haggard and thin, with sweat all over their faces, like fish out of water, panting and with mouths open. It was really a time when no village in front nor town after them was in sight, and not a drop of water was available. How to cover this lengthy road in the loess area? Caocao, riding on his horse, was very anxious at heart. Suddenly, an idea struck him. He pointed his horsewhip, and said to the soldiers, "Brothers, let us hasten! Before us, there is a plum grove with large ripe plums on the branches, tart and sweet, which will help quench our thirst!" Caocao's words inspired and raised the soldiers' morale. Thinking of the sweet and sour plum, everyone's mouth began to water. Their spirits thus aroused, their march began to quicken although, as a matter of fact, for many miles no one actually saw any plum grove. In the end, they had found the source of water instead, and the soldiers were happy because they could now have the cool and sweet water to drink.

414. A Hot-tempered Person

The margius of Lantian, Wang Shu, was a hot-tempered man. Once, he was eating a hard-boiled egg. He tried to pick it up with the chopsticks but did not succeed after several attempts. He lost his temper and, grabbing the egg with his hand, he threw it on the ground with all his strength, stamping his foot on it. But the egg rolled away, and the first stamp missed its target. This so infuriated him that his eyes nearly started from his head. He picked up the egg with his hand, put it into his mouth, bit it into small pieces, spat them out before tossing them onto the ground.

*

Tales of the Dead and the Living
By Liu Yiqing, the same author who wrote *Old Tales Retold*.

415. Falcon

When he was young, the king Wen of Chu loved the sport of hunting. Someone presented him with a falcon. The king noticed that the claws of that falcon were distinctly different from other falcons as they were very sharp. He brought his falcon to the Yunmeng Marsh to hunt. He put up traps as dense as dark clouds in the sky, and raised a fire in the wasteland, causing the flames and smokes to fill all over the place. At that moment, all the other falcons fell over one another trying to catch their preys, but this falcon was devoid of any fighting spirits, for it only stretched out its neck, and stared with wide eyes. The king Wen of Chu asked the man who presented the falcon, saying, "The other falcons caught quite a number of preys, but the falcon you presented did not even move. Have you lied to me?" The falcon presenter replied, "If this falcon only catches pheasants and hares, how dare I present it to Your Majesty?"

Not long after that, a monster was seen gliding through the clouds. Its body was white throughout, but its form was not so defined. At that moment, the falcon spread its wings and, as swift as lightning, shot up to the sky. A little while later, feathers fell like snow flakes and blood poured down like rain. A big bird dropped to the ground; its wingspan measured tens of *li* in width. Nobody regarded it as a bird. But a very learned man told the king Wen of Chu, saying, "This is the young of the *roc*." Thereupon King Wen rewarded the man generously.

416. The Wooden Pillow of Jiaohu God Temple

The man who took care of joss sticks and candles in the Jiaohu God Temple had a cypress wooden pillow. The pillow had been in his possession for over thirty years, and there was a crack in the form of a small opening at its back.

A trader named Tang Lin from the county passed the place and went into the temple to pray for a blessing. The caretaker asked him, "Are you married? If you are, you can lie down near the opening of the pillow and take a nap."

The caretaker then let Tang Lin enter the opening of the cypress wooden pillow. Once inside, he saw vermilion gates, magnificent palaces and luxurious balconies, all out of this world. Tang Lin met the supreme government official in charge of military affairs, and the latter helped bring about his marriage, from which he had six children, four boys and two girls. First, Tang Lin was selected to be a secretariat official; then he was promoted to be a palace official. While he was inside the cypress wooden pillow, Tang Lin never thought of his native land. Later, he experienced some unhappy event, and the caretaker of joss sticks and candles let him out. Then he saw the cypress wooden pillow again.

The caretaker of joss sticks and candles said, "Although you had passed many years inside the pillow, but in reality it was only a little while!"

Confirmation
By the same author who wrote *Old Tales Retold* and *Tales of the Dead and the Living*.

417. The Parrot Put out a Fire

Once upon a time, a parrot flew to another mountain, where all the birds and animals received it with great hospitality. The parrot thought, although it was happy there, it was nevertheless not a place to stay permanently, and so it decided to leave. A few months later, there was a conflagration in that mountain, and the parrot saw it from a distance. It plunged into the water to get its feather soaked, and flew to that mountain to spray the water down onto the fire. A celestial being saw what it was doing and said, "Although you mean well, but your action will avail nothing in view of the raging flames." The parrot replied, "I know my action will not extinguish the fire, but this is the mountain I once lived. The birds and animals here were all friendly to me, we were like brothers, and I cannot bear to see them suffer!" The god was moved by the parrot's kind-heartedness and forthwith proceeded to put out the fire.

*

*The Garden of Strange Happenings
By Liu Jingshu (c.390-470 A.D.), a writer of Song, one of the Southern Dynasties. He was originally from Pengcheng (Xuzhou, Jiangsu Province). *The Garden of Strange Happenings*, which he authored, was a collection of short stories about ghosts and spirits and tales on the subject of Buddhism.

418. Dancing Pheasant

Pheasant treasured its own feather. Whenever it saw its reflection in the water, it would dance.

At the time when Caocao of Wei was in power, someone from the South presented him with a pheasant. He tried every way to make it dance but did not succeed. His son, Cangshu, asked someone to put a large mirror before the pheasant. When the pheasant saw its own reflection in the mirror, it began to dance without stop.

The History of Song, One of the Southern Dynasties
By Shen Yue (441-513 A.D.), a writer of Liang, one of the Southern Dynasties. He was orginally from Wukang, Wuxing (Deqing, Zhejiang Province). Many sections and chapters of the book were incomplete by the time of the Song Dynasty, and several sections of it were made up with materials from *the History of Southern Dynasties* written by Li Yanshou. It was regarded as the official history by later generations.

419. The Maddening Spring

Once upon a time, there was a country in which there was a spring called Maddening Spring. Inside the country, whoever drank from that spring, there was none who would not become insane. Only the king, who had dug a well and used water from his own well, was able to escape insanity.

Since all the people inside the country were mad, they all thought it was the king who was crazed. They gathered together and planned secretly to have the king captured in order that they could cure him of his madness. They used moxibustion, gave acupuncture treatment with a long needle, poured bitter medicine into his mouth and, as a matter of fact, all possible methods were used. Finally, the king was unable to withstand the mental and physical suffering, and went to get water from the spring to drink. Having drunk the maddening spring water, he too, became mad. Thus the whole country, the king and his subjects, young and old, everyone without exception, became insane. From then on, they were all very happy.

*

Stories by Yin Yun
By Yin Yun (471-529 A.D.) styled himself Guan Shu, a writer of Liang, one of the Southern Dynasties. He was originally from Changping, Chenjun (northeast of Sihua, Henan Province). *Stories by Yin Yun* originally contained thirty volumes, but by the Sui Dynasty (581-618 A.D.) only ten volumes remained. During the Ming Dynasty it could still be seen but, later, it was lost. Some fragments were found in various reference books with material taken from diverse sources and arranged

according to subjects. There are more than one hundred and thirty items collected in Lu Xun's *Salvaged Stories of Ancient Origin*. The stories made use of historical materials and legends from Zhou and Qin Dynasties to Southern Qi, rather rich in content.

420. Drill a Fire

Kong Rong of Eastern Han fell seriously ill at midnight and ordered his disciple to drill a fire quickly. No fire was seen lighted for a long time and, somehow, he couldn't help voicing his displeasure at the delay. It was an extremely dark night and his disciple thought it was an injustice to blame him and said unhappily, "Your blame was not justified. It was pitch-dark, and why don't you shine the light over here? Even if you are impatient, still you have to wait till I find the apparatus before a fire can be drilled." As he heard this, Kong Rong said, "That's fair enough. I should not blame people without a proper cause!"

421. The Dream of Yangzhou

Several guests gathered to chat, and agreed on telling their wishes. The first man would like to be the governor of Yangzhou (because Yangzhou was richly endowed, and the weather and scenery were both fine; the governorship would be a lucrative post); the second man said he wished he were a millionaire; the third man desired to become an immortal and rode a crane to soar in the sky. At this juncture, another man opened his mouth, wishing that he were "a millionaire riding a crane for Yaangzhou", and that was of course having all the benefit the previous three had hoped for in one sentence.

People in later generations used the phrase to denote aspiring for something unrealistic and, in time, the phrase was reduced to its quintessense in a few words, "the dream of Yangzhou".

422. World of Fantasy

A destitute man with only enough money for a earthen jar bought and entered it to resist cold. He reckoned in his mind, "If I sell this earthen jar, I'll be able to double the capital and with this doubling of my money, I can then buy two jars. Two jars can become four jars in the same way, and again get twice the interest. If this goes on and on, the profit will be endless; the more it is repeated, the larger the amount accumulated . . . ." He was so delighted that he danced with joy. In so doing, however, he broke the earthen jar.

423. Emperor Xiaowu's Notion of Donkey

The Emperor Xiaowu of Eastern Jin had never seen a donkey in his life. One day, Councillor Xia An, one of the three highest-ranking officials in the imperial court, asked him, "Will Your Majesty please imagine what a donkey looks like, and what animal does it resemble?" The emperor Xiaowu smiled with his mouth covered, "It is of course very much like a pig."

*

A House of Gold
By Xiao Yi (508-554 A.D.), the emperor Yuan of Liang. He was the seventh son of the emperor Wu of Liang, Xiao Yan, and was bestowed the title king of Xiangdong. Later, because of his part in quelling the rebellion of Houjing, he was put on the throne as emperor. He was emperor for three years, but then Western Wei began to attack Liang, and he was stranded in Jiangling. When the city fell into the enemy's hands, he was killed. He had been a good learner and wrote well, being a prolific writer. *A House of Gold* originally had ten volumes with fifteen chapters, but was lost by the time the Ming Dynasty came into being. The extant book was compiled using material culled from *The Yongle Canon* (*The Yongle Canon*, compiled by 2,000 scholars and completed in 1408 A.D., was the world's earliest and biggest encyclopaedia, which contains 22,937 volumes bound into 11,095 books with a total of 370 million Chinese characters). It contains six volumes, fourteen chapters.

424. The Rich Man Wants Another Sheep

There was a rich man in the land of Chu. He kept ninety-nine sheep but hope to have one hundred. To fulfill his desire, he went about contacting acquaintances in the neighbourhood. One of his neighbours, a poor fellow, had only one sheep. When the wealthy man came to know of it, he called on the poor man, saying, "I've ninety-nine sheep and, if you will give me the sheep you own, it will bring the number of my sheep to one hundred, which is the number that will give me satisfaction."

425. Saving the Drowning Man

There was a man whose son had fallen into the water. He knew that the people of Yue in the South were good swimmers, and so he went over a thousand *li* to get there, intending to ask someone to save his son.

It was true the people of Yue were adept in swimming, but there could be no doubt also that his son would drown.

426. A Scented Room for the Stuffy Nose

There was a man in Jade Pond State, whose looks were extremely unsightly. His wife, however, possessed surpassing beauty. The only regret was that she had a stuffy nose and unable to distinguish fragrance from stench. The man, knowing that he was ugly in appearance, tried every means to please his wife, but his wife refused to live with him throughout. He spent a lot of money to buy a very special and expensive incense from the Western Regions and had the house scented from wall to wall. Having done so, he tried to persuade his wife to move into the room. It was a pity he forgot that his wife had a stuffy nose, and could never appreciate it.

In this world of ours, there are always people who do not care whether the actions he takes match the objective, but who insists on his own method in his attempt to attain the desired result. This was what the ugly husband had done, and the consequence could well be expected.

*

*Liuzi
By Liu Zhou (514-565 A.D.) styled himself Kong Zhao, a writer of Northern Qi Dynasty (550-577 A.D.); a native of Fucheng, Bohai (Jiaohe, Henan Province). He was assiduous even as a boy, but failed in the civil service examinations despite his frequent attempts. *Liuzi*, otherwise known as *New Thesis of Liuzi,* is an eclectic work, in which a number of fables derived from ancient books are recorded.

427. Appraising Jade

It so happened two men were appraising a piece of jade together. One said, it was a piece of good jade; the other believed it was of low quality. They argued for a long time without reaching a conclusion.

Both of them insisted, "If you view it from the position of my eyes, you will be able to distinguish whether it is of high or low quality."

The jade had a definite shape, but the position of a man standing might vary, and so would the result. That was why one should not negate the other's judgement offhandedly, for it might only be a matter of views.

428. Yiqiu Lost a Chess Game

Yiqiu was a *go* or encirclement chess player of national stature. Once, while he was playing chess with an opponent, a man passing nearby was playing the reed pipe wind instrument. The music was so pleasing to the ear that Yiqiu couldn't help listening, and his attention was divided. At this juncture, the game had reached a critical stage, for a large portion of his chess pieces were about to be encircled and removed. When asked how he was going to deal with the situation, he was at a loss to understand. Actually, it was not because the composition of the chess game became complicated and hard to comprehend, it was only because Yiqiu had been distracted by the beautiful music and could not concentrate on the chess game.

429. Miscalculation

Lishou was a man most adept in computing. Once, when he was calculating, a wild goose honked and flew over his head, which caused him to pull the bowstring in preparation for shooting the wild goose. At that moment, someone asked him, "How much is three times five?" This computing wizard was at a loss to know the product. It was not because three multiplied by five was difficult to calculate, it was because the wild goose had distracted his attention and made him temporarily muddle-headed.

430. The Big Tripod

During the Spring and Autumn Period, the state of Qi attacked the state of Lu with intention to seize the *cen* tripod, a symbol of dynasty. The state of Lu craftily offered a counterfeit tripod to Qi in exchange for concluding a treaty of alliance. The duke of Qi was a little sceptical. He had heard that Liuji of the state of Lu was a man of his word, and that he conducted his life with honesty. He said, "If Liuji will confirm that this tripod is the big *cen* tripod, that will be enough for me." The duke of Lu, therefore, made up his mind to send Liuji to Qi to present the tripod on behalf of the state of Lu, but Liuji told the duke of Lu, "The *cen* tripod is the symbol of Your Majesty's dynasty, and honesty and trust, like the *cen* tripod, are what I rely to get on in life. You want me to sacrifice my reliance on life to save the *cen* tripod, the symbol of your dynasty. I'm afraid I'll not be able to accomplish it." As the duke of Lu could not find words to refute Liuji, there was nothing he could do but to send the genuine *cen* tripod over to the state of Qi.

431. Stone Cows Excrete Gold

The monarch of the state of Shu was an avaricious man, and the king Hui of Qin availed himself of his vulnerable traits, intending to annex the territory of Shu. However, the narrow paths of Shu (Sichuan) were difficult to traverse, as there were precipitous mountains and streams which the army must overcome. In view of the situation, taking it by storm was not an option, and the avarice of the duke of Shu thus provided an opportunity for the king Hui of Qin to use a well-thought out strategem. He ordered the craftsmen to carve some stone cows; behind those cows, he placed gold and silk while spreading the rumour that those were the excrement of the cows. When the cows were sent to the duke of Shu, the avaricious duke, as expected, was taken in. He ordered the blasting of cliffs, the levelling of valleys and the construction of roads before sending the able-bodied men and soldiers to transport the stone cows, which were sent to him as gifts. At this opportune moment, the people of Qin led their troops quietly behind, and occupied the state of Shu without a hitch. In the end, the state of Shu was defeated and the duke himself killed, becoming the laughingstock of the world. This came about because the duke of Shu was penny-wise and pound-foolish, seeking small gains while incurring big losses.

The History of Wei
By Wei Shou (506-572 A.D.) styled himself Boqi, a historian of Northern dynasties (386-581 A.D.), and a native of Xiaquyang, Julu (west of Pingxiang, Hebei Province). He had served successively in Northern Wei, Eastern Wei and Northern Qi in charge of secretarial duties, while supervising the compilation of national history. The book consisted of one hundred and thirty volumes, but quite a large portion had been lost by the time of Northern Song. Liu Shu, Fan Zuyu and others made up for the loss with material culled from Li Yanshou's *The History of Northern Dynasties*. The extant book has one hundred and fourteen volumes; in all twenty-six volumes had been lost. The book was considered the official history in later years.

The following was selected from The Biography of Tuguhun in The History of Wei.

432. Breaking Arrows

The chief of Tuguhun, A-chai, had twenty sons, and he said to his sons, "Each of you presents me with an arrow." As he received the arrows, he broke them one by one, and threw them to the ground.

After a while, his younger brother, Muliyan, entered, and A-Chai ordered Muliyan, "Get an arrow and break it." Muliyan did as he asked. A-Chai pointed to the nineteen arrows left and said to him, "Break them all at the same time." But Muliyan could not do it.

A-Chai then said to his brother and sons, "Did you see it? A single arrow is easy to break, but not many arrows put together. You cannot break them. Provided you stand together, our country will be impregnable!"

*

The History of the Southern Dynasties
By Li Yanshou, dates of birth and death not known, a historian of early Tang. He was originally from Anyang, Xiangzhou (Henan Province). His father, Li Dashi, had endeavoured to compile the history of Southern

and Northern Dynasties, but died without completing them. Yanshou followed in his father's footsteps, and on the foundation of his father's old manuscripts, single-handedly finished compiling the two books, *The History of the Southern Dynasties* and *The History of the Northern Dynasties,* after sixteen years. It was classified as Official history later.

The two fables below were selected from The Biography of Lu Sengzhen and the Biography of Gu Huan respectively in The History of the Southern Dynasties.

433. A Chosen Neighbour for the Price of Ten Million

After being dismissed from the post of magistrate of Nankang Prefecture, Jiya bought a house with a courtyard contiguous with Lu Sengzhen's residence.

Sengzhen asked how much he had paid for the house.

"Eleven million cash," Jiya replied.

The high price surprised Sengzhen very much.

Jiya added, "I bought the house for one million cash, and ten million cash for a neighbour of my choice."

434. Different Names for the Same Bird

Once upon a time, there was a swan flying across the sky. As it flew extremely high, it could not be seen very clearly. The people of Yue thought it was a wild duck, while the people of Chu said it was a swallow. However, although the people did not live in the same place, and their views were quite different, the bird which flew across the sky remained a swan; it did not change an iota despite their different views.

*

*The History of the Northern Dynasties
The two fables below were selected from The Biograthy of Chang Sunsheng and The Biography of Wang Hao repectively in The History of Northern Dynasties.

435. Killing Two Eagles with One Arrow

The eagle is a very large and ferocious bird. It often wheels around in the sky, but will dive down suddenly and use its hard, sharp claws to catch the hare, the goat, or even the venomous snake, and skin, tear up, and eat them alive.

During the Southern and Northern Dynasties, Chang Sunsheng of Luoyang, Northern Zhou Dynasty, was in Tujue in the northwest on official business. He was an adept in archery, and a superb rider on horseback. People there all said the sound produced by his bow and arrow was like thunder and his horse galloped as fast as lightning.

That day, Chang Sunsheng and the king of Tujue, Shetu, were hunting in the prairie. Suddenly they heard the attendant cry out while pointing his horsewhip at the sky. They looked up and saw two large eagles overhead rolling up and down together. Looking more closely, they discovered the birds were fighting for a large piece of meat. The king of Tujue, Shetu, immediately handed two arrows to Chang Sunsheng. With only one word in response, Chang Sunsheng took over an arrow. He gave free rein to his horse while putting the arrow on the bowstring. "Whiz!" an arrow flew past, and the two eagles were pierced through as one and fell down. Everyone was dumbfounded, but they soon burst into thunderous applause.

436. Wang Hao lost his Horse

Wang Hao styled himself Jigao, was weak in character and dull, like his elder brother. One day, he rode a claret horse and followed emperor Wenxuan of Northern Qi to the battlefield. The weather was very cold when they rose in the morning, and the horse was covered with frost so that he could not recognize it. He declared that he had lost his horse, and the official in charge of forests had to look everywhere on his behalf, but even then he could not find it. A little later, the sun came out, and the frost on the horse melted. They discovered then that the claret horse was safely tethered in front of the tent. At which time he said, "My horse is there still."

*Tales of Funny Jokes

By Hou Bai styled himself Junsu, dates of birth and death unknown; a native of Linzhang (now part of Hebei Province). He lived in early Sui Dynasty. During the reign of emperor Wen of Sui, he took part in compiling the national history, receiving official salary of the fifth rank, but died soon after. Author of *Story of the Strange Banner*, *Tales of Funny Jokes*, and so on, but the original books were all lost. A few items were found in reference books like *Extensive Collection in the Reign of Peace*, *All Rivers Flow to the Sea of Learning*, *Analogy*, etc., which were culled by later generations. Handwritten copy was also discovered in Dunhuang. *Tales of Funny Jokes* followed *The Jokes Forest* by Handan Chun as another early book of jokes in the history of China. Not a few meaningful allegories were found, which may be treated as fables.

437. An Amnesiac

In Hu County there was a forgetful man. One day, he brought with him an axe to work in the field, and with him was also his wife. Arriving at the field, he felt the urgent call of nature, and so he put the axe on one side. When all was done, he suddenly discovered the axe, which delighted him, and he said, "I've come by an axe." Involuntarily, he danced for joy. Because he was careless, he stepped on the faeces, and he said, 'This axe must have been left by the man who defecated here." His wife, seeing that he was so muddle-headed and forgetful, told him, "A while ago, you brought this axe here to cut firewood with and, as you had an urgent call of nature, you put the axe on the ground. Why have you forgotten so soon?" The man looked intently at the face of his wife and murmured, "What's the name of this lady? I seem to have met her somewhere, or have I?"

438. Purchasing a Slave

In the Hu County there was a village called Dongzishang Village, where all the inhabitants were stupid. An old man sent his son to the marketplace to buy a slave, bringing with him not a small amount of money. Before setting out, he told his son, "I've heard that in the capital, people do not let the slaves know when their masters will sell them. They will conceal the slaves in a secret place while the price is being discussed and the transaction ironed out. It is said in this way one will be able to get a good slave."

As his son arrived at the market, he passed through the section that sold mirrors. The traders displayed their mirrors on both sides of the corridor. From one of the mirrors he saw his own reflection. It was young and strong, and he thought it must be the good slave which the trader was selling and which was concealed inside the mirror on purpose. So he asked the shopkeeper, pointing at the mirror, "How much do you sell this slave?" The trader knew he was a fool and deceived him by saying, "It is worth ten thousand coppers." Cheerfully he paid the price, carried the mirror in the bosom and went home.

As he reached home, the old man asked his son, "Where is the slave you bought?" "In my bosom," he replied. "Why don't you get him out and let me see?" his father said. "All right." And he fumbled out a mirror and handed it to his father. His father took over the mirror, looked at it, and saw an old man with silvery eyebrows and beard, while the dark face was etched with wrinkles. He flew into a rage at once and wanted to beat his son, saying, "How can you spend ten thousand coppers to buy such an old slave?" As he was saying, he raised his stick to beat his son. His son was terribly frightened and went to tell his mother. The mother, with a little girl in her arms, came over and said to her husband, "Pass over and let me see it myself." When she looked at the reflection, she too flew into a rage, saying, "You silly old fool, my son only spent ten thousand coppers and got both mother and daughter. How can you say it's expensive?" When the old man heard this, his mood changed at once. As they put down the mirror, no one saw any slave around, but they all thought the slave must have hidden in the mirror.

At that point of time, their neighbour to the east was a witch. The villagers, to a man, believed her words were gospel truth, and so the old man went to seek her opinion. The witch said, "You old man and old woman are all advanced in years. You must have heard that when spirits do not get good food, and money do not come together, the slave will hide himself and refuse to come out. You must therefore choose an auspicious day, prepare more sacrifices before you ask the help of the spirits." Thus the old man spread a feast and invited the witch. The witch, having arrived at the old man's house, hung the mirror above the door, and began to sing and dance, gyrating wildly. The whole village turned out to watch, and those who had looked into the mirror said, "This family will surely have a bright future, as they have bought a good slave!" Unfortunately the mirror was not hung securely, and it fell to the ground breaking into two halves. The witch picked them up, held them in her hands, and looked. She saw in each a reflection of herself and was delighted, saying, "The gods have blessed your family, as one slave has turned into two." Having voiced her opinion, she began to sing, "Let the whole family celebrate their good fortune. Applaud together, spread out the sacrifices, and invite all the gods to come and enjoy. Buy one get one; paid for a slave and got a maidservant free. It was one at first, but now it becomes two."

439. The Tiger and the Hedgehog

A tiger was looking for food in the wilderness, where it saw a hedgehog lying on its back, and basking in the sunshine. The tiger thought it must be a delicious meat ball, its mouth grooling with greed. Hastily, it snatched it with one bite. The hedgehog stiffened its prickles all of a sudden and rolled firmly onto the tiger's nose. The tiger was shocked but could not break loose, and it felt so painful that it roared, running and leaping wildly into the deep forest.

It soon became exhausted with the exercise and, throwing itself on the ground, it fell into a deep slumber. The hedgehog, meanwhile, availed itself of the opportunity, loosened up, and ran to hide in the tussock. When the tiger woke up and discovered that the abominable object on its nose had disappeared, it was simply delighted. It went under a large oak tree, where it saw acorn cups all over the place, each with hard thorns. The sight brought shivers to his consciousness, and he retreated a few steps to take a closer look with his body leaning sideways. It thought the thorny circular things were quite similar to the one he had had a little while ago, but their heads were smaller. Could these be the sons? Thereupon the tiger respectfully spoke to the little thorny balls, saying, "I met your father not long ago, and I've learned the lesson. May it please the young masters to let me pass."

440. Boat Tower

Liu Daozhen, a man who lived in the Jin Dynasty, was rendered homeless by war and had to come to the riverside to earn his living as a boat tracker. He saw an old woman on a boat, working as a sculler.

Liu Daozhen derided the old woman, saying, "You are a woman. Why don't you stay by the loom and weave? Why must you scull on the river?"

Tit for tat, the old woman replied, "As a real man, why don't you go to the battlefield, ride a horse and fight? Why must you come to the riverside and become a tracker?"

Liu Daozhen could not find words to refute her.

441. Play on Words

Houbai of Sui Dynasty was quick-witted and articulate, and had a facile imagination. Once, he and Yang Su rode together bridle to bridle, and saw a locust tree (sophora japonica) at the roadside which had almost withered and died.

Yang Su said, "Scholar Hou, as you are adept in exposition and argumentation, can you bring this tree to life again?"

Houbai replied, "It's simple. Just hang a locust seed on the withered branch, and it will revive."

Yang Su asked why he said so.

Houbai replied, "In *The Confucian Analects* there is a sentence which says, 'As the master (*zi*) is still alive, how dare Hui (speaker) talk of death!'"

(*The Chinese character *zi* has various meanings, including son and seed. It is also an ancient title of respect for a learned or virtuous man. In the text it refers to Confucius, but it is an expression with double meaning.)

442. The Fifth Sage

Yin-an, a recluse scholar, was originally from Xindou, Jizhou (Ji County, Hebei Province). Once, he told an official surnamed Xue, saying, "From ancient times to the present, there are only five persons who can truly be called sages."

Thereupon he bent one of his fingers and said, "Fuxi drew the Eight Diagrams (eight combinations of three whole or broken lines formerly used in divination), which revealed the universal laws of nature. He is the first sage."

He bent another finger and continued, "Shennong introduced agriculture and ensured the livelihood of people in their hundreds of millions. He is the second sage."

He went on, "The duke of Zhou enacted the rules of rites and music, and ushered in a new era of moral principles and civilization. He is the third sage." Having said that, he bent the third finger.

"Confucius was a man of great learning and a profound scholar; he was well-versed in history, and could predict the future. Among the scholars, he always stood out from the rest. He is the fourth sage." Having said that, he bent the fourth finger.

Finally he said, "After Confucius, nobody has the qualification to be called a sage and deserves the bending of a finger." He paused for a moment to think, and added, "Plus myself. It's the fifth." And he bent the fifth finger.

443. An Earthern Hat for a Fool

During the Liang Dynasty, which was one of the Southern and Northern Dynasties, there was a family, and in that family everyone was crazy. The old man of the house asked his son to buy a hat for him in the market, adding, "I've heard that a hat must be able to hold the head. When you buy the hat, make sure that it can hold my head."

Wherefore his son went to the market to look for a hat. The haberdasher recommended him a hat made of black silk fabric. As the hat was folded, he thought it could not hold the head and walked away. In this manner, he walked for the whole day, visiting many haberdasheries without being able to find a suitable hat. Finally, he came to a shop selling eartherware and saw a short-necked wide-mouthed earthern jar with an empty belly. He thought it must be a hat and bought it home.

His father put the earthern jar on his head but, as the mouth of the jar reached all the way down to his neck, his entire face was covered by the jar, and he could no longer see anything outside it. Besides, whenever he put the jar on while walking, his nose rubbed against it and became painful. His breathing, too, was not as easy as before, as he felt somewhat stuffy. But he thought it was the attributes of a hat, and so he tried his best to endure the pain caused by the earthern jar. As time went on, his nose had been rubbed so often that a boil grew on it, and his neck, too, became callous. Despite all the discomfort, however, he refused to take it off. In the end, he had to sit still whenever he put the hat on.

444. Salvaging the Black Beans

There was an idiot during the Sui Dynasty. He loaded a cart of black beans to sell in the capital. As he came to the bank of Bashui River (in Shaanxi Province), the cart turned turtle, and all the black beans dropped into the water. The man left his cart behind and went home, intending to ask the people there to come and help salvaging the beans. After he left, the shop people by the Bashui River fell over one another to get the beans from the water with one tool or another. When the man returned, there was not even a black bean left in the river. Only several thousand tadpoles were found swimming to and fro. The man thought the tadpoles were the beans and so he got ready to enter the water and salvage them. However, the tadpoles were frightened by his action and swam away, so that in an instant there was no more tadpole to be found.

The man stood by the water's edge and sighed, saying, "Black beans, why do you pretend not to know me and flee from me? You mustn't think I'll not recognize you, even though you have put on a little tail."

*The Dong Gaozi Collection

By Wang Ji (585-644 A.D.) styled himself Wugong, alternative name Dong Gaozi, a poet of early Tang Dynasty and a native of Longmen, Jiangzhou (Hejin, Shanxi Province). During the reign of Emperor Taizong, he was once a government official, but later resigned his post and became a hermit. The collection of his essays and poems had five volumes originally, but was lost over the years. The extant *The Dong Gaozi Collection* (also known as *The Wang Wugong Collection*) was compiled by later generations. His prose collections *The Northern Mountain Fu* (descriptive prose interspersed with verse) and *In a Dazed State* were better known.

445. The Two Horses of Feilian

Feilian, the minion of Jie, last ruler of Xia Dynasty (c. 21st-c. 16th century B.C.), had two horses. One was white with red mane; Dragon-like skeleton, and a chest similar to a phoenix's. As it galloped, it looked so facile that it was like dancing. Feilian loved it so much that he rode it every day, and the horse was never unsaddled. As it never had a minute of rest, it eventually died of exhaustion. The other horse was born with clumsy shanks, and always held up its tail. Its neck was like that of a camel, and its knees like those of a fox. It bit as well as hoofed, and often gave backward kicks. Feilian disliked the horse, so he abandoned it and let it return to the wilderness. Yet the horse lived in freedom for that reason, and became stout and strong.

*

*The Dharma Park and the Pearl Forest

By Shi Daoshi styled himself Xuan Yun, dates of birth and death unknown, an eminent monk of early Tang. He was originally from Yique, Henan (south of Luoyang). Left home to become a monk, he lived in Chang-an for a long time, and worked on the Buddhist Scriptures with Xuan Zang (596-664 A.D.), a Buddhist monk in the Tang Dynasty, in the translation site. *The Dharma Park and the Pearl Forest* was completed during Emperor Gaozong's reign (668 A.D.). Apart from adducing the Buddhist sutras, he also collected as many as more than one hundred and forty secular documents, and contributed his share of reference material in the study of pre-Tang social customs, anecdotes and legends.

446. Hitting the Mosquito

Formerly there was a bald head who dyed clothes for a living. One day, accompanied by his son, they arrived at the water's edge to rinse the dyed clothes. Having rinsed, wrung dry, and dried them in the sun, he brought them home. It was a sweltering hot day, the man felt tired and drowsy. On his way home, he saw a tree. Using the sack of clothes as pillow, he went to sleep. A mosquito suddenly flew onto his forehead to suck his blood. His son saw it, and berated the mosquito, saying, "You miserable bug! How dare you suck my father's blood?" Thereupon he brought over a thick stick to hit the mosquito. But the mosquito flew away and he hit his father's head instead, who died instantly. Thereupon the tree god composed a Buddhist chant:

Befriend only the intelligent,

But never love a fool.

This foolish fellow wanted to rid his father of mosquito but, instead, killed him with one stroke.

447. Monkeys Rescue the Moon

In the past, there was a state called Jiashi; inside Jiashi there was a city called Bolonai. In the forest where few people trod, there were five macacus monkeys. One day, the macacus monkeys went under a Nijulu tree, where they discovered a well. As the reflection of the moon swayed with the ripples of the water in the well, the leader of the macacus monkeys told his companions, saying, "The moon has fallen into the well today. We should rescue it with our concerted effort, so that the world need not live in the dark every night." The macacus monkeys then talked over the matter. "How can we save the moon?" they asked. The leader of the macacus monkeys replied, "I know what to do. I'll hold onto a branch of the tree and everyone else will hold onto the other's tail, one after the other, and together we'll be able to rescue the moon." And the macacus monkeys followed their leader's instructions and went into action, one holding the other's tail, stringing together like a long cord. However, as they were about to touch the surface of the water, the branch, because it was too small and weak and the monkeys' combined weight too heavy, snapped, and with a splash all the macacus monkeys fell into the water.

448. Jealous of the Reflections

A couple went to the wine vat to get wine, and both saw the reflections in the vat. It became the cause of their mutual suspicion and jealousy, as one believed the other had hidden someone in the vat. Sometimes it even led to fights between them, and the trouble seemed interminable. A man, who understood their trouble well, came over and broke the wine vat. When the wine was gone, there was no one to be seen. By this time, the couple began to see light, and the knots in the mind of each was disentangled. They realized what they were jealous of was only the reflections and felt quite ashamed of themselves.

*

*Preface to the Inscription of the Orangutan
By Pei Yan (?-684 A.D.) styled himself Zilong, originally from Wensi, Jiangzhou (Shanxi Province). During the reign of Emperor Gaozong, he had once served as head of the secretariat. He plotted with Empress Wu (625-705 A.D.) to depose Emperor Zhongzong, but later turned against Empress Wu. He was put to death for incurring the wrath of Empress Wu.

449. Drunken Orangutan

The orangutans lived in the mountain valley. As a rule, they came out in groups of several hundreds when they were on the move. The mountain people knew their habit well. They knew the orangutans liked wine and wine-soused food and to imitate man by wearing sandals and have fun. The people there had devised a method to catch them. They put wine and wine-soused food and a number of sandals strung together with a cord by the roadside. They then hid themselves and waited for the orangutans to come out. The orangutans had become smart over time, as their companions had been captured by the same method before. When they saw the wine and the sandals, they knew these were the traps set for their capture. They also knew the name of the ancestor of the people who set the traps, and would call the devisers names and curse them, saying, "You flunkeys, do you think you can trap me? I'll run away when I see one." After cursing for a while and seeing nothing happen, they would become impatient, and tell each other, "Let's begin to savour the wine." They would then fall over one another in their eagerness to drink. At some point, they would also pick up the sandals and put them on, and start to dance. It would not take long before everyone of them fell over like ninepins and went into a deep slumber. At that juncture, the mountain people would emerge and capture them one by one.

*

*The Complete Record in and out of the Imperial Court
By Zhang Zhuo (c.660-741 A.D.) styled himself Wencheng, a native of Luze, Shenzhou (Shen County, Hebei Province). A writer of the Tang Dynasty, he was the author of *Roving the Fairyland*, a novel. Originally *The Complete Record in and out of the Imperial Court* had thirty volumes, but was later lost. The extant copy was compiled by collecting what could be salvaged of his writings. There are two versions, one consists of six volumes, and the other, three volumes. They are mostly about events from early Tang to the time of Emperor Xuanzong, with roughly seven-tenth of its content on Empress Wu.

450. The Key is Here

Long, long ago, there was a man who went to the capital to sit for the screening examination. While he was there, his leather bag was stolen.

Yet the silly fellow still rejoiced, for he said, "The thief has stolen my bag, but he will never be able to get the things inside it."—Someone asked him why was it so.

He replied, "The key is still fastened to my belt. What is he going to open the bag with?"

451. The Lion King and the Jackal

Formerly there was a lion which occupied a mountain and declared itself king. It caught a jackal in the deep mountain, and was about to eat it. The jackal implored the lion, saying, "I beg Your Majesty to please let me present you with two deers in my place." The lion was pleased at the suggestion, and agreed to it. After a year, as the jackal still had not sent the deers, the lion was angry, and said to the jackal, "You have snuffed out not a few lives, and today it is your turn to die. You have probably expected it, or aren't you?" The jackal had nothing to contradict the lion, so he kept quiet, and the lion nibbled it until it was all gone.

452. Horse Canon

The son of Bo Le went to look for a horse, using his father's *Horse Canon* as a guide. However, he could not find one similar in appearance to the drawing in the *Horse Canon*, and had to return and told his father. His father wanted him to continue the search. He had just gone out of the door when he met a big frog, and he turned back to tell his father, saying, "I've found a horse more or less like the one in the drawing, only a little incomplete." Bo Le asked, "What about?" His son replied, "This horse has a protuberant skull, two sunken eyes, and a taut backbone. But it doesn't seem that its hoofs can stand galloping for a long period of time." Bo Le said, "It seems to me the horse you choose loves more to leap than to be ridden." His son smile, but no longer went to look for a horse with the *Horse Canon* in hand.

*

*A Li Xiashu Prose Collection
By Li Hua (?-c.766 A.D.) styled himself Xiashu, a writer of the Tang Dynasty; originally from Zanhuang, Zhaozhou (Hebei Province). He advocated prose written in the classical literary style, and against rhythmical prose style marked by Parallelism and ornateness. His prose masterpiece *A Message of Condolence for the Ancient Battlefield* was widely read by later generations. The author's work *The Li Hua Prose Collection* comprised Book One, ten volumes; Book Two, twenty volumes, all of which were lost to the world. The four-volume *A Li Xiashu Prose Collection* was compiled by later generations.

453. The Osprey Catches the Fox

I once saw with my own eyes a queer bird fighting a big fox in the wilderness. The eyes of the bird sparkled like the stars in the sky; its wings spread out as clouds across heaven. It swooped down like thunder and lightning, and the tremendous momentum could be compared to the grass killing frost, for the fox was rendered motionless. The queer bird pecked and nibbled with its sharp beak the liver and brain of the fox and, using its claws it raked out the fox's entrails. Assuming a victor's posture, it threw its head back and looked around, awe-inspiring, and as happy as the cat that ate the canary. Suddenly it spread its wings, which caused a gale, and, as quick as lightning, it was nowhere to be seen.

I asked the farmer in the field, what kind of bird was it? The farmer replied, "The bird's name is yellow gold osprey. Watching it fight and kill the fox, it really filled my heart with joy!"

I said, "A man should have sympathy and a kind heart. Watching the fox die so miserably, one would have expected some compassion. Why have you felt joyful instead?"

The farmer explained, "The fox has caused a lot of harm. It had never stopped doing mishief. It frightened people of my clan and relatives, disturbed my neighbours and village, cunningly evaded the weapon of the hunter, and no arrow could frighten it. All the villagers hated it but could find no way to deal with it. Now that its iniquities are full, god has sent this yellow gold osprey to get rid of it. If I do not feel happy for the elimination of this scourge, what else am I to feel happy for?"

Ah! One in high position may fall from power easily; food with strong flavour may contain poison. Even people who follow the correct path may meet with disaster, let alone those who abuse their power and commit crimes against humanity. How can they avoid the wrath of heaven? Those who occupy official positions should have their heart cleansed, their evil thoughts purged. Evils must be completely eradicated before they can earn the blessing of heaven. If they do not wake up, their fate may even be worse than that of the fox, and the time shall come when they will surely shiver and die before the yellow gold osprey's formidable force.

454. The Fledgling and the Old Ox

A fledgling, holding onto the nest, was becoming fully-fledged, and began to learn the skills of flying from its mother. Unfortunately it was frightened by a hawk and fell from the sky to the road. A wealthy young lady sitting inside a magnificent carriage happened to pass through the spot at that moment. The wounded fledgling aroused her compassion, and she brought it home, keeping it in a cage of carved white jade while feeding it with the rare paddy rice from Qingjiang. Why was it so? It was because the bird was small. Its value lay in the fact that it could be kept as an object of admiration and enjoyment, and that it did not require very much effort.

The ox, which pulled the big cart, looked like a moving mountain from a distance. It lived in this world for the sole purpose of pulling a heavy cart, going over a long distance, to benefit people. When it died, its tendons, its horns, its skin, its bones, all could be made into useful utensils. It did not matter whether it was flood or drought, in scorching summer or freezing winter; it had to endure the lashes of men's whip bestowed upon its fatigued body while climbing up one hill after another, and getting itself up again even if it fell down on the road or dropped into the mire, so tired out that its hoofs came off, its bones broken, exhausted, and fell ill on the ground, with only the eyes which could still move about looking at people. At that juncture, the robber-like crow would fly over, scratch the ox's back with its sharp claws, nibble with its beak the flesh of the ox. Nor was it all. Besides crowing wildly, it would call all its kind to come and enjoy together. A flock of wild dogs would also gather. They dug into the belly of the old ox, tore its entrails and ate, barking ceaselessly and fighting for a piece of meat. Carriages to and from the thoroughfare were in the thousands and tens of thousands, but no one would stop and look at the sad spectacle of an old ox being dismembered. Why? The ox's body must have been the problem. Even if people should want to help it up and revive it, it would be difficult to do so. Yet if people could overlook the transitory trouble and bring it to life again, the reward deriving from its existence would surely be great.

How sad it was! A big timber became an encumbrance and a small timber, valuable. This was against the established principle and logic, and the damage had been serious. If the sovereign who ran the world could see the point and brought order out of chaos, it would not be long before the country became a well-administered, just and benvolent one.

*The Collection of Yuan Cishan

By Yuan Jie (719-772 A.D.) styled himself Cishan, originally from Luoyang; a writer of Tang Dynasty and a successful candidate of the national civil service examination held at the imperial capital in former times. During the rebellion of An Lushan and Shi Siming (755-763 A.D.), he took refuge in a region south of the Yangtze River. Because he lived in Yixu Cave, he called himself Yixuzi. Later, he organized volunteers to fight against Shi Siming, for which meritorious service he was appointed the governor of Daozhou. Framed by influential officials, he resigned his position to become a hermit. His works reflected his sympathetic attitude towards the sufferings of the people, and his opposition to wind, flower, snow and moon—romantic themes. He was the author of *The Collection of Yuan Cishan*. His prose collections *On Begging* and *Changed into a Tiger* were better known, however.

455. In Praise of the Tiger and the Snake

To escape the chaos caused by war, Yixuzi hid himself in a cave in a region south of the Yangtze River. The local people told him, "The cave you now live was originally the palace of the tiger king, and the hillock behind the cave was the forest where a big snake occupied."

Yixuzi lived there for three months, and everything was quiet and fine. He knew then the tiger king behaved like an ancient gentleman, and the big snake was similar to a distinguished man. It was truly so! As Yixuzi took possession of the palace of the tiger king, the tiger king left without coming back; as Yixuzi invaded the forest of the big snake, the big snake slithered away to another place.

The gentle, modest, restrained and magnanimous noble quality they exhibited was more worthy of admiration than that found in those people who, for their own interests, killed each other. Can I not sing the praises of the tiger and the snake by writing an article?

*

*Dream on the Pillow

By Shen Jiji (c.750-800 A.D.), a writer of the Tang Dynasty. He was originally from Wu (south Jiangsu and north Zhejiang), Suzhou. He was the author of *The True Story of Jianzhong* and legends such as *The Biography of Madam Ren* and *Dream on a Pillow*, the latter being more widely known.

456. Gold Millet Dream

In the Tang Dynasty, a scholar, whose surname was Lu, went to the capital to sit for the civil service examination. On his way he stayed in an inn at Handan, where he met the old man Taoist Lu. He sighed at his own extreme poverty and, because of that, he could not enjoy rank and wealth. Old man Lu heard his exclamation, and presented him with a blue china pillow to sleep on. Scholar Lu was tired out by the arduous journey, and went to sleep as soon as he got the pillow. At that moment, the innkeeper was just cooking a pot of millet. Scholar Lu entered the dreamland the moment his head touched the pillow. He dreamed he married a beautiful woman surnamed Cui. He was a successful candidate in the highest imperial examinations in the second year. Then he became an official, and was promoted to ever higher positions until he reached the rank of prime minister. As his official position reached the top, there were people who machinated to harm him, and it almost cost his head. Later, he was able to clear himself, and became the duke of the state of Yan. He had five sons, all of whom were high officials. He enjoyed all the wealth and rank possible, and lived to the ripe old age of over eighty before he died. However, when he turned over in the bed, he found himself still lying in the inn, the Taoist priest sat right by his side, and the innkeeper's millet was still not done. Everything seemed familiar. Scholar Lu was greatly surprised and sat up. "Am I dreaming just now?" he said. The old man Taoist Lu told him, "It has been a dream all your life." Thereupon scholar Lu had a great awakening.

*

The Liu Hedong Collection
By Liu Zongyuan (773-819 A.D.) styled himself Zihou, a writer of the Tang Dynasty. Originally he was from Jie, Hedong (Jiezhou Town, Yuncheng, Shanxi Province). He took part in Wang Shuwen's political reform, which failed, and was demoted to be the head of Yongzhou. Later, he became the governor of Liuzhou. Together with Han Yu, he initiated the ancient Chinese prose movement, and became inseparable as the name Han-Liu had shown. Both belonged to "The Eight Great Men of

Letters of the Tang and Song Dynasties" He had written many fables, fresh in style and sharp in language, to deride the social ills of his time.

457. The Hunter Plays Wind Instrument

The deer had a great fear of the *chu*, the *chu* was afraid of the tiger, and the tiger dreaded the brown bear. The brown bear's body was covered by a layer of brown, long hair. It could stand up and walk like a man. It was huge, possessed tremendous strength, and could do great harm to man.

In the southern region of Chu, there was a hunter who could play the wind instrument in such a way as to produce the sounds of various animals. He quietly brought his bow and arrow, water jar, and kindling material as he went into the mountain, where he played the wind instrument to produce the sound of deer. As the deer heard it, it came along, and the hunter killed it. But who would expect the *chu* to have heard the sound of deer also. It thought there were deers around, and so came over to find its prey. The hunter was frightened, and he played to produce the roar of tiger. The *chu* ran away, but in its place came the tiger. When the hunter saw the tiger, he was even more frightened, and so he produced the sound of the brown bear in order to drive away the tiger. However, as the brown bear heard the sound, it came around to meet his companion. Failing to see its kind, it was infuriated and seized the hunter, tore him from limb to limb, and ate him.

458. The Biography of *Fu Ban*

Fu ban was a kind of small insect mentioned in ancient Chinese literature. It delighted in carrying things on its back. As it crawled, it would pick up anything it discovered on the way and put it on its back and, with its chin up, crawled ever forward. In this manner, the load on its back became heavier and heavier. But, however tired it might be, it kept on crawling. Its back being dry, the load would not slip easily, and in time it would weigh the little thing down, making it hard to get up. People might pity it and try to remove the load on its back but, as soon as it was able to move, it would pick up things on its way as before. It liked to climb up to high places too. While all its strength might be used up, it would not stop, unless it fell to its death.

459. Drowned for Money

All the people in Yongzhou were good swimmers. One day, all of a sudden, the river rose sharply. At that moment, there were five or six persons in a boat. They were half way across the river Xiang when the boat abruptly sprang a leak, and everyone on board jumped into the water and swam towards the opposite bank. Among them was one who was unable to go fast enough despite his utmost effort. His companion was surprised. "You are a good swimmer, why do you lag behind today?" they asked. He said, "There are one thousand coppers tied around my waist. It is too heavy, and that is why I lag behind." "Why don't you throw away the coppers then?" his companion urged him. He shook his head. Gradually he slowed down even more. Those who arrived at the opposite bank shouted to him, saying, "Muddle-headed idiot! You are about to lose your life. What good will the money do?" But he again shook his head. Soon after, he was submerged and drowned.

I was deeply saddened by the incident. Judging from what happened, wasn't it possible for some big bugs to get drowned on account of far greater amount of money?

460. The Elk of Linjiang

A hunter in Linjiang got an elk and intended to keep it at home. No sooner had he entered the door than the dogs in his house began drooling, wagging their tails in the air and circling around. The man got angry and drove the dogs away, but became worried. From that day on, he took the little elk in his arms everyday and carried it to the dogs so that they could become better acquainted. He let the dogs watch the little elk but not frighten it and gradually allow the dogs to play with it.

After a long period of time, the dogs began to obey the wish of their master. In the meantime, the little elk slowly grew up and forgot it was an elk. In its mind, it was convinced that the dogs were its friends. They knocked against one another, now prostrate, now flat on their backs, and became very intimate. In obedience to their master, the dogs seemed in good terms with the elk and played together with delight, but they also licked their lips and smacked their tongues at times.

A few years later, the elk went out of the house, and saw in the street many dogs that belonged to some other families rollicking. It went closer, wanting to play with them. At the sight of the elk, the dogs were both irritated and glad. They showed their teeth, circled around, then bit the elk to death before having it eaten. What remained of the skeleton was thrown in the street in wild disorder. Until its death, the elk did not understand why it had come to such a sorry end.

461. Tricks of the Guizhou Donkey

In ancient times, the district of Qian (Guizhou Province) had no donkey. An officious fellow transported a donkey to the place and put it at the foot of the mountain. A tiger, which had never seen a donkey before, discovered this colossus, and felt greatly amazed, so it hid in the forest and took a peep at it. After a while, the tiger slowly came nearer to take a closer look. But it was unable to decide what kind of animal it was, and so it dared not take any drastic action.

One day, the donkey brayed. This so frightened the tiger that it fled to a distant place. It thought the donkey was going to have it eaten. However, it soon discovered that the donkey did not pursue it, and it returned to continue its observation. The observation led him to believe that the donkey did not have any special skill and, besides, the bray of the donkey had become nothing startling. Despite all this, the tiger did not dare to attack.

As time wore on, the tiger was getting braver in front of the donkey. By way of sounding out, it tried to provoke the donkey by teasing it, leaning against it, scratching it, or simply bumping against it. The donkey was very angry at the affront, and it raised its hind legs to kick the tiger. The tiger was delighted in discovering the nature of its ability, and it said gleefully, "That's your only ability after all!" Thereupon it pounced upon the donkey, broke its throat with one bite, and finished it off before it left.

462. Mice

An Yongzhou Man had a superstitious fear on matter of omens concerning the twelve divisions of a day named after the twelve Terrestrial branches. He was especially careful not to commit any mistakes during the anniversary of his ancestor's death. As he was born in the year which belonged to the first of the twelve Earthly Branches, when the mouse was the reigning god, he was very respectful to the mice by logical extension. He did not keep cat and dog in his house, nor did he allow his servants to catch them. He opened his granary and kitchen to the mice, allowed them to do as they pleased, and never bothered to interfere. For that reason, the mice spread the news to all their kind, and one after the other arrived at his house, where every mouse could eat to its heart's content and live peacefully. As a result, there was not even one utensil in the house that was intact, not a dress on the clothes-stand that was in good condition, and the food the family consumed were mostly the leftovers of the mice. During the day, the mice walked about in groups with family members, and at night, they were even more unbridled: biting, nibbling, and fighting without constraint. The noises they made were sharp, jarring, and caused people to sleep with difficulty. But that family never considered it bothersome.

A few years later, the mice-loving family moved to other prefecture, and another family moved into the same house. The mice were as unscrupulous as before. The new master of the house said, "The mice are the scoundrels in the dark corner. They eat and steal, perpetrate every conceivable evil. I wonder how have they become so reckless?" He borrowed five or six cats from someone and put them in the room with all the doors and windows tightly closed. He had the tiles of the house taken off and let water be poured into their holes. In addition to all these measures, he had also hired several casual laborers to help eradicate the mice. It was not long before the mice that were caught and killed became a small hill. The master had the mice thrown away in a remote place, where their dead bodies became decomposed and emitted an unbearable stink that lasted for several months.

Well, the mice once believed they could eat their fill and live in peace forever!

463. The Dogs in Guangdong Bark at the Snow

Formerly I heard that in places south of Guangdong and Sichuan, it was always cloudy and drizzling, sometimes for days on end, and sunny days were hard to come by. Occasionally when the sun did come out, flocks of dogs would bark at it. I thought at that time this was exaggerating.

In the winter of my second year in the southern region, I was fortunate enough to encounter a heavy snowfall, which was extremely rare in Guangdong. At that time, snow fell all over the hills and dales, and covered several prefectures and counties. In view of the dazzlingly white snow, which the dogs of all those places, big and small, had never experienced before, and they were thrown into a panic. In confusion, they bit and barked, running helter-skelter in all directions. The phenomenon of dogs becoming crazy continued for several days, and normalcy was restored only after all the snow had melted. By that time, I was convinced what I had heard before was true.

464. Globefish

There was a kind of fish in the river called globefish. One day, a globefish was swimming between the piers of the bridge and bumped against one of them. It did not blame itself for not keeping away from the pier but, instead, angrily accused it for the accident. It opened its two gills, raised its two fins, and floated on the water in a blow-up without moving for a long time. At this juncture, a hawk flew over, grabbed the globefish, tore open its belly and ate it.

The globefish loved to swim but did not know when to stop and, because it was addicted to swimming, it knocked against the bridge piers. It did not chide itself but gave vent to its anger without rhyme or reason. As a result, its belly was torn open by a hawk and died. How pitiable it was!

465. Fake Medicine

I suffered from what people called a lump in the abdomen, which caused palpitation, and had to see the physician. The physician said, "You should take *fushen* (Poria cum Ligno Hospite)." The next day, I bought *fushen* from the town, and decocted the herbal medicine but, after taking the decoction, my condition worsened. I then went to see the physician again, asking him about the cause. The physician wanted to examine the dregs. Having done so, he said, "Well, it's only some old taro! The herbal medicine seller has cheated you. You have bought the fake medicine out of ignorance. But why do you put the blame on me? You should be ashamed of yourself!" I was greatly embarrassed after knowing the truth. I was angry and sad. Taking the event as an example, I infer there are lots of happenings like this: substitute taro for *fushen*, making the patient's condition worse by delaying the treatment. But who is to judge the right and wrong or the merits and demerits of such cases?

466. The Huge Whale

A huge whale pursued a shoal of sharks, the highly palatable fish, at the shore of the East China Sea. The noise of their activities shook the ocean, and the tossing waves caused even the big islands to jolt. The huge whale could swallow tens of fish each as big as a small boat at a mouthful. Relying on its own boldness and strength, it was insatiably covetous and gluttonous. In the end, it got stranded on the north bank of Jieshi Mountain, and slowly wilted and died there. The positions were now reversed: the fish which had been the object of its pursuit came back to eat its flesh.

467. The Horsewhip Trader

There was a horsewhip seller in the market, whose horsewhip's true value was roughly fifty coppers, but he insisted on being paid fifty-thousand. The buyer counter-offered fifty, and he burst into laughter; five hundred, he was a little irritated; and when the counter-offer reached five thousand, he flew into a rage, and insisted he would not sell unless it was fifty thousand.

It so happened that the son of a wealthy family came to the market to get a horsewhip, and he paid fifty thousand without counter-offer. He showed me this high-priced horsewhip to display his wealth and influence. I examined it carefully and discovered that the end of the whip had shrunk so that it curled over and became uneven; the handle was crooked and not straight; the joint between the whip staff and the whip strip was not fast and tended to get loose. The bamboo joints on the pole were not clear, the grain being blurred. If you pinched with the finger nails, a hollow would be evident, so much so that the nails would sink into it. If you held high and brandished it, it was so light that you would feel as if there were no whip in your hand at all. "Why have you taken such a liking to this whip as to be so generous and pay fifty thousand for it?" I asked. "I like its colour, which is golden, and the gloss. Besides, the seller has told me not a few good things about this whip," he replied. As I heard it, I ordered the servant to boil a basin of hot water and wash it. The result was, as soon as the whip touched the hot water, its shape altered, and there was no lustre to speak of. The yellow colour, which was dyed on, came from Cape jasmine, and the lustre was actually a layer of wax.

The fop was very unhappy when he saw what happened, but still he held on to the whip and used it as long as three years. Later, he had to go to the eastern suburbs of Chang-an, the capital, on some urgent matter, and it so happened that his carriage and another carriage contended for the right to use the road in Changyi Leban, and the horses on both sides began to hoof at each other. The fop lashed his horse so hard that the whip broke into five or six pieces, but the horses continued to kick without stop. He fell from his horse himself. When he looked at the broken whip later, it was all hollow, worthless as dirt, and had no merit to speak of.

Presently there are people who cleverly camouflage his appearance, use deceptive language, in order to obtain an official position in the imperial court. In case his ability is misjudged and he is allocated a position which is beyond his ability to perform, he will be delighted; if his ability is not overestimated, and he is given a position corresponding to his ability, he will be infuriated, saying, "Am I not fit to be a minister?" However, there are still not a few people who become ministers without being seen through. In time of peace and prosperity, these people will not cause serious harm even though they are put on their respective positions for three years; but in time of turmoil, when contributions are required, then their hollow bellies and dirt-like characters will not be able to sustain the responsibilities asked of them. Like the horsewhip mentioned above, they will break down and the serious consequences of falling from the horseback can hardly be avoided.

468. A Dragon Banished from Heaven

Ma Ruzi of Fufeng Prefecture said, when he was fifteen or sixteen, he once played at the postal kiosk in the suburbs of Zezhou. All of a sudden, a beautiful wonder girl touched down from the sky. She was resplendent in her red leather garment. Under it was a shirt of white silk with pattern, and on her head donned a luxurious corona that swung as she walked. She was dignified and graceful, and dazzlingly attractive. She was seen by several fops loafing in the vicinity, who was half frightened and half pleased at the discovery. After some hesitation, they came closer and tried to flirt with her.

The wonder woman was infuriated and berated them, saying, "You mustn't do so! I came from the palace of His Majesty the emperor of heaven, where I used to live, and where the twinkling stars moved around me. I breathed the two airs of *yin* and *yan*. It was because I looked down upon the immortals of *penglai* and *kunlun*, and disdained them to be my friends that the emperor of heaven thought I was too arrogant and conceited, and banished me to earth in anger. I'll go back to heaven in seven days. Although I'm at present suffering humiliation and indignity, you should not think we match each other. Besides, after I shall have returned to the palace in heaven, disaster will surely fall upon your head." And the fops were scared and hastened to leave.

The girl then entered the convent and lodged at the Buddhist Scriptures Hall. On the seventh day, she took out a cup of water, drank it, opened her mouth, slowly blew out the steam, and turned into a multicoloured cloud. As she reversed her leather garment and put it on, she immediately transformed into a white dragon. She circled around before soaring higher into the sky and vanished. Nobody knew what happened thereafter. It was really amazing.

Ah! It is certainly improper to take advantage of one who had been banished from the court in heaven, more so when one side did not belong to the dragon species.

*

*The Han Changli Collection
By Han Yu (768-824 A.D.) styled himself Tuizhi, a writer of the Tang Dynasty; originally from Heyang (Mengzhou, Henan Province). He was once an official of the Department of Civil Personnel. Most outstanding was his achievement in prose, for which he was eulogized by later generations as spearheading the literary resurgence after a decline of eight dynasties which preceded the tang Dynasty. He headed the list of "the Eight Great Men of letters of the Tang and Song Dynasties". His fables were novel in plot, and meaningful in conception. *The Han Changli Collection*, which consisted of forty volumes, with thirty volumes

in essays and ten volumes in verse, was compiled by his disciple Li Han. During the Song Dynasty, another additional ten volumes called *Unofficial Collection* were compiled, with one volume of *Addenda*.

469. On the Subject of Horse

The world must first of all give birth to a Bo Le, an adept in appraising horses, before the pedigreed horses can be recognized. Pedigreed horses are always there, but Bo Le is not. That is why despite the existence of an outstanding pedigreed horse, it will not be discovered in the hands of a mediocre horse keeper and will die of old age in the stable, deprived of the opprtunity to be called a pedigreed horse.

In a drove of horses, the thoroughbred can eat as much as one hundred and twenty catties of grains in one session. As the stableman does not know it is a pedigreed horse, he only rations to it the same amount of feed an ordinary horse gets. Thus it can never eats its fill despite having the ability of a pedigreed horse, and its outstanding feature therefore cannot show itself. In this manner, it cannot even perform what an ordinary horse does, let alone asking it to cover a thousand *li* in a day.

Giving orders not in accordance with the way orders should be given to a pedigreed horse; providing feed not based on its ability and need and, moreover, unable to understand its neigh of grief and indignation, the stableman will hold his horsewhip and sigh, saying, "There are no pedigreed horses in this world!" Well, are there really no pedigreed horses, or is it because no one knows how to tell the difference?

470. The Biography of Mao Ying

Mao Ying was a native of the state of Zhongshan. His ancestor, Ming Shi, once assisted Yu the Great (2276-2177 B.C., founder of the Xia Dynasty) in bringing the eastern region of the state under control. Because he had rendered great service in nurturing all things on earth, he was installed as the feudal lord of the district of Mao, and became one of the twelve gods when he died. He had said, "My descendants are offspring of gods; they are different from ordinary mortals, and should be born from the mouth by way of spitting." Later events showed it was as he had said. The eighth generation of Ming Shi's descendant, Xu, according to the old tradition, lived in Zhongshan at the time of the Ying Dynasty, the later period of Shang, and learned the magic arts of deities, which enabled him to hide in the light and ordered other living things about if he so wished. He even stole the goddess of the moon and rode the toad to enter the moon palace. All the descendants after him lived in seclusion and no longer became officials. The one lived in the eastern region was called hare, an intelligent and fast runner. Han Lu, a strong courser, once tried to race with it and lost. Han Lu was so enraged that it colluded with another hunting dog, Song Que, and plotted to have it killed, resulting in its whole family being hacked to pieces.

During the reign of the emperor Qin Shi Huang, Meng Tian, a senior general, led his troops to the south on a punitive expedition against the state of Chu. On their way his troops stopped at Zhongshan in order to carry out a large scale hunting exercise to intimidate Chu. First, he summoned the left and right counsellors and military officers. Using milfoil, he divined using the link-mountain strategy by means of the Eight Diagrams, and obtained a good omen. The diviner offered his congratulations, saying, "The quarry we capture today will be toothless and hornless. It will be one wearing a short garment, with a moustache that has a break in the middle. There are eight apertures in his body, habitually sitting cross-legged. If a soft hair is plucked from its body, it can be used to write on the bamboo strip. If characters can be unified, won't the great cause of merging all the states be realized then?" Thereupon Meng Tian led his hugh army to encircle the game, and caught every member of the Mao family, had their soft hair plucked, and carried Mao Ying back in a carriage. He presented his captive to the emperor Qin Shi Huang in Changtai palace, and gathered all members of the Mao clan, keeping them under strict control. The emperor Qin Shi Huang ordered Meng Tian to send hot-water to them so that they could all take a bath. He installed them as lords in Guancheng with the title Guanchengzi. As time went on, they gradually became the emperor's favorites and were all assigned appropriate posts.

Mao Ying had a powerful memory, and was alert and resourceful in handling things. From the remote past, when chronicle was kept by tying knots, to the establishment of the Qin Dynasty with its anecdotes and history, he was able to put them all on record. Everything from *yin* and *yang*, the two opposing prinsiples in nature, divination, astrology, medical skill, clan system, geography, lexicon, painting, the nine schools of thought and various schools of thinkers, nature's justice and human affairs, to Buddhism, Taoism, foreign religious heresy and doctrines, he had them all recorded. He was also well-versed in contemporary matters: secretarial services of the government, registration of traders, their merchandise and prices of goods,— everything he did was in accordance with the emperor's instructions. From those on top, the emperor Qin Shi Huang, crown prince Fu Su, Hu Hai, Prime Minister Lisi, Eunuch Zhao Gao, to the common people, there was no one who did not love him and was glad he had been put in an important position. In addition, he was good at knowing the wishes of those who employed him, no matter they be upright or vicious, nimble or clumsy, he always followed his employer's desire. Occasionally he might be abandoned, but he would always try to endure the slight silently without giving vent to his grievances. The only people he disliked were the military but, even so, if invited, he would go as well. Eventually he was appointed head of the secretariat and became closer to the emperor. Once, he was even addressed by the emperor as *jun*, a symbol of respect. The emperor personally decided all matters of the state, and read ducuments and memorials to the throne with remarks. During which time, not even the maids in the palace could fool around. The only persons allowed to accompany the emperor until it was time for him to retire were Mao Ying and the person who took care of the lamp.

Mao Ying and Chen Xuan of Jiang County, Tao Hong of Hong Nong, and Mr Chu of Huiji were good friends. They respected and praised one another and, when they went out, they were always seen together. If Mao Ying was summoned by the emperor, the other three would not wait for any imperial edict, but would go in to see the emperor at the same time, and the emperor did not blame them either. Later, The emperor summoned Mao Ying to the palace with the intention of assigning him a position of responsibility when, as someone by the emperor's order brushed off the dust from his person and, as Mao Ying hastened to take off his hat to show his appreciation, the emperor saw his head was already becoming bald; in addition to that, the painting and calligraphy he copied were not to the emperor's liking, and the emperor said, "My friend, you are old now, and I suppose you are no longer equal to the job. I had assigned you to be the head of the secretariat before but, it seems to me, you cannot do it now." Mao Ying replied, "I've tried my best." Thereafter, the emperor did not see him anymore. He then returned to his fiefdom, grew old and died in Guancheng. His descendants were numerous, scattering inside the country and in the surrounding states, and all of them claimed they were the direct descendants of the Mao clan from Guancheng, though only that branch of the family tree in the state of Zhongshan could carry on the cause of their ancestors.

The chief court historian, Sima Qian, said, "There were two offshoots produced by the Mao clan, one of which surnamed Ji, descended from the son of the king Wen of Zhou, installed in the place called Mao. These were the state of Lu, the state of Wei, Mao Dan, and so on. During the Warring States Period, there were Maogong and Maosui. The origin of the offshoot that formed the state of Zhongshan, however, was unclear, though its descendants were most prosperous of all. The compilation of *The Spring and Autumn Annals* stopped short at Confucius, but that was not the fault of Mao Ying. General Meng Tian hunted in the state of Zhongshan, where he encircled and captured them, and had their soft hair plucked. Later, they were installed by emperor Qin Shi Huang in Guancheng. It was then that their reputation became known to the world. The Ji clan, however, was unknown throughout. Mao Ying was summoned to the presence of the emperor Qin Shi Huang as a captive at the time, though he was later assigned a position of importance. The state of Qin eventually annexed the six states, and Mao Ying had his share of contributions. His reward, however, was hardly commensurate with the merits and pains. Besides, he was being distanced and cold-shouldered on account of his old age in the end. All these showed the lack of grace on the part of the emperor Qin Shi Huang!

*

*The Liu Yuxi Collection
By Liu Yuxi (772-842 A.D.) styled himself Mengde, originally from Luoyang (Henan Province); a poet of the Tang Dynasty. Together with Liu Zongyuan, he had taken part in the failed political reform movement of Wang Shuwen, and got demoted. After his return to the capital, again he incurred the wrath of influential officials and was demoted further. From then on he was transferred from place to place as provincial governor for over twenty years before he finally came back to the capital.

471. Dim Mirrors

The mirror-manufacturer put ten mirrors in a box for display at the shop. When the box was opened, only one of them was clean and sparkling, bright and shining; the other nine were blurred, as if separated by a layer of fog. Someone said after viewing them, "The good and the bad are too disparate to compare!" The mirror-maker smiled when he heard the remark, saying, "Well, it is not difficult to make them all good. In general, all shopkeepers only think of the sale prospect. Now, mirror-buyers will take every mirror and look at it. They will look carefully and choose the one they like best. The bright mirror will reflect every detail, and even blemish as minute as a wheat awn will show. If the buyer is not a perfect person, and blemish is discovered after looking at the reflection, he/she will not blame his/her own ugliness, but will complain that the mirror is not well-made and that he/she does not like it. That's why out of ten mirrors there can only be one that is bright and shining!"

472. Medicine

I led an idle life and fell ill, with the result I had no appetite for food, even though a dish might in fact be delicious and high in nutritious value. In traditional Chinese medicine, this was believed to have been caused by the clogging of the spirit which, being in confusion, brought about a high fever.

A guest of mine said to me, "You have been ill for quite some time now. In the place where I live there is an occultist who practises medicine for a living. People who had nasty sores on his body had been cured by this physician and restored to good heallth before. Even a cripple could run like a rabbit after being treated, let alone an ordinary illness such as yours. Why don't you ask him to have a look?"

I listened to his suggestion, and went to his clinic. He felt my pulse, looked at my complexion, listened to my voice, synthesized the impression, and tried to find a cure. "Your illness was the result of your work-and-rest pattern being disrupted and the negligence of your food and the changes of temperature. Now that the five internal organs (heart, liver, spleen, lungs and kidneys) cannot digest food, and the six hollow (*fu*) organs (gallbladder, stomach, Large intestine, small intestine, bladder and *sanjiao*) cannot produce the digestive and absorptive power, they are only skin bags which, moreover, have grown all over with efflorescence. However, I can cure you," he said. Thereupon he took out a pill about one cubic inch in size. He handed the pill to me, saying, "Once you have taken it, your fidgets will vanish, the clogging of the spirit will be stopped, the hidden cause of your illness inside your body will be eradicated, and the lost vitality will be restored. You must take care though. Stop taking this medicine once your illness is gone, because it is poisonous. Only a small dose can be administered, as an overdose will lead to new malady, and do harm to your vitality."

I took over the medicine, went back and swallowed it. Two days later, I felt my swollen legs more agile and stronger, and where it was numb before felt better. Ten days later, the extreme itchiness all over disappeared and there was no incessant scratching anymore. In one month, my eyes could see thing as minute as a thread of hair; the ears could hear very faint sound; and a rough and rugged road was as easy to tread as a broad level highway. Even coarse food and weak tea tasted as good as delicacies.

Friends came to congratulate me when they learned about it. Everybody tried to get a word in, saying, "The pill you got is simply a miracle drug. It's difficult to come by. Nevertheless, the physician's attitude seems to suggest he is trying to keep some of his skills in order to boost his prestige. Perhaps he is leaving you with some future trouble to get more money from you. Why don't you visit him again and get one more pill? May be that will prove even more beneficial to your health."

A downright fool I was! A stickler for the prescription applied universally, I copied mechanically as before a wonder drug that had been proved efficacious. I doubted the extremely sincere attitude of the physician, and took for granted the rubbish of those ignorant fellows. I followed their suggestion and indeed took several more pills. Five or six days later, the poison showed its effect. My whole body ached and became swollen, fever alternated with chills as in the case of malaria. By then I began to realize the truth and hastened to see the physician again. The physician flew into a rage, and said, "I knew you did not understand what I told you!" He made up an antidote and urged me to take it at once, which brought back to life a dying man like me. After a few days, as I took a few more decoctions, my health gradually came back.

*The Li Wengong Collection

By Li Ao (772-841 A.D.) styled himself Xizhi, originally from Chengji, Shaanxi (Qin-an east, Gansu Province); a writer of the Tang Dynasty. Having successively held the post of provincial governor, his career ended with the governorship of the administrative district of Nandong, Zhongshan, when he was in charge of both civil and military affairs. He was bestowed the posthumous title of Haowen. He had learned prose written in the classical literary style from Han Yu, and was an activist in the Han Yu ancient literature movement.

473. A Rooster without Cockscomb

In the northern side of Lingkou, Li Ao came across a family who kept twenty-two chickens with seven roosters and fifteen hens. They pecked and drank, playful and interesting, and so he grabbed a handful of grains and cast them on the ground while making noise to attract them. Among the chickens there was one rooster with severed cockscomb which seemed to be their leader. When it saw the grains on the ground, it stretched out its neck and crowed, as if calling the flock. The flock heard its call and vied with each other to rush to the grains, but they disliked the rooster with severed cockscomb so much that they attacked it en masse. It was only after the rooster was driven away that they rushed back for the grains. At dusk, all twenty-one chickens gathered and perched on the same beam above the pillars. The rooster with severed cockscomb then came over, looking for a companion to perch together on the beam. For a moment it looked up, crowing gently, but no one took notice; then it looked around, this time giving out a series of loud crows, almost mournful. In the end, it was the same, and it went away in despair. It went to the big tree in the courtyard, crowing sorrowfully and flew from under the tree to a branch at the top and perched there. Li Ao was astonished to witness what had happened because, as poultry, the chickens were known for their five virtues, and one of which referred to the sharing of food with companions, the virtue of righteousness. This rooster with severed cockscomb was such an example. Why was it that the twenty-one chickens called to share the food did not feel fortunate but, instead, they drove away the caller? Was it not requiting love with hate and, by so doing, losing one of the five virtues, the virtue of righteousness? Why did all the others perch together and only the rooster with severed cockscomb was being excluded? As Li Ao was at a loss to understand, the poultry keeper told him, saying, "The rooster with severed cockscomb is only a guest. Originally it belonged to our neighbour Mr Chen. Because his hen died, he let it be kept with my chickens. This rooster is a skilful fighter and very brave. None of the six roosters in my family is its match and has the guts to fight with it individually, so they all hate it and do not like to share food with it. This rooster is, however, hopelessly outnumbered and has no choice but to perch alone elsewhere despite its bravery and skill in fighting. Yet, despite everything, it will call the others when food is found although, in the end, they will drive it away, regardless of who finds the food first. It was always like this before. It does not get the reward it deserves, but never changes its inherent virtue." As Li Ao listened to the chicken-keeper's narration, he sighed with feeling, saying, "Birds are, after all, very insignificant living things, and yet among them, there is no lack of one that is gifted with the vital essence and believes it is duty-bound not to turn back. Take this guest rooster as an example. It is unsurpassingly brave and righteous, even though the rest of the flock has lost their virtue by being jealous. Even birds behave like this, let alone men and between friends. Thus it can be seen, no matter ghosts or spirits, birds or animals, all things on earth change within certain confines. Who can escape these peculiar arrangement?" Thereupon Li Ao jotted down the event as a reminder to maintain vigilance, and perhaps it might also serve as an object lesson to the rest of the world.

474. National Horse and Gallant Horse

A man with an outstanding horse called the "national horse" rode abreast with another man who was on a fine horse called a "gallant horse". All of a sudden the gallant horse gnawed at the scruff of the national horse's neck, which caused the latter to bleed profusely and blood fell all over the place. The national horse, however, galloped on as before, its manner natural and composed, without even looked back, as if it did not know the gallant horse had bitten it. Not long afterwards, the gallant horse followed its owner home. For two days it could not eat, nor could it drink, but just stood in the stable shivering. Its owner was anxious and went to the owner of the national horse to find out the cause. The owner of the national horse said, "It's possible it felt ashamed of itself. Just let my horse went there to explain and straighten things out, and everything will be alright." Thereupon he brought the national horse to the house of the gallant horse's owner. As the national horse met the gallant horse, it first used its nose to smell about, then they began to eat the forage in the stable together. An hour had not passed and the gallant horse's illness was gone.

Anything with four legs and consumes forage might be classified as a horse or a cattle; anything with two legs and can talk is a human being. The national horse had four legs and ate forage, and so it was a horse; looked at its ears, nose and the other members of its five sense organs and facial features, it was a horse; from the viewpoint of its legs and appearance, it was still a horse; moreover, it could not talk, and it was simply because it was a horse. Nevertheless, from its attitude towards the gallant horse from whom it received the bite, it was really no difference from the human being. Being attacked without a proper cause and yet refrained from making a fuss about the matter, it truly deserved to be called a "national horse"; and to be able to correct one's mistakes in time, the other horse was also worthy of being called a "gallant horse".

475. The Phoenix lost Support

The dragon and the snake were both hangers-on of the phoenix. The dragon was an animal born with wisdom and vigour, and high morals. The phoenix knew the dragon could equal himself and became an intelligent animal. That was why it was so respectful and close to the dragon.

As to the snake, it was a vicious and sinister creature. Any animal that incurred its envy and hatred, it would definitely machinate to bring harm. It envied all the animals that were loved and trusted by the phoenix. Not only was it thinking of biting the dragon to death, it was also jealous of the unicorn, the intelligent turtle, and the other animals that were regarded as intelligent. Unless it could kill them all, it would not be happy.

The phoenix knew that if it did not satisfy the snake's desire, the snake would get together a bunch of jackals and wolves and wild dogs to howl and harass. That was why it gave in to the snake, and the food it provided for the snake was far in excess of what it provided for the dragon. The phoenix knew the dragon required more food to maintain its vigour, and tried its best to satisfy the need, but it was afraid the snake would find this a pretext to make trouble, and so it did not have the courage to go further than it had already done, and give the dragon more food.

The unicorn and the intelligent turtle disliked what they saw and composed a ballad to advise the phoenix, which goes like this:

Oh phoenix, phoenix!
How your virtue dips!
What has passed has passed,
But in future mend you must.
Let it go at that!
Let it go at that!

Later, the phoenix was wounded by a snake bite, and lay inside the cave unable to go out anymore, and the intelligent turtle was forced to hold its breath and huddle up by pulling its head and legs into its shell. The snake, having ascertained that the dragon was asleep, launched a surprise attack, endeavouring to bite its throat. The dragon was so frightened that it fled to a distant place, never to return.

By then the phoenix had lost all its assistants and subordinates. Alone, it could not do anything. It drew back its wings and no longer tried to fly out, for it was afraid to show its status as an intelligent bird.

*

The Biography of Prefectural Magistrate Nanke
By Li Gongzuo (c.770-850 A.D.) styled himself Zhuan Meng, a writer of the Tang Dynasty. He was originally from Longxi (eastern part of Gansu Province). During his life-time, he liked to collect stories. He was the author of *The Biography of Prefectural Magistrate Nanke, The Biography of Xie Xiao-e, The Biography of Lujiang's Feng Ao*, etc. Among the short story writers of Tang Dynasty, he was considered quite a conspicuous figure, and *The Biography of Prefectural Magistrate Nanke*, in particular, had won universal praise.

476. A Dream

During the reign of emperor Dezong, Tang Dynasty, titled Zhen Yuan (785-805 A.D.), there was a man called Chun Yufen. He had a strong sense of justice, ready to help the weak, defying trivial conventions, and lived in the vicinity of Yangzhou. To the south of his house there was a large old locust tree. Chun Yufen and his gallant friends often held drinking party under it. It was a summer day, Chun Yufen got drunk and fell into a deep slumber. In a daze he saw two messengers in purple came to him, inviting him to the Great Peaceful Locust State, where he called on the king, married the princess and became the emperor's son-in-law, enjoying glory, splendour, wealth and rank. He was also appointed by the emperor as the prefectural magistrate of Nanke, where he promoted what was beneficial and abolished what was harmful. The achievements of his official career were remarkable. He was at the post of prefectural magistrate for twenty-two years, during which he had five sons and two daughters with the princess. One of his sons inherited his position, and his daughters were all married to the rich and powerful families. Soon after, Chun Yufen received order to repel the invasion of the state of Tanluo. As he was defeated, he had offended the king and had to resign his post. By that time, his wife had died, and he was hit by slanders and rumours, feeling very melancholy. The king allowed him to go back to his native place accompanied by the messenger. He woke up suddenly and realized the experiences covering tens of years were only a dream. Following the dreamscape, he found an ants' nest under the locust tree, which was the Great Peaceful Locust State in the dreamland.

*

A Mixed Collection of Strange Tales from Youyang

By Duan Chengshi (?-863 A.D.) styled himself Kegu, a writer of the Tang Dynasty. A native of Linzi, Qizhou (Shandong Province), he came from a literary family. He had an addiction for books; his personal collection of books contained mostly unusual and rare private editions. And not only was he very widely read, he was also endowed with a powerful memory. *A Mixed Collection of Strange tales from Youyang* was his representative work, of which the first part contains twenty volumes, and the continuance, ten. It is a mixed collection of strange tales and unheard-of phantastic stories as well as the origin and development of the name and description of a thing, textual research of anecdotes, etc. A few fables are found here and there.

477. Flies

Zhang Fen was the hanger-on of Wang Weigao of Nankang Prefecture. On one occasion while a banquet was in progress, another hanger-on was displaying his unique skill in hitting the fly with a single green bean. He used the green beans in the bowl, one green bean at a time, using his fingers as catapult, and each time he was right at the target. Ten times he catapulted, ten times he succeeded, and never once did he miss, thus arousing the astonishment and admiration of all the guests. At this juncture, Zhang Fen stood up and said, "There is no need to waste the green beans" So saying, he stretched out his hand to catch the fly. His fingers were as fast as lightning. They fell exactly on the two hind legs of the fly. He did so several times without fail. Indeed, there is no limit in the universe; however strong you are, there is always someone stronger.

478. Partners in Crime

The wolf and the *bei* were two different animals. The *Bei*'s forelegs were very short and could not walk. Whenever it walked, it had to put its forelegs on the thighs of the wolf. Without the wolf, the *bei* could not walk at all. That was why people used a common name for the two: *langbei* (the wolf and the *bei*).

West of the city of Linji there was an abandoned grave, and packs of wolves made their homes there by digging holes. For that reason, the place was called "graves of wolves". Not long ago, there was a man whose journey took him to the wilderness all by himself. He passed through the vicinity of the graves of wolves, and met with tens of them. The man was terribly frightened. It so happened that nearby was a haystack which the farmers had piled up. He therefore climbed up to the top of it. As the wolves were unable to get up there, they encircled the haystack and howled. Sometime later, two wolves went back to the graves of wolves, and returned with an old wolf on its back. The old wolf looked for a while, and then pulled a few sticks of dry hay from under the haystack with its mouth, which it spat on the ground. The other wolves imitated her at once, vying with one another to pull away the hay, using their mouths. Very quickly the hay under the haystack was all gone, and the haystack threatened to collapse at any moment, putting the man in geopardy. Fortunately just at that juncture a team of hunters arrived, and they drove away the wolves. Later, the rescued man and the hunters acted in concert and went to dig the graves of the wolves together. They caught over a hundred heads and killed them all. People said the old wolf which could not walk was a *bei*.

*

Shenmengzi
By Lin Shensi (?-880 A.D.) styled himself Qianzhong, alternative name Shenmengzi; originally from Changle, Fujian Province. The book *Shenmengzi* has three volumes, eight sections and forty chapters. It deals mainly with Confucian ideology. A few fables are found here and there.

479. A Roadside Well

Someone drilled a well at the high road to help passersby quench their thirst. However, because of its location, some fell into it by accident. People laid the blame at the door of the man who sank the well.

*

The Lize Series
By Lu Guimeng (?-c.881 A.D.) styled himself Luwang, a native of Suzhou, and a writer of the Tang dynasty. After serving as secondary officials in Suzhou and Huzhou, he later retired and lived in seclusion at Fuli (south of Kunshan), calling himself Master Fuli as well as Tiansuizi. He enjoyed equal popularity with Pi Rixiu, hence the designation "Pilu". He authored *The Lize Series*, three volumes, and ten volumes of poetry, six volumes of *fu*, or descriptive prose interspersed with verse.

480. Metamorphosis

The size of the caterpillar in the tangerine tree was more or less comparable to a finger. There were two horns of flesh, or tentacles, on its head, and the body stretched and curled as it crawled. It was very much like the larva of longicorn, except its colour, which was green. It hid under the leaves of the tangerine tree, raising its head to eat the leaves, similar to the hungry silk worm, and the whole process went on with such great speed that only the stems of the leaves were left in an instant. If one touched it with the hand, its tentacles would become erect and its body curled, in a wild and intractable posture to show its anger.

One day, I went to see it. It did not move anymore, just stretching out its body, lying there stiff and motionless with no desire to eat. On the second day, it had cast off a skin and became a butterfly. However, it still appeared tender and weak, and the wings had not been unfolded yet, in appearance much like a man with a black apron and wearing a pair of green detachable sheaths for the sleeves; spots of red and yellow alternated on its wings, while on its belly colour bars were strewn in random. Upon its head two hatband-like slender cirri were evident. At that moment, it seemed drunk and so weak that it was unable to fly.

One day after that, I went to see it again. It had hardened and could now face the wind and step into the dew. It followed the branch and crawled up until it reached the top when, suddenly, it opened up its wings, and lissomly floated up the sky. In an instant, it had flown a long way. One moment it was hidden by the fragrant flowers, the next it had flown to the top of the bamboo tree, circling around it, flying and dancing, rising straight up to the sky, now up and now down, causing the people to forget the fierceness of its past, and be fascinated only by its loveliness. Not long afterwards it bumped into a spiderweb and got caught in the gossamer. The spider immediately came out and produced more treads to bind up the butterfly. It was, as it were, shackled with the instruments of torture, and could no longer move about. Even though people might commiserate with the butterfly, they were in no position to undo the spider treads and help it fly away.

481. The Wild Dragon

Once upon a time, there was a man who loved dragons. He obtained two dragons and kept them in order to study their habit and desire, and he was called the dragon-raiser.

Now, although the dragon and mankind did not belong to the same species, there were similarities between the two in certain aspects of their personality. Thus the dragon-raiser constructed a splendid pool as the dragons' residence, so they need not go to the distant rivers and oceans to swim. He provided the dragons with very delicious food, so that the whales they caught in the ocean were less tasty in comparison.

The two dragons sometimes lay listlessly in the pool resting, sometimes gambolled in it. On the whole, they were so happy that they did not wish to leave the place.

One day, by coincidence, the two dragons came across a wild dragon. They greeted the wild dragon enthusiastically, and invited it to live with them. "Why bustling about? Rushing to and fro all year round between the boundless heaven and earth, living in seclusion in the cave underground when cold, and flying high in the sky when hot. Are you not feeling tired? Certainly it will be much more comfortable if you can come and live with us!" they said.

The wild dragon threw its head back and sneered at the two dragons, saying, "How parochial and shallow your knowledge is! Heaven has endowed us with a strong physique and horns on the head and scales all over the body; bestowed upon us the ability to dive to the bottom of the chasm and the mouth of the spring, and to soar to the highest heavens; gifted us with intelligence so that we can breathe clouds and travel by wind; entrusted us with the responsibilty to relieve drought and moisten the withered seedlings. We are free to go sightseeing in the vast universe, and to take a rest on the unmeasured vastness of the earth, while experiencing the vicissitudes of the world. Is not all this a blissful enjoyment? You are seeking only temporary ease in this tiny pool as large as a hoof-print, with your feet and claws restrained in the small area of sand and mud, and living with the leeches and earth worms, doing whatever pleases your master, all for the leftovers as food. Although we belong to the same species, and possess the same form and appearance, our interests are vastly different! You have obediently allowed man to treat you as a plaything. I am afraid your food will not be free, however. Sometime in the future, man will lay their hands on your throat and kill you before cutting your flesh to pieces to let them enjoy. Probably that day will not be far off. I sympathize with you and am trying to lend you a hand, hoping somehow I may be able to rescue you out of your misery but, instead, you have tried to induce me to fall into the same trap set by man! In future, you probably will not be able to escape the calamity!"

The wild dragon had not gone very long when the king of Xia took a fancy to dragon meat. He ordered the dragon-raiser to contribute the two dragons, which were then slaughtered, made into meat pulp, and presented to the king for his enjoyment.

*

The Pizi Literary Collection
By Pi Rixiu (c.834-883 A.D.) styled himself Yishao and Ximei, a writer of the Tang Dynasty, originally from Xiangyang (Xiangfan, Hubei Province). He lived in Lumen Mountain in his early years, and so gave himself the name Lumenzi. Later, he became a palace candidate. He joined the insurrectionary army of Huang Chao, and served as a Han Lin Academy scholar. *The Pizi Literary Collection* totals ten volumes, the first nine volumes being prose, the tenth, poetry.

482. Mistaken

In the marshes where ponds abounded, a farmer carried his bow and arrow walking along the edge of his cultivated field. In front of him was a stretch of reeds, and the farmer was thinking of going there for a quiet rest. He had hardly reached there when he saw the reeds shaking and the reed catkins flying around windless. He concluded there must be some animals playing inside the reeds. When he examined closer, he found a tiger leaping and roaring. Judging from its appearance, it must have caught something, for it appeared excited and happy. The farmer thought the tiger might have seen him and was aroused by the sight of its prey. He therefore hid himself in the thick growth of grass and shrubs at once while putting an arrow to his bowstring and pulling it, aiming at the target. When the tiger leaped again and exposed the vital spot, the farmer seized the opportunity and let go the arrow, hitting right at the armpit beside the chest. With a loud crash the huge body of the tiger fell to the ground. The farmer waited for a while; seeing that it was motionless, he carefully walked over to inspect. He found that the tiger had actually killed a roebuck and was celebrating when it, in its turn, was killed by him with an arrow and, with its head pillowed on the roebuck, died as well.

*

The Leisure Advocate
By Zhang Gu, dates of birth and death could not be ascertained. He probably lived in the interval between the reigns of Yizong and Xizong of the Tang Dynasty (around 874 A.D.). He was famed for his book *The Leisure Advocate*. The book is a collection of anecdotal stories with only twenty odd items.

483. Money Can Move the Gods

Zhang Yanshang, an eminent, honest and upright official of the Tang Dynasty, was reviewing a legal case. After looking over the file, he felt there were details of a grievance that required investigation, and called in the warder to interrogate him, "This case has gone on for too long," he said. "I'll ascertain the facts within these few days, and have the case wound up."

Early the next morning when Zhang Yanshang arrived at the office, he saw a note on his table, which read : "Will present a gift of thirty thousand strings (a string of 1,000 cash). Please stop reviewing." Zhang Yanshang was furious and went on investigating the case with even greater effort. The next day, there was another note on his table with the words "Fifty thousand strings". This enraged Zhang Yanshang even more, and he ordered the case be closed within two days. On the third day, once more, a note appeared on his table with the words "One hundred thousand strings". Zhang Yanshang heaved a sigh, saying, "As the cash reached one hundred thousand strings, even the gods will be moved, and there is nothing in the world that is irretrievable. If I insist on investigating, not only will the case be impossible for me to reverse, but I am afraid calamity will befall my own head." Thus, he could not but stop the investigation.

*

*Slanderous Talk
By Luo Yin (833-909 A.D.) styled himself Zhaojian, originally from Yuhang (Zhejiang Province). A writer of the Tang Dynasty, he was the author of *The A and B Collection, Slanderous Talk, Double Coincidence*, and *The Luo Zhaojian Collection, which was* compiled by later generations. The book *Slanderous Talk* consists of five volumes, his prose collection.

484. Heavenly Roosters

Mr Ju's son had not learned his father's skill in getting a livelihood, but he knew the chickens' habitus well. The beak and spur of his rooster were not conspicuous, nor were the feathers bright and shining. It seemed to muddle along listlessly, and without even the zeal to vie for food. Yet, as soon as the enemy appeared, it immediately became a hero among the chickens, courageous beyond compare; as a harbinger of dawn, it crowed earlier than all the other roosters. That's why these cocks were called heavenly roosters.

As Ju's son passed away, his son's son again inherited his career as chicken-raiser. The son's style, however, was quite different from his father's. Unless a rooster had bright and shiny feathers, and sharp beak and spur, he would not keep it. Among the roosters in the flock, one could no longer see any that heralded the break of day with its majestic appearance, nor could one espy the valour against a powerful enemy. There were only roosters with tall cockscombs strutting like peacocks, vying with each other to peck at the food day in day out. Alas! The proper way to raise chickens was lost to the world in the hands of this man!

485. The Wizard of the State of Chu

Within the territory of the state of Chu, offering sacrifices to gods or ancestors had long been a tradition of the common folk. There was a wizard who had quite a reputation in the vicinity. In the beginning when he was invited to offer sacrifices, he only asked for an ordinary feast in addition to songs and dances with which either to welcome or send off the gods. The sacrificial rites thus could be an instrument in restoring a sick person to health and enabling the people to reap a bumper harvest. But in later days, when he was invited to offer sacrifices, he had asked for live and fat cattle and lamb as well as plenty of good wine. Yet, despite all these good things, the sick sometimes died, and those asking for bumper harvest had crop failure instead. The local people were deeply indignant, but could not understand the cause of it.

Discussing the matter, a man said, "Formerly when I went to the wizard's house, I never saw anything burdening his mind, and he could devote all his energy to the sacrificial ceremony when he was invited to it, and blessing was accordingly bestowed by the gods and spirits at once. Besides, the wizard always shared the meat with everyone. In later years, the wizard has more children, with the result expenses in his family have also increased. That was why he could not have complete devotion to the sacrificial ceremony, and the gods could not send the blessing down as well. Moreover, he took all the sacrificial meat back to his home. It was not because the wizard was previously intelligent and now becoming stupid, it was because his family was constantly on his mind, and he had no time for the rest of the people."

Even a wizard could be distracted in matter of sacrificial ceremony, let alone those whose professions were different from his?

486. The Old Man of Qi and the Old Woman Next Door

There was once an old man in Shandong who tilled the land in the fertile plain for a living. He entrusted the management of the farm to his sons who took turns in looking after it. There were neither drought nor flood, nor insect pests, but the quantities of grains harvested varied each year. The old man was suspicious, saying, "Is this the consequence of my not trusting people? The old woman next door was originally my servant. Although she has now moved elsewhere, she still can be regarded as a servant of the family." And he invited her to help the eldest son manage the farm. In the meantime, she was asked to keep watch on him.

When the time came for the harvest, the farmhands who tilled the old man's land took up their farm implements, and threatened to beat his eldest son, driving him away. At this juncture, the old woman next door reported to the old man, saying that his son had not managed the farm well; that he had not discharged his duty, and thus aroused the discontent of the farmhands. The old man, therefore, gave his eldest son a good thrashing, and allowed his second son to take over the management. He did not, however, take any action against the farmhands.

After his second son took over the management, the same thing happened, and the old woman next door reported that the discontent of the farm labourers came about because his second son had not discharged his duty well. Again, the old man gave his second son a good thrashing and let his youngest son take over.

At that moment, someone talked to the old man, saying that such thing never happened before, and it was only after the old woman arrived on the scene that his eldest son and second son were beaten. "If you still insisted in employing the old woman, I'm afraid you will not be able to keep your farmland, and your sons will be driven out and beaten all the time!" he said. As the old man listened, it suddenly dawned on him that he had been deceived. He was infuriated, and fired the old woman even as he restored the positions of the two sons. Came the autumn harvest that year, it was peaceful and quiet as it used to be, and that should be illustration enough that it was indeed the old woman who caused the trouble, for how could the farmhands have done it?

487. What the Woman of Yue Said

Zhu Maichen became rich and powerful. He was now a high official of the regime and could not bear to see his divorced ex-wife suffer privations. So he sent people to construct a house, and appropriated some food and clothing for her. The motive, in fact, was regarded as benevolent.

One day, Zhu Maichen's ex-wife told Zhu's attendant, saying, "Formerly when I was Zhu Maichen's wife, I looked after him by his side for many years. Each time we were in difficulty and had to work hard, when we suffered hunger and cold, I often heard him talk of his asperation, saying that if one day he could make his way in the world, he would consider the assistance of the emperor in governing the country as his responsibility, and work for the people's well-being, helping his generation and bringing comfort to the common people. Now that unfortunately I have left him, which was a few years ago, he became a high official as he had aspired for. The emperor has bestowed upon him a very generous official salary and a high position, enabling him to return to his hometown in silken robes as an official, showing off among his fellow villagers. It is indeed a great triumph and honour for him. However, I've not heard him repeat the lofty words, a promise which he once uttered. Is it because peace reigns over the land, and the people are well-fed and well-clothed, which enables him to assume the attitude he now has? Or, is it because he is anxious to be elevated to a higher position, to advance in peerage, and to enrich his family, so that he has no time for the common people? From my standpoint, if he wants to show his benevolence by means of his assistance to me, that is okay. However, since I've not seen him showing the same benevolence to the rest of the people, how can I eat the food he provides with an easy mind?" Having said that, she breathed her last.

*

Notes on the Well-known Paintings of Successive Dynasties
By Zhang Yanyuan styled himself Aibing, dates of birth and death unavailable, originally from Hedong (west Yongji, Shanxi Province). He lived approximately at the period between emperor Xuanzong and emperor Zhaozong of the Tang Dynasty. *Notes on the Well-known Paintings of Successive Dynasties* consists of ten volumes, and was completed in the reign of emperor Xizong of Tang Dynasty (c.874 A.D.) when he was the president of the supreme court. It was the first important comprehensive history of paintings in ancient China. In addition to recording famous paintings in ancient China and commenting on each, it also lists over three hundred and seventy painters and their biographies from remote times to the Tang Dynasty, with not a few legends which are fables in nature.

488. Add the Finishing Touch

During the Northern and Southern Dynasties (420-589 A.D.), there was a famous painter in the Liang Dynasty (502-537 A.D.), Southern Dynasties, whose name was Zhang Sengyou. He was adept in figure painting, genre painting and dragon painting. According to legend, emperor Wu of Liang once ordered him to paint a mural in the Peace and Happiness Monastery of Nanking (Nanjing) to decorate the Buddhist monastery. Zhang Sengyou painted many figures of the Buddha and pictures of religious tales. He also painted four dragons on four walls, which were as vivid as life. All the viewers praised him for doing such a good job, although there was a little blemish in every one of them, and that was, he did not put in the eyes for the dragons. People were surprised at the negligence, as Zhang Sengyou was a great painter, and so they asked him why he did not put in the eyes. "The reason why I did not put in their eyes is to prevent them from flying away. Once the eyes have been put in, they will fly away at once, and you will not be able to see them anymore," Zhang Sengyou explained. People were not convinced, however, and wanted him to try. Thereupon Zhang Sengyou put the eyes in for two of the dragons. He had just did so when dark clouds gathered and rolled in the sky, lightning accompanied by peals of thunder, and the two dragons took advantage of the wind and clouds, lightning and thunder, to soar high up in the sky and fly away. Later, people summarized the story into a four-character idiom with the literal meaning "to add eyeballs to the picture of a dragon", but it can also mean "to add the finishing touch"—to enliven the whole composition by the skilful use of a couple of sentences.

489. Double-barreled Move

During the Tang Dynasty, in the city of Suzhou, there was a famous painter by the name of Zhang Zao. He was skilful in landscape painting, especially the painting of pines and rocks. One day, he went sightseeing in the monastery, and saw a newly whitewashed wall. As the sun shone on it, the white wall appeared even whiter, which aroused his painting mood to such an extent that he asked the monk there for the brush and ink and began to paint. He stood by the wall, each hand holding a brush. The right hand brush painted a pinetree in spring with twigs burgeoning, the pine needles luxuriantly green, full of life and vigour, and flowing with vitality; the left hand brush, on the other hand, painted a pinetree in Autumn, its trunk hoary and old with scale-like specks all over, not a few dry branches protruding, as if it had endured all the hardships of exposure, and yet all the more vigorous and forceful. Viewers were greatly amazed that he could wield two brushes at the same time and, as fast as wind, painted two entirely different pines. There was none who did not applaud. A poet was so impressed that he inscribed a poem on one side of the painting at once; a calligrapher was inspired and wrote a narration on the wall. The tourists told the monks in the monastery, saying, "These three are superb works of art in your monastery. They have greatly broadened our horizons!"

*

Elves and Goblins
By Niu Qiao styled himself Songqing, alternatively Yanfeng, a writer of the Tang Dynasty, originally from Longxi. He became a palace scholar at the fifth year of Qianfu, which was the title of Xizong of the Tang Dynasty.

490. A Seamless Heavenly Robe

According to legend, there was a scholar by the name of Guo Han in ancient times. One year on a summer night, he was enjoying the cool and the glorious full moon when, all of a sudden, there appeared in the sky a multicoloured cloud, on which a little person stood, and slowly it touched down. It was actually a very beautiful fairy, wearing a silken garment with a brocade scarf draped over her shoulders, while her hat was made of green jade and woven gold threads. On her feet was a pair of shoes with decorative design. Following her were two maids, likewise very beautiful. Guo Han knew they were fairies from heaven, and he hastily went down on his knees and bowed.

The fairy said she was the Girl Weaver from Heaven, coming to inspect the human world by order of God. In view of Guo Han's diligence and excellent character, which she noticed, she had come to talk to him.

Guo Han looked closely at the fairy, and was greatly amazed when he saw her garment was seamless. The fairy said, "In heaven, no threads are used in making clothes, and that's why my garment is seamless." They talked all night till daybreak when the fairy swiftly flew upwards and disappeared.

*

Poems and the Stories Behind Them
By Meng Qi styled himself Chuzhong, dates of birth and death unknown. He had once been an official in Wuzhou (Guangxi Province). *Poems and the Stories Behind Them* recorded anecdotes of poets in the Tang Dynasty.

491. A Broken Mirror Joined Together

Princess Lechang, sister of Chen Shubao (553-604 A.D.), the last monarch of the Chen Dynasty, southern Dynasties, was endowed with beauty and brains. She, moreover, attached equal importance to both love and duty. She and her husband, Xu Deyan, deeply loved one another after marriage. As the army of Sui went down south and the state of Chen would soon be conquered, it was evident that disaster was about to strike, causing husband and wife to be separated. They broke a bronze mirror into two, each holding one half of it, and agreed that should they be separated from one another, both would bring the half mirror in their possession to sell in the streets on the night of the fifteenth of the first lunar month, hoping they would be able to come across one another then.

Soon after the state of Chen was subjugated, the last monarch of Chen Dynasty surrendered, Xu Deyan and the Princess Lechang were forced to separate by undisciplined troops. The princess was captured by Yang Su, a high official of the Sui Dynasty. Then came the second year, and, as agreed before, Xu Deyan went selling his half of the bronze mirror on the night of the fifteenth of the first lunar month in the streets of the capital. As luck would have it, an old servant, sent by the princess, also arrived with her half of the bronze mirror. When the two halves were put together, they matched without a hitch. The mirror reminded Xu Deyan of its owner, and all sorts of feelings welled up in his mind. A poem was inscribed on the other half of the bronze mirror, as follows:

Both mirror and its owner are gone,
The mirror returns, its owner does not;
As the lunar goddess has left my home,
The shining moon is left to shine alone.

In time, the servant brought her half of the bronze mirror back to the princess. As the princess read the poem, she knew the inscription was written by Xu Deyan. She felt awfully bad and cried for several days. Upon inquiry, Yang Su eventually came to know about the matter. He sent someone to look for Xu Deyan, and allowed the husband and wife to be reunited.

492. A Charming Face Among Peach Blossoms

One year during the Tang Dynasty, Cui Hu of Boling County was in the capital, Chang-an, for the national service examination and, later, became a palace scholar. He was laudable in physical features as well as in moral character, although he was a lone soul admiring his own purity, and his circle of friends was small. During the Qingming Festival, or Tomb-Sweeping Day, he took a stroll in the southern corner of the capital alone, where he saw a farmhouse. It was only a small place, but it was overgrown with flowers and trees, and was so quiet that it looked as if no humans were around. After knocking at the door for some time, a young girl finally peeked through the crack between the door and its frame, and asked, "Who is it?" Cui Hu gave his full name, and said, "I'm on a spring outing alone and, feeling thirsty because of the wine, I've come to ask for some water." The girl went inside, brought a cup of water, and opened the door. She then fetched a chair, and asked Cui to be seated, while she leaned herself against a crooked branch of the peach tree beside him, full of goodwill and devotion. She was gentle and charming as she revealed her infinite beauty. Cui Hu tried to seduce her with words but she did not reply.

They stared at each other for quite some time before Cui Hu said goodbye to her. The maiden saw him out to the door, apparently full of affection, and entered her house looking disappointed. Cui Hu looked at her for the last time, and left quite reluctantly.

He did not return until the Tomb-Sweeping Day in the following year, when he suddenly remembered what happened a year before. As he was unable to suppress his emotions, he went straight there to look for her. The courtyard seemed unchanged, but the door was locked. Cui Hu then moved to the left side of the door, and wrote down a poem:

Last year today this door inside,
The face of a beauty and peach blossoms
Set off each other in the light.
Today nobody knows where the beauty doth hide,
While peach blossoms still laugh
At the spring breeze with all their might.

He wrote down "an inscription by Cui Hu of Boling" before he left.

A few days later, he chanced to visit the southern part of the city, and took the opportunity to see the place again. He heard someone crying in the courtyard, and went over to knock in order to find out the cause. An old man came out and asked, "Are you Cui Hu, sir?" "Yes, I am," he replied. The old man cried again. "You have killed my daughter," he said. Cui Hu was as astonished as he was grieved. He did not know how to respond to the accusation. The old man continued, "My duaghter had barely come of age, and was knowledgeable in poetry and literary works. She was still a virgin. Beginning last year, she always seemed distracted, as if she had lost something. A few days ago, I went out with her. Upon our return, she saw the poem at the left door leaf. She read it, and felt ill immediately at the entrance. Not a grain of rice entered her mouth since then, and she died within a few days. I am old now, and she was my only daughter. The reason she was not married was because I was looking for a good son-in-law to rely upon as I grew older. Now she is unfortunately dead. Is it not true that you have killed her?" Again, he took hold of Cui Hu and sobbed inconsolably.

Cui Hu too felt greatly disturbed and sorrowful. He asked to be allowed to go in and cry for a while. The maiden was in her bed, and looked as if she were only sleeping. Cui Hu held her head and put it on his thigh as if it were a pillow. He prayed as he cried, "I am here! Oh, I am here!" After a while, quite unbelievably, the maiden opened her eyes, and in about half a day, she revived. The old man was overjoyed, and married his daughter to Cui Hu.

*

Wunengzi
The author's name and life story cannot be verified. Under the classificaton "Works of Taoist content" in *The New History of Tang* (one of the *Twenty-Four Histories*), under the section *Bibliographical Sketch,* it registered *Wunengzi* as contained three volumes, and annotated that he "lived in seclusion among the people during the reign of Guangqi, which was the title of emperor Xizong of the Tang Dynasty". Based on this information, we know he lived in 885-887 A.D., and the book must have been completed during that period. The book originally had forty-two chapters, but only thirty-four remain now. Its content is mainly about Taoism, with a few fables here and there.

493. The Venomous Bird and the Poisonous Snake

The venomous bird, a legendary bird with poisonous feathers, and the poisonous snake ran into one another, and the venomous bird stretched its neck trying to eat the poisonous snake.

The poisonous snake said to the venomous bird, "Everyone in the world said you are a most venomous bird. The word venom brings infamy. The reason you are so notorious is because you have eaten too many of my kind, and inside your body poison has accumulated too much. If you refrain from eating snakes, there will not be so much poison inside you, and you will no longer have the bad reputation of being a venomous bird."

The venomous bird smiled and replied, "Are you not also being hated by people as a poisonous thing? It's absolutely blandishments! How dare you say I am venomous. The spreading of poison on your part is premeditated, and by biting man you cause his death; that's why I must eat you to rid the world of pest like you as a punishment. People know I can kill you and so they keep me in order that you will not bite anymore; at the same time, people also know the poison in your body will be transferred to my body and feathers, and they sometimes use my feathers to kill other people. Actually the venom in my body comes from your body. I hate poison, yet I still suffer the bad reputation of being venomous. It is man who use my feathers to kill other people, and not I. If a man takes up his sword to kill, can you put the blame on the sword, or is it the man who uses it that is at fault? From this example, it is evident that I do not initiate the poisoning of man. Is it not clear enough? Isn't it understandable that people will keep me but not you? I try to rid the world of evil and get the name of evil, but I live on still because of that, for people will not harm me, which means I am not evil at all. As to you, you spread poison on purpose, hiding in the grass and biting people to gratify yourself, and that's why everybody wants to kill you. You come across me today, and that may be called 'heaven's will'. You may try to escape death by sophistry, but is it possible to succeed?"

The poisonous snake had no answer to the allegation, and the venomous bird ate it.

494. The Owl and Omen

Wunengzi lived with a family surnamed Jing in Qin Village. One night, an owl alighted on a branch of the tree in the Jing family yard and hooted. Jing was very worried and prepared to shoot it down with a catapult. Wunengzi persuaded him not to, but Jing said, "The owl is a bird of bad omen. Whenever any calamity is coming to a family, it will be there to hoot. If it is killed, may be the calamity can be averted."

Wunengzi replied, "If the owl's hooting can bring calamity to men, the owl is of course to blame. But since it can bring calamity, even though you kill it, the approaching calamity will not be averted. If it is because calamity will come to a certain family in the future, and it comes to hoot, then is it not because the owl is devoted to men and comes to forewarn people about it? If the calamity does not come from the owl itself and you kill it, are you not then persecuting the faithful and honest? It is especially unjust since you call yourself human, and human beings and birds and animals are all bred selflessly between heaven and earth. The human eyes are horizontal, his toes are square, and can only walk on earth and is not able to fly, and those are the differences between him and the birds. These differences are shaped by nature and are not affected by the love and hate of men. Who has given the owl the authority to decide men's fortune and misfortune? Who is the first to say that the owl is a bird of bad omen? Have heaven and earth ever said so? Or is it the owl itself that says it? If heaven and earth do not pronounce it, and the owl itself does not say so, why must we insist that the owl is a bird of bad omen? Since nobody knows when has the idea of the owl being a bird of bad omen taken root, then we can also say: the phoenix, despite its multicoloured plumage, is not necessarily an auspicious sign; by the same token, the owl is not inevitably a bird that brings calamity."

As Jing listened to Wunengzi, he gave up the idea of killing the owl with his catapult and, needless to say, there was no calamity that befell his family.

495. A Handsome Young Man

The Fan clan had produced a handsome man. He was already over thirty. Sometimes he would go about everywhere with dishevelled hair, sometimes he would stay at home all day long without a word. If he opened his mouth at all, he would call a lamb a horse, and mountain as water. Whatever he called a thing, it was sure to be different from what it was ordinarily known by other people. Members of his family and fellow villagers all believed he suffered from mental disorder and ignored him, not wanting to make a fuss about it.

Wunengzi, too, thought he had mental illness. One day, in a place overgrown with weeds, where trees blotted out the sky and covered the sun, the two met and came together.

Wunengzi sighed with emotion, saying, "A healthy and strong man; tall, of commanding appearance, what a pity to be suffering from an illness of such nature!" The neuropath responded slowly, saying, "I don't have any illness." Wunengzi was surprised at his saying so. He said, "You can't even find the hat and the belt and put them together, your daily life does not conform to tradition, you can't remember the names of articles, forget the customs and manners of your native land, and the condition is what people call mental disorder. How can you say you have no illness?"

The neuropath, however, replied, "How to wear a hat, how to fasten the belt and how to live the daily life surely have their proper tradition; love of one's family, respect one's fellow villagers,—are all those my natural bent? I'm sure there were people in the past who wove those tales at random, and embellished them so that they became customs and manners. In time, people became used to them and accepted them, even to this day. If one insists that weak wine originally tastes mellow and good, and understands it is a mistake to call the weak wine mellow, and one opposes calling it so, people may think in the reverse and call one a neuropath. Do the names of all things exist automatically as they are? What is clear and light and above us is called heaven, what is yellow and below is called earth; what brings light to the day is called the sun, what shines at night is called the moon; and there are such things as wind, cloud, rain, and fog, smoke, mist, frost, and snow; and there are lofty mountains and rivers and oceans, grass, tree, bird, and animal; and Huaxia (an ancient name for China) and the Yi and Di (barbarian tribes in the east and north of ancient China); emperors, kings, generals and ministers, princes and aristocrats; the scholar, farmer, artisan and merchant, slave and servant; right and wrong, good and bad, the crooked and the upright, honour and disgrace,— all these are names woven by people and imposed upon them. As time went on, people became accustomed to them, and the circumstances under which events took place blurred. As they are accepted and put into practice, nobody has the guts to change them. Suppose in the beginning people called what was clear and light and above us as earth, and what was yellow and below as heaven, the celestial body that lighted up the day as moon, and the celestial body that lighted up the night as sun, then they would also be called as such today. Giving everything a name is what man does. It begins with man. But I also am a man. Since ancient men could give names, why can't we? That's why I believe I can do or not do as I please, beginning with the wearing of clothes and hat, and how I live my daily life, and give the names I choose. As to whether I'm a neuropath or not, even I myself am not clear. If those people who do not know call it neuropath, that's perfectly all right with me!"

*

Views and Events in the Tang Dynasty
By Wang Dingbao (870-940 A.D.), a native of Nanchang during the period of the Five Dynasties (707-960 A.D.). He was a palace scholar during the reign of emperor Zhaozong of Tang Dynasty, whose title was Guanghua. Later, he became an official of Southern Han. The book recorded old stories of the imperial competitive examinations which, in a way, made up for the deficiency in official history. In the meantime, it preserved the anecdotes of the men of letters in the Tang Dynasty and put together the scattered poems of the same period.

496. A Pedant

In the Tang Dynasty, there was a man called Zheng Xun, who held the post of *Shilang* in the Ministry of Civil Office. Later, he was transferred to the Ministry of Rites. At that time, one of the chief offices of the central administration had six ministries under it, namely, The Ministry of Civil Office, of Revenue, of Rites, of War, of Punishments, and of Works. The Ministry of Rites was in charge of ceremony, sacrificial offerings and the recommendation of young scholars. In the Tang Dynasty, *Shilang* was the deputy of the Ministry of Rites, who was responsible for the selection of palace graduates through the imperial examinations. When Zheng Xun was the *Shilang* of the Ministry of Rites, he had recommended quite a number of talented scholars of humble origin, but he also made some stupid mistakes. Once, when Zheng Xun was in charge of the civil service examinations under the Ministry of Rites in accordance with tradition, he read the examination papers and saw a candidate by the name of Yan Biao. He mistakenly took Yan Biao to be the descendant of Yan Zhenqin, the duke of Lujun. With a stroke of his brush, he selected him the Number One Scholar. Yan Zhenqin was an eminent calligrapher and loyal official and as such was loved by all the people. The original intention of Zheng Xun in choosing Yan Biao as the Number One Scholar was to encourage the loyal and the honest, urging them to serve the imperial government. But, when asked about his origin, Yan Biao replied, "I am of humble origin, and not the descendant of the duke of Lujun." By then, it dawned upon Zheng Xun that he had picked the wrong man. Someone wrote a doggerel to deride Zheng Xun, as follows:

The *Donghong* deputy of the ministry is a pedant,
Who has mistaken Yan Biao as duke Lu the great talent.

Later, people called a scholar who stubbornly adhered to outworn rules and ideas as *Donghong*, another name for pedant.

*

*Jade Hall Chitchat
By Wang Renyu (880-956 A.D.) styled himself Denian, originally from Tianshui (Gansu Province), a writer of the era of the Five Dynasties. He loved poetry and was the author of *The West River Collection* consisting of one hundred volumes, with more than ten thousand poems. They were lost except fifteen which were compiled into *A Complete Book of Poetry from the Tang Dynasty*. Some chapters of *Jade Hall Chitchat* had been included in the reference book *Extensive Collection in the Reign of Peace*, and are thus preserved until now.

497. A Cangued Tiger

In a place like Xiangliang and its vicinity, beasts of prey that brought great harm to the people were often seen. Thus catching those fierce animals using tools and traps became a profession. One day, a hunter suddenly came to notify the government, saying, "Last night, a beast of prey bumped into the trap and is now in the pit, and we are here to invite His Honour to savour the game." Thereupon the official led his family and subordinates to the place.

As they arrived at the scene, they saw a fierce tiger which had earlier fallen into the pit. Be it the womenfolk of the inner chambers who stayed in tents put up earlier or the common people, all vied with one another to watch how the fierce tiger was captured. They saw the hunter using a big wooden cangue with nail locks, the four corners of which were fastened with ropes before it was lowered into the pit. Then they began to fill the pit with earth. As the tiger took advantage of the mound of earth to get out of the pit, the hunter pulled the ropes, which caused the two parts of the cangue to dovetail into one another. The head of the tiger had just appeared when the ropes were pulled tight and the cangue fastened with nails. At this moment, the men nearby hastened to bind the tiger with ropes, and all the spectators applauded with laughter.

A fierce tiger like that could not be caught bare-handed. Even though you had the strength of a thousand men, the courage of a hundred, how could you bring it under control without some mechanical device? However, when it was cornered and exhausted, it could be easily subdued like a lamb or a dog. Even though it had pointed teeth and sharp claws, how could it hurt people then? In fact, bringing a strong enemy to terms was similar to catching a fierce tiger!

498. Wild Geese

There were flocks of wild geese which lived on the banks of big rivers and the beaches of large lakes, where water grass grew in profusion. Usually their number was in the hundreds and thousands, occupying the whole stretch of land. When they were resting, their leader would stay at the centre of the flock, and the slave goose among them posted as sentry at the periphery.

In the south, people had their own method of catching the wild geese. When there was no moon, and the sky became dark and cloudy, a man who served as the guide would conceal a candle under an earthen jar, while the rest of his team each carrying a stick followed at the back, quietly groping towards the wild geese. As they approached the flock, the man with the candle would hold it up so that the light twinkled, but he would cover the candle light with his earthen jar in the next second.

The slave-goose on sentry would honk loudly to warn its companions, and the leader would also honk in response. However, when all the wild geese were awakened, things had already returned to normal, the surrounding was quiet, and nothing unusual seemed to prevail. So after a little commotion, the wild geese went to sleep again.

A few moments later, the hunters groped forwards to cover another stretch of the road. The leader of the team took out his candle and again let the light twinkle before hiding it for a second time. The wild geese, as before, would make a fuss about it but, as the rest of the flock woke up and saw nothing untoward happened, there being neither light nor apparent danger, they went back to sleep. In this manner, the hunter played with his candle three or four times in succession, which infuriated the leading goose. Thinking that the slave goose was the cause of trouble, it led the whole flock to peck the slave goose. Actually they had unjustly wronged their loyal friend.

The event made the slave goose afraid of being pecked by their companions. Thus, when it noticed the twinkling light again, it would not honk. The time was now ripe for the attack. The hunters took up their sticks, charged into the flock and hit them indiscriminately, often making a good bag.

*

*Petty Talks of Dreams in the North
By Sun Guangxian (?-968 A. D.) styled himself Mengwen, assumed name Baoguangzi, a writer of the period of the Five Dynasties. He had once served under Gao Conghai, king of Nanping, Jingnan, as an official during the period of the Five Dynasties. Later, he switched allegiance to Song, and was assigned the position of Huangzhou governor, but died before he took up the post. He was famous for his *ci*, a type of Chinese classical poetry, which were seen in *A Collection Among the Flowers, Ci of the Five Dynasties and Tang Dynasty. Petty Talks of Dreams in the North* contains twenty volumes.

499. Passing Fish Eyes for Pearls

In Zezhou (the City of Jin, Shanxi Province), a monk called Hong Mi greeted the arrival of Buddhist relics and constructed a stupa serving as depository. Hong Mi fabricated wild tales, tried every trick to mislead the public and deceive the ignorant. He even claimed that he could produced Buddhist relics himself, and passed off all this rubbish as the doctrine of the Zen sect of Buddhism. When he went to Taiyuan to expound the texts of Buddhism, the rich and influential families vied with one another to invite him for sermons on Buddha dharma. Women, out of ignorance, knelt around him. After Hong Mi had finished his sermons and left, the women picked up several hundred pellets of

Buddhist relics under their seats. These were brought to the expert for verification, and found to be the eyes of dried fish.

500. A Sichuan Monk Versus the Mountain God

Inside the border of Hezhou there was a mountain called Bishan (now part of Chongqing). On the mountain, there was a mountain god temple. According to the local people's tradition, a whole ox must be offered as sacrifice each year. Failing that, the mountain god would cause calamity to befall them. In Hezhou, everyone, from the chief magistrate of the district to the common people, was afraid of the mountain god, and the slaughter of an ox each year as sacrifice had to go on which, it would seem, was a burden without end.

At that time, there was a monk by the name of Shanxiao, who once held the post of district chief magistrate himself. Tired of the ups and downs of officialdom, the moving from place to place in connection with the official post, which he felt was difficult for him to cope with, he had left to become a monk, sticking to the Buddhist religious descipline from then on. He roamed about throughout the world and happened to pass through the god temple of Bishan. When he saw local people used a whole ox for the sacrifice, he said, "There are specifications for the rites in sacrificing to heaven and earth, and to the god of the land and grains. As the mountain god is but a spirit, how dare it enjoy the whole ox that is by right dedicated to heaven! Besides, the ox is needed for its labour to plough the land; and you use it as sacrifice. Will it not be asking too much?" Wherefore he picked up an axe and smashed several of the clay scultures. There was only one left when the monk felt tired and stopped to take a little rest. At that moment the Taoist priest who was the caretaker in charge of the temple's joss sticks and candles supplicated the monk to let it off, saying, "This god is a vegetarian." Because of his supplication, the remaining sculture was left alone.

The news of the smashing of the mountain god statues by the angry monk shocked all the military, administrative and government officials. They sent a report to the higher authorities with great dispatch. But despite the destruction of the temple god statues, no calamity had befallen the monk. Probably what the monk had done was just, and the mountain god knew it was in the wrong. For that reason, it dared not send any calamity to harm him.

501. Mai Wang

Ptime Minister Zhang of the Tang Dynasty had many children, among whom a young man. It so happened that this young man came across an item recorded in a book, which said a silverfish once bored into a Taoist classic book and ate up the word "immortal", causing its body to turn multicoloured, and becoming what people called a *Mai Wang*. The book also said that if a man caught a *Mai Wang* and ate it, that man would become an immortal. The young man was confused by it and wrote the word "immortal" on a piece of paper. After cutting it into pieces, he put them inside a bottle, into which he also brought several silverfish. He then waited for the silverfish to eat up the word "immotal" so that he could in turn eat the silverfish. He waited and waited until he finally became mentally ill, an illness which broke out intermittently. There was nothing his family could do but to lock him up.

*

*Recent Events in Southern Tang

By Zheng Wenbao (953-1013 A.D.) styled himself Zhongxian, originally from Ninghua (Fujian Province); a writer of the Song Dynasty. He was once an official in Southern Tang, one of the ten states during the Five Dynasties lasting from 937 to 975 A.D. After he switched allegiance to Song, he eventually became a councillor in the Ministry of War. He was the author of *Talking of Gardens*, twenty volumes; *Notes on Area South of the Yangtze River*, three volumes, and *Recent Events in Southern Tang*, one volume.

502. Beat the Grass to Startle the Snake

In the Tang Dynasty, there was a man who, by boast and flattery, bribed his superior into the position of Dangtu County Magistrate. The moment he assumed office, he began to bend the law, plunder people's property, extort their fat and marrow, act recklessly and receive bribes. As the county magistrate set the example, his subordinates all followed him, and bribery and malpractice for selfish ends became the order of the day. In the same county, there was an official whose job it was to take care of clerical matters, whom people called the Chief clerk. He was even more outrageous than the the rest of the bunch, and the people shunned him like poison. In time, the people's patience ran out, and a petition was signed jointly and submitted to the county magistrate to accuse him. Wang Lu read the filed plaint, and soon discovered that all the crimes enumerated were similar to his. It was as if they were accusing him. As he read on, he was so frightened that he began to shake like a leaf. He managed with an effort to steady himself. By the time he had finished reading the plaint, he did not know what to do, and it was rather baffling why he wrote down the following comment: "Although you are only beating the grass, I am already frightened like a snake."

*

*Record on Passing the Wisdom of Buddha in the Reign of Jingde

By Daoyuan, dates of birth and death unknown, an eminent monk of the Song Dynasty. He was the disciple of Shao Guo, a famous monk of Tiantai. The book dealt with the history of Buddhism as well as the biographies and works of one thousand seven hundred and one Zen masters. Recorded were also the quotations and paeans of the noted masters of other sects. Buddhists used the lamp as metaphor for Buddhist doctrine, which the Zen masters passed it on to their followers. That was what passing the lamp was about. The book was completed in the reign of emperor Zhenzong of Song Dynasty, whose title was Jingde, and that was why it was entitled *Record on Passing the Wisdon of Buddha in the Reign of Jingde*, or simply *Record on Passing the Lamp*.

503. Like a Parrot

The parrot is a bird with round head, whose eyes keep on staring at people, and a beak thick and big, similar to that of a hawk. Its feathers are beautifully coloured, its tongue soft and nimble. After being drilled repeatedly, it can imitate the human voice, as if it could speak. Formerly, there were people who let it perch on a swing hanging from the roof, and taught it to mimic the human speech, and it often said something unbefitting the occasion, making people feel embarrassed, and not knowing whether to laugh or cry.

In ancient times, there was an accomplished monk who presided over the recitation of the scriptures. As he listened and listened again, he finally gave the order to stop. The monks who were reciting asked him, "Why don't you allow us to continue?" "Because," the master monk replied, "your recitation does not have any meaning, just as the parrot, which mimic the voice of man but does not know the meaning of it. The scriptures are the vehicle through which the doctrine of Buddhism is spread. If you do not understand the meaning and only know how to recite, that is only mimicking the language of the scriptures. As far as the disciples of Buddha are concerned, this is not the right way. You have not learned the wisdom of Buddha! That is why I do not allow you to continue reciting like this."

*

*The Ouyang Wenzhong Collection
By Ouyang Xiu (1007-1072 A.D.) styled himself Yongshu, alternative name Zuiweng, a writer and historian of the Song Dynasty. In the twilight years of his life he called himself Retired Scholar Liuyi. Originally he was from Luling, Jiangxi (Ji-an). Posthumously he was bestowed the title of Wenzhong. He took part in the compilation of *The New History of Tang* and, independently, completed *The New History of the Five Dynasties* (one of *the twenty-four histories*). He was good in almost every field of literature, prose, poetry, and *ci*, a type of classical Chinese poetry, especially prose, achievement of which being the highest, and was regarded as one of *the Eight Great Men of Letters. The Ouyang Wenzhong Collection* consists of one hundred and fifty-three volumes, including poetry, *ci*, and other miscellaneous writings. The following are selected from *Go Back to the Farm*, and *Notes of Liuyi*.

504. Practice Makes Perfect

Chen Yaozi, the Duke Kangsu, was an adept in archery. There was none among his contemporaries who could compete with him, and he was rather proud of his achievement.

Once, he was doing target practice in his own garden. An old man, who was an oil-vendor, put down his shoulder pole and loads, and stood there watching him out of the corner of his eye. He did not go away for a long time. Although he had noticed Chen Kangsu hit the target eight or nine out of ten times, but he only slightly nodded his head.

"You know archery, aren't you? Isn't my skill superb?" asked Duke Kangsu.

"It's nothing so terrific. It's just that you are a practised hand," replied the old oil-vendor.

"How dare you look down upon my shooting skill?" Duke Kangsu flew into a rage.

"You can understand the reason by watching me pour the oil," the old oil-vendor said.

Thereupon the old oil-vendor took a gourd and placed it on the ground. He then fixed on the mouth of the gourd a coin with a hole in the centre. Using a dipper, he scooped out some oil and pour it into the mouth of the gourd. The oil was seen flowing into the gourd drop by drop through the hole of the coin, but not a drop touched the edge of the hole. After the display, he said, "It's nothing. It's only because I'm a pracised hand."

Duke Kangsu smiled after watching the display, and the old oil-vendor left without incident.

505. A Leather-like Face

In the early years of Northern Song, Tian Yuanjun was assigned the important post of chief official in charge of finance and revenues. From then on, descendants of the rich and powerful as well as his own clan and friends all came to him one after another, asking for favour. He was thoroughly disgusted with all these people, yet he could not refuse them to their face. He had to put up a smiling face in order to placate or please them, uttering something agaisnt his conscience to send them away.

Later, occasionally when he touched on the subject, he was full of grievances. He said, "For several years since I held the position, I had to give reception to all sorts of people, forcing myself to smile. I had done it so often that my face wrinkled and became as thick as the leather of my boots."

506. A Magic Mirror

Lu Mengzheng, prime minister of the Song Dynasty, had won the trust and favour of Emperor Taizong of Song and, for that reason, every official in the imperial court tried to fawn on him. A junior official had an antique mirror inherited from his ancesters which, according to him, could show its brightness two hundred *li* away. He intended to present the mirror to Lu Mengzheng, the idea being to attract Lu's attention to himself. He knew Lu Mengzheng was clean though, and dared not do it without careful consideration. He asked Lu Mengzheng's brother to broach the subject should there be an opportunity, and Lu Mengzheng's brother promised to do as he requested. Soon the opportunity came, and Lu told his brother Mengzheng in an unhurried manner about the antique mirror's magic power. After listening to his brother, Lu Mengzheng smiled, saying, "My face is only the size of a plate; what use is it for a mirror that can shine over two hundred *li*?" His brother dared not add another word after the remark.

507. The Bell

A asked B, saying, "A bell is casting in bronze, and a piece of timber is pared into a wooden hammer, or impactor. When the latter is used to strike at the bronze bell, it will produce the sound *clang, clang*. Do you think the sound is produced by the wood or is it by the bronze?"

B replied, "If you strike the parapet with the wooden hammer, a sound of that nature will not be forthcoming; only when it strikes at the bronze bell will it produce the sound. That is to say, the sound comes from the bronze."

A disagreed, saying, "If you use the wooden hammer to hit a heap of coins, there will not be a sound like that. Is it true the sound comes from the bronze?"

"A heap of coins is solid, whereas the bell is hollow in the center, so the sound must have come from the object with a hollow center," observed B.

"A bell made of wood or clay will not produce such sound. Can the sound really come from an object with a hollow center?" A was still sceptical.

508. All broke into a Loud Laugh

Both Feng Dao and He Nin were prime ministers during the time of the Five Dynaties. Feng Dao held the post of high official in four of the

Five Dynasties, namely, Later Tang (923-936 A.D.), Later Jin (936-946 A.D.), Later Han (947-950 A.D.) and Later Zhou (951-960 A.D.), wielding great influence. He was experienced and tactful in handling affairs. He Nin, on the other hand, had an irascible temperament and was not cool-headed enough in handling matters. According to legend, both of them were in the secretariat one day, when Feng Dao was wearing a pair of new boots. He Nin saw them and asked him, "I see, you have bought a pair of new boots. How much are your boots?" Knowing that He Nin was short-tempered, Feng Dao played a trick on him as he raised his left foot and said, "I've paid nine hundred." Noticing that Feng Dao's boots were exactly the same as his own, which was also new, he was nettled, and called the junior official who bought the boots for him and asked, "Prime Minister Feng's boots only cost nine hundred, why do I have to pay one thousand and eight hundred for mine?" Thus without thinking and making no distinction between right and wrong, he gave the junior official a good dressing-down. Sitting beside him, Feng Dao, in the meantime, did not utter a word. He waited till He Nin had finished before raising his right foot slowly and said to him, "This one also cost nine hundred." Thereupon all broke into a loud laugh.

*

*The Collected Works of Sima Wengong
By Sima Guang (1019-1086 A.D.) styled himself Junshi, originally from Sushui Village, Xia County (Shanxi Province); a writer and historian of the Song Dynasty. He rose to become the prime minister but died not long after his promotion, and was bestowed the posthumous title of Wen Zheng, the duke of Wenguo, etc. It was also the reason for the book's title, *The Collected Works of Sima Wengong*, consisting of eighty volumes, including one volume of *fu* (descriptive prose interspersed with verse), fourteen volumes of poetry, and others (different types of prose works). There were many other collections on various subjects, the most important being his monumental work on history, *Zizhitongjian*, or *Lessons in Statecraft*, the title of a 294-volume chronicle, covering a period of 1,362 years down to the Period of Five Dynasties.

509. Gathering Firewood

Sima Guang met a bunch of youths gathering firewood on the road, and they agreed on: "Whoever see the firewood and shout first can pick it up, and the persons who lag behind should not argue." All the youths promised in unison. "Agreed!" they all said. Thus they advanced happily together, cracking jokes and poking fun at one another. Suddenly they saw in front of them a twig. One of the youths forestalled the others by a shout and went forward to pick it up. At this juncture, the rest of the young men scrambled forth, and fought with wooden sticks. Soon someone was hurt.

Sima Guang saw it all. All of a sudden, he felt worried and apprehensive. Rushing back to his home in a confused state of mind, he sighed, "Alas! Compared with this small twig, there are too many things of greater importance in this world. If I am not careful and vigilant, associating myself with people on their promise and smiles when all is well, what if somebody gives a shout first and causes a fight, will no one be hurt then?"

510. The Poison of Scorpion

Yu Fu was enjoying the evening cool in the courtyard. As he laid his hand on the trunk of a tree, he was stung by a crawling scorpion. The pain had become so severe that it seemed to penetrate his heart and lungs. His family invited a witch doctor to pray, hoping somehow to relieve the pain. The witch doctor said, "First of all, you must imagine that the scorpion is not an excessively ruthless and venomous thing. Think of it as but a small worm, and look down upon it, saying to yourself, 'How can such a tiny little thing causes any pain?' and your pain will disappear."

Yu Fu followed the advice of the witch doctor and imagined that the scorpion was insignificant and powerless. After a while, he felt the pain gone. He went to thank the witch doctor, saying, "What kind of magic did you use to get rid of the poison from the tail of the scorpion? It disappeared so speedily." "In fact, the scorpion did not cause the pain," explained the witch doctor. "Your pain came from the mind which was afraid of pain in the first place. I did not use my magic arts to exorcise it. It was you who had overcome the fear of pain in your mind, and it helped to remove it. I could not bring about your pain, nor could I get rid of it. It was all determined by your own mental state."

Wherefore Yu Fu sighed with emotion, saying, "Why! Sorrows and joys, gains and losses, they all can cause pain to man, and not only the tail of a scorpion! But first of all it is the mind of man that brings it about and, for that reason, it can also be removed by eliminating it from the mind. Everything is more or less like that in this world."

511. The Food Cart

It had been raining. Yu Fu left home and saw a food cart stop on the path of a mountain slope. He pointed at the food cart and told his disciple, saying, "The food cart will soon turn turtle, It will not be long before you see it."

They were just ten steps away when there arose a hubbub. Turning their heads, they saw that the food cart had already turned over. The disciple was amazed at the accuracy of his master's prediction and said to Yu Fu, "Master, how did you know that the cart would turn over?"

Yu Fu replied, "I deduced it from the way people were accustomed to act. As it had rained, and the roads were all muddy and difficult to pass except this path at the mountain slope, where water did not accumulate and it was dry, and thus provided a place for people to aggregate. The cart owner had not taken into consideration whether it could stand the bustling, and stopped at this narrow and steep slope for such a long time. As it hindered the movement of passersby and thus was subjected to constant pushing and shoving, how could it not overturn? There are other matters of greater moment than this, which may cause calamitous consequences in parallel situation. How can incident of this nature only happen to a small food cart?"

*

Lessons in Statecraft
This was the first annalistic style in historiography in China, a masterpiece of comprehensive history. Sima Guang took charge of the compilation, and was completed during the reign of Shenzong of Song, the seventh year of Yuanfeng (1084 A.D.), after nineteen years of hard work. It recorded the history of one thousand three hundred sixty-two years from king Wei of Zhou in the Warring states Period to the sixth year of Xiande, title of Shizong of Later Zhou in the Period of Five Dynasties. It contains mainly subjects of politics and military affairs, the intention being to provide object lessons for subsequent rulers,

hence the title of the book. It is an immortal masterpiece in Chinese historical records.

512. Will You Kindly Step into the Jar?

When Wu Zetian became empress of Tang Dynasty, she appointed a bunch of cruel officials, among whom the comparatively well-known being Zhou Xing, Lai Zunchen, etc. Those people used to lodge false accusations against, and framed up, civil and military officials. Making one's hair stand on end especially was the vicious and indiscriminate way the brutal corporal punishment was applied.

During the time of Tianshou, someone accused Zou Xing, Lai Zixun, Qiu Shenji, etc., of rebellion, and Empress Wu issued a secret edict ordering Lai Junchen to catch Zhou Xing for interrogation. Lai Junchen sent a messenger to invite Zhou Xing to a banquet, during which Lai Junchen asked him for advice, saying, "If the prisoner does not confess, what method can be used to make him talk?" "That's too easy," replied Zhou Xing. "You have only to put the prisoner inside a big jar, and let charcoal fire be burnt around it. Don't you think he will not own up then?" Lai Junchen at once sent someone to get a big jar and burnt charcoal around it as Zhou Xing had suggested. As the jar became red through and through, he calmly said to Zhou Xing, "I have received a secret edict from the empress to interrogate you. Now, will you kindly step into the jar?" Zhou Xing was so frightened that sweat broke out all over his body and trickled down his back. He kowtowed and confessed at once.

Later, people used the proverb "will you kindly step into the jar" to denote "give somebody a dose of his own medicine".

*

*Random Notes at Xiang Mountain

By Wen Ying styled himself Daowen, originally from Qiantang (Hangzhou, Zhejiang Province). A famous monk of the era of Renzong of Song, his dates of birth and death, however, were unknown. He was Su Shunqin's friend in poetry, and had association also with Ouyang Xiu and others. At the time Shenzong of Song was on the throne, Wen Ying lived in the Jinluan Monastery of Jingzhou. He authored *Random*

Notes at Xiang Mountain consisting of three volumes, with one volume of continuation; *The Unofficial History of the Jade Pot,* ten volumes; and *Random Notes about Zhu Palace,* three volumes.

513. Tradition

In Meizhou, there was a man called Yang Shuxian, a department head. When he learned that the new magistrate of the prefecture had arrived to assume office, he immediately ordered the band lined up with great fanfare to play music. The leading musician made a speech, in which he said, "To repay the officials as well as the people, it is necessary to celebrate so as to remove the bane and usher in good luck."

The magistrate of the prefecture was pleased with the speech, and he asked, "Who has written the speech?" The musician replied, "This is the tradition of our prefecture, and the song is the only one!"

*

*The Collection of Master Guangling
By Wang Ling (1032-1059 A.D.) styled himself Fengyuan, originally from Guangling (Yangzhou, Jiangsu Province), a writer of the Song Dynasty. Unruly when young, later he humbled himself and studied hard. His poems were robust, exhibiting boldness of vision. Struck by his talent, Wang Anshi married him to his wife's sister, Wu Di. He came to an untimely end at the age of twenty-eight. His posthumous work *The Collection of Master Guangling* contains thirty volumes.

514. By Way of Analogy

In the city, there were ten physicians, of whom only one had high medical skill, and the other nine were more in name than in reality. The physician who had high medical skill used his superb technique to treat his patient, the other nine acted according to what the patients wished them to do. How did the physician with high medical skill cure his patient? He would say to his patient, "This illness must be treated by acupuncture; that illness will need a decoction of medicinal ingredients." The patient would complain, "Acupuncture is too painful, and decoction is too bitter. What shall I do?" The physician would say, "If you want your illness to recover, you must either undergo the acupuncture treatment or take a liquid preparation of medicinal herbs. If you are afraid of pain and bitterness, once the illness deteriorates, death will be inevitable." What would the physician who followed the desire of his patient do? He would tell the patient, "This illness must be treated by acupuncture; that illness must be handled with a dose of decoction." His patient was frightened and besought him, saying, "acupuncture is too painful. If it can be cured by a decoction, will you please change it." The physician would say, "A decoction will do just as well. Why must we insist on treating it with acupuncture?" The patient would say again, "It is too bitter to take a decoction. What must I do?" The physician would chime in, saying, "Some herbal medicine is sweet. Why should I give you a bitter decoction?" Because of the manner the nine physicians treated their patients, they were always in demand, while the one with higher qualification had no patient at all.

Later, when the high official of the city fell ill and sent his man to seek a physician with high skill in the vicinity, one of the nine was invited. After several months of treatment, however, his illness did not improve. He therefore invited another one among the nine, but his illness remained as it was before. He changed his physician five or six times without being able to achieve what the physician with high medical skill would have been able to do. The official heaved a sigh, saying, "It looks as if there is no good physician in the city. As the last one is even worse than the first, it is better to ask the first one to come again." Thereupon he invited the first physician who treated him before.

Alas! What a man! Why didn't he think more seriously? If that physician possessed good medical skill, he would have been able to cure him the first time he came, and not waited till several months thereafter. Since he could not cure him before, he would not be able to cure him now. If cure was not expected, then even though you might call him in again, what good would it do to the illness?

One day, because of his chronic disease, the high official felt extremely tired. One of his sons mentioned the physician with high medical skill, but his father said, "It is up to me to decide which physician should treat my illness. What business is it of yours to mention that physician's name?"

What a man! How could his illness get well if he behaved in this manner? He should be thankful if he was not dead.

515. Mistaken a Horse for an Ox

In the district of Dongguo, a young man who had never seen a horse in all his born days thought all domestic animals with four legs and a large body were oxen. One day, he happened to see a horse upon his arrival at the market. He was astonished and shouted, "Why is this ox so tall and strong?" People nearby burst out laughing when they heard him. As the news spread to every corner of the market, everyone derided him for his ignorance. The young man returned feeling perplexed. He asked the elders at home, and learned that the animal he saw was indeed a horse. He was ashamed of his ignorance and for three days felt depressed without uttering a word.

An old man learned of his plight and came to enlighten him. "My child," he said, "Why are you so unhappy? Have you lost something?" "No, that's not it," replied the young man. "I've msitaken a horse for an ox. Now that I know it, I am ashamed of my mistake. I've nothing to say and I don't feel like going to the market again" "Well! It's a horse alright. You have mistaken it for an ox, and that of course is your mistake. The people in the market laughed at you only on that score. Suppose we are not talking of horse but on matters other than a horse, how many people have committed msitakes in nature similar to that of calling a horse an ox. What is the difference between the mistakes people made and your calling a horse an ox? As a young man, you lack experience, and that's all. There is nothing to be ashamed of," said the old man.

*

*The Complete Works of Wang Linchuan
By Wang Anshi (1021-1086 A.D.) styled himself Jiefu. Later, at his old age, he called himself Banshan. As he had received the title "Duke of Jingguo", people also called him Wang Jinggong, or the duke of Jing. He was given the posthumous title Wen, and so was also known as Wang Wengong, or duke Wen. A native of Linchuan, Fuzhou (Jiangxi Province), he was a writer and statesman of Northern Song, and became prime minister during the reign of Shenzong. He initiated political reform; *the new deals* covering agriculture, water conservancy, loan program (under which farmers would get the government loan when they planted rice seedlings and make repayment after harvest, plus a

twenty percent interest), the neighbourhood administrative system, etc., which contributed to the development of production and the strengthening of national defence. He was one of "the Eight Great Men of Letters of the Tang and Song Dynasties", having contributed greatly in poetry and prose. His works were put together by people of later generations, which became *The Complete Works of Wang Linchuan*, or, *The Collected Works of Wang Wengong*.

516. Fang Zhongyong

Jinxi County of Jiangxi Province had a man called Fang Zhongyong. whose family were farmers for generations. Up to the age of five, Fang Zhongyong had never seen the brush, the ink stick, paper and inkstone. One day, all of a sudden, he cried asking for the brush, the ink stick, paper and instone. His father was rather surprised and borrowed them from his neighbour just to give him satisfaction. He wrote down a four-line poem, and gave a title to it. The poem had its theme centered on the support of one's parents and the unity of the clan. It was passed around and read by all the scholars in the village. From then on, when the occasion arose for the composition of a poem, he was asked to do it, and the literary grace and approach of his poem deserved applause as a rule. People of the same county were all amazed at his talent, and slowly his father was treated as a honoured guest, and someone even contributed financial support for him. His father took advantage of the situation and went with Zhongyong to visit every family in the county by turns, to the negligence of his study.

I learned of Fang Zhongyong's affair a long time ago. During the era of Mingdao (1032-1033 A.D.), I returned to my native village with my father, and there I met Fang Zhongyong at my uncle's home. He was then already twelve or thirteen years old. When asked to compose a poem, the result no longer corresponded with his reputation. Seven years later, I came back from Yangzhou and, when I again went to my uncle's home to inquire about him, they all said, "Fang Zhongyong's talent has all but disappeared; he is more or less like anybody else now."

I believed Fang Zhongyong's ability to acquire knowledge was inborn. What he had inherited was much more than he had acquired but, in the end, he was just an ordinary man like all the others, and the reason was he had not received much postnatally. People like him who had received so much innately could, because of negligence in postnatal training, become an ordinary man. Could those who were less gifted, whose natural endowments were but commonplace, catch up with the aptitude of an average man, if they were not diligent?

*

*Mengxi's Sketches and Notes
By Shen Gua (1031-1095 A.D.) styled himself Cunzhong, originally from Qiantang (Hangzhou, Zhejiang Province); a scientist of the Song Dynasty. A Han Lin scholar, he was a man of great erudition, and contributed towards a wide variety of fields: mathematics, physics, astronomy, geology, medicine, etc. He authored more than twenty books. Extant are *Mengxi's Sketches and Notes, Sushen's meritorious Prescriptions,* and *The Forever Prosperous Collection. Mengxi's Sketches and Notes* contains twenty-six volumes. In addition, there are three volumes of *Supplement to Sketches and Notes,* and one volume of *Sketches and Notes, a Continuation,* totalling thirty volumes, being his representative masterpiece. About one-third of the content is devoted to the subjects of natural sciences. It summarizes the achievement in technology during the Song Dynasty and provides important material for the technological history. In the portion covering events and people, there are occasionally fables.

517. Take Advantage of a Loophole

In Dingyuan County of Haozhou, there was an archer who wielded the spear well, and people around him all admired his skill. There was a petty thief, too, who was adept in playing with the spear and stick, and he looked down even on soldiers excelling in martial arts from the government. Only this archer was his well-matched adversary, so he said, "If I ever meet the archer, I'll fight with him to the death."

One day, the archer happened to come to the village on business while the petty thief was drinking in the country fair. It was difficult to avoid meeting each other at the time even if they had intended to, and both began to fight with knife and spear. A crowd of spectators clustered around in a tight ring as they fought and, for a long time, neither could get the upper hand. Then the archer suddenly said, "The military officer is here. Why don't we fight to the bitter end in front of the military officer?"

The petty thief replied, "Good!" And the archer responded by stabbing him, killing him immediately. This, in fact, was what we called taking advantage of loopholes!

518. Dread the Toll of Bell

When Chen Shugu was transferred from his cabinet post to the county magistracy of Pucheng City, Jianzhou, it so happened a man had lost some article, and a few suspects were arrested. The culprit, however, could not be ascertained. Chen Shugu deceived the prisoners by saying, "There is a big bell that can make out who the thief is, said to be highly efficacious."

He had the bell moved to the courtyard attached to the government office, and prepared a sacrificial offer. The suspects were then brought before the bell. "The bell will not toll if you are not the thief," he said. "However, if you are, when you touch the bell; the bell will toll."

Thereupon with great solemnity Chen Shugu led his fellow officials to pray in front of the bell. When the ceremony was over, he had a curtain hung around it, and sprayed the surface of the bell with Chinese ink. After that, he led the suspects inside the curtain where they were asked to touch the bell. When this was done, he examined all their hands, and it was discovered there was only one person whose hands had no stain of ink. This suspect eventually confessed to having stolen the article after interrogation.

The fact was, he was afraid that the bell might toll, and did not dare to touch it.

519. The Selfish Deputy

Li Shiheng was sent by the emperor to Korea as an envoy, and a military officer was assigned as his deputy. Upon their return, the country of Korea bestowed on the envoy and his deputy not a few presents. Shiheng did not care much about presents and left the handling of such matters to his deputy. As there were too many presents, they took a seagoing vessel. The deputy, afraid that his goods might be spoiled by damp if deposited at the bottom of the ship's hold, and so he had Li Shiheng's goods transported first and put them at the bilge before piling his own possessions on top.

As the vessel sailed out to sea, a storm arose, and the ship threatened to turn over. The captain of the ship was very frightened, and requested that the goods in the bilge be thrown into the sea. Failing that, he said, the overloaded vessel might capsize and endanger the lives of those on board. In a state of fear and uncertainty, the deputy ordered the cargo be abandoned. However, as they were half way through this operation, the storm had blown over, and the ship was safe. There was no longer any need to throw away the cargo on board. When an inventory was taken afterwards, it was discovered that all the things thrown into the sea were the deputy's, and those belonged to Shiheng were intact as they were at the bottom of the hold.

520. Miscalculation

Sometime in the past a man ran across a robber and they began to grapple with one another. As the knife and the spear came into contact, the robber suddenly ejected a mouthful of water, which he kept in the mouth in advance, at the man. It was so sudden that it gave the man a start, for he was afraid the water might blur his eyes. For a split second, the movement of his hands and legs bogged down. The robber took advantage of that instant to stab into his chest with the knife round his waist.

Later, a warrior happened to meet the same robber. He had heard of the robber's nasty trick and thus was well prepared for it. The robber, as they fought, stopped again to eject water from his mouth. However, as the water was being ejected, the warrior took advantage of the interval to stab him in the neck.

The robber's ejection of water was similar to the use of straw dogs by the wizard. The secret was already out. How could he still use the same trick. As a result, he was hoist with his own petard.

*

*The Complete Works of the Two Chengs
By Cheng Hao (1032-1085 A.D.) and Cheng Yi (1033-1107 A.D.), philosophers of the Song Dynasty. As they were brothers, the two names were put together and called the two Chengs. Hao styled himself Bochun, and was known as Master Mingdao; Yi styled himself Zhengshu, and was known as Master Yichuan. Both brothers studied

under Zhou Dunyi. They laid the foundation of the Confucian school of idealist philosophy in Northern Song. Apart from holding official posts for several years, they lectured in Luoyang and other places for a period of over thirty years. Their doctrine was later absorbed and inherited by Zhuxi, together they were called the "Chengzhu school" *The Complete Works of the Two Chengs* was compiled by their disciples and Zhuxi, which consists of sixty-five volumes, including quotations, collected works, dialogue on *The Book of Changes,* conversation on the classics, and so on. The fable below was selected from *the Quotations of Cheng Yi,* which appeared in the *Posthumous Papers of the Two Chengs,* under the heading *Quotations,* volume two.

521. Turn Pale at the Mere Mention of a Tiger

During the Song Dynasty, a group of farmers were hoeing the field. When they became tired, they sat down together on the ridge to chitchat, arguing about what was the most dreadful thing in the world. One said, "The ghost is the most frightful." However, no one ever saw the ghost and, although the topic of their conversation had turned to ghost, everyone looked perfectly calm. Later, a man said, "The tiger is the most terrible." He described the tiger as ferocious. When it was hungry, it would go to the village to eat domestic animals and men. He had hardly finished talking when a farmer sitting beside him was so frightened that his face turned pale and his body shivered all over with fear, as if the tiger were already there. The fact was, that farmer had once been bitten by a tiger. Although he was fortunate enough to escape death, he still had a lingering fear, and that was why he turned pale at the mere mention of the tiger.

When the great philosopher Cheng Yi heard tell of the story, he said, "The state of mind of a person with close knowledge and that of a person with general knowledge are different in their approach towards an object. The average man in the street has never seen the tiger, and so he is not afraid when the tiger is mentioned; although he knows that the tiger eats man, the conversation is regarded as a kind of general knowledge. The farmer, who has been bitten and wounded by the tiger, learned through his personal experience and knew the dreadfulness of the tiger, and that is close knowledge. That was the reason why he turned pale when the tiger was mentioned."

*The Seven Collections of Dongpo

By Su Shi (1037-1101 A.D.) styled himself Zizhan, assumed name Retired Scholar Dongpo; a writer, painter and calligrapher. Originally from Meishan of Meizhou (Sichuan Province), he was a palace graduate in the second year of Jiayou, which was the title of Renzong of the Song Dynasty, and had successively held the important positions of minister of the Ministry of Rites, Han Lin secretary, and so on. As he was at loggerheads with the prime minister, he was forced to leave the capital to become the magistrates of Hangzhou, Yingzhou, Yangzhou, etc. in succession. Later, he was further demoted and went to Lingnan and the Island of Hainan. During the reign of Huizong, he was pardoned but on his way back to the capital, he fell ill and died in Changzhou. Dongpo was brimming with literary talent, and together with his father, Su Xun, and his younger brother, Su Zhe, they were called "the three Sus", all among "the Eight Great Men of Letters of the Tang and Song Dynasties". Of the three Sus, Su Shi was the most outstanding. The style of his poetry, *ci* and prose were bold, generous and natural, having broad perspective and with a strong touch of romanticism. His works opened up a new era, with great and profound influence on the literature of later generations. *The Seven Collections of Dongpo* contains one hundred and ten volumes. The first three collections consist of his creative works: poetry, *ci*, inscriptions, odes, literary eulogies, essays, memorials to the emperor, commentaries on classics, etc. The fourth, fifth, and sixth volumes contain proclamations and petitions to the emperor, which he drafted. The seventh volume contains his political essays. As he often expressed his feelings through the things he described or painted, he had created quite a few fables, which he used as instruments to illustrate his views.

522. Analogues

In previous times, there was a man born blind. As a result, he did not know what the the sun looked like. He asked people whenever he happened to meet one. One man told him, the sun was round, like a brass plate, and to illustrate what he meant, he went to get a brass plate for the blind man to touch. The blind man stroke the brass plate which produced the sound of *clang, clang,* and he said he understood already.

One day, the blind man heard the sound of *clang, clang* from a bell nearby, and he thought the sun had come out. People told him, "It was a bell. The sun shines like a candle, although its light is very much stronger than a candle." The man produced a candle and handed it to him. He touched and fondled it, nodded his head and said he understood this time around.

A few days later, the blind man came by a *yue*, which was a musical instrument similar to a flute and, by coincidence, it was more or less the size of a candle. He was very pleased and cried out, "Ah! The sun!" Those around him could not help roaring with laughter.

The sun was too unlike the bell and the flute, but the blind man could not have known it simply because he had not seen the sun and relied only on hearsay.

523. The Cuttlefish

There was a fish called the cuttlefish, which could put out a black inky liquid and caused the water around it to become black. As it swam by the coast, it was afraid ferocious animals might attack it, and the black inky liquid was intended to help conceal itself. A seabird happened to fly over the coast and saw the colour of the water turning black. It became suspicious and looked more carefully. It was sure the cuttlefish had concealed itself in the black water and, ascertaining the position, swooped down swiftly and seized the cuttlefish with its claws. Alas! Knowing only how to conceal the body to play safe, but did not know how to eliminate the vestige of concealing from the enemy, so that the seabird, which knew the unapparent details, could avail itself of the opportunity to attack. What a pity!

524. Body Worms

A Taoist priest said, "There are three worms concealing inside everyone's stomach, which spied upon a person's privacy and recorded the mistakes he made. They waited for the propitious day when their master was fast asleep, and slipped out to calumniate against the man before the God in heaven, enumerating the mistakes the man had made, hoping that God would reward them with a good meal. The God in heaven believed them and, as punishment the man was either banished from the court, or made to fall ill, or die an untimely death.

Liuzi said, "The God in heaven is wise and just, and why should he trust and connive with such insignificant and contemptible little worms who plot a frame-up?"

525. Northerners go Underwater

There were lots of people who could go under water in the South. Ordinarily they lived at the waterside. At five, they walked about dripping wet; at ten, they could float on the water; at fifteen, they could dive under it. Could these people dive without effort? They must have acquired the technique of diving before they did. Frequent contacts with the water for fifteen years enabled them to learn the characteristics of water. For those who did not have the opportunity to even see the rivers at birth, it was natural that they would shiver when they saw a boat in their prime. That was why the courageous Northerners who learned the technique of diving from the Southerners and followed the latter's instructions to go under water would almost be certain to die of drowning in the rivers.

Those who do not learn through practice but only through abstract theory, will definitely fare no better than the Northerners who learn to dive.

526. The Frightful Appearance of Tiger

During the day, the woman left her two children on the beach to play together, while she herself went to the riverside to wash clothes. Quite unexpectedly, a tiger came down from the mountain, and the woman was so frightened that she jumped into the river to save herself. The two children, however, carried on playing to their hearts' content on the beach. The tiger stared at the two for a long time. Then, slowly, it butted against them with his head, as if hoping that the children would take fright, but the two children seemed too simple-minded to be afraid, and the tiger eventually left them alone.

I believe when a tiger is about to eat a man, it will first of all try to threaten him; if the victim is fearless, then the tiger will not be able to give free play to its awe-inspiring appearance.

527. The Shepherd's Dream

A shepherd, on his way back after putting out his herd to pasture, was in a brown study. His thought jumped from his sheep to horse, from horse to carriage, and from carriage to its canvas top. As he arrived at home, he dreamed that he was sitting in a carriage with a bow-shaped top, while on both sides of the carriage, there were bands playing musical instruments: he had already become a member of the nobility.

The gap between a shepherd and a member of the nobility was immense. For a shepherd to daydream of becoming a member of the nobility, wasn't it bizarre enough?

528. Cunning Mouse

It was nighttime, and Suzi sat resting. A mouse was gnawing at something. He banged the bed, and the noise ceased. However, it began to gnaw again after a while. He called the boy in the study to get a candle. In the candle light, he discovered an empty bag, and the squeaky sound came from inside the bag.

"Oh! The mouse must have been imprisoned inside the bag and cannot go out," he remarked.

When he opened the mouth of the bag and looked in, all was quiet. Holding high his candle, he discovered a dead mouse inside the bag.

The boy was astonished, and said, "It was gnawing at something a moment ago. How come it is dead now? What was the noise we heard just now? Could it be a ghost?"

They turned the bag inside out, and emptied the contents. Upon touching the floor, the mouse took to its heels. Even a man with nimble limbs could not have caught it.

"How odd! This is really a cunning mouse!" Suzi sighed with feeling.

529. Dismiss the Physician and Reject the Medicine

A man, who caught cold and was coughing, went to see the physician. The physician diagnosed his illness as due to noxious agents produced by various parasites; if not taken care of in time it would result in death. He was frightened and brought with him a hundred pieces of gold to pay for the treatment.

The physician then dispensed medicine for his illness, which attacked his kidneys, intestines and stomach; cauterized his body and skin by moxibustion; and forbade him from having delicacies. A month later, all kinds of diseases and ailments broke out. He ran a fever, feeling hot inside the body and chill outside, and coughed incessantly. He was gaunt and felt tired, and looked truly like a man suffered from the effect of the legendary venomous insect.

He therefore turned to another physician, who in turn diagnosed his illness as internal heat, and gave him some medicine to counter it. As a result, he kept vomiting in the morning, had diarrhea in the evening, and lost all appetite for food. He became apprehensive, and went the other way round, taking medicine to heat the system up: stalactite, bird's bill, and things like that. Soon ulcers and scabies began to appear all over his body; dizziness, too, had a hold over him. It seemed he had every description of illness now.

He switched physician again for the third time but, however he tried, his illness became graver with each passing day.

An elder in the village instructed him, saying, "This is the fault of the physician and the medicine! How can you have any ailment? The existence of man depends mainly on his vitality and constitution, which must be sustained by the food he eats, whereas you never stop taking medicine. All sorts of bitter and foul smells befuddle outside the body, and hundreds if not thousands of poisonous substances of the medicine fight against one another inside it. The result is the harming of the mainstay, and the cutting off of food as sustenance. This is the root cause of your illness! Take a step back from all these things, rest a little, dismiss the physician, reject all medicine, and eat whatever you like to eat. In this manner, your vitality will be restored, and your appetite return. I believe that's the best medicine you can have. If you take my advice, you will be cured immediately."

He followed the elder's advice and, in a month, all the ailments had disappeared completely.

*

*Dongpo's Sketchbook
Su Shi's literary sketches consist of five volumes, arranged and compiled by his descendants based on his posthumous manuscripts, hence is also entitled *Articles left by Our Forefathers Dongpo*. Its contents include travel notes, comments on historical figures, but also take up stories of ghosts and gods, celestial beings and Buddha, all of which are very meaningful and thought-provoking.

530. Dependent on Others

During the Dragon Boat Festival (the 5th day of the 5th lunar month), every family tied a bunch of Chinese mugwort together in the shape of a man, and fastened it to the lintel, as people believed it could exorcise evil spirits. But the Spring Festival couplets (pasted on the doorposts) were unhappy and excoriated it, "You are only a bunch of weeds. How dare you ride roughshod over me?" The mugwort man refuted them with lowered head, saying, "Don't be so cocky. You have only half a year's lifespan. At the end of the year, you will be ripped clean and new ones will replace you. You are already one foot in the grave. What's the use of struggling for honour?" As the Spring Festival couplets and the mugwort man entered into endless arguments, the door-god on the wooden door frowned on their quarrel, saying, "We are all lowly creatures, dependent on others to get along. Why must we vie with one another for supremacy, and get angry at trifles?"

531. Poor Scholars Talk about their Ambitions

Two shabby scholars happened to meet and each talked about his ambition.

One said, "The thing most ungratified in all my life is not to have a square meal and enough sleep. If I can realize my ambition one day, I'll definitely eat my fill. After that I'll sleep, sleep nice and happy. Then, upon waking up, I'll eat again."

The other said, "I'm quite different from you. I'll eat and eat, eat without stopping. Where can I find the time to sleep?"

532. Longevity

Three elders met, and someone asked their age.

One said, "I don't remember my age now, but I can still recall my youth when I used to be on friendly terms with Pan Gu (Creator of the universe in Chinese mythology)."

Another said, "Each time the ocean changed into a farmland, I recorded it on a chip, and by now the chips have already filled up ten houses."

The third one said, "The divine peaches I've eaten are too numerous to count. Each time I ate one, I threw the peach-stone at the foot of the Kunlun Mountain. By now, the peach-stones must have reached a height comparable with the Kunlun Mountain!"

As I see it, there is no difference at all between these three old men and the short-lived mayfly or the ephemeral fungus!

533. The Merchant of Liang

In the district of Liang, a man went to the south to do business and returned to his native place seven years later. When he was in the south, he used to eat apricot and seaweed, breathe the air of the beautiful mountains and rivers, drink the sweet spring water, and eat clean and good food. As time went on, there was kind of refreshing qualities about his whole person. Time, too, had removed the rough pimples and cysts. The skins of his face and neck seemed to have grown fairer and finer and smoother, and he looked much handsomer than he was before.

As he was tired of his wandering life and returned to his native village, he observed that he was much better-looking in figure and appearance than most people around. He felt proud and self-complacent, thinking he was head and shoulders above the others. He walked about in the streets of his village, puffed up with pride, enormously conceited about his success. In his opinion, more than ninety percent of his fellow villagers did not look as good as he. When he returned to his own house and entered his bed room, he took a closer look at his wife.

Alarmed, he shouted as he ran away from her. "What kind of a monster is this!" he said. His wife expressed her appreciation as they met, but he said, "What have I to do with you?" When she presented him with hot vegetable soup, he was angry and refused to drink. With both hands she respectfully brought him food, but he would not eat. If she wished to speak a few words with him, he would turn his face towards the wall, and sobbed intermittently. His wife therefore put on her scarf and decked herself out before going to see him again, but he spat at her face without even giving her a look. To add insult to injury, he told his wife, "How can you be compatible with me! Go to hell! Quick, go away!"

His wife felt ashamed and lowered her head. Then she lifted up her eyes and sighed, saying, "I've heard that even though a man might have riches and honour, he would not forsake his wife who shared trials and tribulations with him; that a wife who shared the husband's hard lot must never be cast aside even if he had later married a lady of the nobility. Now, only because your appearance has changed, you come home without the pimples on your face, and you have to send me away because my neck has a cyst. Ah, cyst! As a wife, it isn't my fault at all!" However, his wife was expelled from home all the same.

Three years had passed since the merchant returned. All his fellow villagers hated him for what he did. No one would want to marry him. On the other hand, as the natural environment and climate were different, his hair and blood vessel (in which the blood and *qi* circulate) likewise underwent changes; the food he ate too, modified his physique and skin, and his former rough and ugly self returned. He was now at the end of his rope and so he asked his wife to return home. From then on, he treated her as respectfully as he once did.

534. Words Between the Mouth and the Eyes

Su Dongpo suffered from ophthalmia, and someone informed him he should not eat fish and meat that were sliced into small pieces. Su Dongpo intended to adopt his suggestion, but the mouth refused to go along, saying, "I'm your mouth, and they are your eyes. Why should you treat them well, and treat me so shabbily? Why should you deny me the food because they are sick? It won't do." After listening to the mouth's complaint, Su Dongpo vacillated, and could not make up his mind for quite some time. The mouth again told the eyes, saying, "I give you my word that, in the future, if I should go dumb, I will not get in the way when you want to see!"

*

Miscellaneous Literary Sketches about Aizi
It was also entitled *The Miscellaneous Literary Sketches about Aizi of Retired Scholar Su Dongpo.* As the book was not included in *the Complete Works of Su Dongpo,* people in later generations suspected it to be a fake. However, in recent years, textual research has established that it indeed was Su Dongpo's. It is a book of literary sketches, mainly fables in content. The character *Aizi* was created by Su Dongpo. Through the activities of Aizi in the Warring States Period, Su Dongpo allegorized the realities of his contemporary world.

535. Each One is Worse Than the Other

Aizi went to the beach for a stroll, and saw people there caught quite a large quantity of marine products. He noticed a round, flat little thing with many legs crawling about. Aizi asked a local resident, "What's the name of this little thing?" "It's called swimming crab," replied the resident.

Next, he saw another small animal, also round and flat with many legs, but much smaller than the swimming crab. He asked the resident again, "What's the name of this one?" "It's called crab," replied the resident.

Lastly, he saw another small animal. In appearance, it did not seem to differ from the previous two, only it was even smaller. He asked the resident yet again, and the resident replied, "This is called amphibious crab or brackish-water crab."

Aizi learned that, although they were all having two large pincers and eight legs which walked sideways, they were three different species of crabs, each smaller than the previous one. He could not help sighing, "Why, each one is worse than the other!"

536. Same Age Next Year

Aizi was out walking along the Handan thoroughfare. He saw two old women one making way for the other. One of them asked, "How old are you?" The other replied, "Seventy." "I am sixty nine. Come next year, we will be of the same age," the one who asked said.

537. Tracker Half Price

Aizi saw a man hurrying on with his journey on foot, trying to catch a boat from Luliang (the northeast of Xuzhou, Jiangsu Province) to Pengcheng (Xuzhou). He paid the boat owner fifty coppers for the passage. The boat owner said, "The passage to Pengcheng for a passenger without luggage is one hundred coppers. You are one half short. However, if you will track the boat from here to Pengcheng, I'll exempt you from paying the other half."

538. The King of Qi Wants to Build a City

One day, as the king of Qi attended the imperial court session in the early morning, he turned to his attending officials and said, "Our country is situated among several powerful states, and we suffer from having to prepare for war every year. I am thinking of drafting a batch of able-bodied men to build a big city, beginning from the Donghai Sea (East China Sea) all the way through Taihang mountain, Huanyuan Mountain, down to Wuguan, zigzagging up and down for four thousand li. We will then be saparated from the powerful states, and the state of Qin will not be able to cast its eyes on our west. Will this not be of great advantage to us? Although the people will definitely be somewhat overworked but, we will put things right once and for all, and there won't be anymore expedition and enemy invasion after the project has been completed. When the people receive my order, will they not dance with joy and hasten to join in the construction?"

Aizi replied, "This morning there was a heavy snow. When I came here for the morning court session, I saw at the roadside a man with his body exposed to the elements and almost frozen, but still he sang to the sky. I was surprised and asked him why he did that. He said, 'The heavy snow is seasonable. I am glad people will be able to get cheap wheat next year; however, I'll be frozen to death this year.' This is like building the big city which we have been talking about. When the work on the city has been completed, Heaven knows who will be there to enjoy the perpetual peace and happiness?"

539. Gongsun Long finds his Match

Gongsun Long requested an audience with the king Wen of Zhao, thinking that he could use his eloquence to make a show of himself. He talked about the *roc* with a flying range of ninety thousand *li* and the giant who got six huge legendary turtles with his fishing hook, as he attempted to befuddle king Wen.

But the king Wen of Zhao thought otherwise as he listened to his stories. He said, "I've never seen the huge turtle in the South Sea, but why don't you let me tell you an event which happened in our state! In the district of Zhenyang, two boys, one by the name of Dongli, another called Zuobo, went to Bohai Sea together. After playing around for a while, a flock of birds known as the *roc* flew over the sky and soared above the sea. Dongli went down to the sea to catch them at once. In an instant, he caught one. Although Bohai Sea was deep, the water only came up to below his shanks. Now, where could he put the *roc* in? He turned back and looked, the scarf of Zuobo came rather handy, and he put the bird into it. Zuobo was infuriated and a fight broke out between them. The two children fought each other for a long time until they were ordered to return home by their mother, who saw what they were doing. Zuobo was still angry, and he pulled out the Taihang Mountain and threw it at Dongli. Unfortunately, it missed and hit his mother's eyes instead. As his mother's eyes were blurred by the mountain, she used her fingernail to pick it out, and flicked it towards the northwest. The Taihang Mountain was thus broken into two, the piece of rock that was flicked away was now called the Mount Heng. You must have seen events such as these also?" As Gongsun Long listened, he was on tenterhooks, dejected and despondent. As there was nothing he could do, he bowed and slipped quietly away. Hie disciples heard of the incident and said to him, "How wonderful! Master, you have always talked big, showing off yourself. Now that you have got a bitter pill to swallow, it is just as it ought to be!"

540. A Scholar in Yingqiu

In Yingqiu of the state of Qi there was a scholar. Although he had only very meagre knowledge, he liked to argue for the sake of arguing. One day, he paid Aizi a visit, and asked the latter, "Why must there always be a bell hanging from under the carriage as well as on the neck of a camel? What for?"

"Carriage and camel are both huge in size, and they are often on the road at night. In case they meet on a narrow path, it will be difficult for one to make way for the other, and that is why they have bells. It is a kind of early warning system so that the other side can prepare," Aizi replied.

"How about the pagodas? There is also a bell on top of every pagoda. Do the pagodas also walk at night and need to warn people to give way?" the scholar of Yingqiu asked again.

"You are ignorant of the nature of things, how can you compare them in this manner? Everyone knows that birds like to make their nests in high places and the droppings will make them dirty. The bell on top of the pagoda is to frighten and drive away the birds. How can you compare it with the bell on a carriage or a camel," replied Aizi.

The scholar of Yingqiu was not convinced. "The sparrow hawk and the falcon, which the hunter keeps, has also a bell each tied to its tail, is it also because there are birds that go there to make their nests?"

Aizi burst out laughing as he heard him. "It's strange! Why are you so unreasonable? The sparrow hawk and the falcon fly after their prey in the forest, and sometimes the chains on their feet may get entangled with the branches of trees, which prevents them from flying. When its wings flap, the bell will ring, and the hunter can follow the sound of the bell to rescue it. How can you have it associated with the prevention of birds making their nests on their tails?" he said.

The Yingqiu scholar, however, went on, "I've seen the funeral procession where a man guiding the hearse holds a bell in his hand as he sings, is it also because he is afraid he may get entangled with the branches of trees?"

Aizi was angry at his arguing without rhyme or reason, and he replied, "The guide at the funeral procession is leading the way for the dead. It was all because the dead man liked to argue with people for nothing when he lived that the bell was rung, just to make him a little happier."

541. Mistaking a duck for a Falcon

A man, who wished to go hunting, was in need of a falcon to assist him. He therefore went to the market to find one. Unfortunately, he did not know what a falcon looked like, and bought back a duck instead, which he mistook for a falcon.

Later, he brought his duck along to hunt and, as he saw a hare in the open country, he threw the duck into the air, thinking that it would fly and catch the hare. The duck, however, could not fly, and fell to the ground. The man picked up the duck and threw it again, and the duck fell down as before. He repeated this three or four times, and obtained the same result.

At this moment, the duck opened its mouth to speak, saying, "I'm a duck. If you kill me and eat my meat, that will be my obligation; but why don't you do so instead of throwing me here and there and let me endure all this hardship?"

The man replied, "I thought you were a falcon, which would have been able to help me catch the hare, and that was why I'd thrown you up into the air. Who would have thought you were only a duck?"

The duck stretched out its feet and produced a forced smile, saying, "Can a pair of webbed feet like these catch the hare?"

542. A Divine Animal Called *Xie Zhi*

"I've heard that in ancient times there was an animal called *xie zhi*. Can you tell me what it looked like?" The king Xuan of Qi asked Aizi.

"During the reign of Tang Yao, there was a divine animal called *xie zhi*, which knew the difference between right and wrong. It had only a single horn and lived in the palace. Any crafty and evil official, if found, would be butted to death by this beast and eaten," replied Aizi.

He added, "If there is such a divine animal in the palace today, it probably will not go about seeking food to eat anymore."

543. Decapitate the Aquatic Animals with Tails

Aizi was on board a ship. When evening arrived, he berthed it off the coast of a towering stone island. He heard as though someone was crying under the water, but then someone was talking too, so he listened.

One said, "Yesterday the Dragon King (or God of Rain) published an edict, saying: 'All aquatic animals with tails will be decapitated.' I'm a Chinese alligator, and I'm afraid that I may be decapitated. That's why I'm crying. But you are a frog, and have no tail. Why are you crying?"

He heard another one replied, "It's fortunate that I don't have any tail now, but I'm afraid the Dragon King may look into the past when I was still a tadpole!"

544. The Pleasure and Anger of the Dragon King and the Frog

Once upon a time, the Dragon King came across a frog on the beach. After greeting one another, the frog asked the Dragon King, "What does your place look like?" "The place I live in is piled up with pearls and multicoloured shells. It's a majestic and exquisite palace," the Dragon King responded. "And how about yours?" he asked in return. "In my place," replied the frog, "There are green moss and grass, and limpid spring water flowing slowly over the sparkling and crystal-clear white stone." The frog then asked the Dragon King, "What is it like when Your Majesty is pleased or angry?" "When I'm pleased," replied the Dragon King, "I'll cause the rain to fall on time to moist every living thing, so that there will be a bumper grain harvest; when I'm angry, I'll first of all raise a powerful gale Then I'll send forth thunder and lightning which shake the universe. Within a thousand *li*, there will not be a blade of grass left." He then asked the frog in return, "How about you? What is it like when you are pleased or angry?" The frog replied, "When I'm pleased, I'll enjoy the gentle breeze under the moonlight and sing, carefree and content; when I get angry, my eyes will glare at the object of my hatred, then I'll puff up my stomach until it cannot go any bigger before I stop."

545. Like Father, Like Son

In the state of Qi, there was a rich man, whose son was very stupid. One day, Aizi said to him, "Although your son looks fairly handsome, he lacks knowledge of worldly affairs. How can he manage to run a family in the future?"

The rich man was angry when he heard that, saying, "My son is very smart, and possesses a great many skills. How can you say he does not know worldly affairs?"

Aizi replied, "There is no need to test him by any other means; just ask him where does the rice he eats come from. If his answer is correct, I'll confess that I've been talking nonsense."

Thereupon the rich man summoned his son and put the question to him. His son was all smiles, and said, "How can I be ignorant of that? The rice for every meal comes from the sack."

The rich man, hearing this, was enraged, and chided his son, saying, "You are really dull in the extreme. Don't you know the rice comes from the field?"

Aizi was there at the time. After listening to the altercation, he said, "It's absolutely correct to say, like father, like son."

546. Even the Devil is Afraid of the Villain

Aizi travelled by water. On his way, he saw a temple. Although it was a small and low structure, it was nevertheless well decorated and had a solemn atmosphere. In front of the temple, there was a ditch. A man happened to pass that way and, as the water was rather deep, he could not wade across it. He turned his head and looked at the temple; then went over to move the statue of the god, put it athwart the ditch, and stepped on it, thereby getting himself to the other side. At this juncture, another man arrived. He saw the statue of the god being placed across the ditch, sighed incessantly and said, "How can one blaspheme the god so!" And he went over to help it up, used his clothes to clean away the mud which stuck to its body. Then he put it back on the pedestal, knelt and kowtowed three times before he stood up and left.

Not long after that, Aizi heard an imp in the temple said, "Your Majesty, you are the god here and receive the sacrifices people dedicated, but today you have been insulted by an ignorant man. Why don't you bring some kind of disaster on him to serve as punishment?" The devil king said, "If disaster should be meted out, then it must be brought on the second man." The imp was rather perplexed and asked, "The first man stepped on Your Majesty's body to cross the ditch, and there is no sacrilege worse than that, but you do not want disaster to befall him; the second man was pious and respectful, yet you wish him ill. Why is it so?" The king replied, "Since the first man does not believe in god, how can misfortune be brought to bear on him?"

Aizi sighed with emotion, saying, "Even the devil is afraid of the villain!"

547. Opinionated

Aizi had a penchant for hunting, enjoying the pursuit of birds and animals in the open country. He kept a courser, which was good at catching hares, and Aizi would bring it along with him whenever he went hunting. If a hare was caught, Aizi would pluck out its liver and give it to the hound, and let it eat its fill. Generally speaking, whenever a hare was caught, the hound would wag its tail, stare at Aizi, and enthusiastically wait for him to feed it with the spoils.

One day, they went out to hunt as usual, but the hares they came across were exceptionally scarce, and the hunting dog found itself pinched with hunger. Suddenly he saw two hares in the grass, and Aizi let go the falcon. Hares were cunning animals and, as they ran here and there without definite directions, the hunting dog had already caught up with them. With one vault, it pounced on its prey. However, it mistakenly bit the falcon instead. While the falcon was dead, the hares took the opportunity to run away.

Aizi hastily went over and held the falcon in his hands. He was saddened and angry. The hunting dog, however, came near and wagged its tail, enthusiastically waiting for Aizi to feed it as it was wont to do.

Aizi stared at the hunting dog and gave it a good scolding, saying, "I can't understand why you are so opinionated, thinking you are always in the right!"

548. The Wisdom of Meat-eaters

Aizi's neighbours were all uncouth persons from the state of Qi.

Aizi heard one of them say, "Like the high-ranking officials of Qi, I also am a human being, gifted with the intelligence of the three powers—heaven, earth and man. Why is it they are in possession of wisdom, but I'm not?"

Another opined, "It's because they eat meat every day, and we take only the poor men's foodstuff, and that's why we lack wisdom."

The man who raised the question said, "I've several thousand cash with me after selling the grains. Why not let us eat some meat and see the result?"

A few days later, Aizi heard another dialogue between the two men. "After eating meat for some time, I feel clear-minded and intelligent. When I have to solve problems, I feel I've the wisdom to do so. Not only do I possess wisdom, now I can also go to the heart of things," one of them said.

"I now see clearly the advantage of having the insteps pointing forward," the other man chimed in with him. "If they were to point backwards, wouldn't they be stepped on by people who follow behind?"

The other man said, "I've also discovered that it is beneficial for a man's nostrils to point downwards. If they were to point upwards, wouldn't the rainwater fall into them?"

And the two men began to extol their own wisdom.

Listening to the conversation, Aizi sighed with feeling. "Alas!" he said, "The wisdom of meat-eaters is after all only so-so!"

549. The Mouth is the Door of Misery

Aizi fell ill and ran a fever, suffering somewhat from obnubilation. In his dreamy state, he travelled to the nether world, where he saw the King of Hell holding a court trial. Several spirits carried a man in, and one of them went forward to report, saying, "When he was alive, this man often used his knowledge of people's privacy to threaten and blackmail, so that he could obtain their properties. He did it so vigorously that even a man without any blemish would have to bend his will once he was seduced and fell into the trap. There was nothing he could do but to follow his lead to do evil. To deal with such man, it would be absolutely just to put him into a caldron with boiling water, and feed it with fifty billion catties of firewood. He should be released only after he has been severely punished."

The King of Hell agreed to the proposal, and ordered the warder to implement it. The ox-headed demon was designated to carry out the order. The man asked the ox-headed demon privately, "Who are you?"

"I'm the prison officer responsible for the water in the caldron, and all matters related to the boiling of the caldron in the prison are within my jurisdiction," replied the ox-headed demon.

"If you are the prison officer, why do you wear such shabby leopard leather trousers?" the man asked again.

"There is no such leopard leather in the nether world, and only when the people in the world of the living burn it for our sake that it becomes available. As I'm not well-known in the world of the living, there are few who will burn it for me," the ox-headed demon replied.

"My uncle is a hunter, and he has plenty of leather. If Your Excellency could take pity on me, burn a little less firewood and release me, I'll certainly burn ten pieces of leather for your trousers," the man promised.

"I'll eliminate the word 'billion' to delude the spirit, and you will be able to go home very soon. You will suffer one-third less of the boiling misery," the demon of the nether world said, pleased with the man's promise.

And so the man was forked into the caldron to boil. The ox-headed demon often came over to investigate. The spirit understood that the ox-headed demon was bent on protecting the man, and it dared not order the use of high heat to boil the water. Soon it reported that the designated quantity of firewood had been fulfilled.

As the man came out of the caldron and got dressed, the ox-headed demon said to him before he left, "Don't forget the leopard leather you promised."

The man turned his head to look at the ox-headed demon, saying, "I've a poem dedicated to you here:

"Oh, you ox-headed prison officer, listen:
Only Yama can lessen the sentence given;
Reduce the firewood may not be a big offence,
But ask for leopard leather is against the law hence."

The ox-headed demon was infuriated when it heard what the man said and forked him into the caldron anew. In addition, it increased the quantity of firewood designated before, burning him until it was satisfied.

At that moment, Aizi woke up. He told his disciple, saying, "One must believe the saying, 'The mouth is the door of misery'!"

550. A Surprising Move to Transport the Bell

In the state of Qi, there were two venerable senior statesmen, who had served under several emperors, and were very learned and prestigious. They were highly respected by the people, and looked upon as the pillars of the state. One of them was the prime minister, the other the deputy prime minister. Needless to say, they took part in all affairs of the state, and helped to devise plans to solve its problems.

One day, the king of Qi issued an order to move the capital. However, the moving of a precious bell alone required the manpower of five hundred men, as it was five thousand catties in weight. At that juncture, it would be difficult for the state of Qi to mobilize so many men at so short a time. The officials concerned were unable to think of a way to accomplish it, and so they went to report to the deputy prime minister. The deputy prime minister deliberated for quite some time before he slowly expressed his opinion, saying, "What a small matter! Don't you think even a dignified deputy prime minister could not solve it?" And he issued an order to the officials concerned, saying, "Since the bell can be moved by five hundred men, I propose that it be broken into five hundred equal pieces. With only one man, the job will be completed in five hundred days." The officials designated for the work was very pleased at the solution.

Aizi witnessed the event at that time, and he said, "The prime minister's move was wonderful and, of course, none could have thought of it. However, after the bell has been transported to its destination, how much more manpower is required to have it successfully recast!"

*

*A Man of Letters Wielding his Trenchant Pen

By Peng Cheng. The dates of birth and death of Peng Cheng was unknown. However, it was certain he lived during the reign of emperor Zhezong. A writer of Northern Song Dynasty, he authored *A Man of Letters Wielding his Trenchant Pen,* ten volumes, with another ten volumes of *Sequel,* which made up his main works. It contains the anecdotes of the Song Dynasty, and commentaries on poetry and essays, with a smattering of fables here and there.

551. Idolatry

During the Song Dynasty, there was a man called Peng Yuancai. He was a hanger-on of the wealthy and the powerful. On one occasion, he happened to see the portrait of Fan Zhongyan. Being pleasantly surprised, he went forward to do obeisance, saying, "I'm a commoner, Peng of Xinchang County. It's my pleasure today to be able to call and pay my respects." Having performed the ceremony to show his admiration, he looked at the portait for a while and said, "He who has outstanding moral integrity must also have outstanding appearance." Then he took a mirror to look at himself and compare it with the portrait. He stroked his beard and commented, "It looks roughly similar, only that I do not have the few sticks of hair which are inside the revered

Fan Wenzheng's earholes, but that doesn't matter very much. In a few years' time, when I become older, the hair will grow inside my earholes too."

Later, he went sightseeing in Lushan's Peaceful Taoist Temple. He discovered a portrait of Di Renjie, a prime minister of Tang Dynasty. The appearance of Di showed power and grandeur, with his two eyebrows tilted towards the earlocks. He again stepped forward to kowtow, saying, "Peng, a palace graduate, has come to pay his respects." After the greeting, he looked at the portrait for a long time before he discovered that the eyebrows of Di Renjie tilted upwards and were pointing to his temples, whereas his were pointing downwards. He went to see the barber, therefore, asking him to shave away the lower corners of his eyebrows, so that the ends tapering away as if they were pointing towards the temples. When he returned, his family saw his strange looks, and thought it extremely ludicrous.

Yuancai was enraged by their criticism, however, saying, "What's so funny? Some time ago I saw the revered Fan Wenzheng, and hated my not growing hair inside my earholes. Now I saw the revered Di Liang, and dared not spare my eyebrows. There is nothing so funny about all this. The earholes without hair are inborn, which cannot be corrected by any human effort; whereas removing the hair to alter the shape of the eyebrows is humanly possible. A man of noble character should cultivate himself in regard to human affairs and follow the mandate of heaven, why do you think they are ridiculous? I've tried all my life to revive the ancient moral standard and code of ethics, but unfortunately I am not understood by the others. This is what I refer to as sorrowful for being unable to live with the ancients, and sighing that my proposition to revive the old customs and traditions was difficult to realize."

*

*Random Notes in the Governor's Office
By Bi Zhongxun, dates of birth and death unavailable. During the time of Yuanfeng, he was a judge in Lanzhou (Lan County, Shanxi Province). Based on what he saw there, he recorded the events that were weird and interesting, and compiled them into the book *Random Notes in the Governor's Office,* which contains ten volumes.

552. A Horse that Carries Three Thousand *dan*

To safeguard border construction need, the government erected a law, stipulating that anyone contributed three thousand *hu* (*hu*, a dry measure used in former times, originally equal to ten *dou* later five *dou*) of corn could be designated the official rank of TA, or teaching assistant in the administrative division.

A scholar by the surname of Wang from Qishan contributed three thousand *hu* of corn and obtained the official rank of TA. He also bought a fine horse at high price, though he was dissatisfied with the purchase and felt unhappy whenever he thought of it. On one occasion, as he rode the horse across the busy marketplace, Lisheng, the physician with a touch of humour, intercepted and made fun of him as he asked, "How much is your new horse?"

"One hundred fifty thousand cash," Wang replied.

Lisheng praised the horse to the skies for being so "sturdy".

Wang was astonished, and asked him how did he know.

Lisheng replied, "Since the horse could carry three thousand *dan* (*150,000* kilograms) of grain, how can you say it is not sturdy?"

553. "Colleagues"

A certain man surnamed Wang of the Imperial College, who once held the rank of learned scholar, was sent to Fufeng, Shaanxi to be a county magistrate. There a rich man, who had contributed a rather large quantity of grains to the government, was designated an official title in accordance with established practice. This person called Li tried hard to get closer to the man called Wang, calling him "colleague". Wang, however, was displeased for being so addressed and called him to account, saying, "I came from the imperial court, where I was an official, whereas your official rank derived from the contribution of grains. In status, we are entirely different. How can you call me your colleague?"

The man called Li calmly and shamelessly replied, "I know, sir, that you came from the Imperial College where you held the rank of learned scholar, which rank can be abbreviated and called *guobo* in short; as for me, I've contributed a lot of grains and obtained an official rank, which can be called simply as *gubo* (*gu* in Chinese meaning grains; *guo* meaning Imperial College). Since *gu* and *guo* are homophonic, are we not colleagues?"

*

The Collection of Retired Scholar Houshan
By Chen Shidao (1053-1101 A.D.) styled himself Luchang, alternative name Wuyi, assumed name Retired Scholar Houshan, originally from Pengcheng (Xuzhou, Jiangsu Province); a poet of Northern Song Dynasty. Once a student of Zeng Gong, later he became a follower of Su Shi. He was frustrated throughout his life, and died of poverty and cold in his old age. Author of *The Collection of Retired Scholar Houshan.*

554. The Brown Bear

In Shanxi, people went to hunt with their dogs, and very often used five dogs to pursue a brown bear. The brown bear had a huge body, and was ferocious and powerful. It was, moreover, adept in giving full play to its advantage as a powerful animal. The hunting dogs were comparatively weak in strength but was nimble and could act swiftly. When the brown bear pounced on the left, the dog would spring to the right. When the brown bear jumped forward with its claws, the hunting dog would scurry off to its back. Thus provoked, the brown bear had to turn now left and now right, yet never succeeded in catching the dog. Constant turning and fighting soon took its toll. The brown bear with its huge body became exhausted at a distance less than tens of *li* and had to prostrate itself, panting. At this juncture, all the hunting dogs rush forward together and bit the brown bear to death.

*

The Chicken Ribs Collection
By Chao Buzhi (1053-1110 A.D.) styled himself Wujiu, assumed name Gui Laizi, originally from Juye, Shantung Province; a writer of Northern Song. He was regarded highly by Su Shi, being called one of "the Four Scholars of the Su School". *The Chicken Ribs Collection* contains seventy volumes, including poetry, *ci*, and six hundred and ninety-

three essays. In fact, it was his complete works. A few fables were found here and there.

555. Crows

Crows were very smart and cunning birds; ever on the watch for changes in the voice and facial expression of man. They were so vigilant that every detail could not escape their eyes as it served as a warning for them to fly away. That was why it would not be possible to shoot a crow with the catapult. In the central Shaanxi plain, the people knew the cunningness of the crows very well, and they knew too that to catch them, some ingenious scheme must be devised. They carried cakes to the graveyard, spread them out as if holding a memorial ceremony for the dead, and pretended to cry. After the burning of the paper money offering, they would leave the cakes behind. The crows would then come and contend for the cakes. When the cakes were eaten, the people had already moved to another grave site to carry out the same performance. Despite their cunning, the crows had already eaten one meal without any incident and become complacent. They were no longer suspicious, and flocked over crowing for the cakes. Thus, after three or four meals, they relaxed their vigilance, and began to follow the worshippers closely. They came ever closer, forgetting that they were nearer and nearer to the trap set for them. At this juncture, the men suddenly cast the net and, at one fell swoop, caught not a few of the crows.

Nowadays, people in the world are apt to think they have intelligence and resources enough to protect themselves many times over, yet they do not know that disaster is just lurking around the corner. How many can escape the trap of sham crying and betrayal?

*

The Literary Circles of the Tang Dynasty
By Wang Dang, dates of birth and death not available. He probably lived during the last years of Daguan, title of Huizong of Song. Styled himself Zhengfu, he was originally from Chang-an (Xi-an, Shaanxi Province). *The Literary Circles of Tang Dynasty* was compiled from selections of over fifty categories of Tang novels, imitating *New Version of Old Tales,* and classified them into fifty-two headings. It recorded

anecdotes of the Tang Society. The original book was incomplete. The extant one was compiled in the Qin Dynasty.

556. The Tiger Pays a Debt of Gratitude

Once upon a time, while an old woman was walking on a mountain road, she saw an animal, which looked like a tiger. It was bodily weak, and walked on very slowly. It did not come near her, but apppeared as if one of its paws had been wounded. The old woman plucked up her courage and came near, and the tiger raised one of its front paws to let her see. The old woman saw a thorn in its paw, and helped pull it out. After a few moments, the tiger gave out several roars and took leave of the old woman, as if to tell her that it was ashamed not to be able to repay her kindness.

As the old woman returned home, everyday beginning the following day, she discovered all kinds of animals such as elk, deer, fox, and hare thrown from the other side of the wall into her courtyard without interruption. The old woman ascended the wall, and saw it was the tiger she once helped, and she related the whole story to all her neighbours and friends, including people of her own clan, as she was surprised at what happened.

One day, a badly mutilated dead human body was thrown in, and the old woman was seized by the bullies of the village, who accused her of killing people. It was only after the old woman explained to them what had happened that she was released. She then climbed up the wall again to wait for the tiger. When it finally arrived, she said, "Although you had come to thank me, but I beg you not to throw dead body into my home from now on. May I kowtow to you, O king of the forest!"

557. The Cobbler and the Craftsman

A cobbler's family and a craftsman of musical instruments were neighbours. The cobbler's mother had not yet been encoffined after her death, and the whole family was in a state of deep grief. Their next door neighbour, the crasftsman, however, continued to repair musical instruments, and the noise the instruments made never stopped. The cobbler was very angry at heart, and his quarrel with the craftsman led to a law suit. The craftsman, in defence of his position, said,

"Repairing musical instruments is the profession whereby I earn my living; if I stop doing it, I'll have lost the wherewithal to feed and clothe myself." Having heard the explanation of the accused, the official in charge of the case pronounced the following verdict: "Repairing musical instruments is his profession and cannot be interrupted because your family has funeral arrangements. In the future, when there are funeral arrangements in the craftsman's home, you too will not be asked to stop repairing shoes."

558. The Mouth, the Nose, the Eyes and the Eyebrows

The mouth and the nose were arguing about who was more important and meritorious. The mouth boasted, "I can talk about the right and wrong from ancient to modern times, what ability do you have to surpass me?" The nose answered back sarcastically, saying, "Without me the sweet smell of food will not be known." The eyes interrupted them by saying, "I can distinguish things as minute as hair that are near, and objects as vast as heaven and earth which are distant, and so I'm the only one head and shoulders above you all." He looked at the eyebrows and added, "What contributions do you have that can lift you above me?" The eyebrows were fully at ease, saying, "It's true I do not play a decisive role. But, as there are guests in this world which only keep our master busy with no apparent benefit. Without which, however, there will be no traditional rites of welcome and send-off. By the same token, what do you think the face of man will look like without eyebrows?"

*

Dao Shan's Straight Talk
No author's name was assigned to the works. It is a one-volume book, which contains one hundred and thirty-four items, all about events happened in Northern Song Dynasty up to the fifth year of Chongning, which was the title of emperor Huizong of Song (1102-1106 A.D.). The book must have been completed after this date.

559. Ancient Books in Exchange for Bronze Ware

A scholar spent all his money, which amounted to more than one hundred thousand cash, to buy books, and brought those books to the city to sell. He was halfway from his destination when he met another scholar. The latter looked over the titles of the books and fell in love with them, but he had no money to buy them. This man possessed a lot of bronze ware at home, which he planned to sell and used the money to buy the books. Incidentally, the scholar who wanted to sell his books had a long-standing addiction to bronze ware, and was fascinated by the bronze ware the moment he saw them. Thus, he was overjoyed and said, "You need not sell the bronze ware. Let us have them both appraised and exchange one for the other directly."

Thereupon the scholar gave all the books he had in exchange for tens of bronze objects.

Swiftly, he returned home. His wife was amazed by his sudden return, and went to see his luggage. There were two or three pieces of luggage, all bulged with goods, rattling as they were moved. After finding out the real situation, she scolded her husband severely, saying, "As you have exchanged the books for the bronze ware, when are we going to get rice for our meals?"

"He has got my books, so I don't know when can he get his meals either!" her husband replied.

560. Lifelike Painting

Long, long ago, a certain man requested the painter to paint his portrait. After the painting was completed, he thought it did not look like himself, so he asked the painter to paint another one. He was not satisfied with the second attempt either, and the painter had to do it again for the third and fourth time. Finally, the painter was angry and said, "If it is too lifelike, it will be too ugly to look at!"

*

Night Chat in a Secluded Study
By Huihong (1071-1128 A.D.), otherwise known as Dehong, surnamed Peng, though others claimed it was Yu. A high-ranking monk of the Song Dynasty and a poet, he was originally from Yifeng, Jiangxi Province. *Night Chat in a Secluded Study* contains ten volumes, the content of which deals with poets and poetry, and miscellanies, but is thought to be mostly weird and absurd Some, in fact, are fables.

561. Twaddle of an Idiot's Daydream

During the reign of emperor Gaozong of Tang Dynasty, a monk was often seen roaming between the Yangtze River and the Huai River. His action was so unusual that many people thought it weird. Yet, despite his being seen so often, nobody actually knew his name, nor where was he from. On one occasion, someone asked the monk, "What's your surname?" The monk replied casually, "Surname what." The man asked again, "From what country?" The monk replied as casually as before, "Country what." During the reign of the emperor Xuanzong of Tang, Li Yong, who had once held the post of prefectural magistrate of the North Sea, and who wrote very good tablet inscription and calligraphy, had wanted to write a tablet inscription for the monk. He did not understand that the monk was just jesting and wrote down word by word in accordance with what he said, "The Great Master, surnamed what, and a native of what." During the Song Dynasty, Huihong, a high-ranking monk, recorded the event in *Night Chat in a Secluded Study* and, in this connexion, commented on the inscription of Li Yong, "It is indeed but twaddle of an idiot's daydream."

562. The Crane Spoils the Way of Nature

Liu Yuancai had a penchant for pompous and impracticable matter, and loved the weird and uncanny. He once kept two cranes in his house. Whenever there was guest, he would point at the cranes and brag, "These are divine birds! Everyone knows all birds were oviparous, but these divine birds are viviparous."

He had scarcely finished saying when the gardener came in to report, saying, "The crane has laid an egg last night as big as a pear!"

Liu Yuancai was so abashed that he blushed with shame. He scolded the gardener, "How dare you vilify the divine crane!"

Finally, they all went to see what happened. The crane spread its legs and lay prostrate on the ground. Liu Yuancai was astonished and used his cane to frighten it so that it would stand up. At that very moment, the crane laid another egg.

Liu Yuancai heaved a deep sigh, saying, "Alas, even the divine crane violates the moral teachings of the Way!"

563. Prime Minister Zhang's Script Type of Calligraphy

Prime Minister Zhang loved the script type of Calligraphy, but he did not understand the rules. His contemporaries jeered at him, but he remained the same old self and acted as if nothing had happened.

One day, some quotable quotes came his way. He took up his brush and dashed off. All over the paper, only the swift movement of calligraphy was apparent. Having finished writing, he summoned his nephew and asked him to copy the quotable quotes. His nephew did as he was ordered until he came to the indistinguishable right-falling stroke (in Chinese character) and turning stroke, which baffled him. He put down his brush and brought the paper to the prime minister and asked him, "What character is this?"

The prime minister stared at it for a long time, but he could not recognize it either. Still, he blamed his nephew, saying, "Why didn't you come before? It's all your fault, as by now I've already forgotten."

*

*Reading at Leisure in a Secluded Study
By Fan Zhengmin styled himself Dunweng, dates of birth and death unavailable. He lived in the last years of Northern Song Dynasty, and had held the post of county magistrate in Zhouchangxi at one time. The book *Reading at Leisure in a Secluded Study* contained fourteen volumes, but the original had been lost. Some items were found in volume forty-seven of the reference book compiled by Zeng Zao of Southern Song Dynasty. The reference book was completed in the sixth year (1136 A.D.) of Shaoxing, which was the title of emperor Gaozong of Southern Song. Therefore, the carving copy of *Reading at Leisure in a Secluded Study* must have been in circulation before this date. Several items copied from *Reading at Leisure in a Secluded Study* were also found in volume thirty-two of the book *Talking of the Outer City* compiled by Tao Zongyi in the early years of Ming Dynasty.

564. A Matter of Verbal Parallelism

Li Tingyan wrote a poem with one hundred rhyme schemes and presented it to a superior official. In the poem, there was two lines which read:

As my younger brother died south of the river,

My elder brother departed beyond the Great Wall.

After reading the poem, his superior was deeply grieved and said to him, "I simply couldn't believe that your family should be so unlucky as to meet with such inauspicious calamity!"

Li Tingyan stood up at once and explained it away, saying, "Actually such events had never happened. It was so written simply because I wished to take care of the verbal parallelism (antithesis)."

565. Shun the Character "Luo"

A licentiate whose name was Liu Mian had, by disposition, not a few superstitious taboos. Each time the provincial examination took place, he would avoid the character *luo*, meaning *fail* or *fall* in Chinese. His fellow candidates, whoever dared mention the word *luo*, would run the risk of incurring his displeasure, as it would, by association, remind him of his taboo *luodi*, meaning *fail in the imperial examination* and, because of that, he would become flushed with indignation, and have no qualms about using offensive language. If the offender was his servant, that would mean indiscriminate whipping, and so the latter eventually invented a way to get around such embarrassment. His servant would, for example, use *an-kang* (good health) instead of *an-luo* (peace and happiness) to avoid the character *luo*.

One day, all of a sudden, the result of the examination was published, and he hastily sent his servant to see the bulletin. After a while, the servant returned, and Liu Mian stepped forward to meet him and asked, "Have I succeeded?"

"My dear licentiate, you have *kanged*!" the servant replied at once.

Old Stories of Quwei
By Zhu Bian (?-1154 A.D.) styled himself Shaozhang, originally from Wuyuan, Huizhou (Jiangxi Province). He entered the Imperial College at the age of twenty. At the early years of Jianyan, which was the title of emperor Gaozong of Song Dynasty, suggestion had been made to send someone to the Jin Dynasty (1115-1234 A.D.) to pay respects to the two emperors Hui and Qin, who were being kept as prisoners, and Bian offered himself. He showed unyielding heroism, and was released only when peace negotiations were completed. He should have been promoted several grades, but was thwarted by Qin Hui, and soon died. He authored several books, among them *Old Stories of Quwei*. The following was from Su Shi's article entitled *An Account in Dongpo's Own Words as Fancy Dictates* copied by Zhu Bian As it was not found in *the Complete Works of Dongpo*, it was therefore included in *Old Tales of Quwei*, being the earliest source.

566. Accessible from All Directions

A basin of water toppled over, and a small grass floated on it. An ant was stranded on the grass, feeling perplexed, not knowing how to ferry across the water.

A few moments later, the water dried up, and the ant crawled out immediately. As it met the other ants, it cried out, saying, "I almost could not see you guys anymore!"

How could the little ants have known that, in so short a time, there would be roads that would allow two cars to go side by side, and be accessible from all directions? Come to think of it, this is really amusing.

*

Selected Works of Qianyan
By Xiao Dezao styled himself Dongfu, assumed name Old Man Qianyan; dates of birth and death unknown. He was a poet in the early years of Southern Song Dynasty. A palace graduate during the period of Shaoxing, he had once held the post of county magistrate in Wucheng.

He was the tutor of Jiang Kui, a famous poet of Southern Song. He authored the *Selected Works of Qianyan*, which contained seven volumes. There were three additional volumes to the original, and four volumes of *Continuation*. All were lost, however. The following is taken from *Tales of the Departing Guests* by Zhao Yushi.

567. A Runner in the *Yamen* of Wu Prefecture

The people of the prefecture of Wu (Suzhou, Jiangsu Province) were known for their stupidity, and the people of Southern Lanling (Changzhou, Jiangsu Province) had composed a fable to deride them.

In the upper reaches of Huaihe River there was a monk, who lived in the Wu Prefecture. He went to the market to drink everyday. After having a drop too much, he suffered from temporary mental disorder, and would roll up his shirt sleeves and shake his fist at the passersby, which caused people to avoid him like the plague. The runner responsible for the place's public order reported the matter to the official concerned, and an order was issued for his arrest. Eventually he was handcuffed and imprisoned. When the process of documentation was complete, the monk was sent back to his native place, escorted by the runner.

On the way, the runner scolded the monk incessantly, saying, "You crazy bald pate! Thanks to you, I've to trek hundreds of *li* and endure the hardship of an unprofitable job. I must make you suffer for it!" He kicked at the monk to wake him up before dawn every morning, urging him to start off, and shaking the birch in his hand, threatening to hit him. He would hurry the monk on, not allowing him to rest; at night, he tied up the feet of the monk to prevent him from escaping.

That day, they arrived at the town of Benniu Pond (West of Changzhou, Jiangsu Province). The monk shelled out some money and bought wine to entertain the runner. By night, the runner was dead drunk, and the monk took out his knife to shave the runner's head. He took off his own convict's uniform and put it on the runner. In addition, he handcuffed and tied the runner's feet. After all was done, he knocked down a corner of the wall and escaped.

The next day, when he had recovered from the effects of the wine, the runner found there was nobody within sight. Turning his head, he saw the fallen wall and exclaimed, "Alas! The monk has escaped!" He looked at his clothes, they were the convict's uniform, and he was even more surprised to find his head shaved, his hands cuffed and his feet bound. He was unable to move freely, and had to shout for the people in the inn, saying, "The crazy monk is still here, but I've disappeared!"

Passersby used to relate this story whenever they met the people of Wu prefecture, and the latter laughed heartily when they heard it.

Old Man Qianyan said, "The story is not just a fable. I 'm afraid the runner was not the only one who had lost his true features."

*

*Notes and Data by the Only Man Awake
By Zeng Minxing (?-1175 A.D.) styled himself Dachen. He called himself Retired Scholar Floating Cloud, alternatively the Only Taoist Awake, or the Foolish Old Man Reverted to Type. He was originally from Jishui, Jiangxi Province. At twenty, he was disabled and no longer eligible for an official career, so he concentrated all his effort on learning. He authored *Notes and Data by the Only Man Awake*, which was compiled by his son San Ping into ten volumes. The book mainly recorded the anecdotes of the two Songs, supplementing what was left out by the official history. There was tittle-tattle too that served to widen one's horizon.

568. Where Does the Rice Come From?

Cai Jing, who was the prime minister during the reign of emperor Huizong, Song Dynasty, was a well-known treacherous court official. He was very rich, and all his grandsons enjoyed wealth and honour, not knowing the hardship of growing crops.

One day, Cai Jing, while having meal at the same table with several of his grandsons, asked, "You eat rice everyday. Now, can you tell me where does the rice come from?"

"From the mortar," one of his grandsons immediately responded. It turned out he had seen the workers use the stone mortar to pound the rice, and his knowledge derived from the observation. Cai Jing laughed heartily when he heard the reply.

By his side was another grandson. "No, it's not correct," he said. "I've seen rice coming from inside the cattail mat!" At that time, rice was put into the cattail bag to facilitate transportation, and it provided him with the inspiration.

*

On the Intellect of the East
By Zhu Dunru styled himself Xizhen, a writer of *ci* (a type of classical Chinese poetry). He was originally from Luoyang, Henan Province. In the early years of his career, he professed to be above politics and worldly considerations, and forsook official position to become a recluse. After going south of the Five Ridges, he lived here and there with no permanent home. In the second year of Shaoxing, which was the title of emperor Gaozong of Song Dynasty, through someone's introduction, he was bestowed the title of palace graduate, and began his career as an official. He was the author of *A Woodcutter's Songs*, which described the life of a recluse. *On the Intellect of the East* was taken from *Tales of the Departing Guests* written by Zhao Yushi.

569. The Intellect of the East

A man in the east called himself "the intellect"; this man possessed literary talent somewhat above the average. In the depth of his heart, he was as proud as Lucifer. He looked down upon everyone, from the sages and celebrities in days of yore to the high-officials and elders among his contemporaries. Very often he would point out their failings, criticized and ridiculed them. Unfortunately, he had very little landed property at home, and he was not a management wizard either, and so inevitably he had to suffer hunger and cold during the course of an otherwise normal year.

In his village, there was a rich and powerful family, who owned rows of houses, and was regarded as the richest man in the locality. In his house, there were carriages, horses, maids and servants, bells and drums, musical instruments, curtains and draperies, and all sorts of furnishings,—you name it, he had it. One day, the richest man invited the intellect to his house and said to him, "I'm travelling to a distant place for pleasure, and you can live in my house while I'm away. There are complete sets of gold and silver utensils inside the house which you can use without having to pay for them for one year. When I return by that time, you can give them back to me, and that's all."

Having said that, the rich man left in a carriage. The intellect walked slowly with a cane and entered the big house. All the slave girls and servants, singing girls and concubines, came out to meet their new master, kneeling down all over the floor in the great hall. The intellect let them continue their work according to the personnel roster, provided they obeyed orders. The servants referred to him as their "temporary master". The intellect took a tour of all the buildings and rooms in the house, and thought they were no less impressive-looking than the palaces of the kings and marquises; and he felt very happy.

Suddenly, he felt the call of nature, and he went to the lavatory at the eastern side to relieve himself. He looked up and found the lavatory to be small and low, while the ground was depressed and uneven, and he felt rather uncomfortable. He called in the housekeeper, saying, "The house is large and majestic, but the lavatory does not quite match the splendour." The servant said, "Please issue your instructions as to what modifications are required."

The intellect therefore ordered the lavatory demolished and reconstruction be carried out, enlarging the places that are small and narrow, raising the ground where it is too low, and generally made improvements to protect against cold and heat, rain and wind. He had the beams and joists meticulously decorated with coloured patterns, and the porch columns all painted vermilion. As to the articles which were necessary for the lavatory, such as tissue paper, stove ashes, tools for the elimination of flies and maggots, a set of rules had been set up. If some decision in the morning was found to be impractical, it would be rescinded in the evening. In his pursuit for perfection, the intellect sometimes picked up the broom and the axe himself and worked together with the servants, so that his hands and feet became callused, his hair dishevelled, his complexion turned dark, and his meals forgotten, but he still worried about the lavatory being constructed not to his satisfaction. Soon, the one year deadline was approaching. The lavatory was not yet completed, however.

Unexpectedly, the gatekeeper came in to announce, "The master has returned!" The intellect threw away his broom upon the news, and went in front of the main hall to welcome the rich and powerful man. The rich and powerful man extended his regard to the intellect, saying, "Has the stay in my house been a happy one, sir?" The intellect felt as if he had lost something upon hearing this, saying, "Since you left, I've been busy with the construction of the lavatory. I've not been able to appreciate the warmth and abundance of the hall, nor have I known the quietness and pleasant cool of the other mansions. As to the gentle breeze of the waterside pavilion to the north and the moonlight from the balcony of the tower to the south, the luxuriant bamboos and the gorgeous flowers in the two gardens, I've not yet had the opportunity to enjoy. And I've not gone to the backyard, where the singing girls play the musical instruments and dance, to watch and drink. The twenty-five-stringed plucked instrument is already covered with cobweb, and the bell, tripod and autiques on the table, too, were shrouded in dust. I've not realized it was already one year. Since you have come back, I should now leave."

The rich and powerful man walked him to the gate, and bowed to say good-bye. The intellect returned to his own shabby old house, sad and unhappy. Being downhearted, he died soon thereafter.

At the southern end of the marketplace, there lived a man called Yi Liao. He thought it ridiculous when he learned of the event and told the Foolish Old Man in the Northern Mountain. The Foolish Old Man commented, "What is there to laugh about! In this world of ours, there are lots of people who only know how to engage in the construction of lavatories, but never understand issues that are important and urgent. There is really nothing to laugh at!"

*

Sketches Penned in an Old Cottage Study
By Lu You (1125-1210 A.D.) styled himself Wuguan, originally from Shanyin, Yuezhou (Shaoxing, Zhejiang Province). He was born at a time when the country was on the brink of being annihilated, and he wandered with his family from place to place while he was still in the swaddling clothes. Thus the spirit of patriotism had been fostered even at a tender age. As he grew up, he strongly advocated resistance to the Jin Dynasty. During the reign of Xiaozong, he was bestowed the title of

palace graduate, and had successively held the posts of assistant prefectural magistrate in Zhengjiang, Longxing, Kuizhou, and so on. As his lofty asperation to resist the Jin Dynasty was difficult to realize and, moreover, he was never allocated an important position by the capitulatonist clique, he had lived in seclusion in the countryside for over twenty years. During his lifetime, he wrote over nine thousand poems, mainly on the subjects of his political asperations and passionate patriotism. His style was forceful, bold and unrestrained. He enjoyed quite a reputation in his lifetime, and was honoured as the number one poet of Southern Song Dynasty by later generations. Despite his old age, he persisted in learning, and that was why he called the place he lived as *an old cottage study*. *Sketches Penned in an Old Cottage Study* was his main works in his remaining years, the content of which centred on anecdotes of current affairs and the institutions, with some textual research on poetry and essays as well as folktales.

570. The Governor May Commit Arson with Impunity

As Tian Deng, the new Chief magistrate, assumed office, the clerks and *yamen* runners under him often had to endure angry cursing and corporal punishment. As time progressed, people learned that the new chief magistrate had a superstitious fear of people using homophones of his name to write official documents and in conversation. Because of the taboo, the people of the whole district were wary about their word and behaviour, for they might violate the taboo, and so the character "fire" was used whenever "lamp" (the magistrate's name *deng* was a homophone of *lamp, lantern*) was actually meant.

It was the Lantern festival (the fifteenth of the first moon) that year. Previously, the district government used to issue a notice during such occasion that "in the Lantern Festival, there will be an exhibition of lanterns for three days, and people will be allowed to enter the government building to watch and enjoy". That year, however, the notice no longer followed the tradition; instead, it was written in this way, that "according to tradition, the district will have fire lighted for three days". As the official notice was published, there were widespread comments in the street corner.

People used the saying "The magistrates were allowed to burn down houses, while the common people were forbidden even to light lamps" to taunt and expose such savage, unreasonable, despotic and notorious conduct.

571. The Magistrate Called the General Names

During the period of Longxing, which was the title of emperor Xiaozong of Song Dynasty, there was a commanding general, who happened to be the emperor's relative. On one occasion, he told the guests in a banquet, saying, "As the saying goes, 'One's family has to be in the officialdom for three generations ere he learns how to eat and clothe himself.' You may say I've learned all. I intend to write a book to introduce the clothing, the hat and culinary art. I've not yet decided what the title should be, however." The assistant prefectural magistrate, Xian Yuguang, a Sichuan native, was present at that time, and he remarked, "You have just begin your career and are in the course of performing meritorious deeds, and time is what you do not have at the moment. Only when you have achieved success and won recognition will you have leisure to complete this book. It may be wise to give a title to the book though, and call it *The Living at Ease Collection*." The commanding general, however, did not understand the true meaning of his words.

A certain Niu Qianpang, who escaped via the capital's eastern corridor and returned to the Southern Dynasty as an official, and who spoke with a Shandong accent, interposed when he heard the assistant prefectural magistrate, Xian Yuguang, "Anfu, don't listen to him. The assistant prefectural magistrate is calling you names. His true meaning is that you spend your day in food and drink and have an empty head, that you only know how to put on your clothes and eat your fill, enjoying leisure without attending to government affairs. Doesn't it make you look like birds and beasts? What kind of language is this!" When he learned this, the commanding general flushed with anger and shame. The assistant prefectural magistrate, Xian Yuguang, however, was in high spirits, as one could see how pleased with himself he was from the expression of his face.

*

Of Tales in the Stillnes of the Night

By Yu Wenbao, whose dates of birth and death could not be ascertained. He was originally from Guacang (southeast of Lishui, Zhejiang Province) of Southern song Dynasty. Author of *Tales of Blowing Sword, Of Tales in the Stillness of the Night*, and *The Literary Circles of past and Present, an Outline*, his life story, however, was not known. *Of*

Tales in the Stillness of the Night recorded miscellaneous events and anecdotes of the Song Dynasty. The original had been lost. What remains can be found in volume thirty-eight of Tao Zongyi's *Talking of the Outer City,* and *Gu's novels from forty Novelists* by Gu Yuanqing.

572. Waterside Pavilion

During the Northern Song Dynasty, Fan Zhongyan was once the magistrate of Hangzhou Prefecture. He was upright, fair, knew his subordinates well enough to assign them jobs commensurate with their abilities, and valued talents. Among his subordinates, there were not a few who had been elevated to a higher position through his recommendation. There was a certain man called Su Lin who held an insignificant post outside Hangzhou. As he seldom came to the city, he had no opportunity to be close to Fan Zhongyan and, for that reason, Fan Zhongyan did not know him well enough to promote him. Su Lin was a man of talent and excellent character. As those who could not equal his ability got promoted, it was inevitable that he should nurse a grievance. Thus he wrote a poem and sent it to Fan Zhongyan, as follows:

As the waterfront pavilion gets the first moonlight,

The sun-facing flowers savour the earliest spring delight.

Fan Zhongyan read the poem and knew what was in Su Lin's mind at once. The meaning was clear: those who was close to Fan Zhongyan enjoyed a favourable position. Fan Zhongyan did not mind Su Lin's complaint. On the contrary, he wrote a letter of recommendation based on his talent and asperation.

*

*Liu's Old Stories
By Yue Ke (1183-1234 A.D.) styled himself Suzhi, assumed name Juanweng, originally from Tangyin, Xiangzhou (Henan Province); a historian and writer of the Southern Song Dynasty. He was the grandson of Yue Fei. *Liu's Old Stories* recorded historical figures of the two Songs, political affairs, old stories and folktales. It was a sketchbook with a few fables scattering here and there.

573. Fortune-telling Department

In the capital there was a man who made arrows. He lived on the eastern side of Guan Bridge, and opened his shop everyday. At the gate, he hung up a signboard with three words "Fortune-telling Department" on it. He talkied big, and people thought he must be a high calibre fortune-teller. For that reason, many came to find out their fortune, which helped make his business prosperous.

People of the same trade hated the signboard so much that they joined forces, saying, "Department is what a government office should be called. How dare a mediocre person with some pretended abilility calls himself a 'department'! Who ever heard of such a thing?" And, after discussing the matter among themselves, they planned to sue the fortune-teller.

One of the men said, "That will not be difficult, and I've a way to make him take down his signboard." The next day, this man moved his fortune-telling booth to a location just opposite his shop. He also put up a signboard declaring that his was "The Fortune-telling Department Western Branch". Passersby suddenly saw the light and laughed in their sleeves. The fortune-teller was abashed, and took down his signboard at once.

574. The Guest and his Calling Card

Long, long ago, there was an official in the capital who left home to visit friends. It so happened at that very moment, a guest arrived and sent in his calling card. The gatekeeper told him his master was not there, and asked the guest to leave his calling card so that he could report to his master when he returned. The guest, all of a sudden, bawled at him angrily and gave him a lecture, saying, "How dare you behave like this! Generally speaking, when a man has died, we say he is not there. I'm a bosom friend of your master's, and that's the reason I come to see him. Does your master have any taboo? How can you speak of him like that! I'll certainly wait for him and tell him about it, so he can punish you severely."

The gatekeeper made an obeisance and confessed his mistake at once, asking the guest to enlighten him, saying, "I really don't know the taboo, and I beg your pardon, sir. However, all the officials in the capital who visit my master and leave their calling cards, I've always said the same thing. If you think this is not correct, what must I say to send off the guests?" The guest replied, "Since your master was out visiting and has not come back yet, you can simply say the master has gone out." Hearing these words, the gatekeeper knitted his brows, becoming frightened and worried. He said, "It won't do! My master would certainly prefer to die than to pronounce the two characters 'go out', which is his taboo."

575. The Cat and the Parrot

A man bought a cat from his neighbour, and chose an auspicious day to bring it home, hoping that the cat would rid the house of mice. Who would have thought the cat not only did not go to catch the mice but, instead, went to break the cage of the bird, and ate the parrot kept by his master. Can the conduct of the cat be forgiven?

576. Do it Once More

Once upon a time, someone caught a green turtle (*Trionyx sinensis*). He intended to have it eaten, but did not want to be held responsible for the destruction of life, so he made a blazing fire to boil a caldron of water and put a slender bamboo strip on the edge of the caldron. He told the turtle, saying, "If you can cross this bridge, I'll let you live." The turtle knew very well it was a trap his master had set, so it made every effort to crawl ever so careful, and eventually managed to cross it safely.

His master said, "It's really very good you can cross the bridge! Can you do it once more? I'd like to see it again!"

577. Selling Medicine

Long, long ago, there was a man who sold medicine for sole callosity. He hung a horizontal inscribed board at the door, on which was written two Chinese characters "gong yu", which could either mean "for His Majesty" or "preventive medicine". People ridiculed it as being impractical.

The news spread and eventually reached the ears of the emperor. The emperor summoned him to his presence and charged him, but soon thereafter, the emperor thought the man was just being foolish, and pardoned him.

After his release, he added the following characters to the signboard, "once summoned to the imperial court"

*

*Comic Tales

By Shen Chu. He lived at about the time when emperor Lizong of Southern Song Dynasty was on the throne. Dates of his birth and death, however, could not be ascertained. *Comic Tales*, which he authored, were all events of the past. The book was full of witty humour, hence the title. Only the title was listed in *The Si Ku Quan Shu*, or *Complete library in the Four Branches of Literature*. *Talking of the Outer City*, compiled by Tao Zongyi, registered eight items.

578. Beat the Monk

Qiu Jun, a palace high-ranking official once went to a monastery in Hangzhou to visit a monk, whose Buddhist name was Shan, and the monk was very arrogant towards him. After a while, the son of a district military officer came, and the monk immediately went down the steps to welcome him with great respect. Qiu Jun felt indignant for the different treatment and, after the son of the district military officer left, he asked the monk, "Why did you give me a dry reception but display full courtesy towards the son of the district military officer?" The monk replied, "Reception is non-reception, and non-reception is reception." The reply infuriated Qiu Jun. He stood up, raised his cane and gave the monk a few blows, saying, "Will the monk please don't take offence? Beating is non-beating, and non-beating is beating."

Such thing was seldom met with before! And it made the listeners roared with laughter.

*

*The Earth's Famous Historical Sites

By Zhu Mu, dates of birth and death unknown. At first he was called Bing styled himself Hefu, originally from Jianyang (Fujian Province).

He was a student of Zhuxi. *The earth's Famous Histrorical Sites* contains seventy volumes. A general topology, it was completed in the third year (1239 A.D.) of Jiaxi, which was the title of Lizong of Song Dynasty. Based on the administrative division of Southern Song Dynasty, which had seventeen regions, he recorded the conditions of each district and prefecture. Under the heading *Famous Historic and Cultural Sites*, he registered the poetry and songs of past and present, scenery typical of a place, and folklore, all of which in greater detail than were found in other works.

579. Constant Grinding Can Turn an Iron Rod into a Needle

Libai, the great poet of Tang Dynasty, was too fond of play and did not study well in the mountain village school when he was a little boy.

One day, he became fed up with study and cut class to go down the mountain to play. On the way he met an old woman with a head of white hair, holding a thick iron rod and grinding it on a stone with all her might. Libai was curious and asked her what was she doing. The old woman said, "My daughter wants to do embroidery, and I am grinding a needle for her." Libai thought it was ridiculous and said, "How can such a thick rod be ground into a needle for embroidery!" The old woman replied, "Although the iron rod is very thick, if I persist in my effort, not lazy, not afraid of difficulty, and continue to do it everyday, it will certainly become a needle for embroidery one day. Why not?"

Libai was extremely moved, he thought, "The old woman is advanced in years and still takes pains to grind the iron rod into a needle. I'm very young. Why do I think it too difficult to study, and do not want to learn?" As he felt ashamed of himself, he left the old woman and returned to school.

*

*Of Tales in the Field
By Lin Fang styled himself Danweng, or Jingchu, assumed name Shi Tian, and Momoweng at his old age; dates of birth and death unknown. He authored the book *Of Tales in the Field,* one volume, but was lost. The remnants totalling twenty-seven items are found in Tao Zongyi's *Talking of the Outer City.*

580. Loyal Magpie

To the south of Daci Mountain, there was a large tree whose trunk measured two arm spans around. Up on the tree, there were two magpies, each with a nest of its own where little ones were born. An eagle suddenly ran off with one of the mother magpies, and its two little birds were left twittering without their mother. At that moment, the other mother magpie was feeding its chirping young. When it saw the two nestlings, it felt sorry for them and flew over to bring them to her own nest, feeding them as if they were her own.

Why, the magpie was only a bird; it did not possess human nature, yet it was loyal to its friend. Why is it that man sometimes behaves in a way not even as good as a bird?

581. Same Bait Different Style

I once went past Hengxi River, and saw two old men squat on a rock angling. The first old man had successfully hooked many fish, and it appeared he got them easily; the second old man, on the other hand, did not get even one fish the whole day. Disgusted, he angrily threw down his angling rod and asked the first old man, saying, "We use the same bait, and angle in the same river; why has the result been so different?"

"When I hurl my line into the river," explained the first old man, "I concentrate on myself and do not think of the fish. I do not even blink my eyes and change my expression. This convinces the fish that I'm not here to get them, and they gather to eat the bait. On the other hand, you are thinking all the time of hooking the fish, and fix your gaze on them. Your expression tells them that you come to get them, and the fish are frightened and run away. How can you get the fish like that?"

Inspired by the other man's talk, the second old man followed the advice. Sure enough, he soon got quite a few fish.

When I learned about it, I heaved a sigh, saying, "That is as it should be! To fulfill one's asperation, the key lies in mastering the laws of change."

582. The Moth Flying into the Flame

One night, Master Lin had a guest for company. They were chitchatting. On the table, a candle was lighted. A white moth flew over, circling the candle and throwing itself into the flame again and again. Master Lin tried to drive it away with his fan. It left, but returned again soon thereafter. This was repeated for seven or eight times. Eventually the moth succeeded in running into the flame and got itself scorched and burned, so that it fell down on the table. Its wings, however, did not stop flapping. All the time it assumed the posture of running against the flame, until it was exhausted and died. There was no one who would not laugh at the moth's foolishness.

What is the difference between the sensual pleasures, avarice and lust in the human world and the candle flame? There are people who, like the moth, will throw themselves into sensual pleasures and avarice and lust without hesitation and regret until they ruin themselves. I am afraid people will laugh at them just as they laugh at the stupidity of the flying moth!

*

Funny tales
By Xing Jushi, who lived in the time of Southern Song. No details of his life story was available. The book contained literary sketches, mostly funny stories. The original was lost. It was found in the block-printed edition of *Comic Stories of Snow Billows.* Under its title were the words "authored by Xing Jushi; compiled by Tao Zongyi". From this, it may be inferred the original was already lost by the last years of the Yuan Dynasty. *Talking of the Outer City* also had this book included, and the author's name was given as Yuanhuai of Song.

583. The Late Prime Minister's Distant Nephew

A distant offspring of the late prime minister came to the city of Suzhou to do some sightseeing. He was in a jovial mood and wrote an inscription on the wall: "The great prime minister's distant nephew once came here to do some sightseeing." A scholar by the name of Li Zhang, who was wont to poke fun at others, read the inscription. He took up the brush and, by the side of it, added "the thirty-seventh generation grandson of emperor Hunyuan, Li Zhang, visited the place immediately thereafter".

Leader of the Five Lamps
By Puji styled himself Dachuan, a high-ranking monk in the last years of Song Dynasty; dates of birth and death unknown. He lived in Lingyin Monastery. The book synthesized the five books, *Passing the Lamp at Jingde, Spreading the Lamp at Tiansheng, Continuing the Lamp at Jianzhong Jingguo, Synopsis of the Union of the Lamps, Popularizing the Lamps at Jiatai,* and compiled them into one, deleting about half the content so that it became more compendious. It was an important Buddhist classic, and valued highly by historians. After the book was published, with the exception of *Passing the Lamp at Jingde,* the other four *Lamps* were less and less in circulation.

584. Danxia Burns the Buddha

It was in the teeth of winter, and heavy snowflakes fluttered about. The monk Danxia was out begging alms. He passed a monastery, whose horizontal inscribed board indicated it was the "Huilin Monastery of Luodong". He entered the door to take shelter from the heavy snowfall and wind. The inner temple was empty, all was quiet and not a soul was to be seen. Danxia's hands and feet were frozen, so he carried two wooden Buddhas from the incense burner table, broke them into small pieces and burned them to warm himself.

The glow of the fire alerted the abbot at the rear temple. He put on the *kasaya* and came out. When he saw what happened, he flew into a rage and reproached Danxia, saying, "You rebel! Why do you burn my wooden Buddhas?"

Danxia poked the ashes with his staff and replied, "Don't be mad at me. I'm just burning it to get the *sarira* or relics of Buddha."

Gasping with anger, the abbot said, "Nonsense! The Buddhas you burnt are made of wood. How can there be any relics left?"

"That's even better," Danxia was all smiles. He added, "Since there are no relics, will the master please get me another two to burn."

The old abbot was so shaken with anger that his eyebrows and beard were almost falling down.

*The Three Theories

By Yao Rong. Neither his deeds nor dates of birth and death were known. A book of fables and short essays, *The Three Theories*, which he authored, was found in *Selected Works from Southern Song Dynasty*.

585. Sierra

There was a species of fish called sierra, or Spanish mackerel. Its skin was silvery grey in colour, its tail as long as a swallow's, and its head as big as that of a one-year old babe. Cut into slices and smoked, they could then be transported to a far distant place. Although some fishermen often dove deep into the sea they could not catch it. It was in the period between spring and summer, the breeding season, that they followed the tides and appeared in between the waves. Taking advantage of the opportunity, the fishermen used a curtain-like big net to catch them. The curtain-like net had large grid meshes and measured several hundred feet long. Fishermen stretched it between two boats and attached iron sinkers to its lower fringes to make it sink to the bottom of the sea. When the sierra swam over, it would try to penetrate the net. However, the more it tried to get through, the tighter the squeeze of the net would become. This would make it even angrier, and it would struggle more and try harder, which necessitate the unfolding of its gills and fins. When these in turn caught in the meshes of the net, it would then not be able to get away. As a matter of fact, if it would retreat when it first came into contact with the net, it could have gotten away very easily.

Its fate was sealed by blindly persisting in charging forward and not taking a timely backward step in order to live. As a result, it suffered the cruel end of being processed into meat paste. How very sad it was!

586. Bees North of the Huai River and Crabs South of the Yangtze River

The sting of the hornet's tail was poisonous, and could cause the death of man. The crab south of the Yangtze River was strong and valiant, and its pointed hard pincers could even serve to defend itself against the tiger. However, the people who took the pupas had no need to fight with the poisonous hornets. By the same token, no one ever heard of the fingers of crab-catchers being hurt.

Generally speaking, beehive was built on either a hillock or in the forest or the crevice of a rock. When people found a beehive, they would come to it with a blazing torch at night. The hornets would swarm out of the beehive, threw themselves against the blaze and be burnt to death. The people then severed it, beehive and all, from its base.

As to the crabs, they generally hid themselves among the cattails and the reeds. The crab-catchers lighted a bright lamp and the crabs would crawl out one after the other in a hurry. The crab-catchers need only bend down and pick them up.

As the hornets and the crabs only aspired after the scorching heat and the blaze, and would not be content to live peacefully in their hideouts, their deaths could not be avoided.

*

*The Annals of the Song Dynasty
By Tuotuo (1314-1355 A.D.) styled himself Dayong, a cabinet minister of the Yuan Dynasty. He had held the post of prime minister during the reign of the emperor Shun of the Yuan Dynasty. He restored the civil service examination system, assigned Jia Lu to bring the Huanghe River under control, and took charge of the compilation of the histories of the three dynasties of Song, Liao and Jin. Later, he led an army to suppress the Red Scarf Rebellion and attacked Zhang Shicheng. Both failed, and he was impeached for belabouring the people and wasting resources. He was exiled to Yunnan and killed with poison. The following fable comes from *The Biography of Yang Shi: The Annals of the Song Dynasty.*

587. Stand in the Snow to wait upon Master Cheng

During the Song Dynasty there was a man by the name of Yang Shi. He became a palace graduate in the ninth year (1076 A.D.)of Xining, which was the title of Shenzong. At that period of time, the two brothers, Cheng Hao and Cheng Yi, both eminent scholars of the Confucian school of idealist philosophy, were giving lectures in Henan. Yang Shi gave up his official post to follow Cheng Hao in order to learn from him. When Cheng Hao died, he went to Luoyang to take Cheng Yi as his teacher. By then, Yang Shi was already over forty years old. Unfortunately, when he arrived at Luoyang and went to see Cheng Yi that day, Cheng Yi was taking a nap in his chair, and did not know someone was at the door. As Cheng Yi was resting, Yang Shi dared not disturb him. He stood outside the door waiting respectfully. It was hard winter, and snowflakes fluttered about outside the door. Despite the piercingly cold weather, Yang Shi continued to wait at the door. When Cheng Yi woke up, the snow outside the door had already accumulated over one foot. His devotion to learning and the respect he showed to his master were held up by later generations as a model and eulogized.

*

Extensive Coverage of Contemporary Events
By Chen Yuanliang styled himself *Immortal from the Moon Palace*, dates of birth and death unknown. He lived between the last years of Song Dynasty and the beginning of Yuan Dynasty, and was the author of *Extensive Coverage of Events throughout the Year,* which contained four volumes, recording stories happened during the year, and which was better known. The original book *Extensive Coverage of Contemporary Events* had been lost. The works seen today was from the reference book, compiled on the basis of Chen Yuanliang's original with new addition.

588. The Five Virtues of Scabies

Chen Daqing contracted scabies and his superior teased him. "Don't make fun of me. This disease has five virtues worthy of praise, and is graded higher than all the other diseases," Chen Daqing said.

"Which five virtues?" asked his superior.

"It's difficult to explain," Chen Daqing replied.

"Try then," the superior urged.

"Scabies will not grow in the face, and that's humanity; it's willing to pass to other people, and that's justice; it makes people scratch with hands folded, and that's propriety; it grows in the crevices between the fingers, and that's wisdom; the itches come at regular intervals, and that's honesty," Chen Daqing replied.

His superior burst into uproarious laughter as he heard the explanation.

589. Scholar Qin Loves Antiques

In the Qin Dynasty, there was a scholar who loved antiques and cultural relics so much that even the price of an article might be very high, he would find way to buy it.

One day, a man carried a worn-out mat and came to his door to inform him in person, saying, "Long ago, the duke Ai of Lu asked Confucius to sit down and talk about matters of government administration, and this was the mat they sat on!"

Scholar Qin was very pleased at seeing the mat. He believed the mat was very old, a real antique, and used his land at the outer city to exchange for the worn-out mat.

Not long after that, another man brought him an antique cane. He said, "This was the stick which the king Tai of Zhou had used when he went to the city of Bin (Xunyi, Shaanxi Province) to seek shelter from the *Di* people (a term given to northern tribes in ancient China). It was several hundred years older then the mat which confucius had sat on. How are you going to reward me?" Scholar Qin gave all the money he had in the house.

Following that, another man came with a broken bowl, saying, "Neither the mat nor the cane could be classified as antique. This bowl was made by Jie, the last ruler of the Xia Dynasty (c. 21st-c. 16th century B.C.). Is it not far more distant than the Zhou Dynasty?" Scholar Qin was convinced of its antiquity, and sold his house to buy it.

He had now the three antiques, but all his famlands and property were gone, and he had no money for clothes and food. His love for antiques, however, had not changed, and he could not bear to throw away the three articles. Thus, he draped the mat of the duke of Ai over his shoulders, leaned on the rotten stick of the king Tai of Zhou, carried the broken bowl of Jie, the last ruler of the Xia Dynasty, and went to beg in the streets, mumbling as he did so, "O benefactor, on your charity my livelihood depends, and, if you have the coins minted by the duke Tai of Zhou for the nine prefectures, please give me one!"

590. Insatiable Appetite for Human flesh

A man kept a tiger. The stripes on its body were extremely beautiful and lovely. Its owner fed it with grains, but it refused to eat; gave it rice, it rejected it; provided it with dishes along with rice, it still declined.

A child passed by and, all of a sudden, it snatched him and ate in one mouthful; an adult went by, and he was eaten with his clothes on.

Its master angrily reproached it, "You beast! I've supplied you with a lot of food, but you refused to eat. It turned out you have an insatiable appetite for human flesh."

591. Love "My Elder Brother"

Lu Bao of the Jin Dynasty once wrote a celebrated essay entitled *On Mammon*, in which he called money as "my elder brother". Since then, people used the phrase "my elder brother" as another name for money.

It so happened that an assistant prefectural magistrate surnamed Zhou was demoted to the rank of county magistrate for corruption. As he assumed office, a petty official in the *yamen* tried to sound him out, not knowing if he was honest. The petty official cast a silver doll about one catty in weight, had it put on the table in the hall of the county *yamen*, and then went to the inner chambers of the county magistrate, saying, "My elder brother is waiting in the hall. Please notify me after you receive him." County magistrate Zhou thought someone had come to send him a present and went to the hall at once, but he saw no one except a silver doll on the office table, so he just picked it up and returned to the inner chambers.

Later, the petty official made the county magistrate Zhou angry because of one thing or other, and the latter subjected him to severe torture. The petty official piteously entreated him, saying, "Please forgive me once for my elder brother's sake." County magistrate Zhou replied,

"Your brother is far too dull. Since he knows I like him, why doesn't he come more often? Our last meeting was the only one. He has never come again."

*

*Bo Ya's Zither

By Deng Mu (1247-1306 A.D.) styled himself Muxin, originally from Qiantang (Hangzhou, Zhejiang Province); a scholar in the last years of the Song Dynasty and the beginning of the Yuan dynasty. After the downfall of Song, he lived in seclusion and refused to take up any official position, calling himself "Outside of the Three Religions (Confucianism, Buddhism, Taoism)". He authored *Bo Ya's Zither*, one volume. Originally there were more than sixty poems and essays, but only thirty-one essays and thirteen poems are extant. The book audaciously exposed and attacked the feudal emperor and the corrupt officials; at times the discontent towards the reign of the Yuan Dynasty took the form of fables.

592. The Man of Yue and the Dog

A man of Yue came across a dog on the road. The dog wagged its tail and lowered its head, speaking the language of man. "I've the expertise in hunting, and am willing to go halves on any quarry we get," it said.

The man of Yue was very pleased and brought the dog home. Everyday he fed it with good food and treated it with the courtesy of the human world. The dog became more arrogant with each passing day after being treated with such great kindness. Whenever it caught any animal, it would eat every bit of it.

Someone jeered at the man of Yue, saying, "You keep the dog, but it eats all the quarry whenever one is caught. What's the use of keeping that dog?"

The man of Yue realized his foolishness and insisted on sharing the quarry with the dog from then on. He did not limit himself to half of it, but would even get a little more.

The dog was furious. It bit the man's head, broke his neck and both his feet. Then it ran away from home.

593. The Scoundrels Attach Themselves to the Demon

A demon came to the state of Chu and told the people there, saying, "The emperor of Heaven has sent me here to administer the place. I'll bring you the blessings from heaven."

The people of Chu were greatly stunned. There was nothing they could do but to offer sacrifices to the demon and did things carefully. They built a temple, presented daily sacrificial offerings, burnt incense and worshipped on bended knees.

Seeing that the demon was very powerful, the local scoundrels hastened to attach themselves and become its slaves and servants. Nor was that all; they brought their wives and daughters along to serve the demon. As time went on, the demon's vital energy seeped into the souls of these people, and the movements as well as the language of the scoundrels became indistinguishable from the demon. Relying on the demon, they turned even more overbearing and oppressive towards the people. Anyone who refused to follow the demon would be framed by the scoundrels and suffer mishap. Thus the people all lived in deep distress.

God learned of their plight, came down from heaven to the world of men and said angrily, "It's outrageous the demon is being offered sacrifices here and housed in a temple, acting like a tyrant, and oppressing the people!" He put the thunderbolt in motion and shook the temple until it collapsed, and some of the scoundrels who became accomplices of the demon were also struck to death. Thereupon the miseries of Chu district ended.

And the Scoundrels had thought the demon could be depended upon for ever!

*

The Master Shan Yuandai Collection
By Dai Biaoyuan (1244-1310 A.D.) styled himself Shuaichu or Zengbo, originally from Fenghua (Zhejiang Province), a scholar in the last years of the Song Dynasty and the beginning of the Yuan Dynasty. A palace graduate, he was once a teacher in the prefectural school. He authored *The Master Shan Yuandai Collection,* thirty volumes, also known by

the title of *The Shan Yuan Collection*, in which a few fables were found here and there.

594. A Talk on Cat

The corresponding aspect of man's disposition can all be found in the mouse, the ox, the tiger, the rabbit, the dragon, the snake, the horse, the sheep, the monkey, the rooster, the dog and the pig, and that is why one talks about the relation of the year of one's birth to one of the twelve animals.

The cat might be the closer to man than the rest of the animals, but it failed to be included in the twelve, and some people could not understand why. The question can be explained away by classifying those animals into the eminent and the humble, but how about the snake and the mouse? Can the cat be inferior to them?

This controversy can be straightened out with the following justification, "The cat likes to eat fat meat, live in a cosy, comfortable place, and it often leaves its old master to attach itself to a new one without rhyme or reason and devoid of good faith. Moreover, it will bite and harm its own new-born kittens, which even the snake and mouse will not do."

*

*Conversation with the Recluse Zhan Yuan
By Bai Ting (1248-1328 A.D.) styled himself Tingyu, originally from Qiantang (Hangzhou, Zhejiang Province). He was a poet in between the two dynasties of Song and Yuan. He was famed for his calligraphy and writings. It was said "his poems equal that of Tao and Wei, while his calligraphy has reached the standard of Yan and Liu" (Tao Yuan Ming, Wei Ying Wu, Yan Zhen Qing, Liu Gong Quan). He became a Qixia Mountain recluse in his last years, and assumed the name of Old Man Qixia, otherwise known as Zhan Yuan. He was the author of *The Zhan Yuan Collection* and *Conversation with the Recluse Zhan Yuan*.

595. Swallow the Dates Whole

"Pear benefits the teeth but is harmful to the spleen; date is beneficial to the spleen but will damage the teeth," one of the guests said.

The words caused a youth, who was somewhat weak in the head, to think for a long time before he declared, "From now on, I'll only chew but not swallow the pear so that it'll not hurt my spleen; as to dates, I'll swallow them whole and not chew so they will not damage my teeth!"

A very intimate friend said to him, "That's truly to swallow a date whole!" the remark made everyone convulsed with laughter.

*

Tales by Nancun at Farming Intervals
By Tao Zongyi (?-1396 A.D.) styled himself Jiucheng, assumed name Nancun, originally from Huangyan, Zhejiang Province; a writer in the last years of the Yuan Dynasty and the beginning of the Ming Dynasty. It was said that when he took up temporary residence in Songjiang, and as he sat down to take a rest under the tree at farming intervals, he would write down anything that came to his head on a leaf and put it in a jar. In time, the leaves accumulated to as many as more than ten jars, which he later copied and compiled into a book called *Tales by Nancun at Farming Intervals*. It was Tao's masterpiece. In addition, he had extracted and compiled from the historical records novels before the Ming Dynasty into *Talking of the Outer City*, which also wielded great influence. There were other works like *The compendium of Histories and their Dynastic Backgrounds, The Nancun Poetry Collection, Omissions of the Four Books*, and so on.

596. Muddle Along

According to legend, in ancient times there was a species of bird in Wutai Mountain, which was known as *hanhao worm*. It was a very strange bird, more than a foot in length, four feet, and had two extremely large wings. It was able to transform itself with the change of seasons. It was not oviparous like all the other birds, but a mammal. Its young had to be breastfed by the mother bird to grow. A fully-fledged bird had multicoloured and beautiful plummage in summer. When spread, the plummage looked bright and pretty, similar to the peacock's. During that period of time, the *hanhao worm* was very pleased with itself, and would cry proudly, "The phoenix is not as good as I! The phoenix is not as good as I!" However, not everyday a Sunday. As summer changed into winter, moulting took place, and only a pair of naked wings remained. It was now like a squab in appearance, ugly and unpleasant to look at. By that time, the *hanhao worm* had lost all its capital to show off to the other birds, and there was no help for it but to cry, "Muddle along, muddle along."

597. A Virtuous Mother Sends Back the Money

Nie Yidao was the magistrate of the county on the right side of the river.

One morning, a villager on his way to sell his vegetables picked up fifteen one-dollar bills and brought them back to his mother. His mother said angrily, "Perhaps you have stolen them and come back to deceive me. And even if someone did lost the money, it would only be two or three dollars, how could there be a whole bundle of it? Moreover, our family has never seen so much money. I'm afraid disaster will befall us immediately. You must make haste to return them to whomsoever they belong, and not be involved in such matter!"

However, despite her repeated warning, her son did not listen to her.

His mother said, "If you insist on keeping them, I'll report to the local authorities!"
The son said, "Since they are picked up on the road, where can I return them to?"
The mother replied, "You should wait at the place you found them, and someone will surely come to claim them."

So the son followed his mother's instructions, brought the money back to where he had found it and waited. Soon after he was there, sure enough, someone came to look for the money. Being a villager, he was naive and honest. He did not ask the man how much money he had lost, but simply gave back the money. Spectators urged the man to reward the finder, but the owner of the lost property was stingy, saying, "I actually lost thirty bills. Since I've only collected half of them, how can I reward him?"

Both sides argued heatedly and eventually they grappled each other before the magistrate. Nie Yidao interrogated the villager, and found he had told the truth. Nie also verified it with his mother confidentially, and their words seemed to coincide. He then ordered the two men each write down a statement. One side claimed he had lost thirty bills, another said he had picked up only fifteen. After the statements were submitted, Nie Yidao said to the owner of the lost property, "They are not your bills. If the number is thirty, it must surely be yours. These bills had probably come from heaven for the good mother as old-age pension. May be you should go and look elsewhere!"

Thereupon he handed over the fifteen bills to the mother and son. When people heard the story, they all clapped their hands in applause.

598. The Golden Hairpin

Mu Baci styled himself Xiying was a man from the western Regions (a Han Dynasty term for the area west of Yumenguan, including what is now Xinjiang and parts of Central Asia). He was big and tall in stature, and people called him "Xiying the Tall".

One day, while he was having meal with his wife, his wife used her little golden hairpin to pick up a piece of meat but, just as she was about to put it into her mouth, there came a guest at the door. Xiying immediately went out to welcome the guest and, as the wife had no time to eat the piece of meat, she left the gold pin with the piece of meat in the food container, and stood up to prepare tea for the guest. When she returned to her seat, the gold pin had disappeared. At that moment, a little servant girl was nearby doing her chores, and the mistress suspected she might have stolen it. However, despite repeated interrogation and beating, she did not confess throughout. In the end, she was beaten to death.

One year later, some craftsmen had been hired to repair the house. As the gutter on the tile roof was being cleaned of its filth, something suddenly fell onto the stone, and the sound of metal was heard. The little gold pin lost before had been found! There was also a decayed bone dropped with it. Investigation showed it must be the cat which came to steal the meat, and the gold pin was taken together with it. As the little servant girl had not seen what happened at that time, she had to die uncleared of a false charge.

Alas! Such things are too many to enumerate in the world. Let us just put it down as a lesson for the later generations.

599. To Bark or Not to Bark

A country maintains its officials just as a house keeps its dog.

For example, a thief comes, and the dog will bark. The owner of the house may not see it at first, and he beats the dog for barking. The dog takes the cue, and will bark no more.

Do you think it is a good dog?

*

*Talking of the Outer City
It was a series of books compiled by Tao Zongyi, gathered from various literary sketches beginning from Han and Wei to Song and Yuan dynasties, but there were also Confucian classics, history, the philosophers and their works, poetry and essays, etc., a few of them with no extant copies. There were others the originals of which were lost and, to make up the number, taken from the reference books. As they were only exerpts compiled from his predecessors, each book only contained the outline of its original. The book had one hundred volumes at first, but thirty of which had been lost. It was supplemented until it reached one hundred volumes again by Yu Wenbo of the Ming Dynasty. Tao Ting of the Qing Dynasty added more so that it became one hundred and twenty volumes, but it was no longer Tao Zongyi's original book.

600. The Spider and the Silkworm

The spider said to the silkworm, "You spend your day in food and doing nothing until you are old when you spin silk mouthful after mouthful, some white some yellow, glittering and dazzling, but in the end just wrapping yourself up. The silkworm-raising woman will throw you into the boiling water, and reel off the silk from the cocoons, which signifies the end of your life. Although you can be called an ingenious craftsman but, at the end of the day, it was just a form of suicide. Is it not a very stupid thing to do?"

The silkworm replied, "Of course you can say I just commit suicide, but the silk I spin will be woven into brocade, from which the imperial robe and the robes worn by officials of all ranks are made. Can they do without me? As to you, you are only looking for food to fill your empty stomach. You spin the silk and weave them into a net. As you sit at the centre, you just wait for the mosquitoes, the gadflies, the bees and the butterflies to fall into the net, which you will then catch, kill and eat your fill. You may say it is a very smart thing to do, and you are very capable, but how cruel it is!"

The spider replied, "One should learn from you if he takes the interests of others into consideration but, if he is doing things for himself, he will certainly follow my example." Alas! In this world of ours, there are too few people who like to become the silkworm and not the spider!

601. The Robe Caught Fire

Yu Chanzi and his friend leaned against the bed and sat around the fireplace. His friend bent towards the table reading, his robe dragged over the fire. The fire was intense.

Gentle and refined in manner, Yu Chanzi calmly went before his friend, and bowed. "I had something to tell you just now," he said, "but I know you are rather hot-tempered, and am afraid you might get excited. However, if I don't tell you, I'll not be loyal to my friend. I hope you will be magnanimous and please don't lose your temper before I dare to inform you." His friend said, "If you have anything to say, will you please say it!"

Yu Chanzi behaved as politely as before, muttered and mumbled several times before he said, "Just now the fire burnt your robe."

Stood up, his friend discovered a rather big chunk of his robe had been burnt. He was so angry that his expression changed, saying, "Why don't you say so earlier? Why do you cling to such outworn rules and ideas?"

Yu Chanzi said, "No wonder people say you are short-tempered. You really are!"

602. Old Woman Wang's Winery

At the foot of Mount Hefu, there was a temple of the Old Woman Wang, but nobody knew which dynasty she belonged. Words transmitted from generation to generation through the ages had it that the old woman depended on her winery for livelihood. A Taoist priest lodged at her house often asked her for wine. He never paid for the several hundred jars of wine he had drunk, but the old woman did not complain either.

One day, the Taoist priest said to the old woman, "I've drunk so much wine and did not pay for it, but I'll dig a well for you." When the well was completed, she found the water gushed out of it was the finest wine. "That can be regarded as payment for your kindness," said the Taoist priest. Then he left. From then on, the old woman no longer made wine of her own. She just sold the spring water gushing out from the well as wine, and the taste was even better than the wine she had made herself. People came to buy her wine one after another, and her business flourished. Three years later, the old woman had accumulated thousands and tens of thousands of cash from the wine she sold, and became a rich woman. Then the Taoist priest arrived again, and the old woman expressed her profound gratitude for what he had done.

"Is the wine good?" asked the Taoist priest.

"The wine is good, but there is no distillers' grains for the pigs though," replied the old woman.

As the Taoist priest listened, he smiled and wrote down a dogerrel on the wall:

Heaven's high is not high enough
In comparison with men's mind.
Though well water is sold for wine,
She still wants grains for the pigsty.

Having written that, he left. From then on, the well never gushed out wine again.

*

The Chengyibo Collection
By Liu Ji (1311-1375 A.D.) styled himself Bowen, originally from Qingtian, Zhejiang Province; a founding father of the Ming Dynasty. A palace graduate in the last years of the Yuan Dynasty, he had once held the post of county magistrate in Gao-an, Jiangxi Province, and as

Confucianist educator-official in Jiangsu and Zhejiang, but soon gave up his post to become a recluse. Later, he assisted Zhu Yuanzhang in military planning, participated in confidential work, and was Zhu Yuanzhang's important adviser. He was bestowed the title of Chengyibo. His poems and essays possessed characteristics of his own and, together with Song Lian, they were called the great literary masters of a generation. He authored *Yu Lizi,* which contained three volumes. It was a collection of fables scarcely seen since the dynasties of Yuan and Ming. His poetry, essays and the two books *Yu Lizi,* and *The Masters of Classics in the Spring and Autumn Period* were combined and compiled into the book *The Chengyibo Collection* by later generations. The following are some of them.

603. Not a Product of Jizhou

The mare of Yu Lizi's family gave birth to a foal very much like the famous *jueti,* or hinny, a fine horse. People who saw it all said, "This is a horse that covers a thousand *li* a day! You should present it to the imperial stable in the palace." Yu Lizi was pleased to accept their suggestion. After the horse was sent to the capital, His Majesty ordered the official in charge of the horses to examine the record of special local products presented by various localities. The official presented a memorial to the emperor, saying, "It is true this is a fine horse. However, it was not a product of Jizhou!" Thereupon, the emperor ordered the horse remove to an ordinary stable outside the palace.

604. Gong Gong Rams the Mountain

When Taiming was the owner of Buzhou Mountain, the Huanghe River used to flow through the cave of the mountain, and a fissure appeared. An old man happened to pass through the place. He noticed the fissure, and was terrified. He went to Taiming and told him, "The Buzhou Mountain is about to break apart." Taiming was enraged, thinking the old man was spreading fallacies to deceive people. The old man again repeated it to Taiming's subordinate after he had withdrawn, but Taiming's subordinate too thought the old man was just talking nonsense. He angrily refuted, "How can a mountain break apart? If the sky and the earth are there, Buzhou Mountain will remain. Unless the sky and the earth fall apart, the Buzhou Mountain will not do so." As he finished his sermon, he even threatened to beat the old man up, and the old man had to flee in haste. Not long after the event, Gong Gong too passed the place. Taiming was lukewarm towards him, and treated him with arrogance. Gong Gong was infuriated and used his head to impact the Buzhou Mountain. The rocks fell like broken ice, filling up all the deep pools. Taiming fled in panic, and died eventually in Kun Lun Mountain. His subordinate too became homeless.

605. Rare Treasure

Gong Zhiqiao came by a piece of the finest firmiana timber, which he pared into a musical instrument. After he put on the silk strings and play, it produced the sounds of metal and stone, harmonious and pleasing to the ear. He thought it was the best musical instrument in the world, and presented it to the chief official in charge of music in the imperial court. The official asked the palace musician to test it, and the musician said, "It isn't old." And the instrument was returned to him.

So Gong Zhiqiao brought his musical instrument home. He consulted the varnisher and had many broken veins put on; then he went to the engraver, asking him to carve an inscription in ancient characters. The instrument was sealed in a box and buried in the ground for a year before he dug it out and carried it to the market to sell. An affluent man came and bought it for one hundred *liang* (*liang*=50 grams) of gold and presented it to the imperial court. The officials in charge of music vied with each other to take a look at it, and they all said, "It is indeed the world's rarest treasure!"

606. The Wizard and the Spirit

Wang Sunru asked Yu Lizi, "Do you know the wizard and the spirit in the state of Chu? The people there worshipped the spirits, and often offered sacrifices to them. At one time, the wizard was fighting with the spirit for the sacred tablet, and caused the image of the spirit to fall down and lie on the floor. The spirit did not know who had done it, so it put the blame on the villagers, and began to cause harm to the people. That same day, an old man from the village went to the ancestral temple to offer sacrifice and, as he noticed the idol on the floor, he prayed reverently and helped it up. The spirit saw what he did, and thought the old man was the one who caused the idol to fall down, so it beat the old man severely, which caused the latter to trip over and die. The manners and morals of the time are very much like the falling idol. One must not help it up. The only thing one must do is to avoid it altogether. To do otherwise is to bring misfortune upon oneself.

607. The Prince of Chu and the Owlet

Zhu Ying, the prince of Chu, kept an owlet. He fed it with firmiana nuts and anticipated it to cry like a phoenix. The prime minister, Huang Xie, titled Chun Shenjun, said to him, "It is an owl born with the characteristics that cannot be altered. Even though you feed it with firmiana nuts, how can the food have any effect?" After listening to what Chun Shenjun had said, Zhu Ying replied, "Since you already know the owl will not change into a phoenix even though it is fed with firmiana nut, why do you still pamper your hangers-on, giving them the best food and shoes inlaid with pearls, expecting them to repay you in the future like the state scholars. After all, they are but a bunch of petty thieves and desperadoes? As I see it, how can there be any difference between what you do and the feeding of an owlet with nuts and anticipating it to cry like a phoenix?" Chun Shenjun was not convinced, however. In the end, he was killed by Li Yuan and, although he had many hangers-on, there were none who would avenge his death.

608. A Pedigreed Horse

Rui Bo received orders from the king Li of Zhou to lead an army to attack *Western Rong* (tribesmen in the western borders in the Zhou Dynasty), from which he came by a pedigreed horse. He intended to present it to the king Li of Zhou, but his youngest brother cautioned him, saying, "You had better release the horse instead. You must know the king is insatiably avaricious. Besides, he hears and believes slanders. You return after victory today and present him with a pedigreed horse, but the courtiers close to the monarch will say you have come by more than one pedigreed horse, and approach you to ask for more. As you are unable to satisfy their request, they will spread rumours in front of the king, and the king will believe them. In the end, you are the one who will suffer." Rui Bo did not listen to his younger brother, and presented the pedigreed horse to the king as he had intended. The duke Rongyi, sure enough, sent someone to ask for a pedigreed horse from Rui Bo. As Rui Bo had no pedigreed horse to give him, he went to tell the king, saying, "Rui Bo has got not just one pedigreed horse; he has hidden all the others."

As the king heard and believed the slanders, he was enraged and expelled Rui Bo.

609. Three Merchants from Sichuan

Three merchants each opened a pharmacy. One of them only bought high-quality herbal medicine and fixed his selling price based on the purchase cost, neither too high nor too low, and might be referred to as just right. Another one purchased all classes of herbal medicine regardless of their quality. As to selling price, it was based on the requirement and choice of each customer; high quality meant high price, and vice versa. The third one never stocked high quality goods; he only purchased low-grade goods in large quantity. However, his goods were inexpensive and, moreover, he would add a little to what had been bought without haggling over triffles. Thus, his business prospered, so much so that the threshold of his shop had to be replaced every month because of the many customers who patronized his business. In the span of just a little over one year, he had accumulated so much money that he became one of the richest men in the locality. The one who based his selling price on the requirement and choice of each customer also became rich after some time, although his business was not as good as the previous one. The pharmacy which issisted on selling first-grade goods was almost deserted and, as there were few customers, it became difficult for the owner even to look after the three daily meals. When Yu Lizi learned about it, he sighed, "Nowadays things are much the same for those holding official positions! Formerly, there were three counties near the border with three magistrates. One was honest but was not appreciated by his superior. When he left his post, he was so poor that he could not even pay for a boat, and everyone laughed at him Another one acted according to the situation, he sought money only when the time was appropriate. Thus, the people were not averse to his action, they even praised him for his competence. The third one took anything he could lay his hands on, and used what he obtained to curry favour with his superior. He treated his subordinates as if they were his sons, and the affluent his guests. In less than three years, he was promoted to a higher position. All the people thought he was a good man. How odd it was!"

610. Servants Contend for Household Management

The struggle for power to manage the household among the servants, young and old, of the Bei Guo family was so intense that it led to the neglect of the house even though it was badly damaged. It was only when the building threatened to fall apart that craftsmen were hired to repair it. The craftsmen asked for some provisions in advance, but the person in charge did not agree, and the craftsmen had to go hungry for two days. As the situation could not go on, they spoke to the man in charge, but the man in charge refused to report to his master. Instead, he asked the craftsmen for a bribe and, as long as the bribe was not forthcoming, he would not report to his superior. Thus, hunger and fatigue drove the craftsmen to declare that they would give up the job. In was the raining season at that time, and the rains continued to pour down for several days on end. What happened was that a pillar in the corridor of the Bei Guo family's house snapped, then the wing-rooms on both sides began to fall down and, inevitably, the damage spread to the central room. At this point, the person in charge responded to the request of the craftsmen, arranged for some provisions, prepared a sumptuous meal, and gathered all the craftsmen around, telling them, "Your request is accepted, and we will not stint money." However, as the craftsmen went to inspect the crumbling building, they found it no longer repairable, and they would not undertake to do the work. One of the craftsmen said, "In the beginning, we asked for some provisons, and you refused. My stomach is now full." Another craftsman said, "Your food smells a bit off, and cannot be eaten!" Yet another said, "All the beams and pillars of your house are rotten now, and there is nothing we can do." As they said this, they all left in a hurry. The Bei Guo family's house eventually collapsed because nobody would undertake to repair it. Yu Lizi remarked, "The Bei Guo family was respected before on the strength of their good faith, and became the richest family in the world. But his descendants are unable even to preserve a building now. How swift the transformation has been! When the management of the household was not in order, and the power passed into the hands of subordinates who received bribes openly, that was what had led to the loss of morale and support. How unfortunate it has been!"

611. The Magpies clamour on Account of the Tiger

The southern side of Daughter Mountain was a fovourite place for the magpies to make their nests. A tiger sprang out from behind a Chinese hackberry tree, and the magpies gathered on the tree to clamour for the tiger to leave. The mynahs heard the clamour, and they, too, came together to make a row.

The jay saw what happened and asked the magpies, "The tiger is an animal that moves about on the ground, what business is it of yours to shout at it?"

One of the magpies replied, "The roar of the tiger will cause wind which, I'm afraid, may bring down my nest.and that is why I clamour."

The jay asked the mynahs the same question, but the mynahs had no answer for it.

The jay smiled and said, "The magpies make their nests on the branches of the tree, which cannot stand the wind, and that's why they are afraid of the tiger. You live in the mountain cave. Why should you follow the others to to raise a hubbub?"

612. Yu Lizi Talks about Wisdom

Zhou Zhiyong asked Yu Lizi, "The mountain engenders clouds, and it becomes even more beautiful and lovable. The fire produces smoke, but sometimes it is extinguished by the smoke. Is it not bizarre?" Yu Lizi replied, "Good question! The wisdom of man may also be likened to the clouds and smoke. Wisdom has its roots from man. If it is utilized sensibly, it can be compared to clouds produced by the mountain; if it is utilized insensibly, it will become the smoke. Cases in mind are Han Fei, who had been imprisoned in the state of Qin, and Chao Cuo, who met his death in the Han Dynasty. In both cases it was as if smoke produced by the fire."

613. Yu Lizi Laments the Crumbling House

Yu Lizi went to the country fair, where he saw a crumbling house, and lamented over what happened. Someone inquired as to whether it could still be restored to its original shape, he replied, "If Lu Ban or

Wang Er were still alive, it might be possible, but since they were no lomger alive, who could make plans to repair it? I've heard that even though a house might fall into disrepair, provided the ridge purlin was in place, it could still be utilized. Now that the ridge purlin and the side beams have all fallen into decay, to the extent that any move will cause the roof to collapse, it is better not to touch them. If they are left alone, may be the ridge of the roof and the rafters can still withstand for a while longer so that the right person can be found to repair it. Any move now will cause it to collapse, a situation nobody can be held responsible. Moreover, new materials are needed for the repair, which must be of good quality. But there are no longer any trees in the mountain. Regulations have been changed so often that there is no standard to adhere to. Craftsmen don't know where to begin, and the trees are being cut down as firewood. Even if Lu Ban and Wang Er were still alive, there would not be a place where they could display their skill; not to say there is no one who can take their place. How can I not feel sorrowful?"

614. A Nine-tailed Fox

In the Qingqiu Mountain, there lived a nine-tailed fox which was bent on playing the devil. Having found the skull of a dead person, it put it on the head, knelt down to pray to the Big Dipper and asked God to bestow blessing upon itself. Thereafter, it arrived at the divine stand of Gong Gong, and stood at the top of the mountain range, where it gathered all the foxes from every mountain, every river, lake and swamp. Finally, they ascended the Yu Mountain and danced like humans.

An old *bei*, a wolf-like animal with short forelegs, advised it, saying, "You have on your head the skull of a dead man. When a man dies, his skins and flesh decay and turn into earth, and only the bones remain, of which the skull is a part. The skull has no feeling, the same as the brick, the tile, the sand and the stones. However, the stinking smell and filth are what the latter do not have. You should not wear it anymore . . . . Besides, this is devoid of proper respect to God! You must not offend the dignity of God. If you do not reform yourself, you will surely meet with great calamity in the end!"

The nine-tailed fox, however, thought otherwise, and so it led the foxes to the ruins of Yanbo. Scarcely had it and its followers reached the destination when the hunters descended upon them en masse to catch and kill them, concentrating their arrows first of all on the nine-tailed fox which wore the human skull. Thus the nine-tailed fox, who played the devil, was eventually killed, and the other foxes, which followed it, could not escape their destiny either. The hunters collected all the dead foxes and burned them. They were heaped up like a mountain over two thousand feet high and burned for three years before its foul smell finally dissipated.

615. The Wizard of Luoyang Arouses the Dragon

In the last years of the Eastern Han Dynasty, Luoyang suffered a severe drought. All weeds withered, and ponds dried up. The wizard of Luoyang told his fellow countrymen, saying, "In the pool of the Southern Mountain, there lived a divine being. Why don't we asked it for a divine manifestation? It will certainly bring about rain." An old man cautioned them, saying, "It's a flood dragon and should not be bothered, as it will cause no end of trouble despite its ability to bring rain." Nevertheless, everyone thought, "Since it is now so droughty, and anything may happen any time, how can we still think of the consequences?" And they went together to the pool side with the wizard of Luoyang, asking the flood dragon to make a divine manifestation. Before three cups of wine were completely offered, the flood dragon was seen meandering out, and powerful wind soon followed. In an instant, thunder and lightning clove the air, and rain fell in torrents, as fierce gale also uprooted the big trees. In this manner, it continued for several days. The Yi River, the Luo River, the Chan River and the Jian River all overflowed their banks, and Luoyang was stranded. By then people began to regret they had not listened to the advice of their elders, but it was already too late.

616. A Fake Tiger Faces a Fiercer Animal *Bo*

A man in the state of Chu had an unpleasant experience with the fox, and so he tried everything possible to catch it, but it was all to no avail.

Someone taught him a way, saying, "The tiger is the fiercest animal in the forest. It will make the soul of any animal almost leave its body in horror if it is seen around, and prostrate itself waiting to die."

The man of Chu therefore had a model of the tiger made, on which he put on a piece of tiger skin, and placed it below the window. The fox came, saw it, cried out loud, and fell to the ground.

On one occasion, a wild boar ruined his crops. He ordered someone to bring the model of the tiger, and lay in wait. His son was sent to guard the main road intersection with a sharp spear in hand, while the men in the field shouted in unison. The wild boar was forced to flee to the forest, where it ran into the model of the tiger and turned towards the main road, and was eventually caught.

The man of Chu was overjoyed. He thought the model of the tiger could vanquish all animals in the world. At that moment, an animal similar to the horse in appearance emerged in the wilderness. Again, he put on the model of the tiger and met it head-on.

Someone advised against it, saying, "This is a *bo*, an animal even fiercer than the tiger! Even a real tiger will not be able to defend itself against it. If you go, you will bring disaster upon yourself!" The man of Chu, however, did not heed the warning.

The horse-like animal gave out a thunderous roar and rushed towards the man of Chu, seized him and bit him. Soon his head was torn open and he died.

617. Anthill

At a bend of the Southern Mountain, there was a big tree; on the tree, a swarm of ants gathered. They ate into the tree and lived there. As the tree gradually rotted, the ants became even more prosperous. They separated and occupied respectively the southern and northern sides of the tree, and there were anthills all over the branches. One day, wild fire spread to where they made their nests. The ants on the southern branches fled to the northern branches, and vice versa; for those who were too late to do so, they simply moved to where the fire had not yet spread. It did not take long, however, when everything was swallowed up by the flame, the big tree and all.

618. The Musk Deer

Musk is a very valuable spice and medicine. In the state of Chu, there was a man whose calling was to catch the musk deer for its musk. When the situation was desperate, and its life in imminent danger, the musk deer would dig out the musk from its navel and threw it on the ground; the catchers would then be left busy finding the musk, thus providing an opportunity for it to escape. Lingyin Ziwen heard about it and sighed with emotion, saying, "It is only an animal, yet there are people who cannot be compared with it. Many men die for money, and sometimes even bring disaster on the whole family. Isn't it true their wisdon is much inferior than a musk deer?"

619. The Stork Moves its Nest

One day, when Ziyou was an official in Wu City, a stork moved its nest from a mound outside the city to a gravestone. The old man who looked after the graveyard noticed it, and reported it to Ziyou, saying, "The stork is a bird that knows when the rain will come. I saw it move the nest suddenly. Is this indicative of the possibility that there will be a flood?" "That may be so," Ziyou replied. He then ordered all the people in the city to prepare boats for salvation. A few days later, sure enough, there was a great flood, which reached the mound. The rain continued to pour down, and soon it threatened to submerge the gravestone, making the stork's new nest a dangerous place to stay. At that juncture, the stork just lingered about crying long and sad, not knowing what to do. As Ziyou noticed the situation, he heaved a sigh, and commented, "It is a sad thing. Although the stork possesses some wisdom but, unfortunately, it does not have a long-term strategy."

620. Be Doomed to the Same Fate

The three men, Xiguo Ziqiao, Gongsun Guisui and She Xu, liked to disguise themselves in different attire and climb over their neighbour's walls together at night. Their neighbour hated what they did, so he dug a pit at the spot where they used to climb in and out of his home, into which he poured excrement and urine. That night, the trio climbed over the walls as they were wont to do, and Xiguo Ziqiao was the first to do it. He fell into the latrine pit. However, not only did he not make any fuss about it, he even signalled Gongsun Guisui to follow immediately. As a result, Gongsun Guisui too fell into the pit. He was about to shout when Xiguo Ziqiao covered his mouth, saying, "Don't make any noise!" In the next moment, as She Xu jumped over, he fell into the same trap. At that moment, Ziqiao began to speak, saying, "My reason for not raising the alarm is to avoid our laughing at each other." Later, when people happened to mention the matter, they all blamed Xiguo Ziqiao for not acting properly. He suffered humiliation himself, but concealed the fact with the malicious intent to also himiliate his friends. It was indeed a cruel and foul thing to do.

621. The Taoist Priest Rescues a Tiger

In the Cang Liang Mountain, where the streams and rivulets converged before flowing into the big river, there was a pious Taoist priest who constructed a house there to practise Taoism. One night, freshets roared down from the mountains, and many houses were destroyed by the rush of water. People either held on to a piece of wood or climbed up the rooftops, and cries for help were heard incessantly. The Taoist priest prepared a large boat, put on his straw rain cape, donned his large bamboo rain hat, and stood on the water's edge, lading a team of swimmers with ropes in hand, ready to rescue those needing help. When anyone was seen coming towards them in the water, they would immediately throw out a wooden plank with a rope attached to it. In this manner, they rescued quite a number of people. The next morning, an animal was seen floating in the water. Its body was submerged and only the head was visible, which turned about looking here and there, as if asking for help. When the Taoist priest saw it, he said, "It is also a living thing, and we must hasten to bring it up." The boatman responded by throwing out a wooden plank. It was a tiger. At first, the tiger was a little dazed. It sat there licking its fur until it was dry. As it arrived at the river bank, however, a wicked light began to shine in its eyes as it stared at the Taoist priest. Then it pounced at him, causing him to fall to the ground. It was only the timely assistance of all the people on the scene that saved the Taoist priest from being bitten to death although, inevitably, he had incurred some severe wound.

622. The Catalpa and the Thorn Bushes

The catalpa said to the thorn bushes, "Why do you grow in clumps, vimineous instead of being tall and straight, and so leafy that you have almost no place to stand on, living among the weeds in the field and bending towards the dark corner, covered by the rotten bamboos without seeing the sun. Are you not feeling worried? Look at me, I'm majestic and tall, even surpassing the high and steep cliff in height. The tips of my branches wave beyond the Ninth Heaven and the most ephemeral clouds, and my roots reach the nether world. As the sun and the moon flit past, they will leave their brilliance; as the the wind and the rain converge, juice and fluid begin to circulate. The nestlings of *yuan* (a phoenix-like bird mentioned in ancient literature) and the emerald *luan* (a mythical bird like the phoenix) echo each other continuously from morning till night. When the weather is fine, the thin, floating clouds will mix with the mist-like vapour. Against evaporation and the swampy ground, coupled by the auspicious clouds and the celestial phenomena portending peace and prosperity, a multicoloured scene is set off. When all this happens simultaneously, it becomes a gorgeous, heterogeneous colour pattern embracing the floating sun, strikingly elegant, and it is as if a Sichuan figured satin freshly washed and lifted out of the Jin River; so bright and magnificent, like spring flowers shine inside the greenhouse. That is why when a great craftsman sees me, he falls in love with me, and wants to use my trunk as the pillar of the hall where solemn ceremonies were held."

As he finished speaking, the thorn bushes gave out a long howl against the wind, shaking the vimens and chanted, "How beautiful you have described it! I've heard, 'When the face is beautiful, it will bring humiliation; when the clothing is gorgeous, it will catch the attention of the thief; when one is talented, it will cause jealousy. Your ability is indeed above the average, but unfortunately your luck has not yet arrived and you have not become the material for the contruction of the building. I'm afraid you may not be the pillar of the ceremonial hall but, instead, get hewed down to make a coffin, and be buried in the gloomy underground together with a rotten corpse. By that time, even though you should want to see a little sunlight, could it be possible? I'm not even an eight-footer and not thicker than a finger, twisted and crooked, with no pattern to speak of. Heaven has bestowed no talent and good looks on me except thorns, which prevented me from being cut down as firewood and the birds from gathering here. It's true I do not have your beauty, but I have no worry either. As it is, I've received quite a lot. What more can I wish for?"

623. The Islanders Eat Snakes

The South China Sea islanders liked to eat snake meat. When they travelled to the mainland, they often brought cured snake meat with them. On one occasion, an islander arrived at the state of Qi. An innkeeper treated him with the utmost cordiality, and he was so happy that he returned the hospitality with the dried meat of poisonous snakes. The innkeeper stuck out his tongue in fright and went away. The South China Sea islander was perplexed, mistaken the behaviour of his host as resentment because the gift was too small, so he sent his servant with an additional present of the largest poisonous snake in his possession.

624. Good-looking Clothes

In Shaanxi, there was a man who liked to wear clothes that are good-looking. In case his clothes were not to his liking, he would feel embarrassed and, unless another suit was put on, he would not feel comfortable.

One day, he went to a certain place. Somehow, one of the sleeves of his smart-looking shirt was dirtied. As he had no idea about it, he continued on his way. However, halfway to his destination, his friend pointed out the stain to him. His mood changed immediately as he sighed with great regret. He tried to get rid of the stain by scratching it with his fingernails. Eventually the stain was gone, but the vestiges of dirt remained. He was terribly upset, and constantly looked at them as he went forward. In the end, he had to go home.

625. A Deserted Son

In the district of Jingzhou, a man ran into a tiger. He escaped, but left his son on the spot. As he was convinced his son must have already been eaten by the tiger, he did not go back to look for him.

Someone saw his son and returned to tell him, saying, "Your son is still alive. Why don't you go and look for him at once?" But he did not believe it was true.

I woodcutter found the deserted son and brought him up as his own.

Many years later, the man met his son. He tried to wrangle with the woodcutter, but the son no longer considered him his father.

626. Doctor Huan

There was a physician by the name of Huan, and people called him Doctor Huan. King Zhao's son fell ill and requested Doctor Huan to come and see him. Having diagnosed the patient, Doctor Huan said, "The illness is serious. Unless expensive medicine, which may cost ten thousand pieces of gold, is administered, I'm afraid his condition will not improve." When he was asked what kind of medicine was required, and how to administer it, he replied, "The ochre from the state of Dai, the jade from the state of Chu, the cinnabar from the Heng Mountain, the *Kongcengqing* from Qingling Yutong, the *Astragalus sinicus* (a grassy plant with purple flowers) from Kun Lun Mountain, the pearl from Hepu, the rhinoceros horn from Sichuan, the precious hare from the three Hans, and the three different jades from Yiwulu Mountain: *xun*, *langgan*, *qi*. Mix all these with mercury and lead, and let the Taoist method of alchemy take over for three years. Once the pill of immortality takes shape, get it out and bury it under the ground for another three years. Unearth and take it then, and the crown prince will definitely be cured." The duke Chun Yu smiled and said, "There is not a shadow of doubt that you are Doctor *huan* (The Chinese character *huan* means slow)!"

627. Zhuangzi Commiserates with the Beggar

Zhuangzi went to the state of Qi, where he met with many beggars, with whom he commiserated. One of the beggars followed him and begged, but Zhuangzi said, "I've gone without food for seven days myself." And the beggar heaved a sigh and remarked, "I've seen many people pass through, and there was none who sympathized with me. You are the only person who expresses sympathy with me but, if you have not been without food for seven days, can you have commiserated with me?"

628. The Respected Old Man of Lingqiu

The old man of Lingqiu was an expert in apiculture. Each year he harvested several thousand *dou* (one *dou*= 10 litres) of honey. His beewax too was famous. His wealth therefore could equal that of the aristocrats, whose manor estate was granted by the monarch.

When the old man died, his son inherited the family business. Before a month had passed, the bees flew away in swarms, yet the son was not at all worried. A year later, he lost about half of his bees. In another year, all the bees had flown away, and the family's financial condition went from bad to worse.

When Tao Zhugong arrived at the state of Qi, and passed by their home, he asked the people there, saying, "The family was prosperous before. Why has it become so desolate and quiet now?"

The elderly gentleman next door told him, "That was alll because of apiculture."

Tao Zhugong wanted to know in greater detail.

The elderly gentleman said, "Formerly, when the old man was alive, there in the garden he built a thatched cottage. Inside the thatched cottage, someone was put in charge. That man would cut open the log and have its centre scooped hollow for the apiary. There was no crack, nor would it decay. The beehives were in rows and the space in between hives could be arranged as desired. Whether it be old or new hives, they were equally well ordered; the location and the direction of the windows were meticulously planned. Every five hives made up a unit with one person in charge, and the condition of the honey bees was under constant observation. The temperature of the apiary was strictly regulated, and the structure of the hives well maintained. Their hibernation and breeding were watched. If they bred too fast and too numerous, it would be necessary to divide them into separate swarms. If, however, the number had decreased, then two separate groups would have to be incorporated into one. But never allowed a swarm with two queens. The spiders and ants should be exterminated, and the harassment of the scoliids and fly-catching spiders stopped. During the summertime, he took care they were not exposed to the sun; in the winter, he guarded against freezing. And they were never left to the mercy of the elements. The wind would not sway them, the rain would not submerge them. As the honey was harvested, he made sure to get the surplus only, and not to exhaust everything the bees earned with their labour. In this manner, the original bees would be able to live peacefully, and the new ones will have the opportunity to rest and multipy. Thus the old gentleman need not leave his home to reap the reward. Nowadays, his son's style is different. The thatched cottage in the garden is not repaired, the dirt and filth are not cleaned up, the apiary is left unattended whether it be dry or wet, and it is closed and opened at will. As the apiary is disturbed, the coming and going of the bees are affected, and the bees no longer wish to stay. In time, the hairy caterpillars come to live with the bees, and ants and mole crickets bore into the hives. As there is nobody to look into it; the quails will peck at the honey during daytime and the foxes steal it in the nighttime. They are all undetected. The son only pick the honey, and that's all. How can the condition not become desolate?"

Turning to his disciples, Tao Zhugong said, "Alas! Those who are monarchs of states and have their subjects under them must never fail to learn from this!"

629. A Broken Promise

South of Ji River, there was a merchant. His boat capsized while crossing the river. He took hold of a bundle of floating straw and cried aloud for help. A fisherman steered his boat over and tried to rescue him. The boat was still some distance away when the merchant shouted, saying, "I'm a rich man living in the vicinity of Ji River. If you can save me, I'll give you one hundred pieces of gold as reward."

After the fisherman picked him up, the merchant, however, gave him only ten pieces of gold. The fisherman said, "You have promised a reward of one hundred pieces of gold, but gave only ten. How could you do that to me?"

The merchant immediately flew into a rage, saying, "You are a fisherman. How much can a fisherman get in a day? You have now earned ten pieces of gold in an instant. Why are you still not satisfied?" The fisherman fell into a depression and left at once.

Sometime later, the same merchant was sailing down the Luliang River with the current when his boat hit a rock and sank. By coincidence, the fisherman was also on the spot, and people asked him, "Why don't you go to save the mechant?"

"This is a man who promised a reward but negated it later," replied the fisherman. And he just looked on and did nothing, watching the merchant drowned in the water.

630. Butting Bull and Neighing Horse

The Duke Yi of Wei adored animals. He was enthralled by bullfight and allocated to the bull-keeper an official salary equivalent to that of a sergeant. Ningzi remonstrated with him, saying, "You should not do that. A bull is raised for ploughing, and not for fighting. If you allow it to fight, then ploughing will be neglected. As agriculture is the mainstay of the country, how can it be left unattended? I've heard that a good monarch will not hinder the people's endeavour to satisfy his own fancy." But the duke Yi of Wei would not listen. Since then, the price of a fighting bull rose to ten times that of a ploughing ox, and cattle were no longer kept for the purpose of ploughing. The official in charge of agriculture was unable to turn the tide.

In the state of Bei, a horse gave birth to a foal which was not good at galloping, but its neighing was music pleasing to the ear. The duke Yi of Wei loved it and had it put into his own stable. Ningzi remonstrated against it, saying, "This is a monster. If Your Highness will not wake up, the country will surely perish. The function of a horse is galloping, and neighing is not its field of endeavour. A monarch's duty is to look after the people entrusted by Heaven and, to assist him, assignments are given to the various officials, each after his own duty. Dereliction of duty is to be punished, and so they must not do things outside their jurisdiction. If the monarch will not lead, then the fountainhead is obstructed; when a monster begins to make trouble, it is as a rule because men court for it. You will see that from now on, there will be more and more farmers who don't know how to work in the field, more and more women who don't know how to operate the loom. By that time, you will certainly regret." Again, the duke Yi of Wei refused to listen. Then the *di* tribes (northern tribes in ancient China) launched an attack on the state of Wei in the following year. As the duke Yi of Wei ascended the chariot to lead his army in an attempt to defend the country, the driver could not find the reins and the bit. As the battle was about to begin, his soldiers could not even hold the bows and shoot the arrows. Eventually, he was defeated in Yingze and killed by the *di* tribes.

631. The Duke Ling of Jin is Fond of Dogs

The duke Ling of Jin loved dogs. He built a dog pen in the district of Quwo, and let the dogs wear embroidered dress. His trusted follower, Tu Anjia, boasted before the duke Ling of Jin everyday about how clever the dogs were, which made the duke Ling of Jin loved his dogs even more.

One night, a wild fox came into the palace, and frightened the concubine of the duke Ling of Jin, Lady Xiang. Lady Xiang was very angry. The duke Ling of Jin let loose the dogs to catch the wild fox, but it was all to no avail. Tu Anjia asked the official in charge of the mountain forests to catch another wild fox, which he presented to the duke Ling of Jin, saying, "The dogs have indeed caught the wild fox."

The duke Ling of Jin was overjoyed. He gave the senior official's food to the dogs, and issued a general notice to the whole city, stating, "Anyone who dares to encroach on my dogs will have his legs cut off." And so everyone in the city was terrified when they saw the dogs of the duke Ling of Jin.

When the dogs entered the market place, they would take liberties with the mutton and pork hanging there. In addition, each of them would carry back in its mouths another piece to Tu Anjia. Thus, all of a sudden, Tu Anjia got a lot of meat. If any senior official wished to submit a memorial against the wish of Tu Anjia, a whole flock of dogs would come out to bite him, making no distinction between right and wrong. Zhao Xuanzi intended to remonstrate with the duke Ling of Jin, but the dogs rushed against him and stopped him from entering the palace.

Later, the dog went to the palace garden of the duke Ling of Jin and ate the lamb he kept. Tu Anjia deceived the duke by saying it was the high-ranking official Zhao Dun's dog which did it.

The duke Ling of Jin was enraged and sent someone to kill Zhao Dun. Zhao Dun's countrymen, however, helped him escape to the state of Qin. In view of the fact that everyone hated Tu Anjia, Zhao Dun's younger clan brother, Zhao Chuan, led a punitive expedition to attack him. He was caught and killed. At the same time, the duke Ling of Jin was also executed in the Peach Garden. The dogs he kept scattered all over the city, which were later caught, killed, cooked and eaten by the people.

632. Hu Lizi Chooses a Boat

Hu Lizi intended to travel back to Southern Guangdong via the district of Wu, and the prime minister sent someone to see him off, saying, "Please choose any government-owned boat you like for your return journey."

On the day of his departure, while the man who was to see him off had yet to arrive, Hu Lizi was already there by the riverside. Off shore, there were approximately a thousand boats there, but it was difficult for him to find which one was a government-owned ship.

By that time, the man to see him off had arrived, and Hu Lizi asked him, "There are so many boats here. How do you know which one belongs to the government?" "That's easy. Just find the one with its awning open, the shaft of the scull broken, and the sail in rags, that will be the government-owned ship we want," replied the man. Following this description, as expected, they soon found a government-owned boat.

Hu Lizi lifted up his eyes and sighed, saying, "Are those in charge of government affairs today take the people as 'government-owned people'? Since too few of them love the 'government-owned people', the people must become poverty-stricken as a matter of course!"

633. Anlingjun

Anlingjun was the favourite of the king of Chu, who was entrusted with the affairs of state. Jing Sui requested Jiang Yi to suggest to Anlingjun that the land of the district of Yunmeng be allowed to rent out to the people, so that they could be self-sufficient and not destitute and homeless. Anlingjun asked for instructions from the king, who acquiesced to the suggestion. One day, Anlingjun happened to meet Jing Sui and asked him how much rental he could get from the land, and Jing Sui said he received nothing. Anlingjun was stunned, saying, "It was because I believed you would turn it to profit the king of Chu that I made the suggestion, and now I realize you only did it as a favour to the people." Jing Sui turned pale as he heard this, and left hastily. He later told people, saying, "The country will soon fall into a crisis. In the court, everyone, up and down, is doing things to profit himself and not the people. It will be dangerous to go on like this!"

634. The Dog as an Analogy

Mi Zixia was at a loss to understand how he had made the duke Ling of Wei angry when the duke Ling of Wei ordered the palace guard to beat and throw him out. He was so frightened that he dared not attend court for the next three days. The duke Ling of Wei asked the high-ranking official, Zhu Tuo, "Do you think Mi Zixia will hate me?" "He will not," replied Zhu Tuo. The duke Ling of Wei asked why, and Zhu Tuo again replied, "I don't know whether you have observed the dog. The dog depends on man for its food. When the owner of a dog is displeased, he will beat it, and it will cry and go away, but when it becomes hungry again and needs to eat, it will approach its master, and forget all about the beating it receives from him. At the moment, Mi Zixia is a dog of yours. He relies on Your Highness to give him food. If he cannot win Your Highness' love even for one day, then he will have to go without food that day. How dare he hate you?" "That's right. This is as it should be," the duke Ling of Wei said.

635. Killing One Horse to Save Another

Hu Lizi went to the district of Ai, where he said to its commanding officer, "I've heard that one of the horses which pull your carriage, the inside left horse, has fallen ill, and the vet said, 'It can only be cured by drinking a live horse's blood.' For that reason, your groom sent someone to ask for my outside horse. This put me in an awkward position, and I did not give it to him." The officer commented, "Killing one horse to save another doesn't make sense. How could he have said it?" Hu Lizi said, "That's why I felt a little perplexed. I'm reassured now by your enlightenment. But there is another point I want to take this opportunity to ask for your instructions. I've heard that the monarch of a country must rely on the farmers to cultivate the land and the soldiers to fight a war, but who can say which one is not the sovereign's subject? If the soldiers are not in sufficient number, the farmers will not be protected; on the other hand, if the farmers who cultivate the land are too few, the soldiers will not have enough food to live on. The relation between the soldiers and the farmers is like the hands and the feet, neither side can be left without. Your soldiers are oppressing the farmers now, and you do not stop them. In case any lawsuit arises between them, the farmers are always on the receiving end. It is as if you only treasured the hands and not the feet. Take for example, your groom knows only that you cannot go without the inside horse, but doesn't care that I too must have the outside horse. Formerly, the legal wife of the duke Hu of Chen, Da Ji, loved dancing, and all the mulberry trees in the vicinity of Wanqiu were rooted out by the people there and replaced with the willows. The current situation makes me feel terribly uneasy for you when I think of it."

636. The King of Song Loathes the King of Chu

The king of Song hated the king Wei of Chu. For that reason, he enjoyed speaking ill of the state of Chu. Every morning when he attended the court, he would made fun of the state of Chu by slandering it, saying, "The state of Chu is incompetent in the extreme. Am I about to take over it?" And all the court officials would echo his view. Their tone was so similar that it was as if spoken by the same man. Anyone who travelled from the state of Chu to the state of Song would of necessity fabricate some story about Chu's failing before he would be allowed to enter the state of Song. In Song, regardless of whether he be an official or a common man, everyone would exaggerate the false story a bit so that by the time it reached the court, the king of Song, as expected, would be convinced that the state of Chu was not equal to Song. Thus the ambition to attack the state of Chu began to take shape gradually in the king's mind. Hua Chou, a high-ranking official, remostrated with the king, saying, "The state of Song is utterly no match for the state of Chu. The difference between the two states is similar to that between the zokhor and the monster bull. Even if the state of Chu were as incompetent as Your Highness had envisioned, still the power of Chu is ten times that of the state of Song. One to ten, that is to say, even if Song were victorious ten times, it must not be defeated even once. How can we stake the fate of our country in an adventurous attempt?" The king of Song, however, turned a deaf ear to his advice, and insisted on starting military action. The army of Chu was defeated at Yingshang, which made the king of Song very proud of himself, and became even more presumptuous. Again, Hua Chou remostrated, saying, "I've heard that when a small country defeats a big country, it is because the big one is neglectful in taking precautions, and although a small country may win a war by sheer good luck, one should not always hope for luck and be complacent because a war has been won, one must not take military action lightly and belittle the enemy. It isn't right to bully a common man, let alone such a large state as Chu. Now that the state of Chu has been defeated, it must have already taken precautionary measures, whereas you have become arrogant and imperious. Disaster may be very near now." The king of Song was infuriated by what Hua Chou had said, and the latter had to flee to the state of Qi. In the following year, the king of Song, still dreaming to defeat the state of chu, again took military action against it. But Chu repulsed it and went on to counterattack until it wiped out the state of Song.

637. The Macaques

A man in the state of Chu earned his livelihood by keeping macaques, and people called him "Lord of Macaques". In his courtyard every morning, he organized the macaques into groups and assigned work for each to do. A senior macaque was ordered to lead the others to the mountain to pick the fruits that grew wild in the forest, of which he only allocated one-tenth for the macaques' daily consumption. He would whip those who could not hand in the assigned quantity, and the macaques hated him for the hardship and beating they had to endure, though no one dared to defy him openly.

One day, a small macaque raised a question, "Are the wild fruits in the mountain cultivated by our master?"

"No, they are not," replied all the macaques. "They grow wild by themselves."

"Isn't it no one can pick them unless permitted by the master?" asked the little macaque again.

"No, everyone can pick them," the macaques replied with one voice.

"In that case, why should we rely on him and be enslaved?" opined the little macaque.

Before the little macaque finished talking, all the macaques had already come to realize the truth. That night, they waited untill the Lord of Macaques was fast asleep. They broke the palings, smashed the wooden cage, carried the fruits the Lord of Macaques had accumulated and, holding each others' hands, they entered the forest, never to return.

The Lord of Macaques eventually died of hunger.

638. A Man of Meng City Berates the Tiger

A man who lived in the City of Meng went to the open country with a piece of lion skin on himself. A tiger noticed it and ran away. The man thought the tiger was afraid of himself. As he returned home, he became conceited and began to brag about it.

The next day, he wore a fox fur coat to the wilderness and met the tiger again. The tiger stopped and cast a sidelong glance at him. He was very angry because the tiger did not run away, and he berated it. In the end, he was eaten by the tiger.

639. Yu Lizi Admonishes Ji Xian

Yu Lizi told Ji Xian, "In my journey abroad, I once came to the vicinity of Ru River and the Sishui River, where I saw a temple for the gods constructed on the outskirts of the village. The main hall of the temple was dedicated to the goddess, while the wings were allocated to the spirits. There was nothing else in the goddess hall except incense and candles, whereas in the halls of the spirits, there were tripods of eatables in rows and musical performances, and candlelights day and night. At present, your gate and courtyard is very much like a country fair, regardless of whether it be rain or shine, cold or heat, the noises of geese, ducks, lambs, and the like make such a din that it is difficult even to listen to what people talk. From the bottom of my heart, I really am afraid that you will not become the goddess but just uncle spirits." Ji Xian was killed in the following year when his armed forces were defeated in the ruins of Paogua.

640. Pangolin as Dragon

Someone presented to Shanglingjun a pangolin, and described it as if it were a dragon. Shanglingjun was very pleased and asked him what must it be fed with, and the man replied, "Ants." Shanglingjun then told his man to raise and train it. Another man said it was only a pangolin and not a dragon, which made Shanglingjun very unhappy when he learned of it, and gave the man a good lashing with his whip. Everyone was frightened and none dared say it was not a dragon. They just followed Shanglingjun's example, and treated the pangolin as a god. On one occasion, Shanglingjun was watching and admiring his so-called dragon, which rolled itself into a ball at times, and at other times stretched out its body. The men around him feigned astonishment, marvelling at its mysteriousness, which brought Shanglingjun's excitement to a new height, and had the pangolin moved to the palace. Quite unexpectedly, the pangolin dug a hole at night and escaped. The people around him hastily reported the incident to Shanlingjun, pretending to be surprised and said, "That dragon is really a marvel. It surprises us all by boring into the rock and left us."

Shanglingjun inspected the trail it left, feeling sorry and heart-broken. He asked people to have the ants ready, hoping that the dragon would come back. Not long after that, thunder accompanied by lightning came with heavy downpour, and the real dragon appeared. Shanglingjun thought the dragon had returned, and brought out the ants to welcome it. The real dragon mistook the gesture as teasing. In anger, it shook the palace until it collapsed. Ironically, it caused the death of Shanglingjun. People commented, "Shanglingjun is much too foolish. He mistook the pangolin as a dragon and, when the real dragon came, he fed it with what the pangolin had before. That infuriated the real dragon and it raised the tremor. He was killed when the palace collapsed, but he had only himself to blame."

641. People of the Dark Valley

In the dark valley, there lived an ethnic group who abhorred the sun and had to reside in a cave away from the sunlight. In that place, a snake which could blow fogs also lived, whom the people of the dark valley respectfully served as, in and out of the cave, all depended on its ability to cover the whole area with mist, day and night. A wizard duped the people of the dark valley by saying, "My god has already eaten the sun, and there is none now." The people of the dark valley believed what the wizard said, and thought there was no longer a sun in the sky. They therefore left the cave and moved to a dry and higher ground. The son of Xihe, on his way to Yanzi, passed the dark valley and said to the people there, "The sun has not vanished. You are only enveloped in mist. Although the moisture of the fogs can block the sunlight, but how can it cause the sun to vanish? The sun exists as long as the sky is there, it will not disappear. I've heard that *yin* cannot conquer *yang*, and evil can never prevail over good. The snake is a monster that hides in the dark. The gods and spirits will question its existence, and the thunderbolt will strike it. It is using the wizard to spread rumour and deceive you so you will follow it blindly. Can it continue for long? The cave is where you habitually lived. If you believe the lies and leave the place, when the mist dissipates following the death of the snake, can you stand the strong sunlight then?" The people of the dark valley then went to the wizard to seek a solution, but the wizard feared that his deception might be exposed and dodged the real issue. Before a month had passed, the snake was struck dead by thunder and lightning, and the fogs dissipated following its death.

The strong sunlight now shone brightly upon the high ground, and the people of the dark valley could only exhale at one another to moisten themselves. In the end they were all scorched to death by the sun.

642. A Fungus

A man in Guangdong found a big fungus in the mountain. It was so big it could fill a large chest. It had a nine-layered cap, yellowish gold in colour, and radiating brilliant light. He brought the big fungus home and said to his wife, "This is what people often referred to as the mysterious glossy ganoderma; if eaten, a man can become an immortal. I've heard that immortality is predestined, and heaven never allow a man to become an immortal without reason. It is something people earnestly hope for but cannot get it. I now come by the fungus without effort, that may mean I'm about to become an immortal." Thus he took a bath and fasted for three days, cooked the big fungus and ate it. Who would have thought that the moment he swallowed it, he was killed by the poison it contained. His son looked at him and remarked, "I've heard that those who attained perfection in Taoism must leave his human body behind in this world. Most people are encumbered with the human body and cannot attain immortality. Now, my father has only shaken of his outer form, and he is not dead." So saying, he too ate what was left of the big fungus, and died. The entire family then ate it, and all were dead.

As Yu Lizi heard about it, he sighed with deep emotion and said, "In today's world, those who aspire to attain longevity but die even sooner all belong to this category!"

643. To Know People

The king of Yue assigned his senior official, Ziyu, to build ships. After he had finished building them, a merchant came to him, asking Ziyu to let him take charge of the crew, but Ziyu refused to employ him. Thereupon the merchant went to the state of Wu, where Wang Sunshuai introduced him to the king. When he met the king of Wu, he told him how the senior official of the state of Yue could not appreciate a man of ability as the reason he decided to come over to the state of Wu. One day, Wang Sunshuai accompanied him to the riverside to view the scenery of the great river. Suddenly a strong wind arose, and the ship in the river began to rock and sway terribly. He pointed at the ships in the river and said to Wang Sunshuai, "This ship will turn over, and that one will not." And, sure enough, the outcome was as he had predicted. Wang Sunshuai was greatly impressed by his ability, and recommended him to the king of Wu. The king of Wu assigned him to be the commanding officer of the fleet. As the news reached the state of Yue, the people all blamed Ziyu for not retaining a talented man, but Ziyu explained, "I understand him well. We had once worked together. He likes to draw the long bow, a megalomania who thinks no one throughout the state of Yue can equal him. I've heard that a braggart is wont to think that he never errs, as he wants people to praise or promote him. He who likes to talk about others being not equal to himself has the habit of picking on the mistakes of others, but does not know that in fact he is not as good as the people he despises. Today, the state of Wu employs him but, eventually, things will go astray in his hands." However, people were not convinced at the time. Not long after that, the state of Wu went to war with the state of Chu, and the king of Wu assigned him to command the flotilla. Leaving the Five Lakes and just reaching the mouth of the three rivers, the battleships capsized and sank. The event proved to the people of Yue that Ziyu after all was sagacious, and they remarked, "If the merchant did not sink and die with his ships, then Ziyu would have been despised as a man who forsook a talented man, and became the joke of the state. If it should come to that, then even Tao Gao, Yao Shun's gifted minister, would not have been able to clear him."

644. Bu Wei Seeks Shelter

The state of Yue was invaded by the enemy. To avoid the catastrophe caused by war, Bu Wei fled to a place called Shan. As he had not a cash in his pocket, he did not have the wherewithal to provide himself with a house. Thus he wandered around the Tianlao Mountain for almost half a day and passed the night under a big tree. On the following day, he picked up his axe, intending to cut down the tree for firewood, but his wife hastened to stop him, saying, "We have no house and on this large tree we depend for our shelter. It protects us from the sunlight, the freezing dew, the wind and the rain, and even thunder and lightning. What can we rely upon for all these? Is it not this large tree? That's why we should protect it like protecting our son, respect it like respecting our loving mother, take care of it like taking care of our own bodies. Even acting in this manner, I still am afraid that it will not grow to be luxuriant in branches and leaves. How dare we hurt it in any way? I've heard that when the spring water shrinks, the fish in it will feel uneasy; when the bell announces the coming of frost, the birds in its nest will feel melancholy. Why? They are afraid that the water in the river may dry up and the trees in the forest may wither! Since even the fish and birds feel that way, how much more should men be?" As Yu Lizi listened, he sighed, saying, "How sad it is! The man's knowledge and experience is far inferior than the woman. Alas! He is not only inferior to a woman, he is not even equal to the birds and fish!"

645. No Differrence Between "Fire" and "Tiger"

In Dongou (Wenzhou, Zhejiang Province) dialect, the Chinese Characters "fire" and "tiger" were homophones. There were no earthern tiles in the locality, and people had to thatch their roof, which, incidentally, often caused fire and, at times, proved calamitous to the residents. At the seaside, there was a merchant who did business in the state of Jin. He heard about a man by the name of Feng Fu, who was good at subduing the tiger. Because of him, there was no threat in the vicinity. After he returned to Dongou, the merchant told Dongoujun about the man, and Dongoujun was very pleased by the information. Thus generous gifts made up of horse, jade, brocade and satin were prepared, and the merchant was assigned as messenger to the state of Jin to invite Feng Fu. Upon his arrival, Feng Fu received the best treatment a guest could possibly get. It so happened the day following his arrival, a fire broke out in one of the families there. Someone came to tell Feng Fu about it, and Feng Fu immediately rolled up his sleeves and followed the man who brought the message to the scene, but he could not find any trace of the tiger, although he had looked for it everywhere. By that time, the fire had spread to the vicinity of the palace and the shops. He was surrounded by the crowd, who went to the scene to help quell the fire. As a result, Feng Fu was burned to death; the merchant too was punished for deceiving the emperor. But for all that, Feng Fu was in the dark up to the time of his death as to what it was all about.

646. Ju Meng Leaves for Yi Qu

A man called Ju Meng had acquired the superb skill to domesticate the elephant, and he came to the state of Yi Qu for the sole purpose of practising his profession. He went to see the king of Yi Qu to seek a corresponding position, but the king did not accede to his request. Dejectedly, he returned to the guesthouse, where he poured out a stream of abuse on the king. The manager of the guesthouse said to him, "Not that the king did not want to give in to your request, but that there is utterly no elephant in this place." The words made Ju Meng feel ashamed as he left the place.

647. Que E Flees to Qin

The relation of Qin and Chu had reached an impasse, and Zuoyin Que E of Chu had fled to the state of Qin, where he kept on talking ill of the state of Chu. The king of Qin was very pleased and intended to bestow on him a high-ranking position.

Chen Zhen said, "Among my neighbours, there was a woman, who fled from her husband, a high-ranking official, and remarried. She told her new husband, with whom she seemed to share the same likes and dislikes, a lot of bad things about her former husband. Later, she again fell into disfavour. As she got divorced and remarried for the third time to a guest from a place south of the city, she again slandered her second husband, just as she had done to her first husband before. When the guest told her second husband about what she said, her second husband burst into laughter, saying, 'What she told you now was what she had spoken to me about before!' Now, Zuoyin came from the state of Chu and spoke a lot of bad things about that state. If he should fall into disfavour some day with Your Highness and flee to another country, he would certainly use the same slanderous words which he used agaisnt the king of Chu." The king of Qin listened to Chen Zhen's advice and did not use Que E.

648. Replacing the Beam

The beam of a big house had been eaten hollow by the worms, and the house was in a precarious state. The owner of the house intended to replace it with a new beam, and invited a craftsman there. The craftsman, after looking into it, told the owner, "The beam is utterly worm-eaten, and it must be replaced. But you must prepare the appropriate materials first. It won't do if the materials are not suitable." The owner could not accept the proposal and so he invited another craftsman, who used a number of small sticks bound together to replace the old beam. In the depth of winter that year, there was a heavy downpour of rain and snow in the eleventh moon, and the replacement snapped. The big house followed suit and collapsed.

649. Cat, Mice and Chickens

A man of the state of Zhao, fearing disaster brought about by the mice, went to the state of Zhongshan to ask for a cat. The people of Zhongshan gave him a cat, but the cat not only caught the mice, it also ate the chickens. After a month, all the mice in the house were exterminated. However, the chickens too were all consumed. His son was very worried and said to his father, "Why not get rid of the cat?"

His father replied, "The how and the why of the matter are beyond your comprehension. Our constant cause of trouble is the mice, and not the chickens. Provided there are mice, our food will be stolen, our clothes torn, our walls bored through, our utensils damaged and, because of all this, we are likely to suffer cold and hunger. Isn't it the situation much worse than without the chickens? We'll only have no chickens for our meal at most if all the chickens are gone, but it is far from having to suffer from cold and hunger. Why should we get rid of the cat?"

650. Coercive Measure

The district magistrate fell ill with a sense of oppression in the chest, feeling giddy and confused, so he invited a physician from the state of Qin to treat him. When his illness was cured, he reported the matter to the king of Chu, and the king of Chu ordered all his subjects to go to the state of Qin for treatment if they should fall ill, forbidding them to go to other places to seek remedy.

Not long after that, a pestilence raged through the state of Chu. Those who were treated by Qin physicians were all dead. So the people turned to the state of Qi for treatment, but the district magistrate was extremely enraged and wanted to seize those who went to see the Qi physicians. Ziliang said to the district magistrate, "That's not the right thing to do because, when a man falls ill and sees the physician for medicine, he is only trying to save his own life!"

651. A Nine-headed Bird

In the big mountain of Nieyao, there was a bird which had nine heads, albeit only one body. When one head got any food, all the other eight heads contended for it, each head opening its big mouth to peck the other heads, so that blood began to shed all over its body, and its feathers set flying all over the place. The food was yet to enter the oesophagus, but the nine heads were all wounded with bites.

The wild ducks in the sea noticed and mocked it, saying, "Why don't you think it over: all the food entering the nine mouths go into the same stomach? Why must you keep on fighting?"

652. Shi Kuang Tunes the Musical Instrument

The duke Ping of Jin made a musical instrument, on which the big strings and the small strings were without distinction, and their length as well as their degree of thickness were exactly the same. He then invited the famous contemporary musician Shi Kuang to give a test but, despite a day's manipulating, Shi Kuang was unable to get a normal tune out of it.

The duke Ping of Jin blamed Shi Kuang for playing it badly. Shi Kuang refused to give in. "The big strings and the small strings in a musical insrument each has its own function," he said. "When they are in harmony with one another, a melodious tune is produced. Now that all the strings are made exactly the same, how can I play it well?"

653. Wu Zhiqi and He Bo Go to War

The god of Huaihe River, Wu Zhiqi, and the god of yellow River, He Bo, were at war with one another. Wu Zhiqi designated Tian Wu as supreme commander, Xiang Yishi as deputy commander, and the gods of wind, rain, cloud and thunder, together with the flood dragon, the cicada, the crocodile and the pangolin as vanguards. They set the waves rolling and advanced towards the vicinity of Jieshi and Qiliang. He Bo was greatly alarmed, and thought of fleeing, but Ling Guxu stopped him, saying, "It's better to accept the challenge. If you should lose, there would still be time to escape." And together they deliberated on the choice of a suitable man as supreme commander. Ling Guxu suggested, "The sea turtle can be designated as supreme commander." He Bo responded by saying, "The other side has Tian Wu as its suprime commander, who possesses eight heads and eight feet, its deputy Xiang Yishi who will assist him has nine heads of his own, and the wind, the rain, the cloud and the thunder each has its ability. Together, they make up the core force, while the flood dragon, the cicada, the crocodile and the pangolin each possesses tail like a sword, mouth like a chisel, and scales and shells as keen as razors. At the shake of a head, the mountain can be destroyed. As each holds erect the dorsal fin, the sea will turn over. How can the sea turtle stand up to such powerful force?" But Ling Guxu affirmed with conviction, "It is precisely because of all this that I recommend the sea turtle. As a supreme commander, he is the head of the three armed services. Only when all the members in the three armed forces follow the instructions of one man that concerted action can be taken. When millions of people united as one man, then there is none under heaven to equal him. Now, Tian Wu has eight heads, and its deputy has nine. I've heard that a man's mind has its focus in the eyes and the ears; when there are too many eyes and ears, the result will be confusion. Now that two minds have the task of mobilizing sixty-eight eyes and ears, the consequence will be topsy-turvy. Moreover, since the wind, the rain, the cloud and the thunder each has its own ability and anxious to show off, how can they coordinate their action? That's why I say the sea turtle is more than capable of shouldering the responsibility. The sea turtle is cool-headed by temperament and will not be swayed either by deception or threat, nor will he be easily enraged and lose his cool. Once his mind is made up, he will fight it out to the bitter end and beat the enemy. We will certainly come out victorious." Thus He Bo designated the sea turtle as its supreme commander, leading the unicorn to meet the enemy head-on. In the end, he gained a complete victory.

654. Chang Yang Learns Archery

Chang Yang learned archery from Tulong Zizhu. Tulong Zizhu said, "Do you want to learn the secret of archery? When the king of Chu went to hunt in the marshes of Yunchu, he first sent the official in charge of forests to drive the animals out. As the animals were driven out, a deer appeared on the left side of king Chu, and an elk ran across the right. The king of Chu was just pulling his bowstring to shoot when a swan suddenly swept past his red crank banner, its two wings stretched out as huge as the drooping clouds. The king of Chu fitted an arrow to the string, but did not know what to shoot. Yang Youji gave the king of Chu a word of advice, saying, "When I was shooting, I would place a leaf of the tree at a distance of one hundred paces, and score ten bull's eyes out of ten without a single miss. If I were to have ten leaves, I would not be so sure I could do it."

655. The Yue Craftsman

In the state of Yue there was a craftsman who was adept in building ships. The king of Yue assigned him to the post, and he proved equal to the job. The king ordered the official of the grain bureau to give him the best provisions. The fellow craftsmen of Yue in the shipbuilding industry also respected him very much. A year later, the craftsman said to the king, "Not only can I build ships, I can also steer them." The king believed what he said and placed him at the helm. In the battle of Junli, a strong wind swept across the Five Lakes; with billows dashing against the sky, the craftsman and the ship he piloted were drawn into the lake and swallowed by the water. The people of Yue felt extremely sorry for him. Yu Lizi commented, "He belongs to the category of people who draw a snake and add feet to it—superflouous."

656. Tu Longzi and Duli Confront Each Other in a Chess Game

The two men, Tu Longzi and Duli, confronted each other in a chess game, and Duli had lost several game in succession. All the people in the inn sympathized with him, and tried to back him up, but he lost all the same. The spectators surrounding them were all amazed at the result, and supported Duli together. The attendant of Tu Longzi urged his master to discontinue, saying, "I've heard the adage 'the few are no match for the many'; now that the other side work and pull together, I'm afraid you may not be able to defeat them, thus wasting all the previous efforts." Tu Longzi, however, objected to the idea, and continued to confront Duli. Once again, Duli was utterly defeated, as there was absolutely no room for him to manoeuvre. The spectators watched in amazement, as they held the chess pieces and blamed each other. Tu Longzi invited them for another game, but no one dared to accept the challenge. Tu Longzi's attendant was overjoyed, and said, "Master, you are miraculously skillful!" Tu Longzi replied, "It should not be viewed in that way. Did you ever seen two animals fighting one another? Of all the animals, the tiger is the most ferocious. If tiger fights with tiger, one tiger is of course difficult to defeat a group of tigers, which is easy to understand. If the opponents are tiger and fox, then even a thousand foxes will be no match for a single tiger. Sometimes, more people will create even greater confusion."

657. Yu Fu

Yu Fu had approached master Ji Rang for advice on the way to make a living, and master Ji Rang passed on to him the expertise of planting lacquer trees. In three years, the lacquer trees had grown up, and Yu Fu began to cut them for lacquer. He harvested several hundred *hu* (one *hu*=ten *dou;* one *dou*=one decalitre), which he intended to sell in the state of Wu. His elder brother-in-law said to him, "I've often done business in the state of Wu, and know that the people of Wu attach great importance to decoration. There are lots of lacquer men, and Lacquer is a hot consumer item. I've seen lacquer sellers cooked lacquer leaves until they turned into paste, and mixed it with the lacquer, which helps to double the profits without being detected." Yu Fu was very pleased with the descovery and followed what his elder brother-in-law had suggested, cooking the leaves of lacquer trees into paste, putting it into several hundred jugs, and transported them to the state of Wu with the lacquer. The state of Wu and the state of Yue were not in friendly terms at that time. As the merchants of Yue could not enter the state of Wu, it was very difficult for the people of Wu to get lacquer. When one of the brokers of Wu knew there was lacquer available, he was overjoyed and went to the suburbs to accompany Yu Fu to the state of Wu. After an exchange of customary greetings, the broker had Yu Fu lodged in his own business establishment. The lacquer proved to be of high quality upon examination, and the broker agreed to take delivery of the goods and pay with gold coins. Yu Fu was delighted, and mixed the cooked lacquer leaves with the lacquer that very night, while waiting for the buyer to take delivery. At the agreed time, the brokcr of Wu arrived punctually. He discovered all the paper seals were new, and suspected they had been tampered with, so he proposed to Yu Fu to wait another twenty days. At the end of twenty days, the lacquer was spoilt, and Yu Fu was stranded in the streets of a foreign country without money and unable to return home. He was starved to death in Wu.

658. Ruo Shi

Ruo Shi was a recluse living in the northern side of Ming Mountain. A tiger was often seen crouch near the hedge and eye his house with hostility. Ruo Shi kept a sharp lookout with his family, beating gongs at sunrise, and lighting the torch at sunset. At night, he rang the bells and kept watch. He planted thistles and thorns around his house, built walls in the courtyard, and dug holes in the valley to defend themselves. A year had passed, and the tiger was unable to get near.

One day, the tiger died. Ruo Shi was overjoyed, believing nothing could harm them from then on. He dismantled the mechanism for defence, pulled down guarding facilities, the crumbling courtyard walls were left unrepaired, and the damaged fences were not mended.

Not long after that, a ferocious animal pursued an elk all the way to a corner of his house. As it stopped, it heard the sound of cattle, lambs and pigs, and it forced its way into the house and ate them. Ruo Shi did not realize it was a ferocious animal and shouted at it, but it did not retreat. He picked up a stone and threw at it. The animal suddenly stood up like a man, and pounced on him with its sharp claws, and he was clawed to death.

People commented, "Ruo Shi has a one-sided view. He was aware of only one aspect and ignorant of the other. It served him right to have come to such an end!"

659. Leopard Cat

When Yu Lizi was living in the mountain, one night a leopard cat came to steal the chickens he kept. By the time he discovered it, it was already too late. The next day, his servant found out the place where the leopard cat slipped in, and placed a chicken there as bait. As expected, the leopard cat came again. As it bit the chicken's neck, it was caught and immediately bound up. Although the leopard cat was tied, it still gripped the chicken with its teeth. The servant beat it while trying to snatch the chicken from its mouth, but the leopard cat would not let go even unto death. Yu Lizi sighed and said, "Those people who die for wealth are really no difference from this leopard cat!"

660. Jue Shu Trice Regrets

Jue Shu was an extremely self-confident man. If people advised him to go east, he would deliberately direct his steps to the west. He did farm work north of Guishan, choosing the high terrain to plant rice, and a low-lying land to grow sorghum. His friend advised him, saying, "Sorghum likes to grow in high terrain, and rice prefers humid low-lying land, but you do just the opposite, which is against their nature. How can you gather any crops?" Jue Shu, however, refused to listen, and continued his habitual practice in farming. For a period of ten years, it was always like that. As a result, his granary had no reserve. He went to see other people, and discovered all his friends cultivated their crops in accordance with the nature of each, and every year they reaped a bumper harvest. So he visited his friend and said, "I know I've committed a mistake." Later, he went to do business in Wenshang. When he saw hot consumer goods, he would go anywhere to get them. But, as the market was full of similar merchandise, his goods encountered poor sales almost as a rule. His friend told him, "A smart merchant buys goods that are temporarily not in great demand and waits for the opportunity. In this way, he will reap greater profit. During the Warring States Period, a wealthy merchant by the name of Bai Gui was such a man, and he became a rich man." But Jue Shu was still not convinced. Consequently, he remained poor in the next ten years. Not only was he not getting any richer, he had lost all his capital. By this time, he began to remember what his friend had said, and regretted. Thus he went to see his friend a second time, and swore before him, saying, "From now on, I'll change my way, and commit no more msitakes." Then, one day, Jue Shu invited his friend to take a sea voyage. He padled his boat towards the east, and soon they reached the deepest part of the sea. His friend warned him, "We already come near the deepest part. If we continue to go forward, we may not be able to get back." But Jue Shu turned a deaf ear to his advice, and persisted in the same direction. As a result, he could only come back after roaming abroad for the next nine years. Even then, he had to take advantage of the surge of billows caused by the enormous legendary fish when it changed into a *roc*. As he returned, his head had already turned white, and he looked haggard, almost unrecognizable. He bowed to his friend as he expressed his regrets, and swore to Heaven, saying, "If I don't repent and start anew, let me die before the day is out." His friend smiled and said, "Your repentence comes too late!" As people talked about Jue Shu, they remarked, "His whole life has been a series of regrets. To avoid being vexed, it is better that he does not do it again."

661. The Man of Qi Curses at Meals

A man of Qi was in the habit of hurling abuses at other people at meals. As the mealtime arrived, he would revile his servants to start with. At times, he even broke the bowls and threw the chopsticks about. He did it everyday. The restaurant owner disliked his behaviour very much but, considering the circumstances, he could only endure it. One day, as the man of Qi finished eating and was about to leave, the restaurant owner presented him with a dog, saying, "The dog will drive away a beast of some sort. It isn't a remarkable present, but I'll give it to you now." The man of Qi was pleased and led the dog away. As he was hungry after a long walk, he settled down in the restaurant for a meal. He hailed the dog around and gave it something to eat too. The dog yelped as it began to eat, and it continued yelping while eating until the meal was over. During the mealtime, only the curses of the master above, and the yelping of the dog below the table were heard. It was the same at every meal. One day, the servant could not help laughing, and the man of Qi discovered he was being made a fool. Yu Lizi said, "The ancients have a saying, 'A man must first disgrace himself before others can humiliate him.' 'He who indulges only in eating and drinking will certainly be looked down upon.' Probably it was this category of people that were being referred to."

662. Xuan Shi is Addicted to Wine

Formerly, Xuan Shi was addicted to wine, and his health was affected. He felt all the five internal organs in his abdominal cavity terribly hot, his muscles and bones like being steamed with a boiling pot, and his entire skeletal framework about to collapse. He had tried many methods of cure but all to no avail, and it was only after a lapse of three days that all the symtoms had gone. He told people, saying, "I now know drinking can kill a man, and I'll never drink again!"

But a month of peace had hardly elapsed when his drinking companions visited him. They said to him, "Try drink just a little." At first, he only had three cups; then he drank five on the second day; on the third day, he took ten. Came the fifth day, he was completely drunken. He had forgotten what he once said that drinking could kill a man. Throwing caution to the winds, he went on drinking. As a result, he died at last.

That's why we say, a cat cannot go without fish, a chicken without worm, and a dog without shit. It is their nature, an inborn desire that cannot be relinquished!

663. As Luck Would Have It

In the outskirts of the city of Juzhang, there lived a farmer. He once covered his fence with straw, and quite unexpectedly heard a chirping sound. As he uncovered the heap of straw, there he found a pheasant. Thereupon he again covered the fence with some straw, hoping to come by another pheasant.

The next day, he quietly approached the heap of grass. He heard the same chirping sound as he did the day before. He uncovered the straw only to find a snake, which bit his hand, and the poison of the snake caused his death.

664. Li Ming Cries Over his treasure

A man by the name of Li Ming came by a piece of agate from the Liangfu Mountain, and thought it was a precious jade. He brought it to the market for sale, and someone told him, "It is only a piece of agate. It looks like jade, but in fact it is not. If you sell it at the price of a precious jade, that will make you a laughingstock. Besides, you will not be able to sell it in the end. Why not dispose of it as a piece of agate? Although it may not satisfy you, at least you will be able to sell it!" Li Ming, however, was not convinced, and so he carried the piece of agate and travelled by sea to the state of Yan. Unfortunately, his boat met with a weird dashing of billows. The boatman was very frightened and said to all his passengers, "There must be someone carrying a treasure, which has been discovered by the dragon king. If any person has it, please don't be closefisted. Bring it out, otherwise we may have to die together." Li Ming beat his chest and cried. When he was asked why he cried so miserably, he said, "To tell you the truth, I have with me a treasure, which must be presented to the dragon king now. How can I not feel miserable?" They all took a look at it and, as they discovered it was only a piece of agate, they all burst out laughing. The boatman too smiled, forgetting all about his dread. He teased the man by saying, "If you are not in the palace of the dragon king, there won't be anyone who knows the treasure!"

665. Man from a Remote District

In an out-of-the-way place in the state of Zheng there was a man who learned to make umbrella. When he had mastered the technique, however, there was a drought that year, and the umbrella was useless. So he abandoned the craft of making umbrella, and learned to manufacture water-drawing equipment instead. This took him three years. By that time, there was continuous rain; the water-drawing equipment became redundant, and so he began to make rain gear. Later, bandits arose in the land, and people all put on military uniform, and there were very few people who used rain gear. He had thought of learning to manufacture weapons but, by then, he was in his sunset years.

666. A Man of Wu and His Ape

A man of Wu kept an ape in the cage for ten years. One day, he suddenly felt conscience-stricken, and released the ape. The ape, however, returned to its cage two nights in succession. The man of Wu was puzzled. He thought he might have to bring it to a place further from his house, so he carried the cage to a remote mountain. As the ape had been kept in the cage for too long, it had forgotten its inborn habits, and did not know how to look for food. In the end, it cried piteously and died.

667. Sincere Advice and Flattering Words

Yu Lizi said, "Everyone knows the cries of crow do not necessarily denote a bad omen. By the same token, the sound of magpie will not bring a happy occasion. Nevertheless, if a crow keeps crying on the roof everyday, then even though happy events are there in the family very often, they will not like the cries. What if the cries come from the magpie then? Even though it may cry everyday outside your room, you will still love to listen despite the fact you have lots of unhappy things in your mind. And not only ordinary people behave in this manner, even men of great erudition are no exception. Why is it so? Is it not because of the sound they make? Everybody knows straight talk is sincere advice, but still no one likes to hear. As to flattering words, they are pretensions and lies, yet very often a man can be deceived. It is only when a man understands talking straight is a prescription beneficial to the body, that he will listen willingly; when he knows flattering words are seasonal febrile diseases that he will categorically refuse to listen. The decision is made contingent on whether or not it is advantageous or disadvantageous to oneself. That is why a sincere person, to be effective in his persuasion, must base his advice on this ground. For those who harbour evil intentions, his deception likewise is based on gains and losses to the man. It is only when a person correctly differentiates the advantages and disadvantages that he can distinguish whether or not the words are sincere or just a pack of lies."

668. The Groom of Si Chengzi

The son of Si Chengzi's groom died of globefish poisoning, but his father had not a drop of tears. Si Chengzi asked him, "Do you have any feeling for your son?" "How can I have no feeling?" replied his groom. Si Chengzi continued, "Since you feel for his death, how come you do not shed tears for him? What's the matter?" The groom replied, "I've heard life and death are preordained and those who are contented with their lots will not play with their lives. The globefish is poisonous and, if one eats it, one will die of poisoning. That is a fact known to all. Having known it, and still insists on eating it—that's to value the desire for good food more than life itself, which is not what a son should do. That's why I did not cry." Si Chengzi listened and sighed, "Is not the pernicious effect of taking bribes similar to that of the globefish? Nowadays those who rush about currying favour for personal gains, reckless in their desperation, are only a bunch of men greedy for good food and do not care for their lives. They are inferior to a groom by far, very far . . ."

669. The King of Wu and the Mynah

Fu Cha, the king of Wu, while having an evening feast, heard the mynah crying in the courtyard. He was disgusted with the noise, and sent someone to shoot it.

"That's a pleasant sound. Why shoot it?" said Wu Zixu.

The king of Wu was puzzled, and asked Wu Zixu why the mynah should not be shot at. "Why should Your Highness be so upset by a mynah? As it is born with a mouth, it will make noise. That's common sense. Why should Your Highness be disgusted with it.?" replied Wu Zixu.

"It's an enchanted bird. Whenever it cries, it brings bad luck, and that's why I dislike it," said the king.

Wu Zixu replied, "Is it true you dislike its voice because it is inauspicious? As a matter of fact, not only the mynah, which has a mouth, makes noises of ill omen, the officials around Your Highness are all extremely eloquent. Some will cover any msitakes Your Highness may have committed; others will cater to your desire; and still others will try their best to offer whatever services they can if they think it helpful. Some will speak what Your Highness like to hear, even though it is not true. They will slander those who do not fall in with them, and praise those who do. Whatever they say, there is a motive behind it, and that's why they can cause pleasure or anger, and you will never guess their true objective. Because of that, the weal or woe of Your Highness' country all tie in with their cries! Although Your Highness may not notice them, is there anything more ominous than their cries? Why don't Your Highness pay any attention to that, but only worry about the cries of a small mynah? Misery and happiness have no door—if either comes, one brings it upon oneself. How can a mynah knows it? If Your Highness believes the mynah's cries are not propitious, then precautionary measures should be taken. In the meantime, you must look for mistakes and correct them. That will be extremely beneficial. As for me, the cries of the mynah are really good to hear.!"

670. Tall Man and Short Man

There was a country called Wangwang, where the people were extremely tall. The length of their calf alone could measure over ten feet. They relied on hunting for their livelihood. However, if their prey prostrated itself on the ground and crawled forward, they would not be able to bend their body and catch it simply because they were too tall to do so, and they often had to go without food.

There was another country called Jiaojiao, where the people were extremely short. Their legs had only three inches in length, and they relied on the cicadas for food. If the cicadas took to their wings, then they would not be able to catch them, and they too often had to go hungry.

Wherefore the people of the two countries went to *Nuwa* (a goddess in Chinese mythology) to complain about their troubles. *Nuwa* said to them, "I made you with clay and, although the sizes might be different, the parts made up the body were the same, neither more nor less. The tall people should take advantage of their tallness, and the short people should also take advantage of their shortness. It is impossible to cut off a node from the tall one, nor is it feasible to add another node to the short one. It is just like the kernel inside a nut; although it is very small, yet the elements of roots, leaves, branches and trunk are all there. To take another example, say, the egg of birds. It is like a ball in appearance, but it is pregnant with feathers, beak, claws, and other organs. As to whether you are going to be the kernel or the egg of birds, it is all up to you, and quite beyond my power to decide."

671. The Tiger and the Elk

A tiger pursued an elk closely behind, and the elk ran for all it was worth. At last it arrived at the edge of a cliff, took a look below and jumped down. The tiger, following its example, also threw itself down the cliff, and both were dead. Yu Lizi commented, "The elk jumped down the cliff because it had no alternative, as there was a cliff in front and a tiger at the back, and it must die either way. To retreat, it would surely be eaten by the tiger, and there was not the slightest doubt; jumping down the cliff, however, he might yet be snatched from the jaws of death, which, after all, was better than being eaten by the tiger. The tiger was in an entirely different situation. It could either advance or retreat at will, as it was not under any pressure, and yet it jumped with the elk. Why was it so? Although the elk jumped to its death, it brought the tiger to die together; if it did not jumped down the cliff, the tiger would not have died. The tiger might be regarded as foolish, but the credit should go to the elk, which had formed a clever strategem. How sad it was for the tiger, but it will forever become the mirror of those who are greedy and cruel."

672. Morbid Impetuosity

Where the two countries, Jin and Zheng, shared a common border, there lived a man with an irascible temperament. If his arrow missed, he would pour his scorn on the target, and smashed it to smithereens; if he lost a chess game, he would vent his anger on the chess pieces, and bit them with all his might. Someone told him, "It is not the fault of the target, nor that of the chess pieces. Why don't you find the cause of your failure in yourself?" But he could not understand such argument, and eventually died of morbid impetuosity.

673. Gongsun Fuji

Gongsun Fuji thought his elderly neighbour was senile, and an evil notion came to his head. He conceived a way whereby he could eat and drink in the old man's home at will. He gathered his fellows and said to them, "My next door neighbour is an old man, rich but stingy. I'm thinking of going there to get a little something to eat and drink." One of his evil companions said, "Although he is rich, but what can we do with a scrooge like that?" "Let's steal," Gongsun Fuji suggested. His fellows all pulled a long face. The next day, they came together again to find a solution. One of them said, "Your suggestion is not so good. Do we have a better way?" "We can force him to do it," replied Gongsun Fuji. About half of those present did not agree to this proposal. A few days later, they gathered again, and Gongsun Fuji put forward another suggestion, saying, "We'll use our own money to hold a banquet and courteously invite the old man to drink. We'll then ask him for as many things as can defray the cost of the banquet; we'll also invite his sons and younger brothers to eat and drink as often as we can. In this manner, we can spend all he has accumulated within a few years. What do you think of that?" Everyone supported the latest idea.

The three proposals of Gongsun Fuji all aimed at getting the property of other people by despicable means. As to those who might or might not agree with him, they were only trying to avoid the disrepute of immorality.

674. The Dodder and the Climbing Fig

The dodder and the climbing fig all grew under the pine and the hackberry tree. They were talking about where and which to attach themselves. The dodder said, "The hackberry is not a useful timber. They grow in cluster, shrouding one another. As to the pine, its roots grow deep into the crevices of rocks and, near its roots also grows the tuckahoe. The tuckahoe is the most valuable of all medicinal plants which both Shen Nong (a legendary ruler supposed to have introduced agriculture and herbal medicine) and Yu Shi (the rain god) had taken and become immortals. Its resin seeps into the earth and turns into amber. Amber, the jade in water and the pearl-like stone in the mountain are all priceless treasures. The pine rises from the valley with its trunk stretching straight up into the sky; its branches strong and intertwined. Its luxuriant leaves come alive and play orchestral music as the wind blows over. As I see it, there is no other place better than the pine to attach ourselves." The climbing fig replied, "The pine you described is really beautiful but, in my opinion, it is not as good as the hackberry. We all know that where the beauty is, there will rivalry be. That's why when gold is discovered, the mountain will be dug into; if jade stone is found, the rock will be cut open; if fish is seen, the lake will be dried; if the thick growth of grass hides wild birds, the same will be cleared. Now, the pine is as tall as a hundred feet, towering into the clouds. It does not grow in the deserted cliffs and valleys, but in the place where all can see. Moreover, there you will find the tuckahoe and amber. I'm certain it will be chopped down soon enough." The dodder did not listen to the advice of the climbing fig, and climbed up the pine tree. The climbing fig, on the other hand, twisted itself up the hackberry tree. It bored through the holes made by the blackflies and grubs, entwined itself around the trunk and branches of the tree, and let its own twigs and leaves spread. Thus the leaves of the hackberry began to wither, as its branches and trunk all became excellent places for the parasitic growth of the climbing fig. Its trunk became hollow, its bark chapped and fell like the scale-like outer skin of a bamboo shoot.

A year later, the king of Qi sent a carpenter by the name of Shi to cut down the pine tree as beams for his Snow Palace. As the pine tree was cut down, the dodder died with it. Only the climbing fig and the hackberry were still there.

675. In Dread of Ghosts

There was a man who dreaded ghosts. When he heard the sound of withered leaves falling from the trees, or of snakes and mice crawling about, he believed it was the ghost. A petty thief learned about it, and climbed over his walls to spy upon him, mimicking the sound of ghosts. The man was thoroughly frightened, and dared not so much as casting a sidelong glance at the source of the noise. The petty thief simulated the ghost by making a few more sounds and then slipped into his house, where he took away all his belongings. Someone deceived him by saying, "All your belongings in the house were truly stolen by ghosts." The man had some doubt about the fact, but in his heart of hearts, he believed it was true.

Sometime later, it was discovered there were indeed ghosts in his house. For that reason, even though his belongings were in the hands of the petty thief, he insisted it was the ghosts which stole and gave them to the petty thief. He would never admit that the man was a pilferer.

676. Stealing the Dregs of Wine

In former times, the people of Lu did not know how to make good wine, and only the people of the state of Zhongshan was capable of making good, strong liqueur, which they called "liqueur for a thousand days". The people of Lu had hoped to get the formula but could not.

A man who held an official post in the state of Zhongshan once drank at the home of the liqueur maker, and stole some distillers' grains. When he returned, he put it into the wine of Lu and told people, "This is from the state of Zhongshan!" The people of Lu drank it, and believed it was indeed the good wine from the state of Zhongshan

One day, the owner of the winery in the state of Zhongshan came. He learned there was wine from Zhongshan and asked for a sip, but he spat it out immediately and laughed, saying, "Ha! This is only the distillers' grains from my winery soaked in your local wine!"

677. Ashamed to Use the Jade Wine Vessel

During the Period of Warring States, the king of Zhao came by a piece of Tian jade and had it made into a wine vessel with three legs and a loop handle. He said, "I'll use this wine vessel to toast to those who have made contributions." When the forces of the state of Qin surrounded Handan, and prince Wei Wuji led an army to repulse the enemy attack and rescued Zhao, the king of Zhao held the jade vessel in his hands and knelt before prince Wei Wuji to propose a taost after the siege was raised. The prince Wei Wuji praised the jade vessel profusely as he returned the toast, and that was why after the battle south of Hao (Bo Village, Hebei Province), when the king of Zhao had no other bestowal to make, he would use the wine vessel to propose a toast to his officers and men, and they were all very grateful. From then on, the people of Zhao regarded drinking from the jade vessel as a greater honour than being rewarded the official salary of ten chariots. Later, the king of Zhao used the jade vessel to toast to his favorite who once licked his hemorrhoid. For that reason, when Li Mu defeated the Qin forces and the king of Zhao once more used the jade vessel to offer toast to the officers and men during the victory meeting, all the officers and men expressed their anger and refused to drink. It was the same jade vessel, when used in an improper way, its beauty turned into ugliness, and the reason was that its user did not know the spiritual value it represented!

678. The Leaves of Legume

To keep away from the bandits, Zheng Zishu fled to the village in the suburbs. The villagers presented him with the soup of legume leaves, and he felt it tasted good. Later, he returned home, and longed for the pleasant flavour of the nectarous legume soup. So he picked some leaves from the pulse plants, did after the same fashion, but felt it was not so good after all. Yu Lizi explained, "Is it because the flavour of the legume leaves different? Not so. It was only because the circumstances have changed. That is why the attitude of those who abandon their wife after becoming rich, or disown all their relatives and friends when they are eminent, are simply making an adjustment to the new environment."

679. The Revered Mr Huang

An Qisheng had attained perfection in Taoism and become an immortal in Zhi Fu Mountain (near Bohai Sea, in Yantai, Shandong Province). He carried a vermilion knife with which to control the tiger. Wherever he pointed his knife, the tiger would run to it as if it were a small child. The revered Mr. Huang of the East China Sea admired it very much, and thought the divine power came from the vermilion knife. So he stole the knife and slung it over his shoulder. One day, he was out on the road and met a ferocious tiger. Swiftly he unsheathed his knife to grapple with it, but he was no match for the tiger, and eventually was eaten by it.

680. A Confucian Moralist

A confucian moralist with a pair of large thick-soled boots on his feet, a hat of the three cardinal guides and the five constant virtues on his head, a garment of human relations according to feudal ethics on his body, his long sleeves swinging as he fiddled with his broad belt, forever reciting the Confucian classics and the Book of Odes, professed himself to be a real disciple of Confucius. He met Liu Xie one day, and Liu Xie was a smart fellow. Thinking that the man's appearance was extremely comical, Liu Xie made up his mind to give him a little taunt, and so he said, "To say the truth, you do not yet understand brother Zhongni." The Confucian moralist was furious. He turned hostile all of a sudden, sprang up and pointed at Liu Xie, saying, "The ancient world would be a long night if Heaven had not brought forth a Zhongni. Who are you? How dare you call the master by his name, and even go so far as to address him as brother!" Liu Xie, pretending to wake up somewhat to his error, said, "No wonder all the sages before the legendary ruler Fu Xi had to walk with their lanterns lighted throughout the day!"

*

*The Complete Works of Song Wenxian
By Song Lian (1310-1381 A.D.) styled himself Jing Lian, assumed name Qianxi, originally from Pujiang, Zhejiang Province. He was one of the founding fathers of Ming Dynasty, and a writer and historian. During the last years of the Yuan Dynasty, he lived as a recluse in Dongming Mountain and devoted himself to writing. Later, he left retirement and became an official again in response to Zhu Yuanzhang's call. He was the chief compiler of *The History of the Yuan Dynasty*. Because of his involvement in Hu Weiyong's case, he was exiled to Maozhou, and died on his way there. During the reign of Yingzong of Ming Dynasty (1436-1449 A.D.), he was bestowed the posthumous title of Wenxian, and enjoyed the reputation of being "the leader of the civil officials". He was a prolific writer. The book had an alternative title called *The Complete Works of A Han Lin Scholar*, mainly poetry and essays, among which, *Tales of Long Menzi* was a book of philosophy, expounding philosophical topics through the medium of fables. *Swallow Book* was

penned in the last years of the Yuan Dynasty when Song Lian was a recluse. It was a special collection of fables, writing in an incisive style to deride the politics of the last years of the Yuan Dynasty and the seamy side of society at large. The following are culled from these two books.

681. Zi Liao Chooses a Mate

Zi Liao was cautious and picky when came to choosing a mate, and so for ten years he was unable to fulfill his desire. He was unhappy most of the time, being alone. In a place called Quni, there was an extremely ugly girl, blind in one eye, and with pearl-like pimples and scars grew all over her face. Besides, she was dark in complexion and weak bodily. The local people did not even cast an eye on her when they happened to meet. The unsightly girl felt resentful, and made up her mind to look for a master who could teach her to play *zhu* (an ancient 13-stringed musical instrument) and to pluck the *konghou* (an ancient musical instrument with 23 strings). After a period of three years, she became a consummate player. In addition to her expertise in playing the musical instruments, she was also good at performing lewd dances to confuse the public. Zi Liao fell hopelessly in love with her at first sight, and immediately sent over a generous gift to ask for her hand, giving her the name of *Yuanji* (the number one beauty). Every morning he accompanied her to play the *zhu*, and in the evening he listened to the *konghou* music, snuggling up to, and loving her ardently. Each time he went out, even for just a short period of time, he would scrutinize the expression of her face closely upon his return, and felt more certain than ever that there was nothing amiss, as he laughed at all the other people. At which time, somehow, everyone seemed to have grown one eye too many.

Zi Liao's good friend Wan Ai felt tender and protective towards Zi Liao, and presented to him a dazzlingly beautiful girl from the district of Zhao. People all thought she could compare with Lu Xu and Bai Tai, two well-known national beauties, but Zi Liao would not have anything to do with her and asked her to leave, saying, "What kind of monster is this? How dare she compare with my *Yuanji*!"

682. Bei Gongzhi and the Legendary Luminous Pearl

In Yongqiu, there was a man called Bei Gongzhi, whose livelihood depended on fishing with his small boat. One night, he slept by the riverside and found a luminous pearl, which could light up places within a hundred paces. The local people thought he had gotten a rare treasure, and vied with one another to slaughter a pig or a lamb to congratulate him, saying, "From the moment you came to live in Yongqiu, leaving home to paddle a boat, berthing it upon your return, with only worn-out clothes to put on, coarse food to eat, you may say all the poor people in the state of Song, no one has fared more badly than you did. Today you have come by a rare treasure, and being rare, it is precious. What more do you desire?" A high official in the government also heard the story and came to congratulate him, saying, "The monarch is looking for ten precious pearls to decorate and illuminate his carriage. He has obtained nine at present, and has issued an order to find the tenth everywhere wihtin the state boundary, but as yet no one came to present it. Now that you have chanced upon it at the riverside, you must wrap it up with elegant silk, and put it into a box inlaid with gems. I'll go west with you to the capital and present it to the monarch. Glory, splendour, wealth and rank will soon come your way." As Bei Gongzhi was about to set out, his father returned from the state of Qin, and Bei Gongzhi told him about his imminent departure to present the treasure. His father wept, saying, "We have lived here for ten generations! There has never been any mishap while we go fishing with this little boat. Now that you go to present the precious pearl, you will have wealth and rank; but wealth and rank can make a man arrogant and wilful, arrogant and wilful can cause a man to be ruthless and tyrannical, and ruthless and tyrannical can bring about disaster. The consequence of disaster is death. By that time, even though you would want to return to the peaceful life of fishing in a small boat, could it be done? What do I want this precious pearl for! What do I want this precious pearl for!" Thereupon he smashed the pearl to smithereens.

683. Dou Ziban the Hypocrite

In the state of Chu, there was a man called Dou Ziban. He was grave in appearance, serious in words, and whenever he opened his mouth, he must first of all mentioned how the late king said this and did that. Thus throughout the state, everyone thought he was a man of virtue and high moral character.

One day, he was drinking in Wei Qijiang's house, and Shen Yinshou and Shi Qili were also present. As Shi Qili conversed with Shen Yinshou, he said something somewhat lewd in content. Dou Ziban heard it and became very angry, saying, "If you sink into extravagance, and are fond of women, that will be similar to the mayflies going in and out of the dirty soil, and even ghosts will forsake you. How dare you brag unblushingly in a banquet?" Everybody present was discomfited and in dejection.

But before he had finished talking, a beautiful woman passed in front of the door. Dou Ziban said he had to go to the restroom, and went out. After a while, a man holding a knife was seen following at a rapid pace. Everybody went out to see what happened, and discovered that the man being chased after was Dou Ziban. The fact was, Dou Ziban and the woman had committed adultery. The woman knew he was drinking in Wei Qijiang's home, so she came to tip him a wink. Dou Ziban followed her in response to her hint, but did not expect to have been discovered by her husband.

684. The Duke Jing of Qi

The duke Jing of Qi castigated extravagance and preferred thrifty and simple life-style. All his high officials were steeped in extravagance and lewdness but were afraid that the duke Jing might come to know it, so they pretended to be thrifty and simple to deceive him. When they went to court everyday, they would use plain unadorned carriages pulled by half-starved horses, attire themselves in worn-out costume, and even the hatbands were so old that it seemed they would snap at any moment. The duke Jing of Qi took all this as real, and showed tender affection for them.

One day, the duke Jing of Qi gathered all the high-ranking officials and said to them, "I'll bestow on each one of a you a belt, a brocade dress, a knife carried by the guard of honour and a set of jade ornaments for the sheath of the knife. Deck out and show your status. From now on, you need not be too frugal."

All the officials replied, "Your subjects rely on the authority and sacredness of Your Highness and follow behind the high officials. Though we do not eat polished rice, we are not starved; we do not wear luxurious clothes, yet we do not suffer from cold. We wish Your Highness forever own this territory, and live a long life, so that numerous descendants could enjoy the frugal style of Your Highness' beneficent rule. It is said in *A Commentary on the Spring and Autumn Annals,* 'Thriftiness is the sum total of all virtues.' When the monarch and his subjects practise frugality together, there will be harmony in every aspect of life. Frugality will bring about peace and happiness, and peace and happiness will provide the people with a joyous atmosphere. When things are in harmony, there will be good coordination between superiors and subordinates. Wish Your Highness would take your time in coming to a decision." The duke Jing of Qi was very pleased.

One day, the duke Jing of Qi went sightseeing and, it so happened the high officials were having a feast in the district of Lumen, so he went over to inspect. He noticed that their carriages were all bright and shiny, the horses were all strong and prancing. The dress was extravagant, and the food rich and plenty, clean, exquisite, palatable, and it dawned on him as to the facts. He realized they had deceived him, and scolded them in his rage, saying, "What! All of you are my subjects, and you have the audacity to do things like that!" He had them all put into prison and executed.

The learned and virtuous man said, *"The Book of History* says, 'You take great pains to eradicate it, but deception still goes from bad to worse with every passing day.' What it referred to here was the high officials of Qi!"

685. Big Talk

In the state of Qin, there was a man called Zun Lusha. He liked to indulge in verbiage and big talk and, very often, hoax became truth as he did so. The king of Qin laughed at him, but Zun Lusha replied with all seriousness, "Don't tease me!" he said. "I'm going to expound the doctrine of administering a country to the king of Chu!" Having said that, he set out on his journey to the south, carefree and content.

As he arrived at the border of the state of Chu, and as the sentry guarding the pass was about to tie him up, Zun Lusha said with a severe countenance, "Don't tie me up. I've come here to be the teacher of the king of Chu." Thus the official in charge immediately sent him to the capital. The high court official who was responsible for the reception put him up in the guesthouse before asking him, "Sir, you do not look down upon our country, and come from a thousand *li* away for the sole purpose of making our country powerful and prosperous, for which I hold you in high esteem. However, as we have just been acquainted, I dare not wear my heart upon my sleeve. I'll therefore not talk about anything except the matter of your going to be the king's master. May I ask what is it all about?" In rage, Zun Lusha replied, "That's something you should not know!" As the high official could not get anything from him, he sent him to Minister Xia. Minister Xia treated him as a VIP, and asked the same question. Zun Lusha expressed even greater rage, saying that he would take his leave immediately and go home. Xia was afraid the king might come to know of it and put the blame on him, and so he reported the matter to the king of Chu.

The king of Chu urged Zun Lusha to see him. Zun Lusha deliberately refused to go. Not until the king sent his man three or four times to invite him did he agree to enter the palace. As he stood before the king, he did not kneel down, but simply made an obeisance by cupping one hand in the other before his chest, and called the king by his name, saying, "Your country, the state of Chu, is facing the state of Wu and the state of Yue in the east; the state of Qin in the west; the state of Qi and the state of Jin in the north. They all eye you with hostility. Recently I passed the border of the state of Jin on my way and learned that Marquis Jin has already formed an alliance with the other princes in preparation for the attack on the state of Chu. They killed a white horse, and place it in the pearl tray and the jade receptacle, while smearing blood as a sign of the oath (an old Chinese practice, lick blood and swear), saying, 'Unless the state of Chu is defeated, we'll never see each other again!' In addition, they threw a round flat piece of jade with a hole in the centre (used for ceremonial purposes in ancient China) in the river as sacrifice to the river god, and prepared to cross the Yellow River and dispatch the troops to the south. How can Your Highness still sleep without any anxiety?" The king of Chu was shocked by the revelation, and stood up to ask him for a plan to repulse the enemy. Zun Lusha pointed at the sky and said, "If you will bestow on me the position of minister, I'll make the state of Chu powerful and prosperous. I swear to the sun I will." The king of Chu said, "That's exquisite! May I ask what should be our first move?" Zun Lusha replied, "That cannot be explained to you in the abstract." And the king said repeatedly, "Right, right, right!" Thus an edict was issued and Zun Lusha became a minister.

Three months had passed, and Zun Lusha did not accomplish anything of note. The huge army of the alliance led by the state of Jin had advanced near to the border of the state of Chu. The king was panicky, and hurriedly summoned Zun Lusha for a plan to defeat the enemy. Zun Lusha stared at the king with both eyes without saying a word. When hard-pressed by the king, he replied, slowly and calmly "The Jin troops have come in full fury and can't be held back now. For Your Highness' sake, I propose that you give up the territory and ask for peace." The king of Chu was infuriated and ordered Zun Lusha be imprisoned for three years before cutting off his nose and expelling him from the state of Chu.

Zun Lusha later told people, saying, "From now on I know talking big can cause catastrophe." Thus he no longer dared to draw the long bow. Whenever he was itching for boasting, he would touch his nose with the fingers and restrain himself.

686. The Crow and the Chicks

In a place called Tunze, a man kept a chicken of the species that came from Sichuan. The markings of its plummage was beautiful, and the feather around its neck was red in colour. A flock of pheasants accompanied it to find food as they chirped together. Suddenly, a ferocious bird of the eagle species flew over their heads, and the Sichuan hen hurriedly covered the chicks with her wings. As the ferocious bird could not snatch the chicks, it flew away.

It was not long before a crow came. It mixed with the chicks and pecked around together. The Sichuan hen stared at the crow and saw it getting along well with the young chicks like brothers, pecking and playing, friendly and harmonious, and felt at ease. But, all of a sudden, the crow carried off a chick in its beak and flew up the sky. The Sichuan hen looked up, and did not know what to do. It seemed to regret that the crow had deceived it.

687. Liezong Zihong

In the state of Cai, there was a man called Liezong Zihong, who loved cleanliness to a fault. He had an especial aversion to the smell emitted from other people's mouth. Whenever he talked with people, he would stand at a distance. While he was engaged in conversation, he would spit incessantly. As people advanced an inch, he would retreated a foot. When he bathed, he must change the hot-water ten times. To rid himself of water after bath, he would not use a towel, but would just let the wind blow his body dry. He dug a pit on the floor as latrine, then excavated a canal with a small house above it. The canal was connected to the river, so that bodily waste could immediately be carried away with the water. When he wanted to sleep with a woman, he would carry either spring or well water to have the woman's body thoroughly washed with no allowance for extenuating circumstances, even though it might be a day with heavy snowfall. Thus his wife caught cold and died because of it.

But, strangely enough, he liked the smell of women's foot-binding cloth.

The cloth for foot-binding was like the puttee. It must wrap a woman's legs three rounds, and be pressed tightly against the arch of the foot. It was easily soiled. Periodically when it was unwrapped, it emitted a strong smell assailing the nostrils. Anybody came in contact with the smell would want to vomit. Only Liezong Zihong liked it, and often praised it before other people, saying, "The smell of that thing is as fragrant as the tulip, as warm and humid as borneol, and as rich a perfume as the orchid!" Very often he carried the foot-binding cloth with him in the sleeves. Whenever the food he ate was not delicious enough, he would smell it; when he felt depressed, he would smell it; when he could not suppress his anger, or had to divert himself from boredom, again he would smell it.

On his deathbed he summoned his son to his side, and said, "I'm about to die! I do not ask you to offer corn or any other delicacies as sacrifices but, if you can put some foot-binding cloths in front of my coffin at regular intervals, I will consider it your greatest filial piety!"

All the high officials in the state of Cai who learned about his addiction could not help laughing at him. The learned and virtuous commented, "There was an ancient saying, 'One who is hygienic to a fault in one aspect will be found to be extremely filthy in the other aspect.'"

688. The Cat and the Leopard

Yi Zigao learned that Wei Shaoshi had a leopard which was also a good hunter. He used a pair of precious white jades, which were round and flat, each with a hole in the centre (used for ceremonial purposes in ancient China), in exchange for the leopard and brought it home. Thereafter, he held a feast, inviting all his friends and visitors. Amidst drinking and celebrating, he led the leopard before all his guests to show off. He looped a metal chain and hung beautiful silk ornaments on the leopard, feeding it with meat which was cut from other animals. Sometime later, a mouse happened to run across the eaves, and Yi Zigao hastened to release the leopard so it could catch the mouse. However, the leopard seemed indifferent to what happened. Yi Zigao was annoyed and scolded the leopard rather severely. A few days later, another mouse ran across the room and Yi Zigao again released the leopard to catch it. The leopard was as unmoved as on the previous occasion, and Yi Zigao was even angrier. He lashed the leopard with his whip. The leopard howled aloud, and Yi Zigao thrashed it harder still. In addition to whipping, he tied the leopard up with a thick rope, and shut it inside the palings meant for cattle and sheep. Everyday he fed it only with coarse food and dregs, and the leopard became dejected and cried piteously.

Yi Zigao's friend Anqi Zilun learned about it, and reproved him, saying, "I've heard that the famous sword, *Juque*, when used to mend the shoes, was not as handy as a chisel, although it was unequalled in sharpness. A brocade with beautiful pattern, though magnificent, was not as good as a foot of white cloth when used as facecloth. Despite the ferocity of the leopard, it is no match for the cat when it comes to catching the mouse. Why so daft? Why don't you let the cat catch the mouse and let the leopard capture its prey?" Yi Zigao was enlightened, and followed what Anqi Zilun had suggested. Soon the mice in the house were all caught, and innumerable animals such as deer and the like were captured. People with high moral accomplishment commented, "Although animals are adept in hunting, still each species has its own special skill. When it comes to choosing the right person for the right job, why is it ever so often it is done contrary to the principle of 'from each according to his ability?'"

689. The Bear of Yangdu

There were deep mountain ridges in the district of Yangdu, where bears gathered. By disposition the bear abhorred seeing blood. Now, a bear happened to pass a perilous valley, where its costal region was cut by the thorns of the bushes. The cuts appeared like moistened red threads stuck to the skin. The bear scratched them with its claws, and they bled even more. It continued to scratch until a hole was dug on its body, and the blood flowed like a spring. As the bear could not stop the flow, it tore away the skin with the flesh on it, but the flow of blood could not be staunched. Finally, it clawed out all its entrails and died.

690. Quails

Most places in Jingchu produced quails which were good fighters. When they fought, they intertwined with one another as if they were glued together, so inextricably entangled. High official Li loved to keep quails. Occasionally, he was sent to foreign countries; during which time he would take his quails along with him. The people under the king of Han reported this to their leader, and the king was thrilled and curious, so he ordered quails be gathered to fight with those of high official Li. However, he was unable to score a victory. The monarch thought there were no quails of high calibre locally, and asked senior official Li to turn over his quails as a gift.

Wu Gou, another senior official of Han, remonstrated with the monarch of Han, saying, "The quails are birds that can be found everywhere. How can the state of Han be short of good species? As to whether they can fight, it all depends on selection and training. Now, birds with brown plummage and stripes are called quails; birds with long neck feather and markings like fish scales, short tails, are called quails; and birds with beaks as pointed and sharp as knife and sword are also called quails. They are all quails, but how many of them are dexterous in fighting, and how can they be found? Still, this may not be enough to explain things, how about those who wear round hats, square shoes and, imitating Yao Song, walk in a hurry, and who call themselves scholars,—how many of them can overcome difficulty and eliminate anxiety for the monarch? Talents differ, some high, some low, some superior, some inferior. It is all up to the monarch to discover capable people and assign them to suitable posts, as the problem is not in the objects themselves." The monarch was greatly pleased with the talk, and through careful selection, he was able to choose those that were good in fighting to compete with the quails of senior official Li and won. By the same token, the state of Han also learned a lesson in the way it chose its officials.

Those with high moral accomplishment said, "There is an ancient saying, 'Born a lamb and put on the fur of a tiger. It is pleased at the sight of grass, but shivers at the sight of jackals and wolves.' Today, there are very few officials who do not belong to this category. Are there no real 'tigers'? Not so, it is only because the monarch is not good at discovering and putting them in suitable posts."

691. The Pinworm and the Ascarid

The reason the pinworm and the ascarid can survive is because they hide inside the body of man, and suck and eat the blood plasma and fat of their host all the time. As time progresses, man catches infectious diseases and dies from them. As the host dies, the pinworm and the ascarid will, of course, perish also.

692. Drowning of the Mice

It was the habit of mice to steal grains at night. A man of Yue put the grains in a jar and let the mice eat as much as they liked, paying no attention to their presence. The mice, therefore, called all their companions to come and get into the jar. As a rule, they were able to eat their fill before leaving.

Thereafter, the man of Yue emptied the grains and put in water instead. He then poured brans onto the water, which floated on the surface. The mice, however, did not detect.it. At nightfall, they again called all their companions to slip into the jar one by one. The result: all the mice were drowned.

693. The Human Exterior Conceals the Nature of a Monkey

The monarch of the state of Ji was fond of monkey, and so he assigned a monkey tamer to teach the monkey a few stunts. The monkey tamer, Tuo Tu, dressed up the monkey as a man. He put a nine-mountain tall hat on its head, attired it in clothes knitted with rosy clouds, and let it wear a pair of shoes emboidered with phoenixes. No matter it ascended the hall or descended the stairs, advanced or retreated, or expressed courtesy between guest and host, it was exactly like a man. When it stood and bowed, sat, lay, or knelt down, it was no difference from a man. The monkey tamer reckoned it could now be called to render its services, and so he presented it to the monarch of the state of Ji.

The monarch of Ji was very pleased upon seeing it, and raised his wine cup to offer the monkey a drink. After drinking, the monkey suddenly sprang up, tore off its hat and garment and ran away.

It all began with the idea of dressing it like a man. As its heart remained a monkey, any unforeseen circumstances would cause it to show its true colours!

694. A Beast in Human Clothing

Xi Wangxu of Qi possessed the expertise to do business abroad, and had travelled to numerous towns and cities in Funan and visited homes of various Dunsun tribes, bringing back a variety of precious articles such as hawksbill, agate, etc. On one occasion, he encountered strong wind at sea, and the boat turned turtle. Xi Wangxu took hold of a broken mast, and drifted on the sea for a long time before he was fortunate enough to reach the shore. With his wet clothes on, he wandered in the valley north of Yishan. The valley was deep and quiet, and the sun could not penetrate, and it was as if heavy rain were about to fall. Xi Wangxu believed he would not be able to survive, and so he went looking for a mountain cave where his remains could be preserved and not eaten by the crows and kites. Before he entered the cave, however, an orangutan suddenly emerged from it. It looked up and down at the newcomer. As if feeling sympathetic, it re-entered the cave to get beans, radish, ears of grains and other food items, and re-emerged to invite him by sign language. Xi Wangxu's hunger was just becoming unbearable, and he ate them with relish. There was a small hole on the right side of the cave, in which there was a bed of sorts, spread with bird feathers over a foot thick, and looked very cosy. The orangutan vacated it for Xi Wangxu to sleep, while it moved outside to the mouth of the cave, despite the biting cold. Although it did not speak the language of man, the sound it made morning and evening seemed to indicate it was trying to comfort him and help him get over the difficulty. In this manner, he spent a year there. Then, quite unexpectedly, a big boat arrived and dropped anchor at the foot of the mountain. The orangutan held him under its arm and hastened towards the ship. By accident, the boat was owned by his friend, whom Xi Wangxu recognized at once as he came aboard. The orangutan stood on the shore for a long time watching as the boat sailed away.

Xi Wangxu said to his friend, "I've learned that the blood of orangutan can be used to dye felt, which will not fade even for a hundred years. This animal is a fat one and, if you kill it, you will probably get over two gallons of blood. Why don't you go ashore and capture it?"

His words infuriated his friend, who excoriated him, saying, "The orangutan is only a beast, but acts like a man; you are a man, but act like a beast! If I don't kill you, what will your life be good for?" Thereupon he took a bag and filled it with stones. Then he hung it on the neck of Xi Wangxu before pushing him into the river, where he was drowned.

695. Oxtail Civet

The Yue Mountain produced a kind of oxtail civet, whose fat and meat alternated, making it highly palatable. In autumn, when the fruits in every tree ripened and civets were provided with abundant food, their fur turned smooth and sparkling, and extremely good-looking. The civet knew it would be the object of jealousy, and so it found a cave as its home, erected a shed with stones, and gathered some bamboo leaves to stop up the mouth of the cave, which also served as walls. During the daytime, it hid in the kennel, and came out to look for food at night, leaving no room for man to exploit.

An experienced hunter instigated his dog to follow the civet by tracing its footsteps, smashed its shed, flattened its walls and lighted a fire to smoke its kennel. The civet could not stand the stifling smoke, so it shut the eyes and rushed through the flames to get out; the hunting dog then followed and bit it to death.

696. A Fish-loving Man of Zheng

There was a fish-loving man in the state of Zheng, who had devised quite a number of methods to catch fish, but it was all to no avail. The only way open to him, therefore, was either to use fishing apparatus or collect a pool of rain water to lure the fish, or else weave a tube-shaped cage with bait in it to capture them. He placed three basins in the courtyard, filled them with water, and whenever he came by any fish, he would put them in the basin and raise them.

After the ordeal in the net, the fish were all tired out and, with their white bellies up, they either floated on the surface of the water or opened their mouths wide above it to take a few gasps of air. Another day went by before their fins and tails began to move again.

The man of Zheng carried the basins out to have a closer look. "Can the fish be wounded?" he wondered.

After a few moments, he put grains of cooked rice and wheat bran to feed his fish. Then, taking the fish out of the basin, he asked them, "Have you eaten your fill?"

Nearby, someone reminded him, "The fish depend on the vast expanse of water in the river to live. Now that they had only a ladle of water to play with and, in addition, had to be your plaything, declaring all the time, 'I love the fish, I love the fish', I believe the likelihood of their survival is pretty small!"

The man of Zheng refused to listen. Three days later, all the fish shed their scales and died. By then, the man of Zheng began to regret that he did not follow the advice.

697. A Scholar Fire Fighter

The house of a man of Zhao, Cheng Yangkan, caught fire, and he tried to put it out. As there was no ladder to help him go to the upper floor, he sent his son, Cheng Yangnu, to borrow one from his neighbour, Mr Ben Shui.

Cheng Yangnu made himself spruce, calm and unhurried, and walked towards Mr Ben Shui's home. He bowed three times with hands clasped before he passed through the hall and entered the inner chambers, and sat down beside the pillar at the western porch. Mr Ben Shui ordered the receptionist to give a feast, presenting dried meat, fish paste and good wine to entertain Cheng Yangnu. Cheng Yangnu stood up, raising his wine cup to savour the flavour of the wine, and repeatedly returned his host's compliments. After the wine, Mr Ben Shui asked him, "You have honoured my humble home today. May I ask what have you to instruct me?"

Cheng Yangnu responded by saying, "Heaven has caused a serious disaster to fall upon us. A fire is causing trouble at the moment, and raging flames are spreading. We have to go higher to spray water on the fire but unfortunately we have no wings, and can only look on and cry. We have learned that you have a ladder which can help us ascend a higher place. Can you please lend it to us for once?"

Mr Ben Shui stamped his feet upon hearing what he said. "What pedantic views you have! What pedantic views you have!" he cried. "When one sees a tiger while having a meal in the mountain, one should immediately spit out his food and flee; when one notices a crocodile in the river while washing one's feet, one must immediately throw away the shoes and run. Since you have a fire at home, how can you still bow with your hands clasped?"

Thereupon Mr Ben Shui picked up the ladder and followed him. However, when they arrived at the scene, the house had already turned into a heap of ashes.

698. Two's Company

Jia Fushi and Gong Shishi of the state of Yue had close relation with one another. Jia Fushi was good at planning but incapable of taking strong decision, and Gong Shishi was decisive but careless. When the two of them put their strong points together, there was nothing they could not do successfully. There were two men, but only one heart and one mind. Later, on account of verbal disagreement, they quarrelled and went their several ways. From then on, their handling of government affairs often met with failure.

Mi Xufen cried pleading with both of them, "Have you ever heard of the jellyfish in the sea? The jellyfish has no eyes and depends on the shrimps' assistance to move about, and the shrimps, on the other hand, get food with the jellyfish's help. They are interdependent, one cannot do without the other. But let's put aside the jellyfish for a moment, and allow me to ask you whether you have ever heard of an animal called the *suoji*. It is said that inside its stomach hides the crab. When the crab is hungry, it must crawl out to find food; and when the crab returns, the *suoji* will be full. If not for the mutually beneficial arrangement, the *suoji* would be starved, and the crab would also lose its hideout.

That is why one cannot live without the other! Now, again, let's put aside the *suoji* for a moment, and let me ask you if you have ever heard of Mount Xiawu's kicking mouse? It lives closely with *Qiongqiong Juxu*, and picks licorice for *qiongqiong juxu*. When danger occurs, *qiongqiong juxu* will carry the mouse and flee. That is another example of mutually beneficial arrangement. Now, let us again put aside the story of the kicking mouse, and let me ask you if you have ever heard of the life-sharing bird? One body, two heads, jealous in disposition, and the two heads will peck one another when it is hungry. As one head goes to sleep, the other head will get poisonous grass to harm its counterpart although, as the poisonous grass goes down the throat, the two heads will die together. Ironically, this illustrates the insaparability of the two! The above are all about animals in the mountain and sea, and it is not at all surprising. In the world of men, there are similar examples. Up north, there is a class of men with shared shoulders; they take turns eating and watching while on the road. To be deprived of one partner means both are dead, and that's an example of one cannot lose the other! Now, you are very much like the examples cited above. The difference lies only in one aspect, and that is you are not of the same life-form, although in essence it is really the same! Why should you go your several ways?"

Having listened to the eloquence of their mutual friend, the two of them looked at one another and said, "Had it not been for the advice of Mi Xufen, we would have fallen on even harder times!" Thereupon they became reconciled.

699. Disguise

At the foot of Putian County's Mount Hu, there existed a road that led to the seashore, where most travelling traders passed through it.

In the spring of A.D.1367, a villager put on a tiger skin, and armed with the claws and teeth forged from the iron awl with hammer. He practised the spring of the tiger until his posture closely resembled it. Then he went to haunt the place where water weeds grew. He sent an accomplice to scout around from the vantagepoint of the treetop. If anyone carrying luggage likely to contain valuables was seen coming his way, the man on the treetop would whistle a signal, and the "tiger" would spring out to seize him by the throat and kill him, tearing him to pieces as if it had been bitten by a tiger. He then opened the luggage and picked any articles of value found inside before sealing the bag again to make it appear as if it was never touched so that people would not suspect. As time went on, people began to tell one another that at the foot of Mount Hu there was a tiger, which would not eat man, but only suck his blood, and described what happened as mysterious and incomprehensible.

Later, the disguiser went on a journey for one reason or another, and his wife was left guarding the mountain cave. She heard the whistling signal from the treetop, and thought some treasure must have come their way. Putting on the tiger skin, she pounced ferociously on the trader and bit him. However, the trader put up a desperate fight, and the woman proved not his match. She was frightened and fled. The trader discovered the footprints were those of a human being. When he returned home, he discussed it with his neighbours, and they all agreed to go pursue the "tiger". They traced the footprints all the way to the cave, where they found large quantity of gold, silk and valuables, but the villager had already fled.

Ah! Are there no other human tigers apart from this villager in our world today?

700. Harness the Pig to Plough the Land

Shang Yuzi's family was extremely poor, so poor that he did not have an ox to plough the land. He therefore harnessed a big pig, and drove it towards the east. But, as the big pig was not accustomed to being harnessed, it would struggle to get the yoke off its neck as soon as it was put on, with the result he spent the whole morning trying to plough a single ridge-bordered plot without success.

Mr Ning Wu stepped over to his field and blamed him for it, saying, "That's all your fault! Ploughing is the job of an ox, because the ox has greater strength and can turn over the clods of earth more easily; its hoofs are solid, and able to sink into the mud without fear. A pig may be plump, but how can it plough the field?"

Shang Yuzi was as cross as a bear and did not answer.

Mr Ning Wu said, "Has it not been said in *The Book of Odess* that 'let your companion know that pigs are caught in the pigsty'? That is to say, pigs are good as food. Now, you replace the ox with a pig to plough the field. Is not this turning the world upside down? I only am sympathetic with you, but why do you direct your anger at me and refuse to talk to me, for what reason?"

Shang Yuzi replied, "You think I turn the world upside down, but I'm convinced it is you who have turned things upside down. Do you think I don't know ploughing the land is for the ox, just as managing state affairs is the job of able and virtuous men? To dispense with the service of an ox, although detrimental to the land, the harm is but small. Whereas if able and virtuous men are not enlisted for the administration of the governemnt, all the people will suffer. Why don't you direct your blame to the officials whose job it is to govern the people instead of directing it to me?"

Mr Ning Wu turned to his disciples and said, "I see. The heart of this man is replete with indignation!"

701. Wu Qi Abides by his Word

Once, Wu Qi met his old friend while he was out somewhere, and he invited his friend to have meal together at home. His old friend said, "Good." "I'll be expecting you then," replied Wu Qi.

His old friend did not come, although it was already dark, and Wu Qi continued to wait for him. The next day, he sent someone to look for his old friend. When his old friend came, they then sat down and ate together.

The reason for Wu Qi to wait for his old friend was to show he could be trusted. He was trustworthy, and that was why he could lead the three armed services. To expect the three armed services to obey orders, the Commander-in-Chief must first of all abide by his word.

702. To Tell a Lie

A man called Zizhi became the prime miniser of the state of Yan. On day, he told a lie while remained seated, saying, "Whose white horse is it that has just left through the door?" Those around him replied that they did not see any. But one of them hastened to go out and returned to report, "It's a white horse alright!"

That was actually the method Zizhi used to test the honesty of those around him.

703. An Arrow-maker

There was an arrow-maker who had been in the profession for a long time. The arrows he made were not straight, nor was the weight of the feathers uniform, and the arrow heads were brunt and not sharp. But he was convinced he had acquired the technique of making arrows comparable to that of the famous arrow-maker, Mou Yi, and felt very proud of himself.

Nearby, a man flattered him, saying, "You are indeed an expert. There is no one throughout the Qin and Han Dynasties that could compare with you. Not only were they not able to surpass you in technique, I'm afraid there were lots of people whose skills are much inferior than yours. I believe you should raise the price of your arrows." This made the arrow-maker even prouder.

A certain general Song happened to pass that way, and he picked up the arrows to take a look. However, it only made him spit with contempt and walk away. The arrow-maker did not wake up to his limitations. On the contrary, he thought the general was just being jealous, and he said angrily, "People praised my arrows as comparable to those of the Qin and Han Dynasties, and I don't think that was said lightly. Your present behaviour shows that your are jealous of my achievement. General Song, you are really very unkind."

Someone told Long Menzi about what happened. Long Menzi said, "It is not necessary to overcriticize the arrow-maker. Nowadays many scholars behave in the same way!"

704. Vanity

In Fujian Province there was once a licentious girl. Confident of her beauty, she yearned to get a handsome young man as husband Her Prince Charming, however, did not appear for a long, long time. Because of that, she became extremely irritable and almost lost her will to live.

One day, a man came from the South China Sea. His hair was as black as lacquer, his eyes and brows as good-looking as a painting, and his skin as white as snow. In a word, every movement of his touched a deep chord in one's heart, and everything about him was lovable and graceful. When the girl heard of this handsome man, she was madly excited and, although it was getting dark, she arrived at the man's home alone with a lantern in hand. As the young man came out to welcome her, she found him wearing a hat embellished with precious stones, a brocade robe embroidered with multicoloured design, and a belt around his waist studded with white jades. The girl was filled with elation and amazement, and wished only that she could throw herself into the embrace of the man. She managed to steady her nerves and said to him, "I've admired you for a long time. I'm afraid I don't fit to be your handmaid and attend to your needs. If you will pity and accept me, I'll never forget your kindness even though I might die in doing so." The man was pleased to have her. The girl was respectful and obedient, afraid lest she could not get along well with him. When the man said, "Mealtime", the girl would hand over a spoon and a pair of chopsticks; when the man said, "Bedtime", she would tidy up the pillow and the mat, spread the bedding, and even carry the bedpan for him. Yet she did not feel regrettable nor humiliated.

It looked like the man had a skin ulcer on his left arm, which had a plaster applied to it all the time, and it remained so even after a year. The woman asked the maid in secret, "Is it possible that skin ulcer cannot be cured? It's already twelve months, and the condition remains unchanged. There must be a reason for it." To find out, she tried her best to persuade him to take away the plaster so that she could examine the skin ulcer. The man pretended to be angry, saying, "My skin ulcer is almost healed. I heard people say all women carry poison on their back. If I let you see it, it will fester further and become incurable." Anyway, he would not allow her to see, which made the girl even more suspicious. Because of her suspicion, she got him drunk and, taking advantage of his drunkenness, she took away the plaster on his arm and had a look. It turned out the man was once a thief and, because a crime had been committed, his arm was tattooed, marking him as a criminal. As the cat was finally let out of the bag, she was so angry that she fainted on the spot, and it was a long time before she came to. She held the maid's hands and cried bitterly, saying, "The reason for marriage is to get wealth and rank with a man's help, but I've gotten into such a plight instead. Even if I want to remarry, no notable family and great clan will have me, as I've married once to a criminal, and the common people of the street are not the ones I like to submit myself. If I return to my parents' family, I don't think they will be happy to receive me. If I take a sharp knife to cut my own throat, I'm too weak and timid to do it. Suppose I swallow the humiliation and live out this life, but the mark I saw today is sure to make my broken heart forever broken." Having said that, she again gave way to tears. From then on, the girl was unhappy all the time, and died soon thereafter.

As Long Menzi learned about it, he sighed, saying, "One should take this as an object lesson. What will be the consequence when a girl fails to conduct herself with dignity, and trusts a man lightly! But, are things of this nature only confined to women?"

705. Perspicacity

A man from the district of Wei was noted for his erudition and expertise in appraising antiques. By chance, he found an ancient bronze object at the riverside, which looked like a wine cup but with a hole on each side of it. The pattern on the bronze object was extremely beautiful.

The man of Wei was delighted to have gotten the bronze object, and he invited some friends to his house to admire and enjoy together, saying, "I've come by an ancient object of the Xia Dynasty (c. 21st-c. 17th century B.C.) and am very glad to invite you here to view it together. I'll pour wine into this ancient object, and let everyone take turns to have a sip." However, before they fell to, a man of Choushan entered. He was stunned to see what happened, saying, "Why use it this way? This is called a bronze crotch, which the wrestler placed on his private parts to prevent injury!"

The man of Wei was embarrassed and threw the ancient object out of the house without the courage to cast another look.

And there was another scholar in the district of Chuqiu, whose fame for appraising antiques were not in the least inferior to the man of Wei. One day, he also got an ancient object, which looked very much like a horse, complete with mane and tail but, on its back, there was a hole. He asked the natives far and near, but nobody knew the name of that object. A scholar expressed his opinion by saying, "In ancient times the object was used to hold wine when sacrifices were offered, and was called a sacrificial vessel. If it was in the shape of an elephant, it was called an elephant vessel; I believe this one might be called a horse vessel."

The man of Chuqiu was pleased, and he had a wooden box made to keep it. Whenever there was a banquet, he would use it as a wine vessel and toast to the guests. It so happened that the man from Choushan was again there as a guest. He was flabbergasted and said, "Why use it that way? This is an urinal for the imperial concubine. It is called the young beast."

The man of Chuqiu was abashed and threw it away as the man of Wei did before him. Anyone who heard the story could not help laughing.

Long Menzi heard it and sighed, "In this world of ours, there are many people who lack high perspicacity and, relying only on a smattering of knowledge, confound concept and objective being at will. Whoever has the leisure to make fun of these two scholars?"

706. A Hundred Thousand for the Precious Jade

A merchant from the Western Regions brought a gem for sale. It was a kind of precious jade called *lan*, pure red in colour, like a red cherry, one inch in length, and its value surpassed several hundred thousand.

"Can the *lan* ward off hunger?" asked Long Menzi. "No," came the reply. "Can it cure diseases?" "No," came the same reply. "Can it drive away pestilence?" "No." "Can it make people respect their parents and obey their elder brothers?" "No." "Since it is useless, why spend several hundred thousand just to own it?" Long Menzi asked again. "It is because the thing is found only in remote places which are difficult to reach," came the final answer.

Smiling, Long Menzi went away. He told his disciple Zheng Yuan, saying, "The ancient people have a saying, 'Gold is a precious object, but it will also cause a man's death if he swallows it. When the gold dust enters the eyes, the eyes will become blind.' The precious jade has nothing to do with me for a long time. I've within me a most precious object, which is more than several hundred thousand in value. It cannot get wet, nor drowned; the fire will not burn it, the wind will not flutter it, and the sun will not scorch it. Its application will stabilize the world;

its non-application will benefit one's own well-being, and yet nobody knows that it should be pursued day and night. Instead, people look upon the gold as the only precious object worth seeking. Is not this going after the far-away at the expense of the near-at-hand—foolish? People have long abandoned their asperations! People have long abandoned their aspersations!"

707. Mr. Shu

In the state of Wei, there was a man surnamed Shu, who had no other hobby apart from raising cats. The cat was an animal instrumental in catching mice. He kept over a hundred of them and, around his neighbourhood, all mice had been caught and killed. As the cats had nothing to eat from then on, they began to howl all day long, and Mr Shu had to go and buy fish in the market for them to eat. The cats produced their young, which in turn produced another generation and, because they often had meat supplied to them, began to forget there was such animal species as mouse. What they were accustomed to was to cry when hungry and, as they cried, they would get meat. After their meal, they simply walked around leisurely, carefree; cheerful and light-hearted, living a life of ease and comfort.

To the south of the city, there was a scholar, whose home was experiencing an invasion of mice at the time. The mice ran hither and thither in large numbers, sometimes even fell into the water jar, and so he hastened to borrow a cat from Mr Shu. As the cat noticed that the mouse had a pair of upright ears, bulged eyes which sparkled like black lacquer, red beard and, as it squeaked in confusion, the cat thought it must be some kind of monster, and dared only to follow behind, crawling slowly, without the courage to advance and catch them. The scholar was enraged and pushed the cat to the swarm of mice. The cat was so frightened that it cried in front of the mice. Soon the mice discovered that the cat had no skill worthy of note, and began to bite its feet. Consternation drove the cat to summon up all its strength and, with a tremendous spring, turned and ran away.

708. Burn the House to Rid it of the Mice

There was a bachelor in Western Yue, who used reeds and cogongrass to build a simple thatched house for himself. Farming his small plot of land diligently, he was able to get his daily needs in food. As time went on, such things as soya beans, grains, salt and vinegar, and other condiments, were self-sufficient and did not have to rely on anybody else.

What caused him no end of worry was the infestation of mice, which scampered in swarms around the house even in daytime. During the night, they squeaked as they bit everything at will, all the way till it was dawn. Thus the bachelor was filled with indignation.

One day, he was drunk when he arrived home. He was just lying down when the mice began to play every trick imaginable, which irritated him so much that he could not even close his eyes for a little peaceful moment. The man was wrathful, so he lighted a torch and went everywhere to burn and kill them. As expected, the mice were all scorched to death, but his thatched house was also burned to the ground. The next day, when he became sober, he was at a loss as to what to do. He looked around and found nothing but emptiness, and he had no place to make his home.

Thereupon Long Menzi came to console him for his misfortune.

The man said, "A man should not bear grudges! In the initial stage, I only hated the mice, but then I only saw the mice and forgot my own house. In the end, the disaster came about without my ever considering it. Ah, a man should not bear grudges!"

709. Right and Wrong

Shen Tudun, a commoner who lived in Luoyang, had an ancient cooking vessel, which he obtained from a deep riverbed in Chang-an. Engraved on the surface of the vessel was a yellow dragon soaring in the clouds with its body leaning to one side, painted in gold in dazzlingly bright designs. His western neighbour, Mr Lu, was fond of it when he caught sight of it, and hired a coppersmith to make a similar cast, using a kind of special chemical to temper, and burying it under the ground for three years. Time and the chemical combined to erode the bronze, which became rusty, and looked more or less like Shen Tudun's vessel. One day, Mr Lu presented his vessel to an influential aristocrat, who loved it very much, and who had a feast spread to receive the invited guests. During such occasion, Shen Tudun was sometimes invited. He knew perfectly well the vessel in Mr Lu's possession was an imitation, and so he said, "I've a vessel very much like this one, but I can't say which is the real thing!" The influential aristocrat requested Shen Tudun to bring it there for a look. After scrutinizing it for a long time, he finally pronouced, "This one is not authentic!" All the guests echoed his view and said, "This vessel is not genuine!"

Shen Tudun was very resentful and continued to argue with them without giving ground. However, all the guests rose up against him, trying to put him to shame, and Shen Tudun was no longer in a position to speak. Back in his home, he sighed, saying, "From now on I know that even right and wrong can be altered by the majesty of infuence and power!"

As Long Menzi came to know of it, he smiled and said, "Why did Shen Tudun sense it so late? In commenting a piece of writing, the scholar has acted in the same manner!"

710. Carve the Thigh to Hide a Pearl

There was a treasure mountain in the middle of the sea, on which various kinds of jewellery scattered, and white lights of the precious gems shone all over the place. A seafaring man found a pearl one inch in diameter and intended to bring it home. But the ship had just covered less than a hundred *li* when a strong wind arose, and mountains of rolling waves surged. The ship jolted badly as the flood dragon appeared, and the situation was extremely precarious. The man at the helm told the man with the precious pearl, "The flood dragon sees the the light issuing from the precious pearl and wishes to take possession of it. Please throw the precious pearl into the sea, or else we will all die because of it."

But the seafaring man could not bear to part with the precious pearl. The situation was desperate, however, and he was in no position to bargain. He deliberated for a moment, then carved a hole in his thigh, and put the pearl into it so that the light from it would not be seen. That had proved to be an efficacious move, for the sea immediately became peaceful ad calm, and the seagoing vessel was safe. As he returned home, the man retrieved the precious pearl from his thigh, but the wound had festered and became incurable. He eventually died from it.

*The Su Pingzhong Collection

By Su Boheng styled himself Pingzhong, dates of birth and death unknown, originally from Jinhua, Zhejiang Province. He was a writer in the early years of the Ming Dynasty. A widely read man, he was especially good in ancient Chinese prose. During the last years of the Yuan Dynasty, he was recommended to the imperial court by the local government of his native village. Later, together with Song Lian and Liu Ji, he was called up by Zhu Yuanzhang to be the compiler of the Han Lin Academy, but soon asked for leave to go home to pay respects to his parents, and never returned to his post again. When Song Lian resigned, Boheng was recommended to take his place, but he refused on ground of ill health. *The Su Pingzhong Collection* totals sixteen volumes, among which one contains fables.

711. The Cats of Mr. Dongguo

Mr Dongguo kept a large number of cats, which gathered in his courtyard in packs and bands, leaning or resting, their feet mutually caressing, their tails wagging and playing, their tongues sticking out licking one another, and generally behaving in a very affectionate manner.

A mouse was thrown on the floor, and the cats sprang up very swiftly when they noticed it, and dashed towards the mouse. The foremost cat snatched it, left the band and went to one side. Those failed to grab it followed, some in front to intercept, others pursued at the back, still others howled on the left, while the remaining tried to snatch it from the right. Thereupon they began to fight, and even bite one another in cold blood.

712. The Ears and the Earrings

A western neighbour, a young woman, lost her earrings, and the old woman who was her eastern neighbour came over to console her. The young woman said, "Why do you come to comfort me?" The old woman replied, "I've learned that you lost your earrings, and want to comfort you." The young woman asked her, "Do you still see my ears there?" The old woman replied, "Yes." The young woman said, "I've lost my earrings, but not my ears. Though I've lost my earrings, I do not feel sorrowful. To bother a grand old woman like you to come and comfort me, it seems a bit overdone." The old woman replied, "Your pair of earrings is made of jade and gold, jade and gold are valuable and precious objects. Now that you have lost them, how can you not feel sorrowful?" The young woman explained, "The ears can hear sound, therein lies their value, and not because of the earrings on it which are made of gold and jade. The loss of my earrings does not increase or decrease any part of my ears. Why should you feel sad because of it?"

Ah! Isn't one's body corresponding to the young woman's ears? And isn't it the rank of nobility like the earrings on the ears?

713. Wisteria and Vine

In the interior of Quwo there was a temple of the gods. Inside the temple there were clumps of trees. Many of the trees were very big, and creeping plants such as wisterias and vines climbed along their trunks. The gods in the temple had some misgivings about the future prospect, for the wisterias and the vines might continue to grow and spread, and wished they were eradicated. So the gods told them, "The ancients said, 'There is no fine grass under the big tree.' That is to say, the good grass were hurt by the dense shade of the tree. Now, the trunks of the trees are several arm spans around, but the vines do not even reach one inch. Why? It is because their leaves obstruct your growth by shading you from the sun!"

The wisterias and the vines also noticed that their vines were not as big as the trunks of the trees, and felt very jealous of them. Thus, they conveyed the message through a dream, in which the villagers were told, "Disaster did not come because of the gods, it was the big trees that were the roots of the trouble." And the villagers began to cut down all the big trees. As the big trees were felled, the wisterias and the vines no longer had the tree trunks to attach themselves to, and they withered away.

714. The Golden Pheasant

The king of Chu went to hunt in the swampy land of Yunze. When the animals and birds saw his huntsmen,—be it tiger or rhino, ape or monkey, deer or boar, wild goose or cormorant, bald eagle or oriole, *sushuang* (a kind of wild swan) or swan—all without exception would hasten to hide themselves. Those good in speed would run as far and fast as they could, those adept in flying would soar high above the clouds, and those without any special skill would select a bush wherein they could safely conceal themselves without being discovered. There was only one, a golden pheasant, which, because it had just stuck out its multicoloured silken bag under its throat, did not run away. The king of Chu happened to arrive at that very moment. When he caught sight of the golden pheasant with its colourful silken bag—so peculiar and pleasing to the eyes—, he was enthralled beyond words. The attendants at his left and right had their bows and arrows ready, but the king stopped them from shooting it. Instead, he said to the official in charge, "The golden pheasant must be captured alive." After the golden pheasant's capture, the official in charge gave order to surround the place, and the birds and animals in the forest either died in the claws and mouth of the eagles and dogs, or under the knives and swords of the soldiers, while the rest were wounded in the trap. The golden pheasant was the only one which had escaped being wounded or death.

The next day, the king said to Song Yu, "The golden pheasant, on account of its beautiful silken bag, was able to save its own life. By the same token, it was because of its colourful silken bag that it had been shut up in a cage for the admiration of men. If we take the scholars as comparison, how should they behave to benefit themselves?"

Song Yu replied, "The only thing the golden pheasant has is the multicoloured silken bag. If it were to conceal it inside its throat and soar high into the sky, how could Your Highness see its beautiful ribbon and direct your official concerned to capture it? The reason it could not escape the fate of being imprisoned in a cage was not due to its silken bag, it was because it stuck it out. That's why a scholar should not flaunt his talent."

*

*The Xunzhi Studio Collection
By Fang Xiaoru (1357-1405 A.D.) styled himself Xizhi or Xigu, originally from Ninghai, Zhejiang Province. He was the disciple of Song Lian. During the period of Jianwen, which was the reign title of emperor Hui of Ming, he had once held the post of associate secretary in the central administration. When the capital was taken by the

emperor's uncle, who later usurped the throne in Nanking, Xiaoru was killed for being unyielding. He was the author of *The Xunzhi Studio Collection*.

715. The Wizard of Yue and the Demons

In the state of Yue, a wizard used to falsely allege that he was good at driving out the evil spirits. If someone was ill, he would build a platform for sacrificial rites, upon which he sounded the bugle or rang his magic bell, while leaping about here and there, singing and shouting, and performed a kind of gyrating dance from the Western Regions. According to what he said, this would help drive the demons away. If the sick person by chance became well again, he would be presented with a feast by the patient's family, and receive a reward ere he left. If the patient did not recover from his illness, he would find a pretext to evade responsibility. One thing he never did was to confess that he obtained money by fraud. He often boasted in front of people, "I'm best in dealing with demons. Against me all spirits and demons are powerless."

A few mischievous, unconventional and unrestrained young men, disgusted with the wizard's absurd conduct, met to discuss a plan whereby they disguised themselves as spirits and played a dirty trick on him. One night, as the wizard returned home, the five or six young men hid themselves separately up in the roadside trees with a distance of one *li* in between. When the wizard walked past under the trees, they would hurl down stones and sand. The wizard was taken by surprise when he saw stones and sand coming down from the sky, and thought he had met with spirits and demons. He turned round and round sounding the bugle, trying to frighten them away. He was in a daze and did not know where he was going. Just when he was feeling a little easier because there was a temporary pause, another storm of stones and sand hit him anew. This frightened him even more, and he hastened to sound the bugle. But, being in panic, he could not play the correct tune. Involuntarily, he ran faster and faster, shivering with fear and gasping for breath. He had now lost the strength to sound the bugle, and unknowingly let it slip from his trembling hands. He tried to ring his bell, but the bell, too, fell to the ground. The only thing he could do now was to run and shout. As he did so, he heard the sound of his own steps, the rustling of leaves and the howling of wind coming from the valley. He mistook all this to be the work of the spirits and demons, and cried miserably. He was in an extemely pathetic state.

It was midnight ere he reached home. He knocked at the door as he continued to cry. His wife was shocked and asked him why, but he was so scared that his tongue had become paralysed. Pointing at the bed, he could only say, trembling as he did so, "Quick, quick, let me lie down. I've seen the ghosts, and I'm about to die!"

His wife help him to the bed, but he had already died of fright, and all his skin turned blue as a result. All this had nothing to do with the spirits and demons, of course. But the wizard did not know it even at his deathbed.

716. Knowledge of Vehicle

In the state of Yue, people relied mainly on the boats as means of transportation. A man travelled to various places between the states of Jin and Chu found an abandoned vehicle which was already damaged. All the parts in the axle had decayed, the wheels were broken, the crossbar at the end of the carriage pole had snapped, and the shafts too were fractured. It was, in fact, totally unusable. Still, because the man of Yue had never seen a vehicle, he loaded it into a boat and brought it home as a novelty, just to show off to his fellow villagers and neighbours, to whom he bragged about how the vehicle was able to transport both passengers and goods, and could also be used in case of war. Those who saw it believed him, and thought all vehicles looked alike. Soon there emerged a large group of people who built vehicles for a living based on the same model.

Sometime later, visitors from the states of Jin and Chu came to know what they did with their vehicles, where all the parts were incomplete, and felt rather amused. They commented that the people of Yue were too clumsy, and that the vehicles they built were not serviceable. The people of Yue, however, believed it was meant as a deceptive tactic, and ignored what they said. Later, the state of Yue was invaded, and the people used their vehicles in the battlefield. When the vehicles broke down, the armed forces of Yue suffered a crushing defeat. Despite all the setback, they remained ignorant as to what a proper vehicle should look like.

Armed with only a superficial knowledge albeit with an unshakable conviction, and proceeded to put it into practice, that was the mistakes some scholars had often committed.

*

The Biography of Aliu
By Lu Rong (1436-1494 A.D.) styled himself Wenliang, assumed name Shizhai, originally from Taicang (Jiangsu Province). By disposition he showed great love and devotion to his parents. Read with avidity, he was very learned and well-informed. Once a Zhejiang official, he was later dismissed from office for incurring the displeasure of the powerful and influential. His book *Miscellaneous Tales of the Beans Garden*, fifteen volumes, was considered the best chronicle of events pertaining to the Ming Dynasty. *The Biography of Aliu* was his masterpiece, written in prose, about the servant Aliu, who was slow-witted to the extent of idiocy, constantly making a fool of himself, but he was later found to possess the talent for painting. After he was taught the technique of it, he became a painter.

717. Looking for a Leg of the Bed

A bed was short of one leg and Aliu was sent to cut a forked branch to fix it. Aliu picked up an axe and a saw and went to the wooded land, where he walked back and forth, looking for it the whole day. In the end, he returned empty-handed. Putting out two fingers to illustrate his point, he said, "All the forked branches are growing upwards, and none pointing downward."

718. Aliu and the Saplings

The Zhou Yuansu family had just planted several willow saplings in front of their house and, to prevent the children of neighbours from shaking them, Aliu was asked to look after them.

It was time for Aliu to go home and take his meal, but he was afraid the children might come to spoil the young trees, and so he pulled up all the newly planted willow saplings. After keeping them in a safe place, he felt at ease, and went home to have his meal.

The Dongtian Collection
By Ma Zhongxi (1446-1515 A.D.) styled himself Tianlu, assumed name Dongtian, originally from Gucheng (Hebei Province). A palace graduate in the reign of Chenghua, he was a writer and had once held the post of the right chief censor. Later, on account of a false accusation that he connived at Liu the Six and Liu the Seventh's peasant uprising, he was arrested and put into prison, where he died. Still later, it was discovered to be an injustice, and his official position was restored. *The Dongtian Collection* totals fifteen volumes, of which five volumes are prose, and ten, poetry. *The Biography of Zhongshan Wolf,* rumoured to have insinuated the event of Li Mengyang and Fu Kanghai, enjoyed a very great reputation, and was known within the country and abroad as an outstanding fable.

719. The Biography of Zhongshan Wolf

Zhao Jianzi went to Zhongshan to conduct a large scale hunting activity, led by an official in charge of the forests and hunting affairs, and followed by the falcons and hunting dogs. As arrows flew, innumerable flying birds and ferocious animals fell to the ground. Only a wolf, which stood like a man, blocked the way and howled. Zhao Jianzi spat on his palm, ascended the hunting carriage, and made an effort to pull the famous bow, *Wuhao*, while clamping the arrow, *Sushen*, between his fingers, and shot. The arrow went deep into the body of the wolf, and even the feathers attached to the end of the arrow disappeared into it. The wolf howled wildly, and fled. Zhao Jianzi flew into a rage, and immediately sped his hunting carriage to pursue it. Cloud of dust covered the whole sky, and the noise from the horses and carriages was earth-shaking. Beyond ten paces, it was almost impossible to distinguish between men and horses.

At this juncture, one Master Dongguo, who embraced the doctrine of Mohism, was on his way to the north to seek an official post in Zhongshan. He rode on an emaciated donkey with a bag full of books. Pushing on with his journey very early in the morning, he had lost his way. As the dust spread all over the sky, he shuddered with fear. Just then, a scurrying wolf suddenly appeared before him, stretching its neck as it turned to say, "Sir, isn't it you like to help other people? In former times, Mao Bao released the white turtle and was able to go across the river and survive, Sui Hou rescued the big snake and was rewarded with a bright pearl. The turtle and the snake by nature were not as smart as the wolf. Now that I've met with this misfortune, why don't you put me in your bag as fast as you can, so that I can survive this dire danger? At such a moment, if I can safely emerge from your bag, your kindness, sir, will be as if you were to rescue me from death and enable the bare bones to grow flesh, how can I not imitate the sincerity of the turtle and the snake and repay you?"

Master Dongguo said, "Aya! But if I have you concealed, I will offend the high officials and infuriate the rich and powerful, which will mean disaster. How dare I still expect such thing as your gratitude? However, as we Mohists uphold the doctrine of love without distinction, I must rescue you no matter what. Even though in doing so, I may face immediate calamity, I will not decline to do it." Thus he emptied his bag, took out the books, and with care helped the wolf to get into it. However, he soon discovered that, if he put the wolf head first into the bag, its claws might trample on the drooping flesh under the chin; if he put the lower part first, its body might weigh down on the tail, and he tried it three times without success. But while he was slow in action, being still undecided as to what to do, the pursuers were already getting nearer and nearer.

The wolf implored him, saying, "The matter is urgent! Are you really going to bow and greet, sir, before a drowning man or one in the fire? Or, ring your bell when the right thing to do is to hide from the robber? I'm now relying on you, sir, to think of a way to save me!" The wolf curled its four legs to enable Master Dongguo to tie them up; bent its head all the way down till it touched the tail; arched its back to cover the drooping flesh under the chin. The whole body now looked like a hedgehog, round as a ball, similar to a looper with its body curled up, or a snake twisted its body into a coil, or a turtle with its head recoiled into its shell. It left everything to Master Dongguo now. Master Dongguo did in accordance with what the wolf had indicated and put it into the bag, tied the bag's mouth tightly, and shouldered it to the donkey's back before he retreated to the roadside to await Zhao Jianzi's followers and their horses to pass.

In a moment, Zhao Jianzi was standing beside him. He did not inquire as to the whereabouts of the wolf but, with extreme fury, he unsheathed his sword and broke the shaft into two as he swore, "Anyone who fails to disclose the hiding place of the wolf, his end will be like this shaft."

Master Dongguo lay on his stomach, crawled forward and knelt before Zhao Jianzi, and said, "Your humble servant is very dull, but he still wishes to do a few things in the world. I've travelled a long distance and lost my way. How can I know where the wolf has gone and give direction to your falcons and hunting dogs? But I've heard people say, 'The main road has many sideroads, and that's why the sheep are apt to get lost.' A sheep can be brought under control even by a child and, if an animal as meek as a sheep can get lost because there are forked roads, how much more so for a wolf, which cannot be compared to a sheep. In Zhongshan, there are many forked roads, and plenty of opportunities for a sheep to get lost! If you only look for the wolf in the main road, will it not be very much like standing by a tree stump waiting for a hare or climbing up trees to look for fish? Besides, matters about hunting are under the jurisdiction of the official in charge of hunting and forests, and you should go and ask those officials. We, who hurry on our journey, have nothing to do with it. Moreover, even though I am stupid, that is not to say I can't even recognize a wolf? The wolf's nature is greedy and cruel, it colludes with the jackal to do evil things. Should I not do my part and contribute to your success if you are going to get rid of it but, instead, try to conceal the facts from you?"

Zhao Jianzi remained silent for a while; then, turning his carriage around, he was on his way again. Master Dongguo, too, spurred his donkey on, quickened his pace and went forward.

Some time later, Zhao Jianzi's banners gradually disappeared, the din that came from the carriages and horses died down, and the wolf reckoned Zhao Jianzi must have covered quite a long distance away from them. So it said to Master Dongguo from inside the bag, "Sir, please listen carefully. Release me from the bag, untie the rope, and pull out the arrow on my arm, as I'm about to leave!"

And so Master Dongguo lifted his hand and released the wolf. The wolf howled at him, saying, "A moment ago I was pursued by the hunters; it was fast and urgent, but fortunately you came to the rescue. I'm extremely hungry now. A hungry person is not choosy about his food. Besides, it is actually far worse to die by the roadside and be eaten by the animals than at the hands of the officials in charge of hunting and forests and become the table delicacy of the aristocrats! Sir, since you have devoted your life to the Mohist doctrine, defying hardship, without consideration for your own safety, willing to do some good to benefit the world, why should you now value your body? Why not let me eat you to preserve my insignificant life!" Thus it began to bare its fangs and brandish its claws as it pounced on Master Dongguo.

Master Dongguo hastened to raise his hands and hit the wolf in defence. In the meantime he retreated behind the donkey, circling around it to keep away from the wolf. As Master Dongguo tried his best to defend himself, the wolf was unable to hurt him after all. In the end, both were exhausted and gasped for breath, Master Dongguo at one side and the wolf at the other side of the donkey.

Master Dongguo said, "The wolf has let me down, the wolf has let me down!" "It's not my true intention to let you down," the wolf defended itself. "But then your kind are destined to be our food!"

For quite a long time, both sides refused to budge. The shadow of the sun began to sink gradually in the west, and Master Dongguo reckoned, "As it gets darker, it is possible the wolves will come in packs and bands. By that time I'll be dead for sure!" So he concocted a ruse by saying, "According to customary practice, one must ask for advice from three elders whenever any problem arises. Let us visit three elders. If they say I must offer myself up for you to eat, then go ahead; if they believe you must not eat me, then the matter will have to be dropped!" The wolf was pleased and went forward with Master Dongguo at once.

They walked for some time, encountering nobody on the way. The wolf's greed soon became unbearable and, finding an old tree standing bolt upright by the roadside, it said to Master Dongguo, "Let's ask this old tree." Master Dongguo refused to get along, saying, "Grasses and plants have no feeling; what's the use of asking them?"

The wolf disagreed, "Just ask," it said. "It will have something to say."

Against his will, Master Dongguo stepped forward, saluted with joined hands, and related the whole story from beginning to end. After that, he asked, "Under the circumstances, should the wolf eat me up?"

From within the tree came a booming voice directed to Master Dongguo, "I'm an apricot tree. In those days, when the old man who cultivated trees planted me, he needed only a single apricot pit. In one year, I began to flower; in another year, I began to bear fruit. In three years, I grew so thick that one can barely get one's hands around; in ten years, I've already grown to two arm spans in thickness. Twenty years had now passed. During those years, the old man who planted me ate my fruit, his wife and children ate my fruit and, from the guests who came from outside to the servants, all ate my fruit. Not only that, they also took the nuts to sell in the market for profit. I have contributed much to the old man who planted me. But now I'm old and can no longer flower, nor bear fruit, and so the old man has a grudge against me. He begins to cut the branches and leaves, and intends to sell me to the carpenter for money. Ah! A tree like myself is of no use now. In my sunset years, it will be impossible to avoid being cut and felled with all sizes of ax. What have you contributed to the wolf? How can you expect it to let you off so easily? To tell the true, you should be eaten up!" As the old tree finished speaking, the wolf again bared its fangs and brandished its claws as it pounced on Master Dongguo.

"The wolf failed to keep its promise!" said Master Dongguo. "Originally we agreed on asking the opinions of three elders, but we have just met an old tree. Why must you force me like this?" The wolf had no alterantive but to go forward with Master Dongguo.

In time the wolf became even more impatient. From a distance they saw an old cow basking in the sunshine behind a crumbling low wall, and the wolf said to Master Dongguo, "Let's ask this old cow!"

Master Dongguo replied, "A moment ago it was an ignorant plant which muddled things up by its absurd allegation. Now this is only a cow, an animal. Why must we ask it?"

"Go ahead and ask. If you don't, I'll bite you to death!" The wolf was adamant.

Master Dongguo had no choice but to approach the old cow and saluted it with joined hands while relating to it about what happened. The old cow knitted its brows, stared with its big eyes, licked its nose, opened its big mouth and said to Master Dongguo, "What the old apricot tree said is not at all absurd! Take for example, although I'm only an old cow, yet when my new horns were only as big as a cocoon or a chestnut, when I'm strong in muscles and bones, the old farmer sold a knife to get me, and put me with the other oxen to help plough the farm. As I reached the prime of my life, the other oxen gradually became old and weak, and I had to shoulder all the heavy work. If he went to hunt, I had to lower my head, pull the hunting carriage, find a shortcut and run as fast as I could; if he went to the farm, I had to get my harness off, go to the distant suburbs to help him get rid of the weeds and reclaim the waste land. The old farmer relied on me much as he needed his right hand. I supplied everything from clothing to food. The marriage arrangemnts of his children required my help, taxes and rents were paid with my assistance, and the granary needed my effort to fill. Sometimes I inferred I might get a mat, like what the horse and the dog had gotten, to wrap myself up when I died. Previously, he did not even have one hundred and twenty catties of grain as reserve, but now, as the harvest season of wheat arrives, he usually has ten times more than that amount. In past years, he lived a hand-to-mouth life, nobody came to care for him and comfort him. Nowadays he can swing his hands and go about in the village community, either to pay a visit or take a stroll. Previously, his wine bottle was covered with dust, his lips were dry and chapped, and the earthen jar where wine was stored had never been touched in half a lifetime. Nowadays, however, he can even use millet to make wine himself, and brag about his wine cup and wine pot before his wife and concubine. Formerly he had only coarse cloth jacket to wear, and concerned himself only with wood and mud. Neither did he know how to salute with his hands nor learn with his mind. But now he carries a book, puts a bamboo hat on his head, a leather belt around his waist, and wears loose and comfortable clothes. Every inch of thread and every grain of rice the old peasant owns are all the fruit of my labour! But, because I've grown old and weak, he is now sick of me and drives me to the wasteland and the wilderness, where cold wind hurts my eyes, and the winter sun casts my lonely shadow. I am but a mere bag of bones now, my tears fall like rain; I can't help slobbering, my limbs suffer from convulsion and cannot hold straight; I've lost all the hair attached to the skin, and the wound that was the result of whipping cannot be healed. The old farmer's wife is jealous and cruel. Day in day out she speaks thus to the old man, 'Nothing on the old cow's body is waste material. The meat can be cured, the hide can be tanned to make leather, the bones and horns can be ground and polished into utensils.' Pointing to his eldest son, she said, 'You have learned the skill from the master many years now. Why don't you sharpen your butcher's knife and do it?' All indications point to an extremely grim prospect, and I don't know how I'll die! I've contributed so much and they are so heartless. I'm certain misfortune will soon befall me! What have you contributed to the wolf that you expect yourself to be let off so easily?" As the old cow finished speaking, the wolf again bared its fangs, brandished its claws and pounced on Master Dongguo.

"Don't be so impatient!" said Master Dongguo.

In the distance, an old man leaning on a pigweed staff came towards them. His beard and eyebrows had both turned grey. Dressed in good taste, he seemed a man of moral integrity. Master Dongguo had mixed feelings of joy and dread. Leaving the wolf behind, he stepped forward to meet the old man and knelt down crying and supplicating, "I wish you, my esteemed elder, will say something to save my life!"

The old man asked why, and Master Dongguo said, "This wolf was driven into a corner by the hunting officials, and asked for my help. I helped it survive, but it wants to eat me now. Though I have begged it not to, but it was all to no avail. It looks like I must die in its hands. As a delaying tactic, I made it agree to ask three elders prior to making any decision. First, we met an old apricot tree and the wolf urged me to seek its judgement. But, as plants are ignorant things, I almost lost my life. Later, we met an old cow, and again I was forced to ask for its opinion. As animals are also ignorant, I almost lost my life a second time. Now, we have met you, my esteemed elder, isn't it true Heaven does not end a scholar's life just like that? I wish you would say a word or two to save me!" Having said that, he kowtowed repeatedly by the old man's pigweed staff, his head bowed, waiting for instructions.

As the old man heard the story, he sighed again and again. Finally, he touched the wolf with his pigweed staff and said, "You are wrong! To betray a benefactor is the most inauspicious thing to do. The

Confucianists believe one who receives a kindness and does not betray the benefactor is likely to be a filial son. They also say, 'Even the tiger and the wolf know such thing as love and duty between parents and children'. Since you are devoid of gratitude, the feelings between parents and children no longer exist in you!" He then flayed the wolf aloud, saying, "Wolf, get away from here! If not, I'll hit you with my pigweed staff until you die!"

The wolf tried to explain, saying, "My esteemed old man, you have only a one-side view. Let me relate the whole story, and please listen carefully. It began with my asking Master Dongguo to rescue me. When he tied me up hand and foot, sealed me up in his bag, where his books of poetry weighed down upon me, I had to arch my body and stop breathing. Later, he talked lengthily to Zhao Jianzi on something quite unrelated to my safety. I guess his intention was to suffocate me in the bag so he could get all the benefit. How can a man like that not be eaten?"

The old man turned towards Master Dongguo and said, "In that case, you have also committed some mistakes!"

Wherefore Master Dongguo, in his indignation, related the whole story in detail as to how he had put the wolf into his bag on account of the compassion he had for the wolf. While Master Dongguo was thus engaged, the wolf continued to quibble and refute what he said.

"Your words are not sufficient to convince me!" the old man said. "Why not let's put the wolf into the bag again, so that I can see for myself whether or not his condition was indeed difficult to endure at that time?"

The wolf was pleased to accept the suggestion, and it stretched its legs towards Master Dongguo. Master Dongguo therefore tied up the wolf once again, put it into the bag and shouldered it to the donkey's back. Throughout the whole operation, however, the wolf did not know what was in the old man's mind.

The old man pressed close to Master Dongguo's ears and asked him in a low voice, "Have you a dirk?"

"Yes," Master Dongguo replied.

And he took out the sword. The old man hinted to Master Dongguo with his eyes to stab the wolf.

"Will that not kill the wolf?" Master Dongguo asked.

The old man smiled and said, "Such an ungrateful beast and you still cannot bear to kill it! That of course shows you are a kind-hearted man who loves all men but, nevertheless, a little too foolish. Following one who falls into the well to rescue him from danger, taking off one's clothes to help a friend who is frozen, all this may seem beneficial to the man waiting to be rescued, but that is also going to one's own death! You are such a man, sir! When a man loves others to the extent of foolishness, that's something gentlemen will not be able to agree to!" He laughed uproariously as he finished talking, and Master Dongguo laughed too. Thereupon the old man went into action, helping Master Dongguo kill the wolf with the dirk. They then cast the dead body of the wolf on the road and left.

*

The Manuscript With Seven Subjects
By Lang Ying (1487-1566 A.D.) styled himself Renbao, originally from Renhe, Zhejiang Province (now Hangzhou). A writer of the Ming Dynasty he, however, remained a scholar without an official career. He was born with extraordinary talent, widely-read, accumulated what he learned and observed and compiled them into *The Manuscript With Seven Subjects,* which totals fifty-one volumes, divided into seven categories, namely, astronomy, state affairs, the princple of righteousness, dialectics, poetry and essays, matters and events, and marvellous jokes, of which one thousand two hundred fifty-seven items are devoted to events, as the author endeavours to strike a balace between the miscellaneous notes and researches. The category *Marvellous Jokes* are notes and sketches mixed with fables.

720. Play the Jackal to the Tiger

According to tradition, when a man was eaten by a tiger, his soul would follow the tiger, and would not dare wander elsewhere. In the dictionary, the phenomenon is described as "a ghost believed to lead a tiger to its human victims", that is, he becomes an accomplice.

Whenever a tiger went out, the ghost controlled by the tiger would walk in front to clear the way for the tiger, thus enabling it to avoid danger. That was why when the hunter went for the tiger, he would put such things as a bowl of soup, a lunch box, clothing, shoes, and so on, before it arrived. As the ghost saw these things, it would stop to enjoy them, while the tiger, ignorant of what happened, would continue to go forward, and thus fall into the hunter's trap. If it were not for this strategem, the ghost controlled by the tiger would have disrupted the plan, and all the hunter's scheme would be to no avail.

After the tiger had been captured, the ghost controlled by the tiger would go to the place where the tiger met its fate and cry piteously throughout the night, and it was because it thought leading the tiger to catch a man for food was no longer possible.

721. The Game is Up

According to legend, during the time of the Southern Song Dynasty, Qin Hui, the treacherous court official who turned traitor for personal gain, had conspired to kill the famous general, Yue Fei, who resisted the Jin invasion. Qin Hui was afraid his secret might be exposed, and plotted with his wife nee Wang under the east window. After his death, Qin Hui was thrown into the inferno on account of the crimes he had committed and the murdering of the faithful and honest. He had to suffer all kinds of tortures in the inferno, and so he appeared in nee Wang's dream, asking her to help expiate his sins, so that he might be released from the purgatory. To free him from the suffering, Qin Hui's wife, nee Wang, invited a Taoist priest to do whatever was necessary. When the Taoist priest arrived, nee Wang, because she missed her hsuband so much, begged him to exercise his magic power so she could go to the inferno to see her husband and to console his soul. The Taoist priest let loose his hair, held a sword in his hand, gave free play to his magic arts, and played a trick in front of nee Wang. He told nee Wang that he had met with Qin Hui, who informed him, "Please convey this message to my wife, 'The game is up.'" What Qin Hui meant to say was, "Please inform my wife, 'the conspiracy to kill Yue Fei, which was hatched under the east window, had been exposed.'" The event had given birth to a Chinese idiomatic expression equivalent to "The game is up".

722. A Poet Who Has Lost All Sense of Shame

Recently I came across a friend from Jinhua; he was accustomed to wandering around looking for opportunity in the name of poetry. His real intention was to meet with the high officials and bigwigs. He possessed a personal seal engraved with the following Chinese characters: "A white cloud atop the mountain peak where hibiscus grows." From the way he described himself, it could be seen how pure and aloof he considered himself.

A friend called Gao Luzhi teased him, saying, "This cloud flies into the halls of officials everyday!"

The remark caused everyone to be convulsed with laughter.

*

*Tales of Life's Journey
By Xu Wei (1551-1593 A.D.) styled himself Wenqing, later Wenchang, assumed name The Holy Man of Tianchi (lakes atop the Tianshan Mountain and the Changbaishan Mountain), Qingteng (sinomenium acutum) Recluse, and so on, originally from Shanyin (Shaoxing, Zhejiang Province). Despite frequent attempts, he failed in the civil service examinations in his early years. Later, he became the house guest and adviser of a high official. He had been imprisoned for the crime of manslaughter committed against his wife. As a boy, he was called a child prodigy, full of wits, and the folklore *The Story of Xu Wenchang* circulating in Zhejiang and its vicinity was widespread. He was adept in poetry, traditional Chinese operas, and famed especially for his painting of flowers and birds in traditional Chinese style. He authored *The Xu Wenchang Complete Collection* and the traditional Chinese opera *The Four-toned Ape*, etc. *Tales of Life's Journey* was a book of miscellanies, recording events in different dynasties. Because the title was identical with a book by Luo Mi of the Southern Song Dynasty, it was given an alternative title called *Tales of Life's journey by the Qingteng Recluse.*

723. A Goose Feather Sent from a Thousand *li* Away

During the Tang Dynasty, the leader of the minority nationality in Yunnan, whose family name was Mian, intended to present the native bird, the precious white swan, as a tribute to the emperor, and a messenger called Mian Bogao was sent with several of the birds to the capital Chang-an. When he came to the Mianyang Lake, Mian Bogao noticed it was hot, suffocating, and dirty inside the cage, so he unfastened the cage door and released the swans into the lake for a bath. But how could the swans understand his good intention? As soon as they were out of the cage, they flew towards the sky and disappeared. Thus Mian Bogao had lost his tribute. He was terribly frightened and gave way to tears.

Just as he was in dire desperation, feeling so helpless, Mian Bogao discovered several pure, white swan feathers on the ground. A bright idea suddenly occurred to him. He picked up the feathers and continued his journey to the capital. As the messengers from various places presented their tributes, Mian Bogao had only a few feathers to contribute. The emperor and the other high officials were all stunned. Mian Bogao, however, unhurriedly sang a song:

I was going to pay tribute to the emperor,
The mountains were high and the distance long;
In the Mianyang Lake I lost my swans,
And lay on the ground I gave way to tears.
May I ask the Son of Heaven, emperor of Tang,
Can you forgive Mian Bogao, the messenger?
The gift itself may be light as a goose feather,
But sent from afar, it conveys deep feeling.

As the emperor listened, he was moved by the sincerity of Mian Bogao. And, not only was Mian Bogao not punished, he was given a handsome reward.

*

*Quanzi
By Geng Dingxiang (1554-1596 A.D.) styled himself Zailun, originally from Huang-an, Huguang (Hong-an, Hubei province). He had once held the position of minister in the Ministry of Revenue during the period of Wanli (1573-1620 A.D.), which was the title of emperor Shenzong of Ming, but later asked for leave to go home. Thereafter he lived in Tiantai Mountain as lecturer until he died. He authored *The*

Collected Works of Tiantai, and others. *Quanzi,* one volume, was one of the earliest books which used jokes and fables to caution mankind against impending disasters.

724. The Elegance of One's Gait

A scholar was having a leisurely stroll outdoors in his measured gait with the toes pointing outwards when, all of a sudden, it began to rain hard. Instinctively he quickened his pace and ran for shelter. Having covered over a *li* in distance, he was seized with an unforeseen regret in his heart. He thought, "I ran in a hurry, and thus lost the elegance of my gait as a scholar! Since I've made a mistake, it is but right I should have it immediately corrected."

Thereupon he braved the rain and returned to where he was before, and began anew, walking leisurely in his measuured gait with toes pointing outwards.

725. In Search of a Master

Shang Jizi loved Taoism and used to bring money with him to study abroad. Whenever he met with a Taoist priest wearing a yellow hat, he would knelt down and asked for advice.

A crafty fellow who wanted to cheat Shang Jizi out of his money approached him with fine words and an insinuating countenence, saying, "I've already mastered the magic arts of Taoism. If you follow me and learn from me, I'll certainly pass on my knowledge to you." Shang Jizi then followed him and with all sincerity tried to learn from him. The opportunity the crafty fellow waited for did not come for a long time. Meanwhile, Shang Jizi kept urging him to pass on to him the knowledge of Taoist magic arts. One day, as they arrived at the riverside, the crafty fellow thought the opportunity had arrived, and he deceived Shang Jizi by saying, "The magic arts you wish to learn is here." "Where?" Shang Jizi asked. "It's at the masthead," the man replied. "You will get it if you climb up there." Following his instruction, Shang Jizi deposited his wallet at the foot of the mast, and began to climb up. The man below clapped his hands, urging him to go on. "Climb up some more," he said. Suddenly, Shang Jizi woke up to reality, and embraced the mast with both hands while shouting with great enthusism, "I've got it! I've got it!" Down below, the crafty fellow seized the golden opportunity, picked up the wallet and fled.

Down from the masthead, Shang Jizi was as happy as ever. One bystander said, "Tut-tut! Why are you so stupid! That crafty fellow has run away with your wallet." "He's my master, indeed he is! He did it by way of teaching me!" replied Shang Jizi.

726. The Scarecrow and the Water Birds

A certain man had a pond, which brought nothing but vexation, as teals came and stole his fish all the time. He therefore made a scarecrow, donned it with a straw rain cape and a bamboo hat. Using a bamboo pole he had it put in the middle of the pond to scare the waterr birds.

The first time the water birds saw it, they just circled around in the sky, and did not come down at once. But, later, when they knew what it was all about, they came down again to peck at the fish. As time went on, they even alighted on the bamboo hat in a leisurely, contented manner, and were not in the least afraid.

Someone saw what happened and quietly took away the scarecrow. In its place, he put on himself the straw rain cape and the bamboo hat. Holding a bamboo pole, he then stood in the middle of the pond. The teals came to eat the fish as they were wont to do, and touched down on his bamboo hat. The man stretched out his hands and grabbed the legs of the water bird whenever it perched there. As the teal was unable to extricate itself; it fluttered its wings and cried "Jia, jia" (homophonous with the Chinese character "bogus"). "It was 'jia' (bogus) before, but how can you say it's 'jia' now!" The man said.

727. Admiring the Moralists

Once upon a time, there was a man who admired the fame of the moralists and tried to imitate them. One day, he was out walking on the road. Whenever a padestrain paased him, he would respectfully made an obeisance by cupping one hand in the other before his chest, and made a bow with hands folded in front. Every step he took was strictly in accordance with the old ways.

In so doing, however, he felt extremely fatigued, as he had been doing it for a long time, so he called his attendant. "Look back and see," he instructed. "Are there any padestrain behind us?"

"None," replied his attendant.

He immediately loosened up and rambled along at ease once more.

728. The Peacock and its Tail

The long tail feathers of the peacock shone with beautiful hues and patterns; its brightness dazzled the eyes. It was not something the painter could depict with his brush and colours. The peacock was jealous by nature, and even though it might be domesticated for a long period of time, whenever it saw children dressed in brocade, it would follow closely behind to peck them. When it perched in the hilly area, it would first of all find a place to hide its tail before thinking of settling its body. Even though it rained, its tail got soaked, and the bird catcher with his net was arriving, because it loved its tail so much, it would not flutter and soar high. Thus eventually it was caught by the hunter.

*

Follow-up Tales of Aizi
By Lu Zhuo, dates of birth and death unknown, originally from Changzhou, Jiangsu (now Suzhou). The book imitated Su Shi's *Miscellaneous Tales of Aizi*. In the preface, he said, "In 1576 A.D. I visited Nanking and, feeling bored away from home, I selected the outstanding ones and compiled them into a book to append to its predecessor, which was authored by the revered Su Shi". From this it can be inferred he must be a man of letters in dire straits outside the official circles. The book was probably completed in the fourth year of Wanli (1576 A.D.).

729. Being Serious

Aizi was doing some sightseeing in the suburbs with his two disciples, Tong and Zhi. Aizi was in dire thirst, so he sent Zhi to a farming family to ask for a little hot water. Arriving at the door, Zhi saw an old man reading by the light that came from outside the house. Zhi made a bow with hands folded in front, and asked the old man for a little hot water. The old man pointed at the Chinese character *zhen* and said, "If you know this character, you can have the water." Zhi said, "This is the character *zhen*." The old man was very angry, and did not give him any.

Zhi returned and told Aizi about what happened. Aizi said, "Zhi is not familiar with the ways of the world, so Tong should go." Tong went to see the old man, and the old man asked him the same question. "These are two characters, *zhi* and *ba* (two characters, *zhi* and *ba*, make up the character *zhen*)." The old man was extremely pleased, and offered Tong his best home brew. Aizi tasted and found it to be excellent, and he said, "Tong is very smart! If he is as serious as Zhi, I'm afraid I may not even have a ladle of it."

730. Unblushing Exaggeration

An occultist who loved to talk about immortality was in the habit of telling exaggerated stories, and Aizi taunted him by asking him, "Sir, how old are you now?"

The occultist was all smiles as he replied, "I've forgotten how old I'm now. As I recall, when I was still a child, I once went with a group of children to Mi Xi's home to watch him draw the Eight Diagrams (eight combinations of three whole or broken lines formerly used in divination). I discovered then he was actually a monster with human head and a snake body. I was so frightened that, when I returned home, I fell ill with epilepsy. Fortunately, Mi Xi gave me some herbal medicine, which cured me and enabled me to survive. At the time of Nuwo, the sky tilted to the northwest, and the earth caved in from the southeast. But I was living in the middle region, which was stable and not affected by the disaster. When Shen Nong began to sow, I was no longer eating the five cereals, and that's why I did not eat any of his grains. Once, Chi You attacked me with the five weapons he manufactured, but I raised one of my fingers and wounded his forehead, and he fled, as all his face was covered with blood. Originally Cang Jie was illiterate. He came to learn from me, but I believed he was stupid and did not respond to his request. Qin Dou was pregnant for fourteen months before giving birth to Yao. Yao invited me to attend Qin Dou's birthday party once. Emperor Shun was maltreated by his parents. With his face towards the heavens he wailed at the top of his voice. It was I who wiped off the tears for him. I comforted and encouraged him, enabling him to become a filial son known to all. When Yu the Great (2276-2177 B.C., founder of the Xia Dynasty) was regulating the rivers and watercourses to prevent floods, he once passed by my home. I presented him with a cup of wine as a sign of respect, but he firmly declined. Kong Jia gave me a piece of dragon meat, which I ate without much thinking at the time, and even now my mouth still retained remnants of the stinking smell. Cheng Tang used nets to catch birds and animals. I once made fun of him, calling him a glutton of game animals. When Lu Gui forced me to have a booze-up with him, I refused. For that reason, he tortured me by ordering me to walk on a slippery metal beam kept hot by coal underneath. Yet after seven days and seven nights, I went on talking and laughing as if nothing had happened, and he released me. The little boy of the Jiang family, Lu Shang, used to present me with the fish he caught in the Wei River, some of which I fed to the yellow crane in the mountain. When the Son of Heaven, emperor of Zhou, and the king of Mu, went to the fairyland to attend the festival held on the 3rd day of the 3rd lunar month in honor of the Grand Old Lady of the West Heaven, I was seated at the head of the table. Later, when the news of king Xu Yan's rebellion was brought to his attention, King Mu left the banquet and returned in an eight-horse carriage. The Grand Old Lady of the West Heaven urged me to stay on until the end of the banquet, which I did. Because I had too much nectar to drink, I became dead drunk. Fortunately, the two maids of the Grand Old Lady of the West Heaven, Dong Shuangcheng and E Luhua, supported me and helped me home. From that day onwards, I felt dizzy and sleepy all the time. I'm not entirely out of the wood yet, and really don't know what year it is now!"

Having heard what he said, Aizi nodded his head repeatedly and, after expressing his admiration, he left.

Not long after that, the king of the state of Zhao happened to fall from his horse and hurt his costa. The physician said, "Blood of a thousand years' duration must be applied to the wound to effect a cure." Wherefore the king of Zhao had to look for blood that had existed for a thousand years. He ordered no stone unturned to find the blood. But despite all his efforts, the search was fruitless.

Aizi, therefore, went to inform the king of Zhao, saying, "There is an occultist, who has lived over several thousand years. If he is killed and his blood taken to apply to your wound, you will immediately be cured."

The king of Zhao was overjoyed, and he sent someone secretly to have the occultist caught, while getting ready to take his life.

The occultist knelt down kowtowing, and sobbed as he supplicated, "Both my parents had just passed their fiftieth birhtdays yesterday, and my eastern neighbour brought wine to congratulate them. I had a drop too much and was talking through my hat. Actually I do not live over one thousand years. Master Aizi is an adept in telling lies. I hope Your Highness will not listen to him.!"

The king of Zhao heard what he said and gave him a good scolding, but later released him.

731. I'm the Rice

The wife of Li Ji of the state of Yan was beautiful but loose in morals. She had committed adultery with a young man whose family was her neighbour. When Li Ji heard about it, he decided to make a sneak raid.

One day, Li Ji hid himself and watched them on the sly. He saw the young man entered the house and bolted the door, and so he stood up and went to knock.

Thrown into a panic, his wife said, "It's my husband. What shall we do?"

"Is there any window?" the young man asked.
"There is no window here," replied the wife of Li Ji.
"Any hole in the ground?"
"No hole here," replied Li Ji's wife.
"How can I get out of here then?"
Li Ji's wife saw the sack on the wall and said, "That will be enough."

Thereupon the young man entered the sack, which was then left standing near the bed. He said, "If asked, just lied the sack is filled with rice."

The door was then opened to let Li Ji in. Li Ji searched every corner inside the room, but the young man was nowhere to be seen. Slowly he came near the bed, where he saw the sack. He tried to raise it. It was terribly heavy. He questioned his wife, "What is it inside?"

His wife was so frightened that she just muttered and mumbled without being able to say anything clearly. As Li Ji's scolding was relentless, his interrogation without end, the young man was afraid their affair might soon be exposed, and unconsciously he answered from inside the sack, saying, "I'm the rice."

Thus Li Ji caught the young man and beat him to death. Even his wife was unable to escape the same fate.

When Aizi learned about it, he smiled and said, "Formerly I heard the rock in the state of Jin could speak. Now, the rice in the state of Yan, too, can talk!"

732. Amnesia

There in the state of Qi was a man who suffered from amnesia. When he walked, he was apt to forget where to stop; when he lay down on the bed, he often failed to remember he had to get up. His wife was deeply worried about him, and advised him to see Aizi, saying, "I've heard Master Aizi is both humorous and learned, and that he can cure chronic illnesses. Why don't you ask him for advice?" "O.K.," he promised.

So he rode a horse, carried his bow and arrow, and set out. Having covered less than thirty *li*, he felt an urge inside him. He dismounted from his horse and looked for a place to relieve himself. First, he stuck the bow and arrow on the ground; then he tethered the horse to a tree. Having moved his bowels, he stood up to find the bow and arrow on the ground at his left side and exclaimed, "How unsafe it is! Where comes the sniper's shot, almost right on me!" However, when he discovered the horse tethered to the tree at his right, he was delighted, and said to himself, "Though I have to endure a terrible shock, at least I come by a horse." As he said this, he began to untether the horse. While doing so, he inadvertently stepped on his own shit, which infuriated him, and he stamped his foot and scolded, "What luck! I've stepped on a heap of dog dung, and my shoes were soiled!" And he vaulted onto the horse, brandished his whip, turned around, retraced his steps and went home.

Soon he arrived at the front door of his own house. He was uncertain and asked himself, "Whose house is this? Isn't it possible this is Master Aizi's residence?" At that moment, his wife came out. At the sight of her husband, she knew his amnesia had relapsed, and couldn't help chiding him. He was at a loss to understand what happened and complained, "I've never met this young woman before, why must she use bad language to insult me?"

733. Marriage Between a Child and an Old Man

Aizi had a friend whose name was Yu Ren. The man's daughter had just turned two, clever and lovely, and Aizi liked her very much. So on behalf of his son, he negotiated an engagement between the two.

Yu Ren was rather pleased too, and he asked, "How old is your beloved son?"

"Four," Aizi replied.

"What!" Yu Ren pulled a long face. "Do you want my daughter to marry an old man?"

Aizi was unable to make head or tail of what he said.

"You still feign ignorance," Yu Ren said brutally. "Your son is four years old, and my daughter two. That is to say, your son is twice as old as my daughter. Let's suppose my daughter is married at twenty, by that time your son will be forty. If, unfortunately, her marriage is delayed until twenty-five, then your son will be fifty. Isn't it you intend to marry my daughter to an old man?"

734. Crying in Advance

The king Xuan of Qi asked Chun Yukun, "How many thousand years will the universe take to complete a cycle?"

Chun Yukun replied, "I've heard the master said, 'Heaven and earth begins their number at ten thousand years, and one hundred and twenty thousand years is the grand total. At the year when the grand total takes place, the cycle will have been completed."

Upon hearing this, Aizi burst into tears.

The king Xuan of Qi was flabbergasted, and asked him, "Master, what are you crying for?"

"I'm crying for the people who might be living in the one hundred nineteen thousand nine hundred and ninety-nineth year before the cycle!" Aizi stopped crying and said.

"Why is it so?" the king Xuan of Qi asked again.

"I'm worrid that when that year shall have arrived, where must they go to keep away from the holocaust!" Aizi replied.

735. Biting Dogs

Aizi, having breakfasted, was taking a stroll in front of the house. His neighbour toted two family dogs with a carrying pole and proceeded towards the west. Aizi greeted him and asked, "Where do you tote the dogs to?"

"For sale to the butcher's," replied his neighbour.

"Aren't they we called dogs? Why should you have them slaughtered?" Aizi asked.

The neighbour pointed at the dogs and began to curse, saying, "The beasts ! Last night, robbers came to loot us, they were so frightened that they just concentrated their attention on eating their fill, and did not dare even to utter a bark. Today, we opened our door, but they could not differentiate between a friend and a foe, and launched a collective attack against my guest of honour, wounded him with their bites, and that's why I'm going to have them slaughtered."
Aizi said, "Good!"

736. Castrating a Ram

Aizi kept two sheep in his backyard. The ram was bellicose: whenever it saw a stranger, it would chase and butt at him. Aizi's disciples considered it a nuisance as they made frequent visits to their master's house. They entreated Aizi, saying, "Master, the ram you keep is very ferocious. It will be better to castrate it to make its disposition gentler."

Aizi smiled and replied, "Don't you know people without the male organs today are even fiercer?

*

Hunranzi
By Zhang Chong styled himself Ziyi, dates of birth and death unknown, originally from Liuzhou, Guangxi Province. A palace graduate in the tewnty-second year of Jiajing (1553 A.D.), he had successively held the posts of president of the Supreme Court, the vice-ministers of the Ministry of War and the Ministry of Punishments. He authored *Hunranzi*, or *Master Hunran*.

737. A Gift from God

A peasant in the state of Qi was so poor that he had nothing to live on. He discussed the dire situation with his wife, saying, "I've heard that the god in Mount Taishan is miraculous. Why don't we go to pray and ask for a blessing." They then sold the only old leather garment they had, bought the sacrificial pig and lamb, and proceeded to Mount Taishan to pray. When they returned to their field in the suburbs of Linzi, the capital of Qi, they found, while hoeing the land, a lot of gold pieces, which made them rich and prosperous over night.

The son of the Dongguo family, who lived in the eastern suburbs, learned that the man's gold came about as a result of his praying in Mount Taishan. Following the latter's example, he also sold his leather coat, bought the sacrificial pig and lamb and proceeded to Mount Taishan to pray. Upon his return, however, he met with a tiger and a leopard at the field in the suburbs of Linzi. As a result, he was eaten.

Someone brought forth this matter and asked for the opinion of Hunranzi. Master Hunran said, "... The lesson of the event is: a man with wealth and virtue must not tempt fate by praying for blessings from God. He must not rely on other people. Only in his own gifted talent and labour should he trust to win the right to live in happiness."

738. On Cultivation

A peasant was seen working with a hoe on a piece of farmland. He did it slowly and, with every stroke of his hoe, he breathed several times. A passerby noticed it and criticised the peasant. "You are too slow!" he said. "The land is so big, but you only move your hoe once while you take several breaths. I'm afraid you will not be able to finish hoeing, not even until the end of the year!" The peasant, upon hearing the criticism, greeted the passerby. "I've been tilling land all my life, and am getting old and will soon die in this piece of land, but I still don't quite know how to do it properly. Can you set an example and show me how I should work?"

The passerby took off his coat, stepped into the field, and hastened to brandish the hoe. He executed several strokes as he breathed once, and every stroke was done with all the strength he had. Very soon, the man was exhausted, sweat ran down his cheeks like raindrops, and he had to gasp for breath. He was too breathless to talk, and his legs were so weak that he could hardly stand, so he lay down on the field at once. After resting for a while, exasperatingly slowly he said to the peasant, "I only know it today that farm work is strenuous!"

The peasant replied, "Farm work is not really very hard, but if you move up-tempo, as you have just done, it will be difficult to carry on. If you try to effect several strokes before the next breath, you will inevitably become exhausted. As a result, you must take a little rest before you begin again. On balance, you spend more time resting than working. As for me, I breathe several times in between two strokes of my hoe, but I continue to work without having to pause for breath. In taking stock of the merits and demerits of the different styles, rest more and work less, or work more with little or no rest, it will be evident which is faster, more relaxing and less tiring?"

As the passerby listened, he was convinced the peasant was right. Thereupon he put on his overcoat and left.

*

An Evening Conversation in the Mountains
By Li Zhi (1557-1605 A.D.), original name Zai Zhi styled himself Zhuowu, assumed name Hongfu, also called Retired Scholar Manling and the Longhu Old Man, a native of Jinjiang, Quanzhou, Fujiang Province. A thinker and writer of the Ming Dynasty, he had successively held the posts of councillor in the Ministry of Punishments, magistrate of the district of Yao-an, Yunnan Province, and so on, but resigned at the age of fifty-four to lecture in the city of Ma and its vicinity. He authored *Book Burning, Book Collection, On History*, and so on. He was also inclined to comment on popular novels. There were editions of *The Romance of the Three Kingdoms, Outlaws of the Marsh*, and others, with his comments.

739. In Dread of the Steamed Bun

A certain scholar had never seen the steamed bun. He longed for it but could not get it.

One day, he saw what he believed to be steamed buns put out for sale in the market, so he gave a yell and fell to the ground. The shopkeeper was greatly alarmed, and stepped forward to see what happened.

"I dread the sight of buns," said the destitute scholar.

"How can it be?" the shopkeeper had his doubts, but he prepared over a hundred buns, vacated a room and shut him into it; then he waited patiently outside to see what happened.

Quite a long time had gone by, but it was all quiet inside the room, and not even the faintest noise was audible. The shopkeeper dug a small hole in the wall and peeked in. He saw the scholar putting a bun into his mouth, half of it had already been consumed. He hastened to open the door and questioned the scholar as to why he acted thus. The destitute scholar said, "At the sight of all these things, I suddenly lost all my fear." The shopkeeper knew he had been deceived and berated the scholar severely, saying, "Is there anything else you dread?" "Oh, yes, I do. I still am in dread of two cups of the year-end tea!" replied the destitute scholar.

*

*A Sketchbook
By Liu Yuan Qing (1544-1609 A.D.) styled himself Diaofu, originally from Anfu, Jiangxi Province. During the period of Wanli (1573-1620 A.D.), he had once held the post of director in the Ministry of Rites. Later, he fell ill and returned home, where he devoted his time to writing. He authored *The Liu Pingjun Collection, The Case of the Confucianists*, etc. *A Sketchbook* is a book of sketches, under sixteen headings, in which two categories, *metaphors* and *Humours*, have a rather large number of fables recorded. Most of which, however, overlap with those found in other books, and it is conjectured that they are probably compiled from various sources, not originals.

740. Hard Time for the Blind

A blind man passed a brook which had dried up. He was careless and fell from the bridge. Holding the handrail with both hands, he trembled with fear lest he should drop into the swift current of the deep chasm. A bystander told him, saying, 'Don't be afraid. Down there very near you is dry land." He did not believe the bystander and continued with his firm grip on the handrail while crying for help. This went on for some time until he was exhausted by his effort and, losing hold,.fell to the ground. By way of consoling himself, he said, "Hey! If I had known that below me is dry land, I should not have to suffer like this."

The highway is broad and smooth. He who indulges in daydream and glories in being alone, or understands only one aspect of a thing and becomes smug, should come to his senses after reading this story.

741. Dispute over the Wild Goose

Once upon a time, a man saw a flock of wild geese in the sky and brought his bow and arrow to shoot them. As he did so, he shouted, "Shoot it down and cook." His brother, who was standing by his side, disagreed, saying, "The slow-flying geese should be cooked, those fast-flying ones should be roasted." As neither could convince the other, they went to ask the opinion of Uncle She. Uncle She proposed they went halves, cooking one part and roasting the other. However, as they finally came to a consensus, the wild geese had already flown away.

742. To Scratch the Itching Spot

Once upon a time, there was a man whose body itched and asked his son to scratch it. His son tried three times to locate the itching spot, but failed. He then asked his wife to do it. She tried five places, but all proved to be wrong. The man became angry and said, "My wife and my son are the most intimate persons. Why can't they find the itching place in my body?" And he stretched out his own hand, and located it immediately without the slightest difficulty. Why? Because he knew the exact itching spot and could not have missed it.

743. The Chinese Character for Ten Thousand

In the district of Ru, there was an old man. He was the head of a wealthy farming family. However, for generations none of the clan members had ever learned so much as a literary jargon. For that reason, he engaged a scholar one year from the district of Chu to be the teacher of his son. The first thing the scholar of Chu taught his son was the correct way to hold a writing brush and to copy the calligraphy model, one stroke representing the character "one", two strokes, "two", and three strokes, "three".

The son of the old farmer felt extremely proud and self-satisfied after learning the three characters. And, throwing away his writing brush, he went home to tell his father, saying, "I've learned all! I've learned all! There is no need to bother the master anymore. It is not necessary to spend so much money to engage a master. Let's discharge him politely!"

His father was overjoyed and did just as he had suggested: dismissing the scholar from the district of Chu.

Not long after that, his father wished to invite a relative surnamed Wan (the character for "ten thousand") to come for a drink, and asked the son to write an invitation. The invitation was not completed for an unusual long time, and his father tried to press him.

His son resented, saying, "There are so many family names in the world, why should he choose "wan"? Beginning this morning until now, I've just finished doing five hundred strokes!"

A scholar, who had just been imparted the rudimentary knowledge, felt complacent and smug, and began to boast that he had learned eveything there was to learn. Might this be one of them?

744. The Tiger Cat

There was a cat in Qi Yan's family, which he believed to be rather extraordinary, and nicknamed it "tiger cat".

One of his guests said, "The tiger is surely a ferocious animal, but it is not as mysterious and profound as the dragon. Why don't you change the name and call it the 'dragon cat'?"

Another guest disagreed, saying, "The dragon is of course more mysterious and profound than the tiger, but the dragon rises to heaven with the help of the clouds. Doesn't that mean the cloud is mightier than the dragon. I think you had better call it the 'cloud cat'."

Yet another guest opined, "The thin, floating clouds may cover the sky but, when the wind blows, it is scattered, and that's why I say the cloud is no match for the wind. Please call it the 'wind cat'."

Another guest differed from all the above, "Provided you build a wall, even a strong wind can be blocked," he said. "How can the wind be compared with the wall. I suggest you name it the 'wall cat'."

Yet another guest argued, saying, "Even though a high wall may be solid and strong, yet the mouse can dig a hole in it. In time when there are many holes, the wall will collapse. That is to say, the wall is not as good as the mouse. In my opinion, you must call it the 'mouse cat'."

The old man of Dongli derided them. "Dear me!" he exclaimed. "To catch the mice is what the cat does, and a cat is a cat. Why should you make it lose its true features?"

745. Stuttering Girls

In the state of Yan, there was a man who had two badly stuttering girls. One day, a matchmaker made an appointment to come and arrange their marriages, and father warned his two daughters, saying, "Be sure to keep your mouths shut, and don't talk. Once you open your mouths, you will no longer be eligible!" Both daughters promised to comply by nodding their heads.

A moment later, the matchmaker arrived and they sat down together. In the midst of their conversation, the elder daughter's clothes suddenly caught fire from the heating stove, and the younger sister stuttered, "Elder sister, your clothes have caught fire!"

The elder sister stared at her and stammered out, "Dad has instructed you not to talk. Why do you still open your mouth?"

Eventually, the two daughters' stuttering could not be covered up, and the matchmaker ended her visit and left.

746. Too Many Things to Worry About

Shen Tunzi and his friend went to the country fair together, where he heard a clapper talk (story recited to the rhythm of bamboo clappers). According to the storyteller, "Yang Wenguang is surrounded inside the city of Liuzhou, within there is insufficient provisions and funds for the troops; without, no reinforcements." After listening to the story, he became nervously restless, often stamping his foot and sighing incessantly.

His friend pressed him to return. But, having heard the story, he thought of it day in day out, saying, "Wenguang is in such a wretched situation. Can a way be found to help raise the seige!" On account of depression, he became ill. Members of his family urged him to go to the suburbs for a stroll so that he could be relieved of his anxiety.

On his way to the suburbs, he saw a man carrying bamboo poles on his back to the country fair and he was worried, saying again and again, "The pointed end of the bamboo is very sharp. Pedestrians will get hurt for sure!" When he came home, his melancholia turned even worse.

His people could not think of any other way except to consult the sorcerer. The sorcerer said, "I've turned over the pages of the births and deaths register, your next samsara will be a woman, and your husband will be a muslim surnamed Maha, who is extremely ugly in appearance." As Shen Tunzi heard the pronouncement, he was even more worried, and his illness became a matter of grave concern.

Relatives and friends came to visit and make cautious inquiries. "You must try to take things easy, so that your illness will improve," they all tried to say a few comforting words.

Shen Tunzi replied, "You all want me to relax but, unless Yang Wenguang's seige is raised, the man carrying the bamboo poles has returned home, and my husband Maha has granted me a divorce, how can I be free from anxiety?"

In fact, those sentimental people in this world of ours who worry unnecessarily and hurt themselves are no different from Shen Tunzi!

747. Two Blind Men on a Collision Course

The New City had a blind man from the state of Qi, who was hot-tempered. When he went begging in the street and met with people who did not make way for him, he would be ablaze with anger and cursed, "Are you blind?"

People knew he was blind, and generally would not quarrel with him.

Later, there came another blind man from Liang, who had an irascible temperament. He was begging in the street too. They happened to knock against one another and both fell to the ground. The blind man from Liang originally did not know the other person was blind. He got up and, in a rage, called the other man all manner of names, saying, "Are you also blind?"

Full of noise and clamour, they railed at one another furiously, while the city people watched and smiled.

Alas! When one muddle-headed tries to enlighten another muddle-headed, denouncing one another, unwilling to let the matter drop, are they not similar to these two blind men?

748. The Monster Put a Coat of Paint on the Mirror

On the southern slope of Junfang Mountain in Jinan, there used to be a bright stone mirror about thirty square feet in size. The reflection of the mountain monster was clearly seen in the mirror, and it was impossible for it to dodge. By the time of Southern Yan Dynasty, the mountain monster became disgusted with the mirror, which caught its image so vividly, snd put a coat of paint on it. From then on, the mirror was no longer bright. As the stone mirror had been daubed with paint, the mountain monster became active even in the daytime, and traces of human presence died out.

749. A Book of Model Paintings for Tian and Yang

Tian Sengliang, Yang Qidan and Zheng Fashi of the Sui Dynasty were all famous for their paintings. Zheng Fashi knew his own paintings were not on a par with Yang Qidan's, so he tried to get the latter's original sample, but Yang Qidan would not give him. One day, Yang Qidan brought Zheng Fashi to the imperial court hall and pointed at the palace view, the dress, the people and the carriages, which were all material objects, and said, "These are all my original samples! Don't you know now?" Zheng Fashi drew inspiration from what yang Qidan had said and, from then on, his techniques improved with each passing day.

750. The *Nao* Scratches Where it Itches for the Tiger

In the animal kingdom, there was a species called *nao* (a kind of monkey mentioned in Chinese ancient literature). It had a small body and agile in tree-climbing, and its claws were very sharp. Whenever the tiger felt its head itchy, it would ask the *nao* to scratch for it. The *nao* made use of the opportunity to suck the tiger's brains on the sly, and even presented part of the leftovers to the tiger, saying, "By chance I've got some meat. I dare not keep it for myself but present it to you." "The *nao* has a heart of complete dedication! He loves me so much that he even forgets his own desire for good food," said the tiger. Thus the tiger ate its own brains without knowing it.

As time went on, the tiger's entire brains were almost gone, and he suffered a great pain. He tried to pursue the *nao*, but the *nao* had already climbed up a tall tree and hidden itself. The pain was so unbearable that the tiger jumped and roared before it died.

People in the world think those street-performers and singers carrying musical instruments in Handan City very much like the *nao* but, can you also say only the street-performers and singers are vey much like the *nao*?

751. Portrait and the Man

The people of She County (in Anhui Province) had a tradition of doing business abroad. There was a scholar, whose father left home to do business in Shaanxi and Gansu when he was in the prime of life. For over thirty years, he had been abroad. At home, what was left of him was only a portrait on the hall.

Then, one day, the father returned. His son had some doubts about its facticity, and tried to compare the man with the portrait. He was convinced they were absolutely different. So he denied him by saying, "In the portrait, my father is fair and fat, but you are dark and thin; my father has hardly a beard, but you are the opposite, and greying at the temples. Even such things as the hat, the dress, the shoelaces are entirely different!" His mother emerged from her room and commented, "Hey! It's really not the same, not by a long shot."

Thereafterr, father and mother talked about the past in detail, touching on the portrait painter's name and the whole course of getting the portrait done. After the discussion, his mother became affectionate and said, "He is truly my husband." Then the son stepped forward to acknowledge his father and greet him.

Now, husband and father are the most intimate of all relations, but, due to their rigid adherence to the details of a portrait, even the wife and son became sceptical. There are scholars, who do not understand that the Confucian classics and histories are just like the portrait, that when they adhere rigidly to the text and forget the ideological essence, the blood and flesh, of the sages, it is just like the rigid adherence to the portrait and denying the real father!

752. A Man of Chu Learns to Pilot a Ship

In the state of Chu, there was a man who was learning the skills of ship-piloting. The lessons began with following the direction of the instructor to turn left or right, to go forward or astern. When the preliminary skills had been mastered, the next step was to put what he learned into practice by cruising around the islets and sandbars in the river. As the skills to change course and to go forward or astern were satisfactory, the learner thought himself to have learned all the skills and dismissed the instructor. In his excitement, he steered the ship full speed to the deep water. Unfortunately, he met with a storm, quite sudden and unforeseen. He felt helpless, looking around in fright, his oars falling and his rudder lost, and he was at a loss as to what to do. Was it not because he was lucky at first in being able to steer the ship, which caused him to become complacent, that the danger later occurred?

753. Ten Families as Neighbours

In ancient times, there once lived together ten families as neighbours. It became their customary practice to go to the market place to sell the grains they had bought, and let their own fields lie waste just to earn a little money for their daily expenses. A peasant in the vicinity advised them, saying, "How can this compare to reliance on your own diligence in cultivating the field and reaping the reward?" Two of them followed the suggestion, abandoning the business of buy-and-sell, and returning to cultivate their own land. The other eight families tried to dissuade the two, saying, "How can we wait till the harvest in Autumn?" One of the two, however, continued to work with diligence in his field in spite of what they said, and was later counted among the well-off. The other had fallen into temptation and left his field anew. He was destitute throughout his life.

754. The Quilt on the Face

A destitute man, whose home had not even a sizable straw mat with which to cover themselves in bed, thought it would be far better to expose the hands than the feet. He lied to other people though, saying, "Don't you see, have we left the brush and the inkstone for a moment? Even in sleep, we still hold our fingers outside as if they were brushes."

The destitute man had a son who was not sensible enough. When he was asked, "What have you to cover yourself at night?" he would answer, "Straw mat." The destitute man thought his son had disgraced the family and gave him a good beating, warning him, "From now on, if people should ask you the same question, just answer, 'covered with a quilt' when we sleep."

One day, as the destitute man went out to meet a guest, a straw from the mat happened to stick out in his beard, and his son shouted at him from behind, saying, "Hurry, and do away with the quilt from your face!"—This is an example of the so-called "fare worse and worse for all one's scheming and pretension."

755. Addicted to Broth of Entrails

A friend of so-and so generally stuck to a bland diet and did not like food that was strong and thick with meat and fish. However, he had an addiction, that of broth made with pig's internal organs. It was common knowledge that most of the butchers' booths in the market place were unhygienic. One day, he invited some of his guests to his home to drink, and bought pig liver, tripe, and lung for broth. He instructed the chef not to wash them too thoroughly so as not to take away the original flavour. When the broth was ready, the foul smell assailed the nostrils, and it took courage to put one's nose anywhere near it. He tasted it first, and gave out loud shouts of applause, saying, "Delicious! Delicious!" His guests thought he was a food connoisseur, who knew what he said, and all followed him and expressed appreciation of the broth, forgetting about hygiene. Some of the guests he invited even remembered the recipe and made the same broth later.

*

In Praise of Jokes
By Zhao Nanxing (1550-1627 A.D.) Styled himself Mengbai, assumed name Chaihe, or Clean Capital's Sloppy Guest, originally from Gaoyi, North Zhili (now belongs to Hebei Province). A palace graduate of the period of Wanli, he had once held the post of minister in the Miniastry of Civil Office. He was a leading figure in the Donglin Party, enjoying tremendous reputation throughout the country, and often at loggerheads with the eunuch, Wei Zhongxian. Together with Zou Yuanbiao and Gu Xiancheng, they were regarded by his contemporaries as comparable to the three gentlemen (Chen Fan, Du Wu, Liu Shu) in Eastern Han's interdiction of party activities, and were also called "the three gentlemen". He was later arbitrarily banished by Wei Zhongxian to

Daizhou, where he died. After the death of Wei Zhongxian, Nanxing was bestowed the posthumous title of "Zhongyi", or the faithful and indomitable. He authored many books, such as *The Zhao Zhongyi Collection, History in Verse*, etc. *In Praise of Jokes* collected fables and jokes totalling seventy-two items.

756. Mispronounce the Characters for Life

A scholar pronounced the three Chinese characters Taihangshan, or Taihang Mountain as "Daixingshan". Another scholar, out of kindness, told him, "It should be pronounced as 'Taihangshan". But the former refuted him, saying, "I've been to the foot of the mountain personally, and saw the tablet inscription with my own eyes." Each stuck to his position. The former said, "Let's bet, and the loser should stand treat. There is an old pedant, who has a reputation of being the most knowledgeable about characters. Let's go and ask him." At their meeting, the old pedant was adamant, "It should be pronounced as 'daixing.'" The loser complained that the old pedant did not tell the truth, but the old pedant said to him, "Although you lost and have to stand treat for once, but you can make him mispronounce the characters for life."

The Ode said: What a cruel plan the old pedant cherished in his mind. He caused the scholar to be ignorant of "Taihangshan" for life and, in addition, believed the whole world to be illiterate. Nevertheless, if he were to speak the truth, the scholar would not have been convinced, because he insisted he had seen the tablet inscription with his own eyes.

757. The Three Sages

There was a man who worshipped Confucianism, Buddhism, and Taoism at the same time. He first moulded a statue of Confucius, then one of the very high lord, Lao Zi, and one of Sakyamuni.

A Taoist saw what happened, and moved the statue of the very high Lord to the centre.

A Monk came, and he moved the statue of Sakyamuni to the centre. A Confucianist arrived, and he restored the statue of Confucius to the central position.

The three sages said to one another, "We are all safe and sound originally, but these people moved us here and there, and put everything out of order."

The Ode said: The three sages each has his own disciples. As everyone of them respected his own master, who would yield to the others? Actually a single place could not have accomodated three persons. A disciple of Confucius, surnamed Guan, insisted on letting Sakyamuni occupy the seat of honour. His feeling was entirely different from that of the other disciples.

758. Wearing a Felt Cap on a Hot Summer Day

A man pushed on with his journey in a rush, wearing a felt hat on a hot summer day. When he came to a big tree, he stopped to enjoy the cool in the shade. As he took down his felt hat to fan a little wind, he complacently remarked, "Had it not been for the felt hat, I would have suffered a heatstroke."

759. A Scholar Buys Firewood

A *xiucai*, or scholar, wished to buy firewood, and he said, "Firewood vendor, come here."

The vendor heard the words "come here" clearly, so he carried the firewood before the scholar. The scholar then asked, "What's the price?"

He heard the word "price" clearly, so he named the price.

The scholar said, "It looks solid outside but is actually hollow inside. Please reduce the price."

The vendor did not understand what he said, so he put the firewood on the shoulder and left.

The Ode said: Scholars prefer to speak like a book, but what have they accomplished? How the scholars have misled the people! An official went to the countryside and asked the elders there, saying, "How are the *lishu* doing?" The elders replied, "The pear trees are growing well this year, although worms have eaten away some of them." It seemed this official was no difference from the *xiucai*, or scholar.

(*lishu*, which means "the people" in classical Chinese, is homophonous with 'pear tree')

760. An Unlined Jacket and a Lined Jacket

A poor scholar wore a double-layered jacket in the winter, and somebody said, "It is so cold, why do you still only wear a double-layered jacket?" The poor scholar replied, "It would be even less warm if I put on a garment with no lining."

The Ode said: A lined jacket is better than a garment without lining. If one can view it in this way, one will be content with his lot in poverty and devote his life to things spiritual. There was a man who, for fear of being looked down upon, put on an unlined garment and went to visit a friend. His friend asked him, "The weather is so cold, why do you still wear an unlined garment?" He replied, "I've one shortcoming all along, and that is I cannot stand the heat." His friend knew he was only telling lies, so he detained the man until it was dark, and sent him to pass the night in the pavilion, where he could not stand the cold and had to flee. On another day, his friend met him again and asked him, "I kept you for the night the other day, why didn't you stay and see me the next day?" The man replied, "I was afraid when the sun came out it would be too warm, so I took advantage of the cool in the morning and left in a hurry."

761. To be Blind Has its advantage

Two blind persons, as they walked together on the road, said with complacency, "In this world the blind are in the best position. Those with eyes have to bustle in and out throughout the day, and the peasants are even worse. How can they compare with us, who live a life of leisure and comfort?" Just then a group of peasants heard what they said. Pretending to be government officials, they accused the two blind men of obstructing the road, and gave them both a good beating with their hoes. Thereafter, the blind men were berated and told to go away quickly. The peasants then followed them, eavesdropping their conversation. One of the blind persons said, "After all, it is still advantageous to be blind, for those who were not blind would surely have been seized and incarcerated in addition to being beaten!"

The Ode said: Up north, the blind persons are addressed as teacher, which means they must have their merits. In this world of ours, those who do things that are against reason and nature, breaking the laws and committing evils, are all with perfect eyes, and never a blind person is found among them.

762. A Monk and a Sparrow

A hawk pursued a little sparrow. In its haste and confusion, the sparrow wormed its way into the sleeve of a monk. The monk held it tightly with his hand, and said, "Amitabha, I'll have a piece of meat today." The sparrow closed its eyes and remained motionless, and the monk thought it was dead. However, the moment he relaxed his hold, the sparrow took to the sky and flew away. The monk put his palms together and said, "Amitabha, I'm setting you free now!"

(Amitabha, the Buddha of infinite qualities—an imaginary being unknown to ancient Buddhism, possibly of Persian or Iranian origin, who has eclipsed the historical Buddha in becoming the most popular divinity in the Mahayana Pantheon.)

*

Shu Juzi
By Zhuang Yuanchen styled himself Zhongfu, assumed name Master of Pengchi, originally from Songling (Songjiang, Shanghai); dates of birth and death unknown. He was known to be alive during the period of Wanli. The book *Shu Juzi*, a miscellany expounding the "principle", is divided into two parts, in and out, and contains eight volumes in all. The metaphors and allegories entail the use of fables.

763. The Myna and the Cicada

The myna grew up in the south of the country. People there caught it with net, and trained it to use the tongue. With patience, it could learn to speak like man. However, what it could imitate was only a few words and there it stopped. All day long, it could only repeat them.

As the cicada sang at the treetop, the myna listened and went to jeer at it.

The cicada told the myna, saying, "You can learn to speak the language of man, that is of course very good. But the few words you utter are not your own, and it is tantamount to saying nothing. How can it compare with what I do. I sing out what's in my mind without constraint of any kind!"

The myna felt ashamed and bowed its head. From then on, it never again tried to imitate the speech of man!

764. Black Pearl

In former times, it was rumoured that there were black pearls in Chishui River, and everyone dived to the bottom of the water to fish for them. Some got mollusk with spiral shell, others picked up clam, still others found oval stones and broken tiles, and all were very pleased, thinking they had come by a precious pearl. As Xiangwang heard about it, he could not help laughing, although he tried to cover his mouth. People were enraged, and they all came forward to attack Xiangwang. Xiangwang had to flee to the emperor and hid there. For three years, he dared not show himself in public.

765. Release a Beast to Test its Nature

The hunter caught an animal and did not know whether it would bite or not, so he brought it to the country fair and released it. Unless he was sure it would grab and eat man, he would not shut it up in a cage. Whenever an animal was caught, he would follow the same practice. After several tests, everyone in the country fair was frightened and fled.

766. To Be Original

Once upon a time, a man called Wang Dan went to offer his condolences to a friend, where he met Chen Zun, a chivalrous man of great reputation, who was also there to pay his last respects. The gifts Chen Zun brought to the funeral were rich and generous and he was conscious of the favour he bestowed, as complacency was written all over his face. In a slow and deliberate fashion, Wang Dan placed a bolt of fine silk on the table and said, "I made this myself with the loom." Chen Zun felt deeply abashed, and hurriedly left.

How many of the scholars nowadays are original in writing just like Wang Dan, who wove a bolt of fine silk himself?

*

Jokes for the Refined Taste
By the Master of Fubai Studio, whose real name and deeds were not known. In the book *Discourse at Random of things Past and Present*, authored by Feng Menglong, an item was recorded, and the title of the book from which the item came was called *The jokes of Chu Studio for the Refined taste*. Since Chuzai, or Chu Studio, was the alias of Xu Zichang, there were people who believed the Master of Fubai Studio is in fact Xu Zichang, but there is no proof of that.

767. On the Strength of the Father-in-Law

There was a man who came out first in the imperial competitive examination on the strength of his father-in-law, and someone wove a story to deride him, saying, "The disciples of Confucius took part in the examination. Before the names of the successful candidates were published, a preliminary announcement was made to the effect that Zizhang came out the nineteenth. People remarked, 'He is handsome, and that might redound to his advantage.' Then another circular arrived, announcing Zilu won the thirteenth place. People commented, "He is boorish, but successful all the same. It might have been his breadth of spirit.' Following that, it was announced that Yan Yuan had the twelfth position. People noted, 'He is supposed to be the sage's best pupil. He has suffered a wrong.' When the news came that Gong Yechang was graded number five, people were amazed, saying, 'This man was not so outstanding in the past but, contrary to what one might expect, he headed the list.' Someone remarked, 'Has it been achieved on the strength of his father-in-law?'"

768. The Dog Has fallen Ill

The revered Mr Yu suffered from eye disease, and was about to go and see the physician. It so happened that a dog was lying on the stairs and, as the revered Mr Yu strode over it, he stepped on its neck quite unintentionally. The dog was exasperated and bit the revered Mr Yu, including his clothes, which were torn. The revered Mr Yu raised the torn dress to show the physician.

The physician teased the revered Mr Yu deliberately, saying, "It looks as if the dog has eye disease, or else how can it have torn your clothes?"

After he returned home, the revered Mr Yu reflected, "For a dog to bite its master is but a small matter, but if it has really suffered from eye disease and cannot look after the door properly, that will be a big problem." Thereupon he had the medicine prepared and given to the dog first, and he took what was left by the dog himself.

769. Gouge Out the Horse's Liver

"The horse's liver is extremely poisonous. It can kill a man. That's why emperor Wu of the Han Dynasty said, 'After Wencheng ate the horse's liver, he died,'" said a guest.

The remark was heard by the revered Mr Yu, and he burst into laughter, saying, "The guest is just lying. Since the liver is inside the horse, why doesn't the horse die?"

The guest teased him, "The reason why the horse does not live to be a hundred is exactly because it has such a liver."

The revered Mr Yu seemed to have been inspired. He had a horse at home, so he gouged its liver out, and the horse died immediately. The revered Mr Yu threw the knife on the floor and sighed, saying, "How right his words are! How venomous the horse's liver! Even though I had gouged it out, the horse still could not live. How could it survive if the liver was still in the belly?"

770. Borrowed Clothes

It was raining, and the revered Mr Yu was wearing clothes which he had borrowed from someone. As the road was muddy, he slipped and fell, hurting one of his arms, and the clothes were made dirty. His attendant hastened to help him up, and stroke the painful spot.

The revered Mr Yu stopped him, saying, "Get some water to wash my clothes first. The wounded arm has nothing to do with you."

The attendant said, "Why do you think of the clothes all the time, but do not care about your own body?"

The revered Mr Yu replied, "The arm belongs to me, and nobody will ask me to return it?"

771. Golden Eyes

Dang Jin asked a painter to paint his portrait. When the work was completed, he looked at it and became very angry. He berated the portrait painter, saying, "The other day I saw you draw a tiger, and you stuck gold foil to its eyes. Why do you think I'm not entitled to enjoy a pair of golden eyes?"

772. A Low Stool

There was a wooden stool at home, extremely low. Whenever the revered Mr Yu wanted to sit on it, he had to put tiles under its four legs to raise it higher. As it was so bothersome, he suddenly thought of a solution, and that was to have it moved upstairs by the servant.

But when he sat down, the wooden stool was as low as it was before, and he said, "People talk about tall building. It turns out they are only talking nonsense!" Thereupon he ordered the building demolished.

773. In Fear of the Flood Tide

In August, the howls of tidal waves from the sea was horrifying to the whole city.

During the last years of the Yuan Dynasty, in the period of Zhizheng, which was the title of emperor Shun of Yuan (1341-1368 A.D.), there was a certain man called Buhua, surnamed Dalu, a Mongolian. It was his first visit to the city. When he heard the howling of the tidal waves at night, he was so frightened that he dared not go to sleep. And he sent for the gatekeeper just to make sure what it was.

The gatekeeper, roused suddenly from sleep, in a slip of the tongue, said, "The tidewater has rushed up the shores!"

Buhua, panic-stricken, entered the inner chambers and called his wife, saying, "Originally I had hoped to be an official to bring glory to the family, but tonight it seems we may have to become water spirits together!" Thereupon the whole family, young and old, began to cry bitterly.

Outside, the night watchman heard the sound of crying, and thought some mishap might have happened. He reported it to the local official in charge and his assistant at once. The news caused all the officials, sloppily dressed, to rush to his rescue. Buhua was afraid the flood water might enter the room and so he had shut the door tight. His colleagues, therefore, had either to knock down the door or climb over the walls to get in. When they did, they found the couple and the servants huddling on the beam crying out for help. After making certain nothing was amiss, his colleagues, holding back their laughter, left.

774. The Cat Offers birthday Congratulations to the Mouse

A mouse hid inside a bottle, and the cat could not reach it. The cat brushed the mouse's nose with its whiskers, which made the mouse sneeze.

The cat greeted the mouse in a friendly manner, saying, "Your Highness?"

The mouse said, "Who will believe you are here to offer birthday congratulations? You only come to trick me out, so that you can eat my flesh!"

*

Fun Garden
By The Master of Fubai. It was probably the same person as the Master of Fubai Studio, though it could not be ascertained. *Fun Garden* was one of ten categories in a book series published in the Ming Dynasty called *A Night's Conversation to Banish Anxiety*. The ten categories of the series are: *Fun Garden, The Jokes for the Refined taste, Riddles, Teasing the Courtesans, Curious Pairs, Folk Songs, Drinkers' Wager Games, The Tunes of ci or qu, Oleander, Cassia Twig.*

775. To Borrow an Ox

A man wrote a letter, and had it sent by a messenger, asking a certain rich man to lend him an ox for a while. At that moment, the rich man was in the hall receiving guests. Upon receipt of the message, he took it out from the envelope, pretending to read so as not to expose himself as an illiterate. Then he turned his head towards the messenger, and said, "I'm aware of it, and will go myself in a while."

776. The Target Helps Win the Battle

A military officer went to war. When he was on the verge of being defeated, a divine army suddenly appeared and helped turn the tide.

The military officer kowtowed to him and asked the deity's name, the deity said, "I'm the god of target."

The military officer said, "What virtue have I that I dare put you to the trouble of coming here?"

The god of target replied, "I'm grateful that you have never hurt me even once in the target range."

777. Confucianist Moralists Revile Each Other

Two men were reviling each other on the road. A said, "You disregard the dictates of your own conscience!" B replied, "You are unconscionable!" A said, "You defy nature's justice!" B replied, "You obstruct the course of nature!"

A Confucianist moralist heard the quarrel and told his disciple, "Listen, these two men are giving lecture!"

His disciple said, "They revile one another. What kind of lecture is this?"

The Confucianist moralist replied, "They refer to 'conscience' and 'nature', what is it if not lecture?"

The disciple said, "Since they are giving lecture, why reviling one another?"

The Confucianist moralist replied, "Just look at the Confucianist moralists today. Is there anyone who can live in peace with the others?"

778. Geomancy

There was a man who believed whole-heartedly in geomancy, and would go to consult the geomancer even on minute matters.

One day, while he was sitting by the wall, it collapsed suddenly. As he was held down by the wall, he cried aloud for help.

His people said, "Be patient. Let me go to consult the geomancer and see whether today is an auspicious day to break the ground."

779. Biscuits made from Distillers' Grains

A man, who was poor and not used to drinking, became a little drunk after taking two biscuits made from the distillers' grains before he left home.

He happened to meet his friend on the road, and the friend asked him, "Did you drink this morning?"

"No," he replied. "I only took two biscuits made from distillers' grains."

When he returned home, he told his wife about what happpened. His wife said, "Better just say you have taken some wine. It will help keep up appearances." The husband nodded in agreement.

When he left home and met the same friend again, he was asked the same question. This time he said he had taken some wine.

"Did you drink it warm, or cold?" his friend asked again.

"It was baked," he replied.

His friend smiled and remarked, "It's the same biscuits made from the distillers' grains."

When he came home and his wife learned about it, she blamed him, "How can you say your wine was baked? You should say you drink it warm."

"I know now," her husband responded.

As he met his friend again, he did not wait for the question, but simply tried to show off by saying, "I drank my wine warm today."

His friend asked him, "How much did you drink?"

"Two pieces," he said, putting out two fingers.

780. The Monkey

A monkey, after its death, went to see Yamaraja, the king of Hell, and requested to be reincarnated in a man's body.

The King of Hell said, "If you intend to be a human being, you must pull out all your monkey hairs." And he called the yaksha, a malevolent spirit, to pluck out the monkey's hairs.

Only one hair had been plucked and the monkey already cried out loudly, because it could not bear the pain.

The King of Hell said, "Since you are unwilling to give up even one hair, how can you become a man?"

781. Cultivate the Land Together

Two brothers cultivated a piece of land together. As the paddy was ready for harvest, they discussed how to share the fruit of labour.

The elder brother said, "I'll take the upper half of the plant, and you get the lower half."

The younger brother was dissatisfied because the allocation was unfair.

The elder brother said, "The problem is not difficult to solve. Come next year, you will take the upper half and I, the lower half, and everything will be all right."

In the following year, when the younger brother pressed his elder brother for seed-grains, his elder brother said, "Let's plant taro this year instead!"

782. Be a Vegetarian

It so happened that the cat had a Buddhist rosary on its neck, and the mice were so pleased with the discovery that they said, "The cat has become a vegetarian!" Thereupon the mice brought all their descendants to pay the cat a visit. The cat uttered a loud cry and ate several of them. The mice fled in disorder. Having escaped the danger, the mice stuck out their tongues in amazement and said, "After becoming a vegetarian, it has turned even more ferocious and cruel."

783. This Monk Eats Shrimps

There was a monk who failed to follow the monastic rules for Buddhists. He bought some shrimps secretly and cooked them. The pains were so intense that the shrimps bounced and sprang in desperation. The monk put his palms together and said to the shrimps, "Amitabha, please have a little patience. When the cooking is over, you will not feel painful anymore."

784. A Table With Dew

A man jokingly wrote down five Chinese characters *wo yao zuo huang di* (I want to be the emperor) with his finger on a table which was wet with dew. His personal enemy saw it, and immediately shouldered the table to the local *yamen*, intending to take up the matter personally and accuse the man of "plotting treason". As it was still too early for the magistrate to hold a court trial, the dew on the table soon dried up in the sun and, with it, the finger-written characters disappeared.

People asked him, "Why have you shouldered the table here?"

He replied, "I've a whole house of tables, and so I carried one here as sample especially for everyone to see. I don't know whether His Honour is interested."

785. Selecting the Desired Numbers

A certain man, who was a complete ignoramus, became an official of the office of the commanding officer, and liked to take part in every gathering. Provided it was music and singing, there would he be found. However, he was afraid people might see through his being a music layman, and so he would rock back and forth with other people to express his appreciation whenever the female entertainers were performing.

He was elected by his colleagues to play the host, and thus was responsible for the invitation of the female entertainers and guests. Before everyone had arrived, he would first of all gather the entertainers who were there, and ask for the titles of the songs. These he jotted down on a piece of paper, which he dropped into a box. The box contained miscellaneous articles. Among other things, there was the physician's prescription. As the guests arrived, he began to select the numbers. But he had mistakenly pulled out the prescription instead of the paper on which he had the numbers. On the prescription, it was written: *aconitum carmichaeli* (the rhizome of Chinese monkshood), one and one half grams, and *angelica sinensis*, two grams. Accordingly, he read, "First of all, let's have the numbers *aconitum carmichaeli* and *angelica sinensis* to entertain our guests." This caused all the guests to be convulsed with laughter.

786. A Fall

A man, who was rather careless, had a fall. He got up immediately but tripped and fell again. Thereupon he said, "If I had known I would fall again, I would simply not have gotten up."

*

*Godly Yu's Personal Stories
By Zhang Yiling. Neither the dates of birth and death nor deeds were known. In Feng Menglong's *Discourse at Random of Things Past and Present*, volume four, under the category *Stupidity*, twenty-four items of the *Godly Yu's Personal Stories* were found. The notes underneath said, "compiled by Zhang Yiling of Wu (Suzhou)", from which information, it was known he came from Suzhou. In the book, many stories were woven around the fictitious character, the revered Mr Yu, whose funny mistakes became a venue through which he rendered his incisive sarcasm at the social ills of the time.

787. Preoccupied with the Lambskin Coat

In the village there was a petty thief. At midnight, even as he went to steal in the revered Mr Yu's residence, the latter came home. The petty thief was very frightened and, in panic, he threw away the lambskin coat he wore, and fled. The revered Mr Yu liked the fur coat very much and, from then on, he thought of fur coats all the time. Whenever he went to the city, he would return home even though it was already deep into the night. As he entered his home and found everything peaceful and fine, he would knit his eyebrows and said, "Why didn't the thief come today?"

788. Husband and Wife

A rich man in the village was holding an engagement party, and a bamboo basket full of cash gifts was carried past the main gate of the revered Mr Yu's house. The Yu couple watched it together, and they said to one another, "Let's guess how many pieces of gold are there in the basket?"

"Two hundred pieces," said the wife.

"It looks more like five hundred," said the revered Mr Yu.

The wife said it could not be, the revered Mr Yu said it must be. As they continued to argue, it soon turned into mutual reviling.

The wife said, "I've exhausted my patience. Just say three hundred pieces. How about that?"

But the revered Mr Yu went on cursing with no end in sight. Then his neighbours gathered to mediate, but the revered Mr Yu said, "There are still two hundred pieces of gold not accounted for. Can you say that's a small matter?"

789. Disgorge at Someone Else's Gate

The revered Mr Yu was intoxicated when he staggered unsteadily home after drinking in his friend's house. As he passed in front of a certain building, he felt a sudden turn in his stomach, and disgorged everything he had eaten at the gate, making a horrible mess of someone else's doorstep.

The gatekeeper, having witnessed what happened, angrily scolded him, "Why must you pretend to be drunk, and throw up muck at our door!"

The revered Mr Yu crawled up, looking askance at him, and said, "Why do you complain? Whoever has asked you to build the gate of your house opposite my mouth!"

"What a scoundrel!" the gatekeeper said. He did not know whether to laugh or to cry. "Do you know when our gate was built? Do you think it is built only today to face your mouth?"

"Humph," tit for tat, the revered Mr Yu pointed at his mouth and refuted him, "Let me inform you. This mouth of mine is also getting on in years!"

790. Collecting the Paper of Song Dynasty

The revered Mr Yu had collected quite a few pieces of refined paper of the Song Dynasty. It so happened that a high official from Suzhou, who was renowned for his painting and calligraphy, arrived there at the time, and someone suggested to the revered Mr Yu with sarcasm, saying, "You have such refined paper. Why don't you present them to His Excellency and ask for some calligraphy and painting in return. You will then be able to appreciate and enjoy them in private?"

The revered Mr Yu disproved him, saying, "Do you want to spoil my paper? The paper I collected was intended for the people of Song to inscribe poems and calligraphy on."

791. Repairing the Leaking Roof

There had been continuous rain for several days, and the revered Mr Yu's roof was leaking. Every night he had to move the bed several times, and there was not a dry spot in the room. His wife and children complained all the time, and the revered Mr Yu hastened to send for the craftsman to have the leaking house repaired. When the work was completed, the weather suddenly cleared up, and remained so for a month. The revered Mr Yu looked at the roof from morn till eve, saying,

"How ill-fated I am! After the roof has been repaired, the rain stopped. Isn't the money spent for the repair and materials all for nothing?"

*

*The Fictions of Xuetao

By Jiang Yingke styled himself Jinzhi, assumed name Xuetao, or the Luluo Recluse, dates of birth and death unknown. He was originally from Taoyuan, Huguang (now Hunan Province). A palace graduate of Wanli, he was the author of *The Xuetao Studio Collection*, a collection of poetry and humorous banters in the form of fables, *The Fictions of Xuetao* as well as *Xuetao's Pleasantries*.

792. Bore a Hole in the Wall to Shift the Pain

A man had a sore on his foot which was so painful that he could hardly endure. So he said to his people, "Please bore a hole in the wall as fast as you can."

After the hole had been bored, he put his sore foot in the hole and let over a foot of it stretch into his neighbour's room. His people felt puzzled and asked him, "What's the meaning of this?" "Let the pain go to our neighbours. It is not my concern now."

793. There is No End to Learning

In the district of Chu there was a man who had never seen the ginger plant, and he said, "Ginger grows on the tree." Someone told him, saying, "Ginger comes from the ground." But the man of Chu was obstinate. He said, "I'll use my donkey as wager. Let us ask the next ten persons, and let them be the judge of that."

It was not long before they collected the opinions of ten persons. They all said, "It's from the ground."

The man of Chu was crestfallen. He said, "I've lost the bet, and this donkey is yours, but I still believe ginger grows on the tree."

A man, who was brought up in the North, had never seen the water chestnut. Later, he became an official in the South. At a banquet, he swallowed the water chestnut, shell and all.

Someone told him, saying, "The shell should be removed before it is eaten."

The man from the North, to cover up his ignorance, declared, "Not that I don't know, but that I swallow it with the shell in order to relieve the latent heat inside the body!"

"Is there water chestnut in the North?" the man asked.

"Of course there is. In front of the mountain, and behind it, where else it doesn't grow?" he replied.

Ginger is a root crop, but it was said to grow on the tree; the water chestnut flourishes under water, but it was claimed to have come from the mountain. All this has its roots in ignorance.... All things on earth have their own ways of existence, which are inexhaustible. If you put them into the same mould, your view would be like a chicken in the jar—defintely shallow!

794. A One-egg Property

A townsman was so poor that he could not make both ends meet. One day, by accident, he came by an egg and told his wife, "I own some property now."

"Where is it?" asked his wife.

The man brought the egg out for his wife to see and said, "Here it is. However, I've to wait ten years before my dream can be realized." Thereupon the couple began to figure it out together. The husband said, "I'll ask our neighbour to let his hen hatch the egg. When the egg has hatched out, I'll select a female chick. Within two years, the hen will lay eggs, and the eggs will become chickens. I'll be able to get three hundred chickens, which are worth ten pieces of gold. I'll exchange the ten gold pieces for five cows. The cows will give birth to cows. In three years, I shall have twenty-five heads of cattle, which can be sold for three hundred pieces of gold. I'll lend out the money and, in another three years, I'll be able to collect five hundred pieces of gold. I'll allocate two-third of it to buy land and house, the remaining one-third to hire servants and get a concubine. By then, I'll be able to live in comfort, and together we shall have an easy life in our old age. Isn't it a very good prospect?"

When the wife heard he had intended to get a concubine, she was greatly inflamed, and smashed the egg with her hand, saying, "I'll not sow the seeds of future trouble!"

The husband was extremely irritated and gave his wife a good beating. He did not stop at that either, for he brought her before the magistrate, accusing her by saying, "In the twinkling of an eye, she has ruined all our family property. The shrew must be punished!"

"Where's your family property? In what way has she ruined it?" asked the magistrate.

The man related how he had picked up an egg and planned to increase the family property with it, all the way to his intention to get a concubine.

The magistrate said, "So enormous an amount of property and the shrew ruined it with one punch. She should be punished severely indeed!" Thereupon he ordered the woman to be put into a caldron of boiling oil.

The wife wailed and said, "Those things my husband talked about were all unfulfilled, why should I be put into the caldron of boiling oil?"

"What your husband said about the concubine was also unfulfilled. Why should you become jealous?" the magistrate refuted her.

"That's true. But isn't it necessary to nip it in the bud?" The magistrate smiled, and released her after hearing these words.

Oh, the man was so bent on getting rich, the root cause being his greed. His wife smashed the egg because she was deeply jealous. Yet all this was but a daydream. Since they knew it was unreal, they should have taken it easy, without extravagant hope, remained indifferent, and with no desire of any kind. Since what happened at present was but a dream, how much more so the illusory future? Oh, in this world of ours, was there only this one man who conceived wild fantasy in his mind and had inordinate ambition, and who planned his future prosperity with one egg?

795. The Surgeon

A man claimed to be a good surgeon. An assistant commanding officer went to battle and hit by an arrow in the battlefield. The arrowhead went deep into his flesh, and the surgeon was invited to treat him. The surgeon took a pair of sharp scissors made in Bingzhou and cut off the part of the arrow shaft which was exposed. Then he knelt down on the floor to ask for a reward. The assistant commanding officer said, "The arrowhead is left inside the flesh still and should be treated at once." The surgeon replied, "That's for the physician to take care of. I've not thought it requires my attention!"

796. A Crafty Disciple's Dream

A certain student, crafty by nature, used to concentrate his attention on deceiving people with his cunning scheme.

The schoolmaster was very strict. Whenever his students acted against the regulations, albeit slightly, he would send someone to bring the culprit to justice and punish him by caning. He would not let him off easily.

One day, the said student happened to break the rules. The master looked for him rather impatiently as he sat in the Yilun Hall in rage, waiting for his arrival. After a few moments, the student arrived. He knelt down before the master on both knees, but he mentioned only one thing, saying, "Your student accidentally came by a thousand pieces of gold, and was trying to handle it in a proper way, and that's why I'm late!"

The master, upon hearing that his student had come by so much money, immediately cooled down and asked, "Where did the gold come from?"

"Dug out from the nether world," the student said.

"How do you intend to do with the gold?" he was asked.

"Your student's family originally was very poor, and there is no property worthy of mention. I've talked the matter over with my wife, and we agreed to allocate it in this way: five hundred pieces of gold to buy land, two hundred for a house, one hundred for the furniture, and another hundred for houseboy, servant, maid and concubine. I'll use one half of the remaining one hundred to buy books. From now on, I've made a firm resolution to study hard. I'll give the other half to my master, to repay your care for my education, and that's all I've managed to do," explained the student in detail.

The master said, "It's good of you to think of me, but I may not deserve it." He ordered the messenger to spread a feast with many good dishes, asked the student to sit down and proposed a toast to him. They chatted and joked during the feast, getting on very well with one another, all of which was very different from what it used to be. They went on drinking until the master was half drunk. Suddenly he asked his student, "Just now you were in a hurry to get here, but did you seal and lock the box with the gold in?"

"Your student had just completed a plan to dispose of it when my wife turned over in bed and acidentally woke me up. Upon waking up, I no longer remembered where the gold was, so the box was not needed anymore!"

The master was astounded and asked him, "Was it only a dream when you talked about the gold just now?"

"That's true, it was only a dream!" replied the student.

The master was displeased, but they had been drinking happily together, gotten on well, and he was not in a position to get angry, so he said, slowly, "You've got a noble character after all. When you had the gold, even though it was only a dream, you had not forgotten your master. I can imagine how much more so if you have really come by some gold." Thus he urged the student to drink again and again, and personally accompanied him to the door.

Look! How this crafty student brought forth the gold in a dream to dissipate the master's anger. Not only had he been absolved of a savage beating, but he had also earned the best treatment of his master. It is obvious that just the name of gold is enough to get a man intoxicated. If it is real solid gold that is presented, how can a man not be pulled into the water? Ah, how dreadful it is!

797. A Mouse's Trick in the Name of the Tiger

In the district of Chu, people called the tiger old worm, while in Suzhou, the mouse was likewise dubbed the old worm. When I was an official in Changzhou County, I once went to Loudong on official business, and lived in the lodge for couriers at night. As I put out the light and went to sleep, I suddenly heard the rustling of dishes and bowls. I asked what the noise was, and the gatekeeper said, "It was the old worm." Originally I was from the district of Chu and the name old worm alarmed me, so I asked, "How can such a ferocious animal come to the city?" "It's not a ferocious animal, but a mouse," the gatekeeper smiled. I asked him, "Since when has the mouse become an old worm?" He informed me it was only an appellation people used, and that was all.

Dear me! The mouse assumed the name of the tiger and almost caused me to flee from it. This was indeed somewhat ridiculous. However, in this world there are not a few who frighten people with an assumed name. They possess a few tricks like the mouse and act in the name of the tiger. If all the officials were mean creatures like the mice, then it would really be worrisome for the world!

798. To Cure the Humpback

Formerly there was a physician who boasted of being able to cure the humpback, saying, "Even though the back might be arched like a bow, or a shrimp, or even curled like a ring, if I should be asked to treat him, he would recover and become as straight as an arrow shaft in the evening if he could be treated in the morning." A certain hunchback believed the physician and invited the latter to cure him. The physician took out two wooden boards, one of which he put on the ground and asked the hunchback to lie on it, and the other he placed on the hunchback's body. He then went up the board and stamped it incessantly, and the hunchback died as the body became straight. The son of the hunchback intended to bring the physician to the magistrate, but the physician said, "It is my profession to cure the humpback, and who cares whether the man dies or lives?"

Alas! There are officials who care only for the taxes, money and grains, and do not care whether the people live or die. Are not such officials hardly different from the physician referred to?

*

*Xuetao's Pleasantries

The book is one of *The Four Little Books of Xuetao Studio*. Collected are one hundred and sixty items of jokes, mostly fable in character.

799. Lonesomeness

During the Song Dynasty, there were two persons called the big Song and the small Song, both passed the imperial examination and beccame officials in the capital. Came the Lantern Festival (15th of the first lunar month), the small Song prepared a sumptuous banquet of lights, which was extreme in its ostentation and extravagance.

The big Song reproached him, saying, "My little brother, do you forget the lonesome life the year before last, when we stayed in the mountain monastery to study?"

"But it was exactly for the comfort today that we had willingly endured the hardship of the year before last," the small Song smiled as he responded to his brother.

Ah! The small Song might be considered an outstanding personality, yet he had talked in this manner. Isn't it too much to ask a man to stay the course, which his lofty aspirations demand, in a changed situation?

800. Sour Wine

It was the birthday of Su Qin's father, and his elder brother stood up and brought a cup of wine with both hands to wish his father many happy returns of the day, his father sighed with feeling, saying, "Good wine indeed!" But when Su Qin brought his cup of wine to congratulate his father, his father found fault with him, saying, "The wine is sour!" Su Qin's wife, therefore, borrowed another cup from his sister-in-law. After drinking the wine, his father still complained, saying, "The wine is sour!" Su Qin's wife said, "The wine has just come from our sister-in-law." But the old man berated her, saying, "You are out of place here, and that's why the wine turns sour when it passes your hands."

801. The Quack Halts the Wind

A monk, a Taoist priest and a physician travelled together by boat, and met with a strong wind in midstream. The boat was in a state of extreme danger. The boatman kowtowed to the monk, saying, "Master, could you please pray to the gods to stop the wind?"

The monk chanted, "Mother Buddha, please exercise your power and dissipate the wind and waves!"

The Taoist priest chanted, "Uncle wind and master rain, each return to your original location, and quick! Follow orders!"

The physician followed with his own incantation, saying, "Mustard, mentha haplocalyx, honeysuckle, azedarach!"

The boatman asked him, "What are these things for?"

The physician replied, "All these ingredients are for the dissipation of wind (ailments supposedly caused by wind and dampness, as rheumatism, etc.)."

Well, this is generally the prescription of a quack.

802. Sing the Praises of Others

There used to be a man who often praised the others as a ploy to advertise himself. Someone teased him, saying, "There was a man who thought his wife was beautiful but, instead of asserting it directly, he would say to others, 'My sister-in-law is an unrivalled national beauty. Standing beside my wife, you will not be able to distinguish who is the elder, and who is the younger sister.'"

803. A Cat to Feed the Young Vultures

An adult vulture wanted to feed its young, but was unable to get food, so it caught a cat, which it put in the nest, intending to feed it to the young. But quite contrary to what it had intended, the cat began to devour the young vultures. One by one, it ate them all.

The old vulture was very angry, but the cat said, "Please don't complain. It was you who invited me in!"

804. Shaving the Eyebrows

There was an odious young man who ran amuck in society. At the close of the year, he found himself without a penny in his pocket. When his wife asked what could they do about it, the ruffian replied, "I'll find a way."

It so happened a barber was passing through, so he invited him in to cut his hair. He said to the barber, "Please shave off my eyebrows."

When the barber had finished shaving one side of his brows, he suddenly cried aloud, saying, "Since the beginning of time, was there any barber who spoiled his client's eyebrows?" He seized and threatened to turn the barber over to the magistrate.

The barber was frightened and offered three hundred cash by way of apology. Thus the young ruffian was able to tide over the new year with the money he got.

His wife, observing that he had only one side of the brows remained, proposed to him, "Why don't you have the other side shaved off as well? That will make you look better."

"That shows you are not resourceful enough. I keep the other half for the Lantern Festival (The night of the 15th of the first lunar month)," replied the young ruffian.

805. The Tiger Dreads Alms Begging

A robber and an alms-begging monk met with a tiger on the road. The robber used his bow and arrow to confront it, but the tiger continue to threaten him. The monk, for lack of a better weapon, took his alms bowl and threw it with all his strength at the tiger, and the tiger ran away in panic.

The tiger's son asked its father, "You are not afraid of the robber, but why do you fear a monk?"

The tiger replied, "To deal with the robber, I can fight; but if the monk asks for alms, what can I give him to send him away?"

*

The Finger Moon Collection
By Qu Ruji styled himself Yuanli, dates of birth and death unknown; originally from Changshou, Suzhou (Jiangsu Province). He was the author of *The Jiangqing Collection, The Finger Moon Collection, Outline of Military Strategy and Tactics,* and so on.

806. Untie and Tie the Bell

According to the record in *The Finger Moon Collection,* volume twenty-three, under the heading of *The Dharma,* in ancient times there was a monk called Qingliang Taiqin Fadeng in Jinling (the city of Nanjing, Jiangsu Province), who was forthright in disposition, neither niggling nor bound by the sacred rules of the religious order. All the monks in the same monastery looked down upon him.

His contemporary, the eminent monk Fayan, however, thought highly of monk Fadeng, believing his foundation was solid, his mind bright, and that all the others could not compare with him. One day, the monk Fayan gathered all the monks before him and asked a question, "Who can take down the bell tied to the tiger's neck?" All the monks looked at one another, and no one knew how to solve the problem. At this juncture, Fadeng arrived, and Fayan repeated the question to him. Fadeng replied, "He who tied the bell on the tiger's neck can untie it." Fayan was satisfied with the answer, and said to the other monks, "Do you hear? He is not to be looked down upon."

Thus "untie and tie the bell" becomes an idiomatic expression, and people use it to mean "the one who creates a problem should be the one to solve it". In *A Dream of Red Mansions,* Chapter Ninety, when Daiyu overheard Zijuan and Xueyan talking about Baoyu's marriage, her illness became aggravated. It took three of them, including Zijuan, to repeat the story deliberately, in order to dissipate Daiyu's suspicion. There was a poem to describe the situation, as follows:

The cure for a broken heart is heartening news;
The knot must be untied by the one who tied it.

*Five Assorted Subjects

By Xie Zhaozhe styled himself Zaihang, dates of birth and death unknown; originally from Changle, Fujian. A palace graduate in the twentieth year of Wanli (1595 A.D.), he had once held the post of assistant provincial official in charge of civil and financial administration in Guangxi. He was the author of *The Poetry Anthology of Xiaocao Studio*, thirty volumes; *The Xiaocao Studio Collection of Essays*, twenty-eight volumes, *Continuation*, two volumes, and others, including *Five Assorted Subjects*, altogether over ten books. *Five Assorted Subjects* contains sixteen volumes, composed of *Heaven, Earth, Man, matters* and *events*, hence the title.

807. Getting Rich With Two Skills

A man, who relied on his skills in sewing and shearing, ran into the emperor as the latter was touring the countryside. The headgear of the emperor broke down accidentally and he was ordered to repair it. When the work was completed, he received a handsome reward in the form of money.

As he returned to the mountain, he saw a tiger prostrated on the ground groaning. When he approached, it raised its paw where he discovered a big bamboo thorn. He pulled out the thorn, and the tiger carried a deer in its mouth and presented it to him as a reward.

Arriving at home, he told his wife, "I've two unique skills which can help me get rich immediately!"

And he put up two rows of big characters: "Specialize in repairing the emperor's headdress, and remove the thorn of tiger as a sideline."

*

*Humorous Buddhist Allegories

By Pan Youlong, dates of birth and death as well as deeds unknown; originally from Songzi, Hubei Province. *Humorous Buddhist Allegories*, which he authored, explained the principles of Buddhism through fables and jokes, which was novel in composition. Every story has three parts: proposition, explanation and conclusion. In "proposition", a viewpoint of the Buddhist principle is brought out in the form of question and answer; in the "explanation" part, the proposition or viewpoint is explained through a fable or joke; the "conclusion" recapitulates the utterances of the master, and points out the essence of a Buddhist chant or hymn.

808. Good Friends

Proposition: a monk said to Xuefeng, "Great master, I beseech you to enlighten me on the Buddhist doctrine." Xuefeng replied, "What are you talking about?"

Explanation: "The friendship of two men, A and B, were deep and profound under normal circumstances. One day, A fell ill unexpectedly, and could hardly stand the distress. B came to express his regards, saying, 'Brother, what is the nature of your illness? And what do you need? Just tell me you need anything, and I'll bring it to you.'

"A replied, 'My illness is the need for silver. Provided I can get about ten to fifteen grams of silver, that will be enough.'

"B pretended not to hear it. In appearance, it was as if he was cautious not to make any noise. Then he asked, 'What are you talking about?'"

*

*Discourse at Random of Things Past and Present
By Feng Menglong (1574-1646 A.D.) styled himself Youlong, or Eryou, assumed name Master of Mohan Studio, alias Long Ziyou. A writer in the last years of the Ming Dynasty; and a native of Changzhou, South Zhili (Suzhou, Jiangsu Province), he attained the rank of senior licentiate in the third year of Chongzhen (1628-1644 A.D.), and had once held the position of magistrate in Shouning County. Later, when the armed forces of Qing crossed the river, he took part in the resistance movement against the Qing Dynasty. Died in the second year of Shunzhi (1644-1661 A.D.) in his native place. He had compiled and written many books: novels, traditional Chinese operas, folksongs and popular literature, etc. He dipped into them all, and achieved tremendous success. *Discourse at Random of Things Past and Present,* also called *Jokes of Past and Present* contains thirty-six volumes, mainly anecdotes

of the past and fables and jokes. It was his masterpiece, which brought him fame. Apart from some, they were mostly culled from old books.

809. Remonstrate Against Twig Snapping

That was the time when Cheng Yi held the post of expositor. He had finished lecturing and was about to leave when the emperor came up by coincidence and leaned agaisnt the corridor to snap a willow twig for fun. Chen Yi remonstrated, "In spring, the season for twigs to grow, they should not be snapped at will." The emperor threw away the twig, and left greatly displeased.

810. A Person of Talent and Virtue Practises Physiognomy

In the time of emperor Suzong of Tang, an imperial edict was issued to solicit men of talent and virtue, and a man who was recommended arrived at the capital before anyone else. Suzong was very pleased, and granted him an audience in order to listen to his political view. The man, however, had nothing to say except to fix his gaze on the face of the emperor. Suddenly he said, "I've some discovery, but is it known to Your Majesty already?" "I've no knowledge of it," replied the emperor. "I've discovered that Your Majesty's face is somewhat thinner than at the time of Lingwu," said the man. "It's because I've overworked day in day out," explained the emperor. At this point, all the officials in the court burst out laughing. The emperor knew too it was only the blather of a mediocre man, but in order not to obstruct the solicitation of men of talent and virtue, the emperor still decided to give him the post of county magistrate.

811. Eating Meat as Punishment

A man named Li Zairen in the Tang Dynasty was a descendant of the royal family. To seek refuge from the war calamity, he joined the big war lord Gao Jixing who occupied Hubei and its vicinity, and became an official. Li Zairen was pedantic and tended to adhere stubbornly to outworn rules and ideas, slow to act, and never had the habit of eating pork. One day, in response to his superior's call, he was about to mount his horse when his attendants began to fight with each other. Zairen was furious, and he ordered large flatbread and pork be brought from the kitchen at once. As punishment, he enjoined the two men to eat them face to face. In addition, he solumnly warned them, "In future, if you still dare to fight, I'll add butter to the pork and punish you severely!"

812. Taboo

Emperor Wen of Song of the northern and Southern Dynasties had many taboos and the inauspicious Chinese characters denoting bad luck, defeat, loss and death were generally avoided. He even took away part of the character "gua", meaning a yellow horse with black mouth, because it shared in part with the character "huo", meaning disaster, and substituted it with another "gua", a homophonous character meaning melon. One day, the wall had to be repaired and, in consequence of which, the bed had to be moved too. He asked some scholar to write a goodwill essay, and prepared the three sacrificial animals, pig, ox and lamb to be offered to the earth god. As Jiang Mi read the characters "white door" (a hint at death), the emperor immediately changed his countenance, saying, "Whiten your own door." Xiao Cha of Later Liang Dynasty disliked the hair of people turning white, and Chen Bojing of the Han Dynasty, a native of Runan, never mentioned the character death as long as he lived.

813. Looking for the Grave of Seventy-two Generations Ago

When Xiong Ansheng was in Shandong, someone deceived him by saying, "There was a grave in a certain village, which belonged to Xiong Guang, Henan General of Jin, and which was seventy-two generations old. There was a tombstone inside the grave, hidden there by the villagers." Thereupon Xiong Ansheng began to dig for the tombstone. He was unable to find it and, for several years, had to go into litigation. Finally, Zheng Dahuan, the official in charge of the case, brought in a verdict, saying, "Seventy-two generations ago, which means he lived before the legendary ruler Fu Xi. During the Jin Dynasty, no title of Henan General existed." Thus Xiong Ansheng had no alternative but to lead his whole clan to the grave and wail together.

814. The Revered Mr Chen Abstains from Alcohol

Chen Gao of Nanjing was a good drinker. When he was a brigade general in Shandong, his father was worried that he might drink too much and hold things up, so he wrote a letter to warn him against it. Quite unexpectedly, he used his own salary to hire a craftsman and make a big bowl with capacity of two catties, and engrave eight Chinese characters inside the bowl, which read, "Father has warned against alcohol, only three cups are allowed". It soon became a standing joke among the scholars.

815. Expose the Town God to the Sun

In the seventeenth year of Wanli, title of Shenzong, there was a great drought in Suzhou. At that time, Shi Chuyang was the magistrate of the prefecture. As a man who had always prided himself on his own honesty and unsullied reputation, he keenly felt the urgency of praying for rain. Thus he had the town god moved to the pray-for-rain platform, while he himself sat opposite it, both exposed to the scorching sun and without any cover overhead whatsoever. As a result, the statue of the town god cracked and Shi Chuyang suffered heatstroke which almost cost him his life.

816. Haunted Houses

When Yuan Jiqian, a physician, was in East Village, he rented a house with a courtyard. Many strange things had happened in the house, often in the evening. When it was windy and the sky overcast, the whole family would be thrown into a state of uncertainty, and dared not leave the house. One night, they suddenly heard a howling sound, coming as if from the jar, a kind of low and deep sound, and it frightened the family even more. They thought it must be the most ferocious of all evil spirits. Making a small hole on the window paper, they took a peep outside. There was no moon that night, being the last day of the lunar month. They saw a dark object in the courtyard walking to and fro, its body looked very much like the yellow dog. However, it was unable to raise its head. They hit it on the head with a piece of iron. Following a big "bang", the head of the family's yellow dog was revealed, and the dog ran away in panic. The event began with the delivery of edible oil from Baisheng Village. The dog had tried to lick the oil that was left in the empty jar, but then it got stuck. The whole family had a good laugh. Relieved, they went back to sleep.

In Hongdou Village (Nanchang, Jiangxi Province) there was a rich and influential family. Their hall was spacious and the building imposing, but a sort of unusual noise was heard nightly, which made the family believe there must be an evil spirit. Because of the suspicion, they vacated the house, and let it remain vacant. It so happened a Taoist priest from the Mountain of Dragon and Tiger arrived there at the time, and the family was pleased to get his help, promising in the meantime a handsome reward. The Taoist priest then entered the house. When night came, he saw a mouse with a tail like a big pestle vaulting into a rotten pillar. The Taoist priest caught it from inside the pillar and killed it. As a matter of fact, the mouse's tail had been hurt by a bite and, as it bled while ran past the sandy ground, the tail got stained with grains of sand. When the blood dried up, the tail became big and stiff, looking like a big pestle. The sound was caused by the tail knocking against other objects. The Taoist priest originally was a seller of fake charms at the foot of the mountain. It was sheer coincidence that he met with such an event. Not only had he come by a handsome reward, but his name had also become eminent.

817. Shen Zhou

The name Shen Zhou was illustrious for some time. It so happened that the magistrate of Suzhou Prefecture was looking for a man adept in painting, and his subordinate recommended Shen Zhou. The prefecture chief issued a red-coloured summons to arrest him. As Shen Zhou arrived at the government office, the magistrate ordered him to stand under the eaves to paint. Thereupon Shen Zhou drew the painting "Burn the Famous Stringed Instrument for Fuel and Cook the Crane for Meat" and showed it to the magistrate. The magistrate did not understand the meaning of the painting, and said, "It is but a run-of-the-mill piece of work." In the following year, the magistrate went to the capital to pay respects to the emperor, and took the opportunity to make a coutesy call on the minister of the Ministry of Civil Office, the duke Shou Xi. The duke asked him, "How's Mr Shi Tian (alias of Shen Zhou)?" The magistrate did not know the name, and could not respond to the inquiry then and there. Upon his return, he asked his subordinate, and realized it was the man he ordered arrested with a red-coloured summons. He felt abashed; regretted, and went to apologize to Shen Zhou in person.

818. He and Yu Befriend One Another with a Bottle of Vinegar

He Wenyuan became the magistrate of Wenzhou recently, and took a small boat to visit Yu Yuanqu. The two of them sat down and talked for quite a while, and longed for a drink, but there was no place to get it in such a small hamlet. He Wenyuan sighed, saying, "It will do even if it's only some unfiltered acidic thing." Thereupon Yu Yuanqu fetched a bottle of newly made vinegar to share with his friend. They talked intimately the whole night and not until daybreak did they part. People called it "He and Yu the Vinegar Friends".

819. Zheng Yuqing

Zheng Yuqing, prime minister of Tang Dynasty, was thrifty and free from corruption. One day, he suddenly invited many relatives and friends to his home for a feast. It caught all by surprise, and everyone arrived early. Zheng Yuqing, however, emerged only when the sun was up in the sky. After an exchange of conventional greetings, they chatted for a little while, and began to feel hungry. Just then Zheng Yuqing instructed his attendant, saying, "Tell the chef to steam them well and do away with the hair, but be careful not to break their necks!" All the guests thought it must be either ducks or geese that had been prepared, and exchanged glances silently with one another. After a while, the servants carried the dishes out. The welcome aroma of seasoning, sauce and vinegar, smelt delicious and pleasant enough. Before every guest, however, there was only a bowl of millet, and a steamed bottle-gourd. They all held back their smile and ate with an effort.

820. Three Hundred Jars of Mashed Pickled Vegetables

When the number one scholar, a certain Wang, had not yet passed the imperial examination, he once got drunk and fell into the River Bian. It was the river god who helped him to the bank, saying, "You still have three hundred thousand cash in the form of official salary that waits to be used. If you die here, how will it be spent?" He became a palace graduate in the following year. There was another scholar, who could not pass the imperial examination for quite a long time, and tried to imitate him, pretending to be drunk and fell into the river. The river god picked him up as well. The man was delighted, and asked, "How much official salary do I have?" The water god said, "I don't know. There are only three hundred jars of mashed pickled vegetables waiting to be picked up."

821. Show Off Before a Superior Man

In ancient times, there was a scholar, who loved books, and possessed some literary talent. On one occasion, he arrived at Caishiji beside the Yangtze River. According to legend, the great poet of Tang era, Li Bai, once went sightseeing on board ship in the Yangtze River. While he was drinking at the bows, he suddenly saw the bright moon in the water. He plunged into the water to get the moon, and was drowned at Caishiji. After his death, he was buried there.

Thereafter, whenever men of letters came to the place, they would visit the site and ponder over the past, sigh with emotion, and write a few lines of not very elegant verse, which took up all the space in front of Li Bai's grave. Calling to mind the greatness of Li Bai as a poet, and disgusted with the persons who doodled in front of Li Bai's grave unaware of their own limitations, the scholar was furious. He composed a poem to taunt those people who wrote the doggerels. The seven-character, four-line poem he wrote was as follows:

Beside the Caishi River a little earth mound,
Where Li Bai's name glistens then as now.
Every Tom, Dick and Harry will come around
To show off at Luban's sacred ground.

822. The Cat with Five Virtues

Bin Shi, a monk in Longevity Monastery, chatted with a guest on one occasion while his cat was sleeping beside him, and he said to the guest, meaningfully, "People all say the chicken has five virtues, but my cat has five virtues too. It will not catch the mouse when it sees one, that's benevolence; when the mouse vies with it for food, it yields from modesty, and that's loyalty to friends; it only emerges during a reception after the banquet table has been set, and that's propriety; it can steal any food and eat it too, even though it has been kept with the strictest safeguard, and that's resourcefulness; in winter, it will lie down on the top of the kitchen range, keeping its body still, and that's trustworthiness."

823. A Nice Guy

A man of Later Han Dynasty, known as Sima Hui, never talked about the shortcomings of other people. When he opened his mouth, he always used the word good, making no distinction as to whether it was true or false. If someone asked him how he was, he would reply, "Good." If someone told him a son had died, he would listen and say, "Very good!" His wife chided him, saying, "People believed in your moral integrity and told you about his son. Why did you say very good when you were told his son had died?" He replied, "What you said just now is very good too!"

What we call a goody-goody, or a nice guy who bears no grudge against the world, derives from the story.

824. To Save a Meal

In Tongcheng, Anhui Province, a certain man surnamed Fang was stingy by nature. When his elder brother arrived from the countryside, he lied that he had travelled to a very distant place just to save the expense of serving him supper.

For that reason, his elder brother had to make do with a temporary bed and went to sleep, believing that his brother was not at home. It so happened that a weasel intruded into the house that night for chickens. Fang forgot he had told a lie, and went out to drive the weasel away. The elder brother recognized the voice of his younger brother, and yelled, "You are at home after all!"

The younger Fang hastened to respond, saying, "It isn't me, it's your younger sister-in-law!"

825. Busy Monks

A certain high-ranking official of the imperial court suddenly had an impulse to go sightseeing in the monastery. Upon receiving the notification, all the monks went busy preparing for the reception three days before the event. Some swept the gate area of the monastery, others prepared wine and dishes for the feast, and the intense work of the past three days left everyone's back and legs aching.

The monastery was situated in the deep mountain area, where the forest was thick and the bamboos tall. With the gurgling of spring, it was indeed a clean and elegant place to be in. The high-ranking official, having toured the place, dined and wined to satiety, was in elevated spirits, and he chanted a Tang poem;

At the courtyard's bamboo grove
I listened to the monks chatter,
And happily spent half a day
Of my floating life in incidental leisure.

As the monks heard it, they all burst out laughing.

"Why do you laugh?" asked the high-ranking official.

"Sir, there can be no doubt you have won half a day's leisure, but we monks have been busy for three days."

*

*The House of Jokes

By Feng Menglong. The book was divided into two parts, part one and part two, consisting of eight categories and one hundred items. In the preface, he said, "The world, past and present, is but a house of jokes. You and me are all in the house, and took part in the jokes. Not being a part of it, then you are not a man; without jokes, you cannot take part in it. The world is not a world without joking and the people taking part in it." Thus it clearly indicated the aim of his book was to use fables as a venue to criticize the malpractice and social ills of the time.

826. Giving Birth to a Child is Easier

A licentiate was about to take part in the examination, and he felt heavyhearted all the time. His wife tried to console him, saying, "Look at you, so troubled by your composition. It is as if me giving birth to a baby."

"It is easier for you to give birth to a baby after all," affirmed her husband.

"What makes you think so?" his wife asked.

"Because, it is already in your belly, whereas mine is empty," the husband replied.

827. Three's Company

Three men slept in the same heatable brick bed used in the North, and one of them in his dreamy state felt his leg being attacked by an unbearable itch, and made a desperate effort to scratch it. However, what he did not realize was he had scratched another man's leg, and so no matter how assiduous he did it, the itch could not be stopped. On the other hand, he had caused the other man's leg to drip with blood. The second man in his drowsy state touched the wet spot of his leg, thought the third man must have been bed-wetting, and urged him to get up. Thereupon tthe third man put on his clothes and proceeded to the door in order to relieve himself. It so happened next door was a wineshop, and the pattering sound of wine coming from the wine cask never ceased, which made him think he was still urinating, and stood there all night until daybreak.

828. New Bed and New Trousers

The male parent of a married couple recently acquired a new bed, which was made with very fine craftsmanship, and looked elegant. He thought, such an exquisite bed must be shown to the other male parent of the couple, or else it would have been sheer neglect. He pretended to be ill and lay in the bed in order that the other parent could come and pay him a visit.

By coincidence, the other parent was eager to show off his new pair of trousers, which had just been added to his wardrobe. When he heard about the illness of his counterpart, he was more than happy to pay him a visit. As he arrived, he deliberately raised one of his legs and let his new trousers beneath the robe be seen before he asked, "My good relative, what illness have you suffered from? Why have you become so skinny?"

The parent who pretended to be ill replied, "In point of illness, sir, we have probably been afflicted with the same ailment!"

829. Teaching and Learning

Father wrote the Chinese character "one", and taught his little son to learn it. The next day, while his son stood next to him as he was wiping the table clean, he took the opportunity to write a big "one" on the table with the wet rag in his hand, and asked his son to identify the character. His son did not know it, and the father said, "That's the word 'one' I taught you yesterday!" The son stared at him with wide-open eyes. "Why has it grown so much bigger overnight?" he said in amazement.

830. Riding a Horse on Board the Ship

A man who loved horseback riding was deceived by people and spent over one hundred and four ounces of gold to buy a horse. It was a nag impossible to control.

The man therefore hired a boat and brought the horse aboard, while he rode on the horseback. After the boat covered more than one *li*, he still complained about its slowness, and said to the boatman, "I'll buy you some wine, and can you please put your back into it. You row faster, and I'll let the horse gallop to my heart's content."

831. Pool Capital

A was discussing with B about pooling their capital to make wine. A said to B, "You will provide the rice, and I, the water."

"If all the rice is provided by me, how are we going to work out the accounts?" said B.

"I'll never deceive you. When the wine has been made, you just give all the water back to me, and the rest is all yours."

832. Shrugging shoulders while walking

A person on the road was wearing a new silk skirt. He was worried that people might not see it, and so he shrugged his shoulders as he walked along. He did it for quite some time before asking the houseboy, "Is there anybody looking at me?"

"There is nobody here," replied the houseboy.

"In that case, I can relax a little for the time being," he said, loosening up his shoulders.

833. Sitting on the Fence

The phoenix held a birthday party, and all birds came to congratulate it, but the bat did not come. The phoenix condemned it, saying, "You are my subordinate, why so arrogant?" The bat, however, replied, "I've four feet, and belong to the animal kingdom. Why should I come to pay my respects?"

On another occasion, the unicorn was cerebrating its birthday, and the bat was again absent. The unicorn denounced it. The bat, however, said, "I've wings, and belong to the world of birds. Why should I pay my respects to you?"

*

**An Extensive Collection of Jokes*
By Feng Yinglong. The book contains thirteen volumes, devided into thirteen categories. It was another book of jokes after *The house of Jokes*, but it was a separate work, and not a revised and enlarged edition of *The House of Jokes*.

834. Fraud

A wealthy family's vulgar descendant, who passed himself off as a scholar, submitted to the county *yamen* a written complaint, accusing a certain man of owing him money, and requesting the government to help collect it. The county official was sceptical because of his coarse behaviour and decided to examine him further. He asked him, "Since you are a licentiate, can you please tell us what is the chapter called 'The Duke Huan killed Zijiu' about?"

The man did not know what the county official asked was in fact part of a story culled from *The Confucian Analects,* but thought it must be a homicide case, and was afraid he might get himself involved. So he exclaimed hastily, "I really don't know what it is all about!" The county magistrate realized the man had never read a book and only passed himself off as a licentiate, so he ordered twenty strokes to be administered as punishment before he was driven out.

After being driven out of the courthouse, the man told his servant, saying, "This county official is very unreasonable. He said Weng Xiaojiu was beaten to death by my guandpa. Because of that, he gave me twenty strokes." The servant said, "What the county official asked is a sentence from the book and, even if you did not know, you should say you understood a little."

The man said, "I only said I didn't know, and got twenty strokes. If I were to say I knew something, might I not have to pay with my own life?"

835. Too Subtle to Learn

A man engaged a family teacher. He instructed his son, "You must follow your teacher's good example from now on, and whatever you say or do must not deviate from his teaching."

The child obeyed his father's instructions to the letter and accompanied the teacher at meals. As the teacher began to eat, he did likewise. When the teacher drank, he drank too. The teacher inclined his body, he hastened to follow suit. The teacher discovered that his student had imitated his every action and could not help laughing. He put down the chopsticks and sneezed.

The student was unable to follow him, so he stood up and bowed to the teacher, saying, "This is too subtle for me too learn, sir. I cannot possibly master it!"

836. On Whom One's Livelihood Depends

A Chinese opera actor dressed up as an official and went to his post just as a man came to submit a written complaint. The official's face immediately lighted up with pleasure and said, "Something good has happened!" He put down the writing brush, stepped down the hall and rendered to the plaintiff a profound bow.

The runner in the *yamen* said, "Sir, this is your subject, who comes to lodge a complaint, hoping you can do something for him. Why should you be so respectful?"

The official replied, "You don't understand. On the plaintiff depends my livelihood. How dare I not respect him?"

837. Going Straight or Walking Sideways

When a prisoner exiled to a distant place for military service newly arrived at a detention center, the warder would, as a rule, try by various means to extort some money from him. He would, first of all, order the prisoner to shout and clear the way. If the latter obeyed, the warder would scold him, saying, "It would seem I was following you!"

Then he would enjoin the exiled prisoner to walk behind him as an escort. If the prisoner did as he was ordered, the warder again would berate him, saying, "In so doing, it is as if I was clearing the way for you!"

The exiled prisoner was frustrated by all this but at a loss as to what to do. Finally he knelt down and asked the warder, "Could you tell me what should I do to conform to the rules?"

The warder said, "Provided you give me a little monthly payment, you may do what you like, be it going straight or walking sideways."

838. Investigation

His Excellency the judicial commissioner was on an inspection tour, and Kuang Zhang, Chen Zhongzi and Qi Ren had all been arrested and imprisoned. Kuang Zhang believed he was a filial son, Chen Zhongzi thought he was an honest gentleman, and they did not ask anybody to intercede for them through the back-door. Only Qi Ren gave away his wife and a concubine to an influential high-ranking official, and asked him to plead for exoneration on his behalf.

The influential high-ranking official, therefore, went to see the judicial commissioner on behalf of Qi Ren. The judicial commissioner enumerated the crimes of the three, saying they were all criminals who corrupted social manners and customs, and explained why he had to investigate them. The influential high-ranking official said, "Kuang Zhang divorced his wife and drove away his son; Chen Zhongzi evaded his own elder brother and left his mother, and it was absolutely correct and proper that Your Excellency should arrest them. As to Qi Ren, he is only the head of a gang of beggars. Why arrested him?"

839. A Taoist Priest Undertakes the Whole Taoist Ritual

A vegetatarian family wanted to invite several Taoist priests to come and perform Taoist rites. A Taoist priest, who was avaricious and did not care about his own safety as he thought only of the money he could get, undertook to perform the whole Taoist rites. He worked day and night, rushing from one thing to another in a great bustle. He was so busy that he did not have time even to take a breather. When the third day arrived for the final ceremony, he fainted on the floor.

The vegetarian family was afraid that matter involving human life might implicate them, and asked the grave digger to move the fainted man outside temporarily, pending further arrangement. The Taoist priest, who was lying on the ground, heard the conversation. He struggled to raise his head and told the master of the house, saying, "Please give me the grave digger's wages. I'll crawl out slowly!"

840. Autumn Cicada

A certain master was very harsh in his treatment of the servant, and often provided his servant with insufficient food to eat and not enough clothes to keep warm. One day, the servant heard an autumn cicada sing and asked the master, "What is it singing?"

"It's the autumn cicada," said the master.
"What does the cicada eat?" asked the servant.
"It inhales the wind and drinks the dew," replied the master.
"Does the cicada wear clothes?" asked the servant again.
"No, it doesn't," the master said.
"In that case, the cicada is the most appropriate candidate for your servant," remarked the servant.

841. The Lotus Root and the Ship

A man entertained his guest with the tip of the lotus root, and kept the thick, large head and rootstock in the kitchen. The guest said, "In the course of studying poetry, I often came across famous lines like this:

"'The lotus flower in the jade well
At Taihua Peak is so big
It reaches a hundred feet,
And the lotus root is as long as a ship.'

"I did not believe there was such a long lotus root before, but today I finally am convinced it is a real thing!"
"Why?" asked the host.
"The tip of the lotus root is already here, but the head of the root is still lying there in the kitchen!"

842. To Prevent Suspicion

The immortal He Xiangu lived in the cave all by herself, and Cao Guojiu came to visit her. Before long, Lu Dongbin arrived too. He Xiangu was afraid if Lu Dongbin saw Cao Guojiu, he might become suspicious. So, to confuse people, she applied her magic arts, turning Cao Guojiu into a divine pill, which she swallowed.

A little while later, The rest of the immortals, Han Zhongli, Zhang Guolao, Han Xiangzi, Tieguai Li and Lan Caihe all arrived, and He Xiangu, to avoid suspicion of the other immortals, entreated Lu Dongbin to change her into a divine pill and swallow her into his stomach.

As only Lu Dongbin was there all by himself, the other immortals asked him, "Lu Dongbin, why are you here all by yourself?"

Lu Dongbin was tongue-tied, and could not find words to respond.

The other immortals smiled and said, "It seems likely not only is He Xiangu in Lu Dongbin's stomach, but there was somebody else in He Xiangu's belly, something quite unexpected."

843. Drop Under the Sedan Chair

A woman was on her way to get married but the bottom of the bridal sedan chair she was in suddenly fell apart, and the sedan chair bearers blamed one another, saying, "The bride cannot go on foot. On the other hand, if we turn back for a new sedan chair, the distance is too long, to and from . . . ."

The bride heard their complaint and said, "I've thought of a way."

Everyone was pleased to hear there was a way out.

"You continue to carry the sedan chair outside, while I walk inside it," she suggested.

844. Tea and Wine

Tea said to wine, "I'm able to overcome sleepiness and help bring about an exalted, poetic mood, whereas you have broken many a home and brought down nations in the past. So why not entertain the guests with tea instead?"

Wine refuted tea, saying, "In the caves of the gods and immortals good wine is indispensible, while my influence is felt also in the settlement of litigation and the arrangement of marriages. In sacrificial rites as well as banquets I've always been the first choice. Whoever heard of using the light yellow soup (tea) in my place!" The two boasted of each other's abilities and went into endless arguments, neither would yield to the other. Finally, water mediated between the two, saying, "To brew tea in the stone pot requires water from the well, and making wine to fill the silver bottle needs the help of the spring. You two gentlemen please don't lose your temper over trifles, for, without me, nothing can be accomplished."

845. Where There is Money There is Life

An old gardener failed to grow his eggplants and was often tormented by it. He went to consult an old horticulturalist, who told him, "By the side of every young plant, bury a coin. In this manner, the eggplant will grow."

"Why must it be done this way?" asked the old gardener.

"You must have heard the saying, 'He who has money shall live, he who has not, shall die'," replied the old horticulturalist.

846. No Transaction on Credit After Death

A villager, through his extreme stinginess, became rich. Later, he suffered a grave illness, his breathing barely perceptible yet unwilling to die. He besought his wife, saying, "Throughout my life, I've been greedy and stingy, bit by bit and with great pains, severing from the six relations (father, mother, elder brothers, young brothers, wife, children) to attain the status of today. When I die, you can get my skin and sell it to the tanner, cut out my flesh and sell it to the butcher, and take my bones and sell it to the lacquer manufacturer." He insisted that his wife promised before he would give up his ghost. Half a day after his death, he revived and exhorted his wife again and again, saying, "People are snobbish these days and human feelings of sympathy are as thin as paper. You must remember never to allow any transaction on credit!"

847. Unyielding

The pair—father and son—were obstinate and unyielding by nature.

On a certain day, the father asked his guest to stay for a drink at home, and sent his son to the city to buy some meat.

The son carried the meat and hurried home. He was just about to leave the city gate when he ran into a man head-on. As neither would willingly yield to the other, it resulted in a stalemate.

Eventually the old man had to go and look for his son. As he saw what happened, he said to the son, "You bring the meat home to accompany our guest at meal and let me persist with the confrontation!"

848. Talking of Giants

In the capital, the selection of generals was in progress and a large crowd looked on.

A certain man from Shandong said, "These people are not big and tall enough. In my hometown, there was a truly big man. When he stands up, his head touches the beam of the house."

A man from Shanxi said, "In my hometown, there is a bigger giant. When he sits on the floor, his head can touch the beam of the house."

Another man from Shaanxi came forward, saying, "All these are nothing. In my hometown, there is a still bigger giant. When he opens his mouth, his upper lip touches the beam, while his lower lip rubs against the ground."

A bystander rebuked him, saying, "Where is the giant's body then?"

The man from Shaanxi replied, "Let's talk only about the man's mouth!"

849. Praises

There was a man who had a fondness for praises. A physiognomist knew his partiality, paid him a visit and offered to tell his fortune. Trying his best to eulogize the man, he said, "Sir, you need only this pair of big eyes to lead an entire life of pleasure." The master of the house was very pleased with his words and kept the physiognomist at home for several days, showering him with gifts. Before he left, the physiognomist drew the master of the house aside and said to him, "There is one more word, which you must remember." The man asked what it was, and the physiognomist replied, "Sir, you should try to do some crafts with your hands, and don't put all the trust in your eyes."

850. Deaf-mute Taboos

A deaf and a mute, both considered their condition a taboo subject. One day, the deaf man met the mute. Eager to show he was not deaf, he asked the mute to sing a song. The mute knew the other man could talk, so he opened and closed his mouth, while pretended to beat time with his hands. The deaf man inclined his ear and listened attentively for quite some time. When he saw the mute man's month cease to move, he smiled and said, "It's a long time I haven't heard you sing, and you have become even better."

*

*Elegant Jokes Chosen with Care

By Zui Yuezi. His life story was not known. From the inscription at the beginning of the book, which says, "selected and compiled by Zui Yuezi of Yuzhang", we know he was originally from Nanchang, Jiangxi Province. There are sixty-eight items in *Elegant Jokes Chosen with Care,* which represents one category of a book series compiled by Zui Yuezi.

851. Move House

A man, whose house was sandwiched between a coppersmith and a blacksmith, could hardly endure the rattle of the hammerblow. He asked someone to intercede for him. The two smiths promised to move as he had requested. The man was overjoyed, and gave a feast to send them off. After they dined and wined to satiety, he tried to sound out where they intended to go, and the two smiths spoke with one voice, saying, "The left moves to the right and the right moves to the left."

Move left and move right, nothing inappropriate. Being in the middle, remain neutral, and avoid leaning to either side.

852. Night Soil

A family, who owned a manure pit, wished to sell it. The asking price was four hundred coins, but the buyer was only willing to pay two hundred. The seller became angry and cursed, "Is the dog's dung in this manure pit really so cheap?"

The buyer was enraged and cursed in return, saying, "Why should you lose your temper? I haven't eat yours yet!"

853. The Hoe

The husband returned from the field, and his wife asked him where had he put the hoe.

The husband replied in a loud voice, "I left it in the field."

The wife hastened to warn him, "Speak softly, and don't let anybody hear it. Be quick, go and get it back," she urged.

When he arrived at the field, the hoe was not there, and he hurried back to tell his wife, saying softly and close to her ear, "The hoe has gone."

854. Taoist Magic Mosquito Repellant

A man, who sold Taoist magic mosquito repellant, blew his own trumpet, claiming his magic figures were so efficacious that wherever it was pasted, all mosquitoes disappeared.

Someone bought the Taoist magic figures from him, and pasted it on the wall inside his house, but the swarm of mosquitoes not only did not decrease, it multiplied. So he returned to the marketplace to lodge a complaint.

The man who sold the Taoist magic mosquito repellant said, "You must have pasted it incorrectly, which made it inefficacious."

The buyer asked him, "In order to be proper, where should I paste it then?"

The seller replied, "You should paste it inside the mosquito net!"

855. Salted Fish

Two brothers filled their bowls with rice, and asked their father, "What have we to go with the rice?" "There is a smoked salted fish hanging above the cooking stove. With every mouthful of rice you can glance at it once." After a while, the younger brother suddenly shouted, "Elder brother has glanced at it more than once!" Their father replied, "That will be terribly salty for him!"

In ancient times, people talked of quenching one's thirst by thinking of plums. By looking at the salted fish, one should also be able make it go with the rice!

856. Stealing an Ox

A man, who stole another man's ox, was put in the cangue and paraded through the streets.

One of his acquaintances happened to see him, "What have you done to deserve being cangued and shown here?" he asked.

"What lousy luck! I was strolling in the street, and saw a straw rope. Thinking it might be useful, I picked it up," the man replied.

His acquaintance said, "How could a trifle like that deserves the cangue and lock?"

The ox-stealer replied, "It's because at one end of the straw rope there was a little calf."

857. Venerable Sir

A band of robbers went to plunder a family. The family was terribly frightened, and addressed them as kings, generals and heroes, but the chieftain did not like any of the titles. The family ventured to ask him, "In order to be appropriate, may we ask how should we address you?"

The robber said, "You can call me venerable sir."

The family asked him why called him venerable sir, and the robber replied, "It's because I've seen people call all the officials as venerable sir!"

*

*The Latest Fad in Jokes
Anonymous. There were forty-seven items found in the appendix of *The Moon of an Autumn Night*, volume one. The fables were meaningful and original.

858. Zai Yu Slept in Daytime

Confucius reproached Zai Yu for sleeping in the daytime, and called him "decayed wood or manure".

Zai Yu was recalcitrant, saying, "I just want to meet Duke Zhou, and why should you blame me for it?"

Confucius refuted him, "Is it the right time to dream of Duke Zhou in broad daylight?"

"But Duke Zhou is not the kind of person who would go out at night!" Zai Yu replied.

859. The Hardest Object

Two men were arguing as to "What is the hardest object in the world?"

"Iron is the hardest," said A.

"No, it's not true. Since iron will melt in fire, how can it be called the hardest?" refuted B.

"In that case, what is the hardest then?" asked A.

"In my opinion, the hardest object is the beard," said B.

"How can the beard be the hardest object?" A was skeptical.

"Because, no matter how thick the skin is, the beard can grow out of it," B said.

860. The Tutor Accepts Bribes

Once upon a time, a licentiate brought a goose as gift to the tutor. The tutor said, "If I accept your goose, there is nothing to feed it with. Will it die then? But if I don't accept it, I'll forfeit my integrity through a breach of etiquette. What must I do?"

The licantiate replied, "Master, please accept it. According to the Confucian school of idealist philosophy of the Song Dynasty, 'To die of hunger is but a small matter, but it would be a major issue to forfeit one's integrity.'"

*

*The Gem of Jokes for a Smile
Anonymous. There were sixty-nine items of jokes, found in the block-printed edition of *New Carving Copy of the Drinkers' Wager Games and Jokes for the Banguet*, volume four, under the *jokinggate* category.

861. Live on Others

Once upon a time, a carp and a catfish were bickering.

"There is nothing special about you. As for me, if there is any transformation in the future, I may go to heaven," said the catfish.

"There are golden stars in my eyes, and golden scales draping my body. When the peach flowers are in bloom, and the spring brings warm weather, I can climb past the Dragon Gate with one leap," said the carp.

"I've no golden stars in my eyes, nor golden scales on my body, yet I need only to open my big mouth to live on others as always," the catfish said.

862. Arrested for Being in the Spotlight

The golden oriole, the mosquito and the wine moth happened to meet, and each tried to impress the others with its own abilities.

The golden oriole said, "In the seventh moon when the weather suddenly turns cold, the five cereals (rice, two kinds of millet, wheat and beans) are gathered and taken to the threshing ground. At that time, the master has not tasted them yet, and I am the only one who eats them first."

The wine moth asked, "When the blueblooded young men shoot you with the catapult, how do you fend for yourself?"

The golden oriole replied, "The ancients have a saying, 'Human beings die in pursuit of wealth, and birds die in pursuit of food.'"

The mosquito said, "In the big mansion, a boudoir filled with spring breeze, where there are hardly any traces of human presence, a quiet evening, all in peace. Inside the red silk mosquito net, a beauty sleeps, and I steal a speck of red blood."

The soft-shelled turtle, who emerged from the water, heard the mosquito talk about its romantic experience and climbed up the bank, asking, "Suppose the beauty wakes up and gives you a slap, how are you going to fend for yourself?"

The mosquito replied, "To have witnessed such a wonderful sight before I die, I'll have no regrets."

The wine moth said, "I'm the first to taste the heated wine. With thousands of good friends gathering around, everyone of whom getting drunk with the golden goblet turned upside down, a talented young man supports me with the hand."

The soft-shelled turtle said, "If the talented young man does not help you up, aren't you going to die of drowning?"

The wine moth replied, "The story of Libai raising his wine cup and entering the water drunk to get the moon has been handed down to us from generation to genration."

Passersby heard the noises and, as they gathered around, the golden oriole, the mosquito and the wine moth all fled hurriedly, and only the soft-shelled turtle was caught. The soft-shelled turtle said, "Trouble is caused by talking too much, and people in the limelight often bear the brunt of the attack."

863. An Ox with Coins

In ancient times, there was an inspector-general, who had no sooner assumed office than he ordered all the hunters within the territory to catch an unicorn as a present to him. The hunters travelled throughout the length and breadth of the mountain and forest but could not find an unicorn, so they caught a water buffalo instead, draping around its body with strings of coins and passing it off as an unicorn, which they presented to the inspector-general.

The inspector-general was furious upon seeing the water buffalo and said, "If not for the coins, this beast is clearly an ox!"

864. Urge People to Practise Virtue

In days of yore there was a monk who tried to induce people to do good. "Benefactor, give alms to a monk," he said. "Be charitable, worship the Buddha and you will not suffer the miseries of the knife saw in hell when you die," he said.

Soon the monk and the benefactor both died. Because he was steeped in crime, the monk had to suffer the agony of the knife saw. As the benefactor saw the monk being tortured, he asked him why. The monk replied, "You don't know the reason, of course. The king of Hell has discovered that monasteries are being abandoned and monks in short supply, so he cuts a monk into two to fill up the vacancies."

*

*A Sea of Million-dollar Jokes
Author unknown. Altogether they were sixty-three items found in the carving copy of *Newly Carved Four People Universal Champion Event of Wanbao*, volume seventeen, printed in the last years of the Ming Dynasty,

865. A Common Pond Frog

A swan pursued a frog, and the frog took refuge under the sponge gourd trellis. The sponge gourd asked, "Why do you hide under our trellis?" The frog replied, "At the moment, an official from the imperial court is looking for an object with three names to mete out punishment, and that's why I've to take refuge in your village." The sponge gourd asked again, "What do you mean by one object with three names?" The frog replied, "That is me. I'm called Shilin, Tianji and frog." As soon as the sponge gourd heard this, it hastened to say, "Hurry, and go away. Don't get me into trouble, for I also have three names: Tianluo, Bugua and sponge gourd." The frog had no other recourse but to hide itself in the water. The water, again, asked why it concealed itself under water, and the frog provided the same answer he gave to the sponge gourd. Thereupon water said, "Don't get me involved, for I've three names too." The frog asked, "Which three names?" Water replied,

"My first name is Jiangshui, the second one is Heshui, and the third one is Haishui." The frog became angry upon hearing this, and said, "I took you as the salt water of the sea, who would have thought you were only the freshwater of the river. If I had known it, do you think I would have taken refuge here?"

*

The Zhang Yangyuan Collection
By Zhang Luxiang (1611-1674 A.D.) styled himself Kaofu, assumed name Nianzhi, originally from the Village of Tong, Anhui Province. He was an educator and writer of the Qing Dynasty. A successful candidate in the lowest level of civil service examination in the last years of the Ming Dynasty, he refused to serve under the Qing Dynasty, and devoted his time giving lectures and writing. People called him Master Yangyuan. After his death, his reputation rose with each passing day, and he was worshipped in the Confucian temple beginning from the tenth year of Tongzhi (1871 A.D.), reign title of emperor Muzong of the Qing Dynasty (1862-1874 A.D.), as a secondary god. He was the author of *Memorandum, Learning Vow, Notes on the Book of Changes, Notes on History, Tutoring the Son, On Assistance to Agriculture,* poetry and essays, and so on, all of which had been compiled into *The Zhang Yangyuan Collection* by later generations.

866. A Country Bumpkin

A rustic old man in the village intended to build a house. All the materials had been prepared apart from the selection of a craftsman. As the old man did not want to hire the skilful, many inferior ones vied with one another for the job, each with an intermediary to put in a word or two. Those around the old man also induced him, saying, "If you hire this craftsman, you will save not only money but time. Moreover, he can do everything according to your wish." The old man did not have ideas of his own, so he hired the recommended craftsman and entrusted him with the whole construction project.

The mediocre craftsman had the summer beam cut and used it as short posts above the beam; he split the horizontal beam in two to make the purlins. The old man was indignant and, after giving him a good scolding, dismissed him. He changed one craftsman after another, but they were all the same, reckless and disappointing. Finally, he tried to approach the skilful craftsman. The latter was unwilling to come at first but, moved by the sincerity and doggedness of the old man, he promised to take the job in the end, bringing along with him his assistant and tools. He did not wrangle over the labour cost, being confident of his own skills. The old man was pleased. However, when the craftsman inspected the materials, he discovered that the shortened posts could no longer be used as beam, nor could the purlins be utilized as cross girders, and he sighed, "Alas! Although I've the skills to build the house, the materials have already been spoiled!" Many times he walked around the house, but eventually had to leave expressing his regrets.

And the old man's house had not been built for many years.

867. Legacy

A man exerted his utmost to expand his land possession and his house with courtyard. The intention was to leave all this to his son as inheritance. He said, "Not doing so, there will not be enough for my son."

After listening to what he said, master Zhang asked him, "How much has your father left you? And how much has your grandfather left your father?" The man replied, "What my grandpa left behind was only a little assets and twelve dilapidated houses. It was my father who began the expansion process, and I've taken it further."

Master Zhang listened and said, "If what you said is true, why should you lose sleep and forget to eat from anxiety to plan for your son?" The man replied, "How can you expect every son to possess talent as well as moral integrity, like my father and I, relying on our own efforts to make our home and establish our business?"

Master Zhang listened and smiled, saying, "Well, you are wrong there, very wrong! How do you know your son has no talent and no moral integrity, who cannot be trusted to establish himself like you and your father, and requires you to lose sleep and forget your meals to plan for him? From what you are doing now, it is as if you anticipated your son to be devoid of ability and virtue. You may leave him with an abundance of property, but in reality you treat him rather harshly! Moreover, since you anticipate your son to be devoid of virtue and talent, how can you expect him to grow into a talented and morally superior person, and eventually be able to preserve what he has inherited from you? For me, I'd rather count on my son's virtue and talent. In this manner, even though I've left him nothing, won't it seem much more generous than you do?"

The man listened but said nothing, and left without a word.

*

Book Shadow
By Zhou Lianggong (1612-1673 A.D.) styled himself Yuanliang, assumed name Liyuan; originally from Xiangfu, Henan (Kaifeng). A palace graduate in the last years of the Ming Dynasty, and a writer in the early years of the Qing Dynasty, he had successively held the posts of deputy minister of the Ministry of Revenue, and the official in charge of land taxes in Jiang-an, Jiangnan, during the the periods of Shunzhi, title of emperor Shizu (1644-1661 A.D.), and Kangxi, title of emperor Shengzu (1662-1722 A.D.). An adept in poetry and an essayist, he was called "Master Lixia" by then scholars. He authored more than ten books, such as *The Collected Poems of Laigutang, Book Shadow of Yinshu House,* and so on. *Book Shadow of Yinshu House,* also known as *Book Shadow,* consists of ten volumes. It is a book of miscellaneous articles, notes and commentaries of poetry and essays, some of which may be regarded as fables.

868. The Parrot and the Crested Myna

In our district Bianliang, there was a street where shops selling mountain products aggregated. One of the shopkeepers there kept a parrot which was very smart. In the East Gate, there was another shop whose owner raised a crested myna, which could talk like a man. On one occasion, both shopkeepers brought their birds together for a competition. The parrot recited a poem first, and the myna echoed. The voices of both birds were equally resonant and pleasant, and neither side had the better of the other.

After the parrot finished reciting the poem, it refused to open its mouth for a second time. No matter how hard the myna tried to provoke it, the parrot simply would not say a single word.

Later, someone asked the parrot why didn't it sing again. The parrot replied, "The crested myna's voice is no match for mine, but its cunning surpasses me. If I open my mouth, it will immediately steal and imitate."

*

*The Collected Works of Tianjian
By Qian Chengzhi (1612-1693 A.D.) styled himself Youguang, or Yinguang; originally from the city of Tong, Anhui Province. A successful candidate in the lowest level of civil service examination, and a writer of the Qing Dynasty, he attained the rank of senior licentiate in the capital for his knowledge of the Chinese classics. Together with Chen Zilong, Xia Yunyi and others, he took part in organizing the Cloud Dragon Society. Later, to evade the disaster resulting from partisanship, he escaped to Fujian and Zhejiang. After the turmoil had subsided, he returned to his native village and became a recluse, calling himself Tianjian the Old Man. He was the author of *The Poetics of Tianjian, Tianjian on the Book of Changes,* and so on. The following fable was selected from his collected works.

869. Strange Tale of a Bird Nest

At the foot of the Southern Mountain, there was a bird nest in the cassia forest, and a sparrow hawk and a turtledove were fighting for its occupation. However, the turtledove was no match for the sparrow hawk. At this critical juncture, the prince of Chu happened to pass the place, and the turtledove stretched out its neck, cried piteously to the prince, and flew to his bosom of its own accord. Thus the prince took the turtledove under his protection. The sparrow hawk, which did not know the turtledove was now under the protection of the prince, continued to stretch its neck and fly forward, crying angrily all the time, as if telling people why it had behaved in this way, and confident of its being right. But the prince was unable to decide the case. His hanger-on, who stood by his side, ventured an opinion, saying, "The sparrow hawk is the stronger party, and the turtledove is the weaker side. A great man should help the weak and remove the powerful." The sparrow hawk responded with a sneer, saying, "It is true I'm a sparrow hawk, but the other side is also a hawk, although it looks like a turtledove. I'm sure in the end it will let you down." The prince did not believe its words and drove the sparrow hawk away. He told the hanger-on to get a ladder, carried the turtledove to the treetop and put it inside the nest.

When it was in the bosom of the prince, the turtledove was indeed a turtledove. However, the moment it was put in the nest, it became a hawk. As the hawk had successfully occupied the nest, it leaned back and, staring with wide open eyes, spoke to the hanger-on with an arrogant air, saying, "I do not need your help. When I give out a cry from the nest, all the birds will fold their wings and obediently listen to my order. The sphere of my influence is enormous! The turtledove has now willingly acknowledged defeat. It's strange that the prince thought I was unable to enter the nest and must rely on your assistance to climb up the ladder and send me here!" This said, it roused every feather of its body, inclined its head, and threatened to strike him down. The hanger-on was greatly frightened and went down the ladder hastily to report to the prince. The prince was stunned, saying, "Oh, what a surprise! At the time when I saw it stretch its neck and cry piteously, it was indeed a turtledove. How could it be a hawk!"

With each passing day, the beak and claws of the hawk grew even stronger, and it went out to hunt for food more often. The nestlings of the sparrow nests in the vicinity were unavoidably grabbed, and the young chicks people kept were snatched if they happened to get out of the chicken coop. People raised a hubbub, trying to drive the hawk away, but the hawk would not leave, and the people vented their anger on the prince of Chu, blaming him for causing all the trouble. The prince heard the complaints and sighed, saying, "Alas! I thought it was a turtledove then. How could I know it was a hawk. I feel ashamed to have driven the sparrow hawk away!"

*

*The Chunhantang Collection of Poems and Essays
By Zhou Rong (1619-1679 A.D.) styled himself Maoshan, assumed name Biweng; originally from Yin County, Zhejiang (Ningbo); an adherent of former Ming Dynasty. He had been a successful candidate in the lowest level of civil service examination under the former system. After the dynasty of Qing replaced Ming, he refused to take official job and became a recluse, given to pleasures among the mountains and waters. *The Biography of Old Man Yu*, which was selected from

The Chunhantang Collection of Poems and essays., harshly attacked the sordid conduct of those scholars who forgot their origin once achieved success in their official career, and who threw themselves at the feet of the enemy.

870. The Biography of Old Man Yu

Old Man Yu was originally from Cishui's Zhu ferry-place. His son left home to work as a hired hand, while the old man and his wife lived at the ferry crossing. One day, a scholar came to take shelter from rain under their eaves. Thinly clad, and soaked to the skin, he looked gaunt and delicate. The old man invited him in and sat down. Subsequently, he learned that the young man had gone to the prefecture for the imperial examination at county level and had just come back. The old man had some knowledge of poetry himself, and he talked with the scholar for a long time. He then asked his wife to cook a pot of taro to entertain his guest. The scholar took two bowls before he had enough. Smiling, he said to the old man, "I'll never forget the taro meal grandpa gives me today." As the rain had stopped, the scholar took leave. Ten years had elapsed, and the scholar of former days had become the prime minister. One day, he suddenly had an impulse to eat taro, and ordered the chef to cook it. Having Tasted a few mouthfuls, he discovered it was not as good as he thought, so he put down the chopsticks, sighed and said, "Why is it this taro does not taste as delicious as the one I had in the house of the old man of Zhu Ferry?" He sent someone to visit the old couple at Zhu Ferry, and took them to the capital in a carriage. When the county magistrate and the military officer and other officials learned that the prime minister and the old man used to be good friends, they all behaved according to the prevailing rules of etiquette when they met. The old man's son, naturally, would not have to work again as a hired hand. As they arrived at the capital, the prime minister, having extended his greetings to the old man, said, "In order not to forget your taro, may I ask your good wife to cook some today." Soon the old woman had the taro cooked and brought to the table. The prime minister took two mouthfuls, and then put down his chopsticks, saying, "Why was it the taro tasted so good before?" The old man replied, "This taro is as good as the one before. It tastes different not because the recipe is different, but because the time and your position have changed. Previously, you had just covered tens of *li* from the perfecture to arrive at my place and was stranded by the heavy rain. As the saying goes, 'hunger finds no fault with the cookery'. It is quite different now. At home, you have all kinds of delicacies and fine dishes, in the imperial court you have partaken of the emperor's food, and enjoyed banquets all the time. Under such circumstances, how can you feel the deliciousness of the taro? It made me happy to know that Your Excellency still remember the past and the taro, although you don't feel it as tasty as before. I've become rather old now, and heard too much about everything. In the southern side of our village, there was an impoverished couple. The wife did the daily chores and provided an environment for her husband to persevere in his studies in spite of hardship. Later, her husband was fortunate enough to achieve success and win recognition, but then he became morally degenerated, married a concubine, and abandoned his wife by the first marriage. Thus his wife eventually died of melancholy. That is to say, he looked upon his wife as the taro, which became tasteless. In the eastern side of the city, there were two fellow students, who used to share an inkstone, light a common lamp, sit at the same window and sleep in one bed. In the morning, they could not even differentiate the clothes and shoes of one from those of the other, and often put on the wrong ones. Later, when B became a provincial graduate and held an official post, while A was still poverty-stricken and without a position, his erstwhile friend looked upon him with a sneer and never again cast an eye at him. As a result, they had severed relations. This was treating his friend like the taro, its taste changed as the positions differed. I've heard of the son of a certain family, who had once vowed that if he should be successful in the imperial examination, he would become an honest official, taking the virtuous and upright officials of yore as examples, loyal and patriotic. In the end, however, he was dismissed for taking bribes and bending the law. This was to treat what he learned before like the taro, the moment he became rich and prosperous, the taste changed. There are more examples that can be cited. There to my west is a school. The master there teaches the pupils about the people and events of the past: generals and ministers, high-ranking officials and governors, prefectural governors, prefectural magistrates, county magistrates,—all important persons either in charge of the golden seal with a purple ribbon, or rode on fine horses, or sat in luxurious sedan chairs. However, in time of emergency, when aliens invaded the country, these people surrendered immediately, vying with one another to bend their knees and welcome the enemy for fear of being left behind. They looked upon the ancestral temples, the state, position, reputation and all the favors the emperor had bestowed upon them, etc. etc., as the taro, all without taste. As I see it, in this world of ours, the reflection of those who forget yesterday because of today is not confined to a pair of chopsticks!"

Before the old man had finished talking, the prime minister could not help being shocked and his clothes wetted with cold sweat. He hastened to thank the old man, saying, "Venerable sir, you certainly understand the great truth!" And he presented the old man with very generous giftrs and sent him back to his native land. Bucause of the event, the old man's reputation spread far and wide.

*

Interpreting History
By Ma Su (1621-1673 A.D.) styled himself Wansi, or Congyu; originally from Zouping, Shandong Province; a historian of the Qing Dynasty. He specialized in ancient history and was called "The Three Generations of Ma". *Interpreting History* contains one hundred and sixty volumes, chronicling the history from ancient times to the end of the Qin Dynasty with abundant materials, detailed research, and effectiveness. The part dealing with the events after the Spring and Autumn Period is even more meticulous in its narration and compilation.

871. Rich Man

Once upon a time, a scholar and a rich family were neighbours. Because he was so desperately destitute all his life, the scholar had always been jealous of his neighbour's wealth and happiness. One day, dressed in his best, he paid a visit to his neighbour and asked for the recipe to get rich.

His neighbour said, "It isn't easy to get rich! You go back and be a vegetarian for three days; then come back and I'll tell you how it can be done."

The scholar did as his neighbour had instructed, and came back to pay his neighbour a second visit. The rich neighbour asked him to wait outside the screen. He then prepared a little high table, put away the gift the scholar brought to honour the master before joining his hands together in salute and asked him to enter. "Generally speaking, in order to get rich, one must first of all get rid of five thieves," he said. "Unless one gets rid of the five thieves, wealth cannot be realized."

The scholar asked him to name the five thieves.

"They are what people refer to as love, justice, propriety, wisdom and honesty, the five primal faiths."

The scholar was speechless after he heard the clarification, and he left hurriedly.

*

*Wu Guan Writes in an Outspoken Manner
By Wu Zhuang (1624-? A.D.), assumed name the Old Man of Sixty-one. A writer of Qing Dynasty, he authored *The Innocent Grass, Wu Guan Writes in an Outspoken Manner*, and others.

872. The Pine, the Bamboo and the Plum

The pine, the bamboo and the plum have all along been called the three great friends. Someone calumniated the bamboo in front of the pine and the plum, trying to drive a wedge between them, saying, "The bamboo is hollow inside. How can it be your friend?" The pine and the plum were infuriated by such slanderous words, saying, "It is worthy to be our friends precisely because it is hollow inside. This is upheld by what people refer to as: 'It remains hollow with nothing inside, in order to accomodate more than several hundred people with pride'!"

873. The Purple Swallow and the Golden Oriole

The purple swallow and the golden oriole soared in the sky together, and the golden oriole asked the purple swallow, "Where are you going back to?" The purple swallow replied, "I'm going back to my room in the hall, where men live." In turn, it asked the golden oriole, "And you, where are you going back to?" "I'm going back to the willow forest," the golden oriole replied.

"In the long run, the willow forest is not as safe as the hall," the purple swallow said.

"That isn't so," the golden oriole disagreed. "The willows grow in nature, while the hall is built by man. In the daytime, I gambol among the soft withies, and at night I can rest on the branches thick with leaves. I can soar at will, and the fear of being driven outside the door or imprisoned inside the room has never occurred to me. I sing with my heavenly voice which is nature to me, and which may even be mistaken as the beautiful music performed with the traditional stringed and woodwind instruments, the flutes and the pipes. While playing in the willow forest, I sometimes wander away from it, but the willow forest is there all the time, whereas you live in the hall of man, and there may be times when you want to get in but cannot and times when you want to get out but being locked inside. If you twitter too much in the hall, you may be blamed for being too noisy. Besides, the owner of the hall may be in prosperity or decline, the house itself may be enlarged or demolished. While the owner is rich and thriving, you may not benefit from it, but when the owner's fortune is in the decline, when he is impoverished, you may be in trouble. Yet despite all these inconveniences, you still feel conplacent for being able to live in the hall. This is ridiculous and you should be sneered at like what people do to the sparrows!"

The purple swallow concurred. "You have spoken well!" it said.

*

*The Book of Great Concentration
By Tang Zhen (1630-1704 A.D.) styled himself Zhuwan, assumed name Putting; originally from Dazhou, Sichuan Province; a thinker in the early years of Qing Dynasty. A successful candidate in the imperial examination at the provincial level in the period of Shunzhi, he had once held the post of county magistrate. *The Book of Great Concentration* contains ninety-seven articles. Its original title was *The Yardstick*, for reason of its similarity in style to Wang Chong's *On Yardstick*. The present title was adopted later. The first fifty articles are mostly on academic subjects and the other forty-seven articles deal with politics. Fables and stories are often used as figures of speech to illustrate his point, and are both interesting and lively.

874. Good Physician

Once upon a time, a man was bitten by a poisonous worm and near death, but a good physician from Huoqiu came to his rescue. At the first treatment of the acupuncture needle, he came to; at the second, he could stand up and move about. After taking five decoctions of medicinal ingredients, he fully recovered. The news spread rapidly, and the physician was held up as a supernatural being descended from heaven. For that reason, the rich would invite him to their home should any family member fall ill. Patients throughout the length and breadth of the territory would come to him for treatment. Some would pay him a visit just to see what he looked like. And he became so busy that he did not have a moment to himself. A visitor praised the physician before Tangzi, saying, "Since you have such a marvellous physician, no illness need be worried about, provided he is there." Tangzi refuted him, saying, "Your words are the medium through which diseases spread, and an axe whereby people are hurt. In future, if people do not take preventive measures against diseases because there is a physician here and get themselves killed, your words will have been the cause of it."

875. An Expert at Planning and Management

A man in Zhenze was known for his expertise in planning and management. With his help, crop would double its yield, silk production would increase two-fold, and business too, would earn twice as much. One day, this man happened to pass the front gate of a rich and powerful family where he saw those employed there wear marten hats and fox fur overcoats. His mind was perturbed and thought, "In the village, I only associate myself with the peck and hamper people, and the businessmen are but hawkers selling fish and salt, mere trifles, which is not the way to get rich. If I can worm my way into this family and, if I'm fortunate enough to get an important position with which I can show my talent in management, I'm sure it will be much more satisfying. Why must I stay in the village, and be a fool for all my pains." Thereupon he sought help from a third party and successfully crossed the threshold into this rich and powerful family. After that, he returned to bid farewell to his neighbour. His neighbour was worried, saying, "You have got the wrong notion. The job in that family may not be suited to your talent. I'd strongly dissuade you from going." But he would not listen, and left all the same. A year later, the neighbour accidentally met with this management expert near the house of the rich and powerful family while on a business trip. The latter emerged from the house with a sickly look, wearing a tattered robe. His neighbour called him to a quiet place and asked him, "What has become of you?" "My talent is not needed here, and that's why," the management wizard replied. His neighbour smiled and said, "So you understand now! This is a rich and powerful family whose wealth derives from plunder. What they require are falcons and hounds—hired thugs. The cereals they consume do not come from their own field, the silks on their body are not produced by the silkworms they reared, and the utensils in the house are not bought. You have hoped to put your talent to good use, but what makes you think they will need it? I've predicted you would, in the end, get into such a plight at the time you left us." Thereupon the planning expert left the rich and powerful family, and followed his neighbour back to the village. Since this happened, people invariably reproved him, saying his ideas were mstaken. Actually, his mistake was not in solving problems, but in not smart enough to know his master.

876. Driving out the Insects from the Mosquito Net

When she was a little girl, Tangzi's wife used to sleep with her elder sister in the same bed. Her elder sister let her drive the mosquitoes from inside the curtain, but she was very reluctant to do so. One night, she simply drove the mosquitoes away from the space she occupied, and laid down the curtain. Her mother asked her why she did that, she replied, "Where can I find time to do things for other people. I can only take care of my own affairs." The Confucian doctrine of serving oneself was very similar to the notion of Tangzi's wife.

877. The Sick Girl Tips the Decoction

On the eastern side of Huiqi City, there was a family surnamed Shi. Their little daughter was ill, and a good physician was invited to treat her. However, many days had elapsed and her illness did not improve, and so the physician had to be dismissed. The little girl's father knew the physician he invited was a good physician with consummate skill, but why was it the illness of his daughter did not appear to improve? One day, he quietly hid himself nearby to watch on the sly. He saw his daughter take the decoction but, instead of drinking, she tipped it under the bed. Suddenly it dawned on him and the famous physician was recalled. The same medicine was prescribed. This time the father made sure his daughter took the medicine. After three decoctions, she recovered completely.

The decree of a state will be ineffectual and useless if not enforced among its people. It is comparable to.the Shi family's daughter taking her decoction.

878. Wu County's Famous Physician

There was a famous physician in Wu County, Jiangsu Province, who dressed himself in pretty clothes, rode in luxurious carriage, and had a ruddy complexion as if painted with red powder. His tongue too was as nimble as a revolving axle, eloquent, and able to achieve success one way or another. People who were ill would insist on drinking only the decoction he prescribed. If recovered, the patient would say, "The physician is skilful indeed." On the other hand, if the patient died, his family would say, "Even though the physician may be outstanding, it is of course impossible to revive a dead man." The physician, needless to say, did not have to be responsible for the death of his patient. His name became even more eminent day after day and the reward, handsomer. This was because people were too credulous and easily deceived by his presentation. midway, he could neither advance nor retreat, his own strength being unequal to that of other people, his legs weaker than most. Under such circumstances, could he lie down and wait for death to come? There was only one way out, and that was to extricate himself from the difficult position through his own efforts.

879. The Good Man of Jiangli

Previously there lived in Jiangli, Sichuan Province, an honest man who was bent on doing good and shunned evil deeds. Sincere and thrustworthy, he had never been found to take advantage of other people. He was respected in his own village and, without even having to sign a certificate of indebtedness, a rich man was willing to lend him a large aum of money. He used the money to do business in Shaanxi and Luoyang, following the same stereotype in his own village. His method, however, was not appreciated, and the people there did not like to do business with him. In three years, he lost all his capital and had to return to his own village.

880. A Man of Chu Contracted Eye Cataract

A man of the state of Chu contracted eye cataract. One day, he said to his wife, "My eyes have recovered, and I can see the big tree above the room of our neighbour." His wife told him, "There is no tree above the neighbour's room." He went to a temple in Xiangshan to pray; again, he said to his servant, "My eyes have recovered, and I've seen a thoroughfare accessible from all directions. Isn't the hubbub caused by the carriages and pedestrians on the road?" His servant told him, "What you see are mountains and water. Where does the thoroughfare accessible from all directions come from?" Seeing tree where there was no tree, seeing road where there was no road, how could he say his eyes had recovered? The truth was, his eyes were abnormal. Now, when one says he knows a thing but actually does not, or says he understands but it isn't true, how can we say his mind is clear. The truth is, something must have gone wrong with his mind.

881. The Skill of Ice Engraving

Formerly there was an ice engraving artist who could carve the ice into a person wearing clothes with red and green articles for personal adornment, which was almost lifelike, and as big as a real man in size. The weather of Peking was extremely cold, and so it would not change shape even if placed at the back of the hall for one or two days. If there were indeed some little changes took place, they could be corrected with minor touches. Everyday there were several hundred people viewing his art work, and everyone was amazed by its ingenuity. One day, he said to the visitors, "I'll pass on the skill of ice engraving to whoever can offer three *dou* (one *dou*= one decalitre) of corn." There was no response. Someone asked the ice carver, "You are indeed highly skillful. But why don't you carve metals and jades, making objects as those seen in the eras of Xia, Shang, Zhou and Han, which can be stored for a long time without being damaged. What you engrave now are playthings. Although vivid and true to life, it will melt very soon. I feel sorry for your artistic talent, superb but without practical value. It can entertain people for a short period of time, but cannot be handed down to future generations!"

882. The Powerful Qin Si is Overpowered by a Guest

When Tang Zhen was young, he once accompanied his uncle to a banquet. Present at the table was a powerful man called Qin Si, who could lift a thousand catties. He had stormed and shattered enemy positions in battle, where none could thwart his advance. He often travelled in the mountains and lakes all by himself, and single-handedly fought on equal terms against a dozen people. Tang Zhen's uncle pointed at a guest and jokingly said to Qin Si, "Despite his emaciated appearance, this guest of mine loves pugilism, and has often yearned to defeat you. Why don't you two have a contest now." Qin Si smiled and said, "Come, come!" Thereupon he laid down the wine cup and left the table. He was still looking around talking with the people and had not yet taken a firm foothold when the guest suddenly gave him a punch, which sent him to the floor, and all the guests applauded.

In point of strength, a hundred man like the guest would not be able to defeat Qin Si. His victory came from the element of surprise. In military operations, surprise attack had always been carried out with remarkable result since ancient times.

883. Han Sheng's Prediction

In the past, because of his perchant for hunting, the king of Qin had often harassed the people. Recently he again gathered the hunters in the northern suburbs. A day before the impending event, people in the northern district began to make preparations for leaving, but a certain Han Sheng dissuaded them, saying, "The king's son has fallen ill for three days, and the king is worried. He will not leave the palace to hunt." What happened subsequently proved his prediction to be correct. Someone asked Han Sheng, "Even I, who is a palace guard on night duty, do not know the king's beloved son is ill. How do you come to know it?" Han Sheng replied, "I've heard that the king's son loves flying kites. Recently I watched the palace from an elevated place, and for three days I did not see the little prince's kite, and that's how I came to know his illness."

From what appears on the surface the subtleties of what within can be known by inference. Based on the knowledge thus obtained, a wise man can draw up a clear-cut plan of action, although the foolish might still be vacilating. If a person can provide accurately the unapparent details of an oncoming enemy as Han Sheng had done, he may truly be called a man of great wisdom!

884. Seedlings and the Rain

I had inspected the condition of the farmland. There had been a long drought, and the seedlings near withered. In Central Wu, labour hands for agriculture were adequate and the sound of waterwheel was heard everywhere. However, by the time the eastern side of the field was irrigated, the western part had already dried up. Even though labour hands might be in ample supply, they still could not cope with the situation. But, as the *yang* element reached its zenith, the *yin* aspect began to take over, and the vapours gathered and clouds formed. In just a matter of less than one morning, the whole space between heaven and earth was taken over by clouds and mists, and rain fell in torrents. The downpour continued and, upon waking up the next morning, all the seedlings had once more stood erect. In the ditches and ridges of the field, the twigs and leaves of the vines and grasses all turned green. Man might be diligent, but the result can hardly be compared to the universality of rain and dew.

885. Human Feelings

In those days long past, Tangzi went abroad to study, and came to Ning Sheng's family school. At that time, he and Ning Sheng were both at their early youth. They slept in the same bed, and prepared and ate their meals together when hungry, as if they were brothers. Upon Tangzi's departure, Ning Sheng accompanied him aboard ship and, as they took leave of one another, their eyes were wet with tears. After the boat had set sail, Ning Sheng was still reluctant to part, and continued to run along the shore in pursuit of the boat until the passenger boat disappeared from sight. Ten years later, when they met again, they became very refined and courteous towards one another, their feelings had already somewhat drifted apart. Then another ten years passed them by when Tangzi happened to stay overnight at Ning Sheng's family school. Incidentally, there was a guest in the house and, at mealtime, the guest sat at Ning Sheng's right, while Tangzi was on his left. During the course of the meal, Ning Sheng invariably helped the guest on his right with the dish as a matter of priority and, whenever a toast was proposed, it was always the right side first. Even when he talked and joked, his face always turned to the right. Came the next day, when Tangzi was about to leave, he excused himself for being engaged, and did not go to see him off. This caused Tangzi to recall the past and sigh with emotion, saying, "A boy does not have the wisdom of a man. Why is it the feelings of man are so simple and honest when young, but weakening and indifferent as he grows older, when they should have increased? It is because a child had not yet come into contact with the society and, consequently, his disposition follows the path of nature. When he becomes older, with his experience in life, his disposition will depart further and further from his natural instincts."

*

*Ten Assorted Subjects
By Wang Zhuo (1636-? A.D.), a bibliophile and writer in the early years of the Qing Dynasty. He was named Fei originally, assumed name Mu An and, alternatively, Danlu and Song Xizi; a native of Renhe, Zhejiang Province (Hangzhou). A successful candidate in the lowest level of cvil service examination of the period of Shunzhi, he was a book lover and widely-read. The books he collected reached tens of thousands. He also block-printed the edition of *The Sandelwood Table Book Series*. Writer of *This Present Life, The Collection of Xiajutang, Ten Assorted Subjects, The Verse of My Humble Cottage East of the Wall*, and so on. *Ten Assorted Subjects* contains ten volumes, one of which being fables.

886. Brambles

In the Zhongnan mountain, there was a trail full of brambles. Those brambles had twigs, which were soft and supple and with thorns as thick as huckleberries. Anyone came into contact with the brambles would be hooked and twined, making it difficult to extricate himself and impossible to avoid being hurt. People were afraid of the thorny pricks and had to make a detour to bypass the trail.

A man, out of righteous indignation, lifted up his garment and went to work with intent to break the brambles one by one so that pedestrians could walk along it. What he did not expect was, when a twig on the left was just being snapped off, his right arm was hooked by another twig, while his trousers were also entangled with the brambles. As a result, he soon became exhausted without being able to do much.

A man of virtue said, "This man should be applauded for abhorring things that were bad. However, he had not used the proper method to do it. If he utilized a big axe and cut the brambles away together with all the roots, would not the brambles be cleared completely?"

887. The Pine Tree

It is the nature of pine tree to grow straight and upright. Even when it is only a few feet high, it tends to be as straight as a ramrod. There are people who transplant them to a flower pot, and display it in a grandiose hall, twisting its twigs and branches here and there, and call it bonsai, or potted landscape. When fertilizer is applied, with proper watering, its branches and leaves will become luxuriant, and grow into the shape of a small umbrella. Not that the bonsai is unfit for appreciation, but that if we compare it with the green pine in the lofty mountain and steep hill, where its branches and trunk point straight towards the blue sky, high up in the air, luxuriantly green, which has withstood the frost and the snow;—if we compare the bonsai with all this, then it will seem how insignificant and unreal it is!

888. A Dog

A family in the east side of the city kept a dog; the dog was thin and weak. One night, the house of the family next door sudddenly caught fire, and the fire quickly spread to the family with the dog. All members of the family were soundly asleep and, despite the howling of the dog, they had not been wakened up. Then the dog began to pull their quilt, but they continued to sleep. Finally, the dog pressed its mouth close to their ears and barked aloud, succeeding in waking them up with a start. Seeing that the entire house was covered with thick smoke, the owner hastened to send his wife and children out of it, but the house itself was reduced to ashes. After the event, the master of the family told his relatives, saying, "We are too poor to let this dog eat enough, and have never expected it to help all the four members of the family escape a disaster like this. What will those who normally enjoy good food of others, yet do not want to share their adversity, think, when they learn about what this dog has done?"

*Random Writings in the Kanshan Pavilion

By Huang Tubi. Neither the dates of birth and death nor his life were known. Block-printed edition existed during the period of Kangxi, which was the title of emperor Shengzu of the Qing Dynasty. Based on this information, he should live in the early years of the Qing Dynasty.

889. Wandering Buffalo

On account of avarice, a big bureaucrat was dismissed from his office and reduced to the status of a common citizen. To save his face, he pretended he resigned his post to become a recluse. He bought a parcel of land in a famous scenic spot with hills and waters and constructed a manor on the hilltop, and there he lived.

Having constructed the manor, he next invited a famous painter to paint it on a scroll, so that he could show off to other people the beauty of his manor of forest and spring. When the painting was completed, the painter added a wandering buffalo by the water's edge beside the forest.

When the big bureaucrat saw the buffalo, he asked, "What's the meaning of drawing a buffalo there?"

"Without a buffalo on it, this scenic spot of mountains and forests would seem too lonesome," the painter replied.

890. The Dongpo Meat

A certain man liked to study Su Dongpo's essays but, despite his diligence, he had achieved very little. His devotion to Dongpo's essays, however, was whole-hearted and complete, as he had put in a lot of effort and never ever slackened. He ate a piece of square meat weighing about two catties a day. It so happened a friend came to pay him a visit at the very moment he was eating it and asked him what was he having? The man replied, "Dongpo meat!" His friend teased him, saying, "Why do you hate Su Dongpo so much!"*

(*The Chinese character *rou* means either flesh or meat. *Dongpo meat* is the name of a dish, while the flesh of Dongpo is another thing.)

891. The Coin's Eye

A County magistrate was extremely avaricious and, whenever he received a written complaint from the people, he would look for an opportunity, however slight, to squeeze some money from the complainant, and he did so by drawing a coin's eye as a sign at the lower corner of the paper on which the complaint was written. As this had been a practice of long standing, all the people knew it was the county magistrate's ground rule. Thus those who got entangled in a lawsuit would come together to inform one another the secret of winning it. They all said, "Our magistrate only focusses his attention on the coin's eye."

892. A Couplet Pledge

A county magistrate hung a couplet on the wall of the *yamen* to advertise himself as an upright and intelligent official. The couplet read, "May Heaven strike me dead if I covet one cash; call me an out-and-out scoundrel if I pracitse favouritism once." However, despite his vow, numerous people continued to bribe him with money and gifts, and he never declined. Whenever the local despotic gentry and the rich family asked for favour, he would, as a rule, bend the law for their benefit. Someone reminded him, saying, "Sir, it's not right. Have you forgotten the couplet in the hall? How can you take bribes and bend the law in such a way?" The county magistrate roared with laughter, saying, "What I've done does not violate the pledge of the couplet. I received more than one cash, and took bribes and bent the law certainly more than once. How can I be struck dead by Heaven and become an out-and-out scoundrel?"

893. Money and Life are Joined

An old man was taking a stroll at the bank of the Qiantang River and saw a coin on the beach, so he stepped over to pick it up. Suddenly the tide rose, swift as a galloping steed and with noise like the thunderclap. The old man was too slow to take shelter and got swept off his feet by the tide and drowned. The next day, his body was seen attached to a big tree floating on the water. As people retrieved the corpse, they saw him still grip the coin firmly in his hand. Spectators all sighed and said, "Surely this man understands the essence of the saying that wealth and life are joined!"

After a Few Glasses of Wine
By Niu Xiu (?-1704 A.D.) styled himself Yuqiao; originally from Wujiang, Jiangsu Province. A writer in the early years of the Qing Dynasty, he was selected to the capital for the civil service examination as an outstanding young scholar in the eleventh year of Kangxi (1672 A.D.), title of emperor Shengzu of Qing. He had successively held the posts of county magistrate in Henan, Shaanxi, Guangdong and other provinces, and was the author of *The Collection of Linyetang*, etc. *After a Few Glasses of Wine* recorded miscellaneous events in the last years of Ming and the early years of Qing. His literary style was deeply beautiful and moving, having the uplifting mood of the novels of Tang authors.

894. When a Ghost Turns Out to be a Leopard Cat

In the Lu Village, there was a family surnamed Yan. It was a famous family of long standing but on the decline. All the pavilions, terraces, and open halls were overgrown with underbrush and crumbling as the family did not have the resources to renovate them.

A guest once came to pay them a visit and was lodged upstairs in one of the extensions, where the handrails were broken, the lattice windows dilapidated and the tables were covered with dust; altogether it was a very bleak and desolate environment. The guest felt uneasy and, when night came, he slept with his head under the quilt. Suddenly he heard steps one story above him, *click-clack*, and he became panicky, thinking it must be a ghost. Gradually, the steps came nearer to his bed, and the guest was so frightened that he ventured to peek from a corner of the quilt. He saw a little devil, short in stature, lift the curtain and go into the bed. This gave the guest a terrible shock and, abruptly, he sprang up, spread open the quilt, and wrapped the ghost with it. Now that the ghost was covered with the quilt, he jumped atop of it stark naked, holding it under, yet all the time feared it might escape. Thus he sat until the day broke, when the host came to see him get out of bed. Together they uncovered the quilt, only to discover it was the leopard cat, which the family kept to catch the sparrows. It was not a ghost after all.

Random Conversation North of the Pond
By Wang Shizhen (1634-1711 A.D.) styled himself Yishang, assumed name Ruanting, or, The Recluse of Yuyang; originally from Xincheng, Shandong Province. After his death, to avoid emperor Shizong's taboo, his descendants had his name changed to Shizheng. During the reign of emperor Gaozong, titled Qianlong, a decree was issued to have the name again changed to Shizhen. A palace graduate in the period of Shunzhi, he was once the minister of the Ministry of Punishments. A major poet in the early years of the Qing Dynasty, he led the literary world for tens of years, and left with a large number of works, the most important being *The Collected Poems of Yuyang, Outline of Yuyang Essays, The Best of Yuyang Recluse, Random Conversation North of the Pond, Notes of Xiangzu*, and so on.

895. The Prime Minister's Grandson

There was a certain prime minister from Jiangsu Province, whose family fortune had declined after his death. On one occasion, his grandson had to borrow rice from another man. Midway on his journey home, he could no longer carry the rice bag and had to hire someone, whom he thought was a pauper, to carry it for him. The hired hand, however, only carried it for a short distance and began to gasp for breath. The prime minister's grandson complained about his slowness and, eventually giving vent to anger, said, "I was born in the prime minster's family and used to live a life of ease. It is, therefore, understandable that I do not have the strength to bear the weight of the rice. You, however, come from a poor family. Why are you sush a useless fellow as well!" The hired hand was furious. He put the bag of rice down and refuted him, "Who says I'm a pauper? I'm the grandson of a minister!"

A Collection of Bizarre Stories
By Pu Songling (1640-1715 A.D.) styled himself Liuxian and Jianchen, assumed name Retired Scholar Liuquan, originally from Zichuan, Shandong Province (Zibo); a writer of Qing Dynasty. At nineteen, he had successively passed the civil service examinations at county, prefecture and district levels, but failed in all subsequent attempts until he was seventy-one, when he became a selected scholar.

Throughout his life, except for one year, during which he served as a high official's house guest and adviser, he stayed in the village as the tutor of a family school for over fifty years. He spent the energy of his whole life collecting popular legends and unusual stories and compiled them into the book *A Collection of Bizarre Stories,* contents of which were mainly tales about fox spirits, which he used as a medium to deride and expose the seamy side of society. Writing in a lively style, with strong flavour of romanticism, it became the most outstanding novel written in classical Chinese and an immortal masterpiece. Quite a few vivacious fables are found in the book.

Apart from *A Collection of Bizarre Stories,* Pu Songling was also the author of *A Collection of Essays in Liaozhai, The Collected Poems in Liaozhai, Folk Songs of Liaozhai, The Canon of Agriculture and Sericulture,* etc., books for popular consumption.

896. Teasing One's Own Daughter-in-law

A village scholar was strolling with two friends on the road when, in the distance, a young woman on a donkey came into sight, and he recited jokingly, "There comes a beautiful lady!" Having thus recited, he turned to tell his friends, "Let's run after her!" Thereupon he spurred his horse forward, giggling as he did so.

Soon he overtook the young woman and discovered it was actually his own daughter-in-law. Instantly the flush of shame spread all over his face and he hung his head, becoming as mute as a fish. His friends pretended ignorance, and continued to remark upon her appearance, alsolutely on the loose.

The scholar felt very embarrassed as he jabbered out, "This is the wife of my eldest son!" At this, the two friends sniggered and separated.

Harm set, harm get. The consequence of frivolous behaviour is apt to recoil upon oneself.

897. Grow a Pear Tree

A villager went to the country fair to sell his pears. His pears were luscious and crisp, but the price was rather high. A poor Taoist priest with tattered clothes came before the pear cart to beg. The pear vendor drove him away, but the Taoist priest refused to budge. The pear vendor became angry and berated him. The Taoist priest said, "There are hundreds of pears in your cart, and I only ask for one. It should not be too much of a loss to you. Why should you be angry?" A spectator also put in a word for the Taoist priest, urging the pear vendor to choose a smaller one and gave it to him so as to send him away. But the pear vendor turned a deaf ear to his plea.

A shop assistant next door, seeing that they kicked up a great deal of fuss about trifles, became impatient and took out some money of his own to buy a pear for the Taoist priest. The Taoist priest thanked him and turned to speak to the people there, saying, "We Taoist priests don't understand why people are so stingy. I've such a delicious pear now; may I present it to all of you here and let everyone have a bite." Someone said, "Since it was given to you, why don't you eat it yourself?" "I only want the kernel as seed," he replied. This said, he began to eat in earnest. When he had almost finished it, he put the kernel in his hand, removed the small iron spade from his shoulder, dug a hole of a few square inches with it, put the kernel inside and covered it with yellow soil. Then he stood up, asking the bystanders to give him some water. An officious person went to a nearby shop and brought out a pot of boiling water. The Taoist priest poured it into the hole. At that moment, everyone's attention was drawn to the hole, where they saw a young shoot twisting its way out of the earth, grew gradually until it became a big tree with luxuriant folliage and spreading branches. In the twinkling of an eye, it began to blossom, and soon it bore fruit. The pears it produced were big and sweet, hanging all over the tree in clusters. The Taoist priest climbed up the fork of the tree trunk, picked the pears, and distributed them to all the spectators. Soon the pears were all gone. The Taoist priest took down his spade and began to chop down the tree. For a long time, only the sound of chopping was heard; then the tree fell down. He put the leafy branches on his shoulder and, calmly and unhurriedly, he walked away.

Now, as the Taoist priest was practising his magic arts, the pear vendor too wormed his way into the crowd and stretched his neck to see the fun, completely forgetting that he was there to sell the pears. After the Taoist priest had left, he recalled what he was there for, and went back to the pear cart, but it was already empty. Suddenly it dawned on him that the pears the Taoist priest distributed were all his. He looked closer, and discovered further that one of the shafts of his cart was broken, and the mark of the breakage was evidently new. He felt very resentful and at once proceeded to look for the Taoist priest. As he turned the street corner, he saw one half of the shaft lying at the foot of the wall. Now he knew the branch chopped down by the Taoist priest was part of the shaft. He became despondently dejected, and remained silent for a long while. By then the Taoist priest had disappeared. As the crowd looked at the pear vendor, they roared into laughter.

898. The Taoist Priest of Laoshan

There was a certain scholar surnamed Wang in the county town, the seventh child of an aristocratic family politically influential for generations. Since his youth, he had always been a devout believer in Taoism. When he heard there were many immortals in Laoshan, he set out immediately with his book trunk intending to seek enlightenment there.

As he climbed to the top of the mountain, he saw a Taoist temple. It was peaceful and secluded. A Taoist priest sat on the cattail cushion, his white hair hanging to his neck, looking hearty and bold in spirit. He stepped forward to pay his respects as he listened to the Taoist priest giving lectures on the abstruse and mysterious Taoism, and requested to be accepted as his disciple.

"My only concern is that you may not be able to endure the hardship, as you are used to a bed of roses!" said the Taoist priest.

"I can endure hardship!" replied scholar Wang.

The old Taoist priest had many disciples, who gathered at dusk. scholar Wang kowtowed to everyone of them, and settled down in the temple.

Early in the morning, the Taoist priest called scholar Wang and handed him an axe as he ordered all the disciples to get firewood from the mountain. Scholar Wang did as he was told.

A month later, his hands and feet were covered with thick calluses. It was hard for scholar Wang to endure such hardship, and privately he began to think of returning home.

One evening, he saw two guests drinking with his master. The sun had sunk below the mountain, but the candles and lamps had not yet been lighted. The master took a piece of paper, cut it into the shape of a mirror, and pasted it on the wall. Soon moonlight flooded the house, and even the minutest hair could be seen clearly. His disciples went hither and thither around him, running errands as instructed.

One of the guests said, "Such a gorgeous day in such beautiful surroundings, we should all have a good drink!" Thereupon he raised the wine pot from the table, and had wine bestowed on all the disciples, urging them to drink to their heart's content.

Scholar Wang turned the matter over in his mind and said to himself, "There are seven or eight of us, and there is only a pot of wine; how can everyone share it?" All the disciples brought their own cups, and vied with one another for the drink, fearing lest the wine might be exhausted. Yet, the wine in the pot was never a drop less than it was before, despite pouring cup after cup. This greatly amazed scholar Wang.

A few moments later, another guest said, "I'm grateful for the moonlight. However, it is rather lonesome to drink all by ourselves. Why don't we summon the moon god here to keep us company?" He picked up a chopstick and threw it into the moon mirror. Instantly there came from the centre of brightness a lady of exceptional beauty. She was only about one foot tall when she first emerged from the mirror, but became as tall as an average person as soon as she touched the ground. She had a slender waist and a pretty neck. Breezily she danced to *The Tune of Colorful Costumes*. When dancing was over, she sang the melody, "Oh, celestial being! Oh, Fairy! Please come back! Why must I be imprisoned in the Moon Palace!" The voice was loud and clear, sonorous and beautiful, as if it came from the flute. Having finished singing, she wheeled around and, as if floating in the air, skipped to the table. As everyone watched in amazement, she became a chopstick again. All three laughed heartily.

The other guest said, "Tonight is most enjoyable of all nights, but we have enough wine for now. Why not move our table to the moon palace?"

So saying, the table began to move, and slowly it entered the moon palace.

And the disciples watched the three men sitting in the moon palace, drinking merrily without stop, and even their brows and beard were clearly seen, as though they were just reflections in the mirror.

Some time later, the moonlight gradually faded, and the disciples lighted the candles. By then, only the Taoist priest sat there all by himself, and the guests were nowhere to be seen. The remains of a meal were still evident, but the moon on the wall was just a round paper mirror now.

The Taoist priest asked everyone, "Have you all drunk enough?"

"Enough," everyone replied.

"Since you have enough to drink, you should all go to sleep so that you may not hold up tomorrow morning's firewood gathering!" the Taoist priest said, and everyone retired for the night.

At heart, scholar Wang admired all this very much and, because he was elated at what happened, he gave up the idea of returning home.

Thus passed another month, and scholar Wang really could not put up with the austerity anymore. Besides, the Taoist priest had not passed to him any magic arts. Scholar Wang would not prolong his stay and decided to take his leave. He said to the master, "Your humble disciple has come from a distance of several hundred *li* in the hope of learning Taoism from my immortal master. Now, even though you could not pass to me the magic arts of immortality, at least let me learn some trifling tricks to make my devotion worthwhile! However, more than two months have elapsed, what I did was only going to collect firewood early in the morning and coming back in the evening. At home, your humble disciple really never had to endure such hardship!" The Taoist priest smiled and said, "I've told you before you would not be able to endure the hardship and today it proved I was right after all. Early tomorrow morning, I'll send you back." "Your humble disciple have been here for many days. Could you at least please teach me some trifling magic arts to make my journey worthwhile!" scholar Wang requested.

"What do you have in mind?" asked the Taoist priest.

"I've observed wherever you go, the walls are no obstacle. If I can learn that, it will be quite enough for me!" scholar Wang suggested.

The Taoist priest smiled and gave in to scholar Wang's request. He then taught him the secret formula, and let him chant it personally. When scholar Wang had finished chanting, the Taoist priest directed him, saying, "Go into the wall!"

Scholar Wang's face was rubbing against the wall but he did not have the guts to go into it.

"Try to go into it," the Taoist priest urged him.

Thereupon scholar Wang proceeded unflinchingly but, when he reached the foot of the wall, he was blocked. "Bow your head and dash in quickly. Don't hesitate!" instructed the Taoist priest.

Scholar Wang retreated a few steps and dash into it. As he entered the wall, it was as if there were nothing there. He looked back, sure enough, he was already at the other side of the wall. Scholar Wang was extremely delighted, and came back to the house to thank the Taoist priest.

The Taoist priest said, "When you return home, you must treat it with a serious attitude and a pure heart, or else it will not be efficacious." He assisted scholar Wang with some travelling expenses for the journey home.

When he was finally home, scholar Wang bragged that he had met with an immortal, and that no matter how solid the wall was, it was no obstacle to his advance. His wife did not believe him. Scholar Wang followed the steps he learned in the mountain, took a few paces backwards, and ran speedily into the wall. As his head came into contact with the solid wall, he fell to the ground abruptly. His wife helped him up and saw, to her discomfiture, a bump as big as a hen's egg.

His wife mocked him, and scholar Wang was ashamed and angry. He cursed the old Taoist priest for harbouring ill intentions!

899. Painted Skin

There used to be a scholar in Taiyuan surnamed Wang. Early one day in the morning, while he was walking along the road, he met a young woman, who carried a cloth-wrapped bundle and hurried on with her journey all by herself. She seemed dead tired, and moved with difficulty. Scholar Wang hastened to go closer and discovered she was actually a very beautiful girl of fifteen or sixteen. Scholar Wang had taken quite a fancy to her. "Why are you going all by yourself so early in the morning?" he asked. But the girl said, "You are but a passerby, who cannot relieve me of my worry. Why should you burden yourself by asking?" Scholar Wang replied, "What's troubling you? I'll not stand by if I can help you." The girl was all sadness and said, "My parents coveted money and sold me to a rich family as concubine. That master's wife was an extremely jealous shrew. She beat me day and night. I could no longer endure her cruelty, and so I fled. It is my intention to flee to a distant place." Scholar Wang asked her, "Which place do you have in mind?" The girl replied, "A refugee has no fixed abode." Scholar Wang said, "I live not far from here. Why don't you go to my house first?" The girl was very pleased when she heard the suggestion, and promised to go to scholar Wang's home. Scholar Wang helped carry her swag, and led the way.

Arriving at scholar Wang's house, and having entered into it, the young girl looked around, and saw there was nobody else there, and she asked, "Why? Are you not married?" Scholar Wang replied, "This is my study. All the other family members are at the back." The girl said, "This is a nice place. If indeed you sympathize with me and are willing to save my life, you must keep it a secret and never divulge my whereabouts." Scholar Wang promsied to do as she wished, and slept with the girl. He hid the girl behind closed doors and for many days nobody knew about it. Later, scholar Wang told his wife on the quiet, but his wife was of the opinion that a concubine who fled from a wealthy and influential family could cause trouble, and urged scholar Wang to send her away. Scholar Wang, however, did not follow her advice.

Incidentally, scholar Wang went to the market one day and met with a Taoist priest, who was stunned by his appearance. "What has happened to you?" he asked. Scholar Wang replied, "Nothing." The Taoist priest said, "Why do you say nothing when you are being influenced by evil spirit from head to foot?" Scholar Wang did all he could to plead innocence, and the Taoist priest left him, but added, "A muddle-headed fellow! There is always such person in the world who is on the verge of death and yet does not come to realize the truth!" Scholar Wang thought the words of the Taoist priest was most unusual, and recalled the event surrounding the young girl, whom he now felt suspicious. But then he thought better of it, saying that the young girl was evidently a gentle and kind beauty, and how can she be an evil spirit? The Taoist priest probably tried to frighten people on purpose by talking big, so that he could get some expel-evil-and-capture-the-demon business to make ends meet.

A few moments later, scholar Wang returned to his study and found the door bolted, so that he was unable to get in. As scholar Wang was suspicious of the young woman, he climbed over the wall from a breach. The door of the room, however, was also bolted from within. Quietly, scholar Wang stepped over to the window and peeped in. He saw a hideous demon, green-faced, with a row of sawtooth-like white teeth. A piece of human skin was spread on the bed, and she was painting the skin with a brush. When she had finished painting a beautiful girl, she threw away the color-brush, picked up the skin, threw it on herself just as wearing her clothes and, by a sudden metamorphosis, she became the familiar young girl. After watching what happened, scholar Wang was terrified. He was so scared that he dropped to the ground and crawled out from the study. Hurriedly he went to look for the Taoist priest, but the latter was nowhere to be seen. Looking everywhere around, he finally located him in the outskirts of the town. He knelt down and begged the Taoist priest to save his life. The Taoist priest said, "I can drive her away, but the spirit has found its stand-in with a lot of trouble, and I cannot bear to take away its life." He handed the fly whisk in his hand over to scholar Wang, and instructed him to hang it on the lintel of his bedroom. Just before parting, they agreed to meet again at the Green Emperor Temple.

Back at home, scholar Wang did not dare to go to the study again. He moved to the inner chambers, and hung the fly whisk above the door of the bedroom. At the first watch of the night, he heard the sound of movement outside the door. Scholar Wang did not have the courage to go and see what happened, and had to ask his wife to peek through the window aperture. She saw the young woman arrived at the door. As there was a fly whisk, she dared not enter, but only stood there gnashing her teeth in anger. After standing there for sometime, she finally went away. She returned a moment later, and cursed, saying, "That Taoist priest just tried to intimidate me! Do I have to spit out that which is already in my mouth?" That said, she stretched her hand to get the fly whisk, which she broke into several pieces. Then she entered the door, directly went to the bed where scholar Wang was hiding, tore open his belly, and plucked out the heart and left. Scholar Wang's wife burst into loud sobs, and the maid hastily lighted the candle and brought it in. Scholar Wang was already dead, and there was blood all over his belly. Scholar Wang's wife, nee Chen, was so frightened that she stopped crying aloud.

In the following day, Scholar Wang's wife sent her brother, Er Lang, to tell the Taoist priest. The Taoist priest was very angry and said, "I've been merciful at first, wanting to leave a way out for her to live. Who would have thought that she became so presumptuous!" He followed Er Lang to scholar Wang's house, but the young woman had disappeared. The Taoist priest leaned back, looked around for a few moments, and said, "Fortunately she has not gone far!" He then added, "Which family does the house to the south belong?" Er Lang replied, "It's my place." The Taoist priest said, "The evil spirit is now in your house." Er Lang was surprised, and could hardly believe there was a demon in his own house. The Taoist priest asked him, "Is there any stranger there in your home?" Er Lang replied, "I was out very early in the morning looking for you in the Green Emperor Temple, and did not know what happened at home. Let me go back and make inquiry." He soon came back to report, saying, "There is indeed a stranger. This morning an old woman came and said whe was willing to do house chores. My family kept her, and she has not yet left my house." The Taoist priest said, "That's it." They then went together to Er Lang's home. The Taoist priest raised his wooden sword, standing in the yard, and shouted at her, "Evil creature, give the fly whisk back to me!" The old woman, who was inside the hosue, was so horrified that her face turned white. She ran out of the door, intending to escape. The Taoist priest followed her and attacked her with the sword, which downed her. The human skin slipped to the ground, and she became a ferocious ghost, lying on the floor howling, which was more or less like a pig's squeal. The Taoist priest cut off her head with the sword, and its body became a black ball of smoke, coiling close to the ground. The Taoist priest brought out his bottle gourd, pulled out the stopper, and placed it in the smoke ball. The gourd sucked the smoke into its belly and, in an instant, there was nothing left. The Taoist priest closed the mouth of the gourd with the stopper, and put it in his sack. He turned to look at the human skin. It was painted with the utmost care, complete with the brows, the eyes, the hands and the legs; in fact, every detail was taken cared of. The Taoist priest rolled up the human skin much as he would a scroll of painting. He put it into his sack and departed.

900. Jia Fengzhi

Jia Fengzhi was a native of Pingliang District. His fame as a gifted scholar surpassed all the other men of letters at the time. However, he had not been successful in all the imperial competitive examinations.

One day, Jia Fengzhi met a licentiate on the road. According to the latter's own words, his surname was Lang. He was natural and unrestrained in manner, tactful and refined, reasonable and to the point in words. Jia Fengzhi invited him to be his guest, and presented to him his eight-legged essay exercises for advice. After reading them, Lang offered no praise, but said, "It won't be difficult for you to succeed in getting a first in the imperial examinations at prefectural and county levels but, if you take part in the provincial and metropolitan examinations, even though you might only wish to get the last position, you still would have to put in some effort." "What must I do then?" asked Jia. "It is difficult to rise high or keep forging ahead in this world, but if you can settle for a second best or yield, everything becomes easy to manage. This is something very plain and does not require further elucidation." He cited a couple of men and essays as examples, about whom normally almost all were looked down upon by Jia. Jia smiled as he listened, and said, "The value of books a scholar writes and the theory he propounds lie in their being flawless, so that they will endure and be handed down to posterity. If by so doing, he becomes a high official with a big salary, people will regard it as fair. Whereas if scholarly honour and official rank must necessarily be based on the few essays you cited as model, then even though one should become the prime minister, it would still be shameful as a matter of fact." Lang replied, "You should not look at it this way. A writer may be able to write perfect essays but, if his position is low, his essays will not endure and be handed down. If you want to live an insignificant life without any accomplishment, then forget it; if you do not, then please look at these examiners. Don't you know with what stuff they got through the examinations? I'm sure they will not have their judgement and conscience changed just to read your essays!" All throughout the conversation, Jia did not so much as express one word of concurrence as regards Lang's views. Lang stood up and smiled, saying, "Young and impetuous!" That said, he bade goodbye to his host. Jia went to take the autumn imperial examination later that year, but failed as usual, and he felt greatly depressed. He recalled the words of the licentiate, and tried to find licentiate Lang's instructions contained in his past essays, and forced himself to recite. But before he finished reading, he had already felt sleepy. His mind was perplexed and anxious, not knowing what to do.

Another three years had passed, and the time for the imperial examination had again come. Licentiate Lang suddenly arrived, and they were both very happy at seeing one another. The licentiate presented the seven topics he had drawn up for Jia to do exercises with. On the following day, Lang asked for Jia's compositions, read them over, and thought they would not do. He wanted Jia to rewrite them. Done, he still thought they would do no good. Jia was now at the end of his rope, so he jokingly selected some shallow, impractical sentences from the failed examination papers, that which would make people blush, and had them put together as a piece of composition, which he let Lang read when the latter came again. Lang was in high spirits after reading it, and said, "This time it's really good!" He wanted Jia to memorized the compositions well, and repeatedly told him not to forget. Jia laughed, saying, "To tell the truth, what was written here was not what I would like to say, and it will easily be forgotten. Even though you might thresh me with a whip, it would still be difficult to get them into my head." Thus Lang had to sit before the writing desk, and forced Jia to recite them. He then asked Jia to take off his clothes and show his back, on which he wrote the Taoist magic figures. Before leaving he said, "Only these will be sufficient, and you can put away all the other books." When Lang had left, Jia examined the Taoist magic incantations and tried to wash them away with water. But it could not be done, because the incantations had seeped into the grain of the skin and flesh. As he arrived at the examination hall, he found all the seven topics he had prepared were in the test papers. As he tried to remember the exercises he had done before, he was at a loss to recall any, and only the compositions he put together as a joke remained vivid in the mind. They still made him blush as he wrote them. He had thought of modifying them, but however hard he racked his brains, he could not change a word, much to his surprise. By that time, the sun had inclined toward the west, and he could only copy the seven compositions he had put together and left the examination hall. Lang had long been waiting outside for him. When he saw Jia he asked, "What takes you so long?" Jia told him the truth and immediately requested him to rub off the Taoist magic incantations. But, when he took off his clothes and looked closely, they were all gone. He tried to recall what he had written inside the examination hall, it was as if it had happened a generation ago, not a word could he remember. Jia was greatly amazed, and asked Lang, "Why don't you do it yourself in the same manner?" Lang smiled and said, "I don't have the desire to keep forging ahead through the imperial examinations and so need not read those illogical compositions." He invited Jia to be his guest the next day, which Jia assented. After Lang left, Jia took out the compositions he had put together and read. He discovered they were not what he had wanted to express. He felt very unhappy about it, and so did not go to visit licentiate Lang as promised. Dejectedly he returned home.

Not long after that, the list of successful candidates was published, and Jia, quite unexpectedly, came out first in the list. He took out the compositions again and read them, and every piece of them caused cold sweat to break out all over his body. At the end of reading the seven compositions, several layers of clothes he wore were wet through. He told himself, saying, "Once these compositions are disseminated, what face have I to see all the other scholars in the world!"

901. Current of Copper Coins

Liu Zongyu of Yihe River said: on one occasion his servant Duhe incidentally saw in the garden a current of copper coins flowing like water in the river, in depth and width both about two to three feet. Duhe was very pleased, and hastened to scoop up a handful with both hands. In the meantime, he lay supine on the current of copper coins. A moment later, he got up and looked, but the current of copper coins had disappeared, only the handful which he held was still there.

902. The Mantis Catching the Python

A man surnamed Zhang by chance walked along the bank of the valley stream, and heard a shrill cry from the mountaintop. He followed the trail to the peak to see what happened. There he saw a python as thick as the mouth of a bowl swinging left and right among the trees, using its tail to strike, and causing tree branches to snap and fall down. Judging from the manner the huge snake moved it was evident there must be some kind of control somewhere, but he could not discover anything unusual. This puzzled him even more, and so he went closer. By so doing, he discovered a mantis, which held the head of the snake tightly with its thorny claws. It would not let go despite the swinging and rolling of the snake. The struggle between the two went on for a long time. Surprisingly, the snake died in the end. The skin and flesh of the its head were torn and broken.

903. Berating the Duck

A resident, who lived in Baijiazhuang Village on the western side of the county town, stole his neighbour's duck, had it cooked and eaten. When night came, strangely enough, his entire body itched all over. At dawn, he found his body covered in fuzz like a duck, painful when touched. He was terribly scared, but could not find a remedy for it. That night, he dreamed a man came to tell him, saying, "Your ailment is the punishment sent by Heaven! Unless the owner of the property gave you a good dressing-down, the duck fuzz will not come off."

The old man next door was, however, broad-minded. He had lost things before, but had never been seen to resent it. Cunningly, the man deceived his aged neighbour by saying, "Your duck was stolen by a certain A. He was very much afraid of being called names. If you can condescend to give him a piece of your mind, it will serve as a warning to him so that he will not do it again!"

"Why should I get angry with a bad man over trifles," the old man replied, smiling, after hearing what he said. He would not get involved in the matter after all.

This put the man in an awkward position, and he was forced to make a clean breast of everything he did. The old man gave him a good scolding and, miraculously, the fuzz disappeared.

904. The Black Beast

When the revered Mr so-and-so resided in Shenyang, he once held a banquet at one of the mountaintops to entertain his guests. As he looked down towards the foot of the mountain, he saw a tiger holding something in its mouth coming his way, dug a pit with its claws, and buried it and left. The revered Mr so-and-so sent a man to find what the tiger had buried, and discovered a dead deer. The man took the dead deer away, but put the earth back in the pit so that it appeared no difference at all from it was before.

After a few moments, the tiger escorted there a black beast with hair several inches long all over its body. The tiger led the way, as if the black beast was a respectable guest. As they arrived at the edge of the pit, the black beast squatted down and looked on. The tiger, meanwhile, clawed open the pit. The dead deer was not there, and it began to tremble with fear, throwing itself down on the ground, not daring to move. The black beast flew into a rage, thinking it had been deceived, and ferociously struck at the forehead of the tiger with its sharp claws. The tiger died instantly, and the black beast left straightaway.

905. Dragon

In the district of Beizhi, a dragon fell from the sky. Its movement was clumsy as it climbed into a gentleman's home. The gate was narrow and could barely allow the dragon's large body to squeeze through. The entire family fled at the sight of the dragon. As they climbed up the tall building, they stirred up a commotion by firing blunderbuss and exploding firecrackers, shaking heaven and earth with the din they created. Finally the heavenly dragon left the house. Outside the door, incidentally, there was a puddle of water left after the rain, less than one foot deep. The heavenly dragon crawled into the puddle and rolled, so that its entire body was covered with a layer of mud. It tried its utmost to soar into the sky, but could only fly a little over a foot high before it dropped to the ground again. There was nothing it could do but to coil itself up and lie on the mud pool, where it remained for the next three days while the damned flies gathered in groups on the scales and shells of its body. Suddenly, down came the torrential rain coupled with loud thunderbolts. The heavenly dragon plucked up its spirits, rose to the sky and flew away.

906. Wolf Eating Human Flesh

A carter was pushing a heavily loaded cart up a slope. Just at this critical moment when it required all the attention and strength he had, a wolf came to bite his hip. If the carter let go the cart, the goods on the cart would fall and break; besides, it might crush him. So he had to put up with the severe pain and continued pushing the cart up the slope. When finally he reached the top, the wolf had already bitten a piece of flesh from his hip and escaped.

Taking advantage of the man when he was not in a position to resist, and stealthily tasted a piece of flesh, it was undoubtedly a cunning but ridiculous behaviour!

907. The Lion Cat and the Big Mouse

During the Wanli Period of Ming Dynasty, the mice became a curse in the palace and one of them became as big as a cat, wreaking havoc and disturbing the peace. The palace people tried hard to find a good cat from among the people. But, instead of catching it, the cat was usually eaten by the mouse.

At this juncture, a lion cat was presented by a foreign country. It was as white as snow from head to foot. The palace people put it inside the room where the big mouse came and left unpredictably. They closed all the windows and doors tightly and, hiding themselves outside the room, they watched on the sly. It was only after the lion cat had crouched there for a long time that the big mouse finally ran out of its hole cautiously. It noticed the arrival of a white cat at once, and rushed at it with a howl. The lion cat dodged it by leaping up to the table, but the big mouse followed, and the lion cat had to go down again. Thus up and down they both did it for almost a hundred times. To the palace people, the cat seemed to be afraid of the mouse, and they all thought it was a bootless cat. After some time, the speed with which the mouse leapt up and down began to slow down, as it was gasping with its big belly heaving, and had to take a little rest on the floor. It was precisely at this moment that the lion cat suddenly swooped down and seized the hair on the head of the big mouse with its claws, tearing the head and neck of the mouse with its mouth. The cat and the mouse rolled together like a ball and fought on for some time, making it difficult to judge which one was the winner. Only the angry miaows of the cat and the mournful cries of the big mouse were heard. The palace people hastened to open the door and look in. They saw the big mouse's head bitten into pieces.

By now, people began to understand it was not because the lion cat was timid that it dodged the mouse initially, it was because it was waiting for the right moment when the big mouse would become tired and slack off. When the big mouse attacked, the cat retreated; when the big mouse stepped back, the cat would advance. The cat was showing its wisdom!

Alas! To be more brave than wise, to draw one's sword and ready to fight at the drop of a hat, can you tell the difference between such a man and the big mouse?

908. Wolf

At dusk, a butcher was driven into a corner by a ferocious wolf when he suddenly saw at the roadside a shed put up by the farmer. He hastened to run into it and hid himself. The ferocious wolf reached out one of its paws into the window where a straw mat was hanging there. The butcher swiftly caught it with all his might and prevented it from drawing back. However, he was unable to think of a way to kill the wolf. He had only a small knife less than one inch long. Using the knife, he cut open the skin of the wolf's leg and stretched the opening, into which he blew desperately. He exerted every ounce of his energy blowing air into the opening until he thought the wolf was no longer struggling. Next, he tied up the opening with a ribbon. When he went out of the house to see, he found, to his delight, the wolf had been blown into an ox, its four legs rigid and straight and could not be bent, and its bloody mouth open and could not be closed. He then carried it on his shoulder and brought it home. Now, if he were not a butcher, how could he think of such a method? The business of killing the wolf, recorded above, was carried out by a butcher. Although it was cruel, it was, nevertheless, used to take the life of a ferocious wolf. As such, it should be considered above reproach.

909. Keeping Louse

A villager once sat under a tree, and found a louse on his body. He wrapped the louse with a piece of paper and deposited it in a hole of the tree before he left. Two or three years later, he happened to pass through the place again. All of a sudden, he remembered the louse, and found the paper wrapper still there inside the hole of the tree. When he opened it, the louse was already as dry as bran. He put it on his palm to scrutinize it more closely. A few moments later, he felt the centre of his palm terribly itchy, and the louse's belly gradually filled up. He released the louse, but the itchy spot on his palm bulged into a big bump. It swelled for several days until he died.

910. Shepherd Boys

Two shepherd boys went to the mountain to look for the wolf's den, and saw two cubs there. After talking it over, they decided to separate them, bringing one each up a tree, the distance between the two being only a matter of tens of paces.

Soon the old wolf came back. Upon entering the den, it discovered the disappearance of its cubs, and became panic-stricken. One of the shepherd boy deliberately twisted the young cub's paws and ears to make it howl. As the mother wolf heard the sound, it raised its head and looked around. Ablaze with anger, it rushed to the tree and made an effort to climb, scratching the tree as it howled unceasingly. At this juncture, the shepherd boy on the other tree did the same thing. Following the sound, the mother wolf rushed to the other tree. Then, as the first shepherd boy repeated the trick, the mother wolf hurried back. Thus, back and forth, running and howling, over tens of times, it eventually became exhausted and slowed down perceptibly, its howls becoming weaker and weaker until at last it fell down, gasping for breath. For a considerable period of time, it remained motionless. The shepherd boys then descended from the trees. They discovered the mother wolf was already dead.

911. A Chivalrous Bird

In Tianjing, there was a monastery. In the main hall of that Buddhist temple, upon the ridge of its roof where there was an ornament in the shape of an animal, a pair of storks made its nest. Above the ceiling, on the other hand, there was a big snake, coiling up like a big basin. At the end of spring and the beginning of summer, when the young birds became fledglings, plump and juicy, the big snake would crawl out and eat them all. At that moment, the old storks could only stay at the roof ridge and watch, crying plaintively for a few days and left. The same thing happened for three consecutive years.

Just when people were guessing that the storks might have learned the lesson and would not come again to make their nest that year, the pair of storks returned. After the eggs had hatched out and the nestlings were about to become fledglings, one of the storks flew away, only to return three days later. It entered the nest and, as usual, fed the nestlings. Its cawing attracted the big snake, and the snake wriggled up the roof ridge. The moment it was near the nest, the two old storks became panicky and cried anxiously as they flew to the sky.

A moment later, a gust of wind arose, making a roaring sound. Suddenly, the sky darkened, as if it were night. People at the main hall were amazed and shocked. As they raised their heads and looked, a big bird was already above them. It was so big that its wings covered half the sky and blocked the sunlight. Like a hurricane, it swooped down and, with its steel-like claws, struck at the snake. The head of the snake, which was as big as a peck measure, came off abruptly. It was so violent that even a corner of the main hall several feet long came crumbling down. The big bird fluttered its wings and flew away, and the two storks accompanied it, as if to see it off.

Because of the turmoil, the nest with its two nestlings had tumbled down from the rooftop to the ground. One was dead, another still alive. The monks sent the living nestling to the top of the belfry. A little while later, the old storks returned, and they continued to feed the young bird until its feather stiffened and could fly by itself. Then they flew away together.

912. Elephant

A hunter south of the Five Ridges (Guangdong, Guangxi and the vicinities) went hunting with his bow and arrow. While on the road, he felt tired and lay down to take a little rest, but unconsciously fell asleep. It so happened that an elephant came, rolled him up with its trunk and carried him away. As the hands and legs of the hunter were encircled by the curled trunk, he could not move, and he thought this time around the elephant would surely kill him.

After a while, the elephant brought the hunter under a big tree, uncurled its trunk and put him down. Then it began to greet him by making a ceremonious nod of sorts, which was followed by a long deep cry. Soon, many big elephants responded to the sound and arrived, circling around the hunter as if they had something to ask of him. The elephant that came earlier lay prone on the ground, raising its head to face the tree as it stared at the hunter, as though begging the hunter to climb up. The hunter understood what it meant, and he climbed up the back of the elephant and got himself to a forked branch high up on the tree and sat there, although he was still at a loss as to why he was being put there by the elephants.

Sometime later, a ferocious beast called *suan ni*, or lion, arrived. At the sight of it all the elephants were terrified and prostrated themselves. The lion approached the strongest adversary, staring and stretching its paws as if going to kill it. All the elephants were shaking with fear, yet none dared run away. They just threw back their heads and looked at the hunter, as if seeking sympathy and help, and it dawned upon the hunter what he was invited there for. He fitted an arrow, exerted his utmost and pulled the bowstring. The arrow whizzed away, fatally wounding the lion, which fell and died. Thereupon all the elephants raised their heads towards the hunter, expressing their gratitude by dancing before him.

As the hunter descended from the tree, the same elephant which invited him again lay prone on the ground, asking him to ride on its back. Accordingly, the hunter climbed up, and the elephant carried him to a place where it uncovered a cave underground, sort of storeroom for the fallen ivory. The hunter dismounted from the elephant and collected several bundles of it, which he put on the elephant's back. The grateful elephant then carried the hunter and the ivory out of the mountain.

*

The Southern Mountain Collection
By Dai Mingshi (1653-1713 A.D.) styled himself Tianyou, assumed name Hefu; a native of Tongcheng, Anhui Province. A palace graduate of the period of Kangxi, he became a compiler of the Han Lin Academy. Possessing strong imaginative power as a youth, he paid special attention to the history of Ming Dynasty. Later, he was impeached by the left vice-censor, Zhao Shenqiao, and put in prison for using the title, Yongle, of emperor Chengzu of Ming. This was the big literary inquisition called *The Southern Mountain Collection case* which reverberated throughout the nation. Dai Mingshi was executed, tens of people were implicated and relegated. The book *The Southern Mountain Collection* was banned. More than a hundred years later, Dai Junheng collected his scattered posthumous manuscripts, compiled them into fourteen volumes, and the book began to circulate.

913. On Birds

There was a cassia tree near my study. Everyday beautiful songs of birds were heard therefrom. As I stepped closer to look, two birds made their nest on the cassia tree's crotch, which was only five or six feet above the ground and could be reached with stretched hands. The size of the nest was more or less like a cup. It was constructed with the blades and stems of slender grass connected to one another, and looked meticulous and strong. The two birds, one male and one female, was no larger than a double handful. Their feathers were bright and spotlessly white, beautiful and lovely, but I did not know what species of bird they were. When the young birds had hatched out, the mother bird covered them with her wings, and the male went out to find food. Each time it found any food, it would stop at the roof for a while, and not come down instantly. I tried to tease it by shaking the nest, the bird watched anxiously and cried. If I shook only slightly, its cry would be low; if I shook more strongly, it would cry much louder; and if I stopped shaking altogether, the cries would stop too. A few days later, as I came back from outside, I saw the nest had fallen to the ground. When I tried to find the two birds and their eggs, they were not there either. I asked people of my family, and they said the birds and eggs were taken away by the houseboy of a certain family. Alas! How lovely the two birds were! Their feathers were so spotlessly white and beautiful, their singing so pleasant and sweet! Why didn't they perch in the mountain and the dense forest instead? It was only because they had chosen the wrong place to entrust themselves that they had been toyed with until they died. It might have been that they thought the manners and morals of the time were very tolerant.

914. The Biography of a Poverty-stricken Fellow

It's not known when the poverty-stricken fellow appeared. During the period of Yuanhe (806-820 A.D.), title of emperor Xianzong of Tang, he began to follow Han Yu. Han Yu and the poverty-stricken fellow coexisted for a long time, and it became unbearable, so he wrote an article called *Sending Poverty Off* to get rid of him, but the poverty-stricken fellow would not leave; instead, he humiliated Han Yu for it. When Han Yu died, the poverty-stricken fellow had nowhere to go, and wandered about in the world, looking for a man like Han Yu to associate with. After searching for over nine hundred years, the poverty-stricken fellow located a certain Mr Bei He somewhere between Yangtse River and Huaihe River, who was of the same class with Han Yu, and so, without proper introduction, he paid a visit to Mr Bei He straightaway, introducing himself, saying, "I had once been a mentor-adviser of Han Yu in the past, and I've heard, sir, you are a man of high morality, and would like to entrust myself as your mentor-adviser, hoping for an opportunity to serve you." Mr Bei He was so terrified at the suggestion that he sprang up from his seat. Stepping back several paces, he nervously said, "What are you doing here?" Then he waved his hand to send the poverty-stricken fellow away, and added, "Please leave! In the past, it was because of his association with you that made him an eyesore to the world. He had incurred their derision and contempt, and became so poor that he did not have even a decent home to fall back on. I've often read his *Sending Poverty Off*. I think you had better go! Don't implicate me, and please look for another person to follow." The poverty-stricken fellow said, "Why do you forsake me? If there were another person whom I could follow, I would have followed him long ago. The reason why I come to you, sir, is because I don't like all the other people. Why should you, sir, look down upon me? Can you please tell me what sins have I committed?" Mr Bei He replied, "The word poverty itself would be enough to make me suffer! From the standpoint of words and deeds, talent and eloquence, friendship and, in fact, every aspect of it, you have caused poverty to stick to me, and it is too much to bear!" The poverty-stricken fellow said, "All this means nothing to you, sir. On the other hand, I've brought what you need. With my help, you can sing at the top of your voice, you can comfort yourself by stroking the table and wail, you can pound the table and jump to your feet, you can bristle with anger, and your imagination can travel in the boundless universe freely without any constraint. The immortality of Han Yu came about with my assistance, and that's why Han Yu was at ease later on, despite his doubts in the beginning. I've roamed about in the world for a long, long time already, and I know nowhere is a home for me to return to. After several thousand years, I came across a Han Yu, and now, more than one thousand years have again passed before I meet you, sir. Is there anybody who ever yearned to come to you, despite your erudition and morality? It is only me who admire and willingly follow you. Have I not treated you with kindness and generosity?" After listening to what he said, Mr Bei He promised the poverty-stricken fellow to coexist with him.

915. A Blind Man's View

In a certain alley there was a blind boy, who practised divination for a living, and who was adept in playing the stringed musical instrument. A scholar, who was his neighbour, summoned him to his presence and asked him, "How old are you now?" "I'm fifteen," replied the blind boy. "When did you lose your sight?" "When I was three." "That means you have seen nothing for the last twelve years. Throughout these twelve years, you have come and gone in the dark, not knowing the enormity of heaven and earth, the lights of the sun and the moon, the lofty mountains and the flowing rivers, the handsome and ugly faces of people, and the magnificent palaces. Is it not a very sad thing? I ask you here so as to express my sympathy!" The blind boy smiled and said, "As I listened to what you have just said, you seem to think only the blind are blind, and not knowing some people who have good eyesight are no less blind. Who says a blind man is blind? Although my eyes cannot see things, yet my limbs and my body with all its parts do not feel any restraint, and the reason is because the eyes do not act blindly. When someone's voice is heard, I know who he is and, from what a person says, I'm able to distinguish what is right and what is wrong. As regards movement, I can evaluate the condition of the road, level or otherwise, before deciding whether to proceed in a slow or fast pace, and never have to worry about falling down. I use all my strength in practising my skill. I do not waste my time with trifles and do not spend my energy on matters which will not redound to my benefit. As to making a living, I depend on my ability in pracising divination to feed myself. In time all these become natural to me, and my blindness no longer means much to me. Nowadays people in the world are wont to do things that do not conform to etiquette, that are of no value and, when events happen, nobody sees them; seeing them, they will not be able to evade them. They are unable to distinguish between the wise and the stupid, the good and the bad, and cannot make head or tail of justice and evil. They are incapable of analyzing the situation, even though it would be in their interest to do so, and do not know the difference between peace and turmoil. They read the *Book of Odes* and the *Book of History* everyday, but they do not really understand the meaning. More often than not, they handle things which run counter to reason and, being muddle-headed, they do not even know why they fall. In the end they walk right into the net or trap. The love heaven has bestowed on men is truly generous and enormous, as it gives every man the organs which enable him to have wisdom and freedom of movement, but men have forgotten the real meaning, using them to do things that are against the laws. As a result, they eventually fall into the deep abyss. Are they all one-eyed men? Those who act blindly, rushing here and there, are they not all blind? Who says I alone am blind? I look down upon all these men, and believe they do not deserve a glance from me. Yet you do not feel sad and express sympathy for yourself; instead, you feel sorry and show compassion for me. I must reverse it, and express my grief and commiseration with you!" These speech put the scholar in an awkward position as he could not find words to refute it.

*

*A Collection of Baihetang's Literary Works
By Peng Duanshu styled himself Yiyi, or Lezhai, originally from Danling, Sichuan Province; dates of birth and death unknown. A palace graduate of the period of Yongzheng (1723-1735 A.D.), he had held the ranks of *Langzhong*, or departmental head, of the Ministry of Civil

Office during the period of Qianlong (1736-1795 A.D.), and intendant of Zhaoluo Circuit in Guangdong. Later, he resigned his position and returned to his home village, lecturing in the academy of classical learning in Jinjiang, Chengdu, enjoying quite a reputation. He authored *A Collection of Baihetang's Literary Works, Talking of Poetry at a Snowy Night, Manuscript of Poetry at Old Age,* etc. *Two Monks in the Remote District of Sichuan* from the essay *To Engage in Studies* was one of the most influential fables.

916. Two Monks in the Remote District of Sichuan

In the remote district of Western Sichuan, there were two monks, one poor, the other wealthy. The poor monk told the wealthy monk, saying, "I've made up my mind to make a pilgrimage to the South China Sea. May I ask what you think?" The wealthy monk asked him, "What have you to rely on for your journey?" The poor monk replied, "Only a bottle and an earthen bowl will be sufficient." The wealthy monk did not believe him, saying, "For several years, I've been thinking of hiring a boat and going with the stream to the South China Sea but, as yet I've not been able to realize it. What do you depend on to get there?"

The next year, the poor monk returned from the South China Sea. He related his experience to the wealthy monk, and a blush of shame overspread the face of the wealthy monk as he heard what the other said.

The journey from Western Sichuan to the South China Sea covered a distance of several thousand *li*. The wealthy monk could not reach it, but the poor monk could get there after experiencing all kinds of hardship. When a man makes up his mind, can he be inferior to the monk from the remote district of Western Sichuan?

*

Have a Good Laugh
By Shi Chengjin (?-c.1736 A.D.) styled himself Tianji, assumed name Xingzhai, originally from Yangzhou, Jiangsu Province; a writer and folklorist of the Qing Dynasty. He was the author of *Family Heirloom,* four volumes. It was an encyclopedia of everyday use for the family,

covering every aspect of the basic necessities of life: clothing, food, shelter (housing), transportation; keeping in good health, proven efficacious prescription, fish culture, growing flowers, and popular jokes, altogether over a hundred categories, which may be said to have included everything. *Have a Good Laugh* is one of the categories in *Family Heirloom.*

917. Black Teeth and White Teeth

There were two prostitutes, one had jet-black teeth, and the other had snow-white teeth. The one with jet-black teeth often tried to cover them, the other with snow-white teeth would attempt to bare them.

Someone asked the prostitute with jet-black teeth what was her surname. She shut her mouth tightly, pouted her lips, and pronounced the surname *gu* between her teeth. Asked how old was she, and she bulged her cheeks roundly and replied, "Fifteen." Asked what could she do and from her throat came the answer, "Beat drums."

The man turned to the prostitute with snow-white teeth for her surname, and she bared her teeth, saying, "Qin." Asked her age, she bared her teeth again, and replied, "Seventeen." Asked again what was her expertise, she opened her mouth wide, and exposed all the teeth, saying, "I can play the stringed musical instrument!"

918. Physiognomy

So said his fellow countrymen, "In your physiognomy practice, you have always been correct. Why is it not so today?"

The physiognomist wore a sad face, saying, "Today it is different from the past. In the past, whenever I saw a man with a square face and a big head, I always concluded that he must be a man of wealth and rank, but today a man with a square face and a big head will be the reverse, and I'll have to say he will be down and out. Only a man with a pointed head and a mouth sticking out can become rich and powerful. It is because they are adept at securing personal gains, and currying favour with somebody in authority. Under such circumstances, how can my face reading be accurate?"

919. Yield to the Mouse and Hornet

The mouse and the hornet decided to become sworn brothers, and a licentiate was invited to officiate the oath-taking ceremony. The licentiate couldn't very well decline, and so he went and did it. He was number three in seniority.

Someone asked the licentiate, "Why is it you have been put behind the mouse and the hornet? Won't you be frustrated in the arrangement?"

The licentiate replied, "The two of them, one can squeeze through a hole, and the other can stab. So I've to give in a little and let it go at that."

920. The Record of Contributions Kept at a Buddhist Temple

A soldier in cloth gown and cloth shoes went for a stroll in the Buddhist temple. The monk thought he was an ordinary tourist, and did not extend to him any special treatment.

The soldier asked the monk, "As I see it, your temple is much too shabby. If you have a plan for renovation, please bring the record of contributions here, so I can write my figures."

The monk was very pleased. Tea was immediately served, and his attitude noticeably changed, becoming respectful and courteous. As the soldier began to write on the record book, he put down the first four Chinese characters *Department of Governor-general*, the monk thought he was a high-ranking official in disguise out to inspect. He was so frightened that he knelt down at once. The soldier, however, added another row of characters, which ran as follows: *Officers and Men under his Command*, and the monk took the characters as indicating he was but a common soldier. He pulled a long face and stood up, and refused to kneel anymore. Then he saw the soldier wrote *Happy to contribute thirty*. He took it to mean thirty onces of silver, and smiles overspread his face as he again knelt down. The soldier completed his writing by putting another two characters *copper coins*. The monk was disappointed because the contribution was much less than he expected. He stood up swiftly and refused to kneel again. After a slight bow, he again put on a grave expression.

921. The Mute Speaks

A beggar pretended to be mute, and went along the high streets and back lanes to beg. He would point at his wooden bowl and his mouth, and said, "*yaya!*" (dumb).

One day, the beggar took out two copper coins to get wine. When he had finished drinking, he said, "Please add some more for me."

The wine shop's owner asked him, "On every occasion, when you came here to beg, you were always dumb. Why can you speak today?"

The beggar replied, "On previous occasions, I've no money, and how can one without money speak? Today I've a few coppers, and naturally I can speak."

922. Burn the Ants, Use the Neighbour's Winnowing Basket

An old woman of a certain family, Buddhist rosary in hand, chanted incessantly, "*Amitabha Buddha, Amitabha Buddha!*" Immediately after her chant, she called aloud, "Er Han, Er Han! There are lots of ants crawling in the pan. I'm disgusted. Quick, get a fire, and burn some of them to death!"

Then she went back to chant again, "*Amitabha Buddha, Amitabha Buddha!*" This was followed by: "Eh Han, Er Han, help me scoop up some of the ashes in the cooking stove. Don't use our own winnowing basket, because it may burn. Go and borrow one from our neighbour Zhang San."

923. Man-eating and Without Spitting Out the Bones

A cat half closed its eyes and crouched there snoring loudly.

From a distance two mice saw what happened and spoke between themselves, "Today the cat has turned over a new leaf; it is chanting the scriptures. Let's go out and look for food." Having said that, they slipped out of the hole. As soon as they were out of the hole, the cat immediately sprang forward, caught one of the mice and ate, bones and all.

One of the mice was able to escape and scurry back into the hole, and it said to the other mice, "I thought the cat was chanting with its eyes closed, and it must now have a kind heart. Who would have thought that when it went into action, it was actually a man-eating one, which did not even have the necessity to spit out the bones."

924. A Square Snake

A man once ran into a big snake. When he came back, he exaggerated that he saw a large snake with a width of thirty metres and a length of three hundred metres. His audience did not believe there was such a big snake, and he had to shorten the length of the snake to two hundred and forty metres, but the others were not persuaded. As a result, he had to go on downsizing it from ninety, sixty, to only thirty in the end. Then, he suddenly awakened to the fact that he had only taken away the length of the snake, but did not subtract the number from its width, and the snake had eventually become a square one.

925. Exchange Fingers

A celestial being came to earth to perform the miracle of touching a stone and turning it into gold in order to test the human mind. He was looking for a man who did not covet wealth and profit to free him from worldly cares and become an immortal. However, he had not been able to find such a man. Those he met invariably asked him to change a big stone into gold and, even though it was granted and done, they still thought it was too little. Later, the celestial being came across a man to whom he pointed at a stone and said, "Let me touch this stone, change it into gold and give it to you!" The man shook his head and said he did not want it. The celestial being thought he rejected it because it was too small, and so he pointed at a big stone and said, "I'll change the biggest stone here into gold and give it to you!" The man again shook his head and said he did not want it.

The celestial being reasoned that it was rare to come across one who did not covet anything. He had in mind to free the man of all worldly cares and help him become an immortal on the spot. So thinking, he asked the man, "Big piece of gold, small piece of gold, you don't like them all. What do you want then?" The man put out his finger and said, "I don't want anything else. I just wish I had the finger you used to touch the stone and turn it into gold just now. Exchange it for my finger, so that I, too, can touch the stone and turn it into gold. By that time, there will be gold pieces too many to count."

926. Uni-leg Trousers

A man wanted to have a pair of trousers made, and went to look for a tailor, but all the tailors he contacted asked for too big a piece of cloth, so he did not let them do it. The last tailor in the lineup understood what was in his mind and said, "I require only six feet of cloth to make your trousers."

The man who wanted to make the trousers was very pleased at the response, and he paid the labour cost to the tailor. When the pair of trousers were ready for collection, he discovered the trousers had only one leg, and it was not easy to put it on. Besides, when it was finally put on, its owner could not move a step. He gave a loud laugh and said to the tailor, "Your trousers certainly save on cloth, but it is becoming impossible to take even a step."

927. The Heart is on the Shoulder

In the course of coaching, a pugilist told his pupil, saying, "Whenever you fight with another person, make sure you do not hit his shoulder because, if you should make a mistake, you might kill him."

The pupil asked, "Why so serious?"

The pugilist replied, "Don't you know? In the beginning, the human heart was hidden inside the thorax and, although some person's thorax is a little flat, it is only slightly so, whereas nowadays, people all put their heart on the shoulder. If you aim your fist at his heart, will it not be fatal?"

928. The Sparrow Entertains his Guests

One day, the sparrow invited the kingfisher and the eagle to feast at home. The sparrow said to the kingfisher, "Since you have put on such beautiful clothes, it stands to reason that you should be seated at the head of the table!" Then he turned to the eagle, saying, "Although you are big and tall, your clothes are old and shabby, so you have to put up with a little inconvenience and be placed at the lower seat." The eagle angrily rebuked it, saying, "You little lackey! Why are you so snobbish?" Self-possessed, the sparrow replied, "Who in the world does not know that I'm narrow-minded and shortsighted?"

People who regard clothing as important and character as negligible are to be found everywhere. May be they have all metamorphosed from the sparrows.

929. Ginseng Soup

The son of a rich and powerful family went out early in the morning, and saw a poor man lying on the ground with his load unable to get up, so he asked people, "Why is this man lying on the ground?"

People replied, "This man has nothing to eat. He is hungry and lies down to catch his breath."

The son of the rich and powerful family said, "Since he has not had his meal, why didn't he sip a little cup of ginseng soup before he left the house? That would be enough to make him feeling full for half a day."

930. Don't Spoil the Tiger Skin

A certan man was carried away by the tiger in its mouth. His son, to rescue his father, brought a knife and hurried forward to kill the tiger.

The man inside the mouth of the tiger shouted aloud to his son, saying, "My son, my son, if you must hack, hack only at the tiger's legs, and make sure not to spoil the skin, otherwise it will not worth much."

931. Stealing a Sheep

A woman stole a sheep from her next door neighbour, hid it under the bed and instructed her son not to tell anybody.

Soon the family next door discovered they had lost a sheep, and shouted curses along the street. The son of the woman who stole the sheep said, "My mother did not steal your sheep!"

The woman blamed her son for implicating themselves. She cast a sidelong glance at her son, dropping him a hint not to continue. The son, however, pointed at his mother and said to the neighbour, "Look at the eyes of my mother, they look exactly like those of the sheep!"

932. A "Crude" Moon

A man, when compared himself or discussed with others, invariably called himself crude, or coarse, to show his modesty. One day, he invited some guests for a drink at home. Unknowingly the moon had ascended to the sky, and his guests became excited and said, "How gorgeous the moon is tonight!" The man, making an obeisance by cupping one hand in the other before his chest, responded, "To tell the truth, that is but a crude moon we have."

When modesty is not real, even though it might only be a way of self-effacing, one would be held to ridicule by other people. Honesty is still the best policy.

933. Playing Musical Instrument

A music master was playing the musical instrument downtown. The city residents all thought it was a play-and-sing performance of the *pipa* (a plucked string instrument with a fretted fingerboard) or *sansian* (a three-stringed plucked instrument), and a lot of people gathered to watch. When they discovered that the sound of the music was dull and tasteless, they gradually dispersed.

There was only one person who persisted, and the music master was very pleased and said, "Good! At least there is a friend who is keenly appreciative of my talent, and who does not let me down."

The man who was still there said, "If not for the table under the instrument, which is mine, I would have left long ago. I'm just waiting for my table."

934. Concealing the Thief's Garment

A thief entered the house of a family covertly to steal. That family, however, was extremely poor, and had nothing but bare walls in the house, apart from a jar of rice near the headboard of the bed. The thief reckoned: The jar of rice would be helpful, as it would become a good meal once cooked. Moving the jar would not be convenient though. So he took off his garment and spread it on the floor before he began to move the jar of rice. His intention was to empty the rice from the jar onto the garment and wrap it up to facilitate transportation.

At that moment, the couple, husband and wife, were in bed, and the husband woke up first. Moonlight shone into the house and, taking advantage of the interval when the thief turned to get the jar of rice, the husband stretched out his hand quietly from the bed, and stealthily took away the garment which the thief had spread on the floor and hid it. As the thief came back to look for his garment, it was nowhere to be found. At this juncture, the wife also woke up. As there were noises, she hastened to ask her husband, "There's sort of rustling sound. Is it possible there is a thief in the house?" The husband calmed her down, saying, "I was awake for quite some time, and did not see any thief."

As the thief heard people talking, he hastened to shout, saying, "Just now my garment, which I put on the floor, was stolen by a thief. Why do you say there is no thief?"

935. A Heaven without the Sun

During the dog days of summer, several senior officials gathered to discuss public affairs. As the talk digressed into the subject of the sweltering hot weather, they wondered where they could find a cool spot to relax. Some said, "The pavilion in the water of a certain park is nice and cool." Others said, "The main hall of a certain monastery is pleasant."

There were many common people around at the time. When they heard the argument, all spoke with one voice, saying, "Venerable sirs, there is no place as nice and cool as the law court in such and such a *yamen*." All the officials were astonished and asked, "How do you know the law court in that *yamen* is nice and cool?" The people replied, "Because there you have a Heaven without the sun, and how can it not be cool!"

936. Expropriating Land

A county magistrate was extremely avaricious and, when his tenure of office ran out and he was on his way home, he suddenly discovered among his family members a redundant old man whom he did not recognize, so he asked, "Who is this man?"

The old man replied, "I'm the earth god of this county!"

The county magistrate asked him, "Why do you come here?"

The old man replied, "Since you have expropriated all the land there, how can I not follow you!"

937. No One to Grind the Ink Stick

There was once a family that had produced public officials for several generations. Their son, who was gifted with great literary talent, came back from the county test, the first of two tests before he became a pupil. His father made him recite his own composition, and thought his son must be able to get the number one place. When the list of candidates was published, however, his name was not there. His father thought it odd, and called the county magistrate to account. The county magistrate glanced through and checked all the test papers, and found the ink of his examination paper extremely blurred, so blurred that it looked like rarefied mists, flickering. Not much, if any, was faintly discernible. His father was very angry when he returned home, and ordered his son to kneel below the flight of steps as punishment, sternly interrogating him as to why it was so. The son replied, "Because in the examination hall, no houseboy was there to grind the ink stick for me, and I had to make do with what little ink left in the inkstone, be content with rubbing my brush against it, and that was why the words are blurred."

938. Writing an Inscription

There was an old woman surnamed Wang, who was rich, conceited and fond of singing her own praises. Being advanced in years, she had prepared for herself a coffin and invited a Taoist priest to write a coffin text, asking him to raise her status as high as posible so that she might shine with uncommon lustre, promising in the same breath to give him a very generous reward. The Taoist priest deliberated for a long time, but could not find a suitable title to fit her station in life. In the end, a rather high official title gradually took shape in his mind, and he wrote it down, which was, "The Coffin of Granny Wang, Neighbour of Han Lin Academy Expositor and Libationer of the Imperial College."

*

The Collected Works of Retired Scholar Meiya
By Zhu Shixiu (1715-1780 A.D.) styled himself Feizhan, assumed name Meiya. A philologist, he was originally from Jianning, Fujian Province (now Jian-ou). A palace graduate in the period of Qianlong, he had once been an instructor of Confucianist doctrine in the prefecture of Funing (Xiapu), Fujian Province. Later, he became the chief lecturer in Aofeng College. He was the author of *The Collected Works of Retired Scholar Meiya*, ten volumes, and *The Unoficail Collection,* eight volumes.

939. The Spider Combing Its Web

Xiaoshao, also known as *xizhu,* is a kind of long-legged spider, which is very ingenious. It uses the silk threads from its own belly to make its home and, even if there is only one thread out of order, it will comb it unceasingly until it comforms to the rest. It depends on the cobweb to catch alien insects for consumption and to defend itself against any invader. *Xizhu*'s entire life is spent in arranging and combing the cobweb. The cobweb it weaves gets bigger and bigger, and it will not stop working even when it is old. That's why as far as *xizhu* is concerned, the older one usually catches more insects than the younger one, and the food hunting as well as the self-defence mechanism is also more comprehensive.

Nowadays people often say: "What do the insects know?" Actually, some insects are smarter than man. For example, the expertise with which the *xizhu* manages its cobweb, isn't it worthy of our emulation?

*

*As the Master Holds his Peace
By Yuan Mei (1716-1789 A.D.) styled himself Zicai, assumed name Jianzhai. He was a native of Qiantang, Zhejiang (Now Hangzhou), but lived in Nanking. A writer of the Qing Dynasty, he had successively held the posts of county magistrates of Jiangning, Lishui, Jiangpu, and so on. Resigned his post at thirty-three, he became a recluse, living in Suiyuan of Little Cangshan in Nanking, hence his alternative name *the Retired Scholar of Cangshan*. Later, in his old age, he had another alternative name, *the Old Man of Suiyuan*, and was regarded as the leader of the poetic society. He was the author of *The Collected Works of Little Cangshan Studio, Suiyuan's Notes on Poets and Poetry, As the Master Holds his Peace*, and so on. *As the Master Holds his Peace*, also called *Jokes Together, New Version*, is a book of literary sketches mainly of ghosts, monsters and fantastic stories, written with ease and grace and in a simple and unadorned style. A few fables are found here and there.

940. The Obsession to Hold a Government Post

According to legend, there was a magistrate of the Nanyang Prefecture in the last years of the Ming Dynasty who died in his official residence. It was said his ghost refused to leave after his death, and that at morning roll-call, he would put on his black gauze cap, have his waistband arranged in proper order, and arrive at the main hall to be seated in the proper place. In case there were *yamen* runners came to kowtow to him, he would even nod his head to acknowledge it, and only left after the sun came out.

During the period of Yongzheng, when a magistrate surnamed Qiao arrived at the place to assume office and heard tell of the story, he smiled and said, "This is a man obssessed with holding a government post! Even though his body might be dead, his spirit still thought he was alive. I've thought of a way to enlighten him!" And he put on his official garb and cap, and forestalled the spirit's chance by occupying the seat first. At roll-call, the ghost was seen arriving in the distance with his black gauze cap. When he saw there was already someone taking over his place, he hesitated, heaved a deep sigh and disappeared. Since then, the bizarre phenomenon had not been seen again.

941. Mr. Perspicacious

Provincial graduate Cai Weigong often said, "The spirit has three tricks: one, to confuse; two, to block; three, to scare." Someone asked him, "What do you mean?"

Cai Weigong replied, "My cousin Lu, a stipendiary of Songjiang County, is bold and unrestrained in disposition, and call himself Mr Perspicacious. He once passed through the western village of Maohu (in Shanghai) at dusk. It was getting dark, and he saw a woman with heavy makeup, carrying a rope in her hand, and hurrying towards him. She noticed Lu as she raised her head, and hastily hid herself behind a big tree, while the rope in her hand dropped to the ground. Lu picked it up and saw it was but a straw rope. He put his nose to it, and felt a gruesome smell. He knew he had met with the ghost of a person who hanged herself. He concealed the rope in his bosom, and walked straight on.

"The female spirit emerged from behind the tree, and blocked his way. As Lu kept to the left, she blocked the left, and obtructed the right as Lu turned right. Lu undertood it was what popularly known as 'a wall erected by the spirit', so he just strode ahead without looking back. The woman ghost was at her wits end and gave a shriek, transforming herself into an unkempt appearance, her face covered all over with streaming blood. She stuck out her over-a-foot-long tongue, and hopped towards Lu. Lu said to her with a severe countenance, 'Previously you put on a heavy makeup in order to confuse me; then you blocked my way, trying to interrupt my journey; now you become an evil spirit to frighten me. You have exhausted all your three tricks, and I believe you are at the end of your resources. You must know I'm called by everyone as Mr Perspicacious!'

"Having listened to what Lu had said, the woman spirit knelt down and supplicated him, saying, 'I was originally a woman of the Shi family in the city. As a result of the quarrel I had with my husband, I took it to heart and hanged myself. Today I've heard about a woman of the eastern village in Maohu who was at loggerheads with her husband, and I was planning to take her place. By accident, I met you on the road, and you took away my rope. I am at a loss as to what to do, and hope you can help me save my life.' Lu asked how her life could be saved. She replied, "Please tell the Shi family in the city to hold Buddhist rituals for me, and invite eminent monks to chant incantations to help me get reincarnated,' Lu smiled and said, 'I'm an eminent monk, and I'll now chant incantations for you.' He then raised his voice and chanted, 'An immense world, open and unblocked. To die and be reborn, why find a pawn? Come and go unencumbered, straightforward and free as a bird!' As the woman spirit listened, she was inspired. She prostrated herself before Lu, then kowtowed and left.

"After what happened, the local people said, 'The place was not peaceful before, but since Mr Perspicacious came here, it was no longer haunted.'"

942. The Tiger Drowned Itself

In the western village of Shaoxing there was a very deep river. A boy, who was playing at the riverside, saw a tiger coming, and jumped into the water. He swam and dove, sometimes under the water, and sometimes afloat, in order to find out the intention of the tiger.

The tiger crouched on the bank, its eyes focussed on the boy in the water. This went on for quite a long time. Eventually the tiger became irascible, and began to drool after the food at hand. It sprang up and pounced at the boy. In so doing, it fell into the river. It rolled and turned in the water, causing the river to seethe like a boiling pot. It tried quite a few times to get up the shore, but failed. Soon it was exhausted. In the end, the boy escaped being eaten by the tiger, and the tiger, on the other hand, was drowned.

Pu Lizi

By Ma Shifang styled himself Chengzhi, assumed name Pingquan, alternatively Holy Man Jianwu, originally from Yuzhou, Henan Province, dates of birth and death unknown. He lived from the period of Qianlong to the period of Jiaqing (1736-1820 A.D.). In the forty-eighth year of Qianlong (1783 A.D.), he took part in the provincial examination, and came out second. He had successively been responsible for the teachings of Confucianism in Fengqiu and Gong County, and died in his post. He was the author of *The Collected Works of Chuixianglou, Pu Lizi, Notes of Poems and Poetry by the Lamp*, etc., over ten books in toto. *Pulizi*, nineteen volumes, was a miscellany of what he learned from reading, covering a wide variety of topics, from the classics and histories, the hundred schools of thoughts, to street gossip and hearsay, what he had read, seen, heard, and the impressions thereof. All of which were put down in writing, and commented. There are many instances where the author made use of fables to expound his viewpoints, the following are a few.

943. The Deer and the Fly

A deer ran into a tiger, and fled for its life. The tiger, seeing that the deer had fled, did not chase it immediately; instead, it crouched there waiting. After some time, the deer discovered that the tiger was not after it, and came back to the same place. When it saw that the tiger was there still, it at once turned and fled again. In this manner, it happened three to five times, and the tiger watched the deer scrambling up the hills, running to and fro until it spent itself. At this moment the tiger, taking stock of the situation, slowly got up and, without much trouble, seized the deer and ate it.

When the flycatching spider encountered a fly, it, as a rule, stealthily attacked the fly without much ado. The fly looked at the spider, pretending not to see. As the flycatcher got closer, the fly fluttered its wings and flew away. From a distance, it fiddled about its two wings, very pleased with itself as it turned its head to look at the spider, and got nearer and nearer, sometimes directly in front and sometimes at its back. As time went on, it was so carried away that it came ever nearer, as if taunting its executioner. Finally, it was unable to take to its heels swiftly enough to escape being caught by the flycatching spider.

Pu Lizi Said, "The tiger cannot equal the speed of the deer, and the flycatching spider is no match for the fly in swiftness. That is evident. If, as the deer ran into the tiger, or the fly encountered the flycatching spider, they would just run away and did not turn back, what could the tiger or the flycatching spider do, even though they were so formidable? Therefore, judging from the above, it was not the tiger which caused the death of the deer, or the flycatcher which did harm to the fly. As a matter of fact, it was the deer and the fly themselves that brought about their own destruction. The deer ran fast and died because of it. The fly could fly and died for having the advantage. Cowardice brings danger, but disaster often happens at the very moment one thinks he has something to rely on and therefore does not need to fear. Cowardice causes anxiety and preoccupation, whereas to be secure in the knowledge that one has strong backing will make one drop one's guard and take the enemy lightly. Therefore, cowardice and complacency are equally the path that leads to death."

944. Carrying Tangerines into the City

A man with two loads of tangerines on a carrying pole intended to enter the city. It was almost dusk, and the sky was getting dark. The man was anxious, and hurried towards the county city with his loads. On the way, he asked someone at the roadside, "Can I arrive at the county city before dark?" The roadside man replied, "Just take your time. You will be there before dark and, even if you could not enter the city, there would be inns outside the city where you can stay for the night." The man carrying the tangerines thought the roadside man was kidding him, and felt very angry, so he walked even faster. A misstep caused him to fall down, and the tangerines rolled all over the place. Looking around at the mess, the man was filled with remorse and shame, but he had only himself to blame. There was nothing he could do but to bend down and pick up the tangerines one by one. He did not put them back nicely into the basket but hurled them from a distance, and some fell into the basket, others outside it, and the tangerines scattered all over the place in great confusion. When he finally picked them all up, the sky had turned dark, and it was no longer possible to proceed as planned. That night, the man with the tangerines had to sleep in the open country.

That is what we call "more haste, less speed".

945. Pigweed Staff

A guest presented Pu Lizi with a pigweed staff. After fondling it for a long time, Pu Lizi declined it.

The guest said, "Although the stick is but a small present, yet from the moment the seed germinated until it grew to more than ten feet tall, it was I who watered it. After it grew into maturity, it was again I personally who felled it, scraped it, painted it, all with the intention of presenting it to you. Why don't you accept it?"

Pu Lizi replied, "The value of your present is to use it. But for my age, I still am not in need of a walking stick, that's why I am asking you to take it back."

"Why don't you accept it for the time being, and use it when the time comes," the guest said.

"By the time I need it, the stick may have already decayed and cannot be used," Pu Lizi replied.

The guest was stunned, and asked him why he said so. Slowly Pu Lizi explained, "You have cut down the tree too early. It has not been tempered by the wind, the frost, the rain and the snow, and so it will rot easily."

The guest was silent.

946. Taming a Horse

My neighbour had a mare. It was a good horse. Later, it gave birth to a foal. The mare gave the foal tender care. Whoever came near it, the mare would hoof him. The neighbour was very angry, and summoned several persons to have the mare tied, and whipped the foal. The mare was exasperated, so much so that its eyes turned red, as if shedding blood. Its mane and tail bristled, knocking the post with its head, crying into the air, and making a vigorous spring, which took it to a height of more than ten feet, causing the rope to snap abruptly in the middle, as if cut with a knife. From then on the mare's temper became even more violent. Everyone was afraid and dared not go near.

The neighbour had a boy. Once in a while, the boy would feed the foal with good forage, playing with it, caressing it with affection. The mare watched calmly, and not at all irritated. A few days later, the condition of the mare seemed gradually returned to normal, and the boy put the halter on slowly, and led it to the open country for a trot. The mare followed the boy quietly, and obeyed his order. Once in a while, the boy even lashed it with the whip, but the mare took it lying down, and never resisted. As the boy got better acquainted with the mare, the mare soon became as docile as before the foal was born. Once again it was a good horse.

Pu Lizi said, "It is the same horse throughout. When it kicked at man with its hoofs, it was because it loved its foal so much that it temporarily lost its inherent quality. The neighbour, in a violent rage, beat the foal. It was an act of revenge because of the mare, and was likewise caused by the temporary loss of his natural instincts. To cope anger with anger, the result was a mess. That's why in dealing with anything, animal or otherwise, one must not take away its love by force, but change it gradually in the light of its general tendency. The neighbour's boy was a smart fellow."

947. Courtship of a Pedant

A pedantic scholar, who was over thirty but remained unmarried, disdained all the go-between's effort to find him a wife. Later, he got wind of a certain virtuous young girl and became infatuated with her. Incidentally, the girl's father esteemed the scholar's moral character, and so the prospect of a successful courtship seemed assured. A few days later, the scholar asked someone to bring up the marriage proposal. To his surprise, the marriage proposal was rejected. The scholar did not lose heart, and continued to send several intermediaries to act as match-maker, but the parents of the bride was even more adamant in their refusal. As it turned out, local tradition demanded marriage proposal first be broached by the bride's family and, only after both sides had come to an agreement, could the bridegroom's family present their betrothal gifts. The marriage proposal, when it was raised by the bridegroom, was regarded as a disgrace. The scholar followed the ancient practice, by which the bridegroom should court the bride first. That insistence crashed with the local tradition and the scholar's action was deemed disrespectful to the existing social customs and habits. As one would not yield to the other, the net result was that the scholar remained single throughout his lifetime.

Pu Lizi said, "Social customs and habits can change a man, and even the sage cannot be exempt. To follow the prevalent customs is not to be devoid of virtue. In actual fact, a man who behaves in conformity with prevalent social customs and habits is considered a virtuous man. Learning the ancient practice is to enable the present to change for the better, and not to go against it. To reverently adhere to the sense of honour of the olden days, yet act in accordance with the current practice, will enable a man to bring about understanding and avoid getting into trouble."

948. Produce Flowers but Bear no Fruits

In the garden a bean seedling unexpectedly sprang up, and Pu Lizi paid meticulous attention to its growth, getting rid of the weeds and watering it everyday. From spring to summer, the bean seedling began to put forth long vines and beautiful flowers, which looked like light morning clouds, shining with a subdued pinkish hue. However, no bean pod had been formed.

Pu Lizi asked for instructions from the old gardener, and the old gardener said, "This kind of bean should be planted in summer and harvested in autumn. The bean needs to interact with the cold weather of autumn before it can form pods and reach maturity. As it is now the dog days of summer, how can it bear fruit?"

"How if I leave it until autumn?" Pu Lizi asked.

"Since the plant is now so luxuriant, its leaves will turn yellow and vines wither when the autumn wind begins to blow, what can you wait for?" the old gardener replied.

"What must I do then?" asked Pu Lizi again.

"You should prune the vines short for now, remove its flowers, and not let the nourishment be wasted by its leaves and vines. If you do that, your bean plant will get boosted with the vitality of heaven and earth earlier than the other bean species, and obtain more nourishment. As a result, it will bear twice as much fruit as the rest," explained the old gardener.

Pu Lizi followed the instructions of the old gardener and, when autumn came, true enough, he was able to reap a good harvest.

To generalize, the same may be said of learning. If one will neither restrain oneself nor put oneself through the mill, one will achieve nothing in the end. The folk adage that "enjoy success when young is the worst danger in life" has its reason based on solid ground.

949. The Proper Way to Love a Man

Someone said, "In my native place, there is an upright gentleman, who treats people with zeal, frank when he talks, and is so eager to take care of others that he often fears he has not done enough."

Pu Lizi said, "There is the word 'manner' in zeal, and the word 'method' or 'way' in one's eagerness to care for others. In former times, there was a cowherd. Because he sympathized with the cow whose body had lice, he poured boiling water onto it. Although the cow lice died as a result, but the skin of the cow was split and its flesh burnt. The old man who was my neighbour had a foal which looked gallant enough and, needless to say, the old man loved it. Everyday, it was fed with chosen good grains. Its hoofs had to be wrapped with a blanket, and it was not kept in an ordinary stable. Instead, it was kept in a room for man. Someone advised the old man, saying it did not conform to the horse's nature, that he should let it have beans and grass, or graze in the suburbs, and gallop. The old man, however, did not follow the advice. As the foal grew up, it could not eat ordinary grass and, when the supply of grains could not keep up with the demand, the horse became thinner and thinner. When the bit and halter were put on, it bounced and skipped like mad, and refused be ridden on. Finally, a horseman with equestrian skill was asked to try it, but it gasped for breath after a few trots. The old man was at his wits end, and had to sell it. The buyer was unable to tame it either, and it had to be killed and eaten in the end."

The two men mentioned above could not be said to be devoid of love, but was that kind of love caring or just the opposite?

*

Consonant Bell
By Shen Qifeng (1741-1801 A.D.) styled himself Tongwei, assumed name binyu, and Ci Expert Red Heart, originally from Suzhou; a writer of the Qing Dynasty. A palace graduate in the period of Qianlong he, however, failed in all subsequent examinations, and devoted his energy in *ci* and *qu* (a type of verse for singing, which emerged in Southern Song and Jin Dynasties and became popular in the Yuan Dynasty) to amuse himself. He had written more than twenty to thirty traditional Chinese operas. Many had been performed, but there was no block-printed edition extant apart from four categories in *Opera Series of Shemota Studio,* which was carved by his friend Shi Yunyu. His literary sketches *Consonant Bell* circulated far wider.

950. Coin Spirit

When my schoolmaster Zhang Chumen was teaching in Dongting Dongshan, Taihu, Yan Aiting, Qian Xiangling had yet to enter the Han Lin Academy, and they studied in the same classroom. One night, when master and pupils were discussing about essays, a spirit popped its head into the big latticework and looked in. At first, the face of the spirit was just as big as a dustpan, then it became a rice pot turned upside down. Later, it grew to the size of an axle, its eyebrows like brooms, its eyes bronze bells, its cheekbones stood out and big, and the dust accumulated almost reaching five *dou* (five decalitres).

Master Zhang looked askance at the thing, smiled, picked up his newly written article *On Tangerine Membrane* and handed it over to let him read, asking, "Do you know these characters?"

The spirit did not utter a word.

Master Zhang said, "Since you are illiterate, why should you assume such a big face before people?"

Master Zhang then put out two fingers to flick its face, which gave out a sound like that from a piece of torn cowhide. Master Zhang burst out laughing and said, "Your skin is so thick, no wonder you are insensible."

The spirit felt ashamed, and its face shrank into the size of a pea instantly.

Master Zhang turned to his students and said, "I know it consistently pretends to be so big and important. It turns out it has not even a face, and just comes here to fool around."

This said, he unsheathed the knife and hacked at it. *clang,* it fell to the ground. Picked up and looked, it was actually only a little copper coin.

951. The Hands of the Spirits

Chen Jingchu of Xiaoshan had lived in Tianjing over a long period of time as a travelling merchant. Later, he packed his things and set out for home. On his way, he passed through the territory of Shandong. It so happened there was a severe drought and many people were starved to death. Business was bad, and the innkeeper was unwilling to accept any traveller. Thus he had to lodge himself in a temple. There were over thirty coffins piled up in the wing-room to his east, while in the western wing, there was only one single coffin with the headboard raised high. At midnight, he saw a hand put out from every coffin, which was dry and yellowish, shrivelled and skinny. The one in the western wing was the only hand which seemed a little fairer and better. Chen Jingchu had always prided himself on boldness, and he looked around and smiled, saying, "You pauper spirits, it seems you must be hard up, and have to come to me for some money!" He loosened his wallet and gave them a big coin each. Thereafter, all the hands in the eastern wing drew back, and the hand in the western wing was the only one which remained outside the coffin. Chen Jingchu said, "I'm afraid you will not be satisfied with one copper coin. Let me add a little more." He increased little by little until the amount reached over a hundred, but the hand still raised high and would not draw back. Chen Jingchu was enraged and said, "This spirit is too disgusting; it is truly insatiably avaricious!" Finally he took two strings of coins and placed it in the palm of the spirit. It was then the spirit withdrew its hand. Chen Jingchu felt rather baffled, and so he brought in a lamp to light up the place. He noticed all the coffins in the eastern wing had the inscription *starved people so-and-so*, but the inscription at the headboard of the coffin in the western wing read, *The Coffin of Prison Warder, the Revered Mr so-and-so of such and such County*, and he sighed with feeling, saying, "The common people have no extravagant desire; they need only one coin to be satisfied; but it has become a habit for big shot like this man to receive bribes and gifts, and he will not be satisfied until the target amount is reached. Failing that he will not withdraw his hand."

After a few moments, the sound of coins knocking against one another was suddenly heard. As it turned out, the crevice of the coffin was too narrow, and the spirit inside the coffin tried to pull but failed to get the two strings of coins in. Then the strings snapped as he used too much strength and *bang*, the copper coins scattered all over the place. The spirit put out its hand again, trying to salvage the coins from both sides of the coffin, but all to no avail, as it could not reach even one coin on the floor. Chen Jingchu gave a side glance and said, smiling, "You are too greedy, and that's why you are empty-handed. You are even worse off than those small people, who at least have a coin each in their pocket!" But the hand from the coffin continued to feel and fish without stop. Chen Jingchu clapped his hands and shouted at it, "If you received two strings of coins before you died, you would sit in the *yamen* and cause someone to be beaten and killed with the staff of great injustice. You were only the running dog of the rich and powerful. How much virtue have you accumulated? Was it worth the trouble to let yourself become so miserable today?" Before his words were finished, he heard the long and pensive sigh of the ghost in the wing-room, and the hand was withdrawn into the coffin.

At dawn, Chen Jingchu mounted his donkey and set out on his way. He gave the coins which were scattered on the floor to the monk in the monastery as rent for the room.

952. The Village of Peach Blossom

In Taicang, Jiangsu Province, there was a scholar surnamed Jiang. At twenty, he was already an outstanding writer. Following traders out to sea for trade, he met with wind and was driven by the current to a place where peaks rose one above the other in the distance like a protective screen, where the river water was limpid and the scenery looked like a picture. There was no city walls. Instead, tens of thousands of peach trees surrounded it, as if it were the capital of a prefectural state. It was midspring, and the air was saturated with the fragrance of flowers. Budding blossoms were waiting to burst forth, but a few were already blooming. They looked like brocade screens and canvasses that had been erected on both sides of the road.

Scholar Jiang was delighted by what he saw. He invited a fellow trader surnamed Ma, and together they went deep into the peach forest. Abruptly they were interrupted by tens of small curtained carraiges coming towards them like a swarm of bees. There were girls inside the carriages, some ugly, some pretty. Among them, there was a girl with hollow cheeks, curly ears, and the few teeth that remained protruded from the mouth. She was richly bejewelled, and seemed to come from an affluent family. Covered her mouth with a handkershief, her face with her sleeve, she behaved in an affected way. Both scholars, Jiang and Ma, could not help laughing when they saw her. Bringing up the rear was a carriage in which sat a young girl with a hairpin from the wood of chaste tree. She had worn only coarse clothes, but she was evidently a born beauty, and even the rarest of flowers like the Hortensia and the cactus could not adequately describe her grace and elegance. Scholar Jiang was greatly impressed, and tried to tail her with scholar Ma. Wheels rattled, and the carriages went past like the wind. Soon they arrived at a government office, and the girls entered it in succession.

Scholar Jiang was puzzled by the phenomenon, and asked the local people about it. Someone explained to him, saying, "The name of the place is called the Village of Peach Blossom. In spring, when flowers are coming out with a rush, it is customary for young males and females to choose their mates. Accordingly, local officials will summon all the marriageble girls here, and have their looks graded. They will also gather the marriageable young men, and assign to each a place in accordance with their literary talent. The next thing they do is to bring together the man and woman in accordance with their grades: man whose talent is graded A will match with the girl whose beauty is rated A, and so on, and so forth. The examination held today is for the girls, and tomorrow one will be held for the men. If you gentlemen are not married, why don't you enrol for the examination?" Scholar Jiang replied courteously, "Good, good." He rented a house with Ma and stayed on. Recalling the girl in the rear carriage, he fell into a reverie. He was sure she was the most beautiful girl in the world. Since he believed himself gifted with above average literary talent, he was convinced he could not fail to grab the first place. Should fate match him with the girl, he would not have travelled across the seas in search of an ideal mate in vain. While he was daydreaming about her, it must be remembered that scholar Ma too, had taken a fancy to the same girl, and had made up his mind to participate in the examination. He went over to discuss the matter with scholar Jiang, but scholar Jiang said, "You are not the literary type, why pretend to be one!" However, scholar Ma had already made up his mind, and Jiang's words fell on deaf ears.

The next day, they both entered the examination hall. Scholar Jiang took up the brush and began to write. Without so much as correcting a word, the composition was soon completed. Scholar Ma could barely cope, but he wrote on just to get it over. After the examination, they returned to their respective quarters. A man, who was sent to transmit the order of the chief examiner, came to ask for three hundred strings of cash from scholar Jiang. He would put him first in the list if the request was complied with. Scholar Jiang was furious at the suggestion, and said, "Apart from short of travelling expenses, and thus I cannot satisfy this avaricious fiend, I would not, even if the house were full of gold pieces, rely on the power of mammon, as it would bring disgrace to my composition, and render me incapable of relying on my own talent to hold up my head." The messenger felt ashamed and went back to his master. Scholar Ma quietly seized the opportunity and followed the man out, handing over to him three hundred strings of cash as requested. When the list of successful candidates were published, scholar Ma was, to everybody's surprise, in the first place. Jiang, on the other hand, was being disgraced and graded last. Scholar

Jiang heaved a deep sigh, saying, "As the examination result is not rated according to merits, failure is nothing to be regretted, but to lose the opportunity of a good marriage because of that, and being made to marry an ugly woman, is something more than I can bear. What shall I do?"

It was not long before the chief examiner matched the men and women according to the position of each in the list of candidates. He ordered the girl who was last in the list to marry scholar Jiang and be his wife. Scholar Jiang thought the bride must be the girl with hollow cheeks, curly ears, and protruded teeth, the ugly monster of a girl he saw before. After the marriage ceremony, he uncovered the headcloth of the bride and, lo and behold, the pitch-black hair of the girl emitted fragance, and the beautiful appearance shone with splendour. It was the young girl he had so ardently admired earlier on. Scholar Jiang was greatly amazed, and asked why it was so. The girl replied, "My family is poor, and often had to pawn personal ornaments to help defray the daily expenses and, even so, it was still difficult to manage. The chief examiner had come to ask for substantial bribes in exchange for placing me at the top of the list, and I sternly refused. Because of that, he harboured resentment in his bosom, and put me last of all." Scholar Jiang smiled as he listened, and said, "When the old man at the frontier lost his mare, who would have guessed it was a blessing in disguise! If I had given the chief examiner the three hundred strings of cash he asked for, and my name was put first in the list, how could I have sat here with the beauty face to face?" The girl also laughed, saying, "Black and white are mixed together, and right and wrong turned upside down. Such is the prevailing practice of the world. Only the people who adhered to high moral principles deserve blessing." Scholar Jiang deeply admired the insight of the girl.

The next day, scholar Jiang went to congratulate scholar Ma. Scholar Ma was in extremely low spirits, and would not utter a word. The woman first in the list of candidates whom he married was the girl mentioned before, who covered her mouth with her handkeerchief, her face with her sleeve, and who behaved in an affected way, the ugly monster of a girl. Scholar Jiang restrained himself from laughing and asked scholar Ma why. It turned out the girl had bribed the chief examiner with a large amount of money and was placed in top position. Scholar Ma too arrived at the top for the same reason, and was awarded this queer character. Scholar Jiang said, laughing, "In straining after the first position, you have done something against your conscience, so you have only yourself to blame. Who else can you put the blame on?" Scholar Ma became depressed after what happened, and returned to his native land in half a year. Scholar Jiang was deeply engrossed in his new life. He did not go back.

953. The City of Dung Beetle

A scholar, surnamed Xun styled himself Xiaoling, who smelt of orchid all over, was acclaimed as a man whose bodily "fragrance lingers on for three days". Once, he embarked upon a merchant ship, drifting along on the sea, when suddenly a strong foul wind arose, and the ship was blown off course to an island. Scholar Xun left the ship and landed on the island, where he detected a stifling offensive smell, which blocked the oesophagus, and irritated the nostrils so severely as to be unbearable. He was just thinking of turning back when he saw an old man bringing along with him a boy with short hair. They walked in his direction, talking and joking as they came. When he saw scholar Xun, the old man was stunned, saying, "Whose dirty disciple are you, and where do you come from? How dare you peek at our Sukhavati (Pure Land)? Are you not afraid of frightening the pedestrians?"

Scholar Xun loathed the bad smell of the old man, and had to step back a few paces before asking the name of the old man from a distance.

The old man too covered his nose with his hand, and replied from where he stood, "My name is Stinking Money Old Man, surnamed Kong, and this is my youngest son called the Smell of the Milk. We moved to this place from the Village of Five Foul Smells for the simple reason that we wished to seek the cave paradise of the immortals whom we admired. Thanks to the tender affection of the proprietor of the Stinking Salted Fish Store, who thought my smell is different from that of the others. He recommended me to a high official who, in turn, assigned me to take charge of the northern gate key of the City of Dung Beetle. You are stinking all over. If you do not hide yourself as soon as possible, the whole village will be polluted. Should the stink build up and spread, and become a plague, what could we do?"

Scholar Xun was thinking of defending himself when the old man and the boy began to vomit incessantly, and he swiftly covered his face with his sleeve and fled. Scholar Xun felt extremely amazed and, in order to verify the truth, he pinched his nose tightly with two fingers and continued to go forward. In front of him, he saw a place where the walls were daubed entirely with muck, and its surroundings full of dung beetles crawling all over the place, which built thmselves up like a long wall. Shaking his clothes, scholar Xun was about to enter it when someone shouted from the city, saying, "Miasma is here! Quick, bring the best perfume to stop it outside the door!" From a distance scholar Xun cast a sidelong glance and saw people heap up cow dung and horse dung into a mound outside the door. This made scholar Xun even more bewildered as he held his breath and walked into the city. When the city people saw scholar Xun, they were all astounded. Running helter-skelter, they dared not even turn their heads to look at him. The only thing they did was to spit. Scholar Xun too detested their filthiness, and retreated to hide himself. People raised a hue and cry to get him expelled from the city. In the confusion, scholar Xun lost his footing and fell into a latrine pit. He tried to prop himself up and stand. Meanwhile, the people came over, touching him from head to foot, smelling again and again. Suddenly they gave a shout of surprise, "Why has he, all of a sudden, become so sweet smelling? That's indeed turning the foul and rotten into the rare and ethereal!" Thereupon they hastened to apologize to scholar Xun, ushering him into the guesthouse. The steps of the guesthouse were built with the stones from the latrine pit, and the walls were daubed with the dirty mud of the gutter. In the courtyard, there was a small pond, the colour of its water was as black as Chinese ink. Scholar Xun took off his clothes to take a bath, but the more he washed himself, the more stinking he became, and he had the feeling that the stench had begun to seep into the organism. He sprang out of the pond quickly, and put on his original clothes.

The next day, an affluent businessman called Ma Tongjia invited him to drink at his home. As he entered the central room, he saw the horizontal inscribed board above the door read "like orchid"; beside it a small room hung a board on which was written "Storing Dirt Room". The study at the back was called "Taking Filth Study". The feast had no other dishes except stinking fish and rotting meat either steamed with scallion or preserved with garlic. After taking the bath, Scholar

Xun had gradually been conditioned, to the extent that he no longer felt those things were stinking, and began to eat like wolf and tiger. A short time afterwards, scholar Xun tried to savour the flavour of the smell coming out of his own throat. He sensed it had filled every corner of the room, but his host clapped his hands and laughed aloud, saying, "How sweet is the smell! Now, the sweet grass can really be put together with the stinking grass."

Old man Kong heard about the event. He could not believe his ears, and had to come to the guesthouse himself to find out. When he saw scholar Xun, he was greatly amazed, saying, "You are indeed a man who refuses to soil his hands. Previously you went about with the stinking smell all over your body, but now the muck has cleaned you up." Thereupon they became friends with complete mutual understanding.

Scholar Xun was afraid that the mechant ship might have waited too long already, and he went to take leave of the old man Kong. The old man Kong held a banquet as a good gesture, and ushered him to the inner chambers, where he saw thirty-six cesspits closely lined up in a row. Inside the pits, there were gold, silver and precious gems. The old man Kong took out several pure gold ingots and presented them to scholar Xun. Then he called out a girl with dishivelled hair and a dirty face but evidently a born beauty, and said to him, smiling, "This is Ah Wei, my daughter,—the filthy Xishi's incarnation (Xishi: a famed beauty of the Spring and Autumn Period). Since you are not married, why don't you bring her along?" Scholar Xun thanked him as he carried the pure gold ingots and brought his wife with him. Having said goodbye to the old man Kong, he returned to the ship.

Scholar Xun had not been seen for half a month, and his fellow passengers had fastened their ship and focussed their eyes, waiting for him to return. When finally they saw scholar Xun walking towards them from a distance, they were overjoyed. However, no sooner was scholar Xun on board, than the stinking smell began to assault the nostrils, which made close contact impossible. Scholar Xun put the pure gold ingots on the table, and the foul smell of which proved to be especially difficult to endure. It was only after Ah Wei went on board that the stench dissipated completely and, with it, ease of mind came back.

Arriving at home, scholar Xun occasionally went out to take a stroll. At the sight of him, people in the streets all covered their nose to let him pass. Only when he was together with Ah Wei was the stench not being offensive. Scholar Xun once brought the pure gold ingots to the market to exchange for money, but the shopkeeper threw them back to him angrily. Three years later, Ah Wei died, and wherever scholar Xun went, he was not well received. He became very unhappy and, embracing the pure gold ingots, he departed this life.

954. Tying Up a Tiger

The mountains of Yizhou were high and steep, and difficult of access, which explained why there were so many ferocious tigers there. Officials there frequently ordered hunters to capture them but, more often than not, the hunters were eaten by the tigers instead.

There was a man called Jiao Qi from Shaanxi, who came to visit his relatives but missed, and had to live here and there without a permanent home. This man was generally very courageous. He once seized with both hands a big stone tripod which was placed in front of the Temple of a Thousand Buddha Statues, and carried it all the way to the left side ridge of the main hall of the temple where the statue of Sakyamuni was housed. Because of this unusual feat, people called him "Jiao Stone Tripod". Jiao knew that in the mountain ridges of Yizhou, there were many tigers, and he entered the mountain by foot in the daytime, killing any tiger he happened to run into with his bare hands. He then carried it back on his shoulder, as was his habit. One day, he entered the mountain and met with two tigers and a cub. Jiao's instinct to kill was aroused, and he despatched both at the same time, which he carried on both shoulders, while the cub was caught alive. People who saw him dodged swiftly to one side, but Jiao Qi himself went on talking and joking as if nothing had happened.

A certain man from an affluent family greatly admired the valour and strength of Jiao Qi, and held a banquet to honour him. During the banquet, Jiao Qi talked about how he caught the tiger, which caused his audience to turn pale with fear. Jiao Qi, on the other hand, got excited and exaggerated too much, gesticulating with hands and feet, and conducting himself in a very proud manner. Suddenly, a cat sprang up the table and grabbed the food, making a mess of the soup and sauce, which splashed onto everybody's clothes. Jiao Qi thought the cat was raised by his host, and so he let it eat its fill and ran away.

The host said, "This is the bastard animal of our next-door neighbour, how disgusting!"

A short time later, the cat came back, and Jiao Qi hastily stood up, raising his fist to strike. All the cups, trays and dishes were overturned and broken, but the cat had jumped to a corner of the window and crouched there. Jiao Qi was furious, and immediately pursued it. The latticework was ruined. The cat, however, sprang to a corner of the roof, staring at Jiao Qi with both its eyes. Jiao Qi was really mad, and stretched both his arms in the posture of seizing and capturing. The cat suddenly gave out a cry, and jumped over to the neighbour's roof, dragging its tail along with it. Jiao Qi was at his wits end, and could only stare at the neighbour's wall blankly. His host clapped his hands and laughed, and Jiao Qi was greatly embarrassed when he left.

People like Jiao Qi could capture tigers but was unable to catch a cat. Was he really brave towards a major enemy but timid in the face of an insignificant one? No, it was only because he did not apply his strength in the proper manner! A cauldron that can cook a cow may not be suitable for a small fish; an arrow that is priced at a thousand pieces of gold may not be the proper weapon to shoot at a small house mouse. Those with skills should bear this point in mind, and those who make use of personnel should grasp this principle even more!

955. Lost One's Position for a Coin

A man from Nanchang lived in the capital with his father, who held the position of assistant tutor in the Imperial College. One day, by chance he passed Yan Shou Si Street, where he saw a young man, who was buying a set of books entitled *The Annals of the State of Lu*. While counting the money, the young man carelessly let fall a coin without being aware of it. Due to his avarice, the man from Nanchang quietly stepped on the coin and, when the young man concluded his purchase and left the place, he bent down to pick it up and put it into his own pocket. Beside the counter sat an old man, who witnessed what happened from beginning to end. He stood up abruptly and asked the man from Nanchang what was his name, sneering as he did so and left. Later, the man from Nanchang entered the transcribing office by virtue of his rank as an imperial college student, and was assigned the post of county magistrate. Before he went to assume office, he sent in his calling card to pay his respects to his superior. At that time, Tang Bin was the governor of Jiangsu Province. Ten times the man from Nanchang asked to see Tang Bin, but Tang Bin refused to receive him. Finally, the governor sent a policeman to transmit his order, saying that the man from Nanchang need not go to assume office, because his name had already been listed in the memorial sent to His Majesty for impeachment. The man from Nanchang was startled upon receiving the news, and hastened to ask for the reason, to which the policeman only replied with one word, "Avarice!" The man from Nanchang thought he had not assumed office yet, where could avarice come from? It must be a mistake. He was all the more anxious to see governor Tang, so that he could clear things up. The policeman, after reporting to the governor inside, came out again to transmit the order of Tang Bin, saying, "Don't you still remember what happened in the bookstore before? When you was only a licentiate, you already loved a coin as if it were life itself. Now that you have become a local official, can you not fleece the people and become a bandit with a gauze cap? Please hand in your official seal at once so that the people will not be crying along the road you pass." The man from Nanchang suddenly saw the light. The old man who asked him for his name in the bookstore at that time was in fact Tang Bin, the gevernor of Jiangsu. He was almost too ashamed to show his face, and handed over the official seal at once as he went away in dejection. To lose one's official position before assuming office was but an incidental event. The reason I put it down in writing here is to warn those who are careless about their words and deeds.

956. Learning the Art of Flattery

During the period of Jiajing (1796-1820 A.D.), prime minister Yan Song arrogated to himself the right to tyrannically abuse his power. One evening, as his adopted sons came to pay their respects one after another, order was given that he would meet them inside the inner hall. They all walked on knees and, when they saw him, they fell prostrate on the ground. The noise of kowtowing was, so to speak, as loud as the mountain falling down. This done, they vied with each other to flatter him. Yan Song was very proud of himself, and he announced, "The position of deputy of the ministry of rites is to be assigned to so-and-so, and the vacancy of censor is to be filled by so-and so." And they all kowtowed again, and thanked him profusely. As they rose from their kneeling position, they exerted their best effort to fawn on him in every manner imaginable. Suddenly, however, they heard the sound of steps on the roof, and one of them said, "There must be a man there." Thereupon they all went out to inspect. They saw someone drop down from above the room and, when a candle was brought, they found a young man with clothes full of patches standing there without a word. Yan Song suspected him to be a thief, and ordered his man to send him to the officials concerned to undergo interrogation. The youth knelt down at once and walked on his knees until he was face to face with Yan Song, when he said, "Your humble servant is not a thief. He is only a beggar." "If you are a beggar, why come here?" Yan Song refuted him. "Your humble servant has troubles which he wishes to keep to himself but, if you will forgive me, I'll now disclose them, and will not regret either." When Yan Song gave his words, the young beggar began to talk. "My name is Zhang Lu, originally from Zhengzhou," he said. "There is another person, nicknamed Baldy Qian. Like me, he is a beggar. Business is good in spring, as traders from all parts of the country gather like clouds. Wherever Baldy Qian went, he was sure to arouse sympathy, and alms in the form of money or grains were given to him in large quantity. I got some as well, but never as much as he did. I asked him why, and he said, 'As a beggar, one should learn to say fine words and to flatter. You've not learned the knack of it, and so you will never receive as much as I do.' I begged him to give me advice, but he declined adamantly. I was thinking that since Your Excellency had many hangers-on, who came here every evening to seek sympathy and favour, their skills in flattery and artful speech must be ten times better than what Baldy Qian could offer. That's why I came from such a long distance and hid myself in the dark corner to listen and observe stealthily for three months. I've learned the rudimentary of the art today, but unfortunately the scheme falls through and I stand exposed now. On your kindness and generosity I now depend. Please forgive my sins." Having heard what the beggar said, Yan Song was struck dumb at first, but then he swiftly recovered and said to everyone present, "Beggars have their own way of doing things. Your skills in flattery and the art of speech really make you their teachers!" Thereupon he forgave the beggar, and instructed his hangers-on to bring him along. Under the tutelage of these men, who took turns in passing on to him their skills of flattery and speech, he mastered every aspect of the art in one year. Since then, Zhang Lu's begging ability was far superior than Baldy Qian's.

*

*Yuewei's Short Sketches from a Humble Cottage
By Ji Yun (1724-1805 A.D.) styled himself Xiaolan and Chunfan, assumed name Shiyun, originally from county Xian, Zhili (now Hebei Province); a writer of the Qing Dynasty. A palace graduate in the period of Qianlong, he had once been the minister of the Ministry of Rites, and the assistant grand secretary in the central administration. He was bestowed the posthumous title of *Wenda*, or *Eminent Man of Letters*, and was once in charge of the compilation of *The Si Ku Quan Shu*, or *Complete Library in the Four Branches of Literature*. He was the author of *The Posthomous Collection of the Revered Mr Ji Wenda, Yuewei's Short Sketches in a Humble Cottage*, of which the latter had enjoyed far greater reputation. It is mostly stories of a bizzare nature, but there are also researches here and there. The language is simple, the narration is lucid and smooth, and it is one of the most important literary sketches in the Qing Dynasty. There are some fables, which are humorous, refreshing and gratifying.

957. An Evil Spirit at its Wits End

The Minister of Revenue, Zhu Xu, narrated the following story:

His elder clan brother, a certain Cao, while going from She County to Yangzhou, passed the house of a friend halfway to his destination. It was the dog days of summer, and his friend ushered him to the study to take a rest. The house was spacious, cool and pleasant, and he had intended to sleep there for the night. His friend advised against it, saying, "The room is haunted; you should not pass the night here." Cao, however, insisted on staying.

At about midnight, a little something crawled slowly in from the crack between the door and its frame. It was as thin as a piece of paper. After entering the room, it smoothed out slowly and took the shape of a human being. In fact, it was a girl. Cao was not in the least afraid. The girl, all of a sudden, had her hair hanging loose, and stuck out its blood-red tongue, apparently the ghost of one hanging herself. Cao said, laughing, "It's the same hair, only a little dishevelled; the tongue too is the same tongue, only a bit longer. What is there to be afraid of?" The girl abruptly took off her head and put it on the table. Cao burst out laughing, saying, "It's not so scary with your head on, let alone a headless ghost!" The female spirit was at its wits end, and vanished without a trace.

When Cao returned from Yangzhou, he chose to sleep in the same room. At midnight, again, a little something was seen crawling in. As its head was just emerging, Cao spat at it, and berated, "Is it the same shameful and disappointing thing?" Eventually, the evil spirit did not come in.

958. Sister Li Disguises Herself as a Ghost

My younger brother's wet nurse, nee Man, was an old woman. She had a daughter called Sister Li married to a young man in the neighbouring village. One day, Sister Li learned that her mother had fallen ill. She was so anxious that she could not wait for her husband to come home and accompany her. Hurriedly she set out all by herself. It was already dark, the crescent moon gave out a faint light. She looked back, and discovered a man trying hard to catch up with her. She thought she had run into a robber or a ruffian. As there was nowhere to turn for help in the wilderness, she took refuge under a white poplar tree at an ancient tomb. Taking off the hairpin and earrings and deposited them in her bosom, she undid the silk ribbon about her and tied it around her neck, let loose her hair and stuck out her tongue, with eyes staring ahead, and waited for the pursuer. When the man came closer, she deliberately invited him to come and sit together. The man took an intent look, and thought he saw the spirit of a woman who had hanged herself. He was so shocked that he fell down instantly unable to get up. Through this ruse Sister Li was able to escape by the skin of her teeth.

As she entered the door of her home, the whole family turned pale with fright. Slowly they learned what had come to pass, and felt indignant yet funny. Before long, it dawned upon them they should pay a visit to their neighbours and tried to get whatever news they could about the event. The next day, all sorts of gossip were in circulation. People said: a young man of a certain family had met with a spirit, and suffered a mishap, and the spirit was still following him. He had gone mad and talked nonsense all the time. Physicians were invited to diagnose the illness and decoctions were administered, Taoist priest too had been called to recite incantations, but all to no avail. It is hard to believe that eventually he died of epilepsy.

959. Jiang Sanmang

In the City of Jing, there was a brave and upright man called Jiang Sanmang. One day, he heard people talk about how Song Dingbo had sold a spirit for money. He was thrilled, and said, "I just come to know that spirit can be tied up. If I can catch a spirit every night, spit on it, change it into a sheep and sell it to the butcher when it takes fright and howls, I'll be able to get enough money for the day's wine and meat." He carried a staff and a rope with him every night, quietly walking among the graves in the wilderness, as if he were a hunter waiting for the foxes and hares. However, he had not seen a ghost. Even the place which had all along rumoured to have spirits was calm and peaceful, though he had pretended to be drunk and slept there just to lure the spirit to come out. One night, he saw several will-o'-the-wisps on the other side of the forest, and he skipped and ran towards them but, as he was about to reach the place, the will-o'-the-wisps had disappeared completely, and dejectedly he went home. A month later, as he had found nothing, he gave up.

960. Empty Words

The descendant of an old and well-known family, while walking deep into the mountain, had lost his way. As he gazed into the distance, he saw a grotto, and thought of going inside to take a little rest. As he was about to enter it, he discovered the deceased Mr so-and-so, his senior, was inside, and he was seized with fear and did not dare to go in. However, his senior the revered Mr so-and-so was hospitable, and invited him in. He did not expect any harm, and so he stepped forward to kowtow and meet the old man. The old man inquired about his well-being, asking him all sorts of questions, just as he used to do when he was alive. Touching briefly on family affairs, they both felt sad and sighed. The scholar followed up by asking, "Your tomb is situated in some other place. Why do you travel here all by yourself?"

The old man heaved a deep sigh and replied, "I did not commit any mistakes when I was alive. However, as a student, I had always followed the others rather than forming an opinion myself. When I was an official, I took care to remain in my proper sphere, and did not have any particular achievement. I've never expected that several years after my death, a large tombstone should suddenly have been erected and, on the legendary dragon's head were the seal characters, which displayed my family name and my official position. What was written in the text itself was entirely beyond my knowledge to comprehend. Even though some of which might be factual, yet it often overshot the truth. Throughout my life, I had been simple and unadorned, frank and straightforward, and so I felt rather uneasy. Besides, sightseers came and went, and when they read it, words of derision were often heard. The ghosts who were there to watch also emitted bursts of jeers. It was unbearable for me to endure such din, so I dodged it by coming to this place. Only at the end of the year, when sacrifices were offered and the grave was swept, did I go back to my tomb, and it was only to see my children and grandchildren!" The scholar tried tactfully to comfort the old man, saying, "A benevolent man and dutiful son will not feel easy without doing something for the glorification of his own parents. Even man like Cai Zhonglang could not refrain from writing an inscription with a quilty conscience, and a famous celebrity like Han of the Ministry of Civil Office stooped to flattery in contributing an epitaph. Such examples were innumerable since ancient times, and why should you take it to heart?" The old man replied seriously, "The matter of right and wrong, the verdict of the masses, are all in the mind of the people. Although one can manipulate public opinion for a period of time but, when I examine my own conscience and ask myself, I feel ashamed of myself. Besides, public opinion is there for all to see, what's the use of pulling the wool over their eyes? To glorify one's ancestors, one must look at their signal successes, why should one use empty words to court condemnation? Don't you know the views of all the Johnny-come-latelies are all similar to this?" Having said that, the old man rose in displeasure, and the scholar felt as if there were something amiss as he left for home.

961. The Ambition of a Wolf Cub

By chance, an affluent man caught two wolf cubs. He kept them with the dogs at home, and it seemed they coexisted rather peacefully. When they grew up gradually they even forgot they were wolves, and remained tame.

It was daytime and the master of the house was sleeping in the hall when he suddenly heard the pack of hounds baying loudly. Startled, he rose and looked around, but there was no one in sight, so he lay down again. The pack of hounds continued to bay aloud. This time he ignored it and pretended to sleep. It turned out the wolves were waiting for him to fall soundly asleep in order to bite his throat. The dogs' ferocious barks were meant to prevent the wolves from getting near him. Thus the master of the house killed the two wolves and skinned them.

962. Tian Buman Upbraiding the Spirit

A tenant peasant by the name of Tian Buman lost his way in the wilderness one night, and entered a graveyard by mistake, where he unwittingly stepped on a human skeleton.

Surprisingly, the skeleton opened its mouth to speak, "Don't tramp on my face, or else I'll cause disaster to descend upon you!"

Tian Buman was an honest and straightforward but intrepid fellow. He upbraided the skeleton, saying, "Why do you obstruct my right of way!"

"It's somebody else who moves me here and not my intention to obstruct you at all," replied the skeleton.

Tian Buman refuted the skeleton, saying, "Why don't you go and harm the person who moved you here?"

"The power and force which supported his fate is strong at present and I cannot harm him," replied the skeleton.

Tian Buman was angry though still smiling, and said, "Then my fortune must be on the decline! You are afraid of the powerful and take advantage of the weak. What kind of logic is this!"

"The power and force that support you are also strong at present, and I dare not cause mischief. I was only saying a few words to frighten you," the skeleton made a few mournful sounds. "Afraid of the powerful and bullying the weak is common in the human world; how can you bring it up just to put the blame on me? If you should sympathize with me, why don't you move me to a hole in the ground. You will be doing me a favor if you do that!" it added.

Tian Buman ignored him and daringly dashed past the skeleton on his way. What he heard was only the mournful cries of the skeleton, but nothing bizarre ever happened, not even afterwards.

963. There's a Limit

A man who gathered firewood met a tiger in the mountain. He took refuge in a stone cave, but the tiger followed him and entered the stone cave also. The stone cave was full of twists and turns, and the firewood gatherer turned hither and thither in order to dodge the tiger. The stone cave became smaller as they proceeded deeper into it, and soon it could barely accommodate the body of the tiger. The tiger, however, was determined to get the firewood gatherer, and it forced its way into the cave. Just at that critical moment, when his life was in imminent danger, the firewood gatherer noticed a small hole beside him, which could only accommodate his body, and he crawled into it like a snake. To his surprise, the winding path led him to a small opening through which light was able to get through from the sky. After walking for a few steps, it was actually possible to penetrate right through the wall and went outside. He then exerted all his strength to transport several large rocks to block up the retreat of the tiger. In the meantime, he put wood and grass on both ends of the cave and burnt them. The smoke suffocated, and the fire scorched, the tiger, so that it roared and caused the whole valley to reverberate with it. It was less than it took to fnish a meal, and the tiger was dead.

The event might well serve as an object lesson to those who do not know where and when to halt.

964. Looking for the Stone Lions

To the south of Cangzhou, there was a temple at the riverside; its main gate had tumbled into the river, while the two stone lions had sunk to its bottom. Ten years later, the monks in the temple were thinking of asking for contributions from the public to rebuild it. They sent men to look for the two stone lions in the river, but were unable to locate them. They all believed the stone lions must have swept by the current and gone down the stream. They padled several small boats, dragging the iron rakes along with them but, after covering more than ten *li* of the river, no trace of the stone lions was discovered.

A lecturer who set up a school in the temple to instruct his students smiled and said, "You people are not knowledgeable about the innate laws of things. The stone lions are different from wood chips; how can they be swept away by flood water? Among the attributes of stone are its hardness and weight, and that of sand are its looseness and mobility. When stone sank into the sand, it would get deeper and deeper into it. If you followed the current to look for the stone lions in the lower reaches, doesn't it seem wide of the mark?" Everyone admired his judgement, and thought that was absolutely right.

Another man, an old river soldier, heard it and said, laughing, "In general, if you throw a stone into the river, you should find it upstream. It is because stone is known by its hardness and weight, and sand, by its looseness and mobility. Water cannot move the stone. The impact of current comes from under it. Water erodes the sand and causes a pit, which becomes deeper and deeper until half the stone is without support below. This causes the stone to lean forward and fall into the pit. In this manner, the current will continue to wash away the sand and the stone will turn against the current continually. That's why looking for the stone downstream or at the bottom will all be fruitless."

They followed the old river soldier's reasoning, going several *li* upstream and, sure enough, the stone lions were eventually located.

From the example cited above, it is evident there are lots of people in this world who know only one aspect of things but not the overall situation.

965. The Tiger Metamorphoses Into a Beautiful Girl

A villager entered the mountain to collect firewood, and saw a beautiful girl in front of the cave. She was extravagantly dressed, and not at all like a village girl. The villager thought she must be a demon, so he hid himself in the thicket, where he could watch her every movement.

At this juncture, a big deer brought her young to the mountain cave for water. The beautiful girl suddenly threw herself on the ground, and metamorphosed into a tiger. The clothes she wore scattered about all over the place, just as the cicada sloughed off its skin. Forthwith she caught the two deers and ate them. A short time later, it changed back into a beautiful girl, put her dress in order, and slowly went away along the mountain path. As she reached the ravine, she stopped to look at her own reflection. Her manner was so sweet and charming that she seemed to have forgotten she had ever been a tiger.

966. Unable to Cope Without Help

The elder Yang Huaiting had a clan uncle, who lodged at a mountain temple in summer in order to concentrate on his study. He was diligent and used to apply himself deep into the night when all the other students were already in bed. As he was dogtired, he had unknowingly fallen asleep. While he was in the dreamland, someone knocked at the windowpane and asked, "Please, sir, may I ask the way to such and such a village?" The clan uncle was surprised. He asked who it could be and there came the reply, "I'm a ghost. The road is full of gullies and ridges, and I've lost my way, being alone. It goes without saying, in the vast expanse of the open country there are few ghosts as a rule and, even if one might chance to meet one or two bored, vulgar ones, I would not want to talk with them. As a matter of fact, they might not be willing to tell me either, even if I should ask them. Although the nether regions and the human world are separated, you and I, sir, are similar in disposition, and that's why when I heard your voice, I came here directly." Thereupon my elder Yang Huaiting's clan uncle told the ghost in detail how to get to the village, and the ghost thanked him and left.

Sometime later, the clan uncle told Yang Huaiting about the incident. Yang Huaiting felt sad and sighed, saying, "Now I know even though you might be a ghost, it would still be difficult to insist on moral fortitude and to defy conventions!"

967. Everything is as One Wishes

A and B were good friends, and A invited B to manage his household affairs. Later, when A became governor, he again asked B to help handle official business in the government. Generally speaking, he always listened to what B had to suggest and asked no questions. This went on for a long time, and B took the opportunity to defraud A of his money and belongings, and A began to understand the craftiness of B, and condemned him accordingly. There were things A did which could be used against him, and B used it to his advantage by making false counter charges. A was furious, and went to the town god's temple to lodge a complaint. That night, he dreamed that the town god said to him, "Since B had been deceitful and ruthless, why did you trust him all along?" A replied, "That was because he did everything as I wished." The town god heaved a sigh, and said, "A man who does everything as one wishes is to be shunned like a plague. Yet you did not dread him, but liked him. Who should he defraud if not you? The cup of his sins is almost full, and sooner or later he will receive divine retribution. For you, however, it is a case of burning your own fingers, and there is nothing to complain about."

968. Drug Presented by a Crafty Man

A man wished to kill his opponent whose interest crashed with his own, but could not find a safe way to do it. A clever but crafty man surreptitiously found out what was in his mind and quietly sent a packet of medicine to him, saying, "Anyone swallow this medicine will die instantly, and there will be no difference as to whether he dies of illness or otherwise. Even if an autopsy is conducted in which the bones are steamed, it will look like he dies of illness." The man was greatly pleased and asked the presenter to stay and have a drink. The presenter died that night after he left for home! It turned out the man had the drug put in his drink to do away with a witness.

969. How the Old Man Catches the Tiger

There were ferocious tigers at the edge of the city, and several hunters were wounded trying to catch them. People in the city said, "Unless you invite Tang Dalie of Huizhou prefecture to come here, you will not be able to rid yourself of the trouble."

So the county government despatched an official to invite Tang Dalie. Soon the official returned to report, saying, "Tang Dalie has selected the two most skilful hunters under him, and they are about to arrive." The two hunters, one was an old man, whose hair and beard were as white as snow, and coughed incessantly; another one was a teenage boy. Everybody was disappointed at sight of the men, yet there was nothing they could do but to welcome them and prepare their meals.

The old man sensed the disappointment of the county magistrate, Ji Zhonghan. Half kneeling, he therefore suggested to him, saying, "I've heard the tiger is less than five *li* from the city. Let's capture it first before coming back for the meal."

The county magistrate sent a servant to guide him to the place. The servant went as far as the mountain pass, and refused to go any further. The old man teased him, saying, "Since I'm here, what are you afraid of?"

Halfway to the mountain valley, the old man said to the boy, "That beast seems to be sleeping still, will you please wake him up!"

The boy mimicked the roar of the tiger and, as expected, the tiger sprang out of the forest at once, and straightaway it pounced on the old man. The old man was holding an axe with a short handle, eight or nine inches in length and four to five inches in width. He stood there as firm as a rock, his arms stretching out. As the tiger jumped towards him, his head inclined to one side, and the tiger vaulted above him. Blood soon spilled all over the ground. When taking a closer look, it was discovered that from its lower jaw all the way to the tailbone, the tiger was split open completely by the old man's axe. The old man was rewarded with generous gifts when he left. According to the old man, he had spent ten years to drill his arms, and another ten years to drill his eyes. His eyes were so well-trained that even a broom would not make him blink, and his arms were so powerful that a man hung overhead would not be able to bend or pull them down with all his strength.

970. A Haunted House Changes Hands

For a period of time, something unusual had happened to the Sima family. At night, bricks and stones were thrown into the courtyard without a cause. Sometimes, there were noises like the howling of spirits. At other times, fire would break out where there were few people around. For over a year, the situation had not improved. Even though monks and Taoist priests were invited to pray or recite scriptures, they were all less than efficacious. Because of all this, the Sima family had decided to sell the house. But before they moved, they had to find another house first.

Initially someone rented the house. But, as he moved in, the same thing happened and, after a short period of time, he too moved out. Since then, nobody ever came to inquire about the house again.

An old scholar, who declared he did not believe in ghost story, bought the house with a mere pittance. Having bought the house, he chose an auspicious day to move in. To everybody's surprise, nothing untoward happened. People praised the old scholar, saying that his high virtue might have helped to suppress the evil spirits.

A short time later, a cunning thief knocked at the door of the old scholar. The two men could not see eye to eye, and wrangling broke out. It was then people began to learn the true state of affairs. The old scholar had bought off the thief, and the two of them colluded to create the ghost story.

971. A Bookworm

A certain Liu Yuzhong of Cangzhou was addicted to ancient books, and his rigid adherence to the interpretation of the classics was such that it almost bordered on supersttion.

On one occasion, he came by a book on the art of war. He bent over his desk reading it for a solid year. He thought he had mastered everything about military affairs, and was capable of commanding a hundred thousand soldiers to do battle. It so happened there was an enemy invasion at the time, and Liu Yuzhong raised an army locally to face the invaders. He had only the knowledge of strategems on paper, and not an iota of actual combat experience. As soon as his army came into contact with the enemy, it was routed instantly, and he himself narrowly escaped being taken prisoner.

Later, he got an ancient book on water conservancy. Again, he bent over his desk reading it for a solid year behind closed doors. He claimed he was capable of turning all the wasteland within a thousand *li* into fertile farmland. The *zhou* or provincial government believed his nonsensical big talk, and allowed him to build water conservancy projects in the village. It was an inauspicious moment, as a period of torrential rain caused flood routing. The surge of flood water followed the channels he constructed but in reverse direction. The whole village was quickly submerged, and the villagers themselves barely escaped with their lives.

972. Two Tutors of Two Family Schools

There were two tutors in two separate family schools who lived in two neighbouring villagers. Both believed it was their responsibility to propagate Taoism. One day, they held a joint lecture together. There were more than ten students sitting below the steps to listen to the two tutors. Just when they were debating with strong terms and a severe countenance about human nature like sages and men of virtue, expounding truth and desire, suddenly a piece of paper, blown there by a rustle of breeze and touched down below the steps. The students picked it up and read. It was found to be the secret correspondence of the two tutors machinating to control a widow's real estate.

973. Black Smoke

An old pedant was walking on the road. Surprisingly, he saw a friend who was already dead. He realized immediately he had met with a ghost. The old pedant was upright in dispostion, and did not feel threatened. He was the first one to ask, "Where are you going?" "I'm now an official of the court under the ruler of the Hades, Yama, and am going to the south village to take a man in. We are going the same direction," the ghost replied. So they walked shoulder to shoulder. As they came to a dilapidated house, the ghost said, "This is the house of a scholar." "How do you know?" asked the old pedant. "All men are busy during the day, and their intelligence is submerged," the ghost replied. "Only when a man is asleep does he not think of anything. During which time his mind is clear, and every character he has learned from the books begins to sparkle, oozing out from a hundred orifices, sometimes evident, sometimes concealed, crisscrossing one another, and so bright it dazzles the eyes. The brilliance of the erudite Zheng Xuan, Kong Anguo and the lustre of the writings of Qu Yuan, Song Yu, Ban Gu and Sima Qian, soar straight up into the sky to vie with the stars and the moon in brightness. The lesser ones will go up tens of metres, others will leap several feet, and the lowest among them will at least glimmer, making their mark on the window. However, the eyes of men cannot see them, and only the ghost can. The light in this house has soared seven or eight feet high, and from that I know it belongs to a scholar." The pedant asked, "I've been a scholar all my life, how high do you think my brightness will be when I sleep?" The question made the situation awkward for the ghost. He hesitated for half a day before he stammered out, though still feeling a little embarrassed, and said, "I passed the family school yesterday when you were sleeping, and saw in your bosom a very thick copy of lecture notes, five to six hundrd pieces of calligraphic works, seventy or eighty pieces of Confucian classics, thirty to forty pieces of expository writings, but every character of which had turned into black smoke, shrouding the entire house. The students there were just like studying in the dense mists and clouds. As I did not see any radiance, I cannot utter a falsehood." The pedant was so enraged that he berated his friend, who was now a ghost. The ghost laughed aloud and left him.

The Collected Works of Qianyantang
By Qian Daxin (1728-1804 A.D.) styled himself Xiaozheng, assumed name Xinmei, originally from Jiading, Jiangsu Province (now belongs to Shanghai). A scholar of the Qing Dynasty, he had successively held the posts of compiler in the Han Lin Academy and official in charge of academic matters in Guangdong. Later, he returned to his native village to mourn his father's death, and did not return. A chief lecturer in the well-konwn colleges of Zhongshan, Loudong, Ziyang, and so on, he was also the author of *Identifying the Discrepancies of the Twenty-two Histories, The Collected Works of Qianyantang*, etc., altogether over thirty books.

974. Two Horses

The master had two horses, one was auburn alternated with white, the other was cinereous. They were more or less of the same age, and both were tame and amenable. But as far as the strength of the legs was concerned, the horse with the colour of auburn alternated with white could cover twenty *li* daily. The master believed it was a good horse, and matched it with a saddle inlaid with gold, which was in turn covered with a saddle cloth made of brocade. It was also being fed from a manger other than the one for the cinereous horse. As the master went hunting, he would ride this horse. As to the cinereous horse, well, it was only used to carry water or forage, works that required heavy manual labour.

Two years later, the horse with auburn and white colours died, and the master turned his attention to the cinereous horse. However, with the master on its back, the cinereous horse refused to move even though it was whipped, and the master could not but give up. Another twenty years had passed, and the cinereous horse finally died in the stable. The master said, "This is an ordinary horse, but it lived much longer than the horse with auburn and white colours. Was it because heaven was wont to be jealous of the talented, or was it because matter of lifespan was predestined?"

That night, the master dreamed that the cinereous horse came to say, "My master, do you really believe I'm not as good as the horse with auburn and white colours? We were both ordinary horses. The only difference was that I had never insisted on doing what I could not accomplish. A gold saddle, or a brocade saddle cloth, they were all useless to me! That's why I would not go all-out to get it, not if I had to sacrifice my life for it. The horse with auburn and white colours paraded its superiority and strove to outshine the rest, forcing itself to do difficult jobs. Because of over exertion, it died young. Accidents whereby my master was thrown off from the saddle had happened two or three times a year since my master rode that horse, whereas I'd never caused any trouble. Why did you say the horse with auburn and white colours was superior?"

When the master woke up, he told the groom about the dream, and the groom said, "The cinereous horse did not know the meaning of life. It only know that to live was to be happy, and did not know that happiness lay in understanding the true meaning of life. As an ordinary horse, the horse with auburn and white colours had the reputation of being a steed, and for that reason it was treated with special care. As a matter of fact, what it rceived greatly surpassed that of the cinereous horse. As to accidents in which the master was thrown off from the saddle and took fright because of it, the master did not put all the blame on the horse. Actually, the horse with auburn and white colours was very smart too!"

975. Spectators Do Not Speak in a Chess Game

I was watching people playing Weiqi (a game played with black and white pieces on a board of 361 crosses) in my friend's home, during which a guest had lost several games, and I teased him for miscalculation, as I gesticulated and tried to tell him how the pieces should be positioned, as if the guest's skill was inferior to mine.

A little while later, the guest invited me to play with him, and I thought it would be easy to deal with a man of his level of skill. I did not expect that only after a few moves, the guest had already occupied a dominating position. Halfway through the game, it was even more difficult for me to assign the pieces, and had to think hard before I could allocate a piece, whereas the guest did it with ease, and was evidently resourceful in dealing with the situation. As the game ended, I lost by thirteen pieces. I was flushed with shame, and could not utter a word.

From then on, whenever people invited me to watch chess games, I would make it a rule to sit beside the players quietly without uttering a word.

976. The Mirror

There was a man who only trusted his own eyes and disliked the mirror. He said, "The thing called mirror reflects the blemishes and add to the suffering of men. I've my own eyes with which to observe everything. Why should I use the mirror?" As time went on, very few of the girls who were regarded as beautiful by others could win his approval, and he could not see the black freckles on his face. He felt at ease, however, thinking there was no one in the world who could surpass him in looks. Those near him often laughed at his ugliness in secret, but he never could wake up to it. How lamentable it was!

*

*The Posthomous Papers of Cui Dongbi
By Cui Shu (1740-1816 A.D.) styled himself Wucheng, assumed name Dongbi, originally from Daming, Zhili (now belongs to Hebei Province); a scholar of the Qing Dynasty. A palace graduate, he had once held the position of county magistrate. Later, he left his post and settled down in Xiangzhou (now Anyang, Henan province), writing behind closed doors for the rest of his life. He was a prolific writer, and especially adept in textual research. His works were compiled into *The Posthumous Papers of Cui Dongbi* by later generations.

977. A Sham Doe Fetus

A travelling trader from Shanxi was known for his ability to appraise the quality of diverse Chinese herbal medicine and to differentiate the genuine from the sham. On one occasion, he passed Huang County on his way to some other place, and stayed in an herbal medicine store. A man brought an ewe's fetus wrapped with a piece of paper and asked him to appraise it, lying to him, "It's a doe's fetus." The guest glanced at it and laughed sarcastically, "It's an ewe's fetus. How can such little toy deceive me!"

After going back to his home, the man told his friend about it. His friend took away the paper wrapper, and used a piece of silk fabric to tightly envelope it. He put this into a brocade pouch before packing it into a small delicately made box. Again, he brought it to the travelling trader from Shanxi and asked him to appraise it. The trader held up the ewe's fetus, turning it over and over again, looking at it for a long time before he said, "This is what we call a genuine doe's fetus. How could the ewe's fetus you asked me to take a look the other day palm off as genuine!"

In reality, this was the same ewe's fetus. Without the wrappings, he laughed at it as bogus; when it is wrapped with silk fabrics, put in a brocade pouch, the attitude of the man immediately changed from disdain to admiration. In today's world, how many people can sustain their facial appearance when confronted with silks and brocades? Under these circumstances, how can a man with a genuine doe's fetus, presenting it without any wrappings, realize his objective?

978. Yang's Tobacco

Of all the traders in the tobacco business, the Yang's in our district town was the most well-known. The price of their merchandise was much higher than the rest, but their business was bustling all the same. Buyers often had to queue up in the street, waiting to get in.

That being the case, the supply of cut-tobacco for pipe smoking fell far short of demand, and the Yang's took advantage of the situation by purchasing products from other tobacco companies, then put the Yang's stamp on the wrapper to make it appear as their own and sold it to the customers. Those who bought from them all praised the quality of the cut-tobacco as excellent. Although they had to pay much more, they never expressed any regret.

From this we can see what people value is but the name, and there are few who can differentiate the good from the bad.

979. The Lotus Root Starch of Cizhou

Cizhou (now Ci County, Hebei Province) produced the lotus root starch known for its superior quality all over the world, and was called "the lotus root starch of Cizhou". Everyone who came to Beijing from places such as Shaanxi, Hubei, Hunan, Henan must passed through Cizhou, and when they did, more often than not, they would buy some lotus root starch made in Cizhou as gift for the high-ranking gevernment officials as well as relatives and friends. Beijing people too thought highly of the Cizhou lotus root starch. But it was precisely because the lotus root starch of Cizhou was so famous that there was more sham than genuine goods in the market.

Inside Cizhou itself, there were tens of business entities selling the lotus root starch. It was mostly made with the mung bean or cornstarch, which was then passed off as lotus root starch, and even the big establsihments with magnificent shop fronts were no exception. Only the Du's of the Southern Gate and the Zhang's of the Northern Gate produced genuine lotus root starch. However, their shops were narrow and humble, and few people knew their locations. There was another family that made genuine lotus root starch located in a certain suburban village. The lotus root starch they produced was even better in quality, but it was only known to a few who lived nearby. People who passed Cizhou from all parts of the land were usually in a hurry, and one could not expect them to make time and check out the quality of the lotus root starch. After all, they only heard about the name of the product. That was why the only thing they did was to find a big establishment. As a result, the bogus lotus root starch was far more easy to sell.

As everybody bought the sham thing, the high-ranking officials naturally seldom got the genuine lotus root starch. Notwithstanding the malpractice, the reputation of Cizhou lotus root starch had not been affected at all in the mind of the Beijing people.

*

*The Collected Works of Jian Songtang
By Zhang Yunao (1747-1829 A.D.) styled himself Zhongya, a native of Qiantang, Zhejiang Province (now Hangzhou); a poet of the Qing Dynasty. A palace graduate, he had once held the position of county magistrate with the reputation of being a benevolent administrator. He was called "Buddha Zhang" and "Upright Magistrate Zhang". Later he resigned his official post and became a recluse, writing to amuse himself. His poems had been highly praised by Yuan Mei and Zhao Yi. A prolific writer, he authored *Jian Songtang's Collection of Poems*,

twenty volumes, *Collected Works*, twelve volumes, and others, altogether more than ten books.

980. A Mad Dog

In a certain city there was a mad dog, which had been driven away by everyone who happened to see it. The dog did not know that it was insane and felt extremely angry for such treatment, biting men in revenge. People loathed it but did not make a fuss of it because they thought it was only a dog. Who would have thought that, as the dog found out that men would not care much about what it did, it became unrestrained and turned even madder than before, biting people ever more often and ferociously. By then people was no longer in a position to deal with it. In this world of ours, where can you still find a man like the courageous warrior Ti Miming, who eliminated all the mad dogs and brought immense satisfaction to the people?

*

*The Luyuan Collection
By Qian Yong (1759-1844 A.D.) styled himself Liqun and Meixi, originally from Jinkui, Jiangsu Province. A painter, calligrapher and a prolific writer, he authored *The Lansen Collection, The Collected Poems of Plum Blossom Brook, Notes on Going Upstairs, On Virtue, The Luyuan Collection, The Study of Bronze and Stone Inscriptions in Luyuan,* and so on. *The Luyuan Collection* contains twenty-three branches of study, recording eight hundred seventy-three events, mostly based on his own experience, but also included what he saw and heard, with the state of affairs in the regions south of the Yangtze River during the early years of the Qing Dynasty in greater detail.

981. The Tailor

In every province there were tailors, but more numerous in Ningbo of Zhejinag than in any other place. At present, most of the master tailors in the city of Beijing originated from Ningbo.

Long, long ago, a man brought a bolt of silk fabrics to the tailor, asking him to make a garment. The tailor inquired about the man's disposition, age, appearance and, in what year did he pass the imperial examination.

But the tailor did not bother to ask for his measurements, the feet and inches. The man was greatly surprised.

The tailor said, "Anyone who passes the imperial examination when young must be very proud of himself. As he walks, he will stick out his chest, and so the lower hem of the garment must be long in front and short at the back. If the man passes the imperial examination at an old age, he will be satisfied and does not have further ambition. He will be sluggish, and poke his head in. Such man should have a longer hem at the back, and a shorter one in front. A fat man's waist will be thick, and a thin man's waist slender. A short jacket is suitable for a hot-tempered man; whereas a sluggard should have a long garment. As to the size of the garment, there are set rules to follow, and need not be asked."

I had the feeling this tailor could be engaged to discuss the principles of tailoring. Nowadays, the tailor habitually obtains the measurements from the old garment, or follow the vogue with a new cut. They do not understand the underlying principles of a garment being short or long. Yet in their mind, the desire to covet a little surplus cloth was ever present. Whether it be the garment of men or that of women, it will be difficult now to have "the perfect fit" as described by Dupu in his poem. Such good tailors are hard to get now.

*

*Newly Engraved Comprehensive Collection of Jokes
By Games Master, life and deeds unknown. There existed a block-printed edition in the fifty-sixth year of Qianlong (1791 A.D.), reign title of emperor Gaozong of the Qing Dynasty, so he must be a writer of the Qianlong period.

982. Patch Up a Lie

A man, who was a habitual liar, used to tell exaggerated stories, and very often his servant had to patch it up for him.

On one occasion, he said, "Our well was blown away yesterday to my neighbour's."

Everyone thought such thing never happened since ancient times, and his servant beside him tried to patch it up, "There's really such a thing," he said. "Our well was close to the neighbour's hedge, and last night the wind was so terribly strong that it moved the hedge to our side of the well. So you see, it is just as if our well had been blown over to our neighbour's."

On another occasion, he said, "Someone shot down a wild goose and lo and behold there was a bowl of rice-flour noodle soup on its head!"

His audience was stunned by what he said, and his servant beside him again tried to patch it up, saying, "That event is also true. My master was just holding a bowl of rice-flour noodle soup in the courtyard when a wild goose was shot down. The head of the wild goose fell exactly into the bowl. See, isn't it true that the head of the wild goose carried a bowl of rice-flour noodle soup?"

On another day, he told people, saying, "There is a tent in my house which can blot out the sky and cover the sun completely without leaving so much as a gap."

His servant knitted his brows when he heard this, saying, "My master has overblown it. How can I patch up such a monstrous lie?"

*

*In Aid of Conversation
By Fang Feihong styled himself Binlai, originally from Wenzhou, Zhejing Province. Neither the dates of his birth and death nor his deeds were known. *In Aid of Conversation* consists of fifty volumes. On the front page of the book there was a foreword by Hu Mengmei dated the fifth year of Jiaqing, and from which it is reasonable to assume that Feihong lived between the periods of Qianlong and Jiaqing.

983. Death by Mistake

The mother-in-law of my eastern neighbour died. According to tradition, an elegiac address at the funeral was required. The family therefore asked the tutor in the family school to write one for them. The tutor readily promised and searched his bookcase for an ancient book, from which he carefully copied a piece in standard script. He never thought he had erred by copying a sacrificial writing meant for the father-in-law instead. As the funeral rites were in progress, someone who was literate discovered that it was an unforgivable mistake. The family was greatly shocked and went to the family school, where they seized the tutor and berated him. The tutor hastened to explain, saying, "The sacrificial writing in the ancient book has a definite style, and it could never be wrong. I'm afraid it was the wrong person that has died in your family."

984. Meeting the King of Hell

There was a scholar who was a sycophant all his life. When he died, he met the King of Hell in the nether regions. The King of Hell suddenly farted, and the scholar hastened to bow and say, "Your Majesty! You raised your respectable bottom and released your cherished wind free from inhibitions. It was as if I'd heard some pleasant music, and smelled a breath of musk and the scent of orchids!" The King of Hell was very pleased and ordered the ox-headed demon to bring him to another hall and treat him with a feast.

Halfway to their destination, the scholar turned to speak to the ox-headed demon, saying, "The two curved horns of yours look very much like the crescent moon in the sky, and your bright piercing eyes are virtually the stars at the bottom of the sea!" The ox-headed demon was extremely delighted with this compliment and it pulled at the garment of the scholar and said, "It's still early for the King's feast. Let's go to my humble abode to have a cup first!"

*

*A Collection of Hearsays

By Le Jun, dates of birth and death unknown. Originally his name was Guan Pu styled himself Yuanshu, assumed name Lianshang. He was a native of Linchuan, Jiangxi Province. A palace graduate of the period of Jiaqing, and a disciple of Weng Fanggang, he enjoyed the reputation of being a man of talent. He authored *The Collected Works of Qingzhishan Studio, A Collection of Hearsays. A Collecton of Hearsays* consists of five volumes, recording miscellaneous events he had heard and seen, among which there are quite a few sharp-witted and profound fables.

985. No Cat is Good in the World

A man hated the mice most of all, and he spent a large sum to get the best cats money could buy, feeding them with fish and meat, and let them sleep on the woollen blanket. Since the cats had a lot to eat and a comfortable place to sleep, they did not have the desire to catch the mice, and sometimes even mixed with them and played together. Wherefore the mice became more reckless than ever. The man was furious, and he stopped feeding the cats, thinking that no cat in the world was good. He put up traps to catch the mice, but the mice kept a distance from them. He placed baits, but the mice did not eat them. He was so mad with the mice that he never stopped thinking of eliminating them, but he was unable to find a way to do it. One day, his house caught fire, destroying the granary, and threatening to burn down his bedroom. He fled outside, and couldn't help laughing aloud. All his neighbours rushed to his aid, trying to put out the fire, but he was angry, and blamed them for what they did, saying, "These mean creatures are about to be burnt to death by the great fire. Why do you come to rescue them?"

986. Cherishing the Donkey

There was an old man, who was very wealthy but extremely close-fisted. He was good at extending loans for interest, and there was not a day he did not receive interest from one loan or another. Later, as he grew older, when even walking became a burden for him, he bought a donkey, so that he could ride instead of walk. However, he cherished the donkey to the utmost. Unless he was tired out, he would not sit on the saddle. The opportunity of the donkey being placed under the old man's hips was at most three to four times a year.

When the weather was hot and the old man had to go a long distance to collect loans, he had no alternative but to bring his donkey along. Halfway on the road, the old man was so tired that he panted for breath, and he had to mount the donkey. After covering a distance of two to three *li*, the donkey, for reason that it had seldom been ridden by a man, was also short of breath. The old man became panic-stricken, and immediately alighted from the donkey and unsaddled it. The donkey mistook its master's intention, thinking that he wanted to let it take a rest, and so it took an about-turn, following the same road and went home. The old man hastened to call it, but the donkey was completely absorbed in running and did not hear the old man's call. The old man tried his best to follow it, but could not catch up. He was afraid the donkey might go astray and get lost. At the same time, he also hated to part with the saddle, so he shouldered the saddle and rushed back.

As he reached home, he asked at once, "Is the donkey home?"

"It is here," replied the old man's son.

Thereupon the old man cheered up. Slowly he unloaded the saddle from his shoulder, feeling as though he had walked with a limp, and his back ached so much that it was as if it had been split open. All this added to the fact that he had suffered heatstroke, and he was ill for over a month.

*

*The Collected Works of Youhuo Studio
By Li Daoping styled himself Zunwang, assumed name Yuanshan, originally from Anlu, Huguang (now Zhongxiang, Hubei Province); dates of birth and death unknown. A palace graduate of the period of Jiaqing, he had once held the position of educator-official in Jiayu County. Because he lived in the upper reaches of Yunshui River, he was called Master Yunshang.

987. The Horse with a Long Mane

A man kept a horse. The horse was tall and big, majestic and powerful, and the mane on its neck was long, so long that it almost completely covered its eyes. The horse keeper once brought the horse to graze in the mountain. All the animals there noticed its tremendous size, and dared not go near for fear of provoking it. At times a tiger came, and the horse stepped forward bravely to fight with the tiger. They usually fought for the whole day, and neither side had the better of the other. People who witnessed the fight reported it to the owner, praising the horse for its bravery. The owner was pleased and said, "The horse is really very strong and brave! It was unable to defeat the tiger simply because its mane was too long, which obstructed its view and prevented it from seeing clearly. If the mane is shorn, I'm sure it will be able to defeat the tiger." And he had the mane cut off.

The next day, he again sent the horse to graze. He followed it to the mountain, confident that his horse would defeat the tiger. As expected, soon a tiger appeared. At the sight of the tiger, the horse shivered with fear. Less than three rounds they fought, and the horse was bitten to death by the tiger.

The owner felt very sorry for his horse, although he had escaped danger himself. He was baffled and thought of it on his way home. When he reached home, he consulted with the experienced elders in the village. The elders said, "You must know success in any endeavour depends on courage, and failure is caused by cowardice. Initially, the horse challenged the tiger without fear because its mane covered its eyes. It did not know its opponent was a tiger. When the mane was cut, it saw the tiger clearly, and it became timid and nervous. As it lost its courage to fight, its defeat was almost certain. Courage begets success, and cowardice causes failure—it is an universal truth. Examples are found everywhere, and not only confined to this horse."

*

A Collection of Poems and Essays from the Yinji Studio
By Guan Tong (1780-1831 A.D.) styled himself Yizhi, originally from Shangyuan, Jiangsu Province (now Nanjing). A palace graduate of the period of Daoguang (1821-1850 A.D.), he was the student of Yao Nai, who was a writer of classical Chinese, and an advocate of the Tongcheng School. Guan Tong himself was famed for his prose. He was the author of *A Collection of Poems and Essays from the Yinji Studio, Notes on the Seven Confucian Classics, A Chronicle of Mencius Life*, etc.

988. Notes on Scorpion

When Guanzi sojourned in Shangqiu, he noticed a teenager in the inn keeping scorpions for fun, and inquired from him about the way scorpions were raised. The teenager said, "When I catch a scorpion, the first thing I do is to get rid of its venomous tail so that it will not sting me. I can then keep it for fun." Guanzi took over the container of the scorpions and had a closer look. He observed there were more than ten of them, all appeared to be tame. If food was thrown in, they would contend with one another for it; if teased, they became frightened and ran away. Judging from their appearance, they seemed to be afraid of men. The teenager was extremely self-conplacent, carrying the scorpions with him as he left laughing.

The guest beside Guanzi said, "The same method may be employed to tame evil men."

989. Notes on Pigeon

Marquis Ye's family came by two pigeons, and they tied the pigeons' wings and kept them in the suburbs. The leopard cat knew the pigeons could not fly, and caught the female pigeon and ate it. The male pigeon was infuriated, and did all it could to peck the leopard cat with its sharp beak. The pain sent the leopard cat howling and fleeing. A few days later, Marquis Ye got another female pigeon, and he kept it with the male as before. The leopard cat came and ate the female pigeon yet again. As the leopard cat had been pecked by the male pigeon on the previous occasions, it pretended to be afraid and stayed away from it. The male pigeon was confident of its own power and did not take precautions. Soon it was also eaten by the leopard.

*

*The Complete Works of Ding An
By Gong Zizhen (1792-1841 A.D.) styled himself Seren, assumed name Ding An, originally from Renhe, Zhejiang Province (now Hangzhou); a writer of the Qing Dynasty. A palace graduate of the era of Daoguang, he advocated political and economical reform, and was one of the forerunners of bourgeois reformism. He had once been the official in

charge of the Ministry of Rites. Later, he resigned his official position and returned to his home town, lecturing in Hangzhou and Danyang. Died of illness two years later in Danyang College. Exposing in depth the corruption and seamy side of the ruling feudalistic clique, his poems and essays were permeated with passionate patriotism.

990. Worrying about the Tree

Wanmo planted a tree. It did not grow well after seven years, which caused him no end of worry. A wise man said to him, "Don't you worry. In time it will certainly grow into a towering tree, and become luxuriant."

Xumo also planted a tree. It took only three days for the tree to stand upright, and as strong as a pillar. Its roots and buds were so full of vigor that it took only one day to put forth shoots, and three days to grow luxuriant branches and leaves. In seven days, it became a huge tree that reached the sky. But Xumo began to worry that it had grown too fast.

A sage said to him, "You are dedicating the love you have for the peach, the plum, the three-bristle cudrania and the *zuo* or oak to this tree. It is not appropriate to compare the speed with which Wanmo's tree grows with that of your tree."

A hundred days later, Xumo was still worrying about the tree he had planted.

When a tree has just been planted, people will worry about whether it will grow up. By the same token, when it has grown into a big tree, people still cannot treat it properly.

991. God's Wish to Bestow Wine Failed

All the celestial beings from every corner of heaven came to pay their respects to God, and God said, "Let everyone have a cup of wine!"

God's minister in charge of wine cups took the bamboo slips to register the names of every celestial being, but he was unable to complete the registration after three thousand years.

God wanted him to explain. The minister in charge of wine cups reported, saying, "Because every celestial being brings his sedan-chair bearers."

God said, "The sedan-chair bearers should be registered also." Thus the job could not be finished after seven thousand years.

God again wanted him to explain, and the minister in charge of wine cups reported, "Because the sedan-chair bearers each has his own sedan-chair bearers too!"

God heaved a sigh in silence, as his wish to give each celestial being a cup of wine could not be fulfilled.

*

Casual Literary Notes of the Studio of Two Kinds of Autumn Rain
By Liang Shaoren (1792-? A.D.) styled himself Jinzhu, assumed name Yinglai, originally from Qiantang, Zhejiang Province (now Hangzhou). A palace graduate of the era of Daoguang, he had once served as secretary of the Imperial Patent Office in the Inner Chancery. His works included *Casual Literary Notes of the Studio of Two Kinds of Autumn Rain* and *A Collection of poems*.

992. Debate about the Stones

There were some clothes as well as quilts put out to air in front of the small tavern. The clothesline was tied to a bamboo pole which, again, was inserted into a wooden roller. In the afternoon, when the wind blew hard, it often caused the wooden roller as well as the clothes and quilts to tumble and fall to the ground.

A certain A noticed it. He took a sip of wine and said, "If the roller is made of stone, it will not move like that."

"Who says stone will not move?" a certain B was not convinced and refuted him. "Let me ask you. Why is it the churn stone of the dyehouse moves from morning till night?"

"That's because man steps on it," A replied.

"What do you mean by stepping on it?" B stared at him with wide open eyes. "Tens of thousands of people go up the Town God Mountain and the Ziyang Mountain to burn incense everyday. Why don't I see the stones move an inch?"

"It's because they are all very big and solid," A explained.

"If what you said is true, how do you explain the stone bridge which spans the city river, where the stones are all small and hollow? Why don't the stones move even though they are stepped on everyday?"

*

Qu Ting's Insignificant Talk
By Shi Cheng (1813-? A.D.) otherwise known as Shi Chun styled himself Mutang, originally from Panyu, Guangdong Province (now Guangzhou). Becoming a palace graduate in the twentieth year of Daoguang, he was the leading lecturer in the Yuexiu College of Duanxi for over twenty years.

993. Phoenix Duck

Our family kept several phoenix ducks. Their feather was as pure and white as snow. They swam in the pond everyday. Beside the pond, there was a small canal. Whenever it rained and the river rose suddenly and sharply, the water would flow into the canal, bringing the small shrimps and fish with it. At that time, the phoenix ducks would swim to the canal to find food. They had no knowledge that the canal was muddy. Once they got in, they would sink into the quagmire and get inextricably bogged down in the mud. As a result, their spotlessly white feather became as black as pitch, and nobody would recognize them as phoenix ducks anymore.

For that reason, I sighed with deep feeling. In today's world, there are those who covet petty gains and forget the consequences, who destroy their own purity for the enjoyment of food. Is the phenomenon only confined to a few ducks?

The Good Laugh Collection
By Retired Scholar Du Yiwo, whose life and name were unknown. The book has an author's preface dated the fifth year of Guangxu (1879 A.D.), reign title of emperor Dezong of Qing (1875-1908 A.D.), which states, "When I was a youngster of twenty, I often fell ill. Each time I had to do composition, I would become ill before a month had passed; and every time I fell ill, it would be more than one month. In 1852 A.D.and 1855 A.D. I was bedridden twice, each time for half a year." From what had been written, it might be inferred that because of health problem, he had given up participating in the imperial examinations. From then on, he spent his time in lyre-playing, chess, calligraphy and painting—fancies of men of letters, to amuse himself. During the course of thirty years, he accumulated enough materials to compile them into *The Good Laugh Collection*, six volumes, with the intention of "ridding worries and eliminating depression only". At the end of the preface, he affixed his name as "Retired Scholar Du Yiwo of Wu (Southern Jiangsu and Northern Zhejiang, and their vicinity)", from which it was surmised he must be a native of Suzhou, and lived between the eras of Daoguang and Guangxu.

994. Ancient Bricks

Bi Qiufan was the governor of Shaanxi and it was his sixtieth birthday, so his subordinates all sent brithday gifts to congratulate him, but he had accepted none of them.

A county magistrate sent someone to bring him twenty pieces of ancient bricks; on each was engraved with the title of the emperor's reign, indicating these were objects of the Qin and Han Dynasties. Bi Qiufan was extremely delighted, and he summoned the manservant who sent the bricks, saying, "I did not accept any of the other birthday gifts. I was pleased with your master's gift, and that's why I accepted it." The servant was overwhelmed by an unexpected favour, and hastened to report, saying, "It was for Your Excellency's birthday that my master had gathered many craftsmen in the government office to manufacture all these bricks. My master personally oversaw the production, and chose the best ones to present them to Your Excellency." As Bi Qiufan listened, he smiled and let the matter go at that.

995. Don't Like Eggs

A man from the South had an inborn aversion for eggs. When he travelled to the North for the first time and went to get his breakfast in the morning, the waiter asked him what would he have, and he asked in return, "Anything palatable?" "We have osmanthus meat," replied the waiter. When the dish was brought in, it was actually scrambled eggs with pork. For fear of being called an ignoramus who did not even know the name of the dish, he could not tell the waiter that he did not like eggs. So he asked again, "Any other good dishes?" "How about fried batter?" the waiter suggested. "Good, very good!" the man said. When the dish was presented, it was omelette. He had now no other recourse but to say he felt rather full and did not have any appetite for food. His servant reminded him, "There is still a long distance to cover. What shall we do if we cannot put up with an empty stomach?" The man said, "In that case, get some dimsum or appetizer." He asked the waiter whether there was any dimsum available, and the waiter said there was steamed fruit. The man said, "Bring more of it." Actually it was another name for steamed eggs. The man was exasperated, and had to endure hunger as he set out.

There are lots of things one does not know. If one must pretend to know what one doesn't know and be a hungry general, that is really ridiculous.

*

The Comprehensive Collection of Jokes
By Cheng Shijue, dates of birth and death unknown, originally from Suzhou, Jiangsu Province. A palace graduate of the era of Guangxu, he did not, however, fare well in his official career. In the preface to *The Comprehensive Collection of Jokes,* he stated, "It is regrettable that I've accomplished nothing. Being advanced in years, I am just like an old horse in the stable. The future offers no prospect, and I'm blocked from climbing up the ladder of success." Therefore, he "closes the

door to visitors, and concentrates his attention in writing". The book is the most influential collection of jokes in Chinese modern history, and shares the same title with Games Master's book, but a different creation.

996. Arresting the Spirits

The Jade Emperor ordered Zhong Kui, the most capable spirit-catcher, to descend from heaven and arrest the spirits. Zhong Kui obeyed His Majesty's order and arrived at the human world with his army of spirit-catchers. To fulfil their task they had brought their swords with them. However, they had never expected the ghosts and spirits in the human world to be more numerous than in the nether regions, and even fiercer. The spirits saw Zhong Kui coming, and acted violently. The harum-scarum rushed forward to wrest his sword, the quick-witted brought their dexterity into play, those asked for money pulled his boots and took off his hat, the obscene loosened his belt and did away with his garment, the discourteous pulled his beard and plucked his brows, the destitute stole his sword and pilfered his knife, the mischievous dug his nostrils and scooped out his eyes, and the drunken talked nineteen to the dozen. Together the spirits wrestled Zhong Kui to the ground, and sat on his body, and the satyr embraced him with both hands. Thus the most capable spirit-catcher and spirit-eater was unable to practise his magic arts, and the bunch of spirits became all the more ferocious, crying and shouting at the top of their voice.

Zhong Kui was at a loss as to what to do when a big fat monk suddenly appeared with his bulging stomach. All smiles, the monk walked towards him. He helped Zhong Kui to his feet and said, "General Demon-tamer, why are you in such a tight corner today?"

"I've not expected the spirits of the human world so hard to tame!" replied Zhong Kui.

"That's all right. Let me catch them for you," said the monk.

As the monk caught sight of the spirits, he burst out laughing.and, opening his big mouth, he swallowed them all into his stomach.

Zhong Kui was greatly amazed and said, "My master, your magic power is really great!"

"You have no idea! The world is full of these evil creatures. There is no need to reason with, or show mercy, to them. The only way to deal with them is to put them inside the big belly!"

997. The Spirit's Choice

The Chinese character for avarice is very similar to the character for poverty as, truly, there never was a man who was avaricious and did not become destitute.

There was a man who was both avaricious and destitute and, because he died of poverty and hardship, his poor spirit had a faraway look and a no-one-to-turn-to appearance when he arrived at the nether regions. The King of Hell expeditiously rendered his verdict, saying, "You evil creature, you were as greedy as a wolf when you were in the land of the living. As a result, you became poverty-stricken. When you were poor, you could not be content with your lot, but allowed your fancy to run wild, coveted an unearned income, and committed all sorts of wicked things. So it is but fair to change you into a beast or insect and the like." The avaricious ghost said, "I've no right to oppose your decision but, if it pleases Your Majesty, could you allow me to choose what kind of beast or insect I would like to change into."

"What do you choose?" asked the King of Hell.

"If you change me into a beast, please let me be Bo Le's horse, or Zhang Guo's donkey. If you change me into a bird, I would like to be You Jun's goose, or Yi Gong's crane. If you change me into an insect, then I think I would like to become Zhuangzi's butterfly, or Zichan's fish."

The King of Hell flew into a rage upon hearing what he said. Pointing his finger at the avaricious spirit, he scolded him roundly, saying, "You evil spirit, you are so picky. What's the difference between you and those choosing good positions from available official vacancies in the world of the living? I'll punish you by changing you into a tortoise. Since you are afraid of destitution, I'll make you always draw back your head; since you are insatiably avaricious, I'll let you drink the wind throughout the year unable to get a square meal."

By that time it began to dawn upon the avaricious spirit, and it said, "Although I've not been an official, I know now the whole officialdom is steeped in crime."

998. A Buffalo Looking for its Phratry

The Cowherd had ten thousand strings of copper coins loaded onto the buffalo as he set out for the palace of the Big Dipper to hand them in, but the Buffalo suddenly escaped and descended on to the earth. As it looked at its own appearance, which was filthy and vulgar, it felt rather embarrassed. But as there was plenty of coins on its back, it believed it would not be difficult for it to join the powerful aristocrats and become one of their kind, or so it thought. It would bring glory to its native village. So thinking, it went to the East China Sea to see the unicorn, telling the latter about his plan. The unicorn said, "My horn and my feet came from the same phratry as the feudal princes. How can I let you, the idiot who knock its head against the wall, to mix with my aristocratic phratry?" And it shouted at the buffalo and ordered it to leave.

The buffalo then went to the Western Regions to see the green lion. Before his name was announced, the lion already noticed the ugly and disgusting appearance of the buffalo. It gave a big roar, which frightened the buffalo out of its wits, and made it run all the way to the wilderness.

Suddenly, the buffalo thought of the donkey who lived in the reeds. In the past, they had pulled the cart together and built up a cordial relationship, and so it went to see the donkey. The donkey said, "In the Southern Mountain, there was a spotted leopard. Although it is a recluse in name, it has a large circle of friends. I'll introduce you to it." Thus they went together to the Southern Mountain. As the donkey saw the spotted leopard, it tried its utmost to praise the buffalo's sincerity and its innate goodness. At first the spotted leopard refused. Later, when it saw the large amount of money on the buffalo's back, it smiled and said, "As I look at your back, it seems plausible for us to share a common ancestry. Besides, the reason why I'm being called the spotted leopard is precisely for the coin pattern on my back! Though you don't have the pattern, it can be created artificially!" As it rattled on, it began to unload the coins from the buffalo's back, divide the hairs on the buffalo's skin, and make a bright pattern with the coins, which was lustrous and glistening with myriads of golden rays. The buffalo had been transformed into an unusual beast. It was very much like a rich man, who contributed money to get an official position, and had a new title to his name immediately. What could be the difference between the two? As the donkey looked on attentively, it smiled and said, "The moment the wallet is opened, you become a handsome beast, and even if you invited the monarch of Jie State, Ge Lu, here, he would not be able to know your voice!" Having said that, it left.

Since then, the spotted leopard treated the buffalo as a member of its phratry, and the buffalo too was puffed up with pride. However, in less than ten days, the coins on the buffalo's back began to come off, and its skin returned to its old looks. The leopard was furious, saying, "Your ugly shape has brought disgrace to my aristocratic ancestry!" Thereupon it drove the buffalo away.

The buffalo was extremely puzzled and did not know what to do, so it returned to the palace of the Big Dipper. The cowherd beat its back with whip and staff, and asked where it had brought the coins to! The buffalo told the cowherd everything truthfully, and the cowherd berated it, saying, "You idiotic beast! The reason why the leopard was willing to share the phratry with you was because you had those coins on your back! Once the money was gone, why on earth should it want to have a member like you, who lived in the mud, as its ancestors' unworthy descendant!"

And the cowherd took a piece of rope and attached it to the buffalo's nostrills. Thereafter, he had it fastened at the back of the shed, or *lao*. That was why later the sacrificial ox was also called *lao* by the Chinese people.

999. A Lazy Woman

There was a lazy woman, who relied on her husband to provide food and drink everyday. She had only to open her mouth to be fed and hold out her hands to be dressed, leading a life of ease.

One day, her husband had to travel to a distant place, and the journey was expected to take him five days. He was afraid that his wife might be starved, and had made a big round flat cake with a hole in the middle, which he looped round the woman's neck. Thinking that it would be sufficient for five days' consumption, he felt at ease and left.

When the husband returned, he discovered the woman was already dead for three days. He was terribly frightened, and tried to find out the cause of her death. He saw the big round flat cake was eaten only at the portion next to her mouth. Her indolence had prevented her from turning the cake around, so that the rest of the cake could not be reached, and she died of hunger as a result.

*

*The Yong An Sketchbook

By Xue Fucheng (1838-1894 A.D.) styled himself Shuyun, assumed name Yong An, originally from Wuxi, Jiangsu Province. A diplomat of modern times, he was once the assistant of Zeng Guofan and Li Hongzhang, and had been recommended with personal guarantee from the two to the position of prefectural magistrate for his meritorious contributions in foreign affairs. Later, he was sent on diplomatic missions to England, France, Italy and Belgium. When he returned, he was assigned the post of left vice-censor. He authored *The Yong An Sketchbook* and *The Collected Works of Yong An.*

1000. The Centipede and the Earthworm

A centipede was crawling back and forth around the hole of the earthworm. The earthworm hid itself inside the hole. Suddenly, it popped its head out and bit off one of the centipede's legs. The centipede, in great anger, tried to enter the hole, but the hole was too small to accommodate it, and so it could only crawl above the hole. Then the earthworm took it by surprise and bit off another leg. Although the centipede was even more furious, it could but guard the entrance to the hole doggedly. Thus the earthworm bit off the centipede's legs one after another. In an hour, all the legs of the centipede had all been bitten off. Although it was still living bodily, it could no longer move about, just as a dead silkworm, lying prone on the ground. At that moment, the earthworm emerged from the hole in an imposing manner, bit open the centipede's belly and ate to its heart's content.

1001. The Spider and the Snake

While the spider was making a web between the walls two to three feet from the ground, a big snake passed under it and raised its head, intending to swallow the spider. However, to reach the spider, it was still a little short, and the snake tried several times without success. At last, it gave up. As it was about to crawl away, the spider suddenly swung down from a dangling thread, threatening to go after the snake. The snake was furious. Raising its head again, it endeavoured to swallow the spider. Expeditiously, the spider contracted its thread and retreated to the centre of the web. A short time later, as the snake was about to leave for the second time, the spider swung down again and, as the snake threatened it, it speedily retreated. In this manner, the same trick was repeated three or four times. Finally, the snake was tired out and lay prone with its head on the ground. The spider seized this opportunity in disregard of its own danger, caught it unawares, and swiftly touched down on the head of the snake. No matter how the snake threw and flung, and bounced madly, the spider stuck there until the snake eventually died. The spider then sucked its brains, and ate its fill before it left.

1002. The Wall Gecko and the Scorpion

A wall gecko and a scorpion happened to meet. The scorpion had no eyes, rushing ahead blindly, and it took the wall gecko with only a little teasing to enrage it and provoke it to sting. The gecko was cunning in disposition and nimble in movement, and it would not wait until the scorpion stung to dodge the attack. The tail hook of the scorpion did not get the gecko, but hurt itself instead. The scorpion was all the more angry because of its failure, and was determined not to rest until it got the gecko. The gecto repeated its trick, and the scorpion again stabbed itself. It died after three unsuccessful attempts. Thereupon the gecko began to eat the scorpion until only its empty shell was left. It was said that the gecko's method never failed. For a long time, the gecko had depended on the scorpion for food, and that's why the gecko was also called the "scorpion-eater".

Recording a Variety of Events
By Huang Junzai styled himself Tian He, originally from Yangzhou, Jiangsu Province. The book contains eighteen volumes, recording a variety of events the writer had seen and heard from the fourteenth year (1834 A.D.) of the era of Daoguang to the twelfth year (1873 A.D.) of the era of Tongzhi, covering a period of forty years, and touching upon the political, economical and diplomatic aspects of those years as well as the Opium War (1840-1842 A.D., 1856 A.D.) and the Taiping Heavenly Kingdom (1851-1864 A.D.). As the materials derived mostly from street gossip and hearsay, they were of limited value. However, there are quite a few novel legendary stories which may be regarded as good fable creations.

1003. Wooden Eggs

In Huai-an, Jiangsu Province, a man surnamed Wu set up an establishment for the egg business, ordinarily with tens of thousands of eggs in the store. At the end of the month when they customarily made an inventory of the stock in hand, it was always found to be a few hundred short. Later, the shop owner decided to draw an inventory every ten days, but the loss of eggs continued.

This led the businessman surnamed Wu to suspect the storekeeper. The storekeeper resented the unredressed injustice, and kept watch day and night. One day, he saw a big snake over ten metres long twine its body around the beam of the room while stretching its head down and opening its big mouth to suck the eggs, which it swallowed. The eggs were over one feet from its mouth, but one by one they went up into it and disappeared. After swallowing more than ten eggs at a time, it would then entwined itself round the beam, put forth its strength and contracted its body to break the eggs inside its stomach before it slithered away. The next day, the snake came again, and the same thing happened.

The storekeeper suddenly woke up to the truth. The missing eggs were all stolen by the snake! He tried to get some hardwood with which he made a number of wooden eggs and mixed them with the real ones. In the following day, the snake came as before, and drew in the eggs.

This time it was a mixture of real and sham eggs. Then it entwined itself round the beam as it had done before, trying to break the eggs in the stomach. It did not work. It tried to contract its body further, shaking and beating its tail, but all to no avail. Finally, it had to slither ouside, where it rolled and leapt on the grass beside the Wu's residence. After three days and three nights of struggle, it died of indigestion.

The storekeeper then invited the owner of the establishment to the scene. When the belly of the snake was slit open, and the wooden eggs taken out of it, he narrated the whole story of how the snake had stolen the eggs. The truth had been brought into daylight, and the storekeeper's injustice was redressed.

1004. Traffic Accident

The pampered son of an influential family went sightseeing in a carriage. He whipped his horse once too often, and the horse dashed forward in pain. The pampered son of the influential family was elated, thinking that all passersby must have admired the speed with which his carriage had been going.

But after joy came sadness, and his carriage, in top speed, collided with a large goods wagon pulled by five horses. The carriage was destroyed and came to a halt. In the meantime, the effect of inertia threw the pampered son out and fell in front of the carriage.

The pampered son, relied on the influence of his father and his elder brother, who were high-officials, demanded that the merchant of the big goods wagon compensated him. The merchant resented the demand, and the pampered son filed a suit with the county *yamen*, expecting the county magistrate to punished the merchant severely.

However, the county magistrate was an upright and incorruptible man. After careful inquiries, he said to the pampered son of the imfluential family, "If, as you said, the big goods wagon rammed your small carriage, then, sir, you must have been shaken out of the carriage and fell at the back. Since you had fallen in front of the carriage, that proved it was your smaller carriage which rammed the big wagon." He pointed out to the pampered son that he was the cause of the collision, and ordered him to be responsible for the repair of the merchant's big goods wagon. The pampered son was unable to dispute the fact and returned home in an angry mood.

*

*A Collection of Merry Talks

By Holy Man Xiaoshi, name as well as date of birth unknown. *A Collection of Merry Talks* is a book of jokes in the form of fables. Most of its content threw out innuendoes against manners and morals of the time. There is a block-printed edition of the book dated the tenth year of Guangxu (1884 A.D.), reign title of emperor Dezong of Qing (1875-1908 A.D.).

1005. The Tortoise and the Magpie Become Sworn Brothers

The Tortoise and the magpie went for brothers, the magpie becoming the younger brother, and the tortoise the elder brother. The sworn elder brother said to the sworn younger brother, "Since our hearts are now linked together, I intend to bring you to the Crystal Palace at the bottom of the sea, so that you can see the halls of the dragon palace and the priceless treasures." The magpie said, "Let me also bring you to the halls of *Lingxiao* in heaven, so that you can see the moon palace and the moon god." As the tortoise listened to the magpie's suggestion, he said, "Why don't you bring me to heaven first. Afterwards I can accompany you to the sea."

The magpie readily agreed.

So the tortoise climebed up the back of the magpie, and the magpie fluttered its wings and flew towards heaven. It so happened just at that moment, a man with a catapult appeared on the scene, and he launched a pellet shot, which fell precisely on the tortoise shell, causing the tortoise to tumble from the sky. As the magpie turned its head and failed to find its sworn brother, it began to look for the tortoise everywhere. After half a day's search, it finally located its tortoise brother, which had fallen into a chimney with its four feet dangling in the air. The tortoise too was searching for its magpie brother in every direction. The magpie alighted and asked, "Elder brother, you must have been shocked. Unfortunately, you have not been able to fulfill your wish. With your head throwing back, you must be very hungry now." The tortoise replied, "As a matter of fact, I do not feel very hungry. Although there is no food here, at least there are a few mouthfuls of smoke to satisfy my craving."

1006. Two Mosquitoes Go for Brothers

Two mosquitoes became sworn brothers. The city mosquito was the younger brother, and the village mosquito the elder brother. The elder mosquito said to the younger mosquito, "In your city, everyday all kinds of delicacies must have entered the mouths of the high and mighty, and delicious food passed through their intestines. No wonder their skin and flesh are delicate, smooth and fat. How long have you been cultivating yourself to deserve such good fortune? Those who supply me with blood are all farmers in the village. They eat wild herbs everyday. Inside their bellies there is only rice bran. Their bodies are lean and have very little blood. What sins have I committed to deserve such bland diet?"

The city mosquito said, "When I was in the city, I always attended banquets and ate delicious fish and meat everyday. I was too full to want to eat anything."

The village mosquito said, "First of all, you must bring me to the city to taste the flavour of those bigwigs' fat and blood. Thereafter, I'll accompany you to the countryside to sample that of the farmers. How about that?"

The city mosquito readily agreed. It brought the village mosquito to the Great Buddha Temple, and pointed at the two sculptured fierce-looking gods, *heng* and *ha*, who were guarding the temple gate, and said, "There you have two important persons. Please go and suck their blood."

The village mosquito flew over, and bored for a long time with its mouth. In the end, it complained, saying, "This important person's body is really very big, but he grudges to let people eat. I drill almost half a day, and not only is it tasteless, but he does not even want to let me have a drop of his blood!"

1007. In a Trance

A man had his shoes mispaired; the sole of one was thick, the other thin. As he walked, one leg was long, the other short, feeling very funny.

The man was surprised and said, "Why have my legs become unequal in length? May be the road is uneven."

Someone told him, "You must have mismatched the shoes!" So the man sent his servant home to get the other shoe. The servant left for a long time and came back empty-handed. He said to the master, "It's useless to change them, because the soles of the other pair at home is also one thick and one thin."

*

With a Laugh
By Yu Yue (1821-1907 A.D.), originally from Deqing, Zhejiang Province. He was a writer and linguist. A palace graduate of the Daoguang era, he had held the position of compiler in the Han Lin Academy and served as a tutor in Henan Province, becoming a lecturer in Hangzhou in his remaining years. A prolific writer, his writings were put together as *The Complete Works of Chun Zaitang*. His collection of jokes *With a Laugh* was included in *The Complete Works of Chun Zaitang*, volume forty-eight of *The Yu Lou Collection of Miscellanies*.

1008. Kill the Mule and Ride the Chicken Home

A guest arrived, and the host prepared a vegetarian feast to entertain him. The guest felt unhappy about it. The host apologized, saying, "My family is very poor, and the town market is such a long way from here. I'm sorry I cannot provide you with meat dishes."

"In that case," said the guest, "please slaughter the mule I rode here!"

"What are you going to ride home then?" asked the host.

The guest pointed at the chicken in front of the steps and said, "I'll ride your chicken home!"

1009. "Tall Hats"

People like to be flattered and toadied to, which phenomenon, in folk language, was said to be predisposed to "wearing a tall hat". There was an official in the capital who was about to be transferred to other part of the country. Before he left for his new post, he went, first of all, to say goodbye to his respected teacher. His respected teacher, to whom he was greatly indebted, exhorted him, saying, "An official position outside the capital is not easy to do well, and you must be cautious."

The man assured him, "I've already prepared a hundred 'tall hats', and will give one to everyone I meet. I believe nobody will make matters difficult for me!"

His respected teacher was annoyed and said, "We are upright people. Why must we do that?"

"But," the man replied, "in this world, how many persons can you find to dislike flattery like my respected teacher?"

"What you said is of course not without reason," his respected teacher nodded his head.

The man, when he emerged from the residence of his respected teacher, said to everyone, "Of my one hundred 'tall hats', there are now only ninety-nine left."

1010. Engaging a Teacher

A man engaged a teacher to give guidance in learning to his son.

When the teacher arrived, the host said to him, "My family is very poor, and may not be able to adequately conform to the rules of etiquette. I hope, master, you will understand!"

"Why must you stand on ceremony?" replied the teacher. "I've never thought much of such things."

"Is it okay if I entertain you, sir, with only plain tea and simple food?" asked the host.

"That's all right," replied the teacher.

"There is no servant at home," added the host. "Can I ask you, sir, to sweep the courtyard and to open and shut the doors and windows for us?"

"That's all right," affirmed the teacher.

"In case my wife and the chidren like to buy a few odds and ends, can you please put up with the inconvenience?" the host asked again.

"That's all right too," the teacher replied.

"That's very good of you to say so, very good indeed," the host was very pleased.

"I've a word to say too," the teacher said. "Hope you will not be shocked."

"What is it?" asked the host.

"I'm ashamed to say I don't learn anything since my childhood," replied the teacher. "And that is what I want you to know."

"You are much too modest, sir!" replied the host.

"I'll not deceive you," said the teacher. "I do not even recognize the character 'big' (the simplest)."

*

*Witticisms
By Wu Woyao (1866-1910 A.D.) styled himself Xiaoyun as well as Jianren, originally from Nanhai Sea, Guangdong Province. He was a writer in the last years of Qing. As he lived in the town of Foshan (now a city), he also called himself Man of Foshan. He went to Shanghai to seek employment when he was over twenty. Later, he lived in Shandong Province, and then travelled to Japan. When he came back to his own country, he became the editor of newspapers and magazines. He was the author of *The Strange Phenomenon I've Seen in the Last Twenty Years*, a type of traditional Chinese novel, each chapter of which headed by a couplet giving the gist of its content, focussing on exposing

the shady deals in the official circle, the metropolis infested with foreign adventurers, the marketplace and the feudal clan. He was also the author of the novels *The History of Agony* and *The Strange Unjust Case Involving Nine Lives*. *Witticisms* is a book of satirical fable stories.

1011. Aliases

Four animals, a monkey, a dog, a hog and a horse, all wanted to get an alias for itself. However, none of them was much of a scholar, and did not know where to start. In the end, they agreed on going to the city, where each would adopt as its alternative name if one was available.

Having come to an understanding, the dog rushed towards the city like mad. Once it was there, it went in front of a temple. Raising its head, it noticed a horizontal inscribed board with *"hua ji ming wan"* (transforming the deeprooted obstinacy), and it adopted this as its alternative name. Following closely, the horse was the next animal to enter the city. Holding its head high, it looked around, but did not discover anything. As it lowered its gaze, there was the characters *"gen shen di gu"* (taking strong root) on a stone tablet, and it said, "I'll use this as an alias." Before long, the monkey, bouncing and vivacious, also arrived. It looked up and pointed to a horizontal inscribed board with the characters *"wu pian wu dang"* (Nonpartisan), and it said, "I'll call myself *'wu pian wu dang'*."

Almost half a day had passed before the hog, in a leisurely manner, staggered along. It searched the whole city without any discovery. The other three animals all laughed at it. The hog said, "Has anyone of you found your alias?" They replied in unison, "Yes, we have." "Why don't you inform me if you have already had your aliases chosen?" said the hog. So each of them announced its alias. When the hog had listened to each one in turn, it laughed, saying, "From time immemorial, an alias has only two to three characters, and I've yet to hear of one with four?" At these words, the three of them were stupefied and, staring at each other, they were speechless.

Observing their perplexity, the hog said, "That really does not matter very much. Suppose each one of you were to give me one character, then I would have an alias made up of three characters. At the same time, each of yours would be reduced to three characters as well."

The three animals were very pleased at this suggestion. After talking over with one another, they said, "Since only the superfluous character is to be given up, why don't we just get rid of the last character?". Thus the dog took down the character *"wan"* (obstinate), the horse gave up the character *"gu"*(strong), and the monkey abandoned the character *"dang"* (partisan), which combined contributed to the hog's alias *"wan gu dang"* (diehard partisan).

1012. Lepsima Saccharina

The silverfish or bookworm consumed a bellyful of books, and its body configuration became shockingly large. For that reason, it became extremely conceited, thinking it was the most learned scholar in the whole world. With its head raised high, it was overweeningly arrogant as it swaggered through the streets. However, when it met the dung beetle, it was bullied; when it met the fly-catching spider, it was again humiliated. The silverfish was both angry and anxious, and he asked people, saying, "I've a bellyful of the *Book of Odes* and the *Book of History*. I consider myself the most erudite person in the whole world, and a scholar with a thorough knowledge of the past and the present. Why is it there are still so many people who like to intimidate me?" People laughed at him, saying, "It's a pity that despite your self-confidence, you suffer from indigestion after consuming a bellyful of the *Book of Odes* and the *Book of Histories*. Even though you might be more learned still, what difference would it make?"

1013. Firestone

The flint and the steel on impact produced spark, which caused the tinder to catch fire. The flint said, "This is the flame which is stored inside my body, and has nothing to do with the steel." The steel resented what it said and refuted, "It is the impact from me which produces the live cinders, what has it to do with the flint?" As both were opinionated, they went their several ways.

One day, the flint thought of starting a fire and dashed itself against the other object, but no spark was forthcoming, although it had tried over a hundred times. The steel also intended to start a fire and impacted against another object but could not produce the anticipated result.

Thereupon they began to understand the significance of interdependence and became reconciled, keeping close to one another, just as they used to do, to ensure the start of a fire at any time. The tinder learned of it, and went to a distant place to hide itself. The flint and the steel on impact did produce sparks but, just like the ephemeral lightning, they would not last for long. Because of that, no fire resulted from their union. From their observation, the morally accomplished people realized that, as a fundamental principle, all objects existed with diametricallly opposed innate characters. For instance, hard and soft complement one another.

1014. The Maggots

The King of Hell was at leisure that day, and so he led the official in charge of the life-and-death register and the other spirits to tour the open country, where they saw many maggots wriggling in a latrine pit. The King of Hell ordered the official in charge of the life-and-death register to put his words on record, saying, "Let them be reincarnated as men." The official in charge of the life-and-death register obeyed and put these words in the register. As they continued their journey, they saw the decomposed body inside a coffin, and the maggots crawling all over it. The King of Hell likewise ordered the official in charge of the life-and-death register to put his words down, saying, "All of them should be sent to the hell of the plough of clay forever." The official in charge of the life-and-death register asked, "They are all maggots, why the difference in reward and punishment?" The King of Hell replied, "The maggots in the latrine pit take what men have discarded and, by so doing, they have made contributions. That is why they should be reincarnated as men. The corpse maggots eat the fat, the blood and the flesh of men. If they are allowed to be reincarnated as men and become officials, will not the people in the world suffer as a result?" The official in charge of the life-and-death register sighed at the King's words, saying, "No wonder the people are so miserable. It turned out many maggots had escaped to the world."

1015. A Snake Seeking Ease and Comfort

There was a snake that yearned to stretch itself. However, the cave it lived in was extremely shallow, and it had to coil itself up to sleep. If it wished to stretch its body, it must crawl outside the cave to do so, but then it was afraid it might meet with man. For that reason, it had been looking for a long and narrow hole. It could not find one for a long, long time.

One day, by accident, it ran into a sleeping elephant. The snake crawled under the elephant's trunk, and discovered that the nostril of the elephant was actually very long and deep and, what was even more to his delight was that it became wider and wider as it went further inside. He felt so happy that it crawled into it, stretched its body, and made a vow to live there forever.

As the elephant was soundly asleep, the sudden itchy feeling in its nostril caused it to stand up, raise its trunk and give a few big sneezes, which resulted in the snake being thrown to a distance of over thirty meters. That tumble caused the whole body skeleton of the snake to fall apart. It felt its body aching all over and could hardly move.

When the other snakes roved past the place and learned of it, they all jeered at it, and said, "This came about all because you had sought excessive comfort!"

1016. The Tortoise and the Crab

The tortoise was born with an outer shell, and the crab too had an outer shell. The difference between the two was that, the shell of the tortoise was thicker, and the crab's shell was thinner. Thus the tortoise could better withstand strong pressure, and the crab could not face heavy blow.

Nevertheless, the crab has two big pincers to protect itself, whereas the tortoise could only withdraw its head and its four limbs into the shell as a defensive measure against danger.

1017. The Earthworm Learns from the Snake

Both the snake and the earthworm had no legs. However, the snake moved very fast, which caused the earthworm to admire it greatly. The earthworm tried to imitate the snake's manner of movement, but it was too clumsy to make any improvement. It therefore hid itself outside the snake's hole, and carefully observed every movement of the snake. It saw the snake twist its body left and right, and slither ahead. The earthworm tried to follow the same style, twisting its body, shaking its head and wagging its tail, but it soon became exhausted, while its speed remained the same. To master the high-speed technique, there was nothing it could do but to engage the snake as its teacher. The snake took its teaching very seriously. Its effort notwithstanding, the earthworm was unable to learn, although it had been taught a hundred times. To find out the cause, the snake carefully examined the body structure of the earthworm, and it sighed when the study was completed, saying, "Although I don't have legs, but I've backbone, which was made up of pieces of bones joined together; whereas throughout your body, inside and out, there isn't even a piece of bone! As it is, how can you go about in this world!"

1018. The Fawning Dog

The dog was an expert in ingratiating itself with the others, and the worst example of bullying the poor and currying favour with the rich. When it saw a man with tattered clothes, it would howl to the best of its ability. One day, it arrived at the suburbs, and saw nobody around. All of a sudden, a spotted leopard came into sight, which the dog noticed when it was still a great distance away. The dog was delighted, thinking, "This fellow has coins hanging all over its body. He must surely be the young master of some wealthy and influential family. I should welcome him respectfully." Thereupon it hastened to go forward, wagged its tail and assumed every imaginable posture to beg for pity. When it was close to the spotted leopard, the leopard suddenly opened its big mouth and pounced on the dog. The dog was terribly frightened. It turned around and ran for its life. Although it had escaped being caught, it was almost scared to death. At this juncture, it met an ox. The ox asked where it came from, and the dog related what had happened a few moments ago. The ox smiled after listening to the story, saying, "You are too ignorant of the ways of the world. Haven't you heard? Presently in this world, the more money a man has, the stronger his desire to eat other people!"